ATONEMENT
OF THE
SPINE CLEAVER

Atonement of the Spine Cleaver is a work of fiction. Names, characters, places, and incidents are products of the author's imagination. Any resemblance to actual persons, living or dead, events or locals is entirely coincidental.

Copyright © 2023 by F. E. Bryce.

All rights reserved.

No portion of this book may be reproduced in any form whatsoever without written permission from the publisher or author, except as permitted by U.S. copyright law.

Paperback ISBN: 979-8-9879188-0-7

Electronic ISBN: 979-8-9879188-3-8

Hardback ISBN: 979-8-9879188-6-9

Cover Design: Krafigs Design at www.krafigsdesign.com

Map Design: Keir Scott-Schrueder at @keir_ss_cartography on Instagram

Chapter Art: Shane Nel at @syrenillustration on Instagram

Editors:

Jennifer Murgia at www.jennifermurgia.com

Hot Tree Editing at www.hottreeediting.com

RATHMORE

N

OSTR

AILTERIA

IRONHAVEN

LAND OF UNGIFTED KINGS

LYONDREA

PRINCIPALITY OF PAZULA

B

GREY

SUNLOCK

THE WORLD OF ILLUS

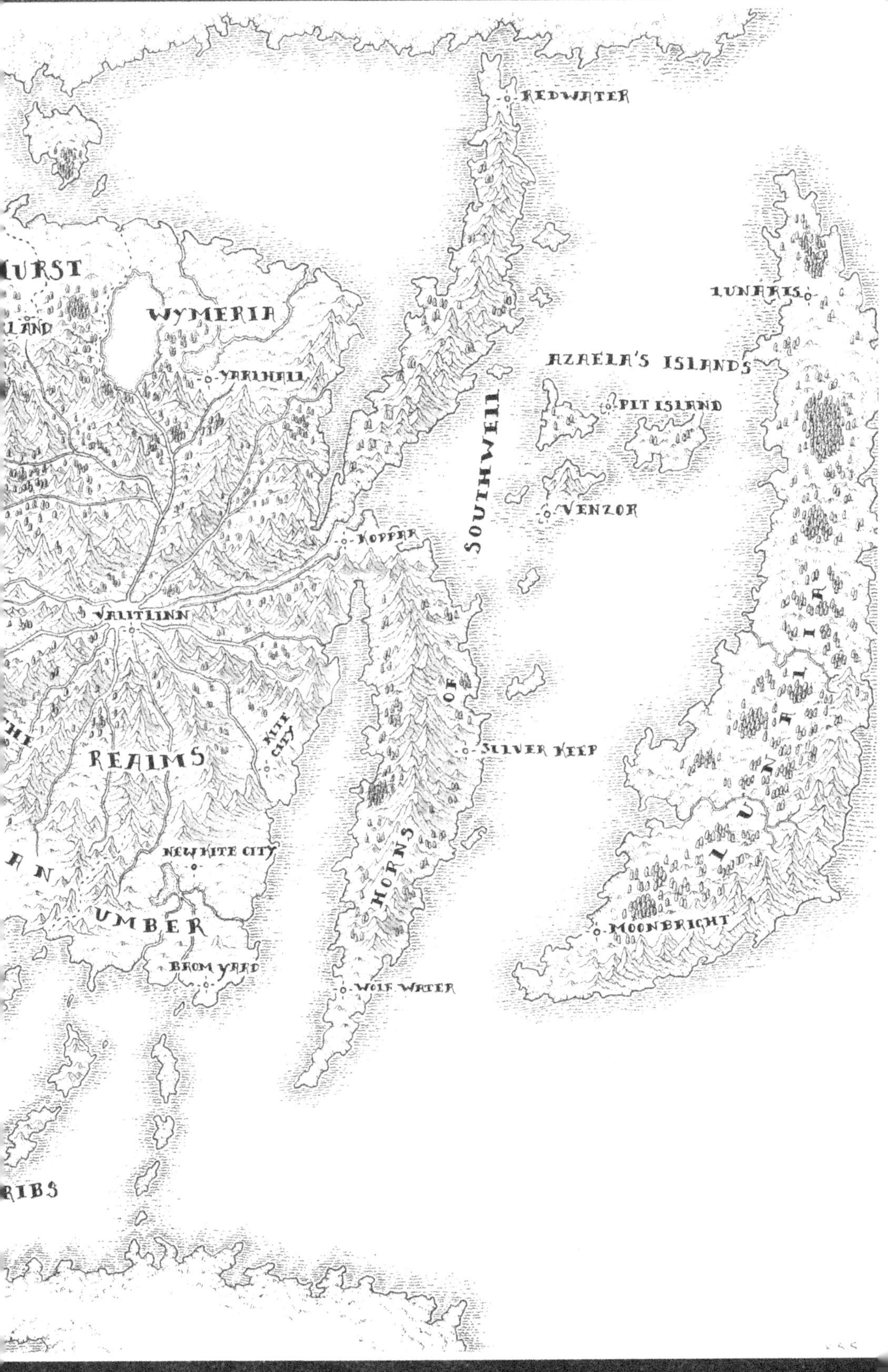
REDWATER
URST
WYMERIA
LAND
YARIHALL
LUNARIS
AZAELA'S ISLANDS
PIT ISLAND
SOUTHWELL
VENZOR
KOPPER
VALITLINN
THE
REALMS
KITE CITY
SILVER KEEP
HORNS OF
LUNARIA
NEW KITE CITY
AN
UMBER
MOONBRIGHT
BROMYARD
WOLF WATER
RIBS

N
LEGEND
TEMPLE
CITY
MOUNTAIN OF THE RED QUEEN
NEW VOLCANO
FLIR
LUXAMAL
THE • REALMS

WHITLE
OLD VOLCANO
DEATH
LIFE
FAUNA
RASIP
PALADIN'S ROAD
SALT STONE CITY
THE NEST
ELUS RIVER
ICE
WATER
LAKE WENSO
YER
ESCRES
AIR
LIGHT
DARK

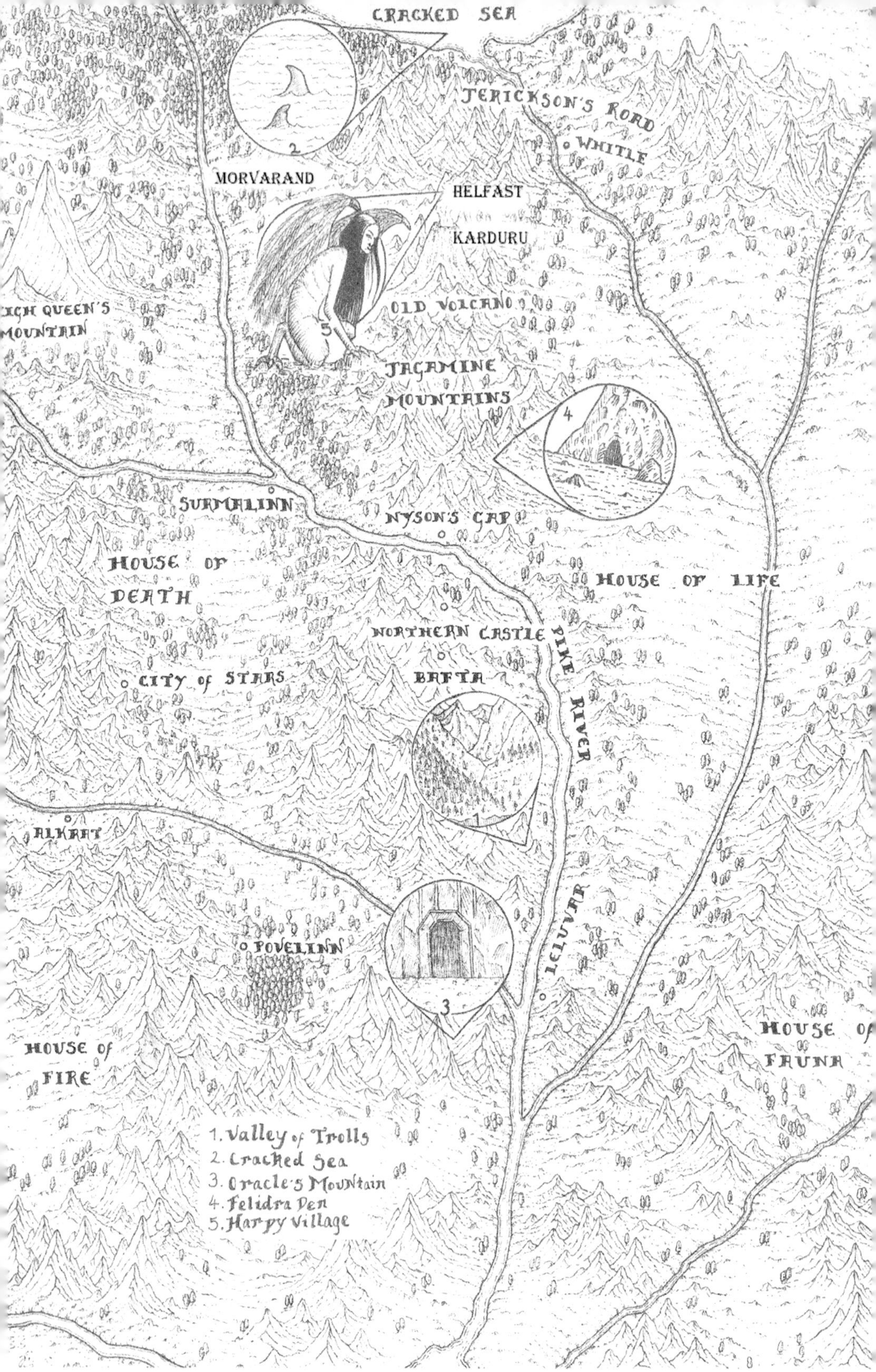

CRACKED SEA

JERICKSON'S ROAD

WHITLE

MORVARAND

HELFAST

KARDURU

IGH QUEEN'S MOUNTAIN

OLD VOLCANO

JAGAMINE MOUNTAINS

SURMALINN

NYSON'S GAP

HOUSE OF DEATH

HOUSE OF LIFE

NORTHERN CASTLE

PIKE RIVER

CITY OF STARS

BAFTA

ALKRAT

POVELINN

LELUVAR

HOUSE OF

FAUNA

HOUSE OF FIRE

1. Valley of Trolls
2. Cracked Sea
3. Oracle's Mountain
4. Felidra Den
5. Harpy Village

To my mom; I couldn't have done this without you.

Well, I guess I could have, but I would have been 1,000 years old. So thank you for pushing me to finish while I'm still in double digits. I love you and appreciate you endlessly.

Author's Note

It is important to note going into this book that Illus is a queer normative world. They are free to love and be who they want.

It is also important to know that power and class structures in their societies are based on power and family, not sex or gender.

There are printable maps and a glossary available on authorfebryce.com to help with any world-building questions that come up throughout the story.

And finally, a content warning to readers; Atonement of the Spine Cleaver contains graphic depictions of violence, profanity, mentions of suicidal thoughts, grief, explicit F/M sex scenes, and an explicit F/F sex scene.

ATONEMENT
OF THE
SPINE CLEAVER

Rorax

10,033 A.R.

PROLOGUE

"Gods above."

Rorax blew out a breath and stepped out onto the terrace, her eyes wide with awe as she grabbed the railing and pressed herself against the cool stone to get a better look. The balcony, stemming off the royal palace's library, had a bird's-eye view of Surmalinn, and the city was absolutely breathtaking.

Against the still black sky, fires she and her soldiers had lit around the city illuminated the dark like tiny fireflies glowing orange against the night. The light from the flames reflected off the surface of the Elus River, basking everything in a soft golden glow.

Vaguely through her admiration, she could hear the House of Death civilians below her screaming, begging, and bartering for their lives and their children's lives.

Their homes.

Their schools.

Their businesses.

All of it would burn to the ground tonight, and in a few hours their whole existence would be turned into nothing more than ash and smoke.

The reminder caused indecision to niggle painfully in her heart.

Rorax gripped the stone railing tighter with her blood-soaked hands as the clock tower burning in the middle of the city center collapsed into a pile of hot coals and shot orange sparks into the night sky as the screaming below intensified.

Something dark grew in her chest as she watched a woman carrying a small child wrapped protectively in her arms sprint down an alley, away from the city center where most of her men were still stationed.

The Wolf had been wrong in coming here.

Rorax's army had broken through the House of Death's defenses in less than twenty minutes, and the only souls awaiting them past the walls were just ordinary civilians. The armies, legendary monsters, and weapons the Wolf had told her were here were nowhere to be found. There was nothing. Most of the people here didn't even have a wisp of death magick. It was just a city.

The House of Death hadn't even stationed a small national defense legion here, for fuck's sake; the only soldiers here had been members of the city guard.

Rorax gritted her teeth, trying to slow her thoughts. Her stomach roiled as blood that wasn't her own trickled down the sides of her face and slid down her limbs. She looked down to where her hands gripped the railing to find they had been soaked with enough blood to leave two crimson handprints on the light gray stone. The stain might as well have been on her soul.

Rorax was nothing more than a butcher here. She could stop this, order her soldiers to pack up and leave, tell them to stop the bloodshed and the burning. They could all be gone within the hour.

As soon as the thought came, however, the note she had carefully folded in her back pocket seemed to burn her through her leathers. Her brother's plea to free him.

No, she couldn't stop the mission.

The blood coating her skin might feel sticky and awful, but if burning Surmalinn to the ground meant she would eventually be able to free her brother, then she was going to do it. She would kill every living soul in this city for him. Rorax owed Darras her life, and in over one hundred years, she had not found another opportunity to free him. This was it.

But would he even want to see her after learning she was responsible for the deaths of so many innocent people?

The blood continued to slide down Rorax's face and hair, falling in fast little droplets at her feet. The sound seemed to urge her to hurry as indecision warred in her stomach.

Whatever she decided, there would be no going back. She was either going to kill her mother, or she was going to kill the queen.

She looked over the beautiful, burning cityscape of Surmalinn once more, hardening her resolve.

Saying a fast prayer to the gods for forgiveness, she pulled her sword out of its sheath and entered the palace once more.

Chapter 1

Rorax

10,081 A.R.

"Oi! You there! Can we borrow your hole?"

The woman—who had been busy digging a grave for the body of the grossly disfigured man lying next to it—let out an unflattering squawk when she looked up and saw Volla and Rorax staring at her from a few feet away.

Volla leaned heavily against a tree and wiped the sweat off her forehead with her wrist. "We can share it even. We aren't picky, and she sure as shit ain't picky." Volla jerked her thumb toward the body draped across Rorax's shoulders. Rorax shifted the heavy weight of the armored corpse from one foot to the other as sweat dripped down her nose.

Usually, Volla would just flame the corpses they needed hidden into ash, but after they had infiltrated and nearly burned the nearest Lyondrean fortress to the ground, her power was precariously close to tapping out.

Volla took a few slow steps closer, and the woman took a nervous step back. Volla had pale white skin, long hair that was currently braided to the middle of her back, and an angular face. Sitting, she wasn't all that intimidating, but when she stood to her full six-foot two-inch height and puffed out her muscular frame, even the biggest men eyed her with the same wary look the woman was giving her now.

"Please? We would really appreciate it," Volla pleaded, attempting to be diplomatic, though they would simply take it if the woman didn't acquiesce.

The woman had a split lip and bruises scattered across her face. Her already pale skin blanched as she nodded fast. "Ye-yes of course. You can use it."

Rorax grunted her thanks before shuffling closer to the empty grave and dumping the body unceremoniously next to the other. The bodies matched—the dead man was donned in the exact same red and orange leather armor of the dead female. Out of the seventy-five soldiers stationed at the fortress, three had escaped their ambush and run off into the woods, and it seemed like one of them had sought refuge with the wrong woman.

"Did you see any other soldiers wearing the same armor run this way?" Rorax asked the woman.

She nodded. "Two more passed through my village, but only this one tried to force his way inside."

"You didn't want to offer him refuge?" Volla asked, raising an eyebrow.

The woman just looked over the soldiers with pursed lips and shook her head. "Got me enough mouths to feed back home."

Volla reached over and plucked the shovel out of the woman's hands. "We'll finish up here. If you want the shovel, come back for it later. We'll leave it here."

Volla Torvik, always so thoughtful, even when digging the graves of enemies and cowards. Rorax would have happily propped the body on a heaping pile of horseshit if it meant they could have immediately started heading back to the rendezvous point, but Volla had insisted on a proper burial for the dead. Rorax didn't think cramming two bodies into the same grave really counted as proper, but she wasn't about to argue. After being recruited by her new Heilstorm unit almost forty-six summers ago, Rorax had learned better than to argue with Volla about what constituted as honor; the definition seemed to change every day.

"K-Keep it." A little color came back into the woman's cheeks. "Thank you."

Volla started digging as the woman turned and scurried back into the woods.

"We just won the lottery. Digging graves takes forever in this gods-forsaken country." Volla grunted, heaving a shovelful of dirt out of the pit.

"I am feeling lucky." Rorax wiped the dripping sweat off her forehead with the back of her hand and eyed the rocky soil Volla was digging into.

Volla pointed a dirty finger at Rorax in between scoops of dirt. "You're always fucking lucky, Ror. Most of the time it's incredibly annoying, but today? I could kiss you."

Rorax grinned. "Maybe some of my luck will rub off on you and you can win your first game of cards in ten years."

Volla huffed a laugh. "Don't get my hopes up. Do you think we'll get to go straight home after this?" Volla straightened her spine and pushed a filthy hand over her long, platinum blonde braid, leaving streaks of dirt and blood in the strands. "I'm sick of being in this shithole country."

Their four-person Heilstorm unit was on loan to House of Weather for a mission a few miles west across the border of Lyondrea. They had been here for over a month investigating rumors that the Lyondrean queen was researching how to open Pits, which was illegal according to the Guardians' Law. They hadn't been able to find any concrete evidence of that yet, and Rorax prayed that the queen wasn't so naïve. The first two Pit Wars had nearly decimated the population of Illus by releasing monsters straight out of hell, and the consequence for opening Pits again would be the queen's execution.

Once again, Rorax prayed to the gods that her brother, Darras, was safe. She'd tried to ease her conscience by reminding herself that prison was probably safer than open exposure to the queen's monsters, but it felt like a lie.

"I would assume so. With this last loose end, we could be released anytime," Rorax mused, holding her hand out to take the shovel from Volla.

Volla handed it over and pulled herself out of the hole as Rorax got in, looking around at the empty woods before wiping her hands on her pants. "I bet we get delayed because of Jia."

Rorax cringed at the sound of the shovel scraping loudly across a big rock in the ground. "Maybe. The king and queen might want us to finish one more mission to test her out again before making our final decision."

"Well, I like her." Volla sat down on the opposite side of the hole from the two corpses, stretching her long legs in front of her and leaning back on her hands. "She's way better than the prat we were working with before."

Rorax snorted, hauling up another scoop of dirt.

There were four of them in their Heilstorm unit, and they were Unit One out of four total units.

Jia Frostguard, the newest recruit, had joined after one of their old team members started getting sloppy and eventually got herself killed. Volla had nominated Jia, knowing how proficient she was in both archery and larceny—and apparently knowing intimately how good she was with her tongue.

Their new team had a different dynamic, but so far it was a good one. A really good one. Jia had a lot to learn until she was up to par, but their unit's potential had both their leader, Sahana, and the King and Queen of Ice excited about the potential. She was a perfect fit for their unit, the "missing piece" Volla said, though Volla had been taking Jia to her bed almost every night since Jia's initiation a few moons past, so her opinion was entirely biased.

"Alright, give me the shovel," Volla sniped. "You're moving at the same speed as those snails over there."

"I am not." Rorax handed Volla the shovel as she eyed four crusty snails climbing the tree next to them. Even the snails looked wrong in Lyondrea, more threatening with black crystalized shells.

Volla was one of the strongest beings Rorax had ever met; her biceps were nearly the same size as Rorax's head. Volla's weapon of choice was a giant broadsword that probably weighed as much as Rorax did, and Volla could swing it with ease like it was nothing more than a short stick. So, she made quick work out of the digging.

Volla continued for a few more minutes before they shoved both bodies into the shallow grave and covered them with dirt.

"Let's get back," Volla said with a sigh, and Rorax agreed. Rorax didn't like the idea of leaving Sahana and Jia alone with Captain Crax for too long. Captain Crax was one of the commanders of House of Weather's armies and was the point of contact while they were on loan to Weather. There was something ruthless about Crax, and she had a slightly unhinged look in her eye that made Rorax uneasy. They traversed back through the forest, back to the small, one-tower stronghold, passing numerous groups of Crax's men digging graves for other dead Lyondrean soldiers.

Rorax and Volla strolled side by side through what was left of the slightly scorched front gates. Crax's men were standing around admiring the damage their unit had left. Blood, scorch marks, ice, arrows, and corpses lay strewn about the crumbling bailey of the stronghold.

On their way to the interrogation room, Volla and Rorax passed by a line of surviving Lyondreans who were shackled and bound, waiting their turn. The line was short; thankfully it wouldn't take long.

They met back up with Crax, Sahana, and Jia in one of the rooms during the middle of a torture session. Crax was administering the torture while Sahana leaned against the wall and watched with indifference. Jia stood next to her with a look of mild interest.

Crax, however, was cutting into her victim with a kind of bloodthirsty glee that made Rorax's stomach churn with unease and disgust.

"Is your queen trying to open the Pits?" Crax dragged the flat edge of a small carving knife up the side of the woman's cheek, along the dark tresses of her curly hair.

"Please... if ya promise this ends here... if ya swear on ya gods that this ends here and that ya will not track down my family, I will... I will tell ya everything I know," the woman begged with haggard breaths.

An oily grin crept over Crax's mouth, and a shiver threatened to shake Rorax's shoulders as she watched. "Sounds like agreeable terms to me. What do you say, Sahana?"

"If she gives us everything we need to know, it is acceptable." Sahana turned to Volla and Rorax. "Is it done?" Sahana, her long black hair pinned up in a smooth bun, gave them a bored look. Her brown eyes and small hoop earrings glinted in the torch light. Even though it had only been the four of them during the takedown of the small fortress, Sahana looked unruffled besides a thin layer of ash or dirt smeared across her light brown skin.

"Yes, Commander," Volla answered, "and we found one of the three men that got away. He's dead."

"Good. Crax brought a few hounds with her to track down the other two, so we will leave them to her since she arrived late enough to miss all the fun."

Rorax eyed the woman Crax had tied to a chair in the middle of the room. This woman had been the officer leading the paltry defense of the stronghold and was now bound loosely to the chair by her wrists and ankles. There was no way she could escape with all five of them standing there, so the bindings were more of a way to keep her upright while Crax interrogated her.

Crax, a pale woman with short-cropped blonde hair and a set of armor in House of Weather's royal blue with yellow lightning sigil on the front, turned back to the officer, gripped the back of the woman's head, and ripped it back viciously. "Talk. Now. Is your queen trying to open the Pits?"

The officer said nothing as her chest heaved in short puffs of breath, her eyes wide and terrified.

Crax let out a little sigh and took a small knife out of a sheath on her belt. "The tip if you would, Volla?"

Even though Rorax knew Volla was exhausted, Volla followed orders, focusing on Crax's knife until the sharp end of the short blade was red-hot, like a live coal. Crax turned and pressed it firmly into the officer's cheek, causing her to scream in agony.

Crax giggled at the sound, like a happy little girl playing with her favorite toy.

Volla and Rorax shared a wary look. They had worked with Captain Crax before, and every time they did, she proved to be bloodthirsty and crueler than before. King of House Weather, Zhang Valk, was a good and kind king, one of the steadiest and most competent kings in the Realms, and one of House of Ice's greatest allies. It surprised Rorax that he trusted Crax enough to represent him and act for House of Weather here.

Next to them, Jia stiffened and went slightly pale as the smell of burned hair and skin permeated the air. After working for nearly fifty years with Volla, one of the most powerful wielders of Fire Magick in the Realms, the smell of burning flesh barely registered to Rorax anymore.

Most people born and bred in House of Ice were familiar with war, including all its smells and the grotesque imagery of death and monsters, but Jia was the top general's daughter in the House of Ice and had been born with a certain amount of privilege that the rest of them had not. Compared to some of their missions, the death toll on this one could be considered tame; Rorax was nearly desensitized to this, and Jia would shortly be too.

Rorax studied Jia as her fellow Heilstorm watched Crax continue her administrations. Jia had long, dark purple hair she had pulled into a tight ponytail, striking phoenix eyes, and normally clean olive skin tone that was currently covered in the same sweat, grime, and blood that the rest of them wore.

Crax pressed the hot blade to a new section of the officer's skin, and the woman shrieked. "YES! Yes, there are rumors she is opening the Pits! Rumors!"

Crax smiled again. "Now we are getting somewhere."

Sahana sighed and turned to Volla and Rorax. "We're going back home tonight. Jia and I will finish up here. Go back to camp and start packing up, both of you."

"Thank the gods," Volla said with a sigh.

Rorax gave one last hesitant look at Crax, who was circling the bound woman like a shark smelling blood in the water. Did she want to leave Sahana and Jia behind with her? Her thoughts must have been written all over her face.

"Rorax," Sahana urged. "We will meet you back at camp."

Rorax nodded and turned around to follow Volla out of the room.

In the corridor, there were a handful of men and women on the rack, waiting to be interrogated. As they left the room, one of the men in chains wheezed for breath while the other struggled violently against his shackles. "You are a monster!" the man snarled, spitting in the dirt at Rorax's boots, yanking his body fruitlessly against his constraints. "In the eyes of the Lyondreans! In the eyes of the gods! You're all monsters!"

Volla wisely ignored the man and continued down the hall, but Rorax gripped the man's face gently, tipping his chin to the side so he was forced to see her easy grin. "I might be your villain, but don't forget that Lyondrea started this when they started opening the Pits and sending their soldiers over the border to kill the Realm's civilians."

The man didn't register Rorax's words as his rage splintered into fear when he stared up at Rorax, his terror plain to see even as he started to tremble under her fingertips. "I... I know you. Spine Cleaver."

"Let's go, Grumpy!" Volla called over her shoulder as she continued to make her way toward the main gate. "And don't play with your food, or you'll never get rid of your shitty reputation."

Rorax gave the shaking man a saccharine smile before slipping away and following Sahana's second-in-command toward the front gates. Crax's men eyed Volla and Rorax with raised eyebrows but kept their mouths firmly shut as they walked out of the front gates and into the woods.

They were silent for a while before Volla sighed. "Ror, what's your opinion of Jia?"

Rorax snorted. "I think it's a little late for that."

"What do you mean?"

"You're asking for my approval after I had to shove grass in my ears in an attempt not to hear you fuck her while I was on watch last night." Rorax's voice was flat, but a little smirk kicked up the corner of her mouth. "If you were that worried about me approving, you should have covered her mouth."

Volla chuckled.

The sun was starting to set, casting a brilliant orange light across the sky and creating a peaceful glow in the forest of pines. Happiness and relief bloomed through Rorax's chest as she breathed in the crisp air. They had been coordinating out of a cave for the past month, and while the weather had been warm enough that the camping wasn't awful, the thought of sleeping in her own bed made Rorax want to moan with pleasure. She held a branch out of Volla's way, and Volla ducked underneath.

"General Frostguard and Ye-Jun can't know. They'll separate us."

General Frostguard and Ye-Jun, Jia's mother and brother, would undoubtedly force Jia into another Heilstorm unit if they found out about them being romantically linked. The general had been reluctant to let her only daughter join the Heilstorms in the first place, but Sahana had convinced her. If the general knew that Jia had the ultimate distraction in the very same unit where she was posted, she would be furious.

Rorax looked over her shoulder at Volla with a raised eyebrow. Her friend was usually stoic and unflappable, especially in battle, but right now she sounded nervous and uncertain. "How serious is it between you two?"

Volla blew out a breath while rubbing at the dirty skin on her neck under her blonde ponytail. "Don't tell her... but I... I think I'm in love."

She couldn't help it. Rorax threw back her head and laughed.

Volla shoved her to keep her walking. "Shut up."

Rorax stumbled forward, still chuckling and wiping a tear from her eye. "You're in love?"

Volla was a rake, famously promiscuous with all the women in the Realms. For her to fall in love was quite a thing.

"Yes. Don't tell anyone, Grumpy, especially not Ye-Jun," Volla said. The serious note in her tone made Rorax look at her again with another raised eyebrow.

"Fine." Hopefully Jia would last longer than Volla's other flings.

"I'm hungry," Volla said in an obvious attempt to change the subject.

Rorax looked back in front of her at the trail and let her redirect the conversation. For now. "Food can wait, I think. I just want a real bed."

"Are you going to spend your first night home in your bed or Ye-Jun's?" Volla asked. Ror could hear Volla's smirk as she pushed through a clump of ferns.

Rorax wrinkled her nose. She hadn't slept with Ye-Jun in years. "You know I'm—"

The earth started to tremble and shake beneath their feet.

Volla swore behind her as Rorax swayed, tripping, then catching herself on a nearby pine tree.

"What the fuck is going on?" Volla bellowed before a wall, an invisible force-field of energy, slammed into them with so much force they both were knocked off their feet and thrown backward into the air.

Rorax's body was thrust into a tree. Needles and branches scraped and cut her skin before she slammed onto the ground so hard the world snapped away.

Rorax's own scream of agony jolted her out of unconsciousness before she could clamp her mouth shut.

Her neck was on fire; someone must have been branding her or taking pliers and plucking out the nerves on the back of her neck one by one.

She clamped her hand around the back of her spine to feel, but there was nothing but hot, smooth skin there. No one was torturing her.

Rorax let out a silent scream into the dirt before she gritted her teeth. The pain was so blindingly hot, the only thing she could do was writhe, taking fistfuls of soil and unclenching and clenching them so tightly she could have been condensing the soil into rocks.

She didn't dare unclench her jaw, because if she did, she would scream in anguish, and she couldn't reveal her position. They were under attack. Weren't they?

Rorax silently listened for any movement in the forest, but she couldn't hear anything except for a few chirping birds. She couldn't think of a single soul who had the power to throw her twenty feet into the air like that, let alone cause her this much pain.

"VOLLA! RORAX?" a familiar voice called out, and when she realized it was Sahana calling her name, a relieved, dry sob ripped out from between her teeth.

"Here," Rorax managed to rasp out, but it was nothing more than a dry whisper. She swallowed hard, ignoring the sharp flash of pain that raced down the back of her neck, and tried again. "Here!"

It wasn't much louder, but before she knew it, Volla was sliding down onto her knees next to Rorax's side. "Rorax, gods, Rorax. Are you okay? Can you hear me?"

All Rorax could manage was a small nod.

"Sahana, Jia, she's here!" Volla called over her shoulder before turning back to Rorax's body to check for injuries.

Rorax only had a few cuts and bruises. She could feel where the scrapes in her back were, but the only thing that was causing her pain was her neck. She whimpered in anguish.

"Fuck, I've never heard you make that sound before, Ror." Volla's hands fluttered uselessly over Rorax's body, her eyes wide in fear. "What's wrong, Rorax? Talk to me."

Jia and Sahana came crashing through the foliage. Volla's head snapped up to Sahana. "What the hell just happened?"

"My neck," Rorax wheezed.

Sahana crouched down next to Volla. Her usually warm brown skin went ashen, and her hands started trembling as she brushed the locks of long black hair away from Rorax's neck.

Through Rorax's pain, a deep sense of foreboding and fear took root in her chest.

She had never seen Sahana look like this before, shaken and scared.

"What's going on, Sahana?" Volla growled, curling her lips over her teeth.

"She's been Marked," Sahana breathed, her shaky voice barely audible. "Rorax, you've been Marked for the Choosing."

CHAPTER 2

RORAX

Six Months Later - in the fifth month of 10,082 A.R.

"That's a kill, Spine Cleaver."

Rorax opened her eyes to find a long blade pressed against her throat. She grunted as her eyes followed the cutting edge up to the face of a familiar, grinning idiot. "Even though you cheat, Volla, I'm still beating you seventeen to eight."

"No," Volla huffed as she sheathed her sword. "We don't officially start counting until we leave the country."

"We started counting the minute we passed the borders of Koppar. Sahana has the official rules we wrote in her bag; go ask her," Rorax said smugly, closing her eyes again. "Now, go away. I want a few more hours of sleep."

"Nope, it's time to get up, Grumpy."

Something grimy and heavy tapped lightly on Rorax's forehead.

"Tell me you didn't just put the bottom of your nasty shoe on my face." Rorax's lips curled over her teeth, and she peeled one eye open again to glare. "What the fuck do you want?"

They were scheduled to have a free day today to gather anything they needed in Sahloo before they crossed the Lyondrean border again tomorrow morning. A free day meant more sleep, and Rorax wanted as much as she could get before she went back to sleeping on the forest floor in Lyondrea.

Volla grinned unapologetically down at Rorax, her curly blonde hair draping down around her face. "Come on, Grumpy, didn't you miss me?"

"Not at all."

"Liar."

Rorax rolled her eyes, pulling her sleeping bag up closer to her chin. "You've only been gone for two days."

"More than enough time to miss me, Spine Cleaver." Volla winked and plopped down on the empty bed behind Rorax, her weapons and armor clinking softly. Volla carried both a longsword and a shortsword with her everywhere.

Rorax had opted for the floor, suspecting there were bugs in the mattress, but since Volla had just pressed her nasty, probably shit-covered boot against her face, Rorax kept her mouth shut about the bugs. In fact, Rorax hoped they bit Volla in the ass.

"Did you get him?" Rorax mumbled, scrubbing her hands over her face as Volla unstrapped her weapons from her back.

Volla and Jia had left two days ago to assassinate a wayward officer in the House of Alloy's army. He had been a low-level officer, and it was a task that was usually below their unit's scope, but they had been the closest in the area and Sahana had volunteered, sending Jia and Volla to give them a chance to be alone for a few days before the unit left on their new mission.

Volla grinned. "Oh yeah. He had a lot to say, too. Jia threatened to shove a shard of ice up his ass, and he gave us everything."

"Congratulations," Rorax mumbled, rolling onto her side and giving Volla her back. "I'll see you in a few hours."

Volla jabbed her boot into Rorax's spine, and Rorax lifted her middle finger over her shoulder.

"Here, I brought you something. There's a little passage about you in here," Volla said. Rorax peeked over her shoulder to see Volla waving around a rolled-up newspaper.

Rorax rolled her eyes. "Just read it to me."

"It's one of the rankings the *Valitlinn Press* does every year." Volla cleared her throat. "'*Ranked at number three on our list of 'The Realms' Most Deadly Warriors' we have listed, the Spine Cleaver. Nothing is known about this elusive warrior other than she took part in the Siege of Surmalinn, has white eyes, and decapitates her victims. She is a known affiliate of the Heilstorms and has over 120 confirmed solo kills this last year alone.*' Damn... that's the third article about you this month. Kiniera is going to be furious." Rorax could hear the smile in Volla's voice. "It's good you finally paid Merosa to fix your rune. Blue is more your color anyway; the white is creepy."

Rorax reached up and absentmindedly brushed her finger over the rune that had been tattooed on the back of her ear. She had it repaired after their last mission in Lyondrea a few moons past. This particular rune shifted the color of her eyes from white to make them appear light blue, and it had cost her a fortune to get it fixed.

"Who else is on the list?" Rorax asked, tucking her hand back into the warmth of her sleeping roll.

Volla hummed. "Sahana was ranked number one, again. And a random man I haven't heard of from the House of Death was ranked number two."

"Did they say anything about their beloved Torch in there?"

Volla pursed her lips and looked the paper over. "No, I'm not even in the Deadliest Warrior rankings, which is horseshit since I could kill you with my eyes closed and my hands tied behind my back. Oh wait, here is something. They said some people hoped to see me in the Tournament of Houses again this year, but some people are calling for 'new blood' and they hope to see someone fresh win it."

She scoffed, set the paper down on Rorax's abandoned bed, and nudged Rorax's back with her boot again.

"Come on, Grumpy." Volla laughed. "I'm serious, get up. I need your help today. But before we go . . . I need to ask you a question."

Rorax groaned from her bag, burrowing in deeper. "What?"

"Will you be my maid of honor tonight?"

Rorax jerked her head around to gape at the blonde so fast her neck twinged. "What?"

Volla grinned. "I asked you to be my maid of honor at my wedding tonight. Karan is going to officiate, and Jia wanted to ask Sahana to be her maid of honor, which leaves you for me."

Rorax's eyes widened as they traced over Volla's face, looking for a lie, but she didn't find one.

Volla had asked her before if Rorax would be her maid of honor when the day came. The answer had always been the same—*of course.* But now the answer meant more than ever.

"No, sorry." Rorax grinned up at the deep scowl on her best friend's face. "I have plans. I'm actually *very* in demand for maid of honor. I've already been booked—" Volla kicked her again, and Rorax grunted on impact. "Fine, *fine.* I'll do it."

Volla rolled her eyes, but there was a little smile threatening the corner of her mouth as she stood up. "Come on, we need to go find the right mushrooms for the marriage draught. Sahana is going to take Jia to find a dress before she gets home, so we need to find them all before she gets back."

Rorax was up in a flash, lifting herself out of her sleeping roll, pulling on her black training leathers, and attaching Glimr's sheath to her lower back before quickly lacing her boots.

Volla threw Rorax a heavy cloak that she found draped over Rorax's travel pack sitting at the foot of the bed. "You're going to need that; it's cold and rainy out still."

"I probably wouldn't need it if we weren't going out at the ass crack of dawn," Rorax grumbled as she fastened the dark cloak under her chin.

"What we do for love." Volla sighed, pushing her way out of the small room, Rorax on her heels.

Jia was lounging in the kitchen, slurping at a bowl of milk and square shredded wheat cubes. Her dark purple hair was the color of rich grape juice, her phoenix eyes matching in the dark purple color. Her deeply tanned skin seemed to glow, even though it was an unholy hour of the morning and she'd probably only gotten an hour or two of sleep.

Volla bent down to kiss Jia on the cheek as she swept past, and Jia beamed up at her. Rorax grabbed some dried jerky and apricots off the counter to eat for breakfast and gently tugged Jia's long purple ponytail. "Congratulations."

Jia turned her starry eyes to Rorax as Rorax followed Volla to the door. "Did you say yes, then?"

"Of course she said yes. Rorax values her life too much to say no." Volla huffed, pausing at the threshold of the open door, twisting her long blonde strands of hair into a ponytail at the top of her head. "How many draught mushrooms do we need to find?"

"Twenty. Ten for you, and ten for me."

"I'll see you at sunset then, *Wife.*" Volla winked at Jia and stepped out into the still-dark morning.

Rorax closed the door behind them, chuckling at the ferocious red that bloomed over Jia's cheeks.

It was raining buckets in Sahloo, the capital city of the House of Weather. This was their second and, thankfully, last night their unit was staying here. Tomorrow morning, they would be moving on, back to Lyondrea.

Rorax smiled up at the sky as water dripped down her face. The magick House of Weather was, predictably, all weather-related. If Rorax had the power to manipulate the weather, it might always be raining where she lived, too.

Volla nudged Rorax as they moved along the sidewalk and pointed at something across the street. "I need to learn how to do that with fire."

Rorax squinted her eyes to see what Volla was talking about. Across the street was a man holding his hands a foot apart, cupping a ball of lighting between them.

But it wasn't just a *ball,* no he was twisting lightning around, the energy crackling in the shape of a baby rabbit. A group of little kids were gathered around the man, clapping and cooing in pleasure as the rabbit hopped in his hands.

"Oh," Rorax hummed, "adorable."

The Realms was the center of magick. All magick branched out from the center city, Valitlinn, so magick was common in the Realms. However, usually only a small amount was held by average civilians, like this man with his small baby rabbit. Anyone who held more magick in them was usually promoted to house armies or more powerful offices. Though, Rorax had to admit the number of hours of practice it would have taken this man to hone the skill necessary to create a rabbit out of lightning was impressive.

"That should be my new party trick," Volla said, tightening her hood around her face against the rain as they watched the lightning rabbit puff out of existence, the man sweaty and pale, but still bowing slightly at the children's enthusiastic applause. Where the man had held only enough magick to keep the rabbit for a few minutes, Volla held enough magick to have it for hours.

"Your *new* party trick? You don't have a party trick."

"Yes, I do," Volla said with an indignant huff.

"Roasting the eyebrows off anyone who flirts with Jia does not count as a party trick," Rorax mumbled as they continued down the streets of Sahloo toward the market street.

Despite the rain, the market was busy this morning. Volla and Rorax had to squeeze in between people, pushing from stall to stall to find what they needed. Rorax bought some more dried fruit and a bar of oat soap she was going to bring with her to Lyondrea. Volla picked up some new bowstrings as a wedding gift for Jia, some food for dinner, and most of the marriage draught ingredients.

As they continued to shop for other various odds and ends, none of the vendors bothered to look under their hoods. Most everyone out today wore some kind of cloak to protect them from the rain, and Volla and Rorax's accents were so well done the vendors treated them as House Weather natives anyway. The few that saw through their accents only ever gave them quick, furtive looks, knowing better than to ask any questions.

The vendor selling the marriage draught mushrooms only had fifteen mushrooms out of the twenty Volla needed. Volla grimaced at Rorax as she shoved the mushrooms into a small linen bag and tucked them safely in her cloak pocket. "I'm glad you decided to come. Looks like we'll be making a trip to the underground market after all. I hope Angelo is there; he's been saying how excited he is to see you in all his letters."

Rorax rolled her eyes, pulling her cloak tighter around her body. "That charismatic little troll is excited to see everyone."

Volla and Rorax made their way down to the familiar dark tunnels underneath the city. To access it, they had to go through a grimy, dilapidated bar and pay a few silver coins to the beefy guard at the door. He grunted as he counted Volla's coins in his palm before bending and opening the hatch down to the tunnels that led to the Underground Market.

Rorax went first, carefully stepping down the rungs of the moss-covered ladder before Volla followed. Instead of using one of the torches lined along the wall for customers to use on their descent into the market, Volla lifted her hand and a small fireball appeared out of thin air, cupped in her palm. The ball of fire illuminated the damp, mossy hall, and Volla took the lead to guide them down.

Once they were well away from the trapdoor of the bar and about halfway to the market, Rorax asked, "Who's all coming tonight? Did either of you invite your families?"

Volla released a deep sigh as she continued to trudge down the deserted hallway. "No. There wasn't time. And the last time I wrote to my family, none of them bothered to answer. Not even my older brother. Both my parents and my sisters are still angry with me, and they wouldn't have come if I asked anyway. We didn't tell Ye-Jun because, if Jia's mother found out about us, she would pull her daughter out of the unit and force us to abandon the mission faster than we could say 'fire.'" Volla looked over her shoulder and gave Rorax a lewd grin. "Maybe we should have invited Ye-Jun, though. Just for you. A good lay would do *wonders* for your temperament, Grumpy."

Rorax huffed but was thankful Volla's little flame wasn't giving off enough light to show off her pink cheeks.

They stopped talking as the damp air started carrying the smells of incense and burning resin. The smells grew stronger as they got closer to the market.

When Rorax and Volla finally entered the room, Rorax had to hide her smile. It always felt strangely like home down here.

A large underground dome made from weathered and mossy bricks constituted the roof of a very large, circular room that housed the underground market of Sahloo.

The market, with all its rickety stalls and worn-down torches, housed sellers of various trinkets, potions, services, and weapons that were illegal or frowned upon by average society. Anything you couldn't find in the open-air market above could be found down here—for an exorbitant price, of course.

Almost every major city in the Realms had an underground market. Sahloo's was one of the smallest markets in the country, seeing as most of the residents here didn't really need anything they could not find above ground.

As Rorax looked around, she recognized almost every single person there from past visits to the market, which meant they knew exactly who she and Volla were—or at least who Volla was. Anyone who had any magick at all could feel the power nearly bursting from Volla.

Shifty-looking sellers and buyers gave Rorax and Volla wary glances as they slid around them. Volla ignored them, focused only on a shop located on the southern side of the room. Rorax followed her closely and couldn't help but run her fingers over the top of her fighting leathers on her neck, thankfully finding the dark fabric was still covering the base of her neck all the way up to her hairline.

Volla bought the remaining mushrooms she needed for the draught and laid them out on her palm, counting them one more time. "That makes twenty. Come on. Let's go before Angelo spots us. I will send him an official invitation once we're above ground—Kään save me. Rorax, is that a felidra?"

Volla pointed over Rorax's shoulder, and Rorax whipped around. In one of the stalls behind her, a merchant selling maps and rare pearls had what looked like a panther cub perched on the table next to him.

Two brilliantly colored wings poked up over the shoulders of the black cub; they were folded close to the cub's back, but the vibrant colors were unmistakable, causing a sharp trill of fear that rocketed down Rorax's spine.

"That man must have a fucking death wish," Rorax muttered. "That thing has another six weeks before it'll rip his throat out."

Movement out of the corner of her eye caught her attention, and she turned to see a short man moving toward them with angry, fast steps, all but throwing members of the crowd out of his path. His curly hair on the top of his head bobbed, his waist-long beard swayed back and forth, and his cheeks were ruddy and pink with anger. Volla didn't need to send an invitation to Angelo; she was going to have her opportunity to do it right now.

A lazy smile crept across Rorax's face. This was going to be fun.

"Vol-la Tor-vik!" yelled the short, stout man, drawing out Volla's name into four syllables.

His hands, clenched into fists, flew to his hips as he glared from the mushrooms laid out in Volla's outstretched palm into her guilty face. "Those better not be *marriage draught* mushrooms for *you know who!"* he bellowed, and not for the first time, Rorax was amazed such a small body could produce so much volume.

Angelo, King of the Underground and one of Volla and Rorax's oldest friends, looked like steam was about to start billowing out of his ears.

"Angelo...." Volla bit her lip, looking to Rorax for help.

Rorax ignored her friend's plea, her smile stretching from ear to ear. "They are, and they're for exactly the person you think they're for, too."

Angelo's face went red as he spluttered angry, incoherent words before turning and motioning for the women to follow him.

Volla shot Rorax a betrayed glare, and it was all Rorax could do not to cackle.

Rorax could just *barely* make out Angelo's angry muttering—something about inconsiderate, ungrateful House of Ice boneheads—as they trailed him into his office, just around the corner from the stall selling mushrooms on the south end of the dome.

Angelo's office was surprisingly neat. There was nothing in it but a large desk, two chairs situated in front of it, and the large underground market sigil—two green king cobras with a white diamond between them—painted on the wall behind the desk. Even his desktop was clean of everything but a few pencils.

Of course, this wasn't Angelo's main hub of operations. He was usually stationed in the Realms' capital, Valitlinn, and was probably here in Sahloo only once every six months.

Rorax sat down in one of the two chairs and finally let loose her grin, leaning back into her chair as Volla shoved the newly purchased mushrooms into the small linen bag.

"Angelo, I didn't think you'd be in town. It's *Sahloo* for gods' sake, you hate it here. And besides, I asked her to marry me only *yesterday*," Volla pleaded, pulling the strings tight and tucking the bag back in her pocket.

Angelo tucked his small body into his chair opposite Rorax and Volla and narrowed his eyes into angry little slits. "You didn't think to send a message through the underground? Or think that Sahana wouldn't have wanted one more information briefing with me and Kiniera before you lot left to Lyondrea for *months*?"

He had a point.

"Well, who's officiating the wedding? Sahana? *You*?" Angelo huffed, pointing a short, accusing finger at Rorax.

Rorax put her hands up in surrender. "Not me. Karan apparently." Her smug grin stretched into a smile as Angelo threw his hands up in exasperation.

"Karan can eat limp lettuce and a sock," Angelo harrumphed. "Two hundred years of friendship with the Torch just went down the drain. She doesn't even invite me to her *wedding*. Her weddin' to my *niece* no less!"

Rorax snorted at the word *niece*. Jia and Angelo were one hundred and ten percent not related.

Volla rolled her eyes. "Jia and I just got back from a mission. You can count this visit as me coming to invite you almost as soon as I could."

Angelo glared. Gods above, Angelo was so *dramatic*, and Rorax loved it.

"Angelo," Rorax croaked, trying her best to hold in her laughter, "they are getting married on our rooftop at sunset. Be there and you can arm wrestle Karan for officiating duties."

"Perfect!" Volla beamed as Angelo's scowl deepened.

He gave them both withering looks, eyeing them back and forth from under his bushy black eyebrows for nearly a whole minute before a little smile cracked over his mouth. "Alright, little lass, I forgive you. Now get yer ass over here!"

Volla unfolded her tall frame from her chair and bent down to give Angelo a hug. Volla was a few inches over six feet tall, and Angelo barely scraped five feet, making the small man appear even smaller as Volla embraced him.

Angelo patted the back of her golden head with his light brown hand. "My Torch is getting married. It's a miracle. Never in my days would I have thought you could ever convince that woman, or any woman for that matter, to say yes."

Volla pulled back to beam down at him, her pride showing through her eyes. "*She* had to beg *me*."

"That's my Torch. Always so humble." Angelo patted her cheek, beaming up at Volla before turning his gaze over to Rorax, a mischievous glint in his eyes. "If I'm bein' honest with ya, a small part of me thought the mushrooms were for you and the new Ice King!"

Rorax's eyes bugged out, and Volla burst out laughing.

"I've tried to tell her, but she's convinced that Raengar would only marry her in her dreams, Angelo," Volla said, wiping a tear from her eye.

Rorax searched her brain for a change of subject and settled on the small cub with butterfly wings they had spotted a few minutes ago in the stalls. "Angelo, did that man out there have a... *felidra cub* on his table?"

Angelo gave her a knowing look before his face darkened. "It is. Apparently, it has a rune from a Life Witch on it that keeps it young and never lets it grow. Tis not the first cub to 've shown up in the underground market in the last few months either. There is a rumor that if you see a felidra when it first hatches, you can soul bond to it. Horseshit if yer askin' me."

"One tiny scratch and that rune will break, and that man becomes second breakfast," Rorax said. "Seems like quite the risk."

Angelo nodded, his eyes still dark as he bent down and opened one of his drawers, pulling out a paper and tossing it on his desk in front of Rorax. "Speaking of runes, I read the paper today. Congratulations on your ranking, *Spine Cleaver*."

Rorax reluctantly grabbed the paper off the desk, reading over the words that Volla had read to her this morning.

Ranked at number three, we have listed: the Spine Cleaver.

"I know you said you have a meeting with Sahana later, but do you have any juicy gossip for us now?" Volla asked.

Angelo pursed his lips and ran his hand slowly over his beard. "With a possible war involving Lyondrea loomin' on the horizon, business has been busy. Don't tell Sahana, but the demand for Starsoot and Rathmore Venom has been through the roof, makin' me a rich man." A *richer* man, he meant. "But it's been mostly quiet in terms of gossip." Starsoot and Rathmore Venom were both drugs that were illegal under the Guardians' Law and only available through the underground market.

Volla's disappointment was palpable. "That's boring."

"Now, now, let me think here." Angelo tugged at the end of his beard in thought. "The Council of the Houses' vote on whether the King of Alloy is committin' treason and plottin' with Lyondrea has been scheduled for next month."

"Is there any word on if it's expected to pass?" Volla asked.

Angelo nodded. "Aye, it's *expected* to pass. King Märr has his claws in about half of 'em, but Kiniera and I have been workin' hard to undermine 'em, and we predict that we will squeak it through."

Rorax's lips curled. "Good."

"Märr is a reeking piss pot," Volla agreed.

"He is, but even if the vote passes through the Council, the trial won't be held until after the Choosin'."

The mention of the Choosing had Rorax's spine straightening. "Why not?"

Angelo shrugged, leaning back in his chair. "The Northern Guardian has deemed herself unfit to help preside over the trial until the Choosing is over. Complete horseshit if you ask me. We have two other Guardians that could preside just fine."

Rorax and Volla shared a look.

"Oh! Speakin' of the Choosing, the King and Queen of Ice put out a statement just last week saying every citizen is required to have their necks checked for the Contestar mark by a city official. They will be the last of the Realms to require such a thing, so hopefully the Contestar is found this time."

Volla stiffened almost imperceptibly. Rorax clamped down on the urge to reach her hand to the back of her neck and brush her fingers over the silver mark. She was forever grateful that Angelo's eyes were on her friend as she composed herself. "The sooner we find her, the sooner we can start the Tournament of Houses. I have been looking forward to this Tournament for *years*; it's been *too* long."

To her credit, Volla didn't look too troubled as she groaned, "It better not happen while we're in Lyondrea. I have a title to defend."

"See, I'm mighty thankful you'll be gone! It'll make the betting *much* more lucrative," Angelo chuckled, giving Volla a wink. "Now, you two wait here! I have to find you a weddin' gift!"

Surprisingly agile, Angelo pushed out of his giant chair and went running out of his office.

As soon as he was out of the room, Volla turned to glare at Rorax, who just gave her an innocent smile. "Thanks for your help back there. On *your* wedding day, I'm going to tell him you want him to bring the goblins."

The smile dropped off Rorax's face. "You wouldn't."

Angelo had a pair of slobbering goblin pets he kept at his house that he liked to bring with him *everywhere,* even though they smelled like death and looked like it, too.

Volla gave her a smug grin that softened into a happy smile as she leaned back in her chair. "Despite him being the most dramatic soul in the Realms, I'm glad he's coming tonight."

Rorax snorted and stretched her legs out in front of her. "You're mooning, Torvik."

Volla shrugged. "I'm excited. I asked her this morning because I wanted to have one night to be... distracted. One night to be together before we cross the border again into Lyondrea."

The smile on Volla's face faded, and Rorax kept her own face solemn even as an excited bubble rose in her chest.

Lyondrea.

They were finally going back to Lyondrea, to not only spend time in the capital city but also the countryside.

She was finally going to be back inside the country that had kidnapped and continually held her brother captive for over a hundred years. Hopefully she would find a clue about him this time. A scrap of information, a whisper, *anything*.

Rorax rubbed her thumb over her ring.

Volla caught the movement and raised an eyebrow. "Tell me." Those big green eyes never missed anything. It was annoying.

Rorax sighed, leaning back even farther into her chair. "I'm actually eager to get out to Lyondrea again."

"To start looking for Darras, I suppose." Volla's face darkened. She reached out to pluck one of the pencils from Angelo's desk and started rolling it between her fingers. "This is the first mission I... the first mission I ever thought about saying no to. It makes me sick knowing Jia will be there, beyond enemy lines, but I know that even if I did say no, she would still go. Even if I refused and defected, she would go without me. After Ye-Jun and Kiniera's latest report, Jia didn't sleep for almost two weeks."

Volla's face went pale, and Rorax could have sworn the pencil Volla was twirling in her fingers started to smoke.

"Those monsters Lyondrea might be breeding? They would be bred for only one thing. To kill, break, and destroy the Realms."

The rumors of the Pits had become serious enough that the Council of Houses, made up of the kings and queens of the Realms as well as all three Guardians, had demanded that House of Ice give them control of the Heilstorms. Within that same week, the Heilstorms had their orders; Unit One was to infiltrate Lyondrea's capital city, Allteria, and find out where the breeding pits were located for the monsters. The second, third, and fourth units' orders were to focus on helping with the border skirmishes that had intensified over the last few months and find information on the movements and plans of the Lyondrea army while offering support where and when Unit One needed it.

Volla and Rorax sat in heavy silence for a long time before Volla tossed the half-burned pencil back onto Angelo's desk and stood up. "Come on, let's go find Angelo. I don't want my wife to divorce me before I even get her to say 'I do'."

CHAPTER 3

RORAX

Volla and Jia's wedding was going to be magickal... or as magickal as they could make it with only eight hours to prepare.

Rorax spent the rest of day picking flowers—mostly daisies and dandelions—on the edge of Sahloo to make bouquets, and she helped Sahana cook the small feast they were going to eat before the ceremony began.

When it was time to eat, the guests slowly started to arrive.

Karan, Sahana's handsome mate, arrived first. After kissing Sahana a sound hello, he moved to kiss both Jia and Volla on the cheek, offering his congratulations.

Angelo arrived in a flurry, as usual, marching right over to Karan without saying hello to any of the rest of them first.

"I am officiatin' this wedding, or I'll give ya both fleas the next time you come down to the market." Angelo pointed his finger threateningly at Sahana and Karan in turn.

Sahana snickered, and Karan good-naturedly put his hands up in defeat. "If you officiate, I'll walk them down the aisle," Karan offered.

"That's a deal." Angelo finally turned his grin to the rest of the room, straightening his tunic and looking over the modest spread of foods they had put on the table. "It smells divine in here! Let's eat!"

"Go get them please, Karan. We are ready to start." Sahana placed the last flower into the wooden arch they had erected and decorated. "Angelo, come here."

Karan, his usual chin-length black hair pinned up in a small bun on the top of his head, grinned at Rorax with excitement before he disappeared behind the door to the rooftop.

"Yes, ma'am," Angelo said, straightening his tunic and smoothing a hand over his meticulously groomed long black beard as he situated himself in the center under the colorful arch. He had been the only one of them, besides the brides, that had been able to really dress up for the occasion. Rorax, Sahana, and Karan were all dressed in various shades of black leather armor.

A soft, cool breeze brushed across Rorax's cheeks. It smelled like the rain from earlier that afternoon. The angry blue and black storm clouds were still on the horizon, but they were now illuminated by the sunset, coloring the clouds a deep orange and purple.

"Mark my words, this will be you next! To the King of Ice, no less!" Angelo informed Rorax, like this was an undeniable fact, as she took her position on his left side. The King and Queen of Ice, Raengar and Isolde, were brother and sister and ruled the House of Ice together. In the years before Raengar and Isolde had taken the House of Ice throne from their father, they had always been close with Rorax. Very close. But the king had always looked at Rorax like another friend, not the way she ached for him to look at her.

"Definitely not." Rorax laughed at Angelo and shook her head. "Crazy old troll," she teased sadly as her longing made her heart palpitate inside her chest.

Angelo gave her a big, sassy wink. "I'm never wrong about these things, lass. Just promise me you'll get married somewhere warm. Koppar makes the snot freeze in my beard."

Sahana and Rorax shared a horrified glance.

The roof where they were holding the ceremony was on a tall apartment building that had been picked out and funded for them by the King and Queen of Weather. It overlooked Sahloo, so they could see the sunset bathing the river and the white stucco city in warm oranges and purples.

Sahana filled in on the opposite side of the flower-covered arch as Rorax hummed in happiness.

"These are so beautiful," Sahana murmured, her brown eyes soft as she took in the flower arch that she and Rorax had decorated together.

Jia, Karan, and Volla finally emerged. Standing in the middle, the beaming women looped on each arm, Karan slowly led them toward the arch and their awaiting friends.

They had found almost-matching silver dresses for Jia and Volla to wear tonight. Jia's purple locks were done in long, intricate war braids, and Volla had opted to pull her unruly blonde curls into a messy bun atop her head.

When they got close, Volla stepped in front of Rorax with a wink, and Jia floated in front of Sahana. Karan fell in line behind his mate.

Jia burst into quiet, happy sobs, and in turn Volla's tears dripped down her cheeks as she held her new wife's face in her hands. "I love you, Jia Frostguard. I love you more than the stars love the sky. More than you love the forest at dusk or the color black." Jia sniffled again. "And I love you more than Rorax loves her gods-damned knife."

Volla didn't look away from her wife's eyes but released her face with one hand to flip Rorax off over her shoulder.

A wet giggle burst from Jia, and Karan threw his head back, erupting with a deep belly laugh. Sahana had to clamp her hand over her mouth, bending over a bit to keep her laughter inside, and Rorax just smiled.

She did love her knife, Glimr, *a lot.*

Angelo held out a knife to Volla and Jia, and they sliced a shallow cut into their palms before they pressed their bloody wounds together. Angelo tied their wrists and fingers with a chord and had them say their vows before Sahana bound them together with an ancient incantation.

Rorax would always remember that evening—the deep, contented happiness she felt in the marrow of her bones, and the image of Volla's forehead pressed against Jia's as they were tangled in each other, right as the sun was descending with orange and red clouds setting fire across the sky.

Jia and Volla took their marriage draught together, gave everyone a hug, and disappeared downstairs.

Angelo gave Rorax a tight hug, his shaggy head pressing against her shoulder. "You be careful over there, Spine Cleaver." He tightened his arms around her waist before he reached up and patted her cheek with a warm hand. "Take care of them all, you hear me?"

Rorax nodded and gave Angelo's shoulders a tight squeeze. "I will."

Karan gave Sahana a deep kiss before he left, brushing his thumb over her cheek. "Make sure you write, love. I'll come after you if you don't."

Sahana swatted his side with a watery grin before she pulled him back into a hug. "You would never be able to find me."

Karan gave Rorax a faint smile over the top of Sahana's head, his eyes warm and thoughtful. "Take care of yourself over there, too, Grumpy."

As darkness fell on them, Karan and Angelo took their leave together.

Rorax and Sahana had decided to give Jia and Volla the apartment alone for an illusion of a one-night honeymoon, so they'd brought their sleeping things to the roof.

Sahana sighed contentedly as she snuggled into her sleeping bag next to Rorax and looked up into the stars.

Rorax was already settled next to her. A warm, gratified, happy feeling ballooned in her chest. The feeling wasn't entirely familiar to Rorax, but it had been happening a lot tonight, and she wanted to keep basking in it. "Tonight was perfect, I think."

Sahana hummed her agreement as she looked up into the stars. "If Karan and I were to renew our vows, I would want it just like that. No one else except the people I love and who love me. I wouldn't let Angelo preside over my wedding though. I would make him be my flower girl."

Rorax giggled as she imagined Angelo walking down the aisle with flowers entwined in his long black beard, pelting everyone with rose petals as he passed them.

Sahana smiled softly and rolled over onto her side to face Rorax. "This unit feels like a family. More than any of my other units that I've ever led before."

Family. The happy balloon in her chest seemed to pop as unwanted memories curled their black fingers into Rorax's heart. She swallowed thickly. "The Wolf used to say that we were a family."

Sahana scoffed loudly. "That dusty cunt wasn't part of your family, Rorax, no matter how many times she told you she was. You are no longer the Wolf's Pup. That name died with her."

The Wolf's Pup or simply *the Pup*, the nickname given to her as a child, a constant reminder of her shame and reckless faith. The name mocked her, reminded her of her failures and her irreparable dishonor.

"That name will never die." Something sour and ugly built in Rorax's chest, bubbling with resentment toward herself and the Wolf. She wiped her fingers down her sleeping bag like she could wipe away the blood that would forever be on her hands.

There was a long silence, and thankfully Sahana let the topic drop. "Will you ever report to the Choosing, Rorax?"

Rorax's back stiffened, and she suddenly wished there was somewhere she could slink away to avoid this conversation. "No."

From what little Rorax knew about the Choosing, it was all but a death sentence. Twelve people went in, and only one survived. She couldn't release herself from the Choosing without taking her life, so her plan was to keep running from it for as long as she could.

Sahana blew out a slow breath. "You would be an excellent Guardian, Ror. You're better suited for it than the Guardian we currently have in the north, and you would have a spot on the Trigonal Throne."

The Trigonal Throne.

The Realms was a country made up of twelve different houses. Each house was tied to one of the twelve main elemental strains of magick: air, fire, water, light, dark, ice, foliage, fauna, alloy, death, life, and ice.

The Trigonal Throne was in the center of the Realms, in the city of Valitlinn, a city ruled by Guardians. It was believed that magick originated in Valitlinn, so it was where the three Guardians of the Realms sat, the three most magickally powerful beings in the world.

The Northern Guardian, the Western Guardian, and the Eastern Guardian. The Northern Guardian was the one stepping down in the Choosing that Rorax had been marked for, so if Rorax won the Choosing, it would put her primarily in charge of the protection of Houses Life, Fire, Fauna, and Death; the very same Realm she had nearly burned to the ground under the Wolf's direction.

Sahana was wrong, anyone would be a better Northern Guardian than she'd be. Becoming the Guardian would also take her away from her home and from the loved ones she had left behind in Koppar.

"Think about it, Rorax." Sahana rolled over, burying herself deeper into her sleeping bag. "If we find out Lyondrea really is trying to open the Pits, I can't think of anyone better to lead us into war."

"What is your name?"

"Rorax Greywood?"

"What does that mean?"

"It means I am a warrior."

Rorax knew it was a dream, it was a dream she had often, but it didn't stop it from feeling real when the Wolf bent down to a seven-year-old Rorax and brushed the snow off her cheeks with warm, soft fingers. "Very good, my little Pup."

The soft voice of the Wolf—the woman who found her and pulled her off the streets of Koppar after Darras was kidnapped, her mother in almost every right, the one who had saved her and fed her—always comforted Rorax in her dreams.

The moment she opened her eyes, the guilt and conflict always made her grumpy, and this morning wasn't any different.

Rorax woke up before Sahana, when the dawn was just starting to brush the night away, the Wolf's voice still in her ears and the phantom touch of her warm fingers still on her cheeks.

But the Wolf was not her mother. The Wolf had used and manipulated Rorax to kill thousands of people. She couldn't forget that.

When her thoughts became too much, she got up and started to shove her things roughly into her pack. When she was done, she sat with her legs dangling off the side of the roof, twirling her knife, Glimr, in her fingers, and trying not to think about the Wolf.

"Another dream?" Sahana asked groggily from where she'd slept.

"Yes," Rorax clipped.

Sahana silently got up and padded to the spot next to her. "I'm sorry, Rorax. I shouldn't have brought her up."

Rorax didn't want to talk about it, so instead she rolled her gaze to the side and asked, "Want to spar?"

They ran two-person drills with their swords, Rorax admittedly swinging a touch too hard, until Volla and Jia finally emerged from the apartment below, pushing open the door to the roof.

Jia was beaming from ear to ear, her skin glowing and her hair up in a pristine ponytail. Volla, with running kohl under her eyes and her blonde hair frizzed out around her face, looked like she had just been pulled out of the gutter.

"Rough night?" Rorax snickered, her dark mood evaporating as she eyed the drool that was still dried up on Volla's chin.

"Nah." Volla threw her arm across Rorax's shoulders, her tall, burly frame leaning heavily down onto her as she winked at Jia. "Best night of my life. I'm pretty sure you could only dream of such a night, Grumpy."

"It better have been amazing for the price you're going to pay once you finally comb out your hair." Rorax eyed the frizzy tangle with a smirk. "You look worse than the homeless guy in Valitlinn who stands on the corner and rubs horse dung through his beard."

Jia laughed, her voice tinkling like silver bells, while Volla scowled.

"I'm going to gather all the hair I find in my ass this week and leave it on your toothbrush, Grumpy. See how you like that," Volla sneered playfully, before releasing Rorax and gathering her golden mess of curls on top of her head.

"Volla," Sahana admonished, rolling her eyes. "Keep your hair to yourself, please. Are you two ready to go?"

Volla and Jia nodded as one.

"Good. Jia, do you have room in your pack for this?" Sahana held out a small, leather wrapped bundle.

"Yes," Jia said, carefully taking the bundle from Sahana's palm. "What's in it?"

"Test vials. Vials to take blood samples and to collect things that might be... *unusual* while we're in Lyondrea. If the queen *isn't* trying to open the Pits, Kiniera thinks there might be large quantities of stagnant magick in Lyondrea that has soured and potentially spawned some unsavory creatures."

"That's just *great.* Pit monsters or stagnant magick monsters," Volla griped.

"That's why Lyondrea is a perfect spot for your new summer home," Rorax deadpanned to the blonde second-in-command. "At least your neighbors would look like you."

Volla snorted before she threw her head back and laughed. "Alright, that was a good one, Grumpy."

Jia tucked the pouch in the top of her pack, and Sahana gave them all a wicked grin. "It's time to take down a monster queen."

CHAPTER 4

RORAX

"You know, Rorax, if you did show up for the Choosing, I could come back with you to defend my title in the Tournament of Houses. I've been thinking about someone else taking my crown, it has me breaking out into hives," Volla muttered.

Rorax laughed. "I think it will be a good thing to humble you."

"This country is a gods-damned shithole," Volla griped as she pushed her way through a tall bush, breaking through the leaves and branches like a bull in a porcelain shop.

"I would rather babysit Angelo's twin goblins for a month than hang out here for *fun,*" Rorax grumbled as they continued to trudge, bushwhacking through the woods.

The Heilstorm's first unit was a lot of things.

Sahana Thorash, their leader, was legendary. She was bursting with Dark Magick and even had a select few Life Magick abilities—like minimal healing and being able to track energy signatures. She was the founder of the Heilstorms and one of the deadliest warriors in the whole House of Ice's army. Her mate and husband, Karan Thorash, had been one of the most notorious pirates in all Illus before he settled down with Sahana in Koppar.

Volla Torvik, aka the Torch, arguably held the most Fire Magick in the Realms. She was like a bomb and was famous in warrior circles for her three consecutive victories in the Tournament of Houses.

Jia Frostguard, the newest recruit to Unit One, held a decent amount of Ice Magick, could shoot the wings off a fly with her bow, and could rob a thief lord blind.

Rorax had no elemental magick like most of the Gifted in the Realms. What made Rorax so deadly was Glimr, a knife that was propelled and fueled by a different kind of magick; Rorax could control Glimr with her mind. Rorax could sever a man's spinal column a half mile away using Glimr. She'd left a trail of so many bodies, decapitated so many adversaries, that papers like *Valitlinn Press* and singers across Illus had dubbed her with the nickname the *Spine Cleaver.*

They were considered the best Heilstorm unit the House of Ice had ever seen. The most deadly, tactile, fluid team they'd had in years. So yes, they were a lot of things; each was deadly and perfect at the job they had been given.

What they did not do well, however, was suffer in silence, especially when they thought their complaining was hilarious.

"I swear to Kään, if I step in deer dung, I'm letting Volla burn the whole country down," Jia groaned, tiptoeing around a particularly large pile of round, juicy deer droppings.

There wasn't a direct road to the village where they were meeting their Lyondrean informant, so they were left to bushwhack through the countryside.

They'd left Sahloo four days ago and would hopefully be at the village by midday.

The House of Weather border patrol had split open the famous lightning wall that crackled endlessly over their Lyondrea border for them, promising not to shock them, and then the last few days, their unit had hiked on foot through the Blackwood at the base of the New Volcano. Blackwood forest used to be part of the Lynxwood, but it had been appropriately renamed after the New Volcano eruption from a time long before Rorax had been born. It had left this part of Lynxwood blackened and burnt. The woods had never returned to their previous state of lush vegetation, and the locals' nickname of the Blackwood became its official title.

After two days of marching through nothing but ash, blackened tree husks, and black dirt around the base of the New Volcano, they finally crossed from the Blackwood and back into the part of the Lynxwood forest that hadn't been burned in the eruption. The air in the Blackwood had been dry and a little smoky, but as they moved north into the Lynxwood toward the Mountain of the Red Queen, the air seemed to shift. The mist started gathering between the trees, a thick fog hovering in the air between the tall, white-barked aspen trees that littered the land here.

For hours and hours, they hiked through endless miles of mist and aspen. Each night Volla used her famous Fire Magick to cook their food, but they hadn't kept a fire going throughout the night to avoid any unwanted attention, so the mist had started to permeate through Rorax's very bones.

Sahana's mother was from the House of Life and had passed Sahana the ability to sense any forms of life around them. She kept a low-grade flow of magick going nearly all the time, keeping an eye out for any approaching soldiers, wolves, or the bloodthirsty lynxes that gave the Lynxwood its name.

The traveling hadn't been all that tough, but Rorax still groaned as she pushed a tree branch out of her face. Cold dew that had accumulated on the round aspen leaves fell on her scalp and down the back of her shirt, and she winced. As if feeling endlessly wet and soggy from all the mist wasn't enough.

"We're close now to the village where we're meeting our informant. Only a few more miles northwest," Sahana told them, looking down at the compass and up at the looming Mountain of the Red Queen.

"Thank the gods," Volla groaned.

"Lyondrea should invest some money into some gods-damned infrastructure," Rorax grumbled.

"Roads never hurt *anyone*," Volla agreed.

"It just feels so... *wrong here.*" Sahana looked around, putting her compass away to rub her hands up and down her arms. The fog had started to thicken around them, creeping up closer and making it hard to see through the trees.

"Is it always so ominous in these woods?" Jia asked.

"I would go to war too if I was stuck living with this fog." Volla pulled back a branch, letting them all pass in front of her, as they stepped from a thick line of aspens into a small clearing.

It wasn't even thirty feet across, but they only made it halfway through the small, treeless meadow when Sahana raised a fist. "Hold."

The unit froze in their tracks.

Sahana's dark eyes scanned in front of them, seeing something through the trees—probably energy signatures—that Rorax could not see.

Sahana widened her stance and pulled her katana out of its sheath. "Draw your weapons."

Rorax unsheathed her sword and rolled onto her toes, ready to move as her eyes stayed pinned on the curling mist in front of her.

Jia drew her bow from behind her, the sound of the tightening string letting Rorax know she had an arrow notched and ready.

"Three souls, moving this way quickly. Nonhuman. Unfamiliar. Large," Sahana murmured.

Volla stepped into Rorax's periphery, her longsword gripped tightly in her hands, a wreath of fire snaking around the intricate blade from hilt to tip.

There was a howl, and a huge body emerged from the mist, parting the fog as the dark beast lunged at them.

It was closest to Rorax, and she just barely rolled away as the creature snapped with long fangs at the air where her head had just been.

A wolf.

Or something wolflike. It was bigger than any of the common wolves they had back home. It was almost the same size as a gods-damned bear.

Jia released an arrow, and the arrow flew over Rorax's head and thudded hard against the wolf's fur before falling uselessly to the ground.

The impact barely caused the wolf to stumble before he was back on his haunches and leaping at his next nearest target, Sahana.

Twigs snapped behind Rorax again, and she turned in time to see two more forms burst through the mist, one coming straight for her.

Rorax sprinted toward them.

"Boost!" she shouted to Jia. A narrow pillar of ice formed from the ground, pushing up toward the sky under Rorax, rocketing her into the air. She flew over the wolves racing toward her, throwing Glimr down at one of them before landing on their opposite side, rolling into a crouch.

Rorax's knife had knocked a wolf to the ground.

The other wolf lunged at Volla, who stood ready for it, her sword raised and still wrapped in fire.

The wolf Rorax had thrown her knife at was on its side in the dirt, squirming and snarling, pinned under the weight Rorax applied with her knife.

Jia had run to the side of the wolf at the same time Rorax had, her bow strapped to her back in favor of two shortswords made of sharp ice.

Rorax scanned the trees and the mist around her for any more threats before focusing on the wolf.

The point of her short, intricately forged knife was pressed tip first against the animal beneath it, but there wasn't enough force to penetrate the wolf's flesh. The wolf struggled under the weight, flailing its limbs and snapping its jaws while Rorax kept it pinned down.

Jia looked over at her, confused. "What are you waiting for, Rorax? Kill it."

Rorax's brow furrowed together. She was already applying enough pressure to kill ten grown men standing back-to-back. Clearly this was no ordinary wolf; otherwise, its body would have succumbed by now. She increased the pressure, enough to kill nearly thirty men, then pushed it to forty men before the pain at the back of her head told her she was close to maxing out.

She couldn't do it. She focused, gritting her teeth, and pressing down until her head felt like it might split.

What in the hell was going on?

The wolf's ribs cracked under the pressure, and it yelled in pain as it reared up, trying to swivel its head to bite at Ror and Jia furiously. When it snapped its jaws up at her, Rorax got an idea.

"Ice its head down."

Without hesitation Jia did as she was told. With a fast wave of her fingers, Rorax snapped the knife from pressing the wolf into the ground and instead sent it rocketing through the wolf's mouth.

The knife exploded out of the back of the wolf's skull with so much force, blood and brain splattered against Jia and Ror's faces, but at last the wolf went still.

"Hey, quit dicking around over there!" Volla yelled, snapping Ror and Jia's attention around to see Volla battling her own wolf, sending blasts and whips of fire at the beast. The flames licked uselessly over the wolf's fur, not finding purchase or anything to burn within the hair. "What the *fuck* is going on!"

Sahana had her wolf temporarily subdued—a thick wrapping of dark shadow covering the wolf's eyes, ears, and nose.

"Go for the insides!" Rorax ran toward Sahana. "Open its mouth!"

Sahana's shadows reached inside the wolf's jaw and pried it open. Rorax sent her knife whizzing over to Sahana's wolf. With a jerk of Rorax's wrist, the knife ripped through the second wolf's skull.

They turned to move toward Volla's wolf, who was nipping at Volla's heels, completely ignoring her fire.

The wolf lunged for Volla's neck, and in a flash of violet, Jia threw herself at the beast, and they rolled over the grass.

The wolf ended up on top, pinning Jia to the ground and snapping its jaws down at her. It was about to wrap its teeth around Jia's throat when Rorax came up from behind, wrapped her left arm around its neck, and jerked its head up. With her right arm, she shoved her knife down into the wolf's gullet just as the wolf bit down into Rorax's arm.

The animal's now lifeless body went limp in her arms, but the wolf's long canines were already deeply embedded into the flesh of her forearm.

"Fuck!" Rorax gritted her teeth as a sharp pain radiated up from her wound.

"Gods above." Breathing hard, Jia looked up at Rorax from under the wolf's carcass. "Thanks."

"Are you okay? Are you okay?" Volla slid in next to them on her knees, her hands fluttering around Jia's face. "Jia, answer me right now. Are you—"

"I'm fine. I'm *fine.*" Jia swatted Volla's hands away. "Just get this thing out of Rorax's arm and then get it *off* me. It's dripping blood on me. Disgusting."

With a grunt of pain, Rorax pulled her arm down and off the wolf's long canines and staggered back as Volla heaved the body off Jia.

Sahana snatched Rorax's bloody arm and pressed her hand over the wound.

Rorax hissed in pain, but instantly the flesh around the wound started to close.

"Good work, Ror," Sahana murmured, her eyes on the wound. "Jia might have been dog chow if you hadn't made it to her."

"That's not funny!" Volla called from over her shoulder, hauling Jia to her feet and wrapping her in a big hug. "That was way too close."

"I'm fine." Jia unwrapped herself from Volla's embrace and moved over to nudge the wolf with her toe. "Are wolves... evolving or something? Since when are they immune to magick?"

"No, this must be what they sent the test vials with us for—what Kiniera meant by *sour magick.*"

"Maybe the Lyondrean Queen *isn't* summoning from the Pits. Maybe it's just this."

Volla snorted, looking down at the wolf with her new wife. "Or maybe Lyondrea is just cursed, and we should go home."

Sahana's sweat dripped down her nose as the wounds on Rorax's arm slowly closed over with pink, angry skin. Rorax gently extracted her arm out of Sahana's grip. "That's enough for now, Sahana. We can heal the bruise and the flesh underneath later."

Sahana held an immense amount of Dark Magick, but only bits of Life Magick. Her healing was for small emergencies only.

Sahana released her, stepping back and wiping the sweat off her forehead with the back of her arm. "Okay, yeah. Let me recharge for a bit."

Rorax nodded and stepped over to the wolf carcass where her friends were already investigating.

Rorax crouched down on her haunches next to the dead wolf, reaching out to feel the thick fur with her fingers. "It just feels like... fur. But Volla couldn't set it on fire, and I couldn't cut into it."

Jia reached down and rubbed her fingers through it, too. "It feels just like my dogs at home. Nothing special."

"I wonder if they hunt this close to the billiards on purpose. Looking for people?" Volla mused.

A far away howl sounded, and all four of their heads snapped up, instantly on high alert as other wolves in the area joined in.

"Let's get out of this gods-cursed forest," Volla growled from under her breath. "I don't know if we would survive another wolf, let alone the *pack*."

Rorax couldn't help but agree with the tall blonde, her instincts telling her to run.

"Jia, take samples. Blood and fur should do," Sahana ordered.

When Jia was done, Sahana handed Volla a compass. "You lead us out. I'll watch out for more energy signatures."

CHAPTER 5

RORAX

They were quiet as they moved quickly through the forest, faster and more silent than before. Sahana's head was constantly swiveling, trying to feel out more wolves, and Volla focused on the compass.

Rorax's arm throbbed painfully with every step. When they finally came to the mouth of the forest that opened to a small, dilapidated village, Rorax let out a long sigh of relief.

Sahana led them to an abandoned home at the edge of the town. Volla pushed her way inside first and coughed as a plume of dust rose in the air.

"Dust." Volla coughed, beating her fist against her chest.

The house was simple, made of weathered logs with nothing on the walls, and nothing was in the room except for a long wooden table.

Two doors led off the main room, and as Volla continued into the house, she opened one of the doors and stuck her head in. "Just a bed in here. Not a bed I would recommend using, though. It smells like mold."

Rorax huffed a laugh and pushed past her on creaky floorboards to open the other door. It led into a small, empty pantry that was covered in cobwebs.

Sahana came up behind her and sighed. "We might all have to sleep on the floor tonight, but at least there's an escape route if we need one." Sahana nodded her head to the ceiling, and Rorax followed her gaze to see a hatch that accessed the roof and a half-broken ladder leading up to it.

Sahana turned away and made her way back into the house. Rorax eyed the broken wooden rungs of the ladder warily before following her commander.

When they came back into the main room of the wooden cabin, Sahana pulled out a chair and collapsed down into it. "Now we just wait for our contact to get here. Rorax, give me your arm, and I'll finish healing it."

Rorax gave her arm to Sahana who immediately went back to work healing the wolf bite. Rorax almost groaned with relief as she felt the muscles stitching back together under her skin.

"Who's coming?" Volla asked, dropping her pack into the corner of the cabin before sitting on a chair opposite Sahana with a groan. "Kään help me, those wolves did a number on me. I've said this before, and the sentiment stands, this country is a shithole."

Jia rolled her eyes, but Rorax smirked at Volla. "Just because you're in terrible shape doesn't mean you should blame the whole country."

"There you go, Rorax." Sahana inspected Rorax's good-as-new arm. "All done."

Movement in the window through the broken shutters behind Volla's head caught Sahana and Rorax's attention. A small group of armed soldiers were outside.

"Motherfucker," Sahana hissed.

Volla and Jia were out of their chairs, and Rorax had Glimr thrumming excitedly in her palm, all of them ready to pounce in an instant.

"Stand down," Sahana ordered them. "My informant must be here. She just has a lot more men with her than I requested."

Volla and Jia shared a look.

There was a soft knock at the door.

"Come in." Sahana opened it just wide enough that a woman could slip past her. The woman carried a cast iron cauldron in one hand, and whatever was cooking in it smelled divine. Rorax's stomach rumbled almost loud enough to shake the windows.

The informant pulled her hood away from her face and gave them all a short nod. Rorax had never met her before.

Her dark brown skin was covered in dirt, but her eyes, dark and observant, were full of life as she took in Rorax and the other women. "Welcome to Lyondrea, Heilstorms. My name is Oba."

Oba spoke to them in the common tongue of the Realms, but her Lyondrean accent was thick.

"Oba." Sahana's shoulders relaxed almost imperceptibly at the name. "Thank you for meeting us here. My name is Sahana, and this is Jia, Volla, and Rorax." Sahana gestured to each of them.

"Sahana." Oba nodded, sticking her hand out for Sahana to shake. "It is very good to put a face to a name. We figured you might be hungry," Oba said, heaving the cast iron cauldron onto the table. "So, we brought you supper."

"Are you eating with us?" Sahana asked as Rorax filled in the seat on Sahana's left, Volla on her right. Jia stayed standing behind Sahana, moving into their natural positions.

The informant shook her head. "I do not have the time to stay."

"What's the plan?"

"You are to meet on the southwestern edge of the Allteria. Ask for directions if you must, but otherwise keep your heads down."

Sahana pressed her palms into the tabletop. "Who are we looking to speak to?"

"Me. There's a tavern on the junction of the Elu River and the Peak River. The owner is a good friend of the assistant to the queen's personal secretary, and he wants the war to end. Badly."

Kään save them. They were going on one of the most important missions since the Slave Wars almost a hundred and thirty years ago, but this time they were getting their information nearly fourth hand.

"Badly enough to work for us?" Sahana asked, narrowing her eyes suspiciously.

Oba nodded. "Said daughter was conscripted to work in the Pit, and is bein' forced to help dig those *things* out."

Volla and Rorax shared a nervous glance. From the reports they'd been given by Kiniera's other spies, monster pits were not compatible with living a long and healthy life. Pit workers were often killed long before they reached old age.

Oba turned her focus to Rorax. "You're Rorax Greywood? The one looking for Darras Greywood."

Rorax hesitated for a moment but nodded. "Yes."

Oba stuck her hand into her long cloak and handed Rorax a small scroll. "This is the address of Darras Greywood's last known work associate. They were working together as recently as one week ago. This man lives in the capital and is known to be... shrewd. But I've been told you have your ways of cracking tough nuts."

Volla snorted as Rorax ripped open the scroll and stared, memorizing the address.

When she finally looked back at Oba, she nodded. "Thank you."

Oba nodded back and motioned to the soup. "Eat, it is good. I need to take my leave for the capital, but some men will stay to escort you to the city."

Sahana nodded and stood to see the informant out. As soon as the door closed behind her, Volla ripped open the lid to the soup. "Finally, some decent fucking food."

CHAPTER 6

RORAX

"Is it too late for you to un-mate with her?" Rorax asked Jia, eyeing Volla as her friend loudly slurped her soup. Volla kicked Rorax's chair, making Rorax tamp down a smile after Jia and Rorax shared a feigned look of disgust.

Jia had grown up in the palaces of Koppar, with endless etiquette lessons and high expectations. Once Jia's mother, General Frostguard, picked up on Jia's preferences as a young teen, Jia's mother had started setting her up on dates with the finest bred women in the Realms, hoping for a political alliance. Rorax was looking forward to the day when the general found out her daughter had married a mannerless heathen.

"No. I'm stuck with her, unfortunately." Jia sighed, fighting a smile as Volla reached over and ruffled her long, purple ponytail.

Volla grunted and wiped her mouth with all the decorum and grace of a piglet. "What's the plan for tomorrow, Sahana?"

"We leave here before sunup and start making our way west." Sahana shrugged. "Oba will have details ready at the next stop."

"Do we have to travel with this lot?" Volla gestured a thumb to the handful of men stationed outside their hut. They hadn't bothered to go out and meet them yet. "They're going to slow us down."

"Or they might keep us alive," Jia said.

"They will bring us more attention," Volla countered.

"If they *have* opened the Pits, and it's still unconfirmed that they have, some of the monsters they've dragged out of the Pits will take more than a four-person unit to fell," Jia protested.

"We are not just *any unit,* Jia Torvik."

"They are offering us *protection*."

Rorax watched them go back and forth, a little headache starting to bloom in the back of her head.

"If I was a hungry mountain troll, I would pick the largest target to eat. Wouldn't you?"

"Volla," Sahana admonished. "They're coming with us, at least until we are almost at the junction of the Pike River where we'll meet Oba—as a sign of solidarity to the Lyondrean rebels if nothing else. If that doesn't work, we'll change the strategy. We have to be inconspicuous enough not to bring the whole country's army down on our heads, but the added protection won't hurt us."

"Fine." Volla's mouth twisted with displeasure, but she wiped her face clean and turned her body in her chair to face Rorax. "Rorax, what was on the note Oba gave you about Darras?"

Rorax swallowed another mouthful of soup as she fished around in her pocket for the tiny scroll before handing it over to Volla. "It's an address in the capital. My search won't begin for Darras until we arrive in the capital city."

Volla nodded, reading the address before she handed the scroll over to Jia, who handed it to Sahana.

"If you were to fall, Grumpy, we'd find him. I promise," Volla said, the determination in her voice warming something deep in Rorax's chest.

Another small ache bloomed in the back of Rorax's head, but she pushed it away as she clapped Volla on the shoulder. "Thank you."

They ate in silence until as pain thrummed in the back of Rorax's skull again. Her instincts prickled, and she stood up to peek through the broken blinds, watching the soldiers outside. They were still lounging around, some of them smoking, some of them eating. They showed no signs that anything was amiss.

Rorax's head throbbed, and this time the magick of her knife grew taught, straining her mind like it was tightening against an outside force.

Or an inside force.

She wrenched her hand away from the blinds and whipped around.

"Stop eating," Rorax snapped at them, smacking a spoonful of soup halfway to Volla's open mouth so hard the spoon and soup splattered all over the floor. "Stop."

Volla blinked up at her but leapt to her feet, her hands already on her blades. "What the fuck is going on, Ror?"

"The food. It has a blocking herb in it," Rorax hissed. "I can feel it affecting my connection to Glimr."

A tasteless blocker, used to cut off anyone from any part of their magick.

The Heilstorms were trained to be able to taste poisons and blockers in their food. Only one—one of the most effective, rarest blockers on the market—had absolutely no taste. Waterlily Rine. It would have been extremely difficult and obscenely expensive to obtain enough Rine to block one person, let alone *four*.

Sahana and Jia drew their weapons and were on their feet less than a second later. Almost as if summoned, there was a heavy knock on the door.

"Heilstorms?"

They looked at each other in horror for a split second before the door erupted, splintering inward under the force of a massive impact. Twenty men rushed into the room before a thick block of Jia's ice closed it shut again. There was banging on it from the other side, and before Jia iced over the windows, too, Rorax saw that all the soldiers who'd been outside were no longer lounging around.

They were armed and ready.

The soldiers started to assault the barrier of ice leading to the inside as the soldiers already inside swarmed the Heilstorms. Rorax wasted no time and threw

Glimr at an oncoming soldier. She decapitated one and then the next, dodging and rolling under blows, hacking men apart with her sword in a blind bloodlust.

"STOP!"

Rorax didn't recognize the woman's voice at first, so she didn't stop. She cut down another man, until the voice thundered again. "I said STOP."

Rorax swung her sword, cutting through a man's neck, and only then did she flick her eyes up to the soldier giving them commands. She went utterly still.

Captain Crax, from House of Weather, stood with a knife pressed to Jia's throat.

Rorax froze, and from the corner of her eye she could see both Sahana and Volla stop fighting as well.

"Drop your weapons and raise your hands, or she dies," Crax hissed as blood dribbled from her split lip into her mouth.

Rorax and Volla looked at Sahana, who gave them both a short nod. Sahana and Rorax dropped their swords to the ground, and Rorax summoned Glimr back to her scabbard. Volla's jaw went tight, and she gave Crax a look that promised death before she grudgingly dropped her own sword.

"If you hurt her, I will filet you alive," Volla promised, her voice cold and unforgiving.

"Hello, ladies. I've missed you," Crax said over the sound of soldiers from the outside trying to beat through the ice that blocked the door. Crax pushed a lock of short blonde hair out of her eyes, then looked between the four of them with a crazed smile. "Seems like just yesterday we were in that shitty fortress together. But Lyondrea offered me something I couldn't refuse, and now I fight for them. A pity, I always liked you. You're just as vicious as me."

Rorax snarled, and Crax smirked as she stepped closer to her, shuffling Jia along with her. "Queen Arkyn of Lyondrea wants to offer you a deal, Greywood. Fight for her, swear allegiance to her, and she will give you your brother. Alive and unbound."

Rorax forgot how to breathe, and her heart seized in her chest. "My brother?"

"Darras Greywood is your brother, is he not?"

Rorax's insides went cold. "Where is he?"

I have to find him.

Crax shook her head. "I don't know. His location is only known by a *very* select few. He is very important to Lyondrea. But that location will be given to you when you swear fealty to the queen."

"I can't. I've sworn a Blood Oath to Sahana Thorash and the Heilstorms." The words felt numb on Rorax's lips.

"Oh yes... well, there is that."

Crax pushed Jia into the arms of a nearby soldier and bent to pick up Sahana's knives where she had dropped them on the floor.

Sahana jerked against her own captors but kept her mouth shut as Crax prowled up to her. "I must admit, I'm disappointed in you."

Crax tsked her tongue. "Letting your unit fraternize with each other, letting them slack off in their training." Crax gestured her knife over to Volla before reaching out with her free hand to push a long lock of black hair behind Sahana's ear. "I expected more."

Volla screamed in warning, but it was too late.

The guard holding Sahana reached back and shoved his blade through Sahana's chest.

Rorax barely flinched as Sahana's body crumpled, her blood quickly seeping all over the floor. Rorax couldn't move, couldn't breathe; she just stared. Her commander. Her mentor. Her superior. Her friend for fifty years lay on the floor with lifeless eyes, staring up at the ceiling. Rorax felt a slight buzzing, and then the Blood Oath that kept her tethered to the Heilstorms, and to Sahana and her unit, snapped.

"Move the body into the other room," Crax griped as a pool of Sahana's lifeblood continued to seep over the floorboards. "The blood makes my work-space slippery."

Free. For the first time in nearly fifty years, Rorax was free from the Blood Oath she had sworn to Sahana. She was free to go and do as she pleased.

But at what price?

Darras. Darras. Darras.

Jia screamed, and Volla tried to struggle desperately against the men holding her back.

Crax stepped over the body, breaking Rorax's eye contact with Sahana. "Now that there is no Blood Oath holding you here, what do you decide, Greywood?"

I have to find him.

Rorax's lips and tongue felt heavy and numb and nearly impossible to move. "You have a deal," she croaked.

The soldiers from outside finally smashed through the ice, and they streamed in, carrying in a tall torture device between them that made Rorax's stomach roll. They set it down in front of Crax, who motioned for the soldiers subduing Jia to place her limbs in the holds that would keep her outstretched arms pinned above her head.

A single tear leaked down Jia's cheek as she jerked her body around to no avail. She tried to struggle, icing her captors and headbutting them desperately, but it was no use as her magick started to fail her.

"Leave us," Crax said to the men. They left the room as Crax gave Jia a chilling smile.

Not one single soldier made a move for Rorax. Why would they? They knew she would never put her mission of finding her brother in jeopardy. Not even for Jia and Volla.

Rorax had to grip the back of her chair to stay upright.

The sounds in the room were muffled, as if they were underwater, and the floor seemed to tilt toward her.

I have to find him. Darras. I have to find him. My brother. My family.

Rorax didn't move as the men around her brushed up against her to bend and pick up Sahana's body. Her eyes followed them as they carried her lifeless corpse into the adjacent room and unceremoniously dumped her body on the bed.

Crax stepped up to Volla, and Rorax finally looked away from her commander to stare as Crax laughed so close to Volla's stricken face, Rorax could see her breath push against the strands of Volla's hair. "*You* will just have to wait to die. I want you to watch this."

Crax stepped away from Volla and looked over at Rorax.

"Wait outside. When I'm done here, I will lead you to my queen."

Rorax nodded numbly and took a few steps back toward the door.

"Rorax, you *fucking cunt*!" Volla shrieked, trying to wrestle away from the soldiers holding her.

Crax smiled wickedly at Volla and turned to Jia. "I am going to have fun with this," she crooned.

Crax pulled out a long, rusted, wicked knife, and the breath in Rorax's lungs hitched.

I have to find him. I have to find him. I have to find him....

Volla tried to lunge forward, probably trying to rip her way out of the Waterlily Rine's grasp and away from the soldiers holding her arms and waist, but even if she could, Volla was too far away. She would never make it.

By the time Volla got to Jia, it would be over and Jia would be nothing. Nothing but a tortured corpse and a ghost to haunt them all.

Rorax swallowed down the lump in her throat. *It doesn't matter what happens. I have to find him. I have to find him. I...*

Jia screamed, and that sound... the five words Rorax had spent the last hundred and sixty years clinging to, the mantra she had used to push her through everything, went quiet in her head.

A part of her pleaded desperately for the words to come back, to keep her on the path that would lead her right to her brother's doorstep.

Slowly, more words found their place in her soul and locked into place.

I will find another way.

Crax ran the knife along the skin of Jia's cheekbone until it raised a thin line of blood.

"NO! PLEASE, STOP!" Volla screamed, her voice hoarse with agony and panic.

The sound cracked through her, and before she knew what she was doing, Rorax pulled Glimr from her back and threw it.

Her knife embedded itself into the back of Crax's neck, all the way to the hilt.

The tip burst out of the front of Crax's throat, splattering blood across Jia's face an instant before Crax's body collapsed to the floor at Jia's feet.

One of the soldiers holding Volla gasped. "What the fuck do you think you just—"

"THE DOOR, JIA!" Rorax yelled as she swept her hand in the air from Crax's body to the guard. Her knife jerked out of Crax's throat, and in a white flash it ran clean through one of the guards holding Volla back.

The other guard let Volla go and reached out to grab Rorax, but she ducked under his arms and lunged over the table, sliding across the smooth wooden surface. Rorax grabbed a butter knife on her way over, and when she was on two steady feet again, she threw it as hard as she could toward the soldier by the door.

Jia raised a palm, and the door was again covered in a thick block of ice.

Rorax bent down and plucked the knife from Crax's dead fingers.

Volla cracked the neck of the soldier that had been holding her hostage at the same time as Rorax cut through the restraints holding Jia to the torture device. Jia stumbled free before vomiting all over Crax's dead body.

Volla rushed for Jia as Rorax sent her knife clean through the last soldier in the room.

Soldiers rushed the building, pounding on the exterior and looking for weaknesses. A soldier outside punched through an iced-over windowpane next to the door, and Rorax used Crax's blade to chop off his hand. The soldier screamed in agony and wisely removed his arm from the window as Jia patched the hole in the window with more ice.

Rorax turned to watch as Volla cupped Jia's face with trembling palms, but her voice was steady. "Are you okay? Are you hurt?"

Jia whimpered out another sob as tears streamed down her face but nodded her head. "I'm okay."

Warm relief settled like stones in the bottom of Rorax's stomach.

The opposite window shattered in a flurry of ice and glass, and this time Rorax sent Glimr spinning into the man.

Rorax pulled it back and sent Glimr through the neck of another soldier, summoning it back yet again as big black spots bloomed in her vision. Her chest was getting tight, and the ache in the back of her skull started to burn in pure agony as the magick she held in her body for Glimr went rigid.

Volla gave Rorax a wide, bewildered stare. "Why?"

Rorax's eyebrows furrowed. "Why?"

"You said—" She was cut off as four soldiers rammed their way in through the door again. Rorax took her knife, leaned back under an incoming sword, jabbed Glimr manually up into the first soldier's neck, then sent it flying through two of the other soldiers' throats, spraying blood everywhere.

"You said you would do anything for Darras," Volla finished.

When the knife was back in its sheath, Rorax felt a wave of unnatural, overwhelming exhaustion settle over her shoulders.

"Move, Ror," Volla commanded, and Ror moved to the side as Jia stood and covered the door again.

Rorax could no longer stand, and slowly she sank to her knees.

The wooden floorboards were cool and welcoming, though the blood that was pooled underneath her was hot and sticky. She couldn't convince her muscles to move out of it though.

Rorax heard Volla say something to her, but Volla's voice sounded like she was six miles away. She could feel the Waterlily Rine settle into her system like an anchor on her consciousness, dragging her down closer toward the depths of a numb darkness.

"Rorax?"

Every drop of power was as precious as gold as the Waterlily Rine gripped her even harder. She took in a shuddering breath through cold lips.

There was another yell and more broken glass, and she raised her head to see another soldier trying to come in through the window. With one lazy flick of her arm, Rorax used her knife to sever his head, and the decapitated flesh fell heavily to the floor.

Rorax summoned Glimr back to her hand just as her head started spinning uncontrollably and her vision started to dim. She took in a ragged breath and pressed her forehead into the blood and the cool wooden planks of the floor below her.

Volla said something to her again, but Rorax couldn't hear her.

"You better get us out of this gods-forsaken country, Volla Torvik," Rorax muttered before falling into darkness.

CHAPTER 7

VOLLA

Shock. Debilitating, overwhelming shock rolled through Volla's body as she watched Rorax collapse into herself on the floor. Volla's throat swelled up, and she wanted to laugh, to cry, and to curse at the same time.

Rorax Greywood.

Roraxiva Greywood had stepped in to save their lives with that gods-damned knife of hers. The same knife that stabbed and cut Volla so many times in training that Volla had started hurling it into lakes, into pits, or off mountains at any chance she had to get rid of it, only to see it dangling from Rorax's fingertips seconds later.

Volla's chin trembled at the same time as a violent thump came at the front door where there was currently a thick frozen barrier. It snapped her back into action.

Jia blinked away her tears furiously. "Can you carry Rorax? We can climb through the back hatch and onto the roof and, hopefully, run around them. There are two horses out there we can steal. I saw them earlier."

There was more yelling, and Volla smelled smoke.

"Quickly!" Jia ran down the hall as Volla picked Rorax up from a puddle of blood on the ground. Rorax's armor, face, and hair were completely soaked with it, and it smeared onto Volla's front as she ran to the back pantry. Jia started up the ladder first, holding her arm out to take Rorax's limp body up from Volla.

Jia started climbing but only made it halfway up when the sound of the ice cracking at the front door had them both looking over their shoulders, and any remaining relief in Volla's heart was washed away with acidic fear. Volla could feel Jia through the mating bond they had secured through the marriage draught not two days before, and she knew all of Jia's magick was tapped out; the Waterlily Rine had emptied her. If she pushed herself any further, she would pass out like Rorax had. Despair and regret, like nothing Volla had ever experienced, filled the new void in her chest.

"Hurry!" Jia hissed to her, stepping up a few more rungs.

As the guards crashed into the door again, Volla selfishly stared up at Jia, soaking up precious seconds to study Jia's perfect features, admiring the beauty and strength held there, even now.

"Volla!" Jia hissed again, Rorax dangling precariously over her shoulder. "Don't you fucking *dare*."

Jia reached her free hand out to Volla, meaning to grab her and pull her up, but Volla trapped Jia's hand in her own and placed a reverent kiss to it before taking a step back.

"Run, my love." Volla took another step away.

Tears streamed down Jia's face. "Volla Torvik, don't you dare."

"Get her out of here. Go, Jia."

"I will not leave you here," Jia choked, her tears now dripping off her chin.

"Don't let anyone see the tattoos on Rorax's neck. They are looking for her everywhere."

Jia shook her head. "*No.*"

"Jia—"

She just shook her head. "No fucking way am I taking *Rorax* over *you*." Her voice broke, and another sob wrenched out of her lips. "I love *you*. I'm going to spend the rest of my life with *you*. *You* are my wife."

Volla's heart broke. It cleaved cleanly in half, and her chest throbbed.

"Listen," Volla hissed. They only had precious seconds before the guards broke through the barrier, and she refused to spend the last minutes of her life fighting with the love of her life.

"Rorax just saved our lives. She saved both of us from pain, torture, and death. *Rorax*. She had the opportunity to find Darras, and yet she threw it away. For you. For *us*. I.... Jia...." A painful cry caught in her throat, and she had to force a steadying breath into her lungs. "Jia... I couldn't save you from Crax. Sahana couldn't save you from Crax. But Rorax did. She made the decision, and she *did*."

Volla pointed to that dark head of hair that was now matted and dripping with the blood of the soldiers she had slain single-handedly. "I can't let her die like this, Jia. I owe her everything, and I refuse to let her die in dirt and filth. I... I can't."

Silent tears dripped down Jia cheeks, and she nodded once. She didn't have to say anything. She knew. She knew that if Volla lived past tonight and Rorax didn't, it would haunt her, destroy her.

Rorax was her friend; she had just proven her loyalty, and Volla owed her a life debt. She would not abandon her now while she was defenseless.

Volla took one step up the ladder, gripped Jia's ponytail, and roughly pulled Jia's lips to hers for one last taste. When they broke apart, Volla brushed her thumb over Jia's lips. "I love you. I wanted to spend the rest of my days growing old with you, and I should have taken you away and gotten started on that the minute you agreed to marry me. I'm sorry."

Jia closed her eyes, and Volla was about to move away when something silver caught her eye. Rorax's knife was back in its sheath. Without thinking, Volla snatched it.

Usually, when Volla touched Rorax's knife, the metal burned, searing the skin of whoever touched the metal besides Rorax. This time it warmed against her palm in a greeting, as if it could sense Volla's sacrifice for its master.

There was another crack at the door, and Volla took a step away. "Go. If I survive, I'll find you."

Jia nodded through her tears and continued up the ladder as Volla sucked in a deep breath and turned to face the soldiers.

The men broke through the door not thirty seconds later. Volla immediately knew why Rorax loved her knife more than she loved anything else.

She could feel its energy pulling her limbs to block here, block there, attack here, and attack there. For what felt like hours, Rorax's knife gave force to her limbs that had started to go numb with exhaustion.

A pile of bodies lay at Volla's feet as she fought her way out of the small house and into the field outside. When she finally looked around her, she didn't see any more soldiers coming at her.

Rorax's knife in Volla's hand disappeared, and a tiny seed of hope grew in her heart, blooming into a magnificent flower for one beautiful moment.

Then there was a bone-crunching thrust, and Volla stared down with horror at the end of a bloodstained steel sword thrusting out of her chest.

She screamed as her knees gave out, but a large, clawed hand grabbed her neck and held her up before she could fall over into death.

"Where is the Contestar?" the man snarled into her ear.

Volla opened her mouth, but she couldn't talk.

And the last thing Volla Torvik saw in this world before she tumbled into darkness were two cloudy eyes.

CHAPTER 8

RORAX

Rorax could vaguely hear Jia screaming, the sound pulling at her consciousness. She slowly blinked her eyes and found herself looking down into coarse, black hair.

Jia screamed again, and Rorax rolled her eyes to the side to see Jia off their horse, falling to her knees and clawing at her chest, her fingernails scraping uselessly against the Heilstorm's black scaled armor.

"Jia?" The ground—no, not the ground, a *horse* shifted nervously under Rorax as Jia's screams cut off into sounds of distress, her fingertips splitting open on her armor, spreading fresh blood over the sharp black scales she clawed at.

"No. No, no, no nonono," Jia sobbed, rocking back and forth on her knees, tears running freely down her cheeks. She stopped digging at her chest only long enough to lean forward and vomit.

Jia had been clawing at her chest like an animal, at a wound that was not there. A phantom wound, a wound she might be feeling through her mating bond.

Volla.

The thought rang through her bones with such clarity, with such finality, it rocked Rorax to her core.

Volla was dead.

Jia's mating bond with Volla had been severed, and Jia felt Volla's last feelings... an injury, a sword, an arrow, or a knife through her heart.

Rorax turned away from Jia, who sobbed, her bloody hands cradled into her chest as she curled up in a ball like a fetus in the dirt.

Rorax shoved her way off the horse, falling to the ground, the sounds of Jia's sobs forcing her body to move. She needed to get away, right now. Rorax half walked, half stumbled through the nearly pitch-black Lyondrean forest until she couldn't hear Jia's cries anymore and collapsed to her knees.

Volla was dead. Volla was *dead*. Rorax and Jia had left her to die alone.

Sahana's words echoed through Rorax's head, making her want to scream. *We're a family. This unit is a family. That's what makes us so good.*

Sahana was dead too.

Rorax's heart cleaved in half as she gripped the soil in her fists. She didn't know how she would ever be able to move again.

"We are stopping."

"No."

"We have to, Jia. We need to recoup."

"I want to keep going. The Realms are only a day's ride away."

"We haven't had any food for over a day. We need to eat."

Jia, who was pressed against her back in the saddle, kept quiet but didn't protest further when Rorax turned the horse toward the dilapidated building. The sign on it read "Dowager's Bed and Breakfast."

Rorax pushed their horse into a trot. A woman was in the yard, already tending to a pair of chestnut horses, so Rorax pulled their stolen stallion next to her and slid off the horse. Rorax turned and faced the woman, her body stiffening as the woman's pair of big, blue eyes looked up at her. *Something* about the woman's gaze was unsettling; it was missing something.... She stared at the woman and found something unfamiliar staring back.

Mortality.

The woman was Ungifted.

The people of Illus were split into three possible lifespans. The Gifted had immortal lifespans, and they could hold magick, even if it was so faint that they could not manifest it outside their body. Those who could not manifest magick were called Lowborns, and those who held enough magick to manifest outside of their bodies were called Highborns.

The Blessed lived lifespans of up to three hundred years before they passed into the afterlife, and the Ungifted aged until they were eighty to one hundred years old before they died.

In the Realms, the center of all magick in Illus, there were rarely ever Ungifted who lived there. She only knew of a small colony of them that lived in Valitlinn under the Guardian's protection. The Blessed usually took residence in Ostr and the Principality of Pazula. To see an Ungifted here, so close to the Realm's border, was surprising. Jarring even.

Rorax was Gifted didn't have any elemental power and therefore couldn't pick out specific magick types a person held, like Sahana could... like Sahana *used* to be able to. She had just enough to be able to sense the lack of threat, the silence, and the complete lack of a magickal wave from this woman, however. Her big eyes were almost completely void of any kind of life, let alone a gift.

Their continent was historically unkind to the Ungifted. When magick was left stagnant in the earth for too long, unused by the Gifted, monsters and creatures were known to spawn. It was dangerous to live on the border of the Realms without some kind of gift to protect yourself. Not only that, but there was a stigma that the Ungifted couldn't be trusted since Blood Oaths needed magick and didn't work on them to force them to be accountable.

Based on the faint lines on the woman's face, she must have been alive for thirty of the Ungifted years.

"What is your business in Lyondrea?" The woman grabbed the reins of the dark stallion.

Rorax's eyes flicked to the wooden inn behind the woman. Except for deep gashes that looked an awful lot like claws had cut deep into the wood of the front door of the inn, it looked safe enough.

Rorax studied the marks as she spoke to the woman. "We are looking for a place to stay the night."

The stallion shifted his weight nervously as Jia slid off his back behind Rorax, but the woman kept his head still, gripping the reins tighter. "We have two rooms available, above the kitchen. Two coppers per night, but there's an extra coin due if we'll need to stable your horse."

Rorax looked back into the woman's big blue eyes. She fished three copper marks and a golden coin out of her back pocket and dropped it in the woman's dirty palm. "That's for your silence."

The woman looked at the golden coin in her palm, then glanced up to Rorax with slightly narrowed eyes. Her teeth bit into the dark skin of her lip as her eyes traced over the handle of Rorax's sword peeking over her shoulder.

"We don't want any trouble here. *Can't* have any trouble here."

Rorax tried to keep from curling her lip over her teeth at the woman's inspection. "If anything, maybe you'll sleep easier knowing you have us around for the night in case whatever made those marks comes back for more."

"Right." The woman seemed to sag a bit at the reminder. "Follow me."

The woman showed them to their room, which was cozy and clean with two small beds.

Rorax nodded to the woman as she left Jia and her alone. Jia immediately curled into one of the beds, her face to the wall, and didn't say a word.

Jia was crying in the bathroom.

She had been locked in there for almost an hour now.

Rorax looked forlornly over at the dinner she had brought up from the kitchen below; it lay completely untouched. She rubbed the back of her neck with her palm, trying to push down the feelings of helplessness and grief rising in her chest, making it hard to breathe.

Jia had slept for a while before taking a bath. And she was still in there, crying. Rorax hadn't let herself cry. She didn't have the time to mourn yet. Just a few more days. She needed to get them on a boat to Koppar first.

Assuming she could peel Jia away from the bathroom tomorrow morning, they would be across the border and back into the Realms in only a day or two. Then they'd be back to Valitlinn in a week if they caught a boat, and back to Koppar in two if that boat would carry them all the way home. Once she was back in her own rooms and she'd reported to the king and told Karan what had happened to his mate, then Rorax could fall apart.

Karan could probably feel what had happened, just like Jia had. He was probably on his way to Lyondrea right now in a storm of grief and anger.

As she sat on the edge of the bed, her forearms on her knees, images of that night started rolling through her mind. The same images, over and over.

The knife in Sahana's chest, Crax's blood speckled across Jia's face, Sahana curled up on the ground in a puddle of her own blood, Volla's golden hair as she stood in between her and Crax's men....

Rorax's stomach roiled, and she absentmindedly rubbed her palm across her chest.

Had Volla died of her wounds? Had she been captured and tortured while they had fled and left her there to fight on her own? The questions whirled violently in Rorax's head until her chest and throat grew tight.

She jerked herself off the side of the bed, knocked on the wooden bathroom door once, and pushed her way inside when she didn't hear a response.

Jia was in her bath, curled up in a ball, her knees pressed into her collarbones protectively.

Rorax squatted down next to the tub. "Jia. Look at me."

Jia's head lolled to the side, and her lifeless eyes slid to Rorax.

Rorax bit her lip to keep from flinching.

No joy. No spark. Nothing but raw agony reflected in her eyes, and it made something ugly and unfamiliar crack open inside of Rorax. Shame. Disgust. Regret. Guilt. Something she had not felt so keenly toward herself in nearly fifty years.

Rorax ignored it, pushing it down. "Can you feel your magick yet?"

"Not really," she rasped.

"I can't either, which means the blocker is still in our blood. We have to take samples to get them back to Kiniera."

Jia nodded, her eyes slowly sliding to her backpack on the floor. "The vials. They're in my backpack."

Rorax grabbed a rag from the bathroom before she manually reached around and unsheathed Glimr from her back. She used her knife to cut a strip of fabric from the bottom of the rag before she sliced it across her palm. She directed the slow stream of blood to fill one of the vials before she turned to Jia, holding out her knife.

She used the strip of cloth to soak up the excess blood as Jia filled her own vial. When both vials were filled and capped again, Rorax rubbed her blood over the tops, where a witch rune was etched into the corks. The blood activated the runes, and Rorax watched as the glasses frosted over. The blood would be preserved there, frozen, for weeks.

Rorax stood, tucking the vials back into Jia's backpack. "You need to eat something."

Jia's purple eyes glazed over, but she nodded, the movement small and pitiful.

"I'm serious, Jia. You need to eat. Promise me you'll try to get something down."

Jia nodded slowly, woodenly like a broken doll.

Then, like a coward, Rorax turned and left the room.

Rorax found herself downstairs in the small tavern below their room.

The woman from last night and a tall man who was drying a mug stood behind the bar.

Four tables in the hall were full of rowdy customers, but the majority sat empty.

Rorax ignored the boisterous customers and made her way to the bar. The girl offered her a tight-lipped smile, but the man put down the mug he was drying and scowled. "We don't want any trouble here, ya hear? No amount of—" His eyes flicked to the tables of customers behind Rorax's shoulder who were now bellowing Lyondrea's national anthem. "*—compensation* would be worth it."

Rorax ignored him but slid a few more copper coins to him over the counter. "Do you have any wine here?"

The man looked Rorax over once more. His lips pressed together in a tight frown, but he used the mug he'd just cleaned and filled it.

"What happened to your friend?" the woman asked as she took the mug from the man and slid it across the bar to Rorax.

Rorax shrugged at the woman, tipped the mug back, and drained the contents in a few gulps. She smacked the mug back on the countertop and wiped her mouth with the back of her sleeve. She couldn't get as drunk as she wanted to, in case she needed to haul Jia and herself out of there but... "One more."

The man looked at the woman, who just shrugged, before filling it again.

Rorax took the mug and sat at the closest table, her back to the table full of idiots who were now arm-wrestling each other.

She nursed her mug of wine, brooding when the Ungifted woman slid into the chair across from her.

"Where did ya get that ring?" She looked down at Rorax's pointer finger wrapped around the mug.

The ring had been cast to resemble the top of a raven's skull.

Two empty eye sockets sat close to her first knuckle; the bird's long, sharp beak ran all the way to her second knuckle toward her fingertip. Rorax had used the long, sharp beak as a weapon many times in battle.

It was made of silversteel. House of Alloy could move and manipulate all metal at will, so the gods had given the Gifted deposits of goldsteel, silversteel, and starsteel (the rarest of them all) into the earth. These metals couldn't be manipulated with magick. The metals were expensive, rare, and dangerous to mine but necessary when anything made of iron, bronze, or steel could be used against you.

"It was a gift." Her heart gave a little lifeless squeeze; it had been a gift from her brother, whom she'd abandoned in exchange for Volla and Jia. Gods, she was *worthless*.

"What does the symbol mean?" the woman asked, her eyes narrowing on the skull.

There was a symbol stamped onto the top of the skull. Three circles stacked up, the largest on the bottom and the smallest closer to the beak with a straight line running through the center of all three.

Rorax shrugged, she didn't know what it meant.

The woman's eyes finally snapped back up to Rorax's face. "What happened to the girl you're with? She looked like she'd been terrorized."

Rorax saw the man out of the corner of her eye. He was staring at the two of them with an unhappy frown. "She has been terrorized. In a certain way."

The woman's eyes narrowed even further. "What does that mean?"

"You're prying now." Rorax took another big swallow of wine as pink blossomed on the woman's cheeks.

"I... I guess I am." The woman bristled, crossing her arms over her chest. "But I've only seen that... look, that pale, scared, *dead* look on two other people before. Once when the creature came who made those marks on my front door, and the other when someone I know lost their mate, and I deserve to know if a monster is on its way to my inn."

The reminder of Volla had Rorax finishing her mug of wine. The woman still looked at her suspiciously, so Rorax curled her lip over her teeth. "It wasn't a monster."

"Oh!" The woman's eyes went wide before going soft. "Oh."

The pity and sadness lying in her eyes made Rorax ache, so she changed the subject. "No one should come looking for us. If anyone does, just tell them the truth."

"And what is the truth?"

Rorax pushed herself up, looking the woman dead in the eyes as she stood over her and told her the eventual truth. "We're heading east."

She turned from the woman, not bothering to look at the man who was staring holes in her back, and pushed outside.

Rorax needn't have bothered misdirecting the innkeeper.

At least thirty armed soldiers stood between her and the stable, all on tall Realm-bred horses; they were all wearing dark brown leather armor with a silver wolf in a black triangle painted on their chests. The silver wolf was the sigil of the House of Dark.

They all had that sigil. All except for one.

A man in front of the pack pushed a raggedy hood away from his face and sniffed the air. He was so pale his skin appeared almost gray, so translucent you could see the veins under his skin. His hair was long, stick straight, and white, falling out of his hood in waves to his lap.

He dismounted his horse, sniffed again, and two sightless eyes fell to where Rorax stood, frozen to the spot.

His eyes were cloudy, but even without any pupils the man managed to stare right at her, causing a shiver to wrack through her shoulders. "The Guardian has summoned yeh to the Northern Castle, girl."

Something was wrong with this man, something *different.* Rorax slid to the side, and his sightless eyes moved with her, like he *could* see her.

He was tracking her with some kind of magick. He was an Elite. And from the looks of his long, white hair, he was an *Elder* Elite.

There were twelve main forms of magick in the world, and Fire, Ice, Weather, Alloy, Air, Dark, Light, Foliage, Fauna, Water, Life, and Death were the Realms that housed them. Anyone that held magick *outside* of those twelve main types were called Elites. Elites that had been alive since the Rip, since the beginning of time, were called Elder Elites. There were less than ten of them still alive in all of Illus, and Rorax was staring at one. She knew it.

"The Guardian can go to Hell," Rorax hissed, reaching back and unsheathing Glimr. "Who are you?"

The Elder Elite didn't bother answering her. Fast as a whip, he charged her. Rorax barely had time to dodge under the sword that arched toward her torso. She twirled, pulling her sword out and clashing it against the man's steel. He pushed her back, making her stumble. She threw her knife at the man as hard as she could.

He knocked Glimr to the side in a shower of sparks, and Rorax was so shocked she didn't have time to do anything as the hilt of the man's blade redirected downward and hit her across the temple.

Rorax blacked out for half a second but came to just in time to feel her face hit the ground, her nose spurting blood. One soldier kicked her in the ribs, then another, and Rorax scrambled and fought, earning herself an elbow or a fist to the face and more blows to her ribs before there was a pressing against her skull of dark magick so tight she couldn't see or hear. Everything went black.

CHAPTER 9

RAENGAR

Erich Sumavari, Prince of the House of Death, was a good-looking man. He had dark hair, a straight nose, and was almost as tall and broad as Raengar himself.

He wouldn't be nearly as handsome, though, after Raengar fed him all his teeth and left him strangled in the woods.

"Come on, Butcher King," Erich drawled over his shoulder as he set a punishing pace on the trail up the side of the High Queen's Mountain. "Keep up."

The nickname grated on Raengar's nerves, made him grind his teeth. Raengar had just flown into Morvarand from Koppar, a city built at sea level. Morvarand had an altitude of 7,000 feet, and the High Queen's Mountain was higher still. At this elevation, the oxygen in the air felt thin and useless, something that never seemed to bother him on a dragon's back no matter how high he flew, but hiking up the steep mountainside with his sword and armor made his muscles and lungs burn with need.

He wanted to stop and rest, to try and pry the oxygen out of the thin air, but he would rather let his pride kill him before he showed any weakness in front of Sumavari. The smug bastard.

"Come on, hurry up, we need to get there before the rain washes the trail away," Erich called, looking up at the dark cloudy sky that had just started to produce a few drops but ominously promised more. Erich wore just as much armor as Raengar and wasn't out of breath, but Raengar was convinced Erich was part mountain goat.

Raengar grunted in response and pushed his body faster still, the burn in his lungs intensifying.

He should have insisted he fly his dragon, Deimos, up here, despite the impending rain and Erich insistences that they climb the High Queen's Mountain on foot.

After the attack the House of Ice had led against Death—the Siege of Surmalinn and the fall of Povelinn—the Guardians had made House of Ice the benefactors and keepers of House of Death for a hundred years as a way to help build and repair the damage they had inflicted on the house. Whatever House of Death needed, House of Ice provided as penance. Food, clothes, gold, soldiers, border security, education, and most of all, training for their soldiers had been provided to the House of Death by Ice in the last fifty years since Raengar had assumed his throne.

Raengar and Isolde, the new co-rulers of Ice after the death of their father, had placed Tag Norvakson in charge of the efforts being made to help Death rebuild. So, a few weeks ago, when Tag sent his Blood Hawk, urging Raengar to come to Morvarand and look at something "troubling" Erich's scouts had found on the High Queen's Mountain, Raengar made the time.

Tag Norvakson was a dutiful soldier, an Ice-Born man through and through with unfailing loyalty to king and country. So Raengar had come, trusting that Tag would not waste his time.

He had also come to meet Erich Sumavari. The House of Death's royal family was famous for being secretive. After most of them had been butchered during the War of Sumavari, they had started to hide their identities from the rest of the Realms. The first time Raengar had seen Queen Rosalie Sumavari was at her coronation. He had grown up with the rest of the princes and princesses of the Realm, but not the Sumavaris. He would not squander an opportunity to meet another Sumavari, who was not only a prince of the House of Death, but the general for House of Death's army.

Raengar had to admit that the novelty of meeting the prince was absolutely not worth his pain and suffering, however. Erich had insisted he take Raengar up here himself. On foot. *The fewer scents on the trail the better,* Erich had said. Whatever the fuck that meant.

They hiked for another thirty minutes, Raengar's quads and glutes prickling with exhaustion, when Erich finally held up a hand. "We're here."

Raengar looked around at the balsam pine trees that looked exactly the same as the other 600,000 balsam pines they'd hiked past for the last two hours. Raengar pinched the bridge of his nose. "We are *where* exactly?"

Erich kept creeping through the woods before falling to one knee in the mud and pointing to something on the ground.

As Raengar got closer, Erich put his hand out next to the tracks.

Hoofprints. Two toes deep, heavy hoofprints that were double the size of the hand that Erich laid next to it.

Giant moose roamed freely around the Jagamine Mountains throughout the Realms, feeding large populations of dragons, felidra, and griffins throughout the country. Seeing tracks like this was not unordinary.

Raengar looked at the track with an eyebrow raised, as irritation made his throat tight. "A moose?"

"No, too big."

"Elk?"

He shook his head.

"A giant cow then?" Gods, Raengar was going to pitch this raggedy son of a bitch off the side of the mountain.

Erich shook his head. "No, it's too big for either of those. We think it's a... we think it's a minotaur track."

Raengar's irritation evaporated, and trepidation took its place. Raengar's head snapped up to look at Erich's face. No obvious lie was detectable in his dark gray eyes, but to say that he thought the tracks belonged to a minotaur was a very serious claim.

Minotaurs didn't belong to the world of Illus naturally. The only record of minotaurs were those that were summoned from hell. They were monsters only spawned from the Pits. Pits were opened when a massive amount of magick was burst in the ground and a bridge of sorts was formed from Hell to Illus. Monsters of all forms would try and flood through the connection, some fighting for the chance to live in a world other than Hell, some fighting for the chance to prey on the people.

There had been two Pit Wars in recorded history; the last one had been a horrific bloodbath for all the countries on Illus.

If a minotaur truly was in these mountains, then it would confirm that a Pit had been opened again, that Lyondrea was summoning them, and that the Realms would shortly be going to war in an effort to close the Pit before too many creatures came through the connection.

Raengar resisted the urge to reach out and grab Erich by the front of his black chain mail armor. "Do you know what it would mean if it *was* a minotaur track?"

Erich reluctantly nodded.

"Have you or your men seen one?"

"No, but the tracks... they go for miles back and forth from here to Lyondrea, and they are too big to be moose; no cattle live this far up—"

"But how do you *know*—"

As if in answer to the question burning on Raengar's tongue, a deep, nightmarish roar ripped through the air behind them.

Raengar was up and around with his sword drawn before the sound pinched off. "Go back, Erich. Fetch Tag. Get Deimos."

"I'm not leaving you here."

"Unless you have a shit ton of Death Magick at your disposal that I don't know about, I want you out of my way. Now."

Erich was dangerous; he was good with his sword and had a mind made for war. There was a reason his sister had named him her general. When it came to hand-to-hand combat, however, Raengar would smear the floor with him. Raengar was taller, burlier, and had been raised by Katalon the Corrupt to become the most lethal man on the planet from the day he was born, six hundred and thirty-two years ago.

"Magick won't work against it. Some Pit monsters have an obsidian circlet—" Erich protested, but Raengar cut him off.

"Erich," Raengar snapped, perfectly aware of what the obsidian circlet meant to him. "Deimos. *Now, Sumavari*."

Sagely, Erich shut his mouth, and Raengar heard him start to run back through the thicket they had just hiked through.

Raengar waited for a minute, maybe two, the blood rushing in his ears and his pulse nothing but thunder in his veins, when the minotaur finally stepped out of the bush.

Half man, half bull, the minotaur was a sight straight from nightmares. It was huge, seven feet tall with horns that spanned out threateningly to each side at least three feet, and a thick black fur that covered it from horn to hoof.

Raengar's eyes locked on the black crystal embedded in the minotaur's forehead and cursed. An obsidian circlet. A gift from the God of Monsters to protect his children against the magick of the Gifted. It made monsters immune to magick and extremely hard to kill.

The minotaur turned to face him, sniffing loudly. It roared before lowering its massive head and charged. Raengar lunged to the right, narrowly missing the minotaur's outstretched arm.

Like most of the Pit creatures, minotaurs had varying levels of sentience, ranging from creature to creature. If Raengar could talk to him and find out what was going on, maybe the minotaur would be an invaluable asset.

"Can you speak?" Raengar yelled at the creature, but he was only answered by a loud bellow. The minotaur was fast enough to grab onto the front of Raengar's tunic but not fast enough to dodge as Raengar sliced his sword up and severed the minotaur's hand off.

Raengar was sprayed with blood as the minotaur bellowed in pain, turned, and ran into the forest. Raengar sent a shard of ice after him, hoping to strike him through the heart, but the shard hit the minotaur's back and splintered away uselessly. The obsidian circlet mounted in the minotaur's head protected the creature from Raengar's magick as it sprinted away on legs much faster than Raengar's own.

The implication sat heavily in Raengar's chest as he watched the beast disappear through the trees.

He didn't have any proof.

There were no other witnesses to see the minotaur in all its fury besides the Butcher King himself.

The Council of Houses in Valitlinn would never accept that as enough proof to send the Realms into war, and yet every day they waited was another day that Lyondrea was dragging Pit monsters out of hell.

That's how Tag and his men found Raengar. He was staring off into the Jagamine forest on his knees, covered in dark red minotaur blood.

"Fetch my Blood Hawk," Raengar ordered, not bothering to look at any of them. "Lyondrea has reopened the fucking Pits."

Tag grunted his assent, and Raengar finally turned to look up at his second-in-command. "And someone tell Erich that I will freeze the balls off the next man who calls me the Butcher King."

CHAPTER 10

JIA

The black dress Jia had borrowed whipped around her calves in the sharp wind blowing over the castle. Dark clouds stretched over the sun and casted everything into shadows. The dark clouds matched her mood.

She stood at the top of the battlements, looking out over the empty fields of the castle grounds. She turned the two letters she had penned over in her fingers, running her fingertips over the cursive names she'd scratched onto the front of each with her quill in black ink.

General Frostguard and Kiniera Kulltoug.

She had spent hours agonizing over the words, debating on what to tell her mother and the House of Ice's spymaster. She had settled on the blunt truth, all of it. A variation of: Volla and I got married and were in love. General Crax and the House of Weather betrayed us, and we were attacked. Sahana and Volla are dead. Rorax is a Contestar. We are trapped at the Northern Castle.

Rorax hadn't yet arrived at the castle where they would be essentially held prisoner. She was probably moving slowly due to the massive number of soldiers the Guardian had sent to ensure Rorax couldn't battle her way free.

Extra guards weren't the only precaution the Guardian had made. Jia's arm was still raw where the Guardian had cut her for the Blood Oath. She'd made Jia swear that if Jia let Rorax run from the Choosing or aided her in any way, Jia would die. Once Rorax heard the terms of the Blood Oath, she would stay.

It was tempting really, more tempting than she would have believed to just pitch herself off the side of the tower where she stood, to both ensure the Guardian held no power over her friend and fellow Heilstorm and to put an end to her grief.

Without Volla, what did Jia have to live for, anyway? The sacrifice wouldn't cost her a thing.

The only knowledge keeping Jia here was a threat from the Guardian. "If you don't stay, I will slit Roraxiva's throat before she can step over the threshold of the castle, and I'll watch as her life blood soaks the earth."

At least the Northern Castle was beautiful—as beautiful as a prison could be.

White granite stones made up the high walls and towers with large windows pocketing the surface every ten feet. When the sun was bright in the sky, the white stones gleamed proudly. The castle had four main towers and a tall center keep, all with four floors of rooms and barracks that connected the tall walls. A large viewing platform split the bailey of the castle in two. The castle guards referred to one side of the bailey as the Contestars' Courtyard because the Contestars would train there, and the other side held the stables. The castle guards also trained and monitored the comings and goings of the castle. Flags of the twelve realms decorated the walls and towers, the vibrant-colored banners whipping around in the wind as hard as Jia's dress.

There was an old Heir Ball arena repurposed for the Tournament of Houses at the back of the castle. The arena held thousands of people, had a grass floor, and the stands were made up of rows and rows of rudimentary white stone benches.

Jia breathed in deeply as she tilted her head to look at the sky. She felt the warning sprinkle that always precluded rain. Her mother was going to be furious when she found out she had married inside her unit. Kiniera would be more so.

Kiniera would also be furious that they had kept the fact that Rorax was a Contestar a secret. Jia should send a letter straight to the King of Ice. She knew how the king felt about Rorax, and he was going to be the most furious of all of them. She thought it might be better to cushion the blow by sending it through Kiniera, who knew the king well and would, hopefully, know what to say.

Jia turned from where she stood and quickly moved to the rookery at the top of one of the four towers. The guards let her in, and she moved right to her Blood Hawk, Pyx, who stood out like a sore thumb amongst the significantly smaller black and white crows the other houses used.

Cobalt blue feathers ran over the hawk's head and down its body. The bird nuzzled into Jia's palm as she stoked her fingers down the bird's head. Jia's fingers trembled slightly as she curled the two letters into the silversteel capsule strapped to the bird's back.

"The first letter is going to Kiniera Kulltoug, the Spymaster of House of Ice. The second goes to General Frostguard, my mother," she told Pyx.

The big bird blinked in confirmation, yellow skin sliding over an electric blue iris, as Jia screwed on the top of the capsule.

Blood Hawks were exclusive to the House of Ice and were the fastest and most secure way to transfer messages in the Realms. The biggest birds in the sky, their feathers were made of ice hard enough to deflect arrows, and they would not release a message until they had tasted the blood of a recipient, ensuring they had the right person and not an imposter. They were born and bred in the Nest, a city in the House of Ice responsible for the breeding of not only Blood Hawks but Ice Dragons as well.

Jia had been at the castle for only a day, and Pyx had shown up the first night, pecking incessantly at her window. She didn't know how the bird had found her, or how she'd known Jia needed her, but Jia had been over the moon to see her, cooing at her and stroking fingers down her frozen feathers.

A sense of ominous dread filled Jia's heart as she watched her Blood Hawk fly into the storm. There would be heavy consequences for their actions and secrets. She hoped they would survive them.

CHAPTER 11

RORAX

When the darkness was finally removed from Rorax's eyes, she wanted blood. She felt a bit feral with how badly she wanted the men around her to die.

Two days.

Two *fucking* days they had kept a group of House of Dark soldiers constantly stationed on her.

From the moment she gained consciousness and had finally been able to crack open one crusty, swollen eyelid, at least one guard had been present at her side.

They had kept a thick, Dark Magick blindfold over her eyes and ear coverings pressed against her ears, effectively blocking out all sights and sounds and dampening any ideas Rorax had of escape.

"Hello there."

Rorax furiously tried to blink, ignoring the sting from her swollen, blood-encrusted eyes, and attempted to comprehend who was speaking to her—or anything going on around her.

She looked over her shoulder at the chains behind her back.

While she had been unconscious, the soldiers had bound, loaded, then pinned her onto the back of a wooden cart.

Her hands had been shoved into two small spherical encasings made of iron. The spheres surrounded her hands and pinned them into fists, and the encasings had been clamped up high on her wrists to ensure they were out of range of her fingers.

Unfortunately, the encasings were *very* effective, making it impossible for her to use her nails or fingers to claw her way out or to pick the lock of the chains they'd wrapped around her.

The spherical encasings were connected behind her back by a short chain bolted down to a wooden seat. They were only unbolted when the six or seven soldiers who were her *personal* guard escorted her to the restroom.

Rorax's bound ankles were also anchored to the floor, and she couldn't move them more than an inch.

She felt her knife still resting in its sheath at her back, and it brought a sliver of comfort that the guards hadn't found it and confiscated it. She blew a long strand of hair out of her face, squinting as her eyes adjusted.

"Hello there," the man repeated, and Rorax finally focused on him. Him. Singular. Only one of them was with her. She looked around wildly to double-check, but there was only one soldier remaining in the back of the cart with her now.

The guard they'd left with her had dark brown skin and eyes the same color as the ocean. The black shield with a silver wolf embroidered onto the chest of his uniform confirmed that he was from the House of Dark.

Fucking fantastic.

The only other guard was the driver of the carriage.

At least *he* wouldn't see his death coming.

"Here." The guard in front of her leaned forward and quickly unhooked the gag in her mouth.

Rorax lunged forward, snapping her teeth at his throat; at the very least she could nip at his fingers. She would even bite his nose off if she was lucky enough.

The guard yelped, pulling his body away from her far enough that Rorax wouldn't be able to get close enough to *really* draw blood. Her bound hands jerked her shoulders back, reminding her that she was still anchored to the seat.

Fucking *fantastic*.

She bared her teeth at the guard, listening to the metal of her chains clink together loudly. It would be the first kiss of luck she'd had in *weeks* if they were made of only iron.

Rorax lowered herself back down. The guard chuckled nervously before giving her a sad, apologetic smile. "I'm sorry 'bout the chains. Guardians' orders."

Rorax bristled. If she could use her hands, feet, or even move forward more than a few worthless inches, she would beat that smile off his handsome face in the most brutal way possible.

"It's nice to finally meet ya, Contestar. I'm Captain Lamonte." The captain held a dark hand out to her before he seemed to realize her hands were encased in iron castings behind her back.

His hand dropped awkwardly back to his lap, and his friendly smile faltered for only a half second before it was back in full force.

Rorax narrowed her eyes and wet the inside of her mouth the best she could with her tongue before asking, "Where are we?"

Her voice was raspy, unused, and it made her throat ache. The captain must have understood her however, because he waved a hand to something over Rorax's right shoulder. Her eyes followed to where he had gestured, and her stomach roiled.

Kään help her, she was going to throw up over the side of the cart.

A giant castle loomed overhead.

A familiar castle.

The Northern Castle.

The home of the Northern Guardian. The one place she had been actively avoiding for six months. They were here.

"*Fuck*," Rorax hissed out from between her teeth, jerking against her immovable chains. She took inventory of where they were and what she could possibly use to escape.

She was in a nightmare.

They were in the middle of a long line of people pushing their way in and around the castle. Merchants with their own carts, people on horseback, even a few livestock pushed forward. She could see the flags of all twelve Realms attached to various carts or carried by countless soldiers or civilians.

Rorax hissed again as she took in more of the scene. Around the castle, the hundreds of yards of forest on each side had been cleared and now grew a carpet of freshly cut green grass.

Slowly that lush grass was disappearing though, under rows and rows of multicolored tents and throngs of people setting them up jovially. Tents and transportable buildings of every color and shape were slowly being erected on the grass around the castle, and people from every Realm in the country were already settling in, roasting pigs over the flames, laughing, and clinking their glasses together in... *celebration.*

They were *happy.*

Excited.

The sick feeling of unease and desperation in her stomach seemed so at odds with the throng's easy joy.

"Have yeh ever been to a Choosin' before? Ever been able to watch the Tournament of Houses?" Lamonte asked, resting his hands on his knees and raising a dark eyebrow as he watched her, pulling her attention back to him.

"Never," Rorax answered, her eye catching on a dark forest green flag with a silver Morningstar in the center that was being raised on a makeshift flagpole over a similarly colored green tent. The House of Alloy was here.

Rorax's blood felt a few degrees cooler than it had before as the dark flag reached its full, glorious height and started flapping gently in the breeze.

"Pity that, lass." Lamonte didn't notice her growing unease, or he chose to ignore it, as he shook his head wistfully. "The people've been waitin' a long time for you to show up. About six months, I reckon. This gatherin' will be the most fun the lot of us have seen since... well, since the last Choosin', I suppose."

Rorax flitted her eyes back to Lamonte and narrowed them as much as the swelling in her face would allow. His hands were still on his knees, relaxed, but a muscle in his cheek twitched under her scrutiny.

"Why are there so many guards in the trees?" she asked him, jerking her chin at the tree line over his shoulder. The Northern Castle was located in the middle of a red oak forest, and currently that forest near the tree line was teeming with soldiers, all in similar uniforms to Lamonte's. They watched from the shade of the trees as the civilians set up their camps in front of them.

As Lamonte looked over his shoulder to what she was gesturing at, she used her ability to fling Glimr straight up into the air.

"Ah, noticed them, did ya?" Lamonte said, his focus returning to her. "Well, lass, they're here for *you*."

Rorax's lips twitched in dark amusement, even as she sent her knife higher and higher into the sky. "Why?"

"The Guardian thinks you'll be needin' the extra protection... and the extra incentive to stay." The captain shrugged.

Rorax tilted her head in agitation.

"Captain Lamonte," Rorax purred, her voice straining just slightly with the effort it took to keep forcing her knife farther and farther into the sky. "Where is my comrade? And where are my weapons?"

"Your comrade was sent on ahead of us, along with your weapons." Lamonte rubbed his hands up and down his pants, drying his palms on the dark fabric, but to his credit, his face stayed calm.

"Lamonte," she said, forcing her voice to be low and calm. "Where in the castle would they hold the rest of my weapons?"

The captain eyed Rorax, wiping his palms up and down on his knees again. "The Guardian will let ya know everything ya need to know once we arrive."

Rorax took a deep breath. The little bloom of pain in her temples grew sharply as she sent her knife higher and higher into the sky. She rolled her jaw, trying to keep her anger and panic under control.

"Where is the Hunter now?" She didn't give a fuck if the Hunter was just some old man, the Elder Elite, or the fucking Creator himself. She was going to shove her knife up through his stomach and rip it out from his throat.

Lamonte shrugged. "I reckon he went home. The Guardian asked him to find yeh, an' he did that. He doesn' seem to like socializin'."

There was no lie in the captain's face, and she wasn't going to get close enough to the Guardian to corroborate his story.

So, with a big exhale of breath, she summoned her knife back to her.

Glimr halted its climb into the sky, flipped the point down, and dropped, barreling back toward her at a breakneck speed.

"What a coward, not seeing me all the way here himself." She leaned forward slightly and crossed her hands so that the chains overlapped, making an X behind her. If her knife had enough speed, and her chains weren't enchanted—she prayed to Kään himself that they were made with only basic iron—she might be able to break both chains in one blow.

Lamonte's brows furrowed. "I like the Hunter. A bit gruff, but I wouldn' say—"

Rorax's knife hit the chain, precisely on the overlap.

The speed of the impact created so much force that it snapped through the two iron links that had been bolted down and barreled clean through the bottom wood of the cart.

As soon as she felt the tension on her wrists loosen, she lunged for Lamonte.

Her feet were still chained to the floor, but she could now move her hands and upper body.

Rorax threw one iron-encased punch at his face, which he dodged gracefully, but he couldn't dodge the swift uppercut she threw with her other hand.

The iron encasing her fist slugged against his nose so hard she felt it crack, but she didn't stop to look at the damage.

Rorax summoned her knife back to her and was about to punch it through Lamonte's heart, when that familiar, sickening black magick engulfed her head, cutting out all sight and sound.

The magick surrounding her head made her hesitate, and that was all the time Lamonte must have needed to get in a blow of his own.

Rorax felt an impact, probably a fist, to the side of her ribs in the exact same spot where the Hunter had kicked her. Her ribs burned in agony. The force of the impact sent her toppling over, and she couldn't catch herself with her feet still chained to the floor. She found herself falling backward—like a tree helplessly falling over on the forest floor—off the wooden cart with a loud thump.

She pushed herself up on the balls of iron attached at her wrists, ready to lunge the best she could at Lamonte, when a cloth sack was pulled over her head.

Rorax thrashed violently but tasted the sleeping powder.

In her last seconds of consciousness, she summoned her knife back to the sheath under her shirt before a different kind of darkness, a sleepy kind of unconsciousness, enveloped her whole.

CHAPTER 12

AYRES

He heard the soft pop of a flare, and Ayres craned his neck up to watch the red, smoky marker fly up into the air.

People started yelling, and the courtyard full of soldiers, which had been peaceful and orderly ten seconds before, descended into chaos.

Ayres dismounted his horse and handed his reins off to a small stable boy. His two guards, Piers and Kaiya, were already off their horses and watching the flurry of commotion. Guards and soldiers barked orders at each other, rushing out from the castle and quickly assembling by the front gate, each of them brandishing arms.

"What in Marras's name is going on?" Piers grumbled, running a hand through his hair, staring up again at the red plume in the sky.

Neither Ayres nor Kaiya had a chance to answer him as a single cart, pulled by two white horses, pulled through the castle gate and into the stone courtyard.

Guards swarmed, closing in around the cart, and cut off the exit with a mass of armed bodies as the gate slammed closed behind them.

Captain Lamonte, captain of the Northern Guardian's guards, jumped down off the cart onto the stone floor of the courtyard. He reached back inside, and with a grunt, tossed a woman's limp body over his shoulder. Blood dripped down Lamonte's face, and the bridge of his nose was split open and now angled awkwardly to one side.

"Gods above, what happened to his face?" Piers muttered.

"Did *she* do that?" Kaiya put her fingers to her lips and sucked in a breath. "Marras, any harder and she could have killed him."

A black sack had been pulled tight over the woman's face and hair, and her hands dangling over her head were encased in round, ball-like iron fittings, designed so prisoners couldn't use their fingers.

One of the encasings was slick with blood, and the chains that usually bound those fittings together had been broken and now dangled uselessly toward the ground.

Ayres eyed the broken chains with growing unease. That must have been the reason for the flare, she had broken out.

Whoever this woman was, she was dangerous.

All the guards at the gate stayed on edge, watching as the woman was carried like a sack of potatoes across the courtyard.

"That must be the last Contestar," Piers muttered, "and the Guardian must be threatening everyone's lives to make sure she doesn't run off again."

When his old friend got close enough, Ayres barked out, "Oi! Lamonte! What happened to your pretty face?"

The friendly House of Dark captain sidestepped over to them with easy grace despite the body over his shoulder. "Boys, Kaiya, don't mind the blood. It's nothin' serious, but I have to say it's 'bout time you've shown up. It's been years since I've seen yer ugly mugs."

Piers clasped Lamonte's free arm with his own, giving him a nod before tilting his head at the cart Lamonte had just arrived in. "We got here just before you did, just in time to see the show."

"Who do you have there?" Ayres asked, stepping back and nodding to the unconscious body. "Is she why every soldier in the castle is armed and guarding the gate?"

"Yes, sir." Captain Lamonte looked around in turn at Ayres, Kaiya, and Piers with a wide grin. The dark brown of his skin—only a few shades lighter than Kaiya's—made the sea green of his eyes stand out. "It's the last Contestar. She's a bit of a flight risk, so the Guardian organized all this just 'n case." He gestured around to the guards who were all watching Lamonte warily.

"I didn't believe it was necessary," Lamonte admitted. "And I woke 'er up a bit early so I could prepare her for all this, but she broke out not even two minutes after I released 'er."

Lamonte shook his head in wonderous admiration, but the unease in Ayres's stomach turned into boiling irritation. *She was trying to run again?*

"Where was she hiding?" Kaiya pushed her long white braids over her shoulders before taking a cautious step closer to the unconscious female.

"They picked 'er up in Lyondrea." Lamonte shrugged the shoulder the Contestar wasn't currently draped over. "The Hunter found her nearly five days ago. I think before that, she was in House of Ice. I don' reckon it was an intentional harborin' though."

"Of course, she's Ice," Piers sneered. "Didn't the King of Ice require all of his subjects to be looked at?"

"Tha's wha' I thought." Lamonte shrugged his free shoulder again. "She must've slipped through."

Piers gave a disbelieving hum.

Ayres stepped over to Kaiya to get a closer look at the Contestar.

Thin, black leather armor encased her body from her boots all the way to the top of her throat where the black linen sack that covered her head was tied. Not an inch of skin showed. As he got closer to her, however, he noticed there were tiny red flecks of dried blood covering almost every inch of her armor.

"Was she injured?" Ayres asked, looking over the rest of her torso for clues, but the only thing he found was the same dark red, dried blood covering almost every square inch of her.

Lamonte shook his head, bouncing the woman slightly to adjust her weight on his shoulder. "The Hunter gave her a beatin', but I donna think what yer lookin at's *her* blood. Didn't see any cuts or injuries on 'er besides a few to her face... but it's hard to know."

Ayres looked over the dried blood again and tightened his jaw, his lip curling over his teeth. How many innocent men had died so she could try and run again?

Lamonte saw the fury on Ayres's face. "None of my men died extractin' 'er; it's not their blood. It musta come before that, so I dunno whose blood it is. I dunno what she was doing in Lyondrea either."

Ayres, Kaiya, and Piers all shared a weary glance. They'd all come to the Northern Castle to help protect whichever Contestar the House of Death chose to protect. Already that task seemed ominous and uncertain.

"The Guardian is waitin' for me in her room, an' I don' wanna be around for when this one wakes up. Once was enough for that." He chuckled softly to himself, reaching up to gently touch over his broken nose gingerly with one hand. "I'll see ya durin' the first feast tomorrow night though, yeah?"

Lamonte carted the woman around them and started across the courtyard toward the main keep.

Kaiya cracked her knuckles as she watched him go, her long white braids swaying down her back. "There might be a good reason why she stayed away so long."

"If there's not, she's not going to make it to the first round," Ayres grumbled, crossing his arms over his chest. He glared after the bobbing Contestar until she and Lamonte disappeared.

Chapter 13

Rorax

There was someone in her room.

Rorax opened her eyes and jerked up, blinking away any extra sleep dust remaining on her eyelashes and cheeks. She was in a big four-poster bed that was so soft it felt like she was falling in through the middle, surrounded by smooth, light gray brick walls. The walls were plain, but the ceiling was intricately carved into patterns of paisley and flowers, providing the only decoration in the room.

Lamonte must have dragged her inside the castle.

Fuck.

Across from the bed was a large stone fireplace with two cozy armchairs nestled in front. One of the two armchairs was occupied by a woman.

Rorax blinked a few more times, sitting up straighter in the bed, the hackles on the back of her neck prickling. Her thoughts felt sluggish and distant, making panic bloom in her stomach.

"Welcome to the Northern Castle, Roraxiva."

Fear crackled in Rorax's stomach at the use of her full name.

Rorax had to blink sleep away a few more times before her eyes finally focused on the woman in front of her. The woman sat with her back stick straight, her hands folded neatly in her lap. Her long, straight, silver hair flowed all the way down to her hips.

Age marks, and the most beautiful wrinkles Rorax had ever seen, donned the woman's skin.

Very rarely did someone who was Gifted release their immortality. Wrinkles were a sign of status in the Realms, a sign of unbending will, and they were highly coveted. Rorax had never seen anyone with so many.

The woman before her smiled knowingly. "When I choose to release my power to engage the new Choosing, I'll also choose to release my immortality. They go hand in hand."

When I choose to release my power to engage the new Choosing.

Rorax was confused.

The woman's smile turned wicked. "My name is Guardian Tomaren. Guardian of the Northern Realms."

Rorax stiffened. "The Guardian?"

The Guardian nodded. "We have been awaiting your arrival for months, Roraxiva."

"Where is Jia, and where are my weapons?" Rorax asked. Glimr was with her and could never leave her unless it was trapped by a witch-box made of black salt. There were only a few remaining in the world, and if the knife was not in such a box, Glimr would reappear in her hands once a certain distance was reached. Right now, her knife was in the bed with her, and she gripped it hard as she peeled the heavy blankets away from her body. She tried to stand but had to support herself on the bottom post of the bed when her head immediately started to spin.

"You won't be able to truly move around for another hour or so. Lamonte thought it prudent to give you three times the recommended dose; you've been out for a few hours."

Rorax gritted her teeth together. "Where is Jia, and where are my weapons?"

The woman pulled up the sleeve of her dress, showing Rorax the inside of her elbow where one little white horizontal scar was raised against her flesh.

"Before I came to your rooms, I stopped for a visit with your friend." The Guardian looked up at Rorax with a wicked smile. "I now have a Blood Oath with Jia that means you are not allowed to leave the Choosing or the grounds of the Northern Castle without permission from me. If you do try to leave the Choosing, Jia will die."

Rorax felt heat and adrenaline burn the panic and fear away from her system as she pushed out of bed and staggered to stand over the Guardian.

Rorax stared hard at the thin line on her skin, fighting the bile rising in her throat.

"Take a seat, Roraxiva." The Guardian pointed to the chair next to her.

Rorax moved slowly to do as she was told. She was still covered in dried blood, still in her Heilstorm leathers, and she cringed.

She pointed a finger at the Guardian. "You will release Jia from the Blood Oath immediately. I will take an oath. I will promise to stay, but she will not be forced into this." Jia needed to return home, to her brother and mother to grieve the loss of her mate.

"I have a small matter of business I must attend to outside the castle, but after I return, I would be happy to make the switch." The Guardian gave her a feline smirk as she leaned farther back into the chair before giving Rorax a once-over. "I assume you know why you're here."

Rorax nodded.

"Good. Then I wanted to welcome you to the Choosing. You are the last Contestar to arrive." The Guardian's smirk stayed firmly on her lips, but her eyes grew fractionally colder. "Though, you surprised me. Considering your position and how readily you sacrifice everything else for your country, I find it difficult to understand why I needed to go to such lengths to find you and ensure your cooperation."

Rorax's brow furrowed together. She didn't understand how her being a Heilstorm had anything to do with her being a Contestar. "I don't understand."

"It is the Gods' Law that as soon as I complete the ritual to release my position, I begin to age. I begin to die. Rapidly." She held her hand out to see the marks of age on the back of it. "From what I have compared from the lives of the Ungifted, my body is 80 summers old. Maybe 90. At the rate at which I am aging, I would estimate that my body has roughly a year left before it deteriorates completely back into the earth."

Rorax couldn't do anything but stare.

The Guardian's smile turned bitter as she lowered her hand back to her lap. "This power requires very careful management, Roraxiva. If I were to die while the Guardian's power hasn't been properly transferred, my power would either be split between the two remaining Guardians, and everything would be thrown out of balance, *or* the power I hold would return to the earth. Both options would be devastating. Especially considering one of the Guardians is closely allied with House of Alloy. If the power returned to the earth, there would be a massive increase of monsters spawning, and the Realms would become even more dangerous than they already are."

Rorax's mouth went dry.

"Vadik, the Guardian of the West, is... *enthralled* by King Määr, and we believe King Määr has been helping the Lyondrean Queen open the Pits and will *continue* to help her fight in her war if she starts one, make no mistake. If we let the Guardian of the West gain more power, *thousands* will die in that war. Or thousands will die from the monsters that spawn if the magick is released into the earth. Either way, we *are* going to complete the Choosing and transfer it properly. We have six months to avoid that fate, and if you do not comply, I will kill you. There is too much to lose."

Rorax gaped at the Guardian. She'd had no idea, *no idea,* that the Guardian was deteriorating.

Rorax snapped her mouth shut. "Is there a way that I can break free of the Choosing?"

The Guardian shook her head, her glossy gray hair reflecting some of the fireplace light. "No. Even if you die and are resuscitated, the power is tied to your very soul. You are a conduit for it until you truly pass on to the next life."

Rorax stared at her.

"The people will have their Tournament and their parties, but then the Choosing will begin, and it will need to swiftly come to an end. We have six months before I project myself to die." The Guardian assessed Rorax, running her eyes over Rorax's armor and face.

Rorax tried her best not to fidget. Her armor was absolutely filthy, and the scent of blood and sweat permeated the air.

"I have been in contact with the Ice King and Queen. They have agreed to send some of your equipment over, and they are also sending funds for you to have a new wardrobe made, along with any other supplies you might need. Hella, the tailor in town, will be coming today to collect your measurements."

Rorax frowned a little.

"Three more things, and I will leave you to get acclimated. The first is I would like to keep your... *occupation* a secret. I believe the knowledge that you are a Heilstorm would cause a disturbance among the other Contestars." The Guardian pinned her with intense yellow eyes. "Two, I want to remind you that you cannot harm the other Contestars. If you kill or even aide in the death of the other Contestars, the magick will leave you and you will die; your body will disintegrate into ash. The other Contestars must die during the trials or by natural causes."

Rorax had to lean against the chair as the magnitude, the truth, of her situation hit her. She was trapped between the Guardianship and her death; there was nowhere for her to go.

"Three," the Guardian continued, "in order for the Hunter to find your magick signature, we had to build it up, make it stronger. To do that, we had to sacrifice one of the other Contestars. Roo Abebe, from the House of Life, was killed so we could find you. Many in the castle believe your unwillingness to follow orders is the reason she is dead. They blame you. Tread carefully."

Rorax felt the breath whoosh out of her lungs like she had been punched in the stomach. The Abebes were the ruling family in the House of Life. If their princess had been sacrificed to find her, the whole house was probably calling for her head.

Every minute that passed made the Choosing more and more foreboding. She would do anything to be safe in the walls of Koppar right now.

"Do... do they know yet if the House of Weather has betrayed the Realms? Captain Crax... she used to work for the King of Weather."

"No, we still don't know who betrayed your unit. If your house has any inclination yet, they have not shared it with me or the other Guardians. House of Weather had reported Crax missing months ago when she initially went into Lyondrea. It is believed that she went rogue while she was there, bought out by the Lyondrean Queen, but we still don't know the truth of it, and there is a possibility that knowledge died with her."

Rorax's teeth ground together as the Guardian finally stood from her armchair and crossed the room to the door. She paused in the doorframe and looked at Rorax from over her shoulder. "The Contestars are gathering at seven tonight in the Great Hall. I expect you to be in attendance to meet your competition."

She gave Rorax one last triumphant smile before closing the door behind her.

CHAPTER 14

RORAX

Devastation made Rorax's movements slow and clunky, and she couldn't get the Guardian's words out of her head.

We still don't know who betrayed your unit.

Rorax rubbed her chest where it ached and turned on the water in the bath, slipping in without even testing the temperature. It was hot, scalding even, but as she felt the water burning and stinging her skin, she didn't move.

She didn't want to. She couldn't.

It felt like a punishment—the hot water searing over every nerve ending on her skin—and yet somehow it eased some of the lingering pain in her chest.

Rorax sat there for a long time, staring at the murky, bloody water until it turned cold.

Eventually, someone came casually strolling into Rorax's bathroom to fit Rorax for her clothes. A woman. She didn't knock and didn't speak at first; she just reached into the water and plucked the drain stopper out of the bottom of the tub.

With soft but firm hands, the woman gave Rorax's shoulders a gentle shove. "Out, girl. I have things to do today, and you being wet isn't going to help none."

"Who are you?"

"My name is Hella Wellbok. I am your tailor. I live in Bafta, and I'm here to help you get your wardrobe in order."

Rorax stood on numb legs and stepped over the rim of the tub into a waiting towel the woman held out for her. She dried off and dropped the towel to let the woman, Hella, hold her measuring tape around Rorax's body.

Hella was slight and pale, with golden hair so curly it draped in ringlets around her shoulders. She handed Rorax a long-sleeved, baggy, black linen shirt and matching pants, taking her bloodstained, sweat-soaked Heilstorm armor to be cleaned at her tailor shop in Bafta, the nearest town to the Northern Castle.

Rorax slowly dressed.

"Now what kind of dresses and clothes do you want for the other days of the Choosin'? You'll have interviews and a few balls to go to, so you'll have to wear a dress, or a nice pantsuit if you prefer, but *no* armor. Your House has put me in charge of your wardrobe while you're alive here, and I will not have any fusses about getting you out of your armor."

The numb fog that had seeped into Rorax's mind seemed to lift just a bit.

"Dresses?"

Rorax had never owned a dress. She'd never needed one. She'd been a soldier her entire life and had almost always been on a mission. But she'd secretly always wanted one, always wanted to be more... feminine.

"Dresses," Rorax croaked. "Mostly dresses."

Rorax spent the next twenty minutes telling Hella what kind of clothes she wanted and what clothes she would probably need. The mental break from thinking about Volla and the Choosing was welcome, and she was excited to have her own clothes that weren't issued from the House of Ice's army. It would be her very first dress.

Hella took notes and scratched on a mini notepad that had surfaced from a pocket in her dress.

They were interrupted by a loud knocking on the door.

"Come get these when I call for you, girl," Hella said, sliding her notepad back into her pocket. "I will have my assistant slide you a note under your door when you are to pick them up. *Don't* keep me waiting, or I'll donate them all to the local pigpen." She left Rorax's room with a flourish.

Hella had left the door open, and one of the Guardian's men stood in the doorway. "The Guardian sent me to fetch you. It's time for the Contestars' first meeting."

Rorax nodded and let the man lead the way through the corridors and down a staircase until they came to a set of intricately carved wooden doors. The doors led into a room that could only be the Great Hall.

The Great Hall was a long, rectangular room with the Guardian's throne seated at one end and tall wooden bleachers set up on each side of the room. It was a spectacular room, with stained glass windows and priceless tapestries. But Rorax was more interested in its occupants.

Ten other women, all dressed in colorful, beautiful dresses turned toward her, but Rorax kept her eyes focused on the Guardian, unwilling to back down from the Guardian's gaze until Rorax made it halfway across the hall.

The women here were diverse, with various skin tones and heights. One in particular caught her eye and made her heart seize in her chest. She was tall, muscular, and had long blonde hair.

Rorax stopped breathing. She stopped walking too, standing utterly still, because if she took one more step forward, she didn't know if her knees would support her.

Standing right in front of her, not twenty paces away was Volla. Volla Torvik was alive.

Volla, her best friend in all of Illus, was *alive.* She was breathing, she was whole, and she was *here.*

"Volla?" Rorax croaked, relief and surprise making her throat so tight she had to whisper the words.

The other women standing with her looked around, confused, and Volla's face transformed from uninterested to murderous, but Rorax barely noticed. She didn't know how this was possible, but she didn't care. She didn't give one single fuck. It was *Volla.*

She was going to be able to tell Jia her mate had *survived.* Rorax's best friend had *survived.*

"Holy shit." Rorax suddenly lurched into motion, and then she was jogging, almost running to Volla as she cried out Volla's name again.

"Stop." Volla held out her palms to stop Rorax. Volla's green eyes flashed in fury, but Rorax continued.

Rorax still couldn't breathe right, and her eyes were burning.

When Rorax was less than five feet away, Volla snarled and took a big step away, pulling out a sharp blade as if fending off an attacker. "If you take one more step toward me, I will rip your throat out."

Volla's snarl finally broke through Rorax's shock, and she halted, frozen in place. She reached up and wiped away her tears with the back of her hand as she stared up into her best friend's beautiful, snarling face. "What?"

"My name is *Isgra* Torvik," the woman sneered, her eyes glittering with vicious intent as she took another step away.

"Isgra..." Rorax's brain felt like it was filled with sludge, and the name felt foreign and wrong on her tongue. "Isgra."

Her words didn't make sense.

Rorax blinked, then blinked again. "You're Isgra... Volla's... twin sister."

Isgra's lip curled in contempt, but she nodded.

Rorax looked her up and down slowly, rubbing her palm against a new throb in her chest but noticing how this woman held herself. So different from Volla and yet... she was the spitting image of Volla, completely identical.

Rorax knew Volla's face almost as well as her own after the last fifty years, and this was it. She was right here.

But Volla had never, *ever* looked at Rorax like that, with such disgust and disdain—even when Rorax had deserved it the most. Rorax's eyes caught on a bright red scar that took up the length of the left side of Isgra's neck—a burn mark that Volla didn't have—and knew it was true.

Volla was still dead.

Rorax wrapped her arms around her middle and had to force her body not to collapse.

Isgra watched, her lips curling even farther over her teeth. "Do not ever mistake me for that murderous cunt again."

"Her wife is here. At the castle." Rorax's throat worked, and her voice sounded haggard and broken even to her own ears.

The news made Isgra's entire body flinch like Rorax had just slapped her across the face. "Her *what*?"

Flames started to crawl up Isgra's arms, licking out toward Rorax with hot orange tongues.

A hand wrapped around Rorax's shoulder, pulling her back a few steps. Rorax was so dazed she complied, almost tripping over her own feet as one of the women—one of the other Contestars—jerked her back and put her own body in front of Rorax's to shield her. "Isgra, *relax*. She's new. She obviously didn't know," the woman hissed.

The woman protecting her was an inch or two shorter than Rorax, with similar long black hair but skin a few shades darker than her own. The woman turned her head to look at Rorax, her large brown eyes wide with concern. "Are you okay?"

Rorax opened her mouth to respond, but the words caught in her throat. *No.*

"Oh, let 'em fight, Enna!" one of the women called from the group, a blonde with chin-length hair, short bangs, and tan skin. There was a long white scar running through one of her eyes, violently marring the side of her pretty face. "We've been starvin' for entertainment 'round here!"

"Ladies," the Guardian drawled at them from her throne. "As *entertaining* as it is to watch, I do have other matters I must attend to this evening."

Rorax looked around to the other women in the room, having forgotten all about them. She found all of them watching her with wary eyes, except for the scarred blonde with an excited glint in her good eye.

The group started to sit down on the long bench, and Isgra turned away, dismissing her. Rorax could only stand there watching her go until some of the other girls snickered.

"Come on," Enna grabbed her arm in a surprisingly strong grip and dragged her to the bench, sitting Rorax down next to her.

The Guardian studied all of them for a long moment until she finally spoke, a smile slowly creeping across her mouth. "*Finally*, welcome to the Choosing for the new Northern Guardian, ladies."

There were some nervous murmurs back.

"As most of you know, the Choosing is made up of a series of trials, each of these trials is made not only to test you, but to kill you."

Rorax curled her arms around her waist again, needing her own strength.

"For the next six months, I hope you enjoy your freedom from the leeches of the Realms. Witches, Priests, Kings, Paladins, the Red Circle, the Ungifted, the Western Guardian, the Eastern Guardian, your families, and all the rest of them are barred from entry to the Choosing."

The Guardian stared at the Contestars, then continued her speech. "According to the Guardians' Law, my staff, an emissary from each house, and ten of their house's soldiers are the only ones allowed to reside in the Northern Castle for the Choosing. No one else is to interfere."

"What about the people coming for the Tournament?" one of the women asked.

Rorax thought about the people who had been in the carts next to her when she had arrived.

"Civilians are welcome to attend the Tournament of Houses, but even they must depart once the Tournament has found its victor. Everyone is required to leave the day after the Tournament ends since the Choosing will officially begin shortly after."

"Why are the emissaries and their men allowed to stay?" the woman, Enna, asked from beside her, a little furrow appearing between her dark eyebrows.

"There are eleven of you still alive. Each of you has been given a piece of my magick that will only be released upon your death. The released magick will divvy itself between the remaining Contestars, making the survivors stronger. However, for a few minutes after the new magick hits you, you will lose yourself to a fit of rage for a brief time. The magick itself is angry that it's been split; it *wants* to be whole. It desperately wants to be reconnected to itself, and it will urge you to fight and kill any Contestars remaining that have a sliver of that power. It will be a burst of uncontrollable rage and violence. This period is known as the influx."

"But the Gods' Law is, if we kill each other, we die?" Enna asked again, wringing her fingers in her lap.

The Guardian gave her a bloodthirsty smile. "Precisely. To protect yourself from that fate, we ask that each House sends an emissary that is tasked with building a team of soldiers and knights to choose one Contestar to protect. They are called your Protectorate House. They will protect you from others, yes, but mostly they will protect you from *yourself.* They will keep you from killing a fellow Contestar during your influxes."

Rorax's head was spinning. All the girls were quiet for a long moment.

"Did you say the Houses choose which Contestar they want to be Protectorate to?" Rorax asked, tightening her arms around her waist, her voice scratchy and hoarse.

The Guardian nodded. "The House that wins the Tournament of Houses at the beginning of the next moon will choose a Contestar to represent first. The second place House chooses second. The third place House will choose third, and so on."

The girls whispered excitedly at that. The Tournament of Houses was legendary. It took place only when a Guardian retired and was one of the most famous events in the Realms, commanding more excitement than any national holiday by far.

"What happens if one of us is successful in killing another Contestar?" Isgra asked, and out of the corner of her eye, Rorax saw Isgra cut her a glare.

"If you kill any of the other Contestars here, the magick will poison you. You will be dead within minutes."

Rorax ground her teeth together. The urge to go home, to be anywhere but here, was so strong she would have been out the door already if Jia's life wasn't at risk.

"As you know, the Guardian's are responsible for the safety of the Realms. You must be up to standard, and so every day at four in the afternoon, you will be required to participate in a training session in the Contestars' Courtyard. We will have trainers, coaches, and sparring partners there. You will be introduced to the emissaries at three tomorrow afternoon in the arena at the back of the castle, and then we will have our first social event tomorrow evening. I recommend you all rest tonight and come in your best dress tomorrow. Do any of you have any more questions?"

When no one spoke up, the Guardian dismissed the girls, and they moved toward the door.

Rorax also stood, feeling completely off balance. She needed to be alone. She needed a drink. She needed another bath. She needed to go for a run. She needed sleep. She needed *something* to calm her thoughts and help center herself again so she could figure out how she was going to survive the Choosing.

Rorax ignored Enna's concerned look and turned toward the exit, but a strong hand gripped her arm and yanked her back.

Isgra was standing so close to her, Rorax had to look up to meet her eyes. She must have been the full six-foot-two height that her sister had been, making her a full eight inches taller than Rorax.

Rorax sucked deep breaths into her lungs, talking herself out of shattering every one of Isgra's fingers that were wrapped so tightly around her arm she was sure to have bruises.

"What do you want, *Isgra*?" Rorax ripped her arm out of her grasp.

Isgra bristled, narrowing her eyes even further at Rorax's tone. "I heard you were a soldier for the House of Ice. How well did you know my sister?"

"She was my commander," Rorax hissed. "I was with her every day."

"I heard Volla died begging for mercy like a coward. It doesn't surprise me. I heard that when she died, she died in disgrace," Isgra sneered. The breath caught in Rorax's lungs. "Just make sure you stay away from me and keep my sister's whore out of my si—"

Rorax backhanded Isgra across the mouth so hard her body rotated around, and Rorax saw where her bird ring had cut open Isgra's upper lip from the line of trickling blood.

"You stupid *cunt,"* Isgra hissed as she touched her bloody lip gingerly with her fingertips.

Her eyes held anger, but for the first time there was a flash of hesitation—of fear—in Isgra's eyes, and something deep within Rorax gloated. All the pain and self-pity in Rorax's blood burned into anger and aggression.

Rorax took a menacing step toward Isgra. She smacked Isgra's hand away from her face so she could reach up and grip her chin. "I have nothing left to lose in this life except Volla's wife, Isgra. If you push me too hard, I would be more than happy to beat your skull in until it's your brain dripping down your face and not just blood."

Rorax smirked, running her thumb through the drop of blood running down Isgra's chin, smearing it across her skin.

"Watch yourself. I will turn you both into nothing but roasted piglets," Isgra sneered, knocking Rorax's hand away from her face. But the fear remained in her eyes. Isgra conjured a ball of flame in her hands and was about to throw it at Rorax when a sharp voice cracked through the air.

"Stop!" Enna shoved her way between them *again*, pushing Rorax back a few steps as another Contestar—the one with the scar and the bobbed blonde hair who had been taunting Enna to let them fight earlier—pushed Isgra away.

"Stop it, both of you," Enna snapped.

"Both of ya are blockheads. Didn't ya hear what the Guardian just said? If we kill each other, we die. Don't trigger an influx with all eleven of us standin' in the same room," the blonde hissed, the scar on her face tightening.

"Stay out of this, Briar—"

"Greywood, come here. Now. Torvik, the rest of you, go back to your rooms," the Guardian snapped from her throne.

Isgra gave Rorax one more scathing look before turning on her heel and sulking away. Enna and the blonde with the scar, Briar, hesitated for only a moment before following her out.

Rorax crossed the room to where the Guardian was waiting for her on a golden throne.

The Guardian looked down her nose at her. "If you're not careful, Greywood, you'll find yourself in an early grave."

In the hour that Rorax had arrived and broken the news about Isgra being a Contestar, Jia's tears hadn't shown any signs of slowing down. She rotated between silently weeping and full-on agonized sobs.

Jia had taken the news of Isgra's presence at the castle hard. She'd obviously already been crying when she opened the door to her room for Rorax earlier, but the news that her sister in-law was the complete antithesis of Volla—while also identical to Volla physically—had thrown Jia over the edge.

Jia was curled up in one of the armchairs in front of the fireplace. The skin around her purple eyes was bright pink and puffy; her usually perfect complexion was red and blotchy over her cheeks and neck. There was nothing left in the angular lines of Jia's face but agony and loss.

Jia's room was just like Rorax's, small but with a big bed and its own closet and bathroom. There was also a fireplace with two identical leather armchairs in front of it where they sat now, watching the fire.

"Jia, I...." Rorax's eyes caught on the new white scar on Jia's forearm from the Blood Oath with the Guardian that was designed to trap her here. Rorax had to swallow down a lump in her throat. "I'll make a new Blood Oath with the Guardian. You should be at home with your family. I'm sorry you're here at all."

Fresh tears tracked down Jia's face as she shook her head. She unfolded herself from her chair and slowly moved to the window, wrapping her arms around her waist and hunching her shoulders over herself protectively. "No. I'm glad you're not here alone." Jia sniffled, wiping her eyes with the back of her wrist. "Even when the Guardian releases me, I'll stay with you. Volla... well, she wouldn't want you to be here alone either."

Rorax had to clear her throat, the selfish part of her so relieved at the words. "Thank you. I'm going to start researching in the library here to see if I can find any books on the Choosing, see if there's anything I can do to get myself out of this mess faster. I need to somehow get the magick to unclasp itself from my soul so we can go home."

Jia's limp purple ponytail swayed as she nodded. "I'll help you. There must be a way out of this. I don't want to see you, or... *her* die, even if she isn't Volla." Her voice cracked, and so did a little piece of Rorax's heart.

"Volla didn't... she wasn't close with Isgra, but she still loved her." Jia's shoulders bowed further and started to shake with silent sobs.

Rorax wasn't familiar with offering comfort, but her instincts pulled her toward Jia. She hesitantly wrapped her arms around Jia's shoulders, pressing Jia's wet face onto her shoulder.

"It's alright. You're okay. I've got you." Rorax's eyes burned with tears too, but she blinked them back.

Later. You'll have time to mourn for them later.

Rorax ran her hand over Jia's hair and across her shoulders, trying to soothe her the way she had seen Sahana and Volla do before. "We can get her out of here. We can make sure she makes it through."

Rorax finally left Jia when her friend all but fell asleep standing up. After getting some directions from a soldier, she found the Northern Castle Library. She stepped through the entrance, and her breath caught in her throat.

After the War of the Wings, Valitlinn had taken damage, so the Guardians decided to move the national archives to the Northern Castle for safekeeping. Hundreds of aisles of shelves holding countless books and scrolls lined the walls of the library. Rorax stood for a moment and breathed in the familiar smells of books and underground musk and took in the endless number of stacks.

The Northern Castle Library had been established in a large, natural cave the original builders of the castle had found when they started construction. Hundreds of stalactites hung down from the forty-foot ceiling, each of various lengths—some long enough that they brushed the tops of the bookshelves, some short enough they could only be the length of her pinky finger.

Her jaw went a little slack at the sight. It was even more beautiful than she had imagined.

"Welcome!"

Rorax's body jerked in surprise, and she twisted around to find a small man with a toothy grin and wrinkled, tan skin perched excitedly at a desk at the entrance.

"Blimy! You must be the new Contestar!"

Rorax's brow furrowed as the man hopped over his desk and scurried over to her. "How did you know that?"

He was almost six inches shorter than her, barely five foot tall, dressed in a loose white linen kaftan. He beamed up at her behind glasses that made his eyes seem three times too large for his face.

"You're one of the only people in the castle I haven't seen yet! Common folk aren't allowed in the castle. My name is Radashan, and I am the Bookkeeper and Master of Gnomes for the Northern Castle Library." He gave Rorax a little bow, and her eyebrows furrowed together with uncertainty.

Should she bow back?

Instead Rorax held out her hand. "My name is Rorax Greywood; it is nice to meet you, Radashan Bookkeeper."

He beamed even brighter as he shook Rorax's hand with one of his small ones.

Rorax tilted her head, running her eyes over the soft wrinkles in his brown skin. "Your wrinkles are beautiful. Did you relinquish the Gift?"

Rorax knew at any time the Gifted could relinquish their gift to their House's Priests to age like the Ungifted. She'd known a few people in her life who had voluntarily chosen to see what was on the other side of the veil after hundreds or thousands of years of life. Rorax had never given much thought to her own death. She'd always assumed she would die on one of her unit's missions.

Radashan nodded eagerly. "Thank you! Yes, I gave it up for fifty years! I reinstated it recently, once I heard the Guardian was... retiring."

Rorax raised her eyebrows in surprise. Relinquishing the Gift took a certain amount of skill, but reinstating it was even harder, almost impossible. "I'm impressed."

Radashan looked down to his toes, blushing. "You're very kind, Rorax Greywood."

Smiling, she turned to the rows and rows of books. There must have been a half mile's worth of stacks in both directions, all under the hanging stalactites that were illuminated by torches anchored onto the ends of each aisle. Tiny gnomes with tall, multicolored hats and clothes scurried in and out of the rows, carrying books, scrolls, and papers back and forth or dusting off the books.

"Does water ever get in here?" Rorax asked Radashan, eyeing one stalactite that was almost as thick around and longer than she was tall.

"No! Ukuros, no! The ceiling has been enchanted and stabilized with runes by witches gifted by Water and Alloy to make sure the stalactites are stable, and the books are protected from the elements." Radashan pointed to a chandelier that held up seven round balls of light. Two chubby gnomes were draped across it, fast asleep. "Those chandeliers are fireless, a gift from the House of Light."

Rorax eyed the orbs of light, the stalactites, and the little gnomes running around, before focusing on the sheer number of books. "It's amazing here."

"Thank you, Contestar." Radashan gave a pleased little shuffle under her praise. "Is there anything I can help you find?"

"What do you have here on the Choosing?"

Chapter 15

Tressa

Tressa Abebe stepped up to the railing and carefully peeled the hood of her cloak away from her face so she could see down to the Contestars' Courtyard below.

She hadn't gone to see where her room was, hadn't bothered to go see her office in the Healer's Hall, hadn't unpacked, or even relieved herself after the trip. She hadn't even gone to find Ren yet.

No.

First, before anything else, Tressa needed to see *her*.

Tressa squeezed the railing of the viewing platform over the courtyard and searched each Contestar's face, looking for the one who was unfamiliar among the women. Six months ago, they had gathered initially, and Tressa had gotten to know all of the Contestars. All except the one who hadn't come.

According to the schedule Ren had given her, the Contestars should still be out training before the dinner bell rang. The Guardian's trainers hovered closely, trying to give the Contestars advice as they moved through fighting sequences and tried out new weapons. Tressa's eyes moved over every one of them until she found her. The only girl dressed in the Contestar leathers who hadn't shown up the first time for the Choosing.

It was *her*.

Tressa was a healer, but not just any healer. She was also the Princess of the House of Life. She was the daughter of Abebe, the old King of House of Life and one of the greatest healers in the Realm's history.

She could hold more than the average amount of healing magick in her. Her friends in the past had always described Tressa as sweet, loving, and kind. War, pain, and death were not part of her nature, but as Tressa studied the girl carefully, her fingers twitched with the need to scratch her nails down that fierce, beautiful face.

Coward, Tressa thought as the girl she watched shifted her weight, keeping her eyes locked on the fight in front of her. Her skin was clear, not sweaty and dirty like those of her counterparts. Maybe she couldn't be bothered to train with the rest of them, maybe she had never fought before, but the Guardian's men were giving her a wide berth, as if they were reluctant to cross over into her bubble of influence, and Tressa didn't understand it. She didn't like it either.

Tressa's upper lip twisted into a snarl.

Two large hands wrapped around her upper arms. "Easy now, lass."

Tressa knew the body behind her as well as she knew her own, knew that voice, and she reluctantly melted into his chest, biting back the groan of pleasure at enjoying the heat of his arms.

Warm lips brushed under her ear, and she involuntarily tilted her head toward his wicked mouth.

Tressa's voice was low and lethal. "If she makes it past the first round, even you won't be able to stop me when I kill her."

Ren laughed softly and tucked one of Tressa's waist-long braids behind her ear. "You assume, Princess, that I wouldn't be with you. I already told you, I want to be an accomplice to *all* your sins."

She hummed in pleasure and rocked back grudgingly into Ren's arms. She hadn't seen him in a month, and the warmth and strength radiating from him was enough to distract her from wanting to water the courtyard stones with the girl's blood.

The girl must have finally felt the heat of Tressa's glare, and two icy blue eyes flicked up to focus on her.

Adrenaline flushed into Tressa's blood, and Tressa pulled her lips up and bared her teeth. *I'm going to kill you in the most violent way I can think of.*

But as the girl studied Tressa, nothing in her face changed. She didn't look confused, annoyed, or even vaguely interested that Tressa was staring daggers into her.

The girl slid her gaze up to look at Ren, her eyes skating over the broad arm he had banded across Tressa's torso, holding her tightly against his chest.

Then the girl blinked. Just once.

One bored, uninterested blink, and that was it.

Tressa let loose a low growl, her snarl deepening, but the girl's expression didn't change, and she didn't look away. There was no shame or remorse or recognition in her gaze, and it shot another jolt of unfamiliar, furious adrenaline through Tressa.

Ren jerked her back a step from the railing. She stumbled back with him, hissing like a cat, but Ren just kept pulling her with him. He was at least three times her size, corded with muscle and brawn, and she felt like a paper doll being dragged behind him.

Using the gifts she had inherited from her mother's side of the family, she could have pulped Ren's brain into nothing more than textured mush, but she would never do that.

Never to Ren.

She would rather pulp her own brain than touch a single synapse in his, and he knew it.

He continued to pull her away, through the door to the balcony and down a corridor before he tucked her into an empty hallway and had her back pressed against a wall. He grabbed her wrists and pinned them above her head.

Tressa breathed so heavily her breasts brushed his chest. She could see with smug satisfaction that he was trying not to look at her flawless, ebony skin visible down the front of her dress.

Beneath her bubbling anger at him for dragging her away, a different heat sparked through her, and her chest arched a bit more into him.

"Woman," he growled, his face getting closer to her, keeping her eyes trapped on him. "Now is not the time."

Tressa bit her lip and arched her breasts farther into him, brushing them against his chest until he growled with lust. "I haven't seen you in a month," she pouted. "Now is *definitely* the time."

"That's not what I mean. We will be getting to *that* as soon as I can talk my way into this thick head of yours." Tressa glared, but Ren pressed on. "The Gods' Law states that no one is to touch the Contestars until after the Protectorates choose. *Now* is not the time to kill her, Tressa." His voice was thick and guttural, and her anger was fading fast. Lust spiraled up in her stomach instead. His familiar heat against her body was becoming something she needed, urgently.

Tressa licked her lips, and Ren's eyes watched her mouth. "Tressa, do we have an agreement?"

Ren slowly looked back at her eyes as he pressed his hard body into her a fraction more. She had to bite back a groan as he ground his hips into her, feeling his cock hot and hard against her stomach.

"Tressa," he warned. "I want to hear that promise straight from your cursed, bewitching mouth."

She rolled her eyes and pulled her wrists out of his grasp to wrap her arms up around Ren's thick, muscled neck. She leaned in and bit down on his trapezius softly, her flat teeth scraping on the muscles that clenched across her tongue. Groaning, he rolled his hips so she could feel him against her again.

"Tressa," he growled, begging, the sound making her nipples harden into points under her dress.

"I promise, Ren. I will wait until the Gods' Law does not protect her." She smiled softly, pressing a palm against the side of his jaw, admiring the contrast between his pale flesh and her own dark skin. It was one of her favorite things about them. So different, and yet exactly the same. She looked up into his eyes to see him watching her, his gaze setting her blood on fire.

Tressa rocked onto her toes to plant a chaste kiss against his lips. "I have too much to lose. I won't risk it on her," she said with a sigh.

Ren smiled, and seeing his green eyes sparkle made Tressa's heart squeeze. He bent down and finally kissed her, his tongue sending delicious shivers down her spine. Kissing him swept away all thoughts about the girl, the girl with ice in her eyes and an unflinching stare.

The girl who Tressa was going to murder to avenge her dead sister.

Chapter 16

Raengar

Deimos Ice-Born was said to be the father of all House of Ice's dragons—their war dragons and carrier dragons alike. According to legend, Deimos had been Kään's dragon, made of nothing more than a fistful of frost, and left behind after the gods left Illus. Even if that was legend and nothing more, he was the largest and oldest war dragon on the continent and had been passed down through the Kings of Ice from father to first born since the Rip, when the beginning of the Gifted's recorded history began over ten thousand years ago.

King Raengar Carbore was arguably the most powerful man in the Realms. He was the King of Ice, Guardian of Elu, Commander of the Iskriger Army, and rider of Deimos Ice-Born. Raengar had won Deimos after he'd killed his father, King Katalon Carbore, and usurped the throne.

Deimos and Raengar were a fitting pair, matched in both spirit and temperament. Soulmates of the platonic, dragon-riding sort.

Currently, they were also matching in other ways, both covered in blood and their temper hanging by a frayed thread.

Deimos's wings pumped and tensed under Raengar's thighs as the great dragon banked to the side, coasting over the glittering city of Morvarand, aiming for a small House of Ice war camp erected half a mile from the city gates. As they landed, his dragon tamers swarmed around them, grabbing the reins from Raengar as he climbed off.

Eshaal, the leader of the second unit of the Heilstorms leaned against one of the poles that kept one of the war tents erect, waiting for him. As he approached her, she gave Raengar a respectful bow but kept her eyes hesitantly on Deimos. Her gaze was full of respect and a healthy amount of fear as she watched Raengar's dragon tamers unsaddle Deimos, feed him two large moose carcasses, and start to wash the encrusted blood off his ice-blue scales and claws.

"Hello, Your Grace." Eshaal offered him a scroll. "Your sister's Blood Hawk just arrived with this. It's probably the Council of Houses' answer about what to do with the minotaur news."

Raengar's mood darkened further, and he rolled his jaw as he took the parchment from her hand and grunted his thanks. He didn't even need to break the seal to know what was inside.

"Do you need anything else, Your Grace? Kiniera just arrived; I wanted to go and welcome her."

Raengar shook his head. "No, but ask Kiniera if we can have our meeting after breakfast. I need a bath and some whiskey."

Eshaal nodded and left him with one last nervous gaze to Deimos.

Raengar pushed into his tent and made his way to his desk. Then he cracked the wax seal of the Council of Houses and read every damned word they had written him.

They would not approve of a war with Lyondrea without proof or reliable witnesses.

Raengar tossed the scroll on his desk in disgust.

He was the King of Ice for fuck's sake, the most powerful House in the Realms by leagues, in every ranking system imaginable.

So why he was putting up with the bureaucratic bullshit or playing the mind games of the Council of Houses and the Trigonal Throne was beyond him. Valitlinn could burn for all he cared. Raengar drummed his blood-encrusted fingertips on the wooden pallets that had been stacked together to make his makeshift desk and started reading over his morning reports of any overnight news. Nothing good awaited him. He had lost three men in an overnight skirmish that still bloodied his skin, but there had been no signs of any more Pit monsters.

Raengar had stationed himself in the gap between the High Queens Mountain and the Jagamine Mountains on the border of House of Death. He wanted to move more men to the border, had wanted to push into Lyondrea with the full force of the House of Ice and completely eradicate the Pits and any Lyondrean foolish enough to think opening the Pits was a good idea. But the matter had been brought to the Council of Houses in Valitlinn and had been rejected.

So, here he would stay at the border with only a small contingent of men, supporting House of Death's small but ferocious army, and putter around uselessly, waiting for Lyondrea to show its teeth.

He rubbed the back of his neck with his palm, trying to soothe the tension away before he poured himself a drink in a glass tumbler. He had the glass to his lips when the flap to his tent ripped open and Kiniera and Eshaal rushed inside. Kiniera Kulltoug, his spymaster, and Eshaal, the leader of the Heilstorm's second unit, were complete opposites. Eshaal had light brown skin, a prominent nose, and bobbed black hair. Her eyes were always warm.

Kiniera was normally so pale her white skin was borderline translucent, showing off the perpetual dark circles she had under her eyes, along with the blue and purple veins at her wrists and elbows. Her long, moon-white hair was nearly the same color as her skin, and even her eyes were almost colorless—an icy pale blue.

Something had happened to drain all the color in Kiniera's cheeks. She looked *ill,* almost corpse-like. In fact, Eshaal looked uncharacteristically pale, too.

Something shiny fell from the corner of Kiniera's eye. A tear?

"What's wrong?" Dread curdled in Raengar's chest. He hadn't seen his spymaster cry in nearly fifty-five years.

"Unit One was attacked," Kiniera whispered, another tear escaping her wide, shocked eyes. "I just received a letter from Jia Frostguard. Sahana and Volla were both killed."

Raengar's whole body froze, like his magick had decided to turn inward and frost his insides into a glacier. Kiniera kept speaking to him, but it was like he was underwater. He could barely comprehend her words.

"We recovered Volla's body, but we were unable to recover Sahana. It was either burned beyond recognition—"

"Where is Rorax?" Raengar interrupted, a low hum starting in his ears. Gods above, he had known. He had *known* it was a bad idea to send her to Lyondrea and had approved it anyway.

When Kiniera and Eshaal shared a glance, the little spark of fear that had been in Kiniera's eyes before was back. "Jia and Rorax are on the way to the Northern Castle as we speak. They should arrive today." Kiniera's throat bobbed.

Raengar gritted his teeth. "Why is Rorax going to the Northern Castle and not coming home?"

Home. Where she belonged. With *him.*

His heart beat so hard he felt it in his fingertips. He was banned from meddling in Lyondrea, but he would create a task force to get her brother back, the Guardians and the Council of the Houses be damned. He would shatter the Guardians' Law and not even ask them.

Rorax was too important, and Raengar felt like he was playing a dangerous game he wouldn't win if he kept playing like this.

"She's going to the Northern Castle... because the Hunter tracked her, captured her, and is taking her there."

Raengar blinked down at Kiniera. That low humming noise grew louder in his ears. The Hunter? The last Raengar had heard, the Hunter had been commissioned by the Guardian to find the lost Contestar.

"Why?" Raengar snapped, hating that he already knew the answer, hating that the most important woman of his life had lied. She had *hidden it from him.*

"Because she's the missing Contestar."

Chapter 17

Rorax

Rorax tried not to grumble to herself too loudly as she crossed the city limits into Bafta. The streets were teeming with people and overly dusty, as wagons full of civilians and merchants gathered for the Tournament of Houses. Anyone who spared her a glance gave her distinctive, golden-trimmed Contestar leathers a questioning look as she passed by, but most people were too wrapped up in their own lives to bother with her.

Every day for the past week since Rorax had arrived at the castle, she woke to train before the sun lit the sky. Today she met a still gaunt Jia in the hallway outside of Jia's room, and together they went out to the empty arena behind the castle. They ran and sprinted laps around the grassy area, warming up and stretching for over thirty minutes before moving into their usual sparring routine.

The castle's two baileys were habitually deserted when they left the arena, but when they returned, usually two hours later, a few of the Guardian's soldiers would be sparring in the Contestars' Courtyard. Today Isgra was out training with them. She pretended not to see either of them, even when Jia had given Isgra a long, lingering look.

Usually, Rorax would take a bath and then disappear to the library after training to avoid the hottest part of the day. She'd search through the mountain of books Radashan always left for her and Jia to rifle through. But when Rorax returned to her room later that day, there was a small note attached to the door for her. She read over it three times *very* slowly to make sure she'd read the neat handwriting correctly, before groaning and snatching the little piece of paper off her door and crumpling it in her fist.

"What is it?" Jia asked, coming to a stop next to Rorax.

Jia plucked the crumpled piece of paper from Rorax's hand and read it over and breathed out a laugh. It was a hollow, sickening sound to Rorax—completely devoid of Jia's usual joy—but it was something. "At least you'll have some new clothes. I've had to resort to stealing mine."

Rorax raised her eyebrows at this, but her thieving friend only gave an unrepentant shrug before walking away.

Rorax only had time to take a quick bath and wipe the sweat off her leathers before she went out the door again.

When she finally stopped on a street corner, she uncrumpled the little piece of paper she'd been fisting the entire twenty-minute walk from the Northern Castle and smoothed it out with her fingers.

Please make your way to Wellbok Tailors before midday to pick up your clothes.

102

3rd Street

South Bafta

When she finally arrived at the little building, she reread the sign twice to make sure she was in the right place before pushing the door open and making her way into the shop.

As soon as the door closed behind her and she could comprehend what she was seeing, Rorax froze and gaped at the rainbow-colored walls around her.

Fabric of every color, pattern, and material was crammed into dark wood shelves that lined every wall from floor to ceiling.

Reds, yellows, blacks, purples, blues, silks, chiffons, cottons, smooth leather, patterned leather... everything Rorax had ever dreamed of was here.

She was still gawking at the room when a hidden door, which had been covered by a shelf so full of fabrics that Rorax hadn't even noticed it, flew open and a blurred shape of a woman came flying out toward her.

"You! You are late! I have been expecting you for *two* days now!" The blur stopped in front of Rorax, and she gaped down at the woman glaring up at her with her hands on her hips before jabbing a stern finger into Rorax's face. "I am not a storage facility, *Greywood.* The next time you can't be bothered to show up on time, your clothes are going straight to the brothel! The orphanage! To my brother's hogs! You will pick them up on time or not at all!"

Rorax knew this woman. Hella Wellbok. She was the one who'd been in the castle when she had arrived. She had helped her bathe and dress when she had been lost to grief and shock. She had taken Rorax's measurements and her Heilstorm armor to clean the dried blood away. The woman had blonde hair that draped around her face in tight ringlets down to her waist and sharp green eyes. Any gentleness she had displayed in Rorax's vulnerable moments had long since left the woman's features, leaving only a ferocious, blonde she-lion.

"I... um...." Rorax frowned down at the woman, suddenly feeling hot and flustered. "I just got your note today. I wasn't aware they were ready to be picked up. I only ordered them three days ago. My usual tailor—"

"Your usual tailor?" Hella shrieked. "Your *usual tailor*? Do I look like your usual tailor to you?"

She opened her arms wide so Rorax could assess her. Rorax looked her up and down, taking in her sparkling purple dress and stylish boots, then swallowed hard before shaking her head. "No, I apologize. I will be here on time next time."

If there ever *was* a next time. Rorax fervently hoped there wouldn't be. The woman gave her a satisfied nod before sticking out her hand for Rorax to shake.

"My name is Hella Wellbok, your personal tailor for your time at the Northern Castle."

Rorax shook her hand. "I remember you. Do you have my black armor here?"

Hella nodded her head hard enough her curly blonde hair bounced up and down. "I do! Follow me."

Hella spun around and walked so fast she became a blur to Rorax again.

Rorax treaded carefully, following the small woman through the fabric-covered door that led to the back workshop. She peered around the doorframe to find another room of similar size housing three massive sewing machines, endless measuring tapes, mannequins, and a clothing rack where her Heilstorm fighting leathers rested on a hanger in the front.

Rorax went to them immediately and ran her fingers over the leather. All the blood had been cleaned away, and the leather had been expertly oiled and shined. They looked like the first day they had been issued to her.

Rorax glanced up to see Hella grabbing a clump of hangers with clothes of various shades off a different rack.

"Other Realms brought in custom tailors for their Contestars," Hella griped as she heaved all the hangers and clothes across the room before hanging them next to Rorax's black armor. "The only ones—the *only* ones—to remember me were the King and Queen of Ice. They paid me a fortune to dress you during the Choosing, so you will have all my attention. You *will* be the best dressed Contestar here while you're alive."

Rorax blinked. Hella clicked her tongue as she flicked through the hangers so fast Rorax barely had time to register what she was looking at.

"Here are all the clothes you'll need for the week. A casual outfit to lounge around in, another set of leathers to wear in case yours get scraped up and dirty again, a few casual dresses to wear." Hella paused. "And your dress for the Emissary Ball."

Hella reached up and grabbed the collar of Rorax's Contestar leathers, yanking her face down so they were eye to eye. "If you casually *lounge around* in this Glitter

Silk dress, I will poke a hole in the front of all your dresses for everyone to see your nipples *for a month*. Do you understand me, Greywood?"

"Okay," Rorax breathed.

"Not good enough. I want your solemn oath!" The woman shook Rorax, using the collar of her Contestar armor.

Rorax didn't understand how such a small woman could send a tendril of fear through her stomach over *clothes*, but she nodded quickly anyway. "Yes, Hella, I understand. No lounging around in the Glitter Silk dress."

"Good." Hella nodded in approval, releasing Rorax before turning away and retrieving a linen sack. She brought the sack over for Rorax to peer inside. "Underwear and bras. You have big tits, so I made you three more fighting bras. You had been taking such bad care of yours that the fabric had almost disintegrated!"

Rorax barely registered the insult as she peered at the fabric inside the sack. Lacy, sheer panties and bras filled most of the bag, along with a few sturdy cotton panties and the three promised fighting bras.

Rorax's throat felt tight as she reached in and gingerly touched the lace.

Never in her whole life had she been given something so beautiful, so *sexy*. The Wolf always said such beautiful things were a distraction, unnecessary for Rorax to have since she was never to waver from her *purpose*.

She didn't know if her blood-soaked hands deserved to touch such elegance.

Rorax released the lace and stepped back, clearing her throat. Hella must have seen something on Rorax's face because her features softened as she reached out and patted Rorax on the arm.

"Everyone deserves beauty in their lives, Greywood. Especially those who haven't had much of it."

Rorax nodded thickly.

"Oh, and before you go, I was instructed to give you this."

Hella held a letter out to Rorax. Stamped in green ink on the front of the pale paper were two king cobra snakes, a faceted diamond between them. The sigil of the King of the Underground.

Angelo.

Shocked, Rorax looked up at Hella, who pressed a finger to her lips. "The King of the Underground sends his regards. If you need *anything* from him or the Underground, just say the words and I'll make it happen."

Rorax's throat suddenly felt tight. "Do you know... do you know if anyone told him about Volla and Sahana?"

Hella's eyes filled with sadness. "He knows, girl, and he wants you to survive this. For them and for Jia."

Chapter 18

Rorax

The King of the Underground sends his regards. It shouldn't surprise her that Angelo had found a way to spread his influence on the Choosing, but it had, and it comforted her to know the little troll was watching out for her.

Rorax watched as one of the Highborn girls sparred with Captain Lamonte, rubbing her fingers over the spots in her shoulder where she had bruises from carrying all her new clothes from Bafta back to the Northern Castle.

This girl looked competent, and she knew what she was doing. The Contestars on the other end of the courtyard weren't faring so well. In fact, most of them looked like they'd never held a physical weapon before.

"Do you think this is a joke? Or have all the Contestars been in a coma for the last six months while they waited for you?" Jia mused.

Rorax winced as one of the other Contestars, a Lowborn named Claira, took an elbow from one of the instructors to her nose so hard it cracked. "Is it sad to say I'm starting to hope it's a prank?"

Claira pressed her hands to her bleeding nose, blood dripping from between her fingers, and rushed from the courtyard.

It was almost Rorax's turn to spar with the instructor the Guardian required the Contestars to work with until they had a Protectorate.

Rorax decided to hide her identity for the present—not because the Guardian had recommended it, but because she thought someone here might know one of her former targets. She didn't want to start conflicts until she had to.

Rorax closed her eyes and took a deep breath in through her nose. The evening summer air was clean and crisp here at the Northern Castle. She was a little sweaty from the warm-up exercises and stretches the instructor had them run through, and her muscles felt prepped and ready for a fight.

"How'd you sleep?" Jia asked.

Rorax snorted, opening her eyes to watch Mairi, another Contestar, timidly step up to the instructor. "Like shit."

Rorax had taken a few books Radashan loaned her to her room. She'd stayed up late reading and rereading paragraphs, combing through the texts Radashan had recommended and looking for any little clues. So far Rorax had come up empty.

Mairi, one of the Lowborns, went through the sequence with the Guardian's men before a different girl, a Highborn this time, with dark ebony skin and waist-length braids tied up in a ponytail, squared up to fight.

"How did you sleep?"

"Also like shit," Jia grumbled, her eyes also on the new girl. "My next-door neighbor not only had a disgusting amount of sex last night, but he also sounds like an ox when he snores."

Ror snickered and watched as the new girl surprisingly kept pace with the instructor.

The instructor had solid skills with only a midrange of expertise. Nothing special, but he was consistent and had a flawless basic technique. He'd taken a few Contestars to the mat and flattened them.

"That girl has had House Alloy Special Forces training, Ror."

Jia was right. The girl was attacking and dodging in a very characteristically Alloy way, and it made Rorax let out a little groan.

Depending on how much training that girl had, and if she knew what she was looking for, she would figure Rorax out.

"That one over there? The Lowborn with the long black braid?" Jia jerked her chin, motioning to two Contestars sparring across the training field. "That one knows the Dance of the Harpy."

Rorax looked over at the girl Jia had gestured to and grunted. "Her name is Enna." The Dance of the Harpy was a defensive sword dance, training the defender to move and evade like water.

They'd stopped teaching it to Heilstorms over 200 years ago because of its inefficiency, but it was still an interesting technique.

Ror moved her eyes back to the girl and the instructor. "What about the girl with the long, violent white scar gnarled down the left side of her face?"

Jia slowly looked from one Contestar to the next. "The platinum blonde girl with the tan skin, the Lowborn?"

"Yeah."

"She's scrappy and has that vicious ferocity only people who've had to fight and claw to survive have. Keep an eye on her."

The door to the keep slammed loudly, and it was only Jia's tiny intake of breath that gave Rorax any warning as she looked over her shoulder.

Seeing Isgra swagger across the courtyard felt like a punch to the kidneys. Isgra, all six foot two of her, was covered in dark brown leather armor. She had a broadsword strapped to her back, and her golden blonde hair was braided to the side of her head.

Just like Volla used to style her hair.

"New blood, you're up!"

Jia elbowed Ror in the shoulder, and her attention snapped to her instructor who was waiting for her, bouncing on his toes.

Rorax wanted to get *something* out of this experience. So, from all the wooden weapons laid out on the rack, she chose a wooden mace.

The instructor raised his eyebrows. "Interesting choice. There wasn't anything else that caught your eye?"

She scrunched her nose at him. “No, everything is made of wood; it barely matters.”

He blinked at her before shrugging and getting into position. Out of the corner of her eye, she watched as Isgra crossed the courtyard to where Jia stood.

Fuck.

Rorax gripped the mace tighter in her left hand, her nondominant hand, and squared up. The instructor made the first move, his wooden sword lunging for her unprotected side. He was slow, almost hesitant, like he was sparring with a child he didn’t want to hurt.

Rorax would have been amused if she hadn’t been so distracted. She raised her mace across her body and blocked the incoming blow. The wooden mace vibrated unhappily in her hands, and the instructor immediately went into an explanation on why a direct block might not be the best choice here, but Rorax barely listened.

Isgra had slid in next to Jia. She was saying something to her, but Ror couldn’t hear what. Rorax looked over to see Jia’s cheeks turn pink as she looked up at Isgra.

“Ready?”

She snapped back to her instructor, trying not to grind her teeth. “Yes, let’s go.”

“Remember to try and dodge or deflect instead of taking it head-on,” the instructor urged.

He lunged again, and this time she dodged backward.

“That’s great.” The instructor beamed. “Let’s try to deflect now.”

Rorax had already turned back to Jia and Isgra in time to see Jia’s face as it crumpled and Isgra’s triumphant sneer.

“Hey, are you ready?” the instructor complained, annoyed he didn’t have her complete attention.

She turned her body back to him, a muscle in her jaw twitching. “Yeah, ready.”

He lunged, and quick as a whip, she blocked him dead-on, twirled, and gave him a swift jab right in his nose. The instructor dropped to the ground like a rock, but Rorax was already halfway across the courtyard where Isgra and Jia were standing before he even hit the ground.

Jia was inches from the grave as it was. Her will to live was about as strong as a single strand of hair, and Rorax knew—could feel it in her bones—that if she let Isgra bite into her here, Jia wouldn't make it. Rorax would lose her, too.

Isgra saw Rorax just as she closed in, her face morphing into a surprised gasp before Rorax smashed the two top knuckles of her fist into the bridge of Isgra's nose.

Tears immediately sprung into Isgra's eyes, and she doubled over in pain.

Big mistake.

Rorax grabbed Isgra's bent head and bashed it violently into her knee.

Isgra screamed in pain and stumbled back. Rorax took the opportunity and used Isgra's already backward momentum to trip her. Isgra sprawled back, and Rorax threw herself on top, straddling Isgra's chest and trapping her arms under Ror's knees.

Rorax had broken Isgra's nose, and the blow from Rorax's knee had cut open Isgra's left eyebrow. The split was now draining blood into her eye. Isgra tried to surge up, to move her torso to unseat Rorax from where she straddled her, but she cowed back down when Rorax threw an elbow like a punch across Isgra's right temple.

"Do you remember what I said to you yesterday?" Rorax hissed, her face savage with anger and pain.

Isgra jerked from underneath Ror, seething. "You fucking crazy bitch."

"Wasn't that." Vaguely, Rorax saw Jia standing guard over them, daring any of the horrified onlookers to try and break up the fight. No one made a move to stop them. "Guess again," Rorax urged.

Isgra kept her mouth shut, so Rorax gripped Isgra's chin hard. "What. Did. I. Say?"

"You can't kill me. You would die," she spluttered, her eyes slightly wild. "Volla would never forgive you for it."

Rorax laughed bitterly, raking one sharp fingernail down Isgra's forehead before pressing her fingers into the cut on her eyebrow. Isgra hissed in pain and jerked her face away from Ror. "If you really think that, then you never knew her. Volla would kill me if she knew I had allowed someone to talk to her mate like that. She loved Jia more than she ever loved anyone. More than she ever loved you."

Isgra went dead still, and Rorax felt Isgra's rage and hurt building in her chest, the skin underneath her getting hot.

Volla had told Rorax a long time ago that Isgra feared her own power, was uncertain of it, so Rorax grinned. "Let it out, little Isgra. Let it out to play. You can't handle me now, so let's see if you can take me on with a little boost."

Rorax winked, and Isgra exploded. Rorax could see it in her eyes the split second Isgra decided to let loose and crossed her arms over her face as Isgra breathed fire at Ror with so much force it knocked her head over heels.

Rorax hit the ground stomach first, the breath whooshing out of her, but pounced up to her feet just in time to see Isgra slugging a fireball straight for her chest.

Rorax flung herself into a back handspring just under the fireball as it blazed overhead. There were screams from the crowd behind her as the fireball hit something, but Rorax didn't have time to look. She pulled two knives out of her hair, danced around two other fireballs Isgra hurled at her, and threw the knives one after the other, aiming for Isgra's feet. Isgra dodged one knife, but the other hit home, and Isgra howled in pain.

Rorax used the distraction to sprint forward, dodged one more fireball, and lunged to tackle Isgra to the ground again.

Isgra's burning hands wrapped around Rorax's biceps, melting through leather and searing into her skin as Rorax bit back an agonized scream of pain.

Who are you? The Wolf's soft voice whispered in her ear.

Rorax Greywood.

What does that mean?

It means I do not feel pain.

Rorax grabbed Isgra's wrists, yanking her hands away, and moved to pin Isgra's arms above her head.

Isgra was too strong for that, and it forced a stalemate. Rorax hovered directly over Isgra's head.

Isgra's green eyes clouded over with the color of flame, and she opened her mouth to breathe more fire directly into Rorax's face.

Rorax jerked away from Isgra's hands and, quick as a snake, walloped her across the cut on her temple again, this time with her fist. Then again.

Isgra screamed at the third impact, Rorax beating against the already present wound, and Isgra's back arched off the ground in agony. With Isgra distracted, Rorax leaned around and plucked her knife out of Isgra's foot and whipped around to press it under Isgra's chin. Isgra stilled mid-scream when she felt the blade under her chin, staring up at Ror with incredulous eyes.

Rorax moved closer. "Back to my question, little Isgra. What did I say to you yesterday?"

"You're a monster. Just like her." She whimpered, barely holding back a sob.

Rorax sliced into the skin under Isgra's chin, and her eyes went wide with horror.

"You... you said that if I... talked to her, you would... you would...." She swallowed, and more tears started to flow down her cheeks.

Rorax gripped Isgra's chin, pressing deep into the skin that was covered in blood so Isgra wouldn't be tempted to bite her. She lowered herself down to Isgra's ear to whisper, "I told you that if you tested me, I would beat your skull until it's pulp."

Isgra's whole body started to tremble underneath Ror.

If Isgra hadn't believed that Ror would follow through with her threat before, there was something about Ror's tone that made her absolutely certain now.

Rorax sat up and looked down at the woman beneath her. "Let me make this perfectly clear for you, Isgra, since you didn't seem to understand me before. You don't talk to me or her." Rorax pointed at Jia. "*Ever*. Leave us alone, and I'll leave you alone."

Isgra sent Jia a venomous glare before her green eyes—the exact same shade as Volla's—snapped back up. Rorax tried to ignore her heart punching painfully in her chest.

"I don't want to hear one more venomous word come out of your mouth, or I will saw your jaw off right before I kill you. I have nothing to lose, Isgra. This is more important to me than death, understand that now."

Isgra deflated under her, looking away. "Okay."

"Okay, *what*?" Rorax urged.

She squeezed her eyes shut. "I will leave you alone."

Rorax patted Isgra on the cheek, and her eyes squeezed shut even tighter. "Good girl."

Rorax climbed off Isgra to find the whole courtyard staring at her with open mouths and wide eyes. Even the instructor, whom Ror had knocked out before attacking Isgra, was sitting up and staring at her. There were black scorch marks on the stone where Isgra's fireballs had hit, but nothing else seemed to have been damaged.

The only one not looking at Ror was Jia, who had tears dripping down her cheeks as she stared at Isgra.

Rorax gripped Jia's shoulder and forced her to turn away just as armed guards barreled into the Contestars' Courtyard from the battlement.

Rorax recognized one as he came to stand toe to toe with her. Captain Lamonte, the Guardian's right-hand man. "We saw a fight; what the hell is goin' on?"

"Isgra," Ror called to her, not looking away from Lamonte's face. "Care to tell Captain Lamonte what was going on?" The threat in her voice was clear as day.

"N-Nothing," Isgra squeezed out, her voice thick with tears she desperately tried not to shed. "Nothing. Nothing's going on. We were practicing. We're fine."

Lamonte eyed Rorax for a long moment before looking over her shoulder at Isgra, then back down to Ror.

"The Guardian's not gonna be happy 'bout this when she hears," he said in a low voice.

"Probably not, but I also think it would take a hell of a lot to make that woman happy."

Lamonte didn't seem to disagree with that statement. She stepped around him, jerking her head at Jia. "Come on."

When they passed by the instructor, she looked down at him. "Still think that Morningstar isn't sexy?"

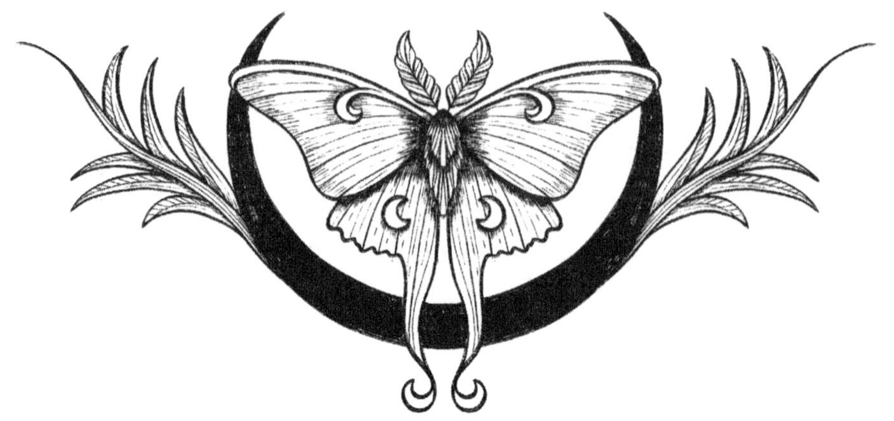

CHAPTER 19

TRESSA

"How are you finding your accommodations?"

Tressa looked up from where she was washing a bloody rag to find the Guardian standing in the doorway to her private washroom, watching Tressa with a glint of triumph in her yellowed eyes. The Guardian was small, shorter than Tressa, but the power the Guardian held seemed to radiate from her in warm waves, like Tressa was standing too close to the sun.

"It's lovely."

"Good. Everything here was remodeled to your sister's liking."

The Guardian had been friends with her father, Darius Abebe. They had grown up in the House of Dark together before Darius married Tressa's mother, becoming King of Life, and the Guardian had won her own Choosing.

As far as battle magick went, the House of Life had none and was the weakest House. It was a tradition long before the Abebes that the Guardians would send soldiers to protect the House of Life borders.

According to the Guardians' Law, when families challenged other families for the Kingship of their House, no other Houses or magick types could compete in the Arena of Rights. Fire Magick holders would fight against other Fire Magick holders.

House of Life was different. Families of different magick types, related by marriage, could fight for them. It was not uncommon to see a family of dark holders fight against a family of Fire or Ice to secure the House of Life seat. The only requirement for House of Life in the Arena was that a holder of Life Magick must sit on the throne and the Council of Houses.

Darius Abebe and his brothers had fought for Tressa's mother, securing her spot on the House of Life throne, and the Guardian had been their biggest ally. She had tied her name to the Abebe house and swore her support, so that if any families thought about fighting the remaining Abebes in the Arena of Rights in Valitlinn, they would fight the Guardian herself. There were always whispers about ambitious families here and there, but no family had dared to challenge them for nearly a hundred years.

When Tressa's father had died, everything changed. The protection was no longer that of a friend—it now came with a price. The Abebes were to offer one member of the family to be always in the Guardian's service. Roo, Tressa's younger sister, had happily taken up the mantle since the position had been stationed in Valitlinn, a city far larger and more cultured than Lulevar, the House of Life capital city.

Tressa had been volunteering for their sister House, House of Death, helping them with their border skirmishes when the news of Roo's death came. She was now required to fill her sister's position of the Guardian's Healer. It had been passed to Tressa since she was the only surviving Abebe besides her mother, the Queen.

Tressa looked around the room, trying to ignore the grief sitting in her soul like a heavy rock. "It's lovely, Guardian. Roo always had exquisite taste."

Something like sorrow flittered in the Guardian's eyes. "She did, if not a bit expensive. But more importantly, she was an excellent healer. Her work was precise—something I expect from her sister as well."

The Guardian eyed Tressa, the implication sitting heavy in the air between them. *Do your job, or my men and my protection will disappear.*

Her mother had not yet taken another husband after her father. If the Abebes were to be challenged and called to fight in the Arena of Rights, it would only be her and her mother to fight. Even with Tressa's other abilities, they would not survive. Tressa swallowed. "I understand, Guardian."

"Whose blood is that?"

Tressa looked down at the bowl. "One of the Contestar's. Claira. She had a broken nose."

"That will hopefully be one of the most minor injuries you treat here, if we hope to cull the Contestars quickly." The Guardian smiled, a cold, dead thing that sent chills up Tressa's spine, before the Guardian turned and left the Hall.

Tressa stood, watching the Guardian, before focusing back down on her hands. The bowl was decorated with gold leaves on the edges and had a ridged interior, specially designed by Master Healers to help scrub linens and fabrics clean.

The bowl wasn't the only thing decorated with gold in the Healer's Hall.

The Healer's Hall had been built perfectly to her sister's specifications and tastes. It was the most beautiful, cleanest, and the most technologically advanced Healer's Hall that Tressa had ever seen. Every inch of the room reminded her of her sister.

Roo had been the Guardian's master healer for over a hundred years before she had been Marked as a Contestar. When Roo had been randomly selected to die so that the Hunter would have a strong enough connection to find the missing Contestar, the Guardian reached out to Tressa and demanded that she take her sister's place.

The Contestars would go through unimaginable trials during the Choosing. It would test their bodies and minds to the very limit; the Hall was more than adequately equipped to handle almost any survivable ailment.

Places where Tressa could heal the sick and wounded were usually havens—her place of refuge and purpose. This place only served as a constant reminder of the sacrifice that had been forced upon her, upon her sister.

Tressa continued to scrub and clean until low voices entered the Hall, and Tressa's head perked up.

She abandoned the bloodied rags in the bowl and turned to wash her hands completely clean. When Tressa finally emerged from the bathroom, she almost tripped and had to hold onto the doorframe for support.

The long-lost Contestar was striding down the center aisle of the beds, her attention focused slightly behind her on the purple-haired woman who was always with her.

The Contestar had the confident walk of someone who was completely familiar with the way her body moved. Her posture was straight, but not stiff, unlike Tressa's own posture, and not like some of the other nobles Tressa knew.

Everything about the Contestar screamed predatory grace, and something about it set Tressa's very soul on edge, her instincts urging her to get away.

Tressa didn't have to give the Contestar any instruction as she sat on one of the beds and peeled her training leather top up and over her head, to better reveal the burned flesh that ran up and down her arms.

The Contestar had obviously been in a healer's rooms before, knew what to do, what would be asked of her.

Why would she be so familiar with the process?

Tressa stared, fingers shaking almost violently at her sides as she fought the urge to reach out and grab the nearest scalpel.

Treat her like a patient. Treat her like a patient. Just until the Selection, treat her like a patient, Tressa intoned silently to herself.

The Contestar finally looked up and over her shoulder at Tressa, catching her stare. Tressa wasn't completely ready, but she steeled her spine and forced herself to walk toward the Contestar anyway.

It wasn't as hard for Tressa to treat the Contestar like a patient as she thought it would be.

Almost as soon as Tressa crossed from the shadow of the bathroom's doorway and into the Hall, the smell of the Contestar's burned flesh filled her nose. She moved to view the wound; genuine horror filled her throat.

"What happened?" Tressa choked out, crouching down by the bed and inspecting the burned flesh. It was red, bloody in spots, and blistering everywhere up and down the Contestar's arms. The skin around her biceps were blackened in the shape of... a handprint. A burned, crispy handprint.

Bile rose in Tressa's throat.

When the Contestar didn't immediately answer, Tressa looked up and found her two clear blue eyes watching her carefully, monitoring every single movement Tressa made.

The Contestar tilted her head. "Training accident."

The Contestar's low, clear voice sent goose bumps down Tressa's spine. There wasn't any kind of agonized inflection or waver in her voice from the pain when injuries like this would send most seasoned soldiers to their knees.

Who was this woman? Could she not feel pain? Had she been tortured and broken?

"Doesn't it... does it hurt?" Tressa stuttered. Her eyebrows furrowed together, and she shifted her weight from one foot to the other in uncertainty.

There was a heavy pause, and Tressa looked up to find the Contestar's companion similarly watching Tressa, analyzing her critically.

The silence was awkward, and Tressa's palms suddenly felt sweaty.

"Yes, as you can imagine, little Healer, it hurts quite a great deal. So, unless you have more questions for me...." The Contestar waved her fingers, gesturing to the burn, and Tressa snapped into action.

"Yes, yes," she muttered, wiping the back of her hand over her brow bone, then focusing on the burn. She started in on the blackened flesh, peeling it away with tweezers and using her magick on the wound until it was blistered and a deep angry red, before moving to the other burns up and down the Contestar's arms.

When she could feel herself straining, she stopped. She'd closed all the skin, but the two handprints wrapped around the Contestar's biceps were still clearly visible.

Tressa had avoided looking into the Contestar's eyes as she worked, even though she could feel the Contestar's gaze on her, heavy and searching the whole time.

Tressa collapsed at the end of the bed, wiping the sweat away from her forehead again and forcing herself to look up to meet the Contestar's eyes. "That's all I can offer you today, and maybe tomorrow, too. More healers will arrive throughout the week, but for now...."

"No, thank you. That was more than enough." The Contestar finally took her eyes off Tressa and reached for the top of her leather armor lying on the bed between them. She should give her a numbing cream, she should offer to cover the wounds, so they didn't ache as much or get infected, but a dark, secret part of Tressa *wanted* it to ache. She *wanted* the Contestar to be in pain.

"Wait!" Tressa blurted, surprising them both. "Let me get some bandages so the blisters don't pop."

She hurried to the storeroom without waiting for an answer, quickly grabbing a salve and some linen strips. Tressa hustled back and sat opposite the Contestar, who offered one of her arms to Tressa, palm up, arm slightly out.

Tressa gently applied the salve, and just as she started with the bandage, the Contestar finally spoke. "Should I know who you are, Healer?"

Tressa's fingers fumbled for just a moment before they were steady again. "No."

The Contestar was quiet until Tressa moved to her other arm. "Well then, who am I to you? I saw you that night on the balcony. Your glare would have killed me if it could have."

Tressa was quiet, silently gathering her courage as she applied the salve and finished wrapping the linen around the Contestar's arm. She piled her supplies in her arms and stood up on unsteady legs to look down into the Contestar's clear blue eyes.

"They call you long-lost Contestar." The words felt like sand in her mouth. "The Contestar they had to sacrifice my sister to find."

"What do you mean?"

"My sister was Marked for the Choosing, too. When you never appeared, they pulled names out of a bowl, my sister was picked, and they sacrificed her so that the magick you held was strong enough for the Hunter to find you."

The Contestar's friend huffed, either in laughter or surprise, Tressa didn't know, because Tressa ignored her, keeping her eyes locked down on the face and the clear blue eyes that remained unmoving and empty. Tressa stared at the Contestar—despite her instincts telling her that this woman was *very* dangerous—and tried to convey her loathing and hatred before finally turning on her heel and walking away.

Chapter 20

Jia

Jia rubbed her thumb over the burn that ran down the length of her knuckles and grimaced. It had blistered painfully the night before, and Jia couldn't keep from touching it, mulling over what she needed to do to be successful in her task today.

She admitted to herself the cook had caught her red-handed. She was a small Fire-Born woman hired by the Guardian to run the kitchen during the Choosing. She was also an admirable opponent and ran a tight and efficient kitchen. So tight that the cook noticed Jia stealing bottles of wine from her rack after only the third bottle and had tried to burn her with a hot poker to force her away.

Jia had been waiting for nearly twenty minutes, crouched in the kitchen broom closet, watching for when the cook turned her back, a familiar thrum in her veins as she waited like a cat for her chance to pounce.

The woman finally disappeared into her freezer, the witch runes on the outside glimmering blue as the door swung open. As quick as a cat, Jia reached around the corner and snatched a bottle of wine from the cook's wine rack.

"Gods!" One of the cook's apprentices yelped, dancing out of the way as he heaved a pot of hot soup away from Jia, trying not to burn her. "How long 've been creepin' in there for?" He was small, barely reaching her chin, but gods, how had she not even noticed him?

"A bit. Excuse me." She didn't wait for him to reply, or for him to rat her out to the cook. She darted around him and out of the kitchen as fast as she could, gripping the bottle tightly around the neck as she ran.

Jia didn't slow down until she was in the hallway and almost to her room. She dug around in her pocket for a corkscrew, pulled the cork free with a soft grunt, and held the bottle out in victory for a split second before taking a deep, long pull of wine straight from the bottle. She kept drinking until the contents were almost gone.

"That's better," she murmured. The liquid seemed to warm her from the inside out and dull the edges of the anxiety and grief plaguing her since she'd spoken to Isgra today. Jia had never seen Rorax so angry before and had never seen someone willfully accept so much pain as Rorax had taken on her behalf today. The wound had smelled awful and had burned Rorax down to the muscles and tendons in her arm. Rorax had always seemed more like Volla's friend than her own, but after what Rorax did today, Jia felt differently towards her. Like their friendship had grown somehow.

The hallways of the castle all faced the inside, toward the two baileys of the castle. Jia took another long drink as she looked out through the windows; she could still see the scorch marks on the stone where Isgra had burned them. Physically, Isgra was so much like her sister, and yet so different.

The wine started seeping quickly into Jia's limbs, and she stumbled to the side, cursing. The bottle slipped from her fingers, crashed on the floor, and glass shattered everywhere.

The remaining wine spread across the ground like a bleeding wound, and as Jia knelt to pick up the glass, a shard nicked her skin, causing real blood to mix into the dark purple puddle.

"Gods!"

Jia looked up to see a woman standing above her. Silvery white, waist-long braids framed a beautiful face, and creamy dark brown skin covered high cheekbones and full lips. The woman's chocolate-colored eyes were rounded with concern as she took in the blood and the wine now running everywhere through the lines of the tiled floor.

In a flash so fast Jia didn't have any time to react, the woman reached down and snatched her wrist, yanking her up to her feet. She was strong, and Jia had to look up into the woman's face, even standing on her own feet.

"You cut yourself." The woman's eyes searched her own, looking for answers. "Are you okay? What happened?"

Jia shrugged. "I dropped it."

"You're bleeding."

Jia looked down and saw that blood was running down her legs, pooling at her feet. It didn't hurt; she could barely feel it through the wine hazing her mind, so she shrugged again. "It's only blood."

The woman blinked several times before jerking her wrist sharply. "Come on."

The woman dragged Jia out of the room and behind her up the stairs to the Healer's Hall. Jia had just been there a few hours ago with Rorax.

A different healer dropped in front of Jia's knees and pressed her fingertips to the skin. Instantly the cut stopped throbbing, but some of the giddy drunkenness dissipated, and the same heavy grief filled its place. She had the urge to pull away, to tell the healer to stop, but instead bit her lip and forced herself to let the healer continue.

"Thank you for bringing me here." Jia looked up at the woman who was standing next to her, watching the healer pick glass from her shins. She tried to sound sincere, even if she wasn't.

The woman's warm eyes flicked to hers, and the corners of her mouth pulled up. "You're welcome. The Tournament of Houses hasn't even started. You don't want to drink the whole castle dry before it starts."

Jia snorted and turned her attention to the healer who was sitting on a low stool in front of her. The healer pulled the last piece of glass free, healed the last cut, and ran her hand over Jia's newly smooth skin.

"All patched up." The healer pushed up from her stool. "You're free to leave."

"Thanks," Jia mumbled.

Jia walked out with the tall woman to the corridor outside the Healer's Hall. She turned—on her way to steal a new bottle of wine—when the woman grabbed Jia's wrist again and forced her around. "Wait. What's your name?"

Jia looked at the woman's face, over the near perfect skin and the faint freckles on her nose, and ran her tongue over her teeth. Her instincts told her to lie but... she shrugged.

"My name is Jia; I'm Ice-Born."

The woman stiffened and dropped Jia's wrist like it had burned her. It was only then that Jia really noticed the woman. She wore leather armor that was dyed black and had silversteel trim dyed red. A goddess was stitched to the front of the leather plate in silver thread, and Jia's chest tightened at the sight. It was the House of Death sigil.

The woman's eyes were no longer warm; they were cold and distant, and the woman's mouth had pressed together into a grim line.

"Have a nice day." The woman nodded briskly and turned away, and this time Jia grabbed her arm to get her to stop moving.

"I'm sorry for what happened to your people." Jia swallowed. "What's your name?"

The woman yanked her arm out of Jia's hold, her eyes remaining cold. "My name is Kaiya Thorn, but you'll hear my people call me Kaiya Whitethorn."

"Why?"

"Because on the day your house led an army into Death, I was the only survivor of a platoon of soldiers defending the Whitewood Forest."

Jia's mouth went dry, and her eyes fell to her feet. "I'm sorry."

Kaiya said nothing.

"If it's any consolation, I am Jia Frostguard. My mother is leading the House of Ice reparations. She is currently in Skavetsia, training your soldiers."

Kaiya said nothing, but the grim set of her mouth softened a fraction.

"Have a nice night. It was good to meet you, Kaiya Whitethorn." Jia turned away to go find more wine.

Chapter 21

Raengar

Raengar watched as Frostflight, his sister's magnificent white dragon, aggressively whipped the dead giant moose clamped in her jaws back and forth, like a dog shaking a squirrel to snap its neck. Blood dripped down the dragon's snow-white scales, staining the creature's long white neck with ribbons of red blood.

"We can't choose her as House of Ice's Contestar, Raengar."

Raengar looked from Frostflight over to his sister, who stood shoulder to shoulder with him. Her blonde hair, the same pale shade as his own, flapped in the wind and whipped around her face. When Raengar had killed their father and taken the throne, Raengar wanted them both to rule together. The Guardians' Law stated that whoever was the strongest in the ruling family would lead, but Isolde was clever, far better at the mundane *ruling* of a country and far more compassionate than he was. He was stronger, more ruthless, and had bonded to the biggest war dragon in the world. They were the dark and light side to the same family coin, so he had made the decision that they would rule Ice together. Most of the time—nearly *all* the time—it worked smoothly. Between the two of them, House of Ice was stronger than they had ever been.

In this moment, however, he wished he had taken the throne for only himself.

"What do you mean, we can't choose her as our Contestar? It's Rorax, Isolde. If we are banned from the Choosing by the Guardians' Laws, then we need to send her our best people to protect her."

Isolde blew out a long, heavy breath. "Do you remember how the Choosing works, Raengar?"

"Twelve Contestars, selected by the gods, fight in trials chosen and organized by the Guardian. The last one standing supplants them."

"What about after they survive the trials?"

"What *about* after they survive?"

Isolde turned so she was completely facing Raengar and folded her arms across her chest. "They not only have to fight in those trials, Raengar; after nine of the Contestars die, the Council of Houses *vote* to approve the final three remaining. If the Council of Houses *doesn't approve* a Contestar, she is *executed*."

Raengar narrowed his eyes at his younger sister. "You don't think she would be voted in?"

Isolde sighed and rubbed her fingers on her temples. "I don't know. What I do know is that the House of Ice runs, protects, and has full control of the Elus River. We control the Azaela's Islands and the Horns of Southwell. We have the biggest army, the only war dragons left in the Realms, the most education, and the most silversteel. To have someone who is Ice-Born be the next Guardian... we might be asking too much. It will eventually get out that Rorax is a Heilstorm, and if you think Määr isn't going to use that to push the votes away from her, you're a fool."

"So, you're going to leave her there unprotected," Raengar bit out, turning to face her completely so that they stood toe to toe.

"Unprotected? Of course not. We'll send Tag as emissary, or Ye-Jun. I'm trying to do what's best for her, Raengar."

Raengar dropped his head back to look up at the sky, his heart boiling, turmoil writhing under his skin.

If Rorax had told them she'd been chosen, they could have planned for this. They would have figured out how to protect her. If she'd just *trusted him*, everything would be different.

"Fuck," Raengar clipped, running aggravated fingers over where his hair was shaved, where the blue head of a dragon was tattooed. "It has to be Kulltoug. We can't send Tag, and Ye-Jun is still overseeing training the House of Death soldiers in Skavetsia. He won't be done in time." And Kiniera held the most magick out of all of them.

Isolde nodded. "Kiniera would protect her."

Raengar turned back to their dragons and rested his hands on his hips, wishing he had a drink or, even better, a smoke rolled from Whitleherb. "When I see Ror next, I am going to skin her alive."

"Get in line," Isolde said. She turned back to their dragons as well, and together they watched them under the setting sun.

"Do you love her?" Isolde asked.

Raengar knew the answer. He knew the answer in the marrow of his bones, but that was between him and Rorax. So instead, he asked, "Why do you think she didn't tell us?"

"Darras. I bet it had to do with Darras. Did they hear anything about him?"

Raengar bit back a groan. Darras Greywood, Rorax's only sibling and one of his father's favorite pets. If Raengar never heard anything about Darras Greywood again, he would die a happy man. "I don't know. Nothing that got reported back to me."

Frostflight crunched loudly on the moose's skull.

"What are we going to do about Lyondrea?"

Raengar reached up and rubbed the back of his neck. Between the Choosing and Lyondrea, a stress headache was starting to form behind his eyes.

Isolde gave him a concerned look and reached over and grabbed Raengar lightly by the wrist. "Raengar, if you think the Pits have opened, then we go to war. We'll send you the men and the dragons you need. You don't have to fight them alone."

"You know as well as I do the Guardians' Law forbids the Realms from going to war unprompted—"

"Fuck the Guardians' Law. How many men must lose their lives before it's no longer 'unprompted'?"

Raengar's eyebrows shot up. Isolde lived her life by a very strict hierarchical system—duty, family, honor—in that order. Every cell in Isolde's body was proprietary, respectful, and composed, and she valued the rules and the laws—both Guardians' and Gods' Laws. The last time he had seen her willing to break those laws was when they'd overthrown their father together, after seeing injuries his father had left on him after a particularly brutal lashing.

"Our ancestors broke the Guardians' Law when they went to war to claim both the Horns and Azaela's Islands, and the Guardians didn't lift a finger against them. I won't sacrifice your life because the Council of Houses decides it wants to see with blind eyes that another Pit War is upon us. I will burn Valitlinn to the ground before that happens."

A bloodthirsty smile crept across Raengar's mouth. "I've always hated that city anyway."

CHAPTER 22

RORAX

"Move over."

Jia eyed Rorax with a raised eyebrow as Rorax climbed the arena steps to where Jia sat.

Jia slid down the row a few inches, and Rorax plopped down next to her, stretching her bare legs out in front of her as Jia looked to the floor of the arena—to the empty chair next to the Guardian and other Contestars that Rorax was meant to sit in—and raised her other eyebrow. "Aren't you supposed to be down there, on display with the rest of the Contestars?"

Rorax just shrugged, leaning back to rest on the row behind her. "This spot has a better view."

Which was true.

From here, Rorax could see over the whole arena but still hear what was being said. She could watch from here but wouldn't *be* watched.

A perfect place to scout.

And the seat meant for Rorax down below was situated between Isgra and the Guardian.

Rorax would rather sit in a pit of hungry rats than spend the next two hours in the middle of those two. After Rorax's fight with Isgra, and then her encounter with the Healer yesterday, she felt drained.

Her arms still throbbed painfully, and she just didn't have it in her to be on the receiving end of any more glares or snide remarks.

Rorax had picked out a simple black dress to wear to the arena.

It was the first dress she ever had that truly belonged to her, and she'd spent nearly ten minutes staring at herself in the mirror after slipping it on. She felt different, a little awkward and a little... *wrong* in it, but she also didn't feel quite the same.

More like just a girl, less like the Pup.

The dress covered the burns Isgra had inflicted on her arms, but she'd asked Jia to go to the Healers Hall to steal another bottle of numbing salve. Now she could barely feel the burns at all.

The only shoes she had were her favorite pair of leather boots and the high heels Hella had given her to wear to the Emissary Ball tonight. She'd been scared to scuff the heels, out of fear Hella would cut the fabric out of her dresses, maybe around the ass, so she'd opted for her boots. Jia "borrowed" a short black dress she'd found on a maid's rack in a corridor to wear.

The sound of cheering and bellows brought Ror back to the present. It felt like everyone in the Realms was crammed in here.

People of every House, who had the means to travel so far, gleefully pushed inside the arena, stuffing themselves into tight nooks and crannies all the way down the stone bleachers lining the long walls of the arena. People had filled in on the stairs next to her, and some grabbed onto the fence at the top of the arena, standing and straining their necks to see the ground floor. Rorax even saw Radashan down there. The little man was squeezing his way into a front-row seat.

"Have you been to a Choosing before?" Rorax asked Jia, keeping her eyes on the people streaming in through the arena entrance.

"No, but my mother got to watch the Guardian win her Choosing. From the stories she told, this is relatively tame," Jia muttered, as they watched two men roll over people already sitting in the stands as they wrestled for a spot.

The Guardian sat on a throne, which had been placed at the opposite end of the arena from the entrance, and lazily watched the wrestling and arguing as people continued to flow in.

At least four more fights broke out, but only when people stopped streaming in did the Guardian's soldiers intervene.

When the crowd had mostly quieted down, the Guardian stood, and even Rorax, who was mostly insensitive to the magick around her, felt her hair stand on end as the Guardian's power prickled over her.

"Tonight, we are excited to welcome all the emissaries and their Houses back to the Northern Castle for another Tournament of Houses and the Choosing."

Her voice was clear, even up to the highest bleachers, and Rorax grinned. The Guardian must be using her House of Air abilities to amplify the sound.

"One Contestar... has chosen to sit out." There were angry and surprised mutters that broke out from all around them, but Rorax stayed focused on the Guardian. "But the rest are ready for their introductions," she said, waving her hand over the ten Contestars seated to her left.

The five Highborns stood up, proud and tall, all wearing beautiful dresses or intricate pantsuits.

"Our Highborns, who come from noble families and already held large quantities of magick in their blood."

The crowd raved until the Highborns were seated once more, the cheering almost blocking out the names of the Contestars.

The Guardian introduced the Lowborns next, but Rorax had no trouble hearing their names called over the crowd this time.

With the Contestar introductions out of the way, the crowd's energy spiked again. This is what they had all traveled so far to see. The Tournament of Houses.

"Now, please help me welcome our Houses and the noble warriors who will be fighting for you and for their realm in the Tournament of Houses!"

The crowd was deafening, overwhelming as everyone in the stadium pushed to their feet and started to cheer.

"Our first house to welcome is the House of Light."

Approximately thirty people entered through the double doors at the opposite end from where the Guardian stood. They wore long, white kaftans with the golden yellow sun sigil of the House of Light stitched on the front.

The emissary strode forward, giving the Guardian a half bow when he reached her. "Guardian. Thank you for hosting us."

"Welcome, Gerald." The Guardian gave him a swift nod before gesturing to the women on the bleachers to her left. "The Contestars."

"Ladies." He bowed again to the Contestars. "House Light is looking to represent a Highborn woman with grace and dignity, who can be a diplomat as well as a warrior during these terrible times."

The five Lowborn Contestars all looked at each other awkwardly, while the five Highborns remained smug.

Gerald bowed once more before the members of the House of Light left the way they came. Rorax gripped her fists so tightly, her nails left little crescent moons in her palms.

There was an awkward silence as another thirty people from a different House filtered in, their clothes colored in scarlet and gold.

Murmurs surfaced in the crowd as some of the people noticed that Volla, the Torch, was not among the Fire emissary's group. She had won the last two Tournament of Houses, but had not come to defend her title? How unlike her.

Jia pointedly ignored the whispers and nudged Ror with her elbow. "Rorax, this is one of the houses."

Rorax squinted, looking over the scarlet and gold cloaks they wore as they streamed through the arena. "The House of Fire?"

"One of the houses that Kiniera recommended to you."

Rorax scrunched her nose in distaste.

The emissary bowed to the Guardian. "Thank you for all of your generosity, Guardian."

The Guardian actually smiled at this man, warm and beaming.

His voice was strong and kind as he turned to the Contestars and bowed to them. "Hello, Contestars. The House of Fire is looking for a Contestar who has the spine to lead us into any potential conflict with the Lyondreans. We want to help develop either a High or Lowborn. We will support whomever we feel will be the most stalwart in that goal."

The man bowed again and turned to leave, oblivious to some people in the crowd staring holes into his back.

The Houses that came next—Foliage, Animal, and Weather—stated they wanted to sponsor Highborns.

The House of Ice was next. They easily had the most manpower thus far, packing the arena with their silver and light blue uniforms and cloaks. Rorax's eyes worked furiously to take in each face, recognizing some of them, but none of Raengar and Isolde's best men or women were among their ranks.

"Holy Mother of Kään. It's Kiniera," Jia whispered. "She's been sending me Blood Hawks back and forth, demanding updates on you and on what happened. But she didn't say that she would *be here*."

Rorax's eyes snapped to the woman leading the group. Kiniera was a slight woman with bony limbs who reached up and lifted a silver and white hood off her head. Rorax immediately had the urge to be both sick over the side of the railing and sit up straight as possible.

As always, Kiniera Kulltoug looked like a ghost. Even from the stands, the dark purple bruise-like bags under her eyes stood out from her chalky white skin, and the bones in her face protruded sharply.

Kiniera swiped her dead eyes over the Contestars, lingering over Isgra for a moment. She bowed, lower than the emissaries before her, and in her raspy voice simply offered, "Thank you for having us, Guardian."

The Guardian's lips pinched, but she gave Kiniera a tight nod. Kiniera turned to the Contestars, searching. Rorax felt the same small urge to be sick again.

It wasn't Kiniera's fault that the very sight of her made Rorax want to pound the nearest bottle of moonshine, but it didn't change the facts. Volla had invented the nickname Ghost Girl for Kiniera, not because of the grayish hue of her skin, but because of the way she had haunted them both.

Gods, she missed Volla.

"House Ice... is looking for someone to lead us through the impending war," Kiniera drawled. "We would be interested in either a High or Lowborn."

There were loud murmurs in the crowd. Everyone had expected Ice to be solely interested in a Highborn. They were the favorites to win the Tournament and were expected to have their pick of the litter, especially with the Torch so obviously missing from House of Fire's ranks.

Kiniera bowed again to the Guardian before slinking back out of the arena.

"I hate to admit it," Jia muttered, "but I can't think of anyone else who would be better at training a Contestar than Kiniera."

Rorax rolled her jaw, thinking of the brutal training Kiniera had put them all through while they were Heilstorms. "Me neither."

The next Houses—Dark, Light, Alloy, and Energy—all claimed to want to exclusively train Highborns.

By the time the final House entered the hall, Rorax's body was stiff, and her stomach growled so loudly people four aisles away turned to gape at her. She just stared them down and shrugged.

"Only Death left." Jia rolled her neck. "Thank the gods."

The House of Death were dressed head to toe in black and red. They were silent and eerie, and the vibes coming off them were deadly.

"Ror," Jia elbowed her again. "This is the House of Death. Kiniera's number two recommendation. Though that man might be a distraction."

A tall, handsome, pale man with impeccable posture and dark hair stepped up and bowed to the Guardian.

Rorax eyed him. "He is handsome."

Jia grabbed Rorax's chin to turn her head. "No Rorax. Him."

Rorax sucked in a breath. The man stood at the back of the pack, his arms folded across his chest. This was a man Rorax really *would* have a hard time keeping her hands off. He had light skin that was deeply bronzed, buzzed black hair, and matching dark scruff. He stood taller than the others around him, and that *face.* He had a prominent eyebrow bone and a straight jaw as sharp as her knife's edge.

His armor covered his chest all the way up to his throat, similar to how Rorax preferred to wear hers now that she had the Choosing's mark on the back of her neck.

Rorax hummed her approval before peeling her eyes away to focus on the House Death emissary.

"Guardian, how could we ever repay you for such extravagant generosity?"

The Guardian smirked. "Prince Sumavari, I do not think you are your House's emissary this year."

The crowd murmured excitedly around them.

"Holy shit," Jia whispered. "An actual Death Prince?"

House of Death's royal family had been hunted after the Sumavari's War in 9431 AR, and since then the family had almost *never* socialized. The only one that was in public was the Queen of Death; no one even knew how many Death siblings there were. Rorax had met one... on the night of the Siege of Surmalinn. That brother had been blonde like his sister the queen.

To see a Sumavari out in society was like seeing an exotic animal, or like an eclipse that only came around once every thousand years, and the crowd was starstruck with him.

"I wanted to take this opportunity to thank you in person; you always throw the best parties." The prince grinned and winked at the Guardian, and the crowd loved it.

The Guardian's smirk bloomed into a smile.

A tall woman standing behind the prince with proud shoulders, long wine-red hair, and matching red lips stepped up next to him and addressed the Contestars. "Ladies," she purred, assessing each one of them individually. "House Death is looking to be a patron for the one who will fight for our country and every single soul in it." The woman's declaration was more nebulous yet more direct than any of the Houses before them. The crowd remained silent at the declaration.

As the House of Death left the arena, the Guardian stood up and clapped her hands together. "Welcome everyone to the Choosing. We have one week until the Tournament of Houses begins, so until then, let the gods bless you with fortune."

Chapter 23

Rorax

Jia and Rorax went straight from the arena to Kiniera's room, getting directions from an Ice guard they saw on the way.

Rorax had to suppress a shiver as she climbed the stairs to the southwest tower where the House of Ice was stationed. Gods, that voice, Kiniera's low, slightly raspy voice—it had made its way into Rorax's nightmares occasionally over the past hundred and fifteen years.

Jia stopped at the door and knocked until Kiniera opened it.

Rorax suppressed her revulsion and unease as she gave Kiniera a nod. "Kulltoug, what a lovely surprise to see you here," she said sarcastically.

Kiniera's ice-blue eyes flashed sharp enough to slice them into ribbons. She said nothing as she stepped back and watched Jia and Rorax slip past her into the room, her fury palpable in the air. A deep sense of foreboding made Rorax's stomach clench.

Emissary rooms were different from the average grunt rooms Jia and Rorax had been given. The front door of the emissary's chambers opened into a meeting room where a long, polished wooden table sat with six chairs around it. The doors to the bedroom and bathroom were at the back.

The room was cold enough that Rorax could see her breath. Ice covered the tabletop, and icicles climbed the stone walls. Kiniera motioned for them to sit, and the foreboding pit in Rorax's stomach dug in even more painfully.

Kiniera was kind enough to wait until they both took their seats before ripping into them.

"You stupid, fucking fools. Mother of Kään. Have you two lost every shred of sanity?" Kiniera hissed, looking at each of them in turn. "Raengar and Isolde are furious, and I think they should just be done with you. They should fucking kill you. Both of you."

Kiniera faced Jia first. "Going on a mission with your *lover.* Your *wife.*" Kiniera snorted bitterly. "We don't allow couples on the same mission for a *reason.* Sahana and Volla might still be alive if Volla's attention hadn't been split in two with concerns for both her unit and her *spouse.*"

With every word, Jia shrunk lower and lower in her chair, shriveling under the truth of her words.

Rorax's jaw got tight at the sight. "Enough, Kiniera."

Kiniera swiveled to Rorax, and it took everything in Rorax not to flinch away. Kiniera couldn't hurt her anymore. She wasn't in charge of making her run "for endurance" until she vomited, or train with swords until her knuckles were bruised and bleeding, or punish her for imperfections, or subjugate her to intense temperature training until she was "calloused" enough to be a Heilstorm. That training had been the most intense, brutal, savage part of her life, but it was *over.* Rorax had survived.

"And *you*, Greywood, putting everything in the world on hold for your mongrel, useless brother. I've never heard of anything so selfish in my life. If you would have died, it wouldn't have mattered. But if you had continued to both survive and evade the Choosing, the Choosing wouldn't have been able to cycle through properly. The Guardian could have deteriorated into death and given Oxana and Vadik her power. Or even worse, the magick could have gotten absorbed back into the land, spawning us more monsters to fight with." Kiniera narrowed her eyes as she looked at Rorax. "Raengar would never let me kill you, but when I found out that the missing Contestar was *you*, I was more tempted than ever to put you six feet underground, and I've been *more* than tempted before."

Kiniera ended her tirade in a nasty hiss, and Rorax believed her. Kiniera would have put an ice stake through her heart in an instant. She might have even deserved it.

"Why are you here?" Rorax asked slowly.

"Because, even though I'm furious with you, we can't let Alloy have a second Contestar under their thumb." Kiniera blew out a breath. Some of the anger drained away from the room, the temperature rising a bit. "And even though I want to kick your ass so hard your tailbone breaks, I also don't want to watch you die. Losing Sahana and Volla was hard enough."

Kiniera turned to Jia. "We couldn't identify Sahana's remains, but we recovered Volla's body. It's being moved to Morvarand right now to where Raengar is stationed. When you are released from your Blood Oath with the Guardian, go there. We were thinking about sending her body back to her relatives in Fire, but you were her chosen family, more than they ever were."

Jia's head hung down, but she nodded her thanks.

"Isgra's resemblance to her sister is... uncanny, isn't it?" Kiniera asked.

"Their faces are exactly the same. Their personalities, however?" Rorax shook her head. "They couldn't be more different. She makes me realize just how lucky we were with Volla."

Kiniera hummed her agreement, looking over at Rorax. "How are you holding up, Roraxiva?"

Rorax looked back at her, blinking. This was probably the first time in all the years Rorax had known Kiniera that she'd asked how Rorax was doing. "I told myself I wouldn't think about it until the Choosing is over."

Kiniera gave her a small nod, the corner of her mouth tipping down as her eyes assessed Rorax's face. "I'm sorry... for both of you. About the loss. I know you two were close, and Sahana will be nearly impossible to replace."

Rorax nodded and almost subconsciously rubbed her palm over that spot in her chest that grieved and ached whenever she thought about her commander and Volla.

That beautiful idiot should have left her to die and ran with her wife.

Kiniera sighed and leaned back in her chair. "I wish I could pull the plug on the other Contestars so we can just go home. The competition is a waste of time."

"What do you mean?"

"I mean that, even though I want to gouge your eyes out and slap you on the back of your head, after doing my research on the rest of the girls here, I would be happy to call you Guardian, Rorax."

"Oh." Warmth tugged at Rorax's heart, but she tried to push it away, rubbing her thumb over the top of her bird skull ring. "Thank you."

"That being said, Raengar and Isolde don't believe they should claim you as their Contestar... officially."

"Officially?" Rorax's eyebrows furrowed. She hadn't thought about what House she wanted to take her on as a Contestar, but subconsciously she'd been counting on the House of Ice. A part of her felt abandoned at the thought of her own country, of Raengar and Isolde, not wanting to be her Protectorate. They must really be furious with her for not telling them about the mark. "They want me to win, but they also don't want to be my Protectorate?"

"They want to be your Protectorate, but they think it will be safer for you to choose a different House, Rorax. House of Ice's public choice of a Contestar will be entirely separate from their 'private' choice. Publicly they want someone who isn't so entangled in our House's bloody history; they want everyone to forget that House Ice led the charge during the Death genocide. They want *you* to appear to be fighting for another House. They would be happy to give that House the benefits of being the Guardian's party, too. They don't need it."

Rorax frowned, not thinking clearly about the hurt.

Kiniera's already tight skin around her sharp facial features seemed to grow tighter as she grimaced. "They want you to win, Rorax. Raengar gave me the authority to do whatever I need to ensure your victory, but they think the Council of Houses will balk at a Heilstorm being led by House of Ice when it comes to vote. And they're right."

Rorax finally understood. The power balance between Ice and the rest of the Realms was already starkly imbalanced. The Council of Houses wouldn't want to see an Ice-Born with Ice-Born Protectorates. It was too much. "I understand."

Kiniera sighed deeply. "I should probably warn you, Rorax. Raengar and Isolde are *disappointed* that you didn't tell them you were chosen."

Rorax opened her mouth to respond, but her words stuck in her throat. *Disappointed* was probably a laughable understatement regarding how Raengar really felt about her deceit. If they didn't come to blows the next time they saw each other, it would be a miracle.

"Before you two leave, you need to know two things—"

Rorax cut her off. "Do you have any news on Darras?"

"No, nothing on Darras. And I'll get to that, it's the second thing on my list."

Rorax bit the inside of her cheek to keep from snapping at Kiniera. Rorax knew Kiniera well, and Kiniera would tell her at her own pace or not at all.

"In my opinion, there are only a few Houses that will be able to handle your influxes, Rorax. I trust you to get a feel for what you need, but I would recommend starting with Air, Dark, Death, and Fire. They each brought their best warriors to the Choosing. Some are only here to compete in the Tournament of Houses, but some will stay. Raengar didn't give me anyone remarkable to compete in the Tournament, except you and Jia, if you should wish to participate. His best men remain with him to help keep the Death border secure."

Rorax nodded. "Okay."

"The Fire emissary has been sniffing around about you. There isn't much for him to find, but we could feed him some information." She shrugged one bony shoulder. "Start there. His name is Elios Delgata, and for all intents and purposes, he seems to keep his nose clean."

Rorax and Jia both nodded their agreement.

"You two also need to be informed that Raengar saw a minotaur on one of his guard tours."

That had Rorax sitting up straight in her chair, almost bounding to her feet. "*What*?"

"Calm down, Rorax. He is fine. Don't forget everything else I just told you. It's important."

Rorax nodded numbly, but she was already mentally past that. "Raengar saw a *minotaur*? *Where*?"

Kiniera sighed in defeat. "He saw one but was unable to get any proof of its existence."

"Is he okay?"

"He's alive and well, but I expect both of you know what this means."

It confirmed that Lyondrea had reopened the Pits.

It meant they were going to war.

CHAPTER 24

JIA

Jia had always loved parties and balls. She loved dancing and drinking and dressing up. Tonight, she was going to dance and drink and forget. She needed to forget.

Jia had thrown herself onto the dance floor, dancing with any women who looked single, or single enough, and drained cup after cup of wine, trying to bury the deep ache.

She plucked another glass of wine from a passing server, twirling with delight. Then she stepped back hard onto someone's toes.

"Oh, I'm sorry. I—" Jia's words froze as she looked up to see Kaiya Whitethorn smile stiffly down at her. Kaiya, the lone survivor of her platoon in Whitewood.

But Jia was too drunk to read the reluctance in Kaiya's face, or to care. She wanted to forget, wanted to relax. And she'd definitely consumed enough wine to achieve that.

"Whitethorn!" Jia beamed, reaching out and pulling on the waist-length white braid that was half up, half down for the dance tonight.

Kaiya wore a black suit and had done her makeup with a skilled hand, drawing a sharp wing on each eyelid. She'd painted her full lips with black lipstick. Kaiya looked mouthwatering, Jia thought, even if Jia was married.

And then she remembered she wasn't married. Not anymore. The reminder jolted her from her happy, drunk haze into grief and darkness. Kaiya looked down at Jia's dress hungrily, and Jia pushed it all away.

Was Kaiya into women?

A small part of Jia, somewhere deep down that hadn't died or been irreplaceably damaged, hoped so. Begged. The corner of Jia's mouth kicked up. "I remember you. You took away my wine."

Kaiya smirked, and Jia was happy to see that the haunted, grim expression that Kaiya had when she found out that Jia was Ice-Born was absent tonight. "It needed to be taken away."

"What a terrible opinion."

Kaiya laughed and stepped further into Jia's space, a faint smile on her lips. "Terrible or not, doesn't make it any less true," Kaiya murmured, her voice low and suggestive. "I saw you dancing tonight. You only dance with women."

Jia knew what she was asking. "I only ever dance with women."

Kaiya was attractive, distractingly so, and just what Jia needed. The booze wasn't helping, and there weren't any drugs at the castle. Maybe she should bury herself in women. Maybe that would help the gaping hole in her heart.

Jia reached out and wrapped her fingers around Kaiya's wrist. "Come on, let's dance."

Kaiya let Jia tug her along until they were on the dance floor, surrounded by other couples eagerly awaiting the next song.

"Are you a good dancer?" Jia asked, looping her arms around Kaiya's neck.

"Maybe you should have asked before you dragged me out here," Kaiya told her, but the confidence in the way she pulled Jia closer made Jia swoon.

Kaiya was tall, but not as tall as Volla, had brown serious eyes, and was an excellent dancer. Everything Volla wasn't and everything Jia needed.

They danced to one song and then another and another. Until the warmth of the wine burned away from the heat that Kaiya was giving her.

"Do you need some help getting back to your room?" Kaiya asked, that hungry look in her eyes, but Jia shook her head.

She wanted to, she did. And maybe that was exactly what she needed to get through this, but she couldn't. She wasn't ready. She wanted one woman on this planet. Her wife. "No, no. I just need… I need another drink."

Kaiya opened her mouth to protest, but Jia was already pulling away, slipping her hand out of Kaiya's warm one and making a mad dash away. Straight to the nearest waiter with a tray full of bubbly wine.

Jia pulled one off a tray and threw back the contents before grabbing another. She weaved in and out of people, looking for Rorax, or maybe Kiniera. Someone she knew, one of her friends… or close enough to it.

She saw Rorax finally—in a black dress that was easily the most stylish and provocative thing Jia had ever seen Rorax wear—and started making her way through the crowd.

Jia continued to move forward, making good progress before a tall blonde in a sleek green suit stepped in her way.

Isgra looked her up and down, but instead of loathing that was so familiar to Jia, a look of want crossed over Isgra's face. It was the same look Volla used to give her. Volla's face. Volla's nose, Volla's eyes, Volla's lips….

Did Isgra taste the same as her sister did?

Maybe it was the wine, maybe it was the tiny spark of lust she felt toward Kaiya Whitethorn, but Jia couldn't help it, couldn't stop herself. She had to know.

She moved forward, put her arms up around Isgra's neck, and pressed her lips to Isgra's. Isgra stiffened, and Jia expected her to shove Jia away, but instead Isgra's arms slowly wrapped around her, bringing her closer, crushing Jia against her chest. Isgra's tongue touched Jia's lips, and Jia opened her mouth. Isgra's palm cupped the side of Jia's face, and she moaned as Jia stroked her tongue with her own.

They did. They tasted the same.

For a split second the lie felt so real, Jia believed it. Everything was right in the world again. Volla was back, kissing her like she meant to do it forever, wrapping her up in her arms. The hole in Jia's heart no longer bled. She wasn't in agony. She was with her love. Her soulmate. Her wife.

Isgra moaned again.

The sound was a lance to the illusion Jia had created. The tone was off, the sound just different enough that everything came crashing down around her. The memory that Volla was dead made Jia push her way out of Isgra's arms, stumbling back. Tears filled Jia's eyes and streamed down her cheeks as she lifted her fingers to her bottom lip. Isgra looked at her with lust and red-hot desire, until she took in Jia's expression of horror, and her face morphed into a mask of pure rage.

Isgra took a step forward, murder in her eyes, but before Isgra could strike, Rorax and Kiniera were there. Kiniera pushed Jia back on her heels so hard she stumbled into Rorax, who enveloped her protectively in her arms and turned her away.

A burst of fire shot out bright and hot, but Jia reflexively extinguished it with a cloud of ice. There was screaming and yelling from everyone around them as the fire and ice displaced several partygoers.

Isgra whispered menacingly at Jia, "If you touch me again, I will roast you from the inside out before Greywood can do anything to stop me. I don't want Volla's disgusting scraps. Now scuttle away back behind Greywood and Kulltoug where you belong."

Then Isgra looked over at Rorax and pointed. "You told me that if I touched her, you'd kill me, Greywood. Keep her away from me. If she kisses me again, I'll strangle her."

Jia flinched, but her heart was already so frayed nothing else could hurt her. Instead, she suddenly felt angry. Volla was gone, and she had left Jia with her motherfucking sister. A sister who looked and tasted exactly the same but was so much less than her.

"That's funny, little Isgra," Rorax taunted. "It looked like you were enjoying yourself before she came to her senses."

Isgra snarled at them. "Keep her away from me."

"Come on." Rorax pulled Jia's arm, but Jia ripped it away.

"No. I'm staying. I need another drink."

CHAPTER 25

RORAX

"Leave me alone, Ror," Jia hissed into her face.

"Absolutely not," Rorax snarled, about to blow the top off her temper.

Rorax had never had such an uncomfortable night in her life.

From the beginning of the evening, men and women from all over the Realms stared at her. There were glances of anger, admiration, lust, and envy, and Rorax had never had so many eyes on her at one time. The extra attention both made her skin crawl with unease and her chest warm with pride.

It was all Hella's fault. The dress was beautiful—made *Rorax* feel beautiful.

Hella had listened to her only request and had given her a thick ribbon to tie around her neck to cover Rorax's Contestar tattoo.

The dress was completely backless, and the only cover on her upper body was the two straps of fabric that had been stylishly sewn from the flowy silk skirt that rested on Rorax's hips up to the ribbon on Rorax's neck. The strips of fabric provided coverage for her breasts, but not much else.

Volla would have loved it. Sahana would have loved it more, and the knowledge made her happiness feel selfish, empty, and slightly vile.

"Tell me, is it you or your beautiful friend here who is the long-lost Contestar?"

Rorax and Jia both turned their heads to the side to find the House of Death emissary, a tall, pale, redheaded woman who stood deceptively casual with her arms crossed over her chest, looking down at Rorax. Her stick-straight red hair draped almost all the way to her waist, and she had swapped out her black armor from when her House had been introduced earlier in the arena for a long black dress and blood-red stilettos.

Rorax stepped in front of Jia slightly. She didn't see a reason to lie to the emissary, and she didn't know if she could do it convincingly right now or not. "It's me."

The emissary looked her up and down slowly, assessing every inch of Rorax from the top of her head to the bottom of her Glitter Silk dress with sharp, assessing eyes before she looked over Jia, too.

"Who are you?" Rorax asked, even though she already knew.

"My name is Milla Garrison. I am the emissary for the House of Death. I will be the one choosing the House of Death's Contestar."

Rorax stepped back, forcing Jia back as well.

"Where have you been for the past six months, Contestar?" Milla asked sharply, raising an eyebrow. "Everyone in Illus has been waiting for you."

Rorax shrugged, watching the emissary carefully as she told the truth. "I don't want the job, and I didn't know the Guardian was deteriorating."

"You don't... want the job?" Milla choked, her eyebrows pushing closer together. "It is your duty as a citizen of the Realms to show up at the Choosing; it's an *honor* to be chosen by the gods for this."

An honor? Rorax wanted to laugh.

"A Lowborn hasn't won the Guardianship in two thousand years," Rorax pointed out. "It feels more like a death sentence."

Milla just blinked at her, staring for so long Rorax couldn't help but swipe her thumb back and forth over the top of her ring a few times. "Well, you will have to excuse me, Emissary, it was nice to meet you."

Rorax managed to take another step back, but Jia tried to free herself again.

"Let *go,* Rorax. I won't let *her* ruin my night. Come on. We need another drink," Jia slurred, rocking back and forth unsteadily, leaning into Rorax for support.

Rorax staggered a bit under Jia's sudden weight, rocking on her high heels and grunting as she tried to turn them both away from Milla's still wide eyes. "Jia, I promise I don't need a drink."

Jia's glazed eyes lifted and focused on Milla. She gave her a sloppy wink. "You," Jia pointed right at Milla, "definitely look like you don't want to go to bed." Jia tried to wink but hiccupped instead.

The emissary's eyes didn't move from Rorax's face, but her shock melted as her upper lip started to curl up over straight white teeth.

Rorax forced Jia back a step, but she backed up right onto someone's toes. Rorax looked up into a pair of angry golden yellow irises and suppressed a gulp. She had just stepped onto the Prince of Death's toes. He could probably rip their lives away with barely a focused thought.

"Excuse us," Rorax mumbled as she hauled Jia off the prince.

"Milla, we came when we saw the fireball. Is there a problem here?" the prince asked the Death emissary, looking over Rorax and then Jia.

"No," the emissary snapped from behind Rorax. "It has been handled. I think I know everything I need to know here."

Rorax kept her face blank and tried to take a step around the prince, still hauling Jia, when two other men trailing behind the prince stepped up. They trapped her and Jia in a circle, surrounding them.

One of the two men towered over Rorax, and when she craned her neck up to get a better look at him, her mouth went dry. It was the handsome House of Death soldier that Jia had pointed out in the arena earlier. The one with the armor like Rorax's own, designed to be tall enough to cover his neck. The black dress shirt he wore now covered most of his neck as well, but Rorax could see the tips of black ink from under the material. The man reminded Rorax of Raengar. Rough, intense, sharp, and though Rorax normally couldn't feel magick signatures from most people, she absolutely felt power radiating from him. It made Rorax want to hold on to her soul with both hands.

Rorax forced herself to shift her attention and take in the other man. He was a few inches shorter than the hulking male in front of her, his skin dark brown. A deep scowl was etched into his face.

As the second man turned to the redheaded Death emissary, Rorax's eyes caught a tattoo under his skin just underneath his left earlobe.

But it wasn't a tattoo at all. No, it was a dark keloid scar—a scar of a ten-pointed star that had been etched into his skin.

Rorax swayed on her feet.

The man started moving his fingers and signing to the Death emissary. ***Who is this? Is she the one that got Roo killed?***

She forced her gaze to the man's hands as regret, despair, and shame rocked through her chest so hard that for a moment she couldn't breathe. The walls felt like they were pressing in on her, and her knees wobbled.

Rorax stumbled to the side, and it was all she could do to stay upright as she watched the man's lithe fingers form the words.

A warm hand gripped her shoulder, but she couldn't look away long enough from the scarred man to see who it was.

She was going to throw up. She could see the siege weapons, see the burning clock tower in the center of Surmalinn....

Since Rorax had been holding Jia up straight, Jia noticed Rorax's reaction.

Jia looked back and forth from Rorax to the man with the scar—not understanding why Rorax's face had lost all its color—before she shoved away from Rorax.

Rorax staggered back, and the man who had a hand on her shoulder guided her safely into his chest for support. She gratefully leaned against him, curled into him, greedily soaking in any comfort and warmth she could find as she numbly watched Jia take two angry steps to stand toe to toe with the man with the scar.

Jia started furiously using her hands to sign back to the man before Rorax could even think to stop her. ***What the fuck did you just say to her?***

"Jia!" Rorax hissed.

The ability to use Language of Hands was incredibly rare.

When the House of Ice had invaded the House of Death, the Wolf had taught them all how to deafen their enemies as a form of torture.

They would blow out their eardrums, pour black salt into the wound, and heal them. The black salt stopped the magick from being able to heal properly, and the eardrums could never be repaired.

Her men had done it to so many people that the House of Death had created a language using their hands, with the help of a few scholars from the House of Ice as an apology to their people.

Under Sahana's direction, the Heilstorms had all learned it, even going as far as developing their own dialect.

She doubted anyone outside the House of Ice knew they could read and use the sign language, but the last thing Rorax needed was Jia giving any additional clues about who she was or what talents they had. Too many clues would lead everyone right to her doorstep.

The man with the ten-pointed star's jaw dropped, and he blinked at her for so long that Jia leaned in closer to him menacingly and started to sign again.

She also knows what you're saying, so I would watch your mouth if I were you. Ask around and find out what she did to Isgra Torvik today; see if what you're spewing is a good idea. Jia put her hands on her hips and gave the man a smug sneer.

The chest behind her stiffened, and she looked up to the dark broody one with the tall-necked dress shirt glaring at Jia. Unease pooled in Rorax's stomach, and she finally found the strength to shove away from him and stand on her own.

She moved forward and gripped the back of Jia's dress and yanked Jia behind her.

The man with the ten-pointed star was now openly gaping at Rorax, his eyes so wide she could probably pop them out with a hard smack to the back of his head.

Rorax looked over her shoulder to find the redheaded emissary also slack-jawed and staring at her. The prince looked just as shocked as the emissary, but the tall one, the one with the intense, beautiful face glowered down at her. Rorax swallowed hard under his stare before focusing her attention back on the man with the scar.

He was still just staring at her, trying to figure her out.

Excuse my friend. She's had too much to drink, Rorax signed back to the man. She grabbed Jia's hand before any of them could say anything and pulled Jia through the crowd and away from House of Death.

Rorax kept a hold on Jia, ignoring Jia's struggles and tugging her along until they reached the opposite end of the room.

She stopped partially behind a pillar and far enough away so no one would be able to hear them speak.

"Jia...." Rorax ground her teeth together, trying to keep her emotions under control. "What the fuck was that? You're going to give us away."

Jia sighed wistfully. "I know. I got carried away. I shouldn't have signed. What did he sign that made you so upset anyway?"

"He didn't sign anything," Rorax shook her head, rubbing her thumb over her ring when Jia just gave her a confused stare. "I just... I haven't ever met anyone who...." A cold, familiar emptiness filled her chest. "He didn't say anything, Jia. It wasn't that. I just have never met any of the people that we... that I tortured like that before."

Jia's purple eyes went wide. "Oh."

Rorax's eyes fell to the white marble tile of the ballroom floor. "Out of everyone in this gods-forsaken castle, the House Death is entitled to think whatever they damn well please about me. They should think worse."

Jia bit her lip and reached out to grasp Rorax's wrist, her eyes full of sad understanding. "One day, Rorax, you're going to need to forgive yourself for what happened there."

Rorax snorted bitterly, knowing it would never happen.

CHAPTER 26

RORAX

The war drums from the Siege of Surmalinn were beating in Rorax's ears as she yanked herself free of her nightmare and threw herself out of bed. She staggered, catching herself on the smooth stone walls of her bedroom as she desperately sucked in haggard breaths.

Fifty years later, she could still see it, the blood on the hands of her soldiers as they carved the ten-pointed stars into the necks of the House of Death guards they had deafened with dull knives, right before rubbing in the black salt to the wound to make sure it scarred forever. It still made disgust, shame, and hatred curl around violently in her stomach. It was all aimed at her. Rorax had brought those men to Surmalinn. She'd broken through the city gates and let the Wolf's army in, and she hadn't stopped what they were doing. Not at first.

Rorax blinked furiously, dropping her head back to stare at the ceiling—but the wooden beams had been carved into beautiful, intricate paisley patterns. It was some of the best sculpture work Rorax had ever seen, a luxury fit for a queen… or a future Guardian.

A faint ringing started in her ears, and the walls seemed to press in on her. Gods, she was going to vomit.

She jerked herself away from the wall and forced her body into her leathers as quickly as she could. She needed to get out, needed some air. Needed to run or fight or climb or scream, *something.*

Rorax wrapped Glimr's sheath around her waist, buckling it just above her hips before she grabbed some of her favorite hair knives and shoved them into the band of the thick braid she'd done up before falling asleep.

She couldn't feel any witch-wards or runes on the window. Her room was only on the second floor of the keep, so she opened the window as far as it would go and stuck her head out. When she didn't spy any guards in the tents below or prowling the wall, she slid out.

Rorax hit the ground in a crouch, rainwater and mud flying up and splattering into her face and eyes. She wiped it off as she looked around for the guards that were supposed to be patrolling the field and tents around the castle, but everything was dark and unmoving, even the late-night revelers had long since gone to sleep.

It was about a hundred yards from the castle wall to the edge of the clearing, and almost every square inch of the grounds was covered in tents or makeshift stalls for merchants. From their haphazard placements, it was obvious that no one had been on the ground organizing where they were supposed to be set up, which Rorax was thankful for as she half jogged through a diagonal pathway. It was easier to slip around unnoticed this way.

Rorax made it to the last tent and paused. She waited for several minutes, searching for movement from the soldiers she had seen swarming the forest earlier, but there was nothing. It was completely still.

She dashed from the line of tents to the nearest tree and pressed her back to the trunk. She listened and waited for a soldier to yell or approach to see what she was doing, but everything remained quiet in the forest around her.

Cautiously, she pushed deeper into the forest, farther away from the tents and the castle, farther away from her prison. She moved slowly through the underbrush to make sure she didn't make any noise or leave any tracks and eventually found a tall cottonwood, with perfectly spaced limbs to climb on, looming over her head.

She grabbed the lowest limb and climbed halfway up the tree until she collapsed onto a limb and sprawled out like a lazy cat.

Rorax considered tying herself onto the branch to keep from rolling off in her sleep but opted for the quick escape in case anything or anyone found her. If she fell from this height, she wouldn't die anyway.

She sighed, taking her first real breath all night, and looked up into the stars, tracing over the familiar constellations.

Volla used to spend hours with her, looking up at the stars and teaching Rorax everything she knew about the cosmos, which was a lot. When Volla had been a girl, House Ice students had been required to go to university to study *something* besides warfare, and Volla had chosen astronomy. That requirement hadn't applied to Rorax going through her education. Through the Wolf's curriculum, the only thing she had ever been required to do was fight, brutalize, and kill.

Rorax closed her eyes and shoved Volla and House Ice out of her head, banishing them into the void.

Moments later she fell asleep.

Yelping, Rorax jerked up straight and gripped the branch underneath her with both hands.

The branch—with her attached—was swinging violently in the air.

She peered down just in time to see a dark band of black-and-red magick wrap around her branch and yank it down. With a loud crack, the wood broke from under her, and Rorax fell hard. She hit one branch with her hip, another raked over the side of her face, leaving a violent scratch over her cheek, before her body slammed down on the ground with a painful thud.

She landed on her shoulder before flopping onto her back. Pain rocketed down her arm as she rolled to her stomach to scramble and get up.

A boot on her back shoved her down into the mud, pressing into her and forcing Rorax to faceplant hard into the ground.

"Gods above, what the—" She moved to turn her neck to see who was shoving her down but froze when a cool blade pressed against her throat.

"Don't move," a male voice above her growled.

The hair on the back of Rorax's neck rose, and her lips curled over her teeth.

"You move even an inch, and I will slit your throat." The man pressed the blade closer to her, as if daring her to try. Her eyes darted around for something she could use, but all she could see was useless dark underbrush.

She tried to summon Glimr, but the sheath had slid up her torso to the middle of her back, and the man standing above her had his boot pressed onto the metal, stepping on it and trapping it in its sheath on her back.

Rorax's fingers flexed into the wet soil, grabbing two handfuls and squeezing tightly. Sticks were poking at the burns that Isgra had made on her arms, and it hurt enough that adrenaline started to pump through her in response, activating the fight in her blood.

She pressed her forehead onto the cool ground and tried to take a deep, calming breath. If she didn't relax, she was going to kill this man the second she got free, before she even got to see who he was.

Her voice was steady, low, and completely lethal as she growled her warning. "Get the fuck off me, or I will bleed you like a pig."

The man above her snickered, and it made her squeeze the dirt in her hands harder. "You are not in a position to be making any demands." As if to prove a point, he pressed more weight onto her back, driving her farther into the earth. "Who are you?"

Rorax grunted at the additional weight. "I'm a guest staying at... the castle." She panted, air pushing out of her lungs.

"Then what in God's name are you doing out here? There's a curfew at the castle for a *reason*."

Rorax tried to struggle against him, to lift or slide out from underneath his boot, but he just pushed down harder, so hard the burns on her arms throbbed in more pain, her breasts started to ache, and her ribs groaned.

"What's your name?" He pressed his blade against her neck until there was a little pinch of pain as he broke skin.

She snarled when the hot, wet drop of blood slid down her throat. "None of your fucking business."

She tried to lurch away, to wiggle just enough that she could free her knife and stab this son of a bitch, but she didn't accomplish anything besides his sword cutting deeper into her skin.

"Name. *Now*," he said through his teeth, increasing the weight he had on her.

She tried to gulp in a breath, but the pressure was too much. She gasped like a goldfish out of water. Her mouth was moving, but she couldn't breathe.

"Gemma!" she wheezed out as black spots started to gather in front of her eyes. "My name is Gemma Sumner."

"Gemma Sumner." the man above her spit, like the name was a rotten fruit in his mouth. "Why are you out here, Gemma?"

He released her a bit, and she sucked in a half breath before telling him the truth. "I was sleeping. I couldn't fall asleep in my room, and I came out here for fresh air."

He paused. "It's dangerous out here, Gemma."

She wheezed a dark laugh from underneath him but said nothing. She was probably the most dangerous thing in this part of the woods, and most creatures knew to stay far away from the Guardian's castle.

The male let out an exasperated sigh as he peeled his sword away from the cut on her skin and sheathed his sword. "Get up. I'll escort you back to the castle. Hurry, I want to get on with my rotation."

He stepped off her.

The second his weight moved off Glimr, she summoned the knife into her hand, twisted her torso up and around, and *sliced*.

She cut into the flesh of his calf as deeply as she could from that angle, his blood splattering across her face as she cleaved into him. He yelled in pain and staggered away from her, freeing his sword from his sheath again.

Rorax rolled away, raising herself into a low crouch, coiled on the balls of her feet. She watched for the perfect opportunity to lunge, ready to throw her knife through the motherfucker's neck.

She was going to cut him into bits. He was going to look like sloppy dog chow when she was done, and it didn't matter who he was. He wouldn't be able to do anything to stop the knife from severing through the tendons, arteries, and bone in the column of his throat.

She was about to throw the knife when she caught enough of the male's face in the dim starlight to recognize him. He was from the House of Death. The prince had called him his "lieutenant."

The House of Death lieutenant took one purposeful step toward her, and she couldn't help but swallow down her sudden unease. He would probably be able to pluck the life right out of her if she gave him too long to use the power he held, but she didn't want to kill him if she didn't have to. He was a friend to the man with the ten-pointed star, and she had caused that man enough pain for one lifetime.

Her survival instincts jolted her forward, and before he could block her, she threw her elbow across his face, the hard bone splitting the skin on his eyebrow. Blood immediately ran down the side of his cheek.

He grunted and blindly reached for Rorax, but she ducked under his arm and watched as he stumbled back a step from the force of her blow.

A dark, deep laugh rattled out of his chest as he reached up with his free hand and slowly untied the black cloak from around his neck.

"I'm impressed. It's not every day that I meet someone quick enough to get the jump on me." His smile was threatening and bloody, and Rorax's hackles rose as he dropped his cloak onto a bush and turned fully toward her. Something about the way he moved, with such confident grace, made her want to sprint, to run to the castle as quickly as she could.

He was injured. The lieutenant would never be able to catch her.

Blood had started to trickle into his left eye, but he didn't seem to care. He just let it run down his face. "I think it's time you tell me your real name, *Gemma*."

Rorax lunged with her knife, but with a loud ring of steel, he deflected her to the side with his sword.

She thrust up again, and again he blocked her, but the blade missed his throat by a mere inch this time.

She took the opportunity to use her other hand to land a solid hook to his stomach with her fist, then stepped back.

He grunted in pain, nearly doubling over as he reached for her, but she slid just out of his reach, his fingers unable to grasp the few strands of hair he managed to brush with his fingertips. The lieutenant used his forward momentum to his advantage, forcing her to dance backward to avoid his blade's reach.

He kept advancing, and Rorax managed to raise her knife to block an incoming blow, but the impact slammed her body against the wide trunk of a tree.

She gasped, shocked by the force of the impact against her spine. With his sword hand—his fingers long enough to wrap around the wrist of her hand holding her knife—he pinned her arm above her. He shoved his knee between her legs, then pushed his knee against the apex of her thighs, using his giant body to effectively pin her to the tree. With his other hand, he grabbed her throat, squeezing just hard enough to warn her.

Rorax's free hand came up to grip the wrist around her neck as he lowered his face down to hers and snarled. The lieutenant narrowed glowing silver eyes at her. His jaw was square and defined, made even sharper by the trimmed facial hair and the hint of dark tattoos that crawled up his neck under his jaw. His face screamed menace, like he could melt her bones away with a look.

Given the fact he was from the House of Death, it might not be far from the truth.

His snarl softened slightly as he took in her face. "Wait, I know you."

Fuck. Adrenaline pumped in her veins, and she tried to buck her hips to push him away. He didn't budge.

His eyes scanned over Rorax's face rapidly, and his head recoiled a bit in shock. "You... you're the one from earlier. From the ball. The woman who knows the Language of Hands." Suspicion and anger deepened in the lines of his face. "Where did you learn the language? Who are you?"

Rorax bared her teeth at him, choosing not to answer his questions. "I'm a guest at the castle. I *told* you that."

"Innocent women don't attack castle guards," he said as he shoved her a little harder against the tree.

She tilted her bleeding neck to the side for him to see the cut he'd made there. "You drew first blood, Lieutenant. I intend to draw the last blood."

Rorax released her free hand holding his wrist and reached up into her hair. His eyes tracked the movement in the dark, but before he could stop her, she plucked out one of the two hair knives, and in a swift move, she plunged it deep into the lieutenant's thigh.

"FUCK!" the lieutenant barked out into her face. He released her throat and used that hand to wrap around hers still holding onto the hair knife embedded into his thigh.

His fingers became instantly slippery with his blood, and it took him two tries to jerk the knife up and out of his quadricep.

Rorax used the distraction to free herself of his grasp and ducked under his arm, twirling away, just out of reach of his bloody fingers.

"I should have snapped your fucking neck," he seethed, taking a stumbling step toward her.

She gave him a sweet, sardonic smile. "I should have aimed for your throat."

The lieutenant snarled, and they clashed blades again, engaging in another dance, this one far more lethal.

Surprisingly, the lieutenant was good, *really* good. From his steady breaths, he was in just as good shape as she, and she grudgingly admitted to herself that his technique was even superior to hers. He had an actual *sword*; the lieutenant was also stronger than she was and just as fast. Gods knew how old he was, and he moved like he had been training for this moment every day of his life.

Rorax was talented, and she was naturally and magickally gifted with a blade. Her knife, for Kään's sake, was literally attached to her soul.

But if she wasn't going to use Glimr, the only advantage she had in this fight, the lieutenant was going to win.

If they both survived this, she would have to ask him for tips. The possibility of her making it out unscathed, however, looked bleak.

She breathed hard and twirled to land a blade through his shoulder, but he deflected her, swinging his sword all the way around his back to simultaneously push her blade away from his body and prepare for his next offensive strike.

He was about to land a high blow. Rorax raised her knife and hair dagger to block him, but he was too strong. He blew through her defenses, and the tip of his sword bit into Rorax's skin, slicing down her cheek and across her collarbone.

Blood started to run down her face, and she looked down in horror as the neck of her shirt started to stain with blood. "This is one of my favorite shirts, you bastard."

"It's going to be a shame when I stab a few more holes in it then, isn't it?" he purred, and her fingers around her knife itched to simply decapitate the fucker.

Rorax bared her teeth, taking a step closer to shove her knife into his chest when he flicked his sword up, locked her knife into the guard of his sword, and sent it flying away into a nearby bush.

The lieutenant took a step back, and the edge of his sword was suddenly at her neck. Again. "You move, you die."

She believed him, she could see the truth of it in his cold eyes as they both glared at each other, breathing heavily.

Her teeth ground together, and she summoned Glimr back to its scabbard. "Fine," she seethed.

The lieutenant jerked her hair knife out of her raised hand before he sheathed his sword. "Get your hands behind your back, you little bitch."

"You bloody bastard." She hissed in pain when he rested the blade against her throat, against the same cut he'd made earlier. But did as she was told and slowly pulled her hands down to her back.

There was a metal clanking sound, and real fear penetrated her mind. His belt—his other hand was undoing his belt. Why was he undoing his belt?

She jerked her hands up to her chest. "What're you doing?" Rorax snapped, ready to bolt, unable to keep a line of panic out of her voice.

He growled. "Put your arms back here *now.* I'm not going to touch you; I don't have anything else to restrain you with to ensure you don't stab me. *Again.*"

Fear still sat heavy in her chest, but she complied. He used his belt to strap her hands together, and when he was done, she wiggled her fingers around, testing his knot. It was secure, but if she needed to, she could unlatch herself in four seconds.

He shoved her forward, and the movement made the knife he still held to her throat slice the skin open again. "Let's go."

"I'm going to kill you one day," she promised. "It's going to be slow and painful, but very, *very* satisfying."

The lieutenant gripped the back of her neck with his hand and squeezed tight in warning. "If you can't keep your mouth closed, I will close it for you."

Rorax bit back a snarl as she started to move forward. He kept his hand wrapped around the back of her neck, and she wished he would put those fingers closer to her mouth so she could bite one clean off.

The lieutenant guided her through the trees and then through the tents, pushing her to enter through the outer gate, which had been left open for vendors and merchants to scurry through mostly unimpeded.

There were torches there, and as soon as they stepped into the light, his hand released her neck and instead grabbed onto her bound hands.

His fingertips brushed over the scabbard holding her knife, and he abruptly halted.

"Is that... the knife you used on me earlier?"

Shit. Rorax glared at him from over her shoulder but kept her mouth shut.

The lieutenant shoved a hand into her hair and yanked her head back, so she was forced to look up into his snarling face. His grip tightened, and a little whimper of pain slipped through her lips before she could trap it. "How the *fuck* did you get that back?"

Rorax bared her teeth at him. "None of your gods-damned business."

He pushed her back into the stone wall, shoving his forearm across the base of her throat over her collarbone. She grunted as her bound hands were smashed behind her back. But he just pressed into her harder, his face inches from hers.

Gods, he was beautiful. It was distracting to have him so close to her. Men shouldn't be allowed to be so handsome; it really didn't seem fair.

"Why did you attack me?"

"Because you held me down, Lieutenant. Because you put your weight on me until I couldn't breathe." She moved into him, becoming the aggressor in *his* space. "And because you made me bleed while I was helpless in the dirt."

Something that looked a lot like shame crossed over the lieutenant's face, but as soon as he parted those perfectly proportioned lips to respond, Rorax used Glimr to slice apart his belt, freeing her hands.

She slammed him in the temple with the hilt of her knife as hard as she could, and the lieutenant's giant form crumpled to the ground at her feet with a loud, violent thud. A little plume of dust flew into the air.

"Fucking bastard." Rorax spit on the ground next to his bleeding face and turned away. She flung the severed parts of his leather belt onto his unconscious body from over her shoulder and didn't look back.

CHAPTER 27

AYRES

"Heeey there, brother. Can ya hear me?" There was a nudge on his cheek, and while Ayres could tell that it was meant to be gentle, his head throbbed.

Ayres groaned as stars popped up on the backs of his eyelids. He swiped a hand at whatever nudged his cheek, but the movement just made everything hurt more. "*Fuck.*"

There was soft male laughter above him. "Ayres, you'd best be gettin' up. If Piers sees ya down here, he'll never le' ya hear the end of it. Heaven forbid Kaiya sees."

Gods, it was like he was hungover on Piers's homemade moonshine, which he wasn't. Ayres tried to remember the last time he drank enough to feel like this. It had been...

He shoved the thought away and let out a pitiful groan. "Marras kill me, I feel like death."

The man above him chuckled again. "Ya look like death, too. That girl sure did ge' you good."

Ayres's body went as tight as a string, his fury making his muscles ache.

That girl.

The girl from the ball, the one who almost fainted in his arms when she saw Cannon. He was going to wring *that girl's* neck with his bare fucking hands.

His head throbbed violently, but he ignored it, sitting up to glare at a familiar dark brown face above him.

Captain Lamonte had come to fetch him.

Embarrassment made the tops of Ayres's ears heat up, but he pushed that away and focused on his anger.

"Where is she?" Ayres snarled.

"There, there now." Lamonte waved his hands placatingly. "No one has seen ya excep' me. No reason to get riled up... excep' for maybe this."

Lamonte held out a calloused palm. Two halves of Ayres belt was draped over it.

His dragon leather belt—the belt he had used to tie the girl's hands up with—was sliced clean in two. He seethed, grabbing the belt pieces from Lamonte. "That was my favorite belt."

"A tragedy," Lamonte agreed as Ayres tucked the belt into a pocket.

Ayres glared at him as he tried to push himself up. His head started spinning again, so he slowly sat back down, sucking in deep breaths.

Lamonte hummed as his gaze moved back over Ayres's eyes. "She was right; she did give ya a small concussion. Yeh should be right as rain 'n 'bout a day or two, less if you stop by the Healers Hall."

Ayres gritted his teeth. "Where is she?"

"She's inside the keep somewhere. I saw her on the stairs. She said she knocked you unconscious out here, and if I was *'feeling so inclined to help out the biggest asshole in the Realms,'* I could find ya here." Lamonte's face lit up like he thought this was funny, like he thought *she* was funny. It made Ayres want to throw something.

"Lamonte," Ayres grunted, throwing a hand up to him, and Lamonte helped him up.

The world tilted slightly, but thankfully it didn't spin this time.

Lamonte walked beside Ayres as he took slow steps toward the castle, his blood boiling. He was going to find her, and then he was going to bury her so far underground that not even House Alloy would be able to sense her.

Lamonte laughed next to him, and Ayres scowled. "I haven't ever met anyone that didn't have that look on their face the first time they met Rorax."

"Rorax," Ayres repeated. "Rorax is the name of the woman? The one with long black hair?"

Lamonte nodded. "That's the one. She's from the House of Ice. A high-level soldier, assistant to the general or somethin'. I've never officially met her... besides durin' trainin' and that one time when we were transportin' her here. She and her companions would come 'n' knock heads together durin' the Solstices and summits at Valitlinn. Gods help us, they were a riot."

Lamonte's eyes glazed over as he walked slowly next to Ayres, smiling faintly like he was remembering the good old days with Rorax and her friends.

He was so deep in his revelry he missed Ayres's scowl. Lamonte patted him on the shoulder and left to find a replacement for Ayres's last few hours of guard duty.

Ayres slowly climbed the tower to his room. He was in the hallway at his door when the door straight across the narrow hallway opened.

"I thought I heard someone coming down the hall. Why are you back so early?" Milla stepped out of her room, pushing a lock of red hair out of her eyes as she squinted at him.

Her eyes went wide with horror. She pressed her hand to her mouth as she took in the blood that was still sticky and damp on the side of his face. "Ayres, oh my gods, are you okay? What happened?"

The memory of that woman, of *Rorax*, made the muscle in his jaw tighten.

Ayres threw his door open and motioned for Milla to follow.

As soon as the door clicked shut behind them, he took off his pants and Milla shrieked.

Ayres turned to her, an eyebrow raised.

He was still in the tight shorts he wore under his leather armor.

Milla was basically a second little sister to him. After spending so much time with her, she sometimes felt like more of a sister than his own did.

Not only were they distantly related, but they'd shared locker rooms in the Military Academy for almost ten years. They'd also gone to battle together countless times. She'd seen him in far, far less. One time, while a Healer had been working with some torn tissue in his groin area, she'd seen it all. Nudity between them had never been an issue. But she had also never stared at him the way she was right then. She looked spooked... and pissed off.

"What?" Ayres asked.

She pointed to his thigh, and he looked down at the open wound. "What in *the Hell* happened out there?"

"Oh, that." Ayres examined the wounds Rorax had given him. They were just barely starting to scab over. "It's nothing."

"*Nothing*, Ayres?" Milla asked, her voice climbing. "*Nothing*? You look like you came from war, not basic guard duty."

"It's not a big deal, Milla." Ayres gritted his teeth against a shot of pain through his temple as he gently ran his fingertips over the bump Rorax had given him.

Milla blew out a breath. "At least tell me you handled it. Any more incidents during guard duty, and you *have to* consider pulling yourself out of Lamonte's rotation, Ayres. You shouldn't be taking risks like this as it is."

Ayres bit the inside of his cheek to keep from snapping at her. They must have had this discussion at least once a day since arriving at this gods-forsaken castle. "Lamonte needs the help, Milla. That's why he asked in the first place, and he *wouldn't* have asked if he didn't have to. You know that."

"So?"

Ayres didn't bother answering and just gave her a flat look.

Lamonte was their friend. He'd been one of the first volunteers in Surmalinn to help them rebuild after the siege, and Lamonte would hold Ayres's secrets until his last breath.

"Fine, Ayr," she huffed, starting to turn toward the door. "I'm leaving. Just make sure you're in the Contestars' Courtyard tomorrow at 9:00 a.m. They're having one-on-ones with Lamonte. It'll be a good time to see what we have to work with."

Ayres grunted his agreement as she pressed the door closed behind her.

CHAPTER 28

AYRES

Cannon made his way across the Contestars' Courtyard toward Ayres and Milla. He took a bite of his berry tart as he looked at the bruising around Ayres's eye with a smirk. Milla told him he'd gotten the black eye during guard duty. The purple and black bruise underneath his eye was indicative of his dark mood.

You'll think it's funny until I give you one to match, Ayres signed to his friend, growling slightly even though Cannon couldn't hear him.

Ayres was grumpy. Even more on edge than usual. He'd woken up not only with a black eye but with a headache to go with it. His morning workout session with Kaiya and Piers had reminded him that all his other injuries that Rorax had given him—his thigh, calf, and palm—were still achy and sore as well. He'd gone to the Healer's Hall, but there had only been a young girl working there this morning, and she only held enough magick to help stabilize him, not completely take care of the injuries. He'd have to go back later and see if Tressa was working.

Ayres kept his eyes trained on the keep, waiting for Rorax to emerge. But so far, she hadn't appeared.

When she finally did show up, however, she didn't come from the keep. She and her purple-haired friend who'd been with her at the Welcome Ball came jogging from the direction of the front gates.

Gone was both the beautiful girl from the ball and the wild girl fighting desperately in the dark last night.

Those versions were nowhere to be found in the woman before him now.

This version of Rorax was a predator.

Rorax moved almost completely in sync with her companion, lithe and agile, and in total control of her body. It was almost eerie how well they moved together. The two small hilts of her hair knives poked out from where her hair was bound at her scalp, and her long braid was decorated with a sharp metal tip at the end. She'd wrapped leather around her hands to protect her knuckles, and her fighting leathers... Ayres recognized that leather armor.

Every Contestar in the square wore a matching set—the distinctive set of armor with dark brown and gold trim.

"*Fuck*," Ayres snapped out, turning his head to Milla. "Did you know that *Rorax*, the girl who knows the Language of Hands from the ball last night, is a *Contestar*?"

"Yes...." Milla looked up at him, her eyebrows furrowed in confusion. "She told me before you found me during the last song."

"She's the one who gave me this fucking black eye," Ayres growled, jabbing a finger at his throbbing, blue and black browbone.

Milla's eyebrows shot up, and her mouth formed a small "o" of surprise. "*Rorax Greywood* is the one who attacked you in the woods?"

Ayres nodded down at her, and Milla gave him a horrified look.

Milla's shoulders tensed. "She's from House of Ice, Ayres. She wasn't hunting you, was she?"

"No, I started it," he grudgingly admitted. "She was asleep in a tree when I found her."

Milla's eyebrows bunched together in confusion. She turned back to look at the Contestar and gasped in horror. Milla pointed at Rorax with one red-painted nail. "Marras help me, Ayres, tell me you didn't give those to her!"

Ayres turned his head and stared at Rorax, then stared some more until Milla burrowed her elbow into his side.

"Ayres, answer me."

Rorax had pulled off her shirt and was standing in only a fighting bra and pants, exposing two red, angry burns that stood out as clear as day against the tan skin of her biceps. Burns that had large, angry blisters over the damaged flesh in the perfect shape of someone's hands. Gods above.

Rorax turned her back to him, and his eyes narrowed in on a blue tattoo that started in between her shoulder blades. He couldn't be sure from here, but he thought it was a dragon.

She bent down and plucked what looked like a tub of salve out of a small leather knapsack at her feet. She stood up straight, unscrewed the top, and started to apply it to the burns on her arms.

Milla nudged Ayres again, breaking him out of his thoughts.

"No," he finally snapped, looking down at his emissary. "I did not fucking burn her."

"She got those fighting Isgra Torvik!"

Ayres and Milla both turned to look over their shoulder to find Piers jogging up to the group.

He gave Cannon a nod of hello before turning to Ayres and Milla. "Sorry I'm late."

"Good morning, sunshine. Where is Kaiya?" Milla asked. "She's even later than you."

Piers shrugged. "Last I saw, she was kicking some random Air-Born out of her bed."

"How do you know Isgra gave those to her?" Ayres asked, his eyes still on the Contestar.

"Lamonte told me. Isgra Torvik has some sort of issue with that girl Rorax is always with, the purple-haired one. Lamonte doesn't know for sure what Isgra's issue is exactly, but Isgra called Rorax's friend some names, tried to push her around, and apparently Rorax wasn't having it."

Ayres looked over to find Isgra, and she indeed sported two dark purple black eyes that matched his own. Marras, soon everyone in the castle was going to have a black eye courtesy of Rorax. They should start a club or maybe a support group.

Ayres's gaze shifted back to Rorax's burns. They looked painful but not exactly fresh. They must have been a week old, unless she had visited the Healers Hall. "When was that?"

"Three days ago?" Piers rubbed his chin. "I think that's what he said."

"Interesting, I didn't know anyone Ice-Born was capable of such loyalty," Milla mused. "And I'm sure you weren't distracted at *all* when Lamonte gave this report to you," Milla teased, rolling her eyes.

Piers just gave her a roguish grin. "Lamonte's the one who has the wicked mouth, Mills. Not me."

Milla laughed, but Ayres kept his eyes pinned to Rorax.

The girl who had almost killed him in the woods and then left him unconscious by the gate was a *Contestar*? Not just any Contestar, but the Contestar that they'd been waiting on for nearly six months. The Contestar that had tried to fight her way free and broke Lamonte's nose on her first day here.

The gods and the magick decided who would be the next Contestars, and they usually had very good reasons for whom they chose. Isgra Torvik had an even stronger gift than her sister, the Torch, did. Some of the other Highborns had exceptional magickal gifts already as well. Rorax felt like a wild card. A wild card he didn't know the first thing about.

Ayres's mouth tugged down at the corners.

"What're you thinking?" Milla asked, nudging him with her elbow.

"I'm thinking that the magick chooses Contestars for a reason, and they have the potential to be the most dangerous beings in the Realms." He watched as

Rorax pulled her shirt back on gingerly. “We need to be careful not to choose a Contestar who will kill us the minute she’s given the Guardian’s full power.”

CHAPTER 29

RORAX

Radashan dumped a new set of books in front of Rorax and Jia. Dust billowed up to the ceiling, and he wiped some from his oversized glasses as he gave Jia and Rorax a wide, toothy grin.

Rorax tried to smile back as she bit back a groan. Several of those books were thicker than her forearm.

"Some ancient tomes that talk about the old Guardians." Radashan beamed, nearly glowing with pride. "The gnomes and I found these in the deep, deep stacks just for you!"

Jia, who sat at the table across from Rorax, gaped wide-eyed with dread at the giant stack.

Rorax and Jia had adopted a table along the far wall of the left side of the library. A huge stalactite the width of a giant pine tree hung from the ceiling and connected into the ground through an equally large stalagmite next to the table. The configuration looked slightly like an hourglass-shaped pillar, and the table was tucked behind the formation, giving them a little bit of privacy in case someone came strolling through the stacks of books.

Rorax swallowed down a big gulp of water from the pint she'd brought with her and eyed the books. She wiped her mouth and felt a grimace tug at the corner of her mouth, but she forced herself to smile brightly at the little librarian before she told him the truth. "Radashan, you are a blessing. Truly. I would be completely lost without you."

Pink covered the tops of the small man's wrinkly cheeks, and he looked at his feet bashfully. "I'm here to help, and it's nice having so much company down here for once."

Jia said her thanks to the librarian, too, before Radashan disappeared back into the stacks with a newly determined slant to his shoulders. Little gnomes with bright-colored hats scurried behind him.

"That man is going to kill me, Rorax." Jia let out a low groan and slumped in her chair. "I don't mind reading, but the only useful thing I've learned today is that trolls store fat in their caves, and if their hoard is big enough, you can blow it up with a little fire."

Rorax smirked as she flipped the page of her own book sitting in front of her. It was titled *The History of the World's Guardians.*

She was only a third of the way in and would never admit it to Jia, but she was bored to tears, too. "Kiniera has all the House of Ice librarians throughout the country researching a way to free the Contestars, but this library is the oldest resource on the continent. There *has* to be something here."

Jia slumped down further and gave Rorax a pitiful, pained stare.

Guilt dug into Rorax's heart as she stared back at her friend. There were still deep, dark circles under Jia's stunning purple phoenix-like eyes, and she had lost weight since they'd arrived at the castle. Her face was a little tighter and more gaunt than usual.

Reading and researching were good for Jia, almost as good as her workouts in the mornings and evenings with Rorax. It got her mind off Volla, off Isgra as well, and ensured Jia didn't waste away.

Jia squinted at Rorax. "Would it really be so bad if you *did* become the Guardian, Ror?"

"Yes," Rorax asserted, not even having to think about her answer. She stiffened in her chair and thought of the best way to make sure she nipped that thought in the bud. "Yes, it sure as fuck would."

Jia tilted her head to the side to take Rorax in and squinted her eyes. "Why? You would have a seat on the *Trigonal Throne.* You would be one of the three most powerful people in the world."

"I do not want to hold the responsibility of the Realms—of the country—in my hands. I want to find Darras. He's been in a Lyondrean prison for *one hundred and fifty-eight years,* Jia."

"But as the Guardian, you would have the resources to build a team to get him back. You could do both—"

"Jia," Rorax snapped, and Jia narrowed her eyes. "Stop. It doesn't make sense for me to be here. I led a siege against my *own people*. My own *country*, and the gods choose me to be an option to *lead it*?"

Rorax suddenly felt sick. She dropped her gaze down to her hands as she ran her finger over the bird skull ring. "I can't. I… I just can't do it, Jia. I let myself be corrupted once. I don't trust myself not to be corrupted again."

"Rorax, that situation…." Rorax looked up to see Jia shaking her head, a different kind of sadness filling her eyes other than the loss of her wife. "That *wasn't your fault*, Rorax."

"That doesn't make me any less responsible." Rorax remembered the man with the ten-pointed star etched on his neck, and her words had never felt truer.

"You would be given the tools to help defend your House," Jia pressed.

"The House of Ice is the most powerful Realm in the most powerful country in the world. It doesn't *need* my protection."

"What about everyone else that lives in the Realms?" Jia asked, purple eyes narrowing.

"What about them?"

Jia huffed disbelievingly. "Gods above, Ror, you can't be serious."

They sat in a heavy silence for a few minutes until Jia made a thinly veiled attempt to change the subject. She picked up a book from the stack. "*History of the Breach, A Guide to the Choosing.*" She picked up another book. "This one, *Ancient Felidra Clan Guide*; I don't care how sweet Radashan is, I'm not reading this." Jia's nose scrunched. "Why would you even need that one?"

A sudden rush of need to be alone hit Rorax so hard she had to bite the inside of her cheek to keep from snapping something she would regret.

Jia had just lost her mate and was here to help her, spending hours of her time searching for a way to survive. But right now, in this moment, Rorax just wanted to be alone to lick the old wounds that suddenly felt so raw.

"I don't know, Jia." Rorax sighed and scrubbed her hands over her face. "I'm going to go get dinner and bring it back here to read some more before the next Contestar training. Do you want anything?"

"No, you stay here. I'll go." Jia gave Rorax a knowing little frown but pushed herself up from the table. "I'll be back."

As soon as she was out of sight, Rorax released a long breath, the tension in her shoulders relaxing.

Would being the Guardian be so bad?

Shame burned in her heart. She couldn't think about protecting anyone else until she'd protected her brother and had atoned for her actions against the House of Death. Even after that, would she even want to be the Guardian? Did she care enough about the Realms to come to their defense?

Rorax sat, lost in thought, for several minutes before she took another sip of water and forced herself to focus on the book in front of her.

"What the fuck are you doing down here?"

Rorax jerked so hard her knee hit the tabletop, the pint of water tipping over and spilling precariously close to the ancient tome she was reading.

"Gods above." She sopped up the excess water off the table with her arm, flinging it onto the ground before it could touch the pages of the book, and glared up to find Lieutenant Jackass standing over her table glaring at her.

She hadn't seen the lieutenant for the last few days, and gauging from the anger flooding her veins, it hadn't been *nearly* enough time to diffuse her fury.

"I'm *reading*, Lieutenant. It may be a difficult concept for someone with the intelligence of an acorn to grasp—" Rorax gritted her teeth, her heart beating furiously as she glared up at him. "—but people usually come to libraries to *study*."

The lieutenant had dark circles under his eyes, but the black eye she'd spotted on him a few days ago at the Contestar training session was long gone. His posture was just as tall and imposing as it had been that night he knocked her out of that tree, and he became even more imposing as he crossed his muscular arms over his chest.

"You're just as sweet as I remember," the lieutenant said darkly. He was wearing a black, long-sleeved, tall-necked shirt, though not as tall necked as the ones he'd worn before. The dark fabric left some of the skin under his jaw exposed, and before she could stop herself, her eyes dipped down to the column of his throat, tracing over the intricate skull and what looked like wings tattooed on the front of his neck.

What are you hiding, Lieutenant?

She pointedly kept her eyes away from his forearms that were exposed, muscled, and also covered in tattoos because the dark fabric was pushed to his elbows. If Lieutenant Jackass *wasn't* Lieutenant Jackass, Rorax would have thought the man an absolute specimen.

"What happened to your arms?" Ayres asked, looking down at her forearms and the burns that, even after a week, still stood out red and angry against her skin.

Rorax bit her lip. She didn't want to talk about Isgra, now or *ever*. Gods, she just wanted to be *alone* for *five gods-damned minutes*. "They were presents from Isgra Torvik."

"What does the Match have against your friend?"

"Hmm, seems like people have been talking."

"It's our job to talk about the Contestars, if we are going to stick our necks out for them."

"The Match and I don't get along. That's all there is to know."

"Is it?" Ayres cocked his head, studying her intently.

Rorax returned his stare with a deceptively lazy one. "Why are you here, Lieutenant? One humiliation wasn't enough?"

A muscle in his cheek jumped, and he took two loaded steps forward. He slapped his palms on the tabletop in front of her and leaned down, looking like he wanted to reach across the table and drag her across the surface by her throat. "If I remember correctly, *I* was the one leading *you* back to the castle by knifepoint."

At his proximity, Rorax's survival instincts prickled, urging her to flee or fight, but she forced herself to stay unmoving in her chair.

The bond she had with her knife strained, reminding her that she could slaughter him if he got too close. House of Death or not, she would punch Glimr through his neck and face the consequences after.

Slowly, she allowed herself to stand until they were nose to nose. "If you want a rematch, just say so. Right here, right now."

"Stop!" Radashan appeared from between the stacks, bookless and without his helper gnomes for once, waving both tan, wrinkled hands in the air. "Stop, *both* of you!"

Radashan pushed the lieutenant away from the table with one wrinkled hand, something Rorax knew the lieutenant was allowing as Radashan only came up to the bottom of the lieutenant's sternum and all Radashan's limbs combined were probably the same width as the lieutenant's bicep. Despite the differences, Radashan stepped between them, raising his arms above his head. They shook so hard Rorax could see them trembling from five feet away.

"Move out of my way," the lieutenant snarled down at the small librarian, his eyes pinned on Rorax with lethal intent.

"The library is a neutral zone! No blood shall be spilled here. It is my job to protect it!" Radashan's voice was barely more than a pleading squeak.

Rorax sneered at the lieutenant. "You heard him, craven. *Shoo.*"

The lieutenant pointed one tattooed finger at her and snarled, "If you don't fucking shut your mouth, I promise you, Rorax, I'll shut it for you."

Rorax gave him a wicked smile. "I'll cut you into ribbons. Right here, right now."

"No!" Radashan squeaked, turning his head over his shoulder with giant, pleading eyes. "No, not here, Ms. Greywood. Please, take this outside!"

"Don't worry, bookkeeper, I have better things to do," Rorax snarled.

The lieutenant looked her up and down slowly with obvious disdain before he turned on his heel and strode away, his angry footsteps echoing off the chalky stalagmites hanging from the ceiling and walls of the library.

When the door slammed behind him, Radashan turned to Rorax, his cheeks pink with distress. "Ms. Greywood! I would have thought you of all people would respect the *library*!"

Shame curled in her stomach as she took in the panic and disappointment on the little man's face, and she bowed her head. "I do, and I'm sorry. It won't happen again. The next time I threaten to kick his balls up his throat will be strictly out of the library."

Radashan's pink cheeks deepened in color, and he pushed his glasses up his nose. "Very... very well."

He took two steps away before hesitating and turning halfway back to her. "A word to the wise, Ms. Greywood. Many Death Magick wielders were killed in the massacre brought on by your people fifty years ago, but not all of them. Maybe you cannot sense magick yet in others, but I can. That man? He reeks of Death Magick, and it would be unwise to provoke him."

Radashan turned away and disappeared without another word, leaving Rorax with a foreboding feeling in her gut that intensified with every one of his quiet, retreating steps.

Chapter 30

Rorax

1. Weather
2. Foliage
3. Darkness
4. Fauna
5. Air
6. Ice
7. Fire
8. Life
9. Light
10. Water
11. Alloy
12. Death

Rorax ground her teeth together as she crumpled the edges of the paper in her hand.

Each Contestar stood in the Great Hall around the Guardian's throne in a semicircle. The Great Hall was deserted except for the Contestars, the Guardian, and Captain Lamonte—who had just handed the Contestars the order in which they were to be interviewed by the House emissaries.

The girls around her whispered, all humming with excited energy as they compared their notes. Rorax stood alone and seethed.

Today was the day they would truly start selling themselves to the emissaries, attempting to prove they were worth their protection. This was the day the Contestars truly began building *connections.*

Rorax would have skipped the whole day just to preserve her peace of mind, but the Guardian had scribbled a note in the top left corner of the paper in red ink:

If you are reported missing from any of the interviews today, I will carve the letters of your name into the bones of Jia's spine.

The Guardian's eyes rested on her, and Rorax felt them hot on her skin.

Rorax crossed her arms over her chest and tried to look bored before she finally glanced up to meet the Guardian's gaze.

The Guardian gave Rorax a smug grin, as if she knew exactly how much Rorax wanted to rake her knife through her skin.

Rorax gave her a chilling smile back. The Guardian tilted her head in surprise for a fraction of a second before Enna and Briar, the blonde with the wicked scar down half of her face, stepped up to Rorax. "Who do ya have first?" Briar asked, snatching the paper out of Rorax's fingers before she could hide it.

Rorax hissed as Briar chuckled and showed Enna the note. "Does the Guardian write ya many love notes like that, Greywood?"

"Gods," Enna whispered. "That's just cruel. She wouldn't really do that, would she?"

Enna was interrupted as the Guardian clapped loudly, demanding their attention. "Girls, as you know, today are the interviews. The order in which you will arrive and where is listed next to the House. You'll have half an hour with each House, with a lunch break after your sixth House."

An excited murmur erupted from the group when the Contestars were dismissed. Rorax didn't give the Guardian or the other girls another glance as she stomped out of the room, plotting the death and demise of the Guardian of the North.

"You seem very interesting, Rorax," the House of Air emissary said, straightening the papers in front of her before looking back up at Rorax. "And it's impressive that you are so close to General Frostguard. I've only heard good things about her, as everyone did when she helped overthrow King Katalon."

The Air emissary, or Allurah, as she'd asked Rorax to call her when Rorax first arrived at her room, let out a heavy mournful sigh. "I would love to ask you to be our Contestar, but my king was very specific that he wants a Highborn if we do well enough in the Tournament of Houses tomorrow." Allurah's cheeks turned a little pink as she picked up the tiny, blue gem on the necklace around her throat, running it up and down the chain nervously. "Even if your fighting prowess is admirable, the king and his advisors want someone who is already adept with their magick. I'm sorry. I know that sounds so... so shallow."

Rorax gave her a tight-lipped smile. The House of Ice had always respected and valued her, but here where people valued elemental magick so much, she had never felt so lowly. It was almost word for word the same speech that each of the first four emissaries had already given her. *No Lowborns.* "It's not. Don't worry, I understand."

"But I did see that fight between you and Isgra Torvik the other day! If we don't manage to perform well in the Tournament of Houses, you would be our first choice of all the Lowborns." Allurah gave her a warm, hopeful smile before getting up and showing Rorax to the door.

"Good luck with the rest of your interviews today, Rorax," Allurah said cheerfully before closing the door in Rorax's face.

Rorax stared at the door, gritting her teeth, talking herself down from breaking the door wide open and showing the emissary just how dangerous she could be.

Instead, she slid back a step, then another, then turned and slowly trudged down the corridor.

Thankfully, her next interview was with Kiniera.

A guard opened the door for Rorax when she got to Kiniera's room, having to use his shoulder to break a thin line of ice that was forming around the doorframe, and Rorax stepped into the room. Kiniera Kulltoug was seated at a table with two large glasses of iced tea in front of her. Rorax decided she'd never been so happy to see her old mentor in her life. One of the first people to train Rorax as a child, and then again when she had joined Sahana's unit, Kiniera held more magick than anyone Rorax had ever met. It was always unknowingly leaking out of her; even now a thin sheen of ice crept up the walls and over the edges of the two drinking glasses on the table. But Rorax had grown up in Koppar, the capital of the House of Ice, and she was used to the cold.

Kiniera sat straight, watching Rorax approach with appraising eyes. She wore a long white robe, which made her skin look gaunter and paler than normal, accenting the purple bags under her eyes and the slightly gray hue to her skin. "Take a seat, Greywood. Get comfortable." Kiniera gave her a knowing smirk as Rorax slid heavily into her seat with a tired sigh. "How has it been going so far?"

"It's been shit," Rorax said as she reached forward to dump a spoonful of sugar into the iced tea in front of her before taking a long drink.

Three of the first five of Rorax's interviews had ended in under fifteen minutes, which didn't speak well for her chances of landing a Protectorate who could benefit her.

Rorax looked up into the pale, hollow-cheeked face of Kiniera Kulltoug over the rim of her cup. "How about yours?"

"Poorly as well." Kiniera's already pale lips went white as her mouth flattened with displeasure. "I need to pick a candidate that will serve as the House of Ice's beacon of hope... but only just long enough for you to kill her."

Rorax snorted and dipped the spoon back into her tea, trying to coax the dregs of sugar on the bottom of the cup to dissolve. "What did you think about the brunette, Enna, from Fauna? Or the small blonde smuggler from the House of Air? Briar?"

"I haven't met with them yet. I met with all the Highborns, but I'm not terribly interested in any of them besides Isgra, and that's only because Volla, *the Torch,* was an icon to the House of Ice." Kiniera sighed, her shoulders slumping as she rotated her glass in her long, bony fingers. "Isgra resents us all, but she won't say no to the strongest house in the Realms asking to be her Protectorate."

Resent was such a polite way to say that Isgra would love nothing more than to put all their heads on a spike.

Rorax huffed a laugh and took a long drink of her tea before setting her glass down and rubbing her thumb over the top of her bird ring. "Any other news or tidbits from Darras?"

Kiniera shook her head. "Your goals and only focus should be to gain a pledge from Death, Fire, or Darkness, preferably in that order."

"Death might be off the table." Rorax picked up her glass again and threw back the rest of her tea, then dropped it on the table with a clatter, trying not to think about the lieutenant. "But I'm going to Fire after this. Hopefully I can convince him to take a chance on me."

Kiniera's silvery white eyebrows furrowed, as though she couldn't possibly understand how Rorax could have already alienated herself from Death this early. But Rorax kept her mouth shut, not offering any additional information.

"Well, Elios, the emissary for House of Fire, has been digging around about you. I dropped enough pieces of intel to his sources that he *should* have put together you're a Heilstorm, but I haven't heard anything more from him. So, either he knows you're a Heilstorm and wants to keep his findings a secret from the other emissaries, which would be a good sign for you, or he hasn't pieced it together yet." Kiniera's lips pressed together again, as though the idea of Elios not connecting her hints would be very disappointing.

Rorax smirked at her current spymaster and old mentor. "Not everyone is as gifted as you, Kiniera." Kiniera waved her small hand, a tiny blush coloring her otherwise colorless cheeks. "Keep those charming words coming, Rorax, or you'll never find a Protectorate at this rate."

Rorax double-checked the number beside the big wooden door and rapped her knuckles against it and waited.

The door swung open, and she had to fight to keep her eyes from widening to the size of moons.

The most beautiful man Rorax had ever seen stood at the door.

He was like the sun—bright, with an unnatural glow about him. His skin, a warm golden tan, contrasted perfectly with his golden blond hair. Unlike some of his counterparts who had interviewed her before, his body language was open and welcoming. He smiled wide and his beautiful blue eyes sparkled with kindness as they took her in.

Kindness.

Rorax took a step back and glanced at the number beside his doorframe to triple-check she had the right door.

She squared her shoulders and hesitantly looked back up at the stunning man. "Um... hello. I'm Rorax Greywood, and I'm here for my interview."

"Hello, Rorax. My name is Elios Delgata, emissary to the House of Fire. It's nice to finally meet you." Elios stuck his palm out to her, and Rorax took it, feeling the unnaturally warm, dry skin under hers as he gave her a friendly handshake. Elios stepped away from the door, motioning her inside his suite. "Come on—"

A door opened down the hall, and a woman with mussed hair and shoes in one hand walked out. Her cheeks were pink, and she had that glorious glow of a girl who'd just been freshly fucked to an orgasm. Probably multiple orgasms.

Jealousy, green and hot, pierced through Rorax's chest. It had been *weeks* since her last orgasm that hadn't been self-induced. *Months*. Now that she thought about it, it had been almost a year.

With a small, wistful sigh, Rorax started to turn away from the girl, but then a tall man wearing nothing but dark pants followed her into the hallway.

Instantly, all the jealousy Rorax felt toward the girl and her orgasm evaporated into nothing, instantly replaced with pity. The poor girl had been tricked into a spider's dark web.

The girl lifted on tiptoe to give Lieutenant Dickbags a quick hug. He awkwardly patted her back with one tattooed hand and stepped back.

The girl disappeared, padding down the hallway barefoot, and the lieutenant turned to see Rorax and Elios watching him. He froze solid, his eyes flickering between them for a moment before focusing on Rorax.

Rorax's mind shuttered when the lieutenant turned his bare-chested body to face her. He had on a pair of loose, low-riding pants, and her eyes greedily traced the gutters of his abdominal muscles up his laterals, over his square pecs, and across his thick trapezoids as she took in his exposed tattoos. Heat bloomed in her core.

She had to clamp her teeth into her tongue to keep from licking her lips. If only that body belonged to a man whose personality wasn't so reminiscent of dirty dishwater.

"Lieutenant," Elios said from behind her, breaking Rorax out of her perusal of the lieutenant's upper body.

"Delgata." The lieutenant nodded to the emissary, his dark eyes flickering to Elios before settling back on Rorax. "What are *you* doing up here?"

Elios opened his mouth to respond, but Rorax was faster. "That is none of your business, but I'm happy to see you're trying out another outlet for your anger besides knocking sleeping girls out of trees, Lieutenant. We both know how well that ended for you last time."

"Careful, Rorax, sounds like a little green monster wants to come out and play." Ayres snorted, crossing his arms over his chest and leaning against his doorjamb. He casually looked her up and down as his lip curled in disgust. "Jealousy isn't a good look on you. Not that anything else would look good on you either."

"I won't be jealous at all if this new development means I might actually get a good night's sleep." Rorax tilted her head at him. "Tell that girl thank you for me, will you, Lieutenant? She is doing the gods' work with all the charity she does. Tell me, Lieutenant, how does a pity fuck feel?"

Elios choked, and the lieutenant moved off the doorjamb to take a few threatening steps closer.

"Come over here and find out?" Ayres smiled maliciously, and she had to fight a shiver of lust and fear from running down her spine. "I'll stoop to your level to help work some of that bitterness out of you. If I can't stomach it, I'll even help you find someone stronger than me to do it."

Rorax saw red, and she took the few remaining steps toward him, so they were toe to toe. Her knife trembled on her back, but she didn't summon it. She didn't want to behead anyone in the hallway, and definitely not in front of Elios.

So instead, she forced herself to smile up at the lieutenant. "I should just go to the brothel in Bafta to get it done. A whore never turned down anyone's gold, and I would put it on your account since this was your idea. But I've heard a rumor that you owe them a small fortune since you've had to pay them to keep quiet about how small you are."

She pointedly looked down at his crotch with pity, even though what she could see from his hastily buttoned pants was far from miniscule.

Behind her, Elios threw his head back and roared with laughter. The lieutenant glowered down at her, his eyes roaming over her face with something that looked a lot like hot loathing as Elios continued to chuckle behind them.

When Elios's laughter subsided, she turned her back on the lieutenant to find Elios beaming at her. Elios waved her inside his room, and Rorax pushed past him without another glance at the lieutenant behind her.

CHAPTER 31

RORAX

The emissary rooms were all built the same. They were much larger than normal lodgings and technically had three rooms. The entry room had a large window, a fireplace, and a long, rectangular table with six chairs around it. The other two rooms consisted of a bathroom and a small bedroom for the emissaries to sleep. Elios's room was no different.

He motioned to the table. "Sit anywhere. I'll be back."

Rorax took a seat on one of the long sides of the table. When Elios came back, he slid in across from her and handed her a folder. It was thin, and when she opened it, she found only a few loose pieces of paper inside.

Time to see if Elios pieced together Kiniera's clues, Rorax thought.

"This is all the information I could find about you."

Rorax felt his eyes on her as she thumbed through the pages slowly. There were fifteen pages in all, most of them reports written by his spies. She could see his scribbles everywhere on them.

"*Roraxiva Greywood. Parents deceased with one living sibling. Trained in House of Ice war camps for nearly fifty years before being recruited as the youngest member in Heilstorm history,*" she read, jerking her eyes from the page to look up into Elios's face, feigning surprise.

"*Eventually became third-in-command of the Heilstorms' First Unit, under Sahana Thorash. Founder of the Special Forces unit responsible for the assassinations of six Lyondrea generals, countless monsters who crossed the border, a few prominent members of Court, and—*" Rorax looked up from the page to study Elios's face. "*—the Wolf during the Siege of Surmalinn.*"

The energy in the room shifted from friendly and amicable to dangerous and sharp.

Rorax's eyes drilled into Elios, a faint buzzing sound in her ears.

As he studied her, the hint of a triumphant smile built at the corners of his beautiful mouth before she returned to reading. "*It was believed that Sahana Thorash made the killing blow against the Wolf, but the most recent autopsy report indicates that the Wolf's injuries are more consistent with some of Greywood's other confirmed kills.*"

She wanted to get Kiniera to destroy the autopsy file, find out how many other people knew about it, and question the man involved. Hopefully Elios hadn't made any copies of the report.

"Everything sounding correct so far?" Elios folded his hands in front of him, his gaze moving up to her again.

Rorax forced her face into a neutral mask and shrugged. "Surprisingly accurate, Emissary. You're the only one all day to have picked up my *occupation*. Everyone else assumes I know how to fight because I'm an army grunt." She shrugged again before asking the only thing that mattered. "How did you get your hands on the autopsy?"

Elios smirked, straightening the papers in front of them. "Don't worry, Contestar. I already had the information destroyed for you."

"Thank you." A little frown forced its way onto Rorax's unwilling mouth. "But that wasn't the question."

"No, it wasn't." His blue eyes glittered in triumph. "My cousin twice removed is the House of Ice mortician in Koppar, and last week I sent him a raven asking him if he'd seen any unclaimed knife wounds that blasted all the way through a body."

The smile faded from his beautiful face, and his eyes got serious. "I won't ever use him as a source again. I won't endanger his life like that by asking him to go between. I ask that you let his life remain… untouched. He didn't even understand what he was looking for when I asked him."

Elios's cousin was a dead man walking. Even if the information was nearly irrelevant to anyone besides Rorax, it was a leak that would need to be swiftly plugged.

Rorax snorted and folded her arms across her chest as feeling slowly started to seep back into her limbs. "Send a raven out today and start finding him a new job. As your House's ice cube maker or something. Anything. When the spymasters of House of Ice find out *any* private information was leaked to another House, they'll come for blood."

Elios tilted his head and gave her a grim nod. "I was afraid of that after what I found. I'll have him on the first ship out tomorrow."

Like that would save his cousin if Kiniera or Rorax wanted him dead.

Elios must have sensed the direction of her thoughts and tried to redirect them. "Your information was by far the hardest to obtain. There isn't anything anywhere else about you. Why is that? Is that because there isn't really anything? Or that House of Ice just destroys it?"

She smiled, but it was far from friendly. "A little of both. I've been training and fighting since I was a child; as an orphan, that was all there was to life." She shrugged, ignoring the flash of pity in Elios's eyes. "Ice also wants to make sure we are as unconnected and as untouchable as possible."

Elios nodded and leaned closer to her. "Even if only half the rumors about you and the Heilstorms are true, you have an impressive resume."

She tried not to make a face at the word *resume*. That word made it seem like the Choosing was a job, not a death sentence or something they were being forced to participate in to the death.

Rorax gave him a tight-lipped smile. "Most of the rumors are true."

"Is that why you didn't report right away to the Choosing? Were you in the middle of an assignment when the Hunter found you?"

"Yes, I was. I can't tell you anything about it, however. It was a highly confidential assignment and is probably still ongoing."

Elios's eyes flashed with disappointment, but it was gone a second later. "I've been trying to see you spar with the other Contestars, but you never do. Why not?"

"There are some members of the House of Alloy's special forces here. I want to keep my identity a secret for as long as possible." Rorax shrugged and looked down at her hands, remembering how the cartilage in Isgra's nose felt as she had crunched it under her fist. "I... uh... also have a ban where I can't spar with anyone until the next moon. I'm sure you heard that I was recently in a fight with the Highborn Isgra Torvik."

Rorax monitored his face, watching carefully to see if there were any sparks of recognition regarding her connection with Isgra, but there was nothing.

Most of Rorax's personal information was still tightly under wraps, and Elios only knew the things Kiniera had been feeding him. Except whom really killed the Wolf. He didn't seem to know of her personal connection to the Wolf or anything about the Siege of Surmalinn, thank Kään.

"To put it mildly, this Choosing's Highborn selection has been disappointing." He rubbed a hand over his clean-shaven face. "My queen urged me to select a Highborn but gave me the authority to choose whomever I deemed fit."

"*Mildly* disappointing?" Rorax couldn't hold back a snort. "Highborns are usually the strongest of the Contestars, the smartest, the fittest, and the easiest to control. I'm undoubtedly biased, but there aren't many of us here who would be able to keep the country safe, let alone rule it. And none of those are Highborns."

"House of Ice is arguably going to be the best Protectorate here. Why not fight for them?"

Rorax rubbed her thumb over her ring. "No one wants to see a House of Ice sponsored Guardian."

Elios hummed in agreement and tilted his golden head to the side, taking her in. "Do you think you have what it takes to become the Guardian?"

Rorax didn't tell him that she had no intention of staying here once she freed herself from the Choosing's hold on her soul.

Instead, the corner of her mouth curled up as she leaned back in her chair and draped her arms across the back. "I have more than enough of what it takes to keep this hellhole safe."

Rorax knocked on the wooden door with the House of Life's insignia on it.

After talking to Elios, she felt more in control. Rorax wanted him to be her Protectorate, and he wanted her to be his Contestar. House of Fire had the manpower to protect her from herself during influxes. It would be a perfect setup.

The door jerked open, and a tall man—a behemoth of a man—stood in the doorway. Rorax gazed up at him, her neck craning.

Kään save her, the man must have been close to the same size as Lieutenant Asshole. Why did all the men that wanted her dead have to be mammoth sized?

The tall, ginger-haired man with a neatly trimmed beard glowered down at her with so much anger and aggression, she was surprised she didn't take a punch to the face right there and then.

Rorax recognized him. He was the House of Life's princess's lover. The healer whose sister had been killed and sacrificed to find Rorax.

Unease coiled in the bottom of Rorax's chest, and she tightened the bond with her knife.

The giant of a man crossed two thick arms over his chest. His voice was as cold as House of Ice. "You here for your interview?"

Rorax nodded slowly, looking for any immediate weapons or threats on his person. She didn't find any, and when he turned his back on her and led the way into his room, she hesitantly followed, shutting the door behind her and moving slowly into his room.

The bedroom door was currently open, revealing heaping piles of clothes and armor that looked like it had been carelessly dumped on the still made-up bed. If Rorax had to guess, the emissary only used this room as a glorified locker and spent most of his time in the princess's bed.

The emissary moved to the opposite side of the table from her, placing it between them, and leaned over as he put his massive hands on the polished wooden tabletop.

His lip curled over his teeth as he looked her over with disgust. "Let's make this fast. The Guardians' Law says I am not allowed to kill you today but know that I want to. That I would. Roo was like a little sister to me, *would* have been my little sister if you had just—"

The emissary's Adam's apple bobbed as his throat worked, the sight barely visible from under his copper-colored beard.

Rorax rubbed her thumb over her ring, something an awful lot like regret tasting in her mouth. "I came here hoping I could clear the air. The looks you and the princess give me make me want to start shopping for a headstone."

The corner of the man's lips twitched, but a shadow passed over his caramel-colored eyes. "Maybe you should."

Rorax shrugged. "Maybe I should. I want to make sure it's a headstone I like if I'm going to be stuck underneath it for all of eternity."

The emissary didn't so much as smirk, so Rorax got to the point.

"I only came here because I want you to deliver a message to the princess for me." And because the Guardian had threatened Jia if she didn't.

The emissary's nostrils flared, and he stood up straight. "Tell me the message, and I will decide if it's worthy to be given or not."

Rorax nodded once, fighting a smile that threatened to cross her mouth. She couldn't help but like men like him, men who protected the people they loved. "I understand why she hates me. If I was in her position, I would feel the same way."

His eyebrows furrowed deeper as he crossed his arms over his chest.

"It's true. But the reason I didn't answer the Court's summons was because I was looking for my brother. He's currently imprisoned. If the roles were reversed and she was looking under every gods-damned pebble in this gods-forsaken land for her lost sibling, the last remaining shred of family she's ever had, would she really have stopped everything to report to the Choosing?"

The emissary's eyes went wide for a split second before he gritted his teeth and looked down. It was quiet for a beat, and when his eyes continued to focus on the bland wooden floor instead of her face, Rorax knew she was right.

"I have another reason for not reporting, but the princess would need to take a Blood Oath of secrecy to hear that reason."

The emissary's head jerked up, and he took a step toward Ror, his eyes blazing. "I would never let her taint her blood with the blood of a coward." He sliced the air in front of her face with his palm. "I don't care what your reasons are; they will *never* be good enough."

"Me not answering the summons gave that girl *five extra months* to live her life."

The emissary barked out a laugh. "How'd you reckon you didn't cost her hundreds of years?"

Because Rorax had the resources to end this fucking competition tomorrow.

Because she was a Heilstorm.

Because she had the most powerful realm at her back.

Rorax stood. "Tell the princess my offer. If she wants answers from me, that's the price. Good luck with the Choosing, Emissary."

The extra knives Rorax hid in her cloak clinked together softly as she made her way up the steps to the House of Alloy's emissary room.

If there was going to be trouble during an interview, it was going to be this one.

Rorax had stopped by her own room to gather some equipment, since she didn't trust the House of Alloy with any fiber of her being.

She knocked on the door, and a man answered.

He stood taller than her by several inches, with dark brown hair slicked back and matching dark brown eyes. The arrogance and entitlement in his eyes were expected as his gaze crawled over Rorax, inspecting her from head to toe. Rorax bit her cheek to not react to his offensive gaze, or to open her mouth and threaten to pluck out his eyes as his gaze lingered on her breasts.

"Hello, Emissary," Rorax ground out, and finally his line of vision lifted to hers.

He smiled an oily smile that only served to put her more on edge as he stepped back and invited her into the room. "Contestar, make yourself at home."

Rorax fought a shiver of revulsion and stepped inside.

Rorax's attention was immediately pulled to a tall, ebony-skinned woman who leaned against the wall, her muscular limbs deceptively loose as she twirled a throwing knife around her finger. The woman's bald head had been carefully shaved to show off the green tattoos marking her scalp. She cocked her head at Rorax as Rorax moved farther into the room and the torch light reflected off her tattoos like they were made of a shiny green metal. The woman had a silver septum piercing, and her brown eyes had a thick line of bright green eyeliner painted sharply on her top eyelids, making her look feline and dangerous.

She stood behind a man seated at the table with auburn hair and tan skin. Rorax's eyes moved to him, taking in his thick arms that were crossed over his chest and the hard set of his jaw. He was watching her, his deep blue eyes looked vaguely familiar.

"Take a seat, Contestar." The woman against the wall smiled, pointing the knife in her hand to the empty chairs at the table. Her smile was far from friendly.

Rorax did as she was told, feeling the man who met her at the door following closely behind, breathing down her neck.

"My name is Niels Wormwood. I am the emissary of House of Alloy. That is Narlaroca, and in front of you is Callum. They're my assistants during our time in the Choosing," the emissary stated as he crossed over and sat in his chair beside Callum. He leaned over the table toward her.

The emissary, Niels, beamed at her for a second longer than was proper. "You are an *interesting specimen*," he crooned, looking her over as if she was not in fact a person but an object. An inanimate soldier. "An interesting House of Ice project."

Rorax did her best not to shuffle in her seat. "It looks like we have three interesting House of Alloy projects here, too," she returned flatly, looking each of them in the eyes.

Niels smiled in delight. "My king has ordered me to select a Highborn, given our small timeframe. He wants someone who already knows how to use her power and is a friend of the House of Alloy." Niels gave her a tight-lipped smile. "You are not a Highborn, but you certainly do know how to fight."

"You beating Isgra's ass was the highlight of my week," the woman, Narlaroca, chimed in from behind the emissary. She smiled wide again to show off slightly sharpened canines. Narlaroca reminded Rorax of a snake, a viper in Alloy colors.

Rorax gave her a tight smile back before turning back to Niels.

"Unfortunately, orders are orders." Niels appeared crestfallen, as he looked over Rorax again. The slow inspection of his beady, black eyes made the hair on Rorax's neck rise. "But if something were to happen in the Tournament tomorrow, if we do not place favorably enough to claim a Highborn, House of Alloy has a special interest in you."

Rorax pushed herself up, eager to leave. "I won't waste any more of your time then."

Niels nodded. "That would be best. Until next time, Contestar."

Rorax looked at each of them one last time before turning and disappearing from the room, her skin crawling over her bones.

Rorax had shown up to the House Death emissary's door to find a tiny little note wedged in the doorframe.

Meet me outside.

-M

That suited her just fine. She craved some fresh air and had taken the opportunity to grab a few coins from her room, with the intention that she would be able to find some food from one of the merchants or vendors that had made camp on the castle grounds.

Rorax had decided that she would go see the emissary before she focused on food, but as she approached a line of tall, black tents, she wished she would have sorted her priorities better.

Unlike most of the other houses who had set up their tents to be in rows, designed to make it easy to socialize and shop with customers from the other realms, Death had set their tents up to resemble a colony, each black tent situated edge to edge, facing inward with only one tent that led in and out of their section.

Rorax dragged her feet, dreading this interview. She was tired, hungry, and wanted to be alone. She didn't have any energy left for another altercation with the lieutenant today. Rorax couldn't see past the wall of tents the Death Court had erected, but she heard the cheering of a crowd.

She approached the House of Death guards standing tall at the entrance. "Excuse me, I have an appointment with the emissary."

The guard looked down his nose at her. "You're early."

"I didn't exactly *click* with my last appointment."

He sneered down at Rorax but turned to the tent and pushed through an opening she hadn't noticed. "Go through there, turn to your left, and you'll see her tent. It's the only tent here with the red flags in the front."

Rorax stepped inside and turned to ask the guard a question, but he had already shut the opening of the tent back up. She scrunched her nose and continued.

When she pushed through the other side of the tent, she saw what the commotion was. A group of soldiers were standing in a circle, taking bets and cheering on a sparring match.

It wasn't just *any* sparring match.

The Prince of Death and the lieutenant were in the center of the humming crowd, swinging swords at each other.

She instantly forgot her exhaustion and her appetite.

Both men were sweaty. Both men were shirtless. And both wore only black leather pants. They exuded confident aggression and testosterone—something that Rorax had always found irresistible—in *palpable* amounts.

Heat rose in her core, and Rorax swallowed to get some moisture on her tongue as the prince landed an elbow into the lieutenant's rib cage. The lieutenant grunted in pain but swiped a foot under the prince.

The prince hit the ground and rolled away, came up in a crouch, and pounced back into the fray.

The lieutenant's personality might have resembled a stinking pile of wild goat dung, but his body....

Gods above.

His tattoos were beautiful.

The same image that was on the House of Death sigil—Marras, Goddess of Death, donned in a white robe—was in the middle of his pecs. A skull with an intricately drawn snake ran down his sides and covered the bottom of his pecs and abdomen. More skulls, snakes, roses, fire, and various weapon designs covered the rest of his darkly tanned skin and the deep V at the base of his other abdominal muscles. When his back turned to her, she saw thin vertical lines tracing down over his spine, starting from the top of his neck and disappearing below his low-riding pants. Images of men fighting bloomed on either side of those lines. Whoever had done the tattoo work for him was a master, skilled beyond reason. She would need to find out who the artist was in case she ever had the time to get another tattoo.

The lieutenant was built thicker than the prince, and he had more muscle packed onto his tall frame. She'd never seen a stronger-looking man.

The prince was leaner and tattoo-less, and as he twisted and turned, she could see almost every muscle and sinew in his upper body. His abdominals, pecs, and laterals strained with the effort of keeping the lieutenant at bay, and it was absolutely delicious.

The lethal dance only became more intense as the men started to tire out. Lieutenant Jackass used a long broadsword he rotated back and forth to catch the dual-bladed blows the prince dealt out.

All around, House of Death soldiers placed bets on who would win. Even Rorax threw in some of the coins she had brought for food to bet on the prince, pointing to the man without any tattoos as she handed the coins to the little man taking bets. Rorax studied the crowd for the man with the ten-pointed star on his neck, but she couldn't find him in the throng. She also didn't see the tall woman with the long white braids.

A flash of red swept into Rorax's peripheral vision as the Death emissary, Milla, stepped next to her, brushing Rorax's shoulder. "They're incredible, aren't they?"

Rorax smirked as the prince landed an elbow to the lieutenant's jaw. "I'll let you know how incredible I think they are *after* I know just how much money I've lost."

Milla chuckled, pushing a long lock of wine-red hair over her shoulder.

"Am I late, Emissary?" Rorax asked, not taking her gaze off the fight.

"No, not at all. I saw you standing over here, and I thought I would come say hello. And tell you that you might want to wipe the drool off your chin before the prince slips in it and falls."

Rorax shot Milla a glare.

Milla took one look at Rorax's face and threw her head back to laugh.

The sound distracted the lieutenant, and he glanced up to look at Milla before his gaze flickered over to Rorax. Recognition flashed in his eyes.

The distraction made the lieutenant falter, just for a split second, but it was all the Death Prince needed to swipe the lieutenant's legs out from under him.

He landed on his back, the air pushed out of his lungs with a grunt, and the crowd erupted. Everyone around Rorax went wild and cheered loudly. Men and women started *rushing* toward the bet taker or pushing to clap the prince on the back. Some went to help the lieutenant up off the ground, giving him conciliatory pats on the back.

Rorax happily made her way to the man who had been taking bets, he returned her money with an additional two coins.

Milla laughed when she saw the smug look on Rorax's face as she made her way back and reached out to nudged Rorax's arm with an elbow. "Follow me, Contestar."

They weaved through the crowd until they came to the emissary's tent. The enormous tent was black with gold-and-red trim.

One solitary guard was posted outside, and Milla paused to speak with him. "Fetch the prince and the lieutenant, please. Tell them the next Contestar meeting has just begun."

The inside was surprisingly well lit because the back of the tent was opened to the forest. It also felt like they had commissioned the House of Light to enchant the space to let in light through the dark fabric. Inside, the space was sparse, completely empty with only a large mahogany table and a few chairs in the middle.

Milla motioned toward the chairs in front of the table as she folded herself into one behind it. "Please, take a seat."

Rorax did as the emissary asked, and for a tense moment, they just stared at each other.

The moment was broken when the prince swaggered into the tent, his arms raised as he pulled his hair into a knot on top of his head. "Sorry I'm late, Rubes. Ayres is cleaning the cut on his eyebrow; then he said he'd be right in."

Rorax took in the shirt he'd donned somewhere after the sparring match with regret.

"That's not a problem. We were just getting started." Milla offered the prince a smile as he plopped down in the chair next to Milla and lounged back.

The prince gave Rorax a short nod, his longish black hair wet with sweat, and his golden eyes gleamed as he took her in. "Hello, Contestar."

"Hello, Prince," Rorax all but purred, tilting her head at him. "Quite a show you put on. Congratulations on your win. You won me a few gold coins today, you know."

The prince's icy expression warmed, and he leaned forward in his chair to rest his elbows on the tabletop. "You were there?"

"She's the reason I lost," came a growling response over Rorax's shoulder.

Rorax's jaw locked up as the lieutenant brushed past her, scowling down at the prince before sitting on the opposite side of Milla. He folded his arms over his chest and glowered at Rorax. The lieutenant had not donned a shirt on the way to the tent, which she was secretly grateful for.

"So, you're a Contestar," he all but snarled across the table at her.

"What an *astute* observation, Lieutenant," Rorax deadpanned, trying not to roll her eyes. "I'm impressed."

A muscle ticked in his jaw, and her eyes locked onto it. Kään save her, even his jaw muscles were impressive.

"You're not fit to lead the Realms, and we're not interested." His usually dark eyes were streaked with a line of silver. "In fact, I should just kill you right here."

The change of color in his eyes must be connected to his mood, connected to how much magick is in his blood, thought Rorax. Plenty of magick wielders' eyes shifted colors as they used the magick they held. With the lieutenant, charcoal was safe, silver meant danger.

Rorax tucked away that piece of information for later.

Rorax's smirk stretched into a smile, and she leaned in closer to him. "I'd like to see you *try*." She would ram her knife through his heart in less than a second.

"Ayres," Milla warned. "I want to ask her a few questions."

The muscle in the lieutenant's jaw twitched again, but he leaned back in his seat.

"The question I want answered the most is probably predictable... where have you been for the last six months?" Milla asked.

"I work for the army in the House of Ice," Rorax said flatly, "and I've been on assignment."

The three of them went deathly still, probably thinking about the Siege. If they only knew, Rorax probably wouldn't get out of there alive.

"What area of the army are you in?" the prince asked.

Rorax slowly slid her eyes from one of them to the next. "I work under General Frostguard."

The prince visibly relaxed, but Milla narrowed her eyes. "Which area are you in?"

Rorax rubbed her thumb over her ring and told Milla the truth. "I'm one of General Frostguard's personal assistants."

All three of them looked at her with renewed suspicion.

"Okay, then." Milla placed her palms flat on the big desk. "Tell us, why should we choose you to be our Contestar?"

Rorax sighed heavily, the exhaustion of the day weighing heavily on her shoulders. "You shouldn't, not if you expect me to win this."

Milla's eyebrows went up, and she shook her head. "I don't understand what you mean."

"I think the Choosing is barbaric. We are sacrificing eleven of the Realms' most formidable women. For what? There *must* be a way out of this. There's the world's oldest library below our feet. There must be something down there that can tell us how to release Contestars from the Choosing, and I want to find it. I want out."

The three of them looked at each other in confusion.

"I have something... something I need to do. Something important that's waiting for me," Rorax said. "So, I don't have the time or the patience to be a bodyguard, especially a bodyguard to a whole *country*."

"That's what you said to me when I first met you. That you didn't want the job." Milla's hands curled into fists on the tabletop. "But why not? If you took Ayres on and managed to land a few blows, you're obviously more than capable of handling your own here. Maybe the magick chose you because you *would* be the best."

Rorax resisted the urge to grind her teeth. "I'm looking for my brother. He was kidnapped by Lyondrea over a hundred and fifty years ago, and I have evidence that they are still holding him there. I want to be able to focus on finding him and getting him out. It could take me months, *years* to extract him, and I don't have time to do both jobs well. Especially not now, on the cusp of war."

Piers let out a low whistle, and as Ayres and Milla shared a look, something hard softened in Milla's eyes. Ayres's face remained the same though as he stood up and stalked toward the front of the tent to the exit. "You know my vote, Milla," he said over his shoulder before disappearing through the flaps.

The prince and Milla shared a long look before she turned back to Rorax. "If Ayres isn't on board with you, then we can't be either. If you can't convince him, then we'll have to choose someone else."

Rorax clicked her ring on the wooden arm of her chair, contemplating them. "If I get him to say yes, then I'm in?"

"Well, you would be closer. We still aren't convinced, and I'd still need to write a letter to our queen to confirm our decision."

Rorax turned to ice in her chair. What would the queen do if she knew Rorax was a Contestar? Would she come to kill her?

Rorax hummed to herself, forcing herself out of her chair.

"Thank you for your time. We will see you in the Tournament tomorrow," Milla said as Rorax exited the tent.

CHAPTER 32

RORAX

The Tournament of Houses was the event of the century—of the quincentenary. The last Choosing took place well over 400 years ago, when the Eastern Guardian had been replaced. The Northern Guardian was always a woman, and only women were ever chosen by the gods to rule here, as the Western Guardian was always a man, but the Eastern Guardian could be either. The last Choosing was still remembered in songs as the Choosing of Terror, said to be one of the bloodiest, horrific Choosings of all time. Rorax prayed to Kään that her Choosing would earn no such nickname.

The Realms would talk about the events that happened here around campfires for years to come. Singers and playwrights would draw inspiration and embellish the brave deeds until it was cemented into the Realms' history. It was the most wagered-on event in the Realms, and even though the Choosing was a closed event to kings, witches, priests, and anyone who was not Gifted and from the Realms, many were rumored to slip their way around guards to attend.

It was the morning of the Tournament, and the energy in the air was palpable. Rorax looked over the half-empty arena, dragged in a deep breath through her nose, and smiled to herself.

The smell of early morning dew and freshly cut grass were some of Rorax's favorite smells, and the excitement in the air was contagious.

Soon the air would also smell of sweat, blood, and competition, adding in a few more of Rorax's favorite smells.

Contestars were only allowed to compete until the round before quarterfinals. From there the Houses would get to compete for their Selection orders. Whichever House won the Tournament would get to choose the Contestar they wanted to represent first, while the losing House would choose their Contestar last.

Rorax bent down and wrapped her arms around her legs, pressing her forehead against her knees, stretching her hamstrings and glutes. She was competing in the first wave and had already completed her warm-up run and spar with Jia. Now they were stretching out on the lawn, watching as the civilians who were camping around the castle filed into the stadium.

Most of them had been waiting hundreds of years for this Tournament. It was a once-in-a-lifetime experience for some of them. All the nation's greatest warriors came together to fight head-to-head. They placed bets, cheered on the warriors from their Realms, and wore their House colors.

Vendors were outside the arena, getting ready to cook meat, sweet buns, popcorn, and various other foods for the masses. Bet takers walked up and down the aisles of the arena, talking to spectators about the warriors in the Tournament, taking bets and giving bet recommendations. Flags, one for each of the twelve Houses and one for the Realm, were erected on the top of the arena bleachers, along with all the mini flags spectators were waving for their Houses.

The energy got more electric as the seats started to fill to capacity, and Rorax felt that energy in her blood, amping her up and making her *yearn* for a good fight. A few soldiers and Tournament entries were similarly stretching and warming up around her, and each were armed to the teeth.

Rorax recognized a handful of Kiniera's House of Ice soldiers from their white and silver dragon sigil, a few of Elios's soldiers in orange and black, and some soldiers from the House of Death wearing black and red: the dark, ebony-skinned male soldier with the ten-pointed star scarred into his skin, and the tall woman with milky brown skin with long white braids pulled back in a thick ponytail were there as well. Only two House of Death soldiers would be competing then, and either those two were extremely formidable or the House of Death wasn't planning on a victory today.

Narlaroca, from the House of Alloy, stood next to a man Rorax didn't recognize, their heads close together as they murmured and watched the growing crowd, her green, metallic tattoos on her scalp glinting in the sun.

Briar and Enna arrived in the arena together and immediately spotted Rorax and Jia on the grass. They made their way over to them, both dressed in the same Contestar armor that Rorax was, dark brown fighting leathers trimmed in gold.

"Oh my god, we should have been here early to get ready." Enna clasped her hand over her mouth. "I didn't even think!"

"Don't worry about it. You won't be in the Tournament long. You'll make it one round, maybe two before you get disqualified." Jia shrugged, one leg bent down in a crouch under her torso, the other fully elongated to the side to stretch the inner muscles of her leg. "Rorax and I, however, might be on the pitch all day." Jia had entered the Tournament to compete for House of Ice.

Enna nodded and made a face like Jia had a good point, but Briar put her fist on her hip, jabbing a finger at Jia. "Oi, just wait until I flip ya on your ass, Jia Frostguard."

A tiny little wisp of a smile made it onto the corners of Jia's mouth. The sight of that little sign of humor made something in Rorax's chest warm with relief, but she rolled her eyes anyway.

"Briar, you're up against fucking Alloy in round one, and Enna is up against one of Kiniera's men. Both of you need to start getting your bodies prepared. Take a few laps and at least get loose."

Eventually the other Contestars started to appear, but none besides the girl from Foliage had a warm-up routine or did any serious before-battle preparations.

The stands filled with people, and when it was time for the Tournament to begin, Lamonte got on the stand where the Guardian's throne usually sat at the end of the arena and started to boom to the crowd. "WELCOME TO THE TOURNAMENT OF HOUSES. YOU'VE ALL COME FAR AND WIDE TO SEE YOUR FAVORITE HEROES COMBAT EACH OTHER TO FIND OUT WHO IS THE TOUGHEST, THE MOST VICIOUS, THE MOST POWERFUL."

A member of the House of Air stood next to Lamonte, boosting his voice, carrying the waves of sound, and amplifying it over the arena. The crowd rumbled, yelling and booing under the swell of Lamonte's voice.

Jia and Rorax made their way to stand with the other Tournament participants scattered along the wall of the arena. And then the fighting began.

Round after round, some of the best soldiers in the Realms fought toe to toe, blade to blade. Sweating and cursing and bleeding ensued as blows landed and were deflected.

Rorax knew it was her turn when Lamonte gave her a worried glance.

"THE NEXT ROUND, WE HAVE RORAX GREYWOOD, ONE OF OUR CONTESTARS, FIGHTING AGAINST NARLAROCA SALT FOR HOUSE OF ALLOY."

Lamonte gave Rorax another worried glance, and Rorax realized Lamonte *pitied* her.

How insulting.

The crowd's reaction ranged from pleased to angry. A mixture of boos for Rorax and cheers from the House of Alloy for Narlaroca filled the air.

"Don't kill her," Jia mumbled as Rorax moved off the wall and started moving toward the center of the arena.

"I'll think about it," Rorax responded over her shoulder, drawing her sword and a knife from her hair, keeping Glimr firmly in its scabbard.

Narlaroca met Rorax in the middle of the arena, her bright green eyes the same color as the bright green accents on her fighting leathers and the green of her tattoos on her shaved scalp. Narlaroca held a wicked-looking spear in one hand, but nothing in the other.

"Good to see you, Contestar." She gave Rorax a wicked smile, showing off her sharp, white canines against her dark skin, as something cold and malicious sparked in her eyes.

"Always a pleasure," Rorax responded flatly, gripping her knife harder in her hand.

"SAME RULES APPLY. THE FIRST TO TAP OUT OR SURRENDER WILL BE ELIMINATED FROM THE TOURNAMENT." Lamonte's voice boomed over the arena again. "NOW YOU MAY BEGIN IN THREE—" Narlaroca coiled on the balls of her feet, her bright green irises flashing brown.

Fuck.

"TWO."

Rorax felt the earth tremble beneath her feet.

"ONE!"

Rorax lunged toward Narlaroca as the ground beneath her split, enabling three spikes to emerge from the ground.

She slid on her knees under Narlaroca's spear as Narlaroca tried to stab her, and Rorax felt the air from the spear kiss over her neck.

Rorax slid until she was behind Narlaroca before pouncing to her feet and kicking out the back of Narlaroca's knees.

Narlaroca collapsed to the ground but thrust her arm up at Rorax, and a spear of earth erupted from the ground.

Rorax swiped her knife at it and just barely managed to slice the sharp tip of the spear before the now blunted end hit her in the chest with enough force to knock her back a few feet.

The breath whooshed out of her chest from the impact, and Rorax gasped for a few seconds before she forced air into her tight lungs.

Narlaroca climbed to her feet, gripped her spear tightly, and threw it right at Rorax with a grunt. The spear rocketed toward Rorax with unnatural speed.

Rorax dodged the spear just in time to find Narlaroca on her with two wicked-looking swords.

Rorax blocked a blow with her sword, then her knife, then repeated the pattern as Narlaroca swung her dual blades mercilessly at Rorax, trying to force the Contestar into making a mistake.

Rorax managed to catch one of Narlaroca's blades between hers, and with a tough *pop,* she yanked Narlaroca's sword out of her hand.

Narlaroca used that free hand to slug Rorax in the face.

Rorax took a few steps back, her head ringing a bit, and Narlaroca used the space to her advantage, flicking her fingers up.

The earth started to tremble under Rorax's boots, so she stepped back quickly. Another spike of earth, like a stalagmite, erupted from the ground, inches away from skewering her.

Narlaroca used her fingers to guide another spike of earth, then another, lashing out with her sword whenever she missed.

Rorax dodged and ducked and spun as she leaned away from Narlaroca, constantly maneuvering herself around the spikes of earth and away from Narlaroca's blade.

Rorax misjudged a spike, and as it erupted it scraped along her cheek, leaving a long scratch of blood dripping down her face instead of skewering her whole.

Rorax hissed in pain, and Narlaroca laughed. "Gotcha, you Ice-Born bitch."

Rorax plucked up one of the throwing knives on her belt and threw it at Narlaroca. The woman leaned a shoulder back, the bright green on her uniform shining in the sun as she effectively dodged the knife. As she straightened, however, Rorax was there.

Rorax backhanded Narlaroca across the face with the blunt end of her sword, grunting with the effort.

Narlaroca's whole body twisted around from the blow, and Rorax took the opportunity to sweep Narlaroca's feet out from under her.

Narlaroca fell like a tree, and Rorax pressed her sword to Narlaroca's neck hard enough to draw blood.

"Tap out, or I will kill you *right here*," Rorax threatened as Narlaroca bared her fang-like teeth up as Rorax. Narlaroca reluctantly reached up and patted her chest three times.

The crowd erupted.

Everyone in the crowd leapt to their feet and started making noise—cheering, screaming, booing, and chanting Rorax's name.

"THE WINNER OF MATCH NUMBER TEN IS OUR CONTESTAR, RORAX GREYWOOD!" Lamonte boomed as the crowd pulsed with energy.

Rorax wiped the blood away from her cheek and took a huge step away from Narlaroca. The crowd's energy pulsed again, and Rorax raised a tentative hand in acknowledgement as she made her way back to her spot next to Jia.

"You need some work on combating and reading Alloy magick, but nice job," Jia told her, not looking away from Narlaroca across the stadium. Narlaroca pushed herself to her feet and stared daggers at Rorax. "You might have just placed yourself on Alloy's radar."

Rorax sighed and leaned against the arena wall, wiping more blood from her face. "Fantastic."

Throughout the afternoon, Rorax continued to stand shoulder to shoulder with Jia as they watched match after match.

Lamonte had left the podium sometime in the late morning, and he carried a clipboard with the Tournament matchups charted out on it everywhere he went, hollering orders to his men while simultaneously announcing who was fighting next.

"NEXT, IN DUEL NUMBER FIFTEEN, PLEASE WELCOME: JIA FROSTGUARD FROM HOUSE OF ICE." Lamonte's deep voice boomed around the arena with the help of his assistant from House Air. Fans stomped their feet and screamed with excitement. "FACING OFF AGAINST RIVER FELLOWS FROM HOUSE OF FIRE."

Jia snorted, peeling herself off the wall next to Rorax, and prowled over to the center of the arena where she would meet her opponent.

Lamonte began the match, and Jia rolled around with the woman, tussling for a few minutes. The soldier was beneath Jia's skill level and didn't have as much experience as her, so Rorax was honestly confused as to what was taking so long—until Jia came back after finally taking her opponent out, dangling a little golden chain with a little red charm in front of Rorax's face. Jia slipped the necklace into Rorax's back pocket. "Got you a gift. I would keep it, but I don't like red."

Rorax snorted, rolling her eyes. Only Jia would steal a necklace during the Tournament of Houses.

Rorax's next adversary in the next round came from the House of Weather, and predictably the first thing her opponent did was shoot a bolt of lightning at Rorax straight from his fingertips. She lunged to avoid the bolt of energy, throwing her body to the side. In a normal battle, she would have just thrown Glimr straight for the man's throat. But she didn't want to kill anyone in the Tournament today and *definitely* didn't want to expose herself as the Spine Cleaver, especially to the House of Alloy.

The man was gearing up for a second lightning strike when Rorax plucked a basic throwing knife from her belt and hurled it. It thudded into the man's shoulder, jerking his body around and sending his next shot wide off mark.

Rorax sprinted toward him while he was off balance and lunged, just barely able to tackle and knock him unconscious before a third lightning bolt could roast her.

"You've got the aim of a blind rat," she muttered to her unconscious opponent at her feet before she jogged back to her place next to Jia.

The packed crowd roared with pleasure. Rorax smiled slightly as the crowd chanted her name. Jia smirked at her as they hit their fists together. "Perfect."

Lamonte silenced the crowd and announced the next round. A Contestar named Serena from the House of Foliage trotted to the center of the arena.

An Alloy Soldier, the Alloy soldier Narlaroca had been speaking to earlier in the arena, stepped forward.

It was a vicious battle. Serena was talented and had obviously trained just as much or more than the House of Alloy man. They fought over the grass, and the man kept the battle light, but Serena was out for blood. In one slick move, Serena cut the feet from underneath the House Alloy soldier and sliced her knife down.

She hesitated, just for a moment, but it was too late. Her knife pierced down into the soldier's chest, and blood spurted everywhere. She must have hit an artery.

Some people in the crowded arena cheered, but most just stared in shock.

Deaths happened in the Tournament of Houses. It wasn't unheard of; in fact, it was even expected, but most people had the sense not to kill a member of the House of Alloy.

Narlaroca and a woman dressed in white—a healer—sprinted toward the man's prone body. It must have been too late, however, because Narlaroca threw back her head and let out an agonized howl, collapsing onto her knees next to the bloody body as the woman in white tried to work.

Lamonte declared Serena the victor, and soldiers heaved the Alloy soldier's body out of the arena. Narlaroca stared at Serena, the promise of death in her eyes.

Serena didn't care. She just stared back at her before turning and making her way back to her spot.

She had to pass by Rorax to do it, and on a high of adrenaline, she must have thought it was a good idea to face Rorax. Serena reached out a hand to Rorax's chest and shoved.

Rorax grabbed her wrist and yanked her closer before twisting Serena's arm and bending it behind her back. Then she shoved Serena face-first into the arena wall Rorax had been leaning on seconds ago. "Try to touch me again, and I'll sever every ligament in your shoulder," Rorax growled in her ear.

Serena whimpered.

"You might feel powerful now, Serena," Rorax lowered her head, so she was close to Serena's ear, "but you just killed Narlaroca Salt's lover—her mate, if I'm not mistaken."

Serena's body turned to ice under Rorax's grip. "You're lying."

Rorax sighed. "I guess we're going to find out, aren't we?" Rorax stepped back and shoved Serena away from her. "You're talented, little Foliage warrior, but you're not nearly as deadly as Narlaroca. Watch yourself."

Serena stumbled, turning back to Rorax with wide eyes.

Rorax just shook her head, then turned her back on her fellow Contestar and continued watching the Tournament.

The man from the House of Death, with the ten-pointed star on his neck, cut down opponent after opponent. As he made his way back to his spot after knocking out his fourth match of the day, Rorax couldn't help but feel admiration that he was so deadly and talented despite what her soldiers had done to him.

The other Death House opponent Lamonte introduced was Kaiya. The tall woman with long white braids and brown skin with the giant, glittering battle-ax was an ace, too. She had the same arrogant swagger that Volla did as she stepped up and took her place in the center of the arena for her next match.

Kaiya had single-handedly disqualified a House of Ice soldier, two House of Alloy men, and three House of Fire soldiers.

After they had been through all their opponents, Rorax turned to Jia. "What's your report going to be?"

Jia breathed out a deep sigh. "Probably the same as yours. Kiniera is going to be disappointed with the showing from Dark and Fire. Ice had a great showing, and so did Death. Death only used two out of their five possible entries, and they're still kicking everyone's ass." Jia slowly turned her head to look Rorax right in the eye. "I hate to tell you this, Ror, but if you can't convince Kiniera to change the king's mind about choosing you as House Ice's Contestar, you're screwed."

Rorax's chest tightened.

Rorax looked over her shoulder, searching for the House of Death emissary in the crowd—only to find the lieutenant, the prince, and Milla already staring at her with assessment in their eyes.

Unease coiled in her stomach. The prince and Milla both flitted their gaze back to the center of the arena, but the lieutenant held her stare.

Rorax scowled, and he scowled back.

Jia followed Rorax's gaze across the arena. "If you could fix your shit with him, he would be an even safer bet than Kiniera. He brought better men here than Kiniera did."

Ayres and Rorax looked away at the same time when someone screamed loudly from the center of the arena.

The same soldier from Death she had been watching earlier, Kaiya, severed a ponytail from the back of a Fire soldier's head with her battle-ax, and then tossed it over her shoulder into the dirt.

"I think the soldier that has the ten-point star—the deaf one—has been gifted by Asepp." Jia used her chin to point to the man standing across the arena with his arms folded over his chest as he watched his female counterpart battle in the arena.

"Why do you think that?" Rorax asked, looking him over. Asepp was the god of House Alloy, the god of metal and earth. He would have very little interest in a deaf Death-Born.

"He moves like he can feel you through the ground, like even though he can't hear any movements, someone is whispering instructions to him."

"What about *her*?" Rorax asked, jerking her chin to the woman who was now forcing her opponent to tap her shoulder three times.

Jia shook her head, leaning back against the wall. "No, she's just good. Not incredibly gifted magickally, but her technique is flawless. She...." Jia swallowed hard, avoiding Rorax's gaze. "She fights the way Volla... did."

They sat in silence, watching as Kaiya was crowned the victor by Lamonte's booming commentary, the rubies embedded in her battle-ax gleaming in the sun.

CHAPTER 33

AYRES

Ayres watched Rorax carefully during every one of her matches. She made his hackles rise.

Her long black hair was clasped in a ponytail high on her head, and war braids were intertwined in the long locks. The way she moved changed from lethal grace to severe brutality. She changed her style in almost every round.

Rorax had taken down Narlaroca and the House of Weather's ace, and she'd barely broken a sweat.

His skin prickled as he remembered the night in the woods when he knocked Rorax out of that tree. If Rorax had a sword or a different weapon that night, the night could very well have ended with his blood watering the trees.

Ayres had underestimated her. He'd thought that no one sound asleep, like a cat in a fucking tree, could possibly have the wits to kill him. He'd thought she was out of her mind.

As soon as Rorax flipped the woman from the House of Water over her shoulder and pressed her sword against her chest, the crowd around them erupted into cheers and bellows.

"*Greywood, Greywood, Greywood!*" They chanted, every word like nails on a chalkboard to Ayres.

Rorax gave them a small wave before slipping back against the wall next to her ever-present friend with the purple hair.

"What are you looking at?" Milla asked, following his gaze to where Rorax stood.

"Rorax." Ayres nodded toward her, wondering where she'd been during the Siege of Surmalinn, if she had done anything to stop the needless slaughter and destruction of his people. Or if she had helped with the Siege, had egged the slaughter on.

The new King and Queen of House of Ice had assured him that everyone involved in the organization of the battle had been killed, but he trusted them as much as he trusted a hungry wolf not to bite him.

Ayres continued to stare at Rorax until she felt his gaze on her, and she looked up and locked eyes with him, her pale blue eyes blazing.

They broke their stare as Kaiya won her next match and the crowd around them roared.

Ayres felt a pull on the back of his neck, at the tug of power there.

Something, *someone* was tugging on the ley lines, using Death Magick.

He swiveled his gaze down to Cannon who was already looking up at him. They had one more day in the arena to go, and Ayres wanted him to win so they would have the first pick.

So, Ayres would go on the hunt this time. Besides, it was his turn.

Chapter 34

Jia

On the second day of the Tournament of Houses, the Contestars were pulled out of the competition. They'd had their opportunity to show the Protectorates what they could do, and it was time for the Houses to battle for the rights of the first pick. Whoever won out of the handful of the entrees that day would be the first to choose the Contestar they wanted to protect.

Jia liked her chances.

It was midday, and the sun was high in the sky as Jia watched round after round from her spot on the wall.

Her first round that day had been a House of Weather woman, whom Jia had quickly knocked out. Her second match was a House of Alloy man, and she'd put arrows through his thigh and shoulder, both places she knew he would recover from, before he went down.

Jia's next match was against Kaiya Whitethorn, and her stomach churned with anticipation. No matter what happened, House of Ice would place either first or second in the Tournament, under House Death, so it didn't really matter. But she was anxious about Kaiya, for a multitude of different reasons.

Kaiya reminded her of Volla. The same charismatic confidence that exuded from Volla lived in Kaiya, too. She resented that Kaiya was here, shining brightly to the crowd who loved her, when Volla's light had been permanently extinguished.

She knew Kaiya would recognize her, but without the music and alcohol to numb her and warm her blood, Jia didn't know where the conversation would go.

When Lamonte called her name over the stadium, introducing her as a fighter for the House of Ice, Jia met her in the middle of the lush green grass that covered the arena floor.

Kaiya looked beautiful, her skin glowing in the sun and her brown eyes sparkling. Her white braids were piled high on her head in a tight ponytail. She had the cockiest grin Jia had ever seen, and that was saying a lot because she'd been Volla Torvik's wife.

The great, ruby-encrusted goldsteel battle-ax twirled in Kaiya's hands, making the jewels glitter in the sun. "Ahh, Jia Frostguard. Fancy seeing you here. When we danced at the ball, I had no idea your skirts hid so much... potential."

Kaiya looked Jia up and down slowly, and Jia's heart thumped a little harder, making her guilt and sorrow swell. It was confusing, conflicting, and she had never been so thankful to hear Lamonte's bellowing voice announcing their names and letting the crowd know the fight was about to begin.

"How about this, if I win, I'm taking you to my bed and making you scream my name until morning," Kaiya said.

Jia didn't want that. She didn't want to go to anyone's bed that wasn't Volla's. The thought made her stomach lurch. But she did love a good bet.

"THE MATCH WILL BEGIN IN THREE—"

Jia's eyes narrowed. "If I win, what do I get?"

Kaiya shrugged, completely confident. "Boasting rights."

"TWO—"

Jia smirked and crouched.

Kaiya mimicked her movements, rolling onto her toes.

"ONE! BEGIN!" Lamonte roared to the screaming crowd.

Jia whipped out her bow and shot two arrows at the House of Death soldier. Twirling her ax almost faster than Jia could track with her eyes, Kaiya knocked them both away and advanced on Jia swiftly.

Right as Kaiya lunged forward with a powerful swing that could have easily cut Jia from shoulder down to navel, Jia dipped under the battle-ax, stuck out her foot, and tripped Kaiya. Kaiya was too lithe on her feet to get knocked down, but she stumbled, then corrected her footing almost instantly.

With a surge of magick, Jia created her own battle-ax, a replica of Kaiya's but made of pale blue ice that was hard as steel, strengthened by her magick. She should fire more arrows; she should use her magick more creatively to make Kaiya slip and slide, or make ice darts or something else that would put her on the offensive, but she didn't want that.

She wanted to feel the blows of this woman directly. Wanted to know how strong Kaiya was. She wanted to feel the exertion of her own efforts, and she wanted to sweat and feel the heavy blade reverberate in her limbs. She wanted to feel alive.

The effort made her breathless, but the look of surprise on Kaiya's face was priceless, especially as she stumbled.

"I don't know if it's brave or ridiculous, taking me on with my own preferred weapon." Kaiya shook her head, laughing right before she struck.

They moved back and forth, whipping their axes at each other dangerously, clashing together again and again.

They continued the dance, much to the crowd's pleasure, but in one sharp blow, Kaiya finally smashed through the sharp edge of Jia's ax and through the strength of her magick in a shower of ice. The force knocked her to her knee. Jia reached for her sword, like she should have done to begin with, but Kaiya jerked Jia into her. Kaiya's chest heaved against Jia's as Jia felt the sharp edge of the battle-ax pressed against the soft skin against the side of her neck.

It was over.

The crowd roared with delight, yelling their pleasure at seeing the House of Ice beaten by a smaller, less-favored House.

Kaiya released her, grinning, soaking up the crowd's joy. "I'll be coming to collect on that debt tonight, Frostguard."

CHAPTER 35

AYRES

"You can't go into the castle looking like that."

Ayres's jaw clenched in irritation, even though Milla was right.

Blood still ran down his forearms and dripped slowly from his fingertips into the dirt. He'd somehow gotten blood matted in his hair, too, and he could feel where the fat droplets had dried and gotten crusty when he ran his hand down the back of his neck and then his face.

Ayres rolled his shoulders. He needed to get moving. He was still a fifteen-minute walk away from cleaning the blood off his skin, and every second he waited, he could feel it staining more of his soul.

Milla tried again. "There's a celebration for the end of the Tournament. Everyone will be there."

Ayres ignored her again and kept walking, pushing branches out of his way. Milla treaded lightly behind him, and he could feel her blue eyes analyzing every step he took.

She obviously wanted him to go tonight. He bit his tongue so he wouldn't snap at her and rolled his shoulders again. "Okay."

"I know you feel like shit. Piers told me about the specs on the situation tonight, but maybe... maybe a distraction could help," she said hopefully. "Piers and I will be there. And Cannon. He won the Tournament today, Ayres. He thinks there's potential in at least one of the new Lowborns, and maybe a Highborn, but at the end of the day, it's yours and the queen's decision. I just want to make sure—"

Ayres spun around and towered over her, his fists clenched at his sides so he wouldn't grip her throat and toss her as far away from him as he possibly could. "Milla, stop," he ground out. "Stop fucking talking. Please."

Milla didn't even flinch; she just looked up at him with sad eyes. "Was it that bad tonight?"

Ayres bit back a laugh. Was it that bad? Was killing an eleven-year-old girl *that fucking bad*? Was constantly being drenched in his people's blood *that bad*?

Tonight, the answer was easy. *Yes.*

But sometimes it wasn't.

Sometimes he looked forward to when the tattoos on his spine felt souls rolling down it—and that made him sick.

Ayres couldn't unclench his teeth. He tried to turn away from her, but she reached out and grabbed his arm.

He ripped free from her grasp, but he could see the blood on his arm had already stained the pale skin on her hands.

"I'm sorry," she whispered, looking down at her crimson-covered hand.

"The Lyondrean soldiers attached a spirit to a girl this time. A *child*, Milla. As if maybe I would spare its life because of a younger host, or maybe because she was a girl...." Ayres's throat got unbearably tight, and he shook his head. He turned away from her again and started walking toward the castle faster, desperately needing to wash the blood away. "Don't touch me again," he snapped at her from over his shoulder.

She kept up with him, and he didn't have to look back at her to know she was crying; he could sense it. "I'm sorry, Ayres. I'm so fucking sorry. But that's why you need a new Guardian. Someone who will help you."

They finally came to a stream. Ayres unsheathed his sword and unceremoniously dumped it on the bank before stepping in fully clothed. The water was only deep enough to come to the top of his shins, so he fell to his knees to submerge more of his body in it.

Ayres stared at the ripples of water swirling around, watching as they gently washed away the blood from his palms. It was soothing, even as agony writhed through his chest underneath his skin.

If he could kill everyone from Lyondrea who thought using Sumavari's books to summon Death Magick was a good idea, he would slaughter every one of them.

"You can't do this alone anymore, Ayres," Milla said.

He watched as more blood swirled away from him in the water and hated that she was right.

Chapter 36

Jia

"I've been looking everywhere for you," Kaiya said behind her.

Jia stood at the edge of the woods, staring into the dark forest absent-mindedly. The tents were full of happy, drunk civilians at her back. She should have been making the rounds, combing through the masses for information and clues to what the other Houses were planning so she could help Rorax and Kiniera, but... she was tired. The hole in her chest threatened to pull her to the bottom of her grief, and in that moment, she just didn't care. Didn't care about Rorax or the Choosing. Didn't care about the plotting and secrets of the Realm's emissaries. She didn't care about any of it. She was empty. Volla was dead and nothing mattered, but something about the dark woods called to her. A balm for her frayed nerves.

At the sound of that warm voice though, she turned to see Kaiya Whitethorn leaning against a nearby tree. She no longer wore her magnificent goldsteel armor but was still dressed in House of Death colors. She wore a black cloak and tunic with red edges, her silvery braids framed her face, and layered necklaces circled her neck. She stood tall, almost as tall as Volla had been. Jia had always been drawn to tall women.

Kaiya's charismatic confidence seemed to wrap Jia up, making her feel a few degrees warmer. Kaiya smiled at Jia with a wicked, triumphant gleam in her brown eyes, like a predator who had finally cornered her prey.

Jia remembered what Kaiya had said. *If I win, I'm taking you to my bed and making you scream my name until morning.*

"Come to collect your debts?"

Kaiya grinned roguishly and stalked forward. "I don't have to take you up to my bed if you don't want. I could fuck you here, as long as you're loud enough that everyone in the Realms can hear, I'll go to bed happy."

At first, the thought of touching anyone who wasn't Volla made Jia wince with distaste, but maybe this was exactly what Jia needed to pull herself out of the abyss, to feel something besides despair and grief.

"You took your time," Jia drawled, turning back to look out at the forest.

"I expected you to be celebrating somewhere. Taking third in the Tournament of Houses is quite an accomplishment," Kaiya said. "You belong out there."

Jia snorted. She had never been part of that crowd, or any crowd except the one that used to follow Volla around. She had belonged then.

There was a heavy silence for a long moment, and Jia wondered if Kaiya had simply crept away before she spoke again.

"I should get back to my guard." Kaiya took a step back, but some broken, desperate part of Jia couldn't let that happen. She needed to try, to try and feel something besides agony and the sharp, painful edges of her shattered heart, and she knew Kaiya could be the person to try with.

Jia turned and moved to the woman with a wicked smile that she hoped didn't look as empty as it felt. She reached out and tugged on Kaiya's collar sharply, pulling her in for a kiss. Kaiya immediately sank her hand into Jia's hair, kissing her back.

Kaiya moaned into Jia's mouth, and despite everything, the sound made Jia's blood go hot.

"Make me feel," Jia whispered into her mouth. "Make me forget."

Kaiya didn't wait. Didn't ask for more permission. She lifted Jia up, and Jia wrapped her arms and legs around Kaiya's waist, kissing her as they walked.

Kaiya carried her blindly into the forest until the sounds of the revelry faded away behind them; then Kaiya broke away from Jia's mouth and set her down. She unbuckled her cloak from around her throat and threw it on the ground for Jia to lie down on.

Jia cupped Kaiya's jaw with both hands and brought her mouth back, slipping her tongue inside and over Kaiya's full, soft lips.

"Gods, you taste good," Kaiya rumbled, and Jia's blood felt like it was on fire.

Kaiya's tongue stroked her back as Jia's fingers went to the ties on Kaiya's tunic, ripping them out roughly until Jia could peel away the clothes from her body. Kaiya kept her hands in Jia's hair and continued kissing her urgently as Jia moved her hand to the back of Kaiya's bra and unlatched the clasp. Jia pulled the garment away, tossing it next to them before she flipped them both over. Jia straddled Kaiya's hips, looking down at the topless woman, drinking her naked form in.

Guilt niggled in her chest, but she pushed it away because *damn.* "Gods help me, your tits are fucking perfect," she growled as she bent her head and sucked a dark brown nipple into her mouth. Kaiya gasped and arched her back more fully into Jia's mouth. Jia switched nipples, sucking the other one even harder, gently scraping her teeth across the tight budded surface.

"*Fuck*, that feels good. Your teeth... *fuck.*" Kaiya gripped Jia's hair tightly, and her hips gave a jerk, and Jia knew Kaiya was wet and ready for her. Just how she liked it.

Jia ripped off Kaiya's pants and parted her thighs, and before any thoughts of Volla could ruin the electricity and lust thrumming through Jia like a live wire, she bent down and gave Kaiya a long lick. Kaiya tasted *divine*. She could easily become Jia's new drug of choice to make sure she got through the Choosing without losing her mind.

Jia stayed there, sucking and biting and rubbing circles on Kaiya's clit, curling her fingers deep inside her wet cunt until the woman started to shake and whimper, her hips gyrating and arching into Jia's mouth.

Jia sat up smugly. She wiped her mouth with the back of her wrist and couldn't help but admire how the moon reflected on Kaiya's pretty, light brown skin.

"Come here," Kaiya whispered, her voice both hoarse and throaty.

Kaiya ripped Jia's clothes off and kissed her hard. Jia moaned into Kaiya's mouth when their breasts rubbed together, Jia's nipples brushing against Kaiya's. So fucking soft.

It was Jia's turn to be on the bottom, and Kään save her, Kaiya was a god with her mouth, and Jia wished she could worship every day. Heat burned as Kaiya swirled her tongue and thrust her fingers into her soaked heat until she came.

Jia came so hard, for a moment she burned like the sun was in her veins.

She pulled on Kaiya's white braids, lifting her up and placing a kiss on her mouth. "Fuck, you are talented," she whispered, and Kaiya laughed.

"Nothing turns me on more than being between a woman's thighs, especially a woman that looks like you." Kaiya gave her a throaty chuckle and slid off her, lying on her back on a spot of the cloak next to her.

They stared up at the stars, but the longer they lay and the more the pleasure faded, the more Jia felt the same heavy devastation weigh her limbs down, so heavy she didn't even know if she could move. A tear slipped down Jia's cheek as she pictured Volla there between her thighs, wishing with everything in her that it was Volla's tongue that had done those wicked things and not a stranger's.

I miss you, she thought to the stars, to whatever world there was beyond where Volla had gone, leaving Jia alone without her. Another tear forced its way from the corner of Jia's eye.

Kaiya turned to her with a smile that dissolved when she saw the tears sliding down Jia's face. "Are you okay, Frostguard?"

Jia heard the Death guard take a few more breaths in the dark before she responded.

"I'm fine." Jia slowly turned away and rolled off Kaiya's cloak.

Chapter 37

Rorax

The infamous night of drinking and partying after the Tournament of Houses lived up to all the rumors—that this was the single most exciting night of debauchery in the Realms. It hadn't disappointed Rorax in the slightest.

She'd never seen ale and wine consumed in such quantities.

Jia had made it all the way to the semifinal round, where she'd narrowly lost to Kaiya Whitethorn.

The man with the ten-pointed star, or Cannon, as Captain Lamonte had called him, had leveled Kaiya, putting her on her back without breaking a sweat. Just like that, he and the House of Death were the new Tournament of Houses champion, taking the title from Volla.

The crowd loved him. Rorax's chest had thrummed with the vibrations of the excited spectators stomping and screaming his name, but he acted like he didn't feel it or couldn't sense that they had been boisterously celebrating his victory and didn't acknowledge them. Even tonight she hadn't seen him yet among the revelers.

Because Cannon and Kaiya had led the standings in the Tournament, House of Death placed first, then House of Ice. House of Fire took third. House of Alloy had placed fourth, and an angry-looking Niels had grabbed the medal for his House and shoved it in a bag.

House of Life had taken dead last, which wasn't a surprise to anyone.

Jia and Rorax didn't participate in the feast, as much as Rorax wanted to. The Wolf had always forbidden her from any kind of sustenance that would impair her performance. She hated to admit it, but it was good practice, especially on a night where so much could be learned.

They circled the grounds all night, looking for any pieces or tidbits of information they could find, watching the Contestars and the emissaries to see who they talked to, who they watched, and where they went.

Rorax saw Kiniera and her spies out on the grounds, keeping themselves hidden in shadows. Anything she and Jia missed, Kiniera would find.

Jia nodded to a group of Weather guards who appeared to be three sheets to the wind. "That's the Wind emissary's second. I'm going to go see if they know anything about what their emissary is thinking concerning the selecting."

She slinked off, and Rorax found a new conversation to listen to.

Unsurprisingly, none of the Highborns stood out to her as someone she would trust with the Realm's most powerful position.

Isgra had gotten absolutely piss drunk within the first thirty minutes of the feast. She hadn't even bothered to socialize with the emissaries or with anyone of any influence who could solidify her position with a Protectorate. She must have thought her showing in the Tournament would be enough, which for some Houses it would have been.

After studying the Contestars for days, Rorax concluded there was only one who may be worthy of being Guardian. Enna Mistvalley, the Lowborn from the House of Fauna, was the only Contestar she could reasonably recommend.

Enna was knowledgeable about the Realms, focused, intelligent, polite, funny, and charismatic. After an hour of watching Enna from the roof of a merchant's temporary stall—endlessly listening to her ramble on about politics with the Air emissary—Rorax knew Enna was the one who she would support and protect to the end of the Choosing.

Enna would be the one she'd champion to become the next Guardian of the North.

Rorax's chest warmed, and a steely determination filled her. It was still early in the Choosing, and Enna could prove to be a coward or a liar, but so far, she was the only Contestar Rorax believed showed the characteristics of being worthy to be the next Guardian of the Realms.

Enna had been mediocre in the arena, but her skill with a blade was something they could work on, and it was too early to know if she had any skill with the magick she would soon hold.

Rorax continued to watch her from the shadows of the rooftop until she felt the hairs on the back of her neck rise, and she knew she was being watched.

She lowered herself flatter against the makeshift roof and looked around before finding two pairs of familiar eyes on her.

Rorax grinned at the befuddled expressions of the House of Death's prince and its redheaded emissary.

The Death Prince didn't smile back, but Milla's face split into a little grin. She motioned Rorax over, so Rorax slipped down from the roof, hitting the ground in a crouch.

She wiped her hands on the back of her leather pants and ignored the startled glances people sent her way as she moved over to them. She put her hands on her hips. "I don't want to like you two, but I've been up there for hours and you're the first to have noticed."

Milla laughed. "Really?" At the same time, the prince grumbled, "What the fuck were you doing on the roof?"

Rorax nodded at Milla, addressing her question first before looking up to the prince.

Why were all the men here so gods-damned mesmerizing? The prince had the most handsome golden eyes Rorax had ever seen. "I am doing some recon on who I want to help through the Choosing to become the next Guardian."

The prince crossed his arms over his chest, squinting down at her. "What are your opinions of everyone thus far?"

Rorax looked between the two, hesitating. They hadn't shown any signs of being openly malicious or openly favorable to any of the Contestars. If Rorax couldn't convince them to be *her* Protectorate, then she needed to try to guide them into protecting someone worthy of their strength. Good thing she knew just the one.

"I've been mostly focused on the Lowborns. The Highborns don't interest me as much."

"Why not?" Milla interrupted, waving her hand vaguely at Enna. "Lowborns aren't as well-connected, barely have any magick, and are usually—with the exception of you—not as well-trained."

Rorax shuffled her feet, unsure of just how much information to divulge. "Well, I think connections are part of the Highborn problem. Stella is from the House of Alloy, and Isgra is from a province of Fire that is largely propped up by Alloy's economy."

Milla hummed, and the prince narrowed his eyes even further. Rorax pushed on. "Lily is from House of Water." Which was an explanation all on its own. "And Serena is House of Foliage—"

Milla cut Rorax off, raising her hand up. "But Foliage is notorious for their hand-to-hand combat and isn't influenced by Alloy. Serena is both educated *and* trained."

The prince silently nodded in agreement.

Rorax wondered how much information she could tell them and how much would damn her and the operatives that Kiniera and Sahana had so painstakingly planted.

Rorax looked back and forth between them, indecision rolling around in her stomach uncomfortably as she rubbed her thumb over her bird skull ring. "Right…."

"Unless you know something we don't?" Milla pushed, seeing her discomfort and raising an eyebrow.

Rorax rubbed her finger over her ring again and took a deep breath. There was a long, awkward pause as Milla waited with her eyebrow still raised, and the prince's eyes narrowed suspiciously at her.

She exhaled the breath she had been holding. Fuck it. "House of Foliage has been smuggling Alloy Star Diamonds out to Bracian to help them defend their borders from Umber for nearly fifteen years now. Just small ones, ones we aren't worried about, but if you want a Contestar who comes from a family who most likely has a House of Alloy agenda, Serena would definitely be perfect for you."

Star Diamonds were used in potions and spells to increase their potency and had been outlawed by the Guardians since the Breach.

The prince uncrossed his arms, and his mouth dropped open. Milla also gaped before her eyebrows furrowed. "How do you know?"

Rorax shrugged. "A lot of intense research."

There were sounds of movement from behind Rorax, and she turned to see the emissary Enna had been speaking to walk away.

"Enna!" Rorax barked out, and Enna's head snapped over to look at them. "Come here," Rorax said, waving her over before turning to the prince and Milla. "She's unaffiliated with any undesirable parties, is extremely educated, and knows at least four types of guerrilla-fighting styles. Most importantly, she's not an idiot."

Rorax felt Enna at her elbow, and she turned to give the Contestar a gentle smile. "Enna, you know Milla, emissary for House of Death, and the Prince of Death." She waved a hand at the two.

Enna's intelligent, caramel-colored eyes narrowed at Rorax in suspicion before turning to Milla and the prince and offering her hand. "Nice to see you again."

Rorax excused herself immediately and turned away when they started discussing the Tournament.

Rorax returned to the dark, unseen edges to watch the crowd some more. She moved around the grounds but didn't see Jia or Kiniera again for the rest of the evening.

When all the major power players—emissaries, Contestars, and prominent Highborns—had long since disappeared back to the castle, Rorax finally emerged from the shadows and sighed.

Rorax started to walk back to the castle. She hadn't learned anything useful to report back to Kiniera.

The Water emissary, Dori Wolfmoon, was sleeping with the Water princess in secret; the House of Air was putting together a fantastic bagpipe band to perform at the capitol parade when the Choosing was over, and the University of Poisons in House of Foliage was getting a new headmaster, were the only useless tidbits she'd gathered during the evening.

The sounds of a scuffle caught her attention, and Rorax ducked in an aisle behind a big tent to avoid being seen before she went utterly still.

Four House of Alloy soldiers dragged an obviously very drunk man by his arms down the aisle.

"Narlaroca will be happy to see ya, Lieutenant," drawled the man who appeared to be the leader of the four soldiers. "We've been looking for a way to get the House of Death to fall in line. Maybe the prince will care about your sorry ass enough to give in."

Rorax took a step closer, trying to see who was being dragged along. She got as close as she dared, creeping past tents to get nearer until the drunk's head rolled on his shoulders. A torch illuminated the unmistakable, strong lines of a handsome face that was bruised, swelling, and bleeding in spots.

She ducked down between two tents, her eyes wide and her heart pounding in her chest.

Fuck.

Fuck.

Lieutenant Dickbags.

"Motherfucker," Rorax swore under her breath, leaning her head back to look at the sky.

Rorax had promised herself she would lie low and try to keep herself out of the crosshairs of the House of Alloy, especially after beating Narlaroca in the Tournament of Houses.

But if the House of Alloy had the lieutenant under their control, it *was* possible the Prince of Death could be coerced by them. It was possible that all the Houses—the whole *Realm*—would fall in line if Alloy secured even one more vote on the Council of Houses. She couldn't let that happen.

Kään help me.

Decision made, she stepped out of the doorway and followed where the men were dragging the lieutenant.

The next aisle had groups of people milling around still and was too crowded to fight the soldiers without possible civilian casualties, so she waited until the next one.

Then the next one.

The next aisle between the tents was deserted, and they were getting closer to the House of Alloy's center. She couldn't wait any longer.

Rorax unsheathed her sword and summoned Glimr to her palm.

The men paused, jerking around when they felt her presence behind them.

"Sorry, boys," Rorax addressed them, gripping her sword in her right hand and Glimr with her left. "The lieutenant is with me."

The leader looked her over with hungry eyes, turning to face her and taking a step closer. His eyes lit with recognition, and his hungry eyes turned violent.

"I know you," he spat out. "Ya went head-to-head with my commander today in the Tournament of Houses. Humiliated 'er, you did."

"Maybe we should teach *you* a lesson in humiliation then. Heard some women like that," another man taunted, and they all chuckled. She could smell the whiskey on their breath from fifteen feet away.

Rorax smirked at the cocky invitation but didn't deign to respond.

Without warning, she sprinted toward them, and they took a startled step back. Rorax threw her knife hard at the man on the far left and lunged with her sword at the one on the far right.

They both fell to the earth, dead before impact.

She recalled Glimr and targeted the third man, but the leader turned to her and stabbed at her with the knife he held in his hand.

She dodged his knife slicing just barely wide of her cheek and shoved her sword through his chest.

He grunted and gurgled up blood that spewed from his mouth all over her arm and chest. She yanked out her sword, shoving the man's body away from her, and cursed at the blood dripping down her front.

She had apparently missed her shot with Glimr, because with a backhand to her face, the third man sent Rorax's head snapping to the side, splitting her bottom lip.

He landed another punch in her abdomen, and with a loud grunt, it rocked her back a few steps. He swung another punch, aiming for her face again, but she deflected the blow, grabbed onto his wrist, and jerked him toward her until his back was pressed to her front before sliding her sword across his throat.

He also gurgled blood onto her leathers before collapsing to the ground, and Rorax scrunched her nose with disgust.

With a quick look around to confirm she was alone with the lieutenant, Rorax bent down to wipe the blood off her sword on the grass. "Fucking disgusting," she growled, summoning Glimr to her palm and cleaning it, too, before sheathing both blades.

Ayres had toppled over, dropping like a rock where the men had let go of him. He now attempted to push himself up on his elbows. He took in the corpses of the men around him with big, confused eyes and swallowed hard. "Did... did I do... this?" the lieutenant asked, slurring all his words.

Rorax snorted. "No, I did."

His eyebrows pulled together, and he looked even more confused than before. "*Why?*"

Rorax ignored Lieutenant Ballsack and looked up and down the aisle of tents for a moment before breathing out a heavy sigh. The aisle was completely empty, everyone here was either, thankfully, too drunk to care what the fighting had been about or smart enough not to get involved. She was just going to leave the bodies here. She didn't have the time or manpower to hide all four.

Where were the lieutenant's men? Where were his people who were always so annoyingly present with him?

Rorax sighed, straightening up and offering him a hand. "Come on, Lieutenant. Let's go. We're going back to your room."

He looked at Rorax's palm like she'd stuck her hand in dog shit before offering it to him.

She shook her mostly clean hand impatiently at him. "Come on. I can't leave you out here for Alloy to kidnap you again, or worse. I hate them more than I dislike you."

The lieutenant's mouth pressed down at the corners, but he reached forward and clasped her palm, letting her haul him up. She grunted loudly when his weight hit her.

He was unsteady at best and leaned precariously forward before she could stabilize him. This man was at least six foot four—probably six foot five—and felt like he weighed as much as a gods-damned horse.

As she struggled to keep him upright, she immediately regretted her decision to save him. "I should have let you die," she grumbled.

The lieutenant just grunted his agreement.

They made their way slowly back to the castle, his weight pressing down on her and making her sweat and stumble with the effort. "Why...?" She grunted, breathing hard. "Why are you so *drunk*?"

"Wanted to forget." Ayres's head lolled, and he shuffled forward. "Bad... bad hunt tonight. Really bad."

Rorax's brows pulled together as she panted. "What... what do you mean, a bad hunt?"

He didn't answer.

Rorax's shoulder sang in agony, and she needed to take a break. She led him over to the side of the castle away from any tents or lingering people and eased him to the ground, propping his back up against the stone wall.

Rorax bent over to put her hands on her knees, sucking in air.

She should just leave him here, or maybe go get Lamonte to pick his ass up again. Saving him from the House of Alloy was more than enough of a good deed for one day.

There were a few people around, most of them too deep in their personal revelry to notice the two of them sitting there next to the castle, but two or three stragglers gave them strange looks that Rorax ignored.

Rorax's hands were splayed out on her kneecaps, and Ayres reached up and tapped the bird ring that never came off her left pointer finger. His head lolled to the side as he looked up at her. "You *do* remind me of... a crow. *Smart.*"

Rorax snorted at the lieutenant's slurred words. It was a shame. It might have been the nicest thing he had ever said to her, and he was too shit-faced to remember it.

"I'm going to call you that... from now on... *Little Crow.*"

Rorax huffed another laugh, and he looked thoughtful for a moment before a shadow crossed his face.

"I... I was drinking tonight because..." The lieutenant swallowed hard, and Rorax could have sworn that silver lined his eyes before he looked down to his tattoo-covered hands lying limp in his lap. "I... killed a little girl tonight."

Rorax forgot her exhaustion. She forgot how to *breathe.*

Her spine straightened. She must have heard him incorrectly. "What did you just say?"

There was no way, *no way*, this self-righteous asshole was out there killing little girls. Somewhere deep in her soul, it just didn't feel right.

The lieutenant shuddered, his head lolling to the side a bit. "They were trying to summon Sumavari's monsters. I felt them pull the magick when it... when they started, but when... when I got there, I was too late." Ayres's voice dropped to a ragged whisper. "It'd already possessed her."

Rorax's heart thundered in her chest so fast she thought it was going to burst. "Sumavari's monsters? But... I thought you needed Sumavari's books to do that. I thought Death had those locked up somewhere."

"They stole them." Ayres's head lolled to one side so violently, he slid down the wall and toppled over. "During the Siege."

Under normal circumstances, Rorax would have snickered at the lieutenant's fucking idiocy, but she couldn't do anything. Horror and shame pumped through her blood like hot lead. The ground underneath her started to sway, so she placed a hand on the stone wall next to her to steady herself.

During the Siege. Fuck. *Fuck.*

Sumavari's monsters were a bedtime tale parents told their children at night to keep them in line. She wouldn't have believed in them herself if it weren't for the museum of bones in Valitlinn, or the countless history books she'd seen in the library confirming their existence.

That must have been why the lieutenant and his men always left the castle randomly, to prevent Lyondrea from using Sumavari's books to summon monsters.

A question she needed to know but didn't want to ask burned on her lips. "Lieutenant, how exactly did they get the books from Surmalinn?" she whispered hoarsely.

"I told you. They stole... during the Siege." the lieutenant answered into the dirt.

"What siege?" Here it was.

"The Siege of Surmalinn."

Her chest felt tight, and she couldn't get any oxygen into her lungs.

Anxiety, fear, guilt, shame, and anger boiled through Rorax's chest so fast she couldn't latch onto anything. She felt like she was spinning out of control, even as she stood on solid ground.

There was a rumble of male voices laughing from somewhere in the sea of multicolored tents, and her head snapped over to look. When she couldn't see any movement, she focused back down on the man who was almost passed out drunk in a heap at her feet and realized how truly vulnerable he was right now.

It suddenly felt critical that Rorax get this burly man tucked away into the safety of his room, and she forced a breath into her burning lungs.

"Up. You have to get up. *Now,* Lieutenant," Rorax snapped.

"Ayres." The lieutenant raised his head from the ground to squint one eye at her. "My name's not *lieutenant.*"

"Get the *fuck* up. It's not safe here." The lieutenant didn't move, so Rorax bent low next to him and used her legs to lift him up. She moaned with the effort, her legs and back aching in protest at his weight. "Kään fucking help me, you're heavy."

They made their way around the castle to the front gates that had been left open for the night and struggled to the tower designated to House of Death. Adrenaline and panic coursed through her veins, spurring her on faster than before. Finally, they came to his room.

Rorax shoved the lieutenant off her in the hallway next to his bedroom, making him use the wall for support. Sweat dripped down her back.

She tried his handle, but it was locked. "Do you have a key?" she snapped at him. He showed Rorax the empty pocket of his damp pants, and Rorax dropped her head back, letting out an exasperated sigh as she looked at the stone ceiling of the hallway.

Rorax needed to be alone, and she needed it now. She needed this beast of a man to be in his bed—*safely*—and then she needed to spend the next twenty years pacing her bedroom as she tried to figure out what to do.

In the only way a giant, deep-voiced beast of a man could drunkenly giggle, he did. "I always... always lock it."

Rorax flipped the lieutenant off without looking back down at him or his gods-damned door.

"Listen," she said, her voice tight as she finally dropped her head to glare at him again, "I need to go to my room to brood, so we need to get inside."

He eyed her but nodded. "Fine."

He lifted a key—that he pulled out of gods knew where—and she snatched it out of his fingers so fast the intoxicated lieutenant blinked at his fingers, confused. She unlocked the door and pushed it open before helping him stagger into his room.

Rorax carefully lowered him onto the bed, and almost as soon as the lieutenant hit the bed, he started to snore softly.

She paced back and forth in his room, her limbs nearly bursting with nervous energy, her mind racing.

Sumavari's books. The Books of Summoning.

The books that could awaken and summon ancient horrors—such as Sumavari's personal pet beasts that he'd used in the war named after him five hundred years ago. The books had been stolen the night *she* had laid siege to Surmalinn. If Lyondrea was trying to open the Pits *and* use Sumavari's pets, they would have an uncontrollable hoard that no man or nation had the strength to repel.

Rorax looked around his room, not really seeing it, at a complete loss for what to do. She wrung her hands together but stopped when she noticed little flecks of blood on them from the men she'd killed earlier and took a deep breath to calm herself.

She should leave. She needed the lieutenant to be safe, and now he was.

Rorax jerked his comforter out from underneath his unconscious form and tossed it over him. Deciding he was going to be fine for the night in his room, she turned on her heel and walked out.

She clicked the door shut behind her before locking it and sliding the key back under the crack of his door.

Rorax took a step away but came to an abrupt halt when she came face-to-face with one of his fellow guards, Kaiya Thorn, the Defender of Whitewood. Rorax could see Kaiya's giant, beautiful goldsteel battle-ax slung over her shoulder, and from the way the woman was standing, Rorax knew Kaiya was seconds away from pulling it out and using it on her.

"What are *you* doing here?" Kaiya snapped, her eyes widened as she looked over Rorax and saw the blood on her leathers. "What happened? Where is he?"

Rorax rolled her eyes. "Nice of you to show up *after* I get Lieutenant Dickbags safe and tucked in." Rorax wiped the sweat off her forehead, trying not to snap at the guard. "He's fine. He's asleep. I just put him to bed."

Kaiya folded her arms across her chest, her long white braids flowing almost to her waist. Her face morphed into a snarl, and she eyed Rorax's split lip suspiciously. "Now tell me what happened and how he got with you."

Rorax ground her teeth, the wish to be alone becoming an urgent need. "The lieutenant got drunk. *Really* drunk. And no one from his fucking fan club was there to defend his virtue from a group of Alloy guards but *me*. They were taking him to Narlaroca to try and ransom him, but I killed them before dragging his sorry ass home."

Kaiya blinked at her, and her bottom lip dropped open like she was at a loss for words, so Rorax turned her back and waved her fingers over her shoulder. "Have fun with his hangover tomorrow morning."

Chapter 38

Ayres

"Get up, *Lieutenant*. You need to go to the afternoon Contestar training, but first you need to take a bath. You smell like a man, and not in a good way."

Ayres popped an eye open and realized it was a mistake, immediately wishing he could slip back into that soft, velvety unconsciousness. His mouth felt like it was stuffed full of sandpaper and dirt as he tried to roll his tongue around in his mouth. He needed to bathe and brush his teeth. As soon as possible.

He tried to push himself off the bed but stopped when his head started to spin.

"Gods above," Ayres groaned into the mattress.

"You'll never believe who dragged your ass home last night."

Ayres carefully cracked open one bloodshot eye. Kaiya Thorn was perched in one of the two leather seats in his room next to his bed. She'd tied her moon-white braids back and seemed to be enjoying a bowl of... oats, or something.

Ayres wrinkled his nose at the benign smell, closing his eyes.

He dragged through his muddled memories, but he could only remember winning an arm-wrestling competition against a House of Air merchant before everything went fuzzy. "I don't know."

He just prayed to Marras his power had stayed at the low rumble it had been when he first went out.

"Rorax Greywood," Kaiya said through a mouthful. "I saw her just as she was leaving your room."

"*What*?" Both of Ayres's eyes popped open, something he immediately regretted.

Kaiya continued to eat her oats, nodding as she swallowed. "I came in here after she left to check on you—you know, to make sure she hadn't left you here bleeding out or something—and found you safe and sound. Your covers were even tucked in under your chin like a little fucking kid."

Ayres bristled and pushed himself to sit on the edge of his bed slowly, resting his elbows on his knees. He was still in the clothes he'd gone out in last night, and they smelled like stale beer and dried blood.

"I hate to say it, but I don't mind her." Kaiya shrugged, setting her empty bowl down on Ayres's bedside table, then leaning back in her chair to watch him. "I think... as far as people from House of Ice go? I think she's okay."

"Yeah, I guess if her House hadn't laid siege to *my Realm*, I wouldn't mind her either," Ayres said pointedly, and Kaiya put her hands up in defense.

Ayres sighed and rubbed the back of his neck. He remembered Rorax's burns, the burns in the shape of handprints that Isgra Torvik had left on Rorax's biceps, and how Rorax had earned them—in defense of her friend.

Truth be told, despite her being a bitch, he didn't mind Rorax that much either. His dick also didn't mind her. The fire of hatred toward her had burned down just a touch, and he didn't like that.

A shot of pain made him see stars behind his eyes. His head *throbbed*, and when he reached up to touch his eyebrow, where a small sharp pain was emanating from, dried flaky blood came away on his finger. "Kaiya, what happened?"

"I don't know, but last night Rorax was covered in a lot more blood than just that."

"What did she do?"

Kaiya's mouth pressed into a little frown. "Well, when she got done dropping you off here last night, she told me House of Alloy had kidnapped you and she had to kill four of them to extricate you. The bodies were found this morning, corroborating her story." Kaiya eyed him up and down. "There were strange tracks leading to the kill sight that looked like something heavy had been dragged there."' Kaiya's eyes flashed, and her chin raised. "I believe her, Ayres. Considering how drunk you were last night when I came in, I think she saved your ass."

Ayres tried to think back, tried to *remember*, but he couldn't. He sighed. "I'll talk to her today, see what she says and if it falls in line with the story she told you."

Kaiya nodded. "Make sure you thank her for us, too, Ayres. Without her, you could be dead or, worse, somewhere deep in the House of Alloy."

She grabbed her bowl and took a few steps toward the door before hesitating. "Oh, and if you ever ditch us again like you did last night, Ayres, I'll find a witch that can etch a tracking rune on your ass."

Chapter 39

Rorax

The morning after the Tournament of Houses, everyone in the mess hall but Jia was still drunk or looked a little green from their lingering hangovers.

Jia eyed Rorax from over a piece of bacon she had pressed between her fingers. "You look like shit, Ror," she said softly.

Rorax cut her a glance but said nothing.

Rorax knew she looked like shit because she *felt* like shit. She felt wrung out and jumpy.

After leaving Ayres's room the night before, she'd all but sprinted down to the library to find a book on the history of Sumavari's monsters.

She needed to know what kind of horrors she could potentially be responsible for releasing into the world. She also wanted to know what she could be facing.

Radashan had already gone to bed for the evening, and the library doors were locked tight. So instead, she'd spent the evening pacing endlessly in her room, spiraling deeper and deeper into a well of shame, anger, and anxiety.

When the sun finally peaked over the horizon, Rorax decided if she was going to pace, she was going to do it outside of the library. Radashan had given her a worried look when he finally arrived to open the doors. "Good morning, Rorax," he said hesitantly, opening the door and stepping inside.

Rorax followed, tight on the librarian's heels. "Show me your section on Sumavari's monsters."

Radashan looked up at her, his already disproportionately large eyes opening even wider. "Why do you need those, Ms. Greywood?"

Rorax didn't have the mental capacity to even try to lie. "I heard someone tried to summon them. I need to know if I should care, and I need to know what I'm up against in case they're successful."

"Good gods." Radashan blinked and pushed his wide, round glasses up his nose. Once, twice, three times he blinked before he gave a short shaky nod. "Follow me."

He turned, and with swift, short little legs he showed her to a small section of books, pointing to one. "This one was written by an old friend. He was alive at the time and survived when Sumavari's creatures were on the loose."

The title read *Surviving Sumavari's Creatures; the Truth Behind the Legends.*

"Thank you." Rorax plucked the book from the bookcase, turned on her heel, and left without another word. She took it back to her room and immediately began to read. Everything she'd read made her more and more anxious.

Jia knocked on Rorax's door a few hours later for their morning workout.

Rorax went only because she needed to do *something* with all her energy. She'd been so distracted in the arena that as soon as they returned to Rorax's room, Jia placed her hands on her hips. "Rorax Greywood, tell me what the fuck is going on with you."

So Rorax told her. She told Jia what she'd found out from a drunk Ayres. About the books and Sumavari's pets, and by the end, Jia looked just as pale and jittery as Rorax. And just as angry.

Rorax rubbed a thumb over her ring, sucking a deep breath in to help calm herself down. The Wolf. The Wolf had caused this. But Rorax had helped her.

But did Rorax care enough about the people in the world to split her focus? She should be spending her attention and energy on finding her brother, on freeing him from Lyondrea. That was her priority. She owed him her life.

But Sumavari's pets were a horror story that even generations later people still remembered. They had killed *thousands* of Gifted and Ungifted alike when they had been unleashed the first time. If Lyondrea was trying to unleash them again... at the same time the Pits were opened... *fuck.*

"I have to help them get the books back," Rorax said numbly, the truth settling on her shoulders like a weight as she stared out her window at nothing.

"They seem to be handling it just fine," Jia said, sitting in one of Rorax's chairs, looking up at Rorax with exhaustion creasing the corners of her eyes. "We have to tell Kiniera, Ror."

So they did.

Kiniera had looked from Jia to Rorax and then slammed her hands on the table violently. "*Fuck*," she exploded so loudly it made Rorax and Jia flinch back. "*Fuck*!" Kiniera pushed up and went to the window, her hands on her hips.

"What does this mean? What's in those books?" Jia asked.

"Creatures that were designed by a madman to help him become the supreme leader of all of Illus," Kiniera growled. "They were designed to be able to kill as many soldiers and civilians as he needed to do it. Warlords, shadow griffons, draugr—hell, I even think the fucking Death Harbinger was one of his fucking pets."

"I thought the Death Harbinger was one of the Sumavaris?" Rorax raised an eyebrow. She had read about the Harbinger in one of her books not too long ago. The Harbinger was only a myth, but the Death Harbinger was *supposed* to be of royal blood with a direct link to Marras herself. One of the most powerful beings in the Realms, if it was true, which the book had seemed to think it wasn't.

"I don't fucking know." Kiniera turned around and stared Rorax down. "What do you want to do about this, Greywood?"

"What exactly is in those books? What could they summon if they were successful?" Rorax asked.

"I don't know everything," Kiniera said, rubbing her fingers into her temples. "But for starters, I know there are books that summon Sumavari's Warlords, monsters made of shadows and fear; one of them can raise the dead, the Death Harbinger, a snake the size of a sea dragon. It makes Pit monsters look like children's pets."

Rorax rubbed her thumb over her ring. "There is only one thing we can do. We need to find them. Sumavari's books are the new priority."

Kiniera nodded. "You were planning on freeing yourself from the Choosing. What about Darras?"

Rorax felt like her tongue was made of lead. "I will keep looking for a way to get out. But he will have to wait, for now."

"The Pits, the books, Lyondrea...." Kiniera's shoulders hunched slightly, and ice began to crawl up her fingertips. "Eshaal is going to step in for Sahana as the new Unit One Heilstorm leader, but I feel Sahana's absence right now like a hole the size of Raengar's bloody dragon. She would know what to do."

Kiniera sighed heavily and turned back to face them, her hands still on her hips. "Go, eat breakfast and figure out a way to force Milla's hand, Spine Cleaver. I want you in the know regarding where those bloody books are at all times."

For the next three hours after she finished her breakfast, Rorax asked around the castle looking for the Death emissary, but no one had seen her.

On Rorax's sixth visit to the House of Death tower, she finally saw the emissary walking down the end of the hall with a handful of guards on her heels.

Rorax jogged after her and came around the corner too fast to evade Milla, as she grabbed Rorax's wrist and the front of her Contestar leathers and shoved her back against the wall.

Rorax blinked once in surprise before giving Milla, who stood in front of Rorax holding a knife at her throat, an impressed grin. "Emissary, I didn't know you had it in you."

"Why have you been looking for me, Greywood?" Milla asked, getting closer and more threatening with every millimeter.

Rorax put her hands up in surrender. "Easy. I just want to talk. Alone." Rorax's eyes flickered up over the redhead's shoulder to the men who watched closely.

Milla's eyes narrowed with suspicion, the knife getting so tight against her skin Rorax knew it would split soon.

"Fine." Milla released her and took a step away. "Follow me," she snapped before turning on her heel and disappearing down the corridor.

Rorax followed, feeling Milla's men glare holes into her back as they turned and headed to Milla's room.

Milla unlocked the door and pushed it open for Rorax. "Stay out here," Milla told the guards.

Rorax moved farther inside the room, and Milla closed the door behind her, leaning back against it. She folded her arms over her chest and gave Rorax a cold glare. "You have ten minutes. I have somewhere to be."

"How generous of you," Rorax drawled. It didn't escape Rorax that Milla stayed next to the door, mere inches from her escape—and potential rescuers—so Rorax moved all the way around and took a seat at the table on the opposite side from Milla, putting the table between them.

She lounged back in her chair and spread her empty hands out on the tabletop, willing the emissary to relax. Rorax wasn't a threat to her.

"If you think that we will choose you as our Contestar because of what you did for Ayres last night, you're wrong," Milla said, her eyes narrowing. "We don't even know if you really saved him, or if you were the one who orchestrated the whole thing. Seems like something Ice would do."

Rorax snorted. "That's not why I'm here. Not exactly."

Milla narrowed her eyes.

"Actually, I'm here because as I was hauling Ayres's ass back to the castle last night, after I killed those men to save him, Ayres told me that the Sumavari's books of Summoning were stolen during the siege," Rorax said, ignoring how Milla's whole body jerked straight with surprise. "He told me Lyondreans are crossing the border into House of Death lands, trying to use the magick in your realm to summon Sumavari's beasts and killing innocent Death civilians to do it. So, I came here to offer my... *talents* to you."

Milla said nothing, *did* nothing. She barely even breathed. So Rorax pressed on, taking the opportunity to make her case.

"I am one hundred and sixty-six years old," Rorax started, her voice low and lethal. "I have been a part of House of Ice's army since I was seven."

The memory of the Wolf bending down in the middle of a snowstorm to her, using soft, warm fingers to caress Rorax's seven-year-old face—to brush the frozen hair out of Rorax's young eyes—burned through Rorax's memories like a comet.

"Come with me, little Pup. I will keep you safe," she had said, and just like that, Rorax didn't live on the streets of Koppar anymore. She moved into the orphan barracks with nothing but Glimr and the bird skull ring her brother had given her on a chain around her neck.

Emotion flickered across Milla's face, but Rorax didn't stop, didn't let her speak.

"I know how to hunt and kill better than almost anyone in the Realms, and Ayres told me you need help doing just that." Rorax leaned forward, keeping her empty and still unarmed hands pinned flat on the tabletop. "So, I will help you with your hunts, help you find all Sumavari's books of Summoning, and help you crown the Guardian of your choice. *If* the House of Death agrees to be my Protectorate, and *if* you try to help me find a way to release myself from the Choosing."

Milla stared at her for so long, Rorax shifted in her chair uncomfortably.

"Have...." The word came out so hoarse that Milla had to clear her throat. "Have you told Kiniera about this?"

"Why do you ask?"

"I don't want her to know. I don't want *any* of the House of Ice knowing that the Sumavari's books are out there on the loose." Milla sliced her hand in the air between them.

"Why? Are you worried they might try to use them?" The thought threatened to tug a sardonic smile from Rorax's lips. House of Ice was not only the most powerful realm in the country, but it was the largest realm geographically. During the War of the Aqueducts, one of King Raengar's ancestors had conquered the Horns of Stromwell and the Azaela's Islands and claimed the land as their own.

They often didn't have enough priests to comb through the magick on the Horns, so monsters and creatures roamed freely. Out of all the Houses, Ice might be the *least* likely to use the books. They couldn't rise any farther up the food chain, and they had their own issues and more than their fair share of their own monsters to deal with.

"Yes," Milla snapped. "I am afraid. I am afraid they will try and use them. I'm afraid that someone would leak the information to the House of Alloy that we lost them. I'm afraid of what the Queen of Wymeria would do if she found out. I don't want to give *any* of them tools that could help them."

"Everyone that was responsible for the attack on House of Death is either dead or in prison on the Ribs," Rorax ground out, thinking of the Realms' most dangerous and secure prison on the southern islands. She pulled her hands from the top of the table so she could fist them in her lap. "House of Ice has the resources to help you. You don't have to do this alone."

"The House of Ice is the reason we are in this predicament in the first place." Milla shook her head, finally coming forward and bracing her hands on the back of the chair directly in front of Rorax. "Why are *you* even offering to help? I don't understand."

Rorax looked down at her hands, rubbing the pad of her thumb over the symbol engraved on the top of her bird ring so hard she knew the symbol would be imprinted on her skin there. She wouldn't lie, and she wouldn't run, not when she had the opportunity to help them. To help *him,* the one with the ten-pointed star. To set her biggest regret to rights. "I have to tell you something, Milla, and I need you to promise that you will stay for the *whole* story. That you won't try and kill me until I'm finished." Rorax finally looked up into Milla's flashing blue eyes. "It's important."

Milla opened her mouth but was cut off by a loud knocking on the door.

"Milla, open the door. I know she's in there with you," a male rumbled from the other side.

Milla snapped her mouth shut and turned to swing open the door for the lieutenant. He stalked into the room, and the look on his face made something like fear wash through the insides of Rorax's stomach. Her heart started thumping in her throat.

He looked miles better than last night, but one of his eyebrows was still swollen; the left side of his face and the corner of his mouth were beginning to bruise.

The lieutenant shut the door behind him, his lip curling over his teeth. "What are *you* doing here?"

"Rorax was just about to tell me something. She's here to volunteer to help us hunt for the books, Ayres," Milla snapped. "The Books she said *you* told her about."

The lieutenant's eyes went as wide as they could under the swelling, and he turned his head to Rorax, swallowing hard. "I did, didn't I, *Little Crow*?"

Rorax huffed a short, nervous laugh. The lieutenant had told her yesterday, *I'm going to call you that... from now on... Little Crow.*

The lieutenant rubbed his hand over his short, cropped hair. "Fuck, it's all coming back to me."

"So, is it true?" Milla asked, raising an eyebrow.

There was a short pause. "Yes, all of it."

"Where was Kaiya?"

"I don't remember."

Milla sighed defeatedly, turned back to Rorax, and frowned. "What were you about to tell me?"

Rorax's eyes flickered back and forth from Milla to the lieutenant.

She couldn't tell Milla that she was the Pup now. She could handle Milla, but the lieutenant.... She wouldn't kill him now, not after what he had revealed last night, and the likelihood she would survive hand-to-hand combat with Ayres without lobbing his head off was slim. She glanced uneasily between the two of them.

There was probably a window in Milla's bedroom that she could escape from if she needed. Hopefully.

Decision made, she dragged in a slow breath, and the words of the Wolf dripped through her mind.

Who are you, little one?

I am Rorax Greywood.

What does that mean?

It means I am not afraid.

Rorax straightened her spine even more and sucked in a steadying breath. She let it out and started her story.

"I was raised by the Wolf in Koppar." Ayres and Milla both stopped breathing. "The Wolf, someone whom I very much considered to be my mother, convinced me to help her by leading an army to lay siege to Surmalinn... about fifty years ago."

Ayres was across the room, faster than Rorax could blink. He yanked her out of her chair by her throat and slammed her against the wall so hard she saw stars. "Who are you? Tell me the truth, or I'll snap this pretty neck. Right here. Right now. Everything."

"My name is Rorax Greywood," Rorax gasped through his grip. "I am also known as the Spine Cleaver." The lieutenant's head jerked back an inch, his fingers flexing tighter around her throat. "I am also...." Kään help her, she was going to die. Right here, right in this shitty, windowless room. He was going to snap her neck; ironic really that the *Spine Cleaver* would die this way.

The lieutenant stared down at her, his eyes fluctuating between bright red and silver. She had been wrong before. Ayres's eyes turning to silver was a warning, but when they turned red? *That* was when there was danger, and she was toeing the line. "You're the Wolf's Pup." Not a question.

Rorax tried not to snarl at the name, her ties to Glimr going tight as the lieutenant's fingers flexed even tighter around her throat. "I *was*. I ripped that title from myself the night of the Siege. The night I decided *not* to kill everyone in Surmalinn." The night she killed the Wolf.

"And *you're* the Spine Cleaver?" The lieutenant's glare bounced back and forth from her blue irises. "But your eyes? The Spine Cleaver has white eyes."

"I have a witch rune that changes the color."

"*Where*?" the lieutenant snapped, and Rorax slowly lifted a hand to point behind her ear.

The lieutenant's hand slid up her neck to cup her jaw so he could jerk her head to the side. He used his other hand to brush her hair up and push her ear to the side, just enough to expose the sensitive skin behind it.

He brought her face forward again. "Show me," he snapped.

"No. Witches are banned from the Choosing. I don't have anyone here to replace it."

"Show me. Now," he snarled, "I want to see."

"Everyone will recognize me, and I went a long way out of my way to make sure that *didn't* happen."

"You'll die here anyway if I don't get confirmation," the lieutenant growled, his fingers flexing.

Rorax sighed in exasperation and lifted her hand with her bird ring to her ear. Using the tip of the beak, Rorax broke through the skin the rune had been tattooed on, just under the tip of her ear.

She didn't feel anything different besides a small trickle of blood down the side of her ear and neck, but the lieutenant's scowl deepened, telling her that her eyes had indeed shifted back from the rune's pale blue coloring to her own natural shade of white.

The part of her eyes where the color should be, her irises, were completely bleached of color. The outer ring of her eye was black, as was her pupil, but where most people had strands of color, Rorax only had strands of various and glittering shades of white.

Eyes of snow for my Ice-Born Pup, the Wolf had always told her.

Her eyes had become famous after the Siege of Surmalinn. Rumors of a white-eyed conqueror made her too easily recognizable, and some missions became more difficult than necessary. So, one day she had gone to the House of Fauna and hired Merosa, self-proclaimed Queen of the Witches, to create a shifter rune to change her eye color. The rune had cost her 2,000 gold marks and days of travel, all of which was down the drain now.

The lieutenant stared at her for several long seconds, looking from one of her eyes to the other. His face betrayed his inner turmoil, like he didn't know what to do. He wanted to kill her, but she had saved his life and was here now begging to help him and his people.

"Lieutenant—*Ayres*—I want to help. I...." She swallowed, her throat suddenly achingly tight. "I'm partially responsible for the fact that Sumavari's books are in the hands of people who plan to use them. I helped do that. I'm part of the reason House of Death civilians are being hunted. I'm part of the reason that you... that you had to kill that little girl."

Ayres's face went completely void. He didn't say anything to her; he barely even breathed as the grip on her neck slackened.

"Ayres, leading that army into Surmalinn that night is my life's *biggest* regret." Rorax clamped her hand around his wrist at her throat, pulling him tight against her again as she tried to will him to see her, to see *into* her as tears escaped from the corner of her eyes. "I'm so sorry. But I can *help* you now. I have all the necessary tools and skills to help you find those books. I can help you save just as many people as I... as I...." Rorax's throat worked, and she watched his expression change. His eyes went from far away to searing into her soul, like they were burning right through her.

"Why haven't you told anyone who you are? You would have all eleven of the other Protectorate's lining up for you, Highborn or not." Milla came to stand by the lieutenant's side, folding her arms across her chest.

"I wanted control over my choice. There are only a few Houses that will be able to truly assist me when my influx hits. I wanted to see and experience for myself who would be the best house for my circumstances, and which houses were under the influence of House of Alloy." Rorax paused and thought for a moment. "Also, I've been hiding or hunting almost every minute of my life, and... I didn't want that here. I wanted something different," she told them, her voice barely above a whisper. Her eyes moved to Milla who was giving her a cold stare. "Until I found out about the books."

Ayres snarled from above her, and he squeezed her neck so hard she started to choke. "Get out. Get out and stay away from me and my House, or I will kill you."

Ayres turned and threw Rorax so hard she flew across the table, skidding across the surface and crashing to the floor on the other side, knocking two chairs over with her.

Rorax achingly pushed herself to her feet, her throat stinging. "Think about it," she rasped, looking from one stony face to the next. "Please."

Then she turned and strode out of the room.

CHAPTER 40

RORAX

Rorax never should have tried to convince Milla and Ayres to accept her as their Contestar. Taking off her rune was one of the worst ideas she'd had in a very long time. Ayres and Milla must have been spreading the word about who she was, and the truth was likely catching like wildfire to a dry grass plane, because for the rest of the day whispers followed Rorax's every footstep. Where she had gone mostly unnoticed before, murmurs, worried glances, and terrified looks haunted her now as more and more people started to recognize the white in her eyes. People stared at her in the mess hall at lunch, walking down the corridor to her room, and when she went to the library for her daily study session. People were talking in low voices and openly staring. Even Radashan balked as if seeing her with new eyes in both confusion and fear.

That evening, Rorax was a few minutes late for Contestar training. The usual crowd who came to watch the Contestars were all there, and when they heard the doors open, they all stopped what they were doing to turn their heads and look at her. Even Lamonte, who was in the middle of a demonstration with a round shield, stuttered into silence.

Her gaze skittered across everyone, settling on Milla and the lieutenant. His fury had obviously not abated, his arms crossed over his chest tightly as he glowered down at her, looking like he wanted to run her through with his sword like an olive on a toothpick.

Rorax kept her shoulders carefully back and her head high, but her cheeks heated under all the attention. She broke eye contact with the lieutenant to approach Lamonte and the other Contestars who had been listening to him teach.

Lamonte stared at Rorax for another beat, the silence in the air heavy and awkward, and only when she raised her eyebrows at him did he snap back to attention.

"Er… right. So, as I was sayin', when you're attacking your opponent with a shield…."

Lamonte was showing Isgra and Enna simple moves using one-handed round shields and wooden swords. He showed them the basic back-and-forth movement of sparring with a shield, and they started to clash back and forth, and Rorax admired how well Enna moved on her feet. She might not *know* the moves yet, they might not be part of her muscle memory, but she was coordinated and smart on her toes. It wouldn't take her long to at least be adequate with a shield.

Enna stumbled on a backward move, the fumble tripped Isgra, who went sprawling face-first onto the ground. Some people in the crowd, momentarily distracted from Rorax, laughed at her. Isgra's eyes tracked the sound, her cheeks blushing a furious shade of bright red. She gritted her teeth and pushed away Enna's outstretched hand to help her up, standing up on her own.

Enna and Isgra started again, moving back and forth in a light spar, until Enna left an opening and Isgra took her shield and smashed it to the side of Enna's face.

Enna stumbled back, reeling, blood trickling down from a cut on her temple. She raised her hands in surrender, but Isgra continued to press into her, swinging her shield at Enna's head again and again until one of the blows sent Enna reeling. Enna stumbled over her own feet and fell over on her hands and knees. Isgra placed a kick to her ribs.

Rorax started to push through the crowd as the people around her murmured with concern.

"Stop," Enna wheezed from the ground, one arm around her middle. "Stop."

"You *Lowborn bitch*," Isgra hissed down at Enna as Enna coughed violently. "Stay down."

Lamonte gripped Isgra's shoulder to pull her away, but Isgra pushed him off and aimed another kick at Enna's side.

Rorax got to Isgra right before the kick made contact, and she shoved Isgra back.

"She said she tapped," Rorax hissed, bending over to offer Enna her hand, helping the bloody Contestar back to her feet.

It was a mistake turning her back on Isgra. Enna gasped, and that was the only warning Rorax got before something smashed into the back of her shoulders so hard, she went sprawling forward onto the smooth stones of the courtyard. She flipped her body around to face her attacker, summoning Glimr to her palm.

The surrounding bystanders who had come that afternoon for the entertainment backed away quickly while Lamonte's soldiers prepared for a fight, grabbing their swords and spears.

Isgra tossed her shield and sword away as she looked down at Rorax, her hands and arms wreathed with flames snaking tightly around her wrist.

"*Heilstorm*," she seethed. "You didn't just *know* my sister. You were in the same unit, weren't you, *Spine Cleaver*?"

Rorax gritted her teeth.

"You were in her unit, and you *left* her. You left her to die in Lyondrea, didn't you, you useless illiterate *cunt?*" Isgra snarled right before she threw a fireball at her head. Rorax rolled to the side just in time, the smell of burnt hair filling her nostrils.

There was a scream from the crowd, and anyone who couldn't defend themselves from the flames scattered, fleeing inside or behind Lamonte's men. Captain Lamonte himself, however, took a few steps closer, shooting Rorax a worried glance.

"Isgra...," Lamonte warned, still gripping the shield he had been using, holding it between them. "You can't kill her without killing yourself."

"It would be a mercy. I would be remembered as a *martyr*, killing an Ice-Born Heilstorm to ensure she couldn't become Guardian of the Realm." Isgra threw another ball of fire at Rorax, who again rolled out of the way.

Isgra used the fire coiling up her arms as whips, snapping at Rorax one after another. Rorax felt like she was dancing, dodging and hopping and twirling away from the long lines of fire, waiting for an opening to attack.

After one miss pulled Isgra's weight off center enough to make her stumble, Rorax pulled one of her knives out of her hair and threw it at Isgra's shoulder.

The woman dodged the knife, leaning to the side just in time, but with Isgra distracted, Rorax sprang forward, taking Isgra's arm and twisting it behind her back so hard the tendons strained in her shoulder.

Luckily, in the stone courtyard, there wasn't much to catch fire, besides the banners of the different house sigils, most of which were engulfed in flames.

"*Calm down*, and we can talk," Rorax muttered into Isgra's ear as she jerked in Rorax's arms to get away. "You're going to hurt someone out here, Isgra."

"Shut your fucking mouth," Isgra snapped.

She tried to jerk herself out of Rorax's arms, but Rorax didn't budge. She caught Lamonte's eye across the courtyard, and he gave her a short little nod.

"You couldn't even save my *sister*," Isgra seethed. "What makes you think you could save the *Realms*?"

Rorax sucked in a breath.

The question cut Rorax to the bone like an arrow straight through her heart, cutting at one of Rorax's deepest insecurities. Her whole body flinched like she'd been burned, and she stumbled back a step and dropped Isgra's arm like a hot coal.

Isgra pressed her advantage and rammed her fist up and across Rorax's brow bone, the force making Rorax retreat even farther.

Gods, she was right. Isgra was *right*. Volla was *dead*. What business did she have trying to save the Realms? Trying to save her brother? Trying to get a Guardian on the throne?

Rorax suddenly felt like she had a band wrapped around her lungs, and she couldn't *breathe*.

"The only reason the gods chose you to be here was so they could ensure your death," Isgra seethed, following her as Rorax stumbled again.

Kään help her, what if Isgra was right about that, too?

What if her failure to save Darras from Lyondrea was another punishment? Something to torment her before she reached her bloody, gruesome end?

Rorax's head spun, and the band around her chest got tighter and tighter until black spots appeared in her vision.

She was going to die here, in the Choosing. She was going to die, and she was going to be forced to abandon Darras to the Lyondrean prison camps. She wasn't going to be able to free Isgra from the Choosing for Volla and Jia. She wasn't going to be able to help protect the Realms from the monsters in Sumavari's book.

Her vision started to swim, and she stumbled back another two steps away from Isgra.

Rorax gritted her teeth and forced breath into her lungs in time for Isgra to approach her again. "You, and the rest of the Lowborn trash, are going to die here, and the world will be a little cleaner for it. Once you're gone, they will be the first ones to go. I'll make sure of it."

Rorax heard someone suck in a breath behind her at the insult. Anger started to boil in her chest, and she tried to grab onto that string, to inflame it.

Isgra laughed, ugly and bitter, sensing that her prey had fallen and was limping. "When I'm done with the Lowborns, I'll kill my sister's bitch wife, too."

Rorax didn't have to pull at her anger this time as adrenaline started to beat in her heart.

Who are you?

Rorax Greywood.

What does that mean?

It means I will do what is necessary for those I love.

Isgra saw the change in Rorax a split second too late, and there was nothing she could do as Rorax planted a swift uppercut into Isgra's stomach.

"What did I *say* about her?" Rorax spat as Isgra doubled over in pain. Rorax took advantage of Isgra's position and kneed her in the forehead. "What did I *tell you,* Isgra?"

Isgra ripped herself away from Rorax, falling to the side on her hands and knees.

Rorax bent down, closer to the fire worker than was smart. "And the next time you spew horseshit about Lowborns, I will break your jaw and smash in your teeth."

Isgra growled and lunged up at Rorax, knocking her over. Rorax prepared herself for the fall, but Isgra's large frame still crushed her into the stones so hard she almost lost her breath.

Isgra landed on top with Rorax on her back, but Rorax pushed herself from beneath Isgra before Isgra could pin her, and she scrambled to her feet.

Isgra waved her arm, and a large burst of fire erupted from her palm, aiming straight for Rorax's face.

To lean back far enough for Rorax to avoid the blast, she had to do a back handspring, and when she came back to her feet, Isgra was up as well, fire in her hands.

Isgra grinned, and Rorax summoned Glimr, then pulled her other knife out of her hair.

She was going to have to kill Isgra. Right here, right now.

Rorax moved her arm back, ready to sling Glimr straight through Isgra's neck, when a violet shadow thudded onto the cobblestones right behind Isgra. A huge chunk of ice clobbered Isgra in the back of her head, and Isgra staggered once before collapsing face-first onto the ground.

The next thing Rorax knew, Jia was in her face, shoving her shoulders so hard she fell back onto her ass.

Jia pressed a boot to Rorax's chest and shoved her over again, so she fell flat on her back.

"You *idiot*," Jia seethed. She leaned down and put her hand on her knees, getting even closer to Rorax's face. "When exactly did you break up with logic so you could fuck stupid, Ror?"

Rorax didn't answer but pushed Jia's booted foot off her chest and pushed up onto her elbows, rolling her jaw with indignation.

"The next time you want to kill someone defending my honor, pick someone who isn't going to kill you in the process. This fucking bitch?" Jia pointed at Isgra's unconscious body lying on the stones twenty feet behind her. "She isn't worth it, Ror. Not worth your time, not worth your attention, and—sure as *fuck*—not worth your life." Jia crossed her arms and straightened up.

Rorax looked around to see that most people had left to find safety inside. Only Lamonte and a few of his men, Elios, some of Kiniera's men, and a handful of Death soldiers remained to see her humiliation.

"What happened to your rune?" Jia snapped, her arms still crossed over her chest.

Rorax ran her tongue over her teeth, debating whether to tell her about her conversation with the lieutenant and Milla.

With a grunt, she got on her feet, brushing dirt and debris off her leathers.

She looked around the courtyard and winced.

There were scorch marks and random little fires everywhere. Lamonte's men were running to put them out, using dark magick to smother them.

Jia started pointing to some of the fires, helping the men put them out with her ice, while Rorax moved over to Lamonte who was busy directing his men.

When she approached, he offered her a small smile.

"I'm sorry," she said, "about interrupting your class. I know it's important to you."

Lamonte's smile got a little wider. "Thank you, Contestar, but no apology's necessary. Ya weren't the one who started all these fires." He waved a hand over the courtyard.

"Good luck with 'er, Rorax, and I'm sorry your secret is out." He gave her a nod, cupping her on the shoulder before moving to give more orders to his men.

CHAPTER 41

AYRES

A name that was becoming *way* too familiar was all it took to obliterate the appetite Ayres had worked up all day.

"I need you to fix your shit with Greywood. I'm going to ask her to let us be her Protectorate."

Piers, who was sitting across the table from Ayres drinking from a mug of ale, choked so hard his drink sprayed out his nose.

Ayres's hands froze midcut, the knife he'd been using to slice apart his steak coming to a standstill.

This wasn't just any steak. It was one of his favorite cuts of meat from his favorite butcher in Bafta. Ayres had even bribed the castle cook with a heavy bag of silver to let him and Piers use his kitchen to prepare the steak perfectly. They were eating in the mess hall on a table in the back corner opposite from where Rorax normally sat, away from everyone's prying eyes and nervous stares.

Ayres ignored Piers's sputtering and narrowed his eyes up at Milla who stood over him with her arms crossed, her expression daring Ayres to argue.

"Have you lost your *fucking* mind?" Ayres growled over Piers's violent coughs.

Conversations ground to a halt at the surrounding tables, and Ayres felt the nervous gaze of at least twenty people.

Milla leaned closer to him and pinned him with a glower.

"Fix. Your. Shit. With. Greywood," she hissed under her breath.

Piers wiped away a tear that had leaked out of the corner of his eye and croaked, "Holy fuck."

Ayres trusted Milla with more than just his life. If he, Rosalie, and then the rest of his siblings were killed, Milla was next in line for House of Death's throne, unless she was challenged by another family. Over her last 400 years, she had become one of the greatest spies, soldiers, and consultants the House of Death had ever seen. Her instincts were impeccable. They had been raised so closely together, she was like another of his siblings.

However, right now, Ayres was more than a little convinced she had lost her gods-damned mind.

"Rorax knows about our mission, and not only are you *not* planning to kill her for it, but you also want to invite her to be our *Contestar*?" Ayres asked incredulously.

"Listen to me, Ayres. Not only could Rorax be an *immeasurable help*, but she is also one of the only Contestars who we know for sure doesn't have a House of Alloy agenda, someone they can't corrupt or buy out."

"Milla, this is the *Pup*. She laid siege to our people. The queen would never agree to it," Ayres snarled.

Milla sat down and folded her hands on the tabletop with excited energy. "Rorax doesn't actually *want* to be the Contestar, and if we agree to be her Protectorate, we will also agree to help her find a way out of the Choosing in exchange for her helping us."

"You're telling me you believe that a fucking Heilstorm doesn't want *anything* to do with the power and the money that Guardians have?" Ayres eyed her. "Right."

"I wouldn't say that it's the power she doesn't want, but the responsibility. Rorax is vehemently against it. She's searching for a lost brother who is currently being held captive in Lyondrea. She just wants to be free so she can search for him."

Ayres couldn't believe he was hearing this.

Milla turned to Piers. "Piers, remember the night of the festival? She sat on the roof, just watching everyone. She came down and told us she was scouting out who she wanted to choose as the Guardian. I thought she must have hit her head too hard, but she was dead serious. She has an insider's view and she's going to make the most of it."

Ayres gave a disbelieving hum, taking a deep swallow of ale.

"Listen, Ayres, I was skeptical, too, but she and her friend—"

"The one with the purple hair who almost beat Cannon in the Tournament?" Piers looked up at Milla with tears in his eyes, his face still bright red after finally having coughed up the ale he inhaled.

Milla nodded. "Yes, that one!"

"Get to the point, Milla," Ayres snapped.

Milla crossed her arms and scowled down at them in turn. "They spend hours every night at the library, digging through old books, trying to find a loophole through the tether that binds Rorax to the Choosing. She's spent *days* in there by now, trying to find a way out of the Choosing without any more bloodshed."

Piers's body jerked forward. "Wait, has she found anything?"

Milla shook her head sadly. "I don't think so. Not yet. They're there right now, though."

"Huh." Piers's eyebrows pulled together, and he looked as confused as Ayres felt.

But as much as Ayres's head told him there was no way in hell a Heilstorm wouldn't want the Guardianship, he trusted Milla's instincts more.

Milla knew what was at stake, and she would have a damned good reason to think Rorax was trustworthy before coming to him.

"So, I think if we helped her figure out how to free herself from the Choosing tether, we could get her to help us direct this competition in our favor." Milla plopped down in the empty spot on the bench next to Piers across from Ayres and slapped her palms on the tabletop. "She could help us choose the best Contestar, be the eyes on the inside during the trials, and help get the Contestar of our choosing to win."

A little frown tugged at the corner of Ayres's lips. "She might not say yes to working with me."

"Don't flatter yourself, Ayres. She doesn't actually care about you." Milla waved her fingers dismissively at him. "But don't push her buttons for gods' sake. Don't fight with her just for fun and don't be your usual asshole self. She *could* kill you, you know. She's dangerous, and we need to assess the risk before we turn our backs."

Ayres's mouth flattened. "My usual asshole self?"

Piers laughed and slapped Milla on the back. "I'm in. I'm interested to see how a Heilstorm thinks. She could teach us some things. Her team broke into our barracks in Morvarand last summer. They were back across the border for weeks before we realized something was even missing. The only reason we knew it was them was because someone found a body whose neck had been—" He dragged his thumb across his throat. "I overheard Elios talking about her though, Ayres," Piers continued. "You might want to mention to him that we're thinking about picking her up. We have first pick at the Selection, thanks to Cannon."

Ayres swore under his breath. Elios wanted her? The memory of seeing Elios and Rorax together in the hallway flashed through his brain, and it set his teeth on edge.

"Does he know she's a Heilstorm?" Piers asked, and Milla nodded eagerly.

"He was telling one of his men to be prepared for a Heilstorm."

Piers laughed. "I bet his man peed himself."

Milla laughed, too, before she noticed the scowl on Ayres's face. "We can handle her, Ayres. Don't worry. The influx makes Contestars more powerful and violent for a few minutes, but it also distracts them. It makes them lose some of their cunning for those minutes, like an angry bull."

Ayres shook his head, waving away Milla's misinterpretation. "It's not that."

Milla looked around to make sure no one was close enough to hear her before focusing on them again. "I also think we should try and recruit Jia for the hunts. One Heilstorm would help, but two? Ayres, we could send a battalion of men back to the front line for Erich. That's a *game changer*. Our reinforcements won't be done training with the House of Ice for another four moons."

His back jerked straight, and he had to bite his tongue to trap the "no" that immediately wanted to burst from his lips.

Milla saw his expression before raising her palms. "Just think about it. Like I said, reinforcements won't get to the front line for another *four moons*. Erich needs the help, and we have an opportunity to recruit the two best stealth soldiers in the *country*."

Piers took another big drink of ale.

A shadow crossed over Milla's face. "You can't keep doing this all by yourself, Ayres. You need help."

Ayres dropped his gaze back down to his tragic, now unwanted steak. "I need some time to think about it, Milla."

She nodded once. "I am going to send a raven to Rosalie to get her approval in case you say yes. The Selection is in seven days."

Chapter 42

Jia

Jia watched the Contestars training in the Contestars' Courtyard. Lamonte and his men were excellent, disciplined, and knowledgeable, but most of these Contestars would need years and years of training before they would be ready for true combat.

Losing a mate was excruciating. It was heavier and more intense than any other kind of grief Jia had ever experienced. Worse than losing her father or her other brother, this loss was vicious and determined to destroy her very soul. Nothing seemed to register to her anymore, not the joy of food or the sun, not the vigor of exercise or sex. The world was empty, yet somehow, she still seemed to be drowning.

However, watching Rorax defend her and that Lowborn Enna against Isgra the other day, that had lit something inside her. Sparked a tiny reminder of the promise Jia had made to Volla.

If Jia was going to survive, she needed to focus on that, distract herself by making sure Rorax made it out of this alive, and not on the gaping hole in her heart that threatened every day to consume her.

Someone edged up to Jia, and she didn't have to look up to see it was the lieutenant from the House of Death. She could feel the power in him, feel the cold fingers of his energy brush over her as if they were asking permission to take her soul away. It made her want to shiver. Jia wasn't sure exactly what happened between Rorax and the lieutenant, but it was a good thing Rorax couldn't feel his magick. She wouldn't be nearly as abrasive to him if she could. Having the lieutenant this close made Jia's skin crawl.

"Tell me about her," the lieutenant said, his voice low and demanding.

"Isgra? Or Rorax?" Jia asked, crossing her arms over her chest.

"Rorax."

"You know everything there is to know about her, Lieutenant," Jia lied.

The man next to her snorted harshly. "Hardly."

Jia watched Lamonte order his men to simply have the burned banners cut down to be replaced and considered the opportunity she'd been given to soften the lieutenant's attitude toward her friend. Milla might be the House of Death's emissary, but something in Jia told her the lieutenant was the one they needed to convince. "What do you want to know?"

"Everything."

It was Jia's turn to snort. "Even I don't know everything about Rorax."

"You know the most out of anyone in the castle."

That was true. But what could she tell him without getting Glimr lodged in her neck?

"She was barely living when the Wolf ordered the Siege of Surmalinn. Even now, she is still learning what it's like to... be a person."

Ayres frowned at her; his eyes narrowed. "What does that mean?"

"The Heilstorms like their soldiers to be soldiers, but Sahana, still let us live. She encouraged us to go out into the world; she wanted us to love and live to have something to fight for." Jia hesitated, shifting on her feet. "But the Wolf, she oversaw Rorax's unit. She recruited her, trained her, and didn't use the same approach as Sahana with her soldiers. Especially because Rorax was so young. I mean, Rorax didn't even know how to *read* until a few years ago. Sahana taught her. After the Wolf died, Sahana offered Rorax the choice of the Blood Oath to continue being a Heilstorm, and she accepted. A few months later, she found out Rorax didn't know what any of the letters meant."

Ayres's mouth tightened in suspicion. "Education is mandatory in Ice."

"Well, the Wolf deemed it *unnecessary* to Rorax's training. She was the Wolf's 'special' case. She trained Rorax to be a weapon for her own use and nothing else."

Ayres's brow furrowed in confusion.

"It wasn't just that." Jia rubbed her hands over her arms, remembering the Wolf always made her skin crawl. "Rorax wasn't allowed to drink, consume unnecessary food—like sweets—read, watch any entertainment, go to balls, or the opera. The Wolf kept her on a short leash and tried to keep her completely indoctrinated in what she was telling her. Rorax was only allowed to go on assassination missions, only on missions where they needed to kill or steal information. She never went on missions where they saved hostages or helped civilians. The Wolf tried to keep Rorax isolated from any other people besides herself, and if Rorax broke any of these rules, she was beaten to within an edge of her life."

Ayres's frown deepened as he listened until he was scowling, the muscles in his jaw tight. "She was groomed."

"Yes. Rorax was controlled, manipulated, and programmed to kill from the time she was seven years old. She became the ultimate weapon for the Wolf to use. The Wolf was successful in some ways... Rorax is virtually unstoppable if she can catch her prey unaware or if she goes against nearly anyone one-on-one. She was in the Valitlinn Press newspaper as the third-most-lethal person in the Realms, and they didn't even know her identity."

Ayres and Jia stood in silence for a moment, watching as one by one the blackened banners of the Houses of the Realms fell to the stone floor, cut down by Lamonte's dark magick and picked up by his men.

"How did she get out? If that was the only thing she ever knew?"

"She hasn't… not all the way. She was a 'secret project' at the military school in Skavetsia. The Wolf kept her isolated, but it was the same school that the king and queen, Raengar and Isolde Carbore, were trained at, and they somehow became acquainted. My brother, Ye-Jun, met her as well, and the four of them became secret friends. They taught her there was more to life than what the Wolf was showing her, exposed Rorax to what was happening to her."

"That's why everyone says she is so close to the King of Ice." Understanding dawned on Ayres's face.

Jia nodded. "When Katalon eventually got wind of how competent Rorax was, he started asking for her to be on his personal assassination missions. She was eventually placed to work with people outside of her unit, like Sahana Thorash and Volla Torvik, and she slipped even further outside the Wolf's control."

Ayres scrubbed his hand over the shadow of his beard. "All of this doesn't excuse what she did."

"No," Jia conceded. "It doesn't. And no one knows that better than she does, Lieutenant."

Jia and Rorax walked side by side to Kiniera's door.

Jia felt free, lighter than she had fifteen minutes ago. The cut on her arm was red and still stinging slightly, but her Blood Oath with the Guardian had been broken.

Rorax had a new cut on her arm in the same place where Jia's had been. It was on the inside of her arm right below her elbow, promising Rorax would stay and compete in the Choosing and not attempt to flee. Jia knew how Rorax felt about Blood Oaths, detesting them with every fiber in her body, but it was still nice to be free—not that she would be going anywhere.

Maybe she should go back to Koppar as soon as possible and start getting Volla's affairs in order. She needed to donate her clothes, armor, and weapons, and sell her apartment, but the thought of going back to that city, where every bench and city corner had memories of Volla wooing her or kissing her senseless made Jia feel woozy and weak. She couldn't do it. Not yet.

Kiniera opened the door and let them inside. "Is it done?"

Rorax nodded, collapsing into one of the chairs around Kiniera's table and scrubbing her face. "It's done."

"Good," Kiniera said, moving to her side of the table across from them. "We have things to do."

Jia sat down slowly. The air in the room was cold, and Jia could feel Kiniera's magick pulsing around her. Kiniera's power was similar to the House of Death lieutenant, and power leaked from her thickly, saturating the air wherever she was. Jia had Ice Magick too, but Jia's was like a thimble of water in Kiniera's ocean.

Whatever the lieutenant did to manage his power was much more effective than Kiniera's technique, or maybe he was just built to hold more. Magick was corrosive, and if too much was held in one body not genetically predisposed to hold it, the magick became toxic.

It was easy to see how Kiniera's magick affected her. She had dark purple bags under her eyes, and her translucent skin stretched over her facial bones a bit too tightly. Jia's mother, General Frostguard, had told her about Kiniera, about the rumors of Kiniera's tragedy with her mate, and she wondered, for about the thousandth time, if any of them were true. She would never ask Kiniera herself. Jia valued her life too much for that, and she doubted Rorax had any idea about the stories or if Rorax would even care.

Kiniera's pale blue eyes drilled into Jia now, as if she could hear Jia's thoughts.

"Frostguard, you will be leaving tomorrow morning and taking a horse up to Nyson's Gap. A ship is waiting there to take you down to Morvarand. Take the samples of blood you have in your witch-vials to Raengar. Tell him I want those vials hand-delivered to the High Acolyte in Luxamal."

Luxamal was the city where the University of Poison was located.

Jia shifted in her chair, frowning. "Kiniera, I... I think I should stay here. With Rorax."

"Don't worry about Rorax, Jia." Kiniera's mouth went soft, and pity warmed her eyes. "We extracted Volla's body. It is waiting for you in Morvarand. We tried to have her brought here for you and Rorax to both attend the funeral, but the Guardian said no. And with Isgra being Isgra, perhaps it's better to have it far away anyway."

The breath whooshed out of Jia's lungs, and suddenly she couldn't breathe. She couldn't see either as tears flooded her eyes. But she did feel Rorax scoot her chair closer and wrap a warm arm around her shoulders.

"Why here?" Rorax asked. "Why not take her back to Koppar?"

Tears flooding her eyes spilled down her cheeks, and the grief that she had momentarily forgotten came crushing down on her.

Volla was dead. The love of her life had died and left her here alone.

"We brought her to Morvarand because Volla loved three things above all else in her life—the Heilstorms, her infernal Blood Hawk, and you, Jia. She wouldn't have cared where she was buried; she would have just wanted you to be there."

CHAPTER 43

ROSALIE

Rosalie Sumavari, Queen of the House of Death, had been staring at the wall for nearly thirty minutes.

The stones in the Royal Palace of Surmalinn were relatively new and still in their perfect and unblemished condition; even the stones on the corners of hallways and doorways were still sharp and unworn.

In fact, the only imperfections you could find to any of the stones in the palace were blemishes and marks that came from the Siege, including the one from which she couldn't seem to jerk her gaze away.

It was barely a hairline fracture down the surface of an otherwise perfect stone, not noticeable unless you were looking right at it. It was the only mark, the only reminder to Rosalie of what had happened to her, of what *could* have happened to her that night.

The stones here had long ago been washed clean of Yansley's blood, back to their natural dark gray coloring, but she would never be able to look at the stones the same way again.

The crack had come from when Yansley, a mammoth of a man who served the Wolf faithfully, had taken Rosalie by the throat and thrown her against the wall. The impact had enough force to make the stone behind her crack.

Rosalie would have died the night of the Siege. She would have died right there by Yansley's hands, with only that small little crack on the surface of an otherwise unblemished gray stone block marking her death.

Instead, Rorax Greywood had stepped in. Rorax had protected Rosalie from being brutalized, violated, and raped before leading her soldiers back out of her city.

If Rorax hadn't decided that House of Death was worth saving and that what her mother was doing was wrong and equated to genocide, Rosalie would have died right there, right against that crack, and the whole of Surmalinn would be nothing but a memory, razed to the ground.

Rosalie might not like Rorax, in fact Rosalie hated her and every memory that she triggered, but Rosalie also trusted Rorax *unequivocally* to choose the right path. Rosalie trusted her to lead them, to protect them, and after all Rorax had been through, Rosalie now trusted Rorax more than ever to make sure that no outside force swayed her into a decision that was not best for the Realms.

"Your Majesty?"

Marras save her. She couldn't believe she was going to choose a Heilstorm, and *Rorax* of all people, to back as the next Guardian.

"Your Majesty?"

There might be other Contestars who were as equally capable. Maybe one who was her equal in strength who *hadn't* almost burned her country down, but would Rosalie trust them as much? Even with Ayres there as a witness?

There was a tug on Rosalie's sleeve, and she jerked her arm away from the wall, jolted from her thoughts to the present.

"Your Majesty?" Rosalie's scullery maid looked up at her with wide, almost frightened eyes, staring from Rosalie to the crack and then back.

Everyone knew what had almost happened to her here. She hadn't let anyone mop up the blood for weeks.

"Go get some paper and an envelope. I need to send a letter."

CHAPTER 44

RAENGAR

"Did you know?" The question tasted like ash in Raengar's mouth, so he swallowed it back with a mouthful of bourbon. He had been drinking a lot lately, enough that Tag had started making worried comments about it, but Raengar didn't care. It was the only thing keeping him from jumping on his dragon and flying to the Northern Castle, breaking all the Guardians' fucking Laws, just to demand answers from *her*. Rorax. *Why didn't you tell me? Do you not trust me?* They were only the beginning.

Out of the corner of his eye, Raengar saw Jia flinch.

She nodded, rubbing a hand down her arm nervously. "Yes. The whole unit knew. We were all there when she was marked."

Something hot seared through Raengar's chest, and he gritted his teeth. The grip on the glass got so tight the glass cracked. Betrayal, anger, disbelief... it was all there.

Raengar wished he could spit ice fire at Jia, and if it was anyone else and at any other time, he would have.

But Jia wasn't whole. She looked even more haggard and fractured than Raengar felt. She'd lost weight while she had been at the castle, her eyes seemed to have sunk into her skull, and any light she might have had when she'd gotten married was completely absent. There wasn't a shadow in her of anything besides desolation and ruin.

Raengar tossed back the rest of his drink, then threw the glass against the wall so hard it shattered into tiny fragments. Jia flinched again, but he didn't hesitate as he turned to her and jabbed a finger in her face. "Tell Rorax if she ever lies to me or hides anything like this again, I will lock her in the dungeon for so long she forgets what the sun looks like. And if *you* ever hide something like this again, I will have you executed for treason. Rorax's actions put the whole fucking *country* at risk, the *world* if this all goes to hell because of her."

"Yes, Your Grace." Jia's face fell.

Raengar stood there, grinding his teeth, breathing like a dragon. Jia needed to get out of his sight before he did something he truly regretted.

"Get out. Have Eshaal take you to Volla's body."

"Wait." Jia ignored him and took one tiny step closer. "Is it true you fought a minotaur in the woods?"

Raengar nodded. "But my testimony was not enough to prompt the Council of Houses into action."

Jia reached into a bag at her side and fished out five vials. Two of them were full of hair, the other three were filled with blood. She stuck her hand out, offering them to him. "Take these. Kiniera said they needed to get to the University of Poison as soon as possible. They're samples of our blood after we—" Jia's voice broke, and she took a long, settling breath before trying again. "They are samples of our blood after we were exposed to the blocker. Kiniera wants to know what it was, who made it, and who ordered it. She thinks the evidence will help convict the Alloy King in his trial. Maybe it will change the Council's mind."

Raengar's eyes widened a fraction, and he took the vials very carefully from Jia's hands. As angry as he was, this evidence was desperately needed. As it was, the trial against Määr hung by a thread.

"Thank you," he murmured.

Jia nodded and turned to leave.

"Everything on Volla's person is yours, as is everything in her apartment in Koppar. Sahana sent the marriage license to us after it was done. I'm sorry… for your loss. Volla was extraordinary, one of the best. Her pyre will be lit tonight at sundown, in the tradition of the House of Fire. You have until then to grieve on your own."

Jia deflated, her shoulders stooped, and her head bowed low. "Thank you."

She took a few more steps to the door before Raengar rasped, "Take care of Rorax, Jia. Get her through this. Please."

Jia straightened and gave him a ghost of a soft smile over her shoulder. "Rorax is the toughest person I know, Your Grace. She will survive this."

Gods above, with every cell in his body he prayed Jia was right. He couldn't lose her.

CHAPTER 45

AYRES

"You're not going to like this."

Ayres looked up from the sword he was sharpening to find Milla standing above him, waving a letter in front of his face.

"Who is it from?" he asked, even as he recognized the beautiful, scrawling penmanship on the parchment.

"The Queen. This is her final decision on whom she wants you to choose to be House of Death's Contestar."

Something in Milla's tone felt ominous, and Ayres's scowl deepened as he tore apart the envelope.

Ayres,

I know you have your reservations about Rorax Greywood, and rightfully so. However, I would like you to choose Rorax as the House of Death's future Contestar.

Use her to help you track the summonings.

Prepare the men, ask for help if you need it to contain her influxes.

This is an order.

I love you.

-Rosalie Sumavari,

Queen of the House of Death, and your most beloved sister

Ayres read the letter four times before he crumpled the parchment up in his fist. He couldn't remember the last time Rosalie had directly commanded him to do anything, and it grated on his skin. She left him to his own devices, let him work with Erich during peace, and hadn't gotten in his way when the summonings occurred and he had to leave to retrieve Sumavari's books. She didn't intervene or even request regular updates but let him work with his guard to stop Lyondrea from summoning anything worse than what they had probably already pulled out of the Pits.

For her to command Ayres, to give him a direct order, it meant something.

Ayres shook his head, clenching the parchment in his fist, and glowered at Rorax, who was across the field of the arena stretching on the lawn. Jia Frostguard, her ever-present companion, was nowhere to be found.

Milla let out a little sigh. "I knew you wouldn't be happy about it."

Ayres narrowed his eyes and looked up at her. "Did you tell the Queen you wanted to pick Rorax?"

Milla shook her head. "No, I *would* have, but she'd already made up her mind before I'd arrived."

Ayres gritted his teeth, shifting his eyes back to Rorax.

How much trouble would he be in with his sister if he said no?

Milla must have been able to read his thoughts because she huffed. "Even you wouldn't go against a direct order, Ayres. Not from Rosalie."

Ayres flexed his jaw but said nothing as he continued to stare a hole in the back of Rorax's head.

Eventually Milla moved. "I am going inside. It's happening, Ayres. Rosalie is my queen, and we follow her orders."

Ayres gritted his teeth even harder but nodded his ascent. Every instinct told him no, told him that choosing her as the Contestar was wrong and dangerous and irresponsible.

"Rorax isn't evil, Ayres," Milla said over her shoulder. "She was just... *misguided* at one time in her life."

His hands curled into fists. Milla was wrong, but she slipped away before he could bite back a response.

Lamonte stood on the side of the arena, sweaty and hot despite the early hour. His hands were up and moving as he used his Dark Magick to conjure and weave a replica of what a real Shadow Wraith would look like—dark, hooded, smoky, with long black fingers and wicked claws.

Rorax was fighting it, bending, and twisting, dancing out of the way of any of the wraith's blows, while dealing her own damage to the shadowed body. For this drill, none of the Highborns were allowed to use their magick to combat it, only their practice weapons, and Rorax had volunteered to go first.

Ayres had known she was talented; he'd seen her in the Tournament of Houses, and Rorax herself told him she'd trained for the House of Ice army since she was only seven years old. But what he watched here made him feel uneasy.

Ayres was one with death. His very life force connected that bridge between worlds, ensuring it was smooth and intact so that souls could pass over into eternity. He could sense death—taste the fear of it—and with the blink of an eye, he could deal death.

He could never be afraid of death; they were old friends.

But if Ayres and death were old friends, Rorax and death were lovers.

Not only was she as willowy as the wind, but she was also tactile, precise, risky—like she knew death intimately and was not afraid.

Movement out of the corner of Ayres's eye made him reluctantly move his gaze from Rorax's display to find Elios making his way to stand next to him.

Ayres gave his friend a short nod, and Elios nodded back as they stood shoulder to shoulder, both watching Rorax battle the black smoky wraith.

She moved gracefully on her feet, and her movements were confident and flowing, like a pre-learned, choreographed dance until she struck out like a viper, utilizing even the smallest opening to hit her target.

"Ayres, if you're not going to ask her to be yours, I'm going to ask her. She could change everything. She would be one of the most powerful Guardians in history. The House of Fire needs someone like that at their back," Elios murmured as Rorax dealt a roundhouse kick to the wraith's head, making it fall back a few feet.

Ayres grunted, trying to ignore how Elios's words made his heart burn in indignation.

Ask her to be yours.

Rorax would never be anything to Ayres.

"Does Milla want to recruit her?" Elios asked.

Ayres's hands clenched tighter around the letter still balled in his fist, and he forced his jaw to unclench. "Yes. And so does Rosalie."

Elios hummed a short laugh before clapping a hand on Ayres's shoulder. "Well, it sounds like you have a Contestar to look after, whether you want one or not."

Ayres let out a resigned sigh as Rorax ducked under an oncoming blow from a clawed hand, one of the claws slicing off a small lock of her hair before she lunged up and used her gods' cursed knife to punch up into the wraith's chest.

The wraith popped into a cloud of dark smoke, and Lamonte threw his head back and laughed. "Very good, Rorax. Very good! Now you all see why you need that endurance training you complain about so much!" Lamonte laughed again, looking at the other Contestars watching from the crowd.

Ayres sighed and rubbed the back of his neck as a small portion of the onlookers laughed with Lamonte and congratulated Rorax. "It looks like I do."

Rorax stood bright-eyed, sweaty, and proud, but under Lamonte's praise she ducked her head a fraction as if the praise made her feel a bit bashful.

Her humble show was almost endearing. *Almost.*

If Rorax hadn't been responsible for the deaths of so many of his people, he might respect her, like her even. As it was, it made him sick not to go over there and snap her neck or run his sword through her heart.

He wanted her to hurt, wanted her to be in *pain* over what she'd done and all the people she had taken from him.

Rorax must have felt his hot gaze on her, because she looked up, her two white irises burning into his soul. Her eyes were striking; the dark circles that surrounded the white irises were only a few shades darker than her pupil. Her Contestar leather armor hugged her body tightly, showing off both the strength in her limbs and the curves of her waist, hips, and breasts. Everything about her was beautiful and strong in an addictive kind of way, and he wanted to put his hands all over her to feel her, to watch her respond to him. It infuriated him.

He bared his teeth at her, but before he went over to use her own knife to gut her, he turned to Elios and gave him his full attention.

"Rorax doesn't want to be the Guardian. Rorax, Milla, and I have talked about it, and we want you to pick Enna Mistvalley as your Contestar when the time comes. Rorax will help her survive through the trials, and we will give you Kaiya or Cannon to help train her," Ayres said.

"Enna?" The corner of Elios's mouth pressed down into a frown. "What about Rorax?"

Ayres shrugged. "Her brother is in Lyondrea in a prison there, and Rorax wants to free him. She doesn't *want* to be in charge of the Guardianship."

The frown on Elios's face deepened. "She doesn't?"

Ayres shook his head. "We are still going to choose her as our Contestar. We want her to help us with some... security problems we're having with Lyondrea, but we don't expect her to win the Choosing. In fact, the deal is she frees herself from the Choosing or she dies at the end."

Ayres would rather let his power go rampant and accidentally pluck the souls out of everyone involved than ever see Rorax as the Guardian.

Elios rubbed his hand over his chin. "But if we choose Enna, then you'll help us win the Choosing?"

Ayres nodded.

"Ice is on board with this?"

Ayres shrugged. "More or less."

Elios pressed his mouth together, thinking for a long moment before he held out a hand, which Ayres shook. "You have a deal."

Chapter 46

Rorax

A knife pressed against Rorax's throat, and her eyes flew open.

"That's a kill." Jia's face hovered above hers, her perfect skin glowing in the dark. "You sleep like the dead."

Rorax scowled and shoved Jia's hands and her knife away from her. "You're a bitch."

Jia huffed a laugh and backed up a step as Rorax sat up in bed, rubbing at her eyes. "You're back."

Jia's face tightened. "Yeah."

Rorax wrapped her arms around her knees, not wanting to ask but needing to know. "What did you find?"

There was a long, heavy silence before Jia answered, her voice broken and haggard. "She was there, her body. Kiniera and Raengar had it moved a few miles north of Morvarand to a war camp where Raengar and his men are. It was burned to almost nothing. I...." Jia's voice broke off, her throat working to swallow her tears. "We had a House of Fire burial ceremony in Morvarand, and Raengar is giving me all her belongings they've found. It... went as well as could be expected."

Jia wiped her cheeks with the back of her hands and bent down to pick up a black leather-bound scabbard that she'd placed on the side of the bed. She carefully unwrapped a blade, one of Volla's shortswords.

Jia handed it to Rorax. "I want to give you this one."

Rorax didn't trust her voice, so she just nodded her thanks as she wrapped her hand around the gold and silversteel handle carefully. The blade was one of Volla's most-prized possessions. A shortsword that had been forged with both goldsteel and silversteel and had been blessed by a fire witch to withstand even the hottest of flames, the perfect sword for the Torch. It had been given to Volla by the King of Fire as a gift for her services in the War of the Wings and had been in her weapons arsenal ever since.

"Thank you," Rorax croaked, her throat feeling scratchy and tight.

"I kept her longsword." Jia's voice was barely audible in the dark as she whispered, "They couldn't recognize Sahana's body in the rubble."

Shame, guilt, and loss pricked tears from her eyes.

"I talked to Raengar. He's furious with you, Rorax. He said if you keep something like that from him again, he will lock you in the dungeons. He told me he would kill me for it if I do it again, and I believe him."

She hunched protectively into herself as another shard of guilt pitted in Rorax's stomach. Rorax placed the blade carefully on the pillow next to her so she could wrap her arms around her knees again, hugging them close. She had betrayed and hurt someone she loved, someone who loved and trusted her in equal measure. He deserved better than her.

Could she die from this feeling? This utter devastation and self-loathing? She wanted to. She felt like her soul had rotted away, decomposing slowly into something so loathsome and foul she didn't know how to heal it.

"I gave him our blood samples and told him what Kiniera said about bringing them to the University of Poison to have them tested. I don't think... I don't think anyone is taking the news of Sahana and Volla's death well. I've never seen him look so on edge."

The news made the already frayed edges of Rorax's heart ache. Raengar meant everything to her, and she wished she could be there to comfort him.

Jia fiddled around with the drawstring on her bag for a moment before she stood. "The Selection is tonight, isn't it?"

Rorax nodded numbly at her. "Yes. After the ball."

"Good, you'll need someone watching your back once the influxes start to hit. Hopefully you get House of Fire. Elios is at least nice to look at."

Rorax nodded but couldn't bring herself to smile as she finally wiped away her tears with her fingers.

"Go back to sleep, Ror. I'll see you at the ball," Jia said, then turned and quietly left the room.

"You're on time. It's a miracle," the Guardian drawled as Rorax gave her a small half-hearted curtsy. She was at least twenty minutes late.

The Guardian had demanded Rorax check in with her upon arrival to ensure her attendance. The overbearing twit.

Rorax forced the corners of her mouth to lift as she straightened. "I wouldn't get used to it, blessed Guardian."

The Guardian sighed and clicked her big, golden, gaudy rings on the wood of her throne. She squinted from one of Rorax's snowy white eyes to the other.

Rorax had sent one of Kiniera's Blood Hawks to Merosa, the Witch Queen, who had been the original caster and had been paid previously to repair her rune. But the damage done to her identity was irreparable. Whispers and fearful glances followed her wherever she went, and even if her eyes were covered again, it was too late. "I heard you had been exposed, Spine Cleaver. I suppose those eyes are hard to hide."

"Unfortunately." Rorax grimaced, looking over her shoulder to find members of the congregation staring at her in fear. "The truth spread overnight. Everyone here knows who I am."

"Fame always did come as a double-edged sword," the Guardian sighed softly, looking Rorax over in her black dress. The dress was deceptively simple, hugged Rorax lovingly, and showed off her arms and shoulders. Her hair was up in a loose bun, and for the first time in the six months since she received it, her Contestar mark was visible for all to see. "Good luck tonight with the Selection."

Rorax refused to give the Guardian another bow, so she just abruptly moved away, scanning the crowd for Jia.

Jia was there, standing on the side of the dance floor, watching people from over the rim of the champagne glass she held. Rorax could see the ever-present sadness in Jia's face, her grief there even as she gave Ror a lazy smile.

With the hand holding her champagne glass, Jia raised her pinky to point to the right, back toward the way Rorax had come. "The Fire emissary is watching you like you're the prized stag of the hunt he wants to claim."

Rorax didn't care about that. She wanted to ask if Jia was all right, but she also knew she wasn't, and Rorax thought the reminder would be unwelcome. So instead, she looked over her shoulder to where Jia was pointing, but she couldn't see the Fire emissary through the crowd.

Jia turned to her left and used her still-raised pinky again to point across the dance floor. "The Lieutenant of Death, however, is staring at you like he wants you stripped and bared for him, but he definitely hates himself for it."

Rorax scoffed but looked across the room toward where Jia pointed. Ayres was hard to miss. He glowered holes in her, his jaw tight.

Rorax narrowed her eyes and tilted her head at him in a challenge. "He wants to kill me," she murmured.

"He definitely does," Jia agreed, taking a deep drink of her champagne. "But he won't. I've heard a rumor that the Queen of Death sent him a letter and commanded him to make you his Contestar."

Rorax halted her staring contest with Lieutenant Jackass to gape at her friend. "Did Kiniera tell you that?"

Jia shook her head. "Milla did."

Rorax blinked, uncomprehending, before a dark shadow crossed in front of her.

Rorax looked up, cranking her neck back to find Lieutenant Jackass had made his way over to her, his face tight with displeasure as he glowered down.

"We need to talk. Come with me," he said abruptly.

He looked handsome, *very* handsome, in his black suit. The neckline was high, and the dark fabric right under his jaw just served to make him even more appealing.

No man has any business looking that gorgeous, Rorax thought to herself ruefully, *especially this one.*

The lieutenant wrapped his big hand around her wrist and dragged her through the throng.

Rorax looked back at Jia, who did nothing to help her except lift her champagne glass to Rorax as if to say, "good luck."

The lieutenant dragged her out into the corridor. When there was a couple there, he turned around another corner and then another before she finally jerked her wrist out of his grasp. "Here is fine."

Ayres growled and spun to face her, crossing his arms over his chest. "Did Jia tell you?"

"Tell me what?" Rorax hedged. She leaned against the wall, but he was so close, so *big*, that the smell of him was overwhelming. It was heady, and her body craved more of it; she wanted to inhale and bask in that balsam pine scent for hours. She moved away from him to lean against the opposite wall.

He turned to face her, and Kään save her, Ayres's shirt being cut so high on his neck made his features seem even more intense, sharper, more dangerous in a way that she wanted to explore.

"Did Jia tell you what my queen ordered us to do?" he growled, and a strand of silver flashed through his dark eyes.

A mix of trepidation and want sparked in her heart. "What did she order you to do?" Rorax asked in a hoarse whisper. Jia had said the queen wanted her as a

Contestar, but Rorax wouldn't be surprised if she had really ordered Ayres to kill her. Maybe that's why he'd brought her so far from the ball.

Ayres, his eyes flashing, stepped closer to Rorax, and she looked up at him, forcing her body to shut down, to stop feeling *anything* but instinct in case he attacked her.

"My queen told us to pick you," he said, shaking his head slowly in disbelief and disgust. "She *ordered* me to choose you as our Contestar."

"What are you going to do?" she asked. She narrowed her eyes at him, but something inside her chest loosened. The Death Queen hadn't ordered her death then.

Ayres took a few more steps forward and pushed her against the wall—his hand on her chest, right under her neck and above her breasts.

"Choose you. Under some conditions."

Rorax's eyes narrowed. "What conditions?"

"We will help you search the library; we will even have our librarians at home search for a way to help you survive this. However, if we fail, and at the end of this it's only you and another Contestar still alive, you have to accept that we will kill you. We won't allow you to become the Northern Guardian."

Rorax swallowed hard, her throat dry. Gods, she was gambling with her life. "I accept."

"And," Ayres continued, "when the Choosing is over, you still have to stay and fight, you still have to help us win the war with Lyondrea."

"No," Rorax said.

Ayres eyes turned into dangerous slits. "No?"

"I will come back to fight for the Realms, but first I have to find my brother. I have to free him from Lyondrea. Once I do that, *then* I will come back to fight for the Realms."

Ayres's eyes grew fractionally softer before he nodded. "Okay."

"Okay."

His gaze dipped down to her dress again, but when they returned to her eyes, he looked angry. He growled down into her face. "Just so we both know, I will pluck your life from your body without a second thought if I even *think* something is wrong, if I think you're working something out behind the scenes to find and use Sumavari's books. My people's lives are on the line, and I will not play games with someone as dangerous as you, Little Crow."

Little Crow. Despite his threats and anger, something about his words made her glow in pleasure. His recognition of her strength and ability, combined with the power and confidence of him—the *force* of him as he pushed against her—it made her core burn.

Gods, this man was dangerous to her sanity.

She shook it off and snapped her teeth in his face, snarling, "If you so much as lay a *finger* on me or Jia with the intent to harm, I will ship your head to your queen in a shoebox."

"I can't fucking believe this," Ayres hissed. He glared down at her, looking back and forth between her snow-white eyes, the energy between them crackling. Despite the way her body reacted to him, the air was heavy, full of anger, hatred, and mistrust.

"For the record, I think this is a fucking mistake," he snapped before stepping away from her and looking slowly down at her body in her dress. Rorax sucked in a deep breath as his eyes hovered involuntarily over her breasts for a split second before he turned and stalked down the hall.

CHAPTER 47

AYRES

"I'm never attending another ball with you and Rorax Greywood in the same room *ever* again," Milla complained from behind him.

Ayres watched as Elios Delgado spun Rorax around the dance floor with grace and expert ease, and he was surprised his back molars hadn't been ground into dust. He'd counted over a hundred ways he wanted to kill his old friend for putting his hands on Rorax, for acting like he had some claim on her. This was their third dance together. And he wished to the gods he could look away.

"Ayres, go find a barmaid to fuck. Please. You *reek* of aggression," Milla grumbled with an exasperated huff.

Ayres ignored Milla, a muscle ticking in his cheek as Elios's hand slid dangerously close to Rorax's ass.

Ayres didn't care. He didn't give a *fuck* whose bed she chose to warm as long as it ended the minute she was named to the House of Death and fell under their protection. If Ayres let his House choose Rorax as their Contestar, she couldn't be in *anyone's* bed but one of their own. He wouldn't risk her accidentally spilling House of Death's secrets like that. No one could know about Sumavari's books. Gods knew, he'd already royally fucked up by telling Rorax about them.

A rustle of movement at his side had him looking away from Rorax momentarily.

"You're looking tense, Lieutenant." Jia Frostguard sidled up next to him, looking at Ayres with a knowing smirk. "I'll trade you a secret for a secret," she purred.

Ayres grimaced, knowing better than to deal in secrets with a fucking Heilstorm, but... "Deal."

"Before the dance started, I got my hands on a list of the songs they're planning to play at the ball tonight before the Selection. We're on song thirty-three, and there's only one more." She held her hand out, and a tiny scroll of paper lay in her palm. Ayres's body went stiff, but he plucked the paper out of her palm and unrolled it. "Delgado looks like he's a starving man out there with her, doesn't he?" she said.

Ayres saw the tiny name of the dance scribbled in the thirty fourth slot, and his body turned to ice.

Jia snickered as Ayres crumpled the piece of paper in his fist.

"What do you want to know, Jia?" he snapped, his body tense, coiled.

Jia's gaze left Ayres and combed over the dancing bodies in the room. "I don't know yet. I'll let you know when there's a secret I'm just *dying* to have."'

Jia winked one of her dark purple eyes at Ayres. She turned and was about to walk away but hesitated and slowly turned back to him. "If you need any more assistance retrieving the *things* that were stolen from you, my *talents* are also at your disposal."

Ayres understood her meaning. She was offering to help find the books, too. He nodded once, and Jia turned away and disappeared into the crowd.

Milla snorted from her spot once Jia left, still perched on the wall behind him. "She just played you like a fiddle. You didn't even make her work for it, Ayres."

Ayres ignored his friend as the song currently playing began to slow, and before Ayres knew what he was doing, he strode across the room, shoving through the throng of people roughly to get to Rorax. Just as she and Elios lifted from their final bows, Ayres stopped in front of her. "May I have the next dance?"

"I...." Rorax stared up at him, her wide eyes flicking back and forth from Elios to Ayres before she gave Ayres a confused nod. "Yes."

Elios frowned slightly, but Ayres grabbed her hand to drag her out to the middle of the dance floor before Elios could say anything.

He positioned her in front of him. Her back to his chest, Ayres leaned his head down to her ear, breathing in her scent. Gods, how could someone so evil smell as good as she did? "Do you know which dance is next?"

"No." Rorax shook her head, a blush covering the apples of her cheekbones at his proximity. Her voice was hard, but there was a tinge of breathlessness there, and he liked it. More than he should. "Do you?"

Ayres hummed in satisfaction as the violins began to play the opening chords of the seksitan.

Rorax gasped as she recognized the melody and looked over her shoulder at him. "A seksitan? You asked me to dance a *seksitan* with you?"

Her voice was uncharacteristically high, and a little bead of sweat appeared on her forehead. Satisfaction seared through him.

"I couldn't let you dance this with Delgado," Ayres said, the corner of his mouth coming up.

"Why? And what if I wanted to dance it with Delgado?" She sounded breathless as he ran his fingers over the skin of her arm, and the masculine side of him hummed.

"Trust me," Ayres purred, ignoring her first question, and noted with some kind of sick satisfaction her heartbeat strumming in her throat.

The music started to play, and Ayres dipped Rorax over his arm, bending her over so far, her long hair brushed the top of his shiny black shoe.

The seksitan was a dance for lovers. It was said to be the dance of sex, and so of course he wouldn't let Rorax dance it with someone who wasn't from Death, Ayres reasoned with himself.

Ayres trailed his fingers from her extended chin down her throat and almost to her cleavage before snapping her back up and all but throwing her into a spin. He guided her through the steps, then draped her over his other arm, trailing his fingers down her throat, then over her collarbones and again almost down to the swell of her breasts as he straightened her up.

Her cheeks were pink, and she looked unsettled. Her involuntary reactions felt like the ultimate victory to him in that moment, and as they started to move together, he pulled her closer than necessary. She took a sharp breath as her backside brushed against his core.

Rorax was beautiful. Her body was perfect as it moved against his. Her red-painted lips were full and looked so soft.

And for one blinding moment, Ayres wished that Rorax wasn't... Rorax. He wished they didn't have this history, this weight on their shoulders. Then he could woo her properly, take her out to the town, kiss her, invite her into his bed....

He flipped her so they were chest to chest, and as they started to move together in the steps of a seksitan, she stared up at him with those beautiful, white eyes.

Marras save him. He dipped her down again, letting his fingers trail over her skin, slower this time. Sensually. Taking in the heat and the soft skin as he brushed over her collarbones.

He brought her up, but this time as they came face-to-face, he felt her hot breath against his lips, and for one foolish moment, he wanted to taste her.

Gods curse him, he needed to sort himself out.

As the last chords of the seksitan faded into the air, the Guardian stood, looking out over the crowd. "Everyone but emissaries and Contestars gather in the back of the room. It's time for the Selection."

Chapter 48

Rorax

People slowly filtered from the ballroom into the Great Hall, most of them drunk and loud.

It took a long time, and Rorax stood at the front of the crowd awkwardly, rubbing her thumb across her ring over and over.

The murmur in the crowd only died down when the Guardian stood up from her throne. "Emissaries, line up next to me here on the left in order of who won the Tournament of Houses, and then the Selection will begin."

The Contestars lined up on the opposite side of the emissaries.

Rorax's heart thumped wildly in her chest as she made her way over to the Contestars' side of the room.

Isgra took one look at the line and chose the opposite end away from Rorax, which suited Rorax just fine. Enna came to stand next to Rorax, and Rorax gave her as confident of a nod as she could. There was still time for the House of Death to change their minds.

The Guardian stood in front of her throne, her arms wide as she welcomed the crowd into the Great Hall. Her hair was long and straight, draping around her face. She was dressed in a long, golden gown with wide sleeves, which made her eyes seem even more bright and yellow than they really were, making them look almost feline.

"Welcome," the Guardian called out to the crowd. "It is time for the Choosing to begin. Tonight, the Realms will make their selections according to their placements in the Tournament of Houses. While the Contestars are alive, the house that chose them are charged with the protection and well-being of their Contestar. At any time, any house can remove their protection from a Contestar or choose to support a different Contestar as a supporting house. When a Contestar dies, the House can choose to stay at the Choosing to continue to protect a living Contestar. They can switch as many times as they like."

The Guardian turned to the Contestars. "Sit on that bench until you are chosen." She pointed a long finger to an empty bench to the right side. "We will start with the House of Death and conclude with the House of Life."

The Guardian sat down and waved her hand impatiently at Milla, who stood in front of the emissary line. Milla stepped forward and offered the Guardian a polite bow before turning to the Contestar line.

Milla's blue eyes burned into Rorax, and relief spread thickly within Rorax's chest. "We have decided to select Rorax Greywood as the House of Death champion."

There was some clapping, more than a few confused whispers, and a few loud, angry bellows from the crowd as Rorax bowed her head and crossed the room to sit with Milla on the long bench.

Some of the Contestars eyed Rorax, and she held each of their gazes until she made it to Isgra. Isgra sneered at her, and Rorax forced herself to give Isgra a flat, uninterested look before she turned away.

The Guardian motioned for Kiniera to step forward, and she did. "The House of Ice has decided to choose one of the relatives of an Ice hero. We would like to choose Isgra Torvik, sister of the late Volla Torvik, as the House of Ice Champion."

The crowd erupted into cheers. It was expected that Ice would choose a Highborn.

Rorax stared at Isgra as a dark look passed over her face, right before she shook it off and beamed back at the crowd, waving as she crossed the floor. Kiniera sat down next to Rorax, and Isgra sat down on the other side of Kiniera.

Elios and the House of Fire were next, and he shot Rorax a brief defeated glance before turning to the Contestars.

"The House of Fire is choosing Enna Mistvalley, for her courage, thorough knowledge of politics, and good heart," Elios stated.

Enna's mouth dropped before a wide, beaming smile overtook her face. The hall erupted into whispers, and the Highborn Contestars looked at Elios, their expressions ranging from shock to anger that they had been passed over for a Lowborn.

When it was House of Life's turn, at the end of the Selection, Ren stepped forward. There were no more Contestars to choose from because Roo had died before the Choosing had even begun in order to find Rorax. It seemed like everyone in the room seemed to remember that at once, and Rorax could feel the heavy weight of a thousand angry stares.

"House of Life chooses to support the Contestar Enna Mistvalley. We are honored to take our position as her second House."

The crowd was unruly, confused, and loud about their confusion on why the House of Life would choose to back a *Lowborn,* but Ren held his broad shoulders tall as he went and took his place next to a bewildered-looking Enna.

When the Selection was over, everyone stood and dispersed into their new Houses.

Enna went with Fire and with Life. Milla led the way over to where the House of Death contingent was seated.

The lieutenant turned to Rorax and crossed his arms over his chest. "Don't make me regret this, Little Crow."

Rorax snorted, looking up at him with narrowed eyes. "Don't make *me* regret this, Lieutenant."

The lieutenant narrowed his eyes, but Rorax turned away to face the Prince of Death, who smiled at her, his golden eyes twinkling. "Glad to have ya on the team, Spine Cleaver."

Rorax rolled her eyes and gave him a cocky grin.

"Let's go play cards with the men on their last night here," the prince said, slapping the lieutenant on his broad shoulder. "I don't remember the last time I robbed you."

Chapter 49

Rorax

"I'm going to need another drink before he steals any more of my money." Milla scowled down at her cards, then at the giant stack of silver coins stacked precariously in front of the prince.

"That's a good idea," Rorax agreed, reaching up and scratching the back of her head between her two hair knives tucked in her hair. She eyed the bastard who'd won her an extra few coins to add to her purse in his victory.

"Peasants," the prince tsked, not even bothering to look up as he shoveled the copper coins into an already full leather coin bag. "As a *prince*, it's my *job* to be able to rob the people."

"Is he always this smug?" Rorax asked the emissary, jerking her chin at the prince.

"Always," Milla grinned.

They were in Milla's room, scattered around the emissary table and chairs. They played poker for nearly four hours after the Selection. Besides the lieutenant shooting her dirty looks between nearly every hand, it had been a calm and peaceful evening. A *fun* evening.

The three of them had slowly eliminated everyone else. The lieutenant had thankfully left the room nearly twenty minutes ago, grumbling about cheaters and card sharks.

Rorax felt strangely comfortable with the two of them, the prince and Milla. It felt like they didn't hate her, even though they *should*.

"Can I ask you something?" she said.

They shared a wary look, but Milla nodded at her. "Okay."

Rorax rubbed her finger along the grain of the wood on the table, unable to look up at them. "Did Surmalinn ever... rebuild?"

There was a heavy silence before the prince blew out a sad breath. "Slowly, but yes. Surmalinn has been fully restored. Povelinn was destroyed beyond repair. Most of the civilians have started a new colony outside the ruins called New Povelinn, or they became refugees in Surmalinn and Morvarand and just melded into the populations there."

Rorax swallowed tightly and finally looked up into the prince's face. His lips were pressed together tightly, the corners of his mouth turned down, but his golden yellow irises were warm. Milla's face was similarly grim, but Rorax couldn't see any traces of resentment or anger in either one of their expressions, so she continued.

"In the library, was there anything else besides Sumavari's books that were stolen? Or damaged?" she asked. She curled her hand into a fist on the table. She had specifically ordered her men *not* to touch the library, to leave it alone. If she found out they'd disobeyed orders, it was never too late to have them court-martialed.

Something softened in Milla's face. "No. Nothing else. The soldiers left the schools, the libraries, and the hospitals completely intact."

Rorax nodded. "Good."

There was one more question she had to ask, one more question that had been burning a hole in her soul, but her mouth felt like it was full of cotton as she tried to form the words. Rorax brushed her fingertips over the skin of her neck, just below her left ear.

"The man... the man with the star tattoo...." She swallowed. "Did he get it the night of the siege?"

The prince's face hardened, and he took a long drink from what was left of his pint of ale.

Milla's expression didn't change at all as she nodded. "His name is Cannon, and yes, he did. It was done by one of the House of Ice soldiers. Your soldiers. He knows exactly who, but you'll have to ask him."

Rorax's throat was achingly tight as she nodded. "Thank you."

Milla gave her a small nod before pushing herself up from the table. "I'll go get us another drink."

Rorax stood after Milla disappeared from the room; she took two steps toward the fire to warm up her hands when the prince spoke behind her. "There was a generous donation to the University of Surmalinn twenty years ago from a House of Ice patron. It was anonymous, but it was signed 'For not doing all that I could.' You wouldn't happen to know where that came from, would you?"

Rorax froze, her eyes wide. She started to turn toward the prince, the half-truth ready on her lips, when something hit her in the chest, absorbing into her flesh, into every cell of her being.

Something hot, something new, and something powerful slithered up her back.

She turned around to face the prince, confused and scared as the feeling consumed her, but before she could say a word to him, a heavy, red mist covered her vision, and then she was too angry to speak. Too enraged to think. She wanted blood.

Rorax looked around, searching for something, for anything. She didn't know *what* she was looking for, but she couldn't find it, so she was going to have to settle on something else, or *someone else.*

Slowly, ever so slowly, she turned back to the prince.

He could give her blood, he could give her a fight, and she was going to take it.

The prince looked at her softly, but when he took in the expression on Rorax's face, he went pale.

"Rorax?" He scrambled to his feet and took one step back, but it was too late.

Rorax grabbed his wooden pint of beer from the table and hurled it at the prince's head. He raised his arms to block it, but the metal edging of the cup sliced into his raised hand.

Rorax pulled both hair knives out of her braid in the same instant the prince snatched the fire poker from the flames of the firepit warming the room.

Rorax lunged. The prince blocked.

They clashed in a shower of hot sparks.

The prince snarled at her from over their locked weapons. "What are you doing?"

She considered him. She could throw Glimr into the prince's neck and be done with it. She wanted his blood on her hands, wanted the dark liquid over her skin, but... maybe the kill would be too fast, not satisfying enough if she just used her knife.

Something in her face must have unsettled him.

With a sharp grunt, the prince shoved her back a few steps and used the distance to move toward the door.

"GUARDS! MILLA!" the prince yelled over his shoulder. "GET AYRES!"

Rorax hissed, launching herself at the prince. He deflected her to the side again in another shower of hot sparks.

"MILLA!" he bellowed over his shoulder as he deflected one, two, three of her lunges in rapid succession as they moved along the long, wooden table. The fire poker was long and effective at keeping Rorax away from the parts of his body she wanted to strike.

"Rorax, what the fuck?" he grunted.

Rorax just hissed in response.

One solitary guard burst through the door.

Rorax hurled one of her hair knives at the soldier. It stabbed the man through his shoulder and pinned him to the wooden door before he could interfere with her prey.

He shrieked in pain and tried unsuccessfully to work the knife out of the wood.

"Gods fuck me, Ror," the prince grunted. Rorax pulled her second knife out of her hair. Fear contorted the prince's mouth before twisting the rest of his features. He stumbled, creating an opening, and Rorax knocked the fire poker out of his hand. It sailed away before hitting the ground and sliding under the table.

Rorax grinned. The prince stumbled again, and using the opportunity, Rorax slammed the butt of her knife into the prince's temple.

He collapsed on the ground at her feet.

She stood above him, looking down on her prey through the red haze still clouding her vision.

Kill him, kill him, kill him, something inside her chanted.

Rorax hesitated and shook her head, trying to clear the red haze from her mind as a hand wrapped around her throat and threw her backward with so much force it launched her into the air. She slammed into the stone wall.

She hissed and rolled, ready to spring onto her toes.

The lieutenant stood above her, breathing hard, his nostrils flaring like a bull. His men followed him in and immediately drew their weapons, but he raised his arm.

"Get him down," he said, pointing to the man still pinned to Milla's door, watching them both with wide, pained eyes. "But do not touch her."

He took another step closer to her, baring his teeth. "You want a fight, Rorax? Well then, I'll give you a fucking fight."

"Finally." She smiled her most wicked smile, the red haze, heat, and adrenaline inside her surging before she launched herself at him.

It was both brutal and raw, and the lieutenant delivered *exactly* what he promised. In a flurry of limbs, angry fists, and barely dodged blades, they fought.

The lieutenant managed to sink his knuckles into her flesh at least ten times and grazed his sword across her skin another twenty, each stroke leaving a scratch, a bruise, or a nick in her flesh.

Her knuckles landed on his ribs, but the light scaled armor he wore sliced open the flesh there, her knuckles becoming progressively bloodier as the fight went on.

The lieutenant swung his arm wide over her head, just missing her with an attempted backhanded blow, and when she saw the opportunity, she tackled him.

He dropped his sword as he hit the ground hard with a loud, painful grunt, and as he tried to push back on top of her, they rolled in a flurry of violent limbs down the long corridor.

She punched him hard, her bird ring cutting open his cheekbone with a small spray of blood. She raised her head, reached for Glimr, and was about to thrust it up into Ayres's neck when he somehow found his way on top of her. He pinned her hand to the ground and headbutted her with his head against her brow bone. The force of it smacked her head against the floor.

It hurt like a *motherfucker* as stars popped in her eyes, but the pain jolted her free of the hot thing writhing in her chest. Her vision cleared, and she took a deep, desperate breath. She felt like she'd been underwater for the last five minutes. The red haze on her vision was gone.

What the fuck just happened?

Ayres's chest was heaving, his silver and red eyes wild like he wanted to kill her. He raised his fist threateningly, but the prince was suddenly there, gripping it before it could strike. "Ayres, stop!"

Rorax blinked a few times, shaking her head clear of any remaining haziness.

She blinked up at Ayres's face and saw nothing but pure, undiluted loathing. Horror crept through her like a poison paralyzing her.

Fuck. *Fuck*, what had she done?

Shame ricocheted around her chest as she heard someone shrieking in the distance, the voice vague and muffled. "Ayres, stop! Don't kill her! She's influxing!"

CHAPTER 50

AYRES

Ayres ripped his arm away from the prince's grasp.

"Milla, talk," Ayres barked. He didn't move his gaze from Rorax even as she closed her eyes. He refused to move off her just because she'd stopped fighting.

He didn't trust her. Not at all.

A tear leaked out of the corner of Rorax's closed and swelling eye, and he bit back a snarl. She hadn't even waited a full day to attack them. If she was trying to get him to feel any pity for her, trying to convince him that she was *sorry* for this bullshit to let her live, she could think again. He should have known she would try and pull something like this the minute he had his back turned.

Ayres wrapped his hand around Rorax's throat, not to cut off her oxygen but to remind her that if she so much as jerked her body a millimeter, he would snap her neck.

Rorax gripped his wrist with trembling fingers.

Ayres tensed, and he waited for her to try and pull him off her, but she didn't.

Instead, she pulled his hand almost imperceptibly tighter against her throat. Like she wanted him there to restrain her.

The miniscule movement eased something in his chest.

"Ayres," Milla barked, suddenly right next to him, panting hard with her hands on her knees. "Are you... listening to me?"

Ayres's head snapped up, but he kept his eyes pinned on the female beneath him. "What did you say?"

"An emergency courier just let us know. The Weather Contestar has been murdered in her room," Milla rushed. "Rorax is influxing, Ayres. She doesn't have any control."

Another tear slipped out from the corner of Rorax's closed eyes, and she pressed her lips together tightly.

"She was seconds, *seconds, Milla,* from killing Piers." Ayres finally looked up at Milla. "I should kill her now and be done with it. I can't wait around for her to just pick us off one by one."

Milla's cheeks burned an even brighter red than they already were, and she jabbed a finger in his face. "Don't you *dare*, Ayres," she snapped. "This would have happened with *any* Contestar we selected. It's *our* job, *our* responsibility to protect her. By selecting her, we *promised,* we gave our *word*. Our *queen* gave her word. Our *House* gave its word. We knew this was going to happen eventually, and we weren't prepared. This is our fault."

Ayres ground his teeth together and looked back down at Rorax.

When Rorax slowly peeled her eyes open, an alarm bell rang through his skull. She looked empty, defeated... and broken.

Ayres had seen some of the same looks in his soldiers' eyes after coming home from war. Some of them came back from it, and some of them didn't.

"Rorax," he snapped. "Look at me."

Her white eyes just stared lifelessly up at the ceiling, looking through him as though he was a ghost, like he didn't exist.

"Rorax," he snapped at her, a little louder this time. "Look. At. Me."

His hand gripping her neck released her, moving up to grip her chin. "Ror."

Milla knelt on her knees next to Rorax. "What the fuck did you do to her?"

"I didn't.... I don't think.... *Shit.*" Something like fear rattled in his chest. He had all but thrown her into the ground. What if he'd caused some irreparable damage to her brain?

Ayres slid off her, kneeling on the opposite side of Rorax's prone body. "Fuck, Rorax, talk to me."

He slid his fingers into her hair, feeling for cuts or damage, but he didn't feel any blood.

The prince disappeared and then reappeared, holding the side of his head with one hand and a pint of water in the other. He dumped it down on her, and she jerked, some of the life returning to her eyes.

"Rorax?" Ayres asked, softer this time, and her eyes moved to him. Thank Marras.

Her gaze slid to Piers, and she winced. She pushed her way to her elbows slowly. "I'm sorry," she whispered to him. "I'm so sorry. I—"

"You just had an influx," Ayres told her, his voice staying remarkably gentle for how conflicted he felt. "If you feel that again, we need to know. You know what to look for now."

Rorax winced and nodded.

Ayres stood, scooped her up in his arms, and looked down at the prince. "I'm taking her to the Healers Hall. Do you need to go?"

His friend shook his head. "Naw, she just gave me a little bump. I'm okay."

"I'm so sorry, Piers," she whispered again, her voice hoarse. "I'm so, so—"

"It's okay," Piers assured her. "I'm not dead. When you get back, you can apologize to Phillip. He's the one you pinned to the door with your knife."

Rorax winced in Ayres's arms and nodded.

Ayres was halfway to the Healer's Hall before she spoke again, making guilt burn in his chest. "Thank you, Ayres, for protecting them from me. The last time I felt that lost in bloodlust, I was in Surmalinn. I... I'm so sorry."

Ayres pressed her tighter. "It's okay, everything's okay."

He said the words but didn't know if he even believed them.

Chapter 51

Rorax

Despite everything that happened last night and not returning to her bed until the early hours of the morning, Rorax was still awake right before sunrise. She pulled on her leathers and boots slowly before gathering her knives and her other effects.

Jia was waiting for her in the hallway, and from the way her purple eyes squinted as they gave her a once-over, it was obvious she'd heard one of the Contestars had been murdered last night. A House of Death guard had been stationed outside her door and eyed Jia warily. Rorax didn't know if she was insulted or flattered they'd only given her one guard.

"Go get some breakfast, soldier," Rorax told the guard. "And go get some sleep. I'm safe with her."

"I'm... not a guard. I'm a messenger." The guard must have seen Jia's performance during the Tournament of Houses because he gave her a wary look. "The prince and the Death emissary have requested your presence for breakfast. They'll meet you in the mess hall."

"Oh," Rorax said wearily. "Understood."

The messenger bowed and scurried down the hall.

"Any word on what happened last night?" Rorax asked as Jia peeled herself from the wall and moved down the stairs with Rorax.

"It was Claira, the Lowborn who was supposed to be under the protection of the House of Water. Kiniera said her throat had been slit while she was in her bed." Jia shook her head. "House of Water is again proving themselves to be useless in all things," she grumbled.

"Does anyone have any idea who did it?" Rorax asked.

Jia shook her head. "No. Fauna couldn't find a scent. So, either Water washed it away to hide something, or the assassin was *very* careful. None of the Guardian's men saw anything or anybody during the time of the influx either. Without any witnesses or scents to identify who was in the room with her, there isn't much that can be done."

Captain Lamonte and his men could ask around, but the Houses would all vouch for each other, providing alibis.

"All of the other Contestars were subdued, and there were no other fatalities," Jia reported.

"If House of Water going to move to another Contestar?"

"They announced this morning they are backing Mo, the House of Earth Contestar."

"*Fuck*," Rorax hissed. The last thing they needed was the House of Earth gaining more power here.

Rorax pushed open the doors to the mess hall and froze.

Lieutenant Jackass, Cannon, and Kaiya all sat around a table in the back of the room on the left side, on the opposite side from where she and Jia usually sat. They all watched Rorax and Jia with wary eyes.

They were each dressed in their fighting leathers, their weapons strapped to them. The lieutenant's fighting leathers crept all the way up to his jaw, but Cannon's... Cannon's leathers stopped at his collarbone, displaying the dark ten-pointed star that scarred his dark, ebony skin.

Rorax's mouth went dry as shame gripped her.

"You certainly know how to pick the warmest, most welcoming crowds," Jia muttered from beside her.

"It's a talent." Rorax sucked in a deep breath and steeled her spine as she walked over to their table.

"Well, isn't this a nice surprise," Rorax deadpanned, taking them all in.

"I see almost killing our prince yesterday hasn't made you any more pleasant, Pup." Kaiya sneered, and Rorax's cheeks went hot.

"We're here because we want to help you train," Ayres cut in, crossing his arms over his leather-clad chest. "You haven't fought in any serious altercations. If the Realms go to war, you wouldn't be of any use to anyone on the front lines."

Indignation made Rorax grind her teeth as she sat down next to Kaiya, opposite Ayres. Jia slid in next to her. "Okay, so what's the plan?"

"Have breakfast with us, and then we will go down to the arena," Ayres told her.

A maid came scurrying to the table, bringing two additional plates of food.

Jia dug in, but Rorax simply stared down at the plate not quite understanding. After last night, were they really going to ensure that she was fed properly before a workout?

"It isn't poisoned." Kaiya pulled her cup up to her mouth. "Not today, anyway."

Rorax gave her a look, then started to peel the orange that had been set in front of her.

Kaiya turned her attention to Jia. "So, we know Rorax is the ruthless contract killer. What was *your* role for the Heilstorms?"

Jia grinned around a mouthful of food. "I guess I'll have to show you."

"She could steal the crown off a greedy king's head," Rorax said.

"Perfect. A butcher and a thief," Kaiya said, sneering. "So, tell me, how did you get into your profession? A young orphan who had to steal to eat?"

Rorax snorted at the same time Jia grinned mischievously at Kaiya. "Neither. I just like to steal."

The Frostguard family was one of the wealthiest and most respected families in the Realms. Rumor was they lived in a goldsteel-gilded mansion.

"Her older brother, Ye-Jun, said the first time he held her she stole the diamond nose ring right out of his nose." Rorax snorted. "He didn't even notice until he found it when he was cleaning it out of her diaper a day later."

Ayres narrowed his eyes at them, and Cannon watched with a smirk.

Kaiya eyed Rorax's plate that had nothing but fruit, meat, and vegetables. "Do you eat like that every day, Contestar?"

Rorax raised an eyebrow. "What?"

"Here, Rorax, try this." Jia reached over and plucked a sweet orange roll off Kaiya's plate. She smiled, and Rorax didn't miss how Kaiya stared at Jia's lips for a second too long.

Rorax had never had an orange roll before. The Wolf had deemed sweets and pastries "unnecessary" to her diet. Sahana had taught Rorax how to read and how to dance and so many things about life, but they had never really explored foods before. They spent most of their time on the road. Hesitantly, Rorax took the roll from Jia, ignoring the sound of protest that Kaiya made. Rorax took a bite, and her eyes went wide as the taste and sweetness rolled over her tongue.

"Wow," Rorax said, mumbling and staring down at the soft, flaky dough with wonder. She was never going to eat anything else ever again. It was *divine*.

Kaiya reached out her hand to take the roll back, but Rorax held it away. "I'm never sharing again."

Around her, they all laughed, and the icy air that hung around the table earlier seemed to melt away into something a bit more comfortable, something that felt like the beginnings of comradery.

After breakfast, they made their way down to the empty arena, and Rorax felt the comfortable feeling fade.

"How much exposure do you have in open-war combat and heavy armor?" Ayres asked, turning to Rorax and holding his arms across his chest.

"None," she told him hesitantly.

Cannon, the man with the ten-pointed star, caught her eye.

How many soldiers have you been paired against in training simulations? Cannon signed with his hands.

Usually, I cap out at five but have been successful against groups of seven, depending on the weaponry, Rorax signed back. She hesitated, rubbing her thumb over her ring, but decided to trust them. ***But I've taken out groups of fifty at a time... using my knife.***

Ayres's eyes flashed. "Your knife?"

Rorax glanced over at Jia, who just gave her a nod. Ayres needed to know, or he would never be able to protect his people from her.

"When I was born, I was connected with one of the Sestera Blades," Rorax said, signing and watching carefully as Cannon and Ayres went pale.

Which one?

"Glimr."

"What is that?" Kaiya asked, her gaze bouncing from Rorax to Cannon and Ayres, and back.

"That first night I met you... in the woods...." Ayres stared, his eyes wide.

"You were stepping on it at first, on my back," Rorax half growled. "I couldn't summon it."

Can we see? Cannon asked, taking a step forward.

Rorax nodded and summoned her knife to her palm. All three of them flinched at its sudden appearance but then moved closer.

"What's a Sestera Blade?" Kaiya asked.

Kaiya reached out to touch it, but Jia stepped forward and slapped her hand back. "Touch it and you'll regret it, I promise."

Kaiya hissed but retracted her hand to her side. "What do you mean?"

"It burns anyone who tries to use it who isn't me," Rorax explained, turning it over in her hands, showing off the intricately welded handle and wickedly sharp edges. "A Sestera Blade is a weapon given to the Gifted by the gods. I can move it with my mind. I don't hold any other magick except for this."

They are made from starsteel, Cannon sighed, his eyes wide. ***There are only three other Sestera Blades that exist. The gods only granted the Gifted four, and it's believed they've all been lost through the ages. Until now.***

"Who bound this to you? Where did they find it?' Ayres asked, his gaze moving up from the knife to her face.

"I don't know where he found it," Rorax shrugged, "but my brother, Darras, is the one who bound it to me when I was born."

Cannon squinted at her. ***Why do they call you the Spine Cleaver?***

Rorax looked at Jia, who grinned back at her. Jia nocked an arrow and shot it straight in the air.

Rorax threw her knife, backhanded and across her body, so she could still use her fingers to point the knife where the arrow flew in the air.

They heard a soft snick, and then the wood of the arrow caught the wind and floated away while the metal arrowhead plummeted straight back down. The arrowhead thumped softly in the grass at Rorax's feet, cleanly severed from the rest of the shaft.

Rorax bent and picked it up, tossing the arrowhead to Cannon before signing again. ***The knife is extremely accurate, so I aim for the neck. For most things—most people—it's a one-shot kill.***

All three of the House of Death soldiers gawked at the arrowhead resting in Cannon's palm.

"What are the limitations?" Kaiya asked, her throat sounding dry and raspy as she looked back and forth from Rorax to the arrowhead. "There *are* some limitations on it... right?"

Jia snorted a laugh behind her as Rorax nodded. "I usually only throw it with the same strength that I would normally throw a knife. I can amplify the thrust behind it with magick, but I only hold so much power. I can sever around fifty spinal columns or penetrate twenty or so chest plates before I get tapped out."

Have you tested its accuracy over long distances? Cannon asked, and Rorax nodded.

"It's accurate for as long as I can see it. Once it reaches around a half a mile though, it gives me a headache." She reached up and touched her temples lightly with her fingers. "I feel the strain here."

Ayres nodded, rubbing a hand over the stubble starting to grow around his jaw. "That sounds like any magick when you're about to tap out."

"How do we defend against something like that? When you influx?" Kaiya asked, worry straining her voice. "It's a miracle the prince survived, that you didn't run him through."

Rorax's cheeks burned with shame, but she looked Kaiya in the eye and agreed. "It *is* a miracle. I wanted to; the influx wanted to... release. It wanted to prove how strong it was. It wanted blood, and it wanted to *kill* the prince," she admitted with a shiver running through her shoulders. "I had just enough cognizance not to do it, but just barely, and the influxes will only get stronger from here."

Rorax looked up at Ayres to find him already watching her, a muscle ticking in his jaw. "Can we lock it in a box?" he asked.

Rorax bit back a despairing groan. "Yes, but it would need to be locked in a black salt box. Otherwise, it will reappear in my hand when I walk away. I don't have one, and I don't even know where to find one."

Ayres blew out a breath. "We have one in the House of Death artifact vault." He turned to Kaiya. "Will you go tell Milla to send a hawk out to the queen? If we want to survive this, we need that box."

Kaiya turned and jogged out of the arena without a word.

"We need to get you fitted for a full set of heavy armor," Ayres said, cracking his neck to the side. "We will go into Bafta tomorrow and get you sized."

Rorax swallowed hard, then nodded her consent.

I'll be spearheading your training, Cannon said from beside Ayres. ***So, get warmed up and then show me what you can do.***

CHAPTER 52

RORAX

Rorax couldn't believe it, but she missed Cannon.

She was convinced Cannon was a sadist, since he'd spent the last week nearly breaking her in half as she ran through all his drills. Rorax ran, conditioned, and endlessly sparred with more opponents and moving bodies than she'd ever faced before. Preparing herself for war was one of the most exhausting things she'd ever done; the only exception was her initial Heilstorm training. That had kept her on the verge of death for months straight.

She'd been fitted for her first ever suit of heavy armor the night before, and the thought of having to run Cannon's drills *in* that suit nearly made Rorax groan out loud.

However, even training in a forty-five-pound suit of armor had to be preferable to *this*. The awkwardness of sitting in a room with all ten of the remaining Contestars as they milled and waited. They were in the opening of a cave that looked out onto a narrow valley between two steep mountainsides. The narrow valley below was split down the middle by a wide, winding river.

The Contestars, the Guardian's soldiers, and some of the emissaries had climbed onto the back of a transfer dragon before dawn this morning. The four massive blue-and-white beasts had flown them all south along the Death and Life border for nearly six hours before dropping the Contestars on top of the towering mountain.

The Guardian had walked them down a narrow trail that led into a cave and turned to look at them all individually with her bright yellow eyes.

"Welcome to the Valley of Trolls. The first trial is here." A few of the Contestars and emissaries groaned despairingly. The Guardian ignored them. "Your job is to find the golden horn and bring the horn to the other end of the valley where my men and I are waiting for your arrival. There are two horns to find, and you will be split into two teams: Highborns versus the Lowborns. The Highborns are to search the valley on the right side of the river, the Lowborns the left side. Your team is to kill the creatures defending the horn, or you will be disqualified."

The wind outside the cave howled ominously, and the fear and anticipation rolled off most of the Contestars.

They'd been given orders to wait there for a red flare to erupt in the sky, signaling the beginning of their first trial. Then after a blue flare, they would make their descent.

"What do you think the point of this trial is?" Serena, the Contestar for House of Foliage, asked from the opposite side of the cave as she inspected the edge of her brutal-looking machete. "The point of the trials is to test us, isn't it? What're they testing?"

Two Contestars next to her both shrugged nervously.

"My Protectorate told me this trial is to test our determination and restraint," a Highborn Contestar named Itzel answered. She sat cross-legged in the middle of the cave, serenely looking out into the forest. She was the House of Dark's Contestar, and they had fitted her with new, shiny black leathers.

Isgra sat next to Itzel, her long legs dangling off the side of the cave's mouth. She leered at Rorax from over her shoulder. "Some of us probably won't make it then."

"Perhaps not." Itzel shrugged, not taking her eyes off the valley below.

Rorax ignored Isgra's jab and eyed the longsword strapped to Isgra's back.

It was the sister sword of Volla's shortsword, the one that Jia had given her the night before the Selection. The weapon had the same intricate pattern carved into the surface of the metal.

Rorax absentmindedly ran her fingertips over Volla's sword that hung at her hip. It had been carved in the same style as Isgra's. Goldsteel and silversteel battled for dominance of the blade in waves, and the hilt was elaborately carved with the House of Fire's firebird sigil stamped into the metal on the handle.

Rorax had first seen Isgra's sword this morning in the Contestars' Courtyard. The Contestars and a contingent of Lamonte's men were gathering and getting ready to depart for the first trial site.

She'd tripped over her feet when she saw the sword, and to her dismay the prince had been the one to steady her. He gave her a concerned look, the black eye she'd given him a week before starting to yellow under his skin. "Don't die out there, Rorax. You owe me that at least," he muttered before clapping her softly on the shoulder and disappearing back into the castle.

He'd been the only one to see her off. Protectorates were not allowed at this trial site, and Ayres, Cannon, Kaiya, and even Jia had left early yesterday morning for a summoning anyway.

Rorax's mouth suddenly tasted bitter.

A red flare shot into the sky in a puff of smoke.

"Five versus five," Stella, the House of Light's Contestar, sneered as the women all rose to their feet. "I feel like Claira dying was a good way to even out the teams."

Rorax fought to keep from growling, but Briar beat her to it. "It's no joking matter. She was fucking murdered in cold blood."

Stella's grin turned wicked. "I know."

A blue flare exploded into the sky, and they took off, the Highborns down the trail out the mouth of the cave to the right, the Lowborns to the left.

All the remaining Lowborns—Briar, Mairi, Enna, and Lily—started jogging down a dirt trail leading to the valley floor, their armor and weapons clinking. Rorax brought up the rear.

When they reached the bottom of the sheer mountainside, they stopped to listen.

There was nothing to hear, except the typical sounds of a forest floor, birds chirping, and the nearby river.

Enna stepped forward, a faint blush visible on her cheeks from exertion. "Let's split up, some of us next to the river, some of us next to the mountain."

"I'll go with you, Enna," Rorax interjected before anyone could pick teams, turning to the other three Contestars. "You three go together. You go down the river, we'll take the mountainside."

Enna shot her a suspicious look, but the three other women nodded and turned toward the river.

Enna and Rorax started to carefully tread over the forest floor. They moved as silently as Enna could and only stopped after an hour or so for water.

"Rorax, can I ask you a question?" Enna asked, peering at Rorax from over the mouth of her waterskin.

Rorax nodded wearily, watching as Enna started to tighten the lid. She already knew what Enna was going to ask.

"Why do you try and help me so much?"

The corner of Rorax's lips tugged up, and she met Enna's stare with a raised eyebrow. "Do you wish I *wasn't* looking out for you?"

Enna frowned, setting the waterskin to the side. "No, but it's confusing. I don't understand it. Why would you help your... enemy?"

"You are not my enemy, Enna."

Enna's head cocked to the side so fast Rorax thought it might pop right off. "What?"

Rorax smiled to herself as she took another small sip from her own waterskin. "Accept the aid."

Enna looked at Rorax for a long moment, confused, before shaking her head. "Do you have feelings for Elios?"

It was surprisingly hard not to spit out the water Rorax had just sipped. She beat a hand against her chest as the water threatened to go down the wrong pipe. "Feelings? Romantic feelings? For Elios Delgado?"

Enna nodded carefully.

Rorax shook her head. "No. Why?"

Enna shrugged. "I think he might have feelings for you. He watches you a lot during training, so I wanted to matchmake him. He's sweet."

Rorax rolled her tongue across her teeth and fought the urge to snap at Enna. Where did she find the headspace to worry about matchmaking? She should be training to be the Guardian and getting herself prepared for when Rorax found a way to release herself from this nightmare. Rorax turned away, scanning the woods.

"What about the lieutenant?"

Rorax's head snapped around. "Absolutely not."

The denial was too fast, and Enna's smug little grin chaffed Rorax's patience.

"I think your eyes are beautiful, by the way. I have never seen another person with white eyes before."

Rorax gritted her teeth as she bent down and tossed her water back into her small pack.

"Can I ask you another question?" Enna persisted.

Rorax grunted.

"You're the Spine Cleaver. How many people have you killed? How old were you when you... when you first killed someone?" Enna swallowed hard, suddenly looking uncomfortable.

Rorax didn't show her surprise or discomfort. She didn't *have* to answer Enna, but... "I was... nine? As for the exact number, I have no idea. The real killing began for me when I fought in the War of the Slaves against House of Air. We were deemed too valuable to leave on the front lines long-term, so we'd only be brought in to assassinate leaders or incapacitate weapons, but sometimes those missions were more... hands-on than others."

Some of the color drained from Enna's cheeks. "I've never killed anyone before."

Rorax didn't know what to say to that, so she stayed quiet. If Enna became the Guardian, she would become as intimately acquainted with death as Rorax was.

Enna seemed to shake herself a bit. "That's what you were doing before, huh? Before you came here, you were on a mission?"

Rorax nodded, pulling her pack onto her back. "I was in Lyondrea when I got the mark. When I got back, the King of Ice informed us we were going deep undercover for our next mission. It was our second or third day on that mission when the Hunter found me."

"You didn't know the Guardian was deteriorating? That you were needed here?"

"No." Rorax turned away from the girl still perched on a fallen tree and took a few steps away, knowing Enna would follow. "We knew the Guardian wasn't helping Death investigate Lyondrea or doing her job, but we didn't know why."

Enna made a thoughtful noise behind Rorax as she also put on her pack. Then they got moving again.

Rorax couldn't see the animal near them, but gods above, she could smell it.

Her lip curled as she breathed in the smell of rotting flesh. Enna raised her hand to her mouth and nose. "What is that?" she whispered.

Rorax turned and gave her a withering look that she hoped communicated, "Shut your fucking mouth." Enna pulled at the collar of her Contestar armor and stayed quiet.

Rorax looked around, sniffing, but she couldn't see anything. She could only smell it. Maybe this was the creature guarding the horn? She needed to find out. She took a handful of steps toward the river before realizing the scent was getting fainter and turning in the other direction.

Rorax summoned Glimr as the scent got stronger.

Enna followed her, sounding like a drunk donkey stomping through the woods.

Rorax turned and raised an eyebrow at her, and Enna just mouthed "sorry" and hurried to catch up to Rorax, making even more noise.

"Stay here," Rorax mouthed.

Enna gave her a sheepish nod, and Rorax crept forward.

She edged toward the smell, coming close to the edge of the valley where the steep mountainside curved up toward the sky, and there it was. A cave.

Rorax approached the opening and peered carefully around the edge.

A torch illuminated the animal who lived in the cave, and her stomach dropped.

A troll. A huge, eight-foot mountain troll with short white fur, long apelike muscular limbs, and claws on each hand that acted like talons and could rip through armor like butter.

Rorax could only see the troll's muscular back, but she knew the face held six total eyes, two in the front, and the other four in a row going back to its ears on either side.

The smell of decay and rot must have been the fat she'd heard trolls collected and stored from the animals they ate. Behind the troll on the floor of the cave was a chest with a small horn carved into the wood on the front panel.

Rorax pressed her back to the side of the mountain again, scared and pissed off. She breathed for a moment before she padded away from the cave and back toward Enna.

Rorax felt a little woozy as she made her way back, and she used the trees to support herself. When she found Enna again, she leaned over and clapped her hands on her knees, forcing air into her lungs. "It's a fucking cave troll. It's guarding the chest."

The color drained out of Enna's face. "You're joking."

Rorax shook her head, and Enna hissed, "We are all going to die. We don't stand a chance!"

Rorax tried to drag a few breaths in, her chest feeling tight.

Almost ten years ago, her Heilstorm unit had downed a troll while they were on a mission. The thing had broken Rorax's leg and almost bashed her skull in. Ultimately, it had taken all four of the Heilstorms at maximum capacity to take it down. All four lethal, specially trained Heilstorms, and not a rabble of Contestars randomly fucking thrown together.

"We have to go back. We have to get the other girls, and we—" Enna's voice was high and so close to panicking that Rorax had to close her eyes and desperately try to calm her own heart.

"Enna. Shut the *fuck* up," Rorax snapped quietly, pressing her eyes together tighter.

Enna closed her mouth so hard her teeth clicked together.

Still bent over, Rorax squeezed her knees in her hands.

Shit.

Then she pushed another breath into her lungs and forced herself to stand up straight.

Who are you?

Rorax Greywood.

What does that mean?

It means I will not be afraid.

New, hot, determination strummed brightly in her chest. She wasn't going to die here.

An obsidian circlet made the trolls immune to magick. Rorax couldn't kill it with her knife alone like she would have done to any other man or monster. She was going to need to use all the tools she could get her hands on to even try to defeat the troll.

Volla's sword, Glimr, four disposable knives, her two hair knives, and Enna's two matching katanas.

That was all she and Enna had. They were so fucked.

Even if Rorax and Enna sprinted to get the others, the Highborns might find their treasure first, and that was unacceptable.

"Can't you just use a knife? You're the Spine Cleaver," Enna whispered, eyeing the trees like the troll was going to barrel through them any moment now.

"A troll's spinal column is not the same as a man's. It's thickened. And trolls have little obsidian crystals they grow on their foreheads. It was a gift from the gods to some of their favorite creatures or something."

Enna blinked. "*What*?"

"It's called the obsidian circlet, and it makes them immune to magick. So, I wouldn't be able to push my knife all the way through his skull without being literally in its arms." The thought made Rorax shiver. If she got that close to a living troll, she'd be beaten to a bloody pulp; her next form would be nothing but beat-up jelly for toast.

She could throw her knife just using her own strength, but the most she would accomplish would be pissing it off. Maybe she could use her knife to skin the crystal off its skull, or if she got lucky, puncture one of its six eyes. That would kill it, wouldn't it?

Rorax closed her eyes and tried to remember what she'd read about trolls the other night in her mystical creatures book.

Trolls could knock down a fully grown oak tree with their bare hands, had the same intelligence level as the silverback gorillas of Umbr, and were as fast as Sumavari's wolves.

Kään save her. Rorax knew she was going to die one day, but she really wished she wasn't going to die from something so fucking *ugly*. Rorax could lure the troll out of the cave, but she couldn't outrun it, and if Rorax climbed a tree, it could climb faster. They were fucked.

Enna chewed on the inside of her cheek. "What about fire? Do they like fire? We could trap it inside its cave and try to burn it."

"It wouldn't just go up in flames, but...." Rorax was on her feet so fast her head spun. "Explosives. Trolls ferment fat."

Enna blinked at her. "What?"

Rorax didn't respond as a plan built in her head faster than she could speak. "Enna, listen to me."

Rorax stepped into the mouth of the cave. "Hey, big guy," she said loudly.

The troll was sitting cross-legged on the ground, playing with two sharp bones in his huge, clawed hands. Its head snapped over to stare at her, its six eyes blinking at her at the same time.

She could almost hear its thoughts as the troll looked her over slowly.

Dinner.

Rorax fought the urge to gulp and instead took another shaky step forward. "Listen, I just need the contents of that chest you're hoarding, and we will be on our way."

The troll ignored her and slowly got to its feet. Drool dripped from its muzzle, like a dog before a meal.

Rorax lunged, and with all her strength, she threw one of her spare knives into one of the hands of the troll, pinning it to the side of the cave.

The troll let out an infuriated roar just as Rorax threw the second knife, pinning its foot.

"NOW!" Rorax yelled, and she heard the scuffs of boots behind her as Enna darted into the cave. Enna had to find that fat deposit, and Rorax had to buy her time.

Rorax threw her third knife, aiming for the troll's other foot, but he took a step back, onto her game now, and the knife clattered uselessly to the ground.

With a roar of pain, the troll ripped his hand off the wall with a cloud of dust and rock. Rorax threw her knife to pin his other foot while he was distracted, and based on another painful roar, Rorax knew she'd hit her mark.

Rorax took a step closer to the troll and pulled Glimr out of her sheath at her back.

The troll bent to pull one of the blades from his foot. With a hard yank, he started to pull it free.

Without magick to aid its course, Rorax took a step toward the troll and threw her knife at the newly freed foot.

It pinned both the troll's foot and its hand to the floor this time, and the troll let out an ear-splitting bellow of anger and frustration, sending a shiver down Rorax's spine.

Rorax had just taken a step forward, putting her in striking distance. Before she could move away, the troll swung.

It walloped her in the side so hard she heard a rib crack, the force of the impact sending her body hurdling straight into the side of the cave where she felt skin at her right temple slice open.

She pushed herself up, staggering back to her feet just as the troll pried her blade out of its hand and foot. It bent to pull Glimr out of its other foot, then slowly looked up at Rorax with a low, angry growl, inspecting his prey.

The troll tossed Glimr to the side, and Rorax summoned the blade back to her palm. She pulled out her sword, her last weapon and line of defense, and ignored the shooting pain across her rib cage.

But then Enna slipped past the unsuspecting troll and right by Rorax, screaming as she went, "The fat is on fire! Run!"

The troll howled in outrage and took two staggering steps toward Rorax before everything exploded.

Chapter 53

Rorax

The explosion knocked Rorax off her feet. She hit the ground hard, right on the side with her cracked rib.

Her ears were ringing, and so much sharp pain lanced up her spine, chest, and upper back the only thing she could do for a few seconds was take deep, ragged breaths and blink up at the treetops in pain.

She got up on her elbows, holding in her groan, and then sniffed the air. Smoke and the smell of burning hair and fat permeated the air so thickly, Rorax coughed before she could stop herself, the action causing her ribs to throb.

Enna came scrambling down the rocks, her eyes pinned on Rorax. Ash streaked the light brown skin on her face.

The caramel-colored horn peeked over Enna's shoulder where it was strapped to her back, and Rorax sighed with relief.

When Enna got a good look at Rorax's face, she stumbled, eyes going wide as she took in all the blood. "Good gods above."

"It's not as bad as it looks," Rorax lied as Enna reached a hand down to Rorax to help pull her up.

Rorax groaned as she got to her feet and braced herself against the nearest tree.

"Are you okay?" Enna's panicked eyes ran over Rorax's body, looking for more injuries.

"I'm fine," Rorax lied again, forcing herself to stand straight.

Enna gave her a look that said she knew she was full of horse shit. "Do you think you have any internal injuries?"

Rorax paused, taking inventory of how she felt, and shook her head. "I don't think so." She just *really* hoped they wouldn't run into any more trolls. Or Highborns.

Rorax debated whether to climb back into the troll's cave but decided against it. Glimr was safe at her back, but her other knives would be stuck under the troll's burning carcass.

"Gross." Enna shivered and shot a disgusted look over her shoulder at the cave and the troll she had just detonated. "Let's go."

Rorax and Enna moved slowly through the forest, choosing to head diagonally across the canyon, simultaneously moving toward the river and the end of the valley. They had to be nearing the end of the valley by now, close enough that Rorax was on the lookout for Isgra.

Rorax moved as fast as she could manage without passing out, but each breath burned in her chest.

She eventually had to stop. She paused with one hand on a tree when there was a loud scream from the other side of the river. Enna and Rorax looked over their shoulders to watch through the trees.

All five of the Highborns were sprinting through the forest toward them, glancing terrified looks over their shoulders as they ran.

Understanding barreled into Rorax. "Motherfucker."

Enna took one look at Rorax's body language and swore. "You're joking."

Almost as if in answer, a loud, ferocious roar bellowed its frustration from across the river.

It was a *very* familiar sound.

Gods save us.

As the Highborns started to cross the river, Rorax whipped around to face Enna.

"Run. Go straight up the river, and once everyone is out of sight, blow the horn. Get Briar to come back for you as protection in case there are more of these things out there, and then you all need to run to the end. Get back to your Protectorates as soon as possible before one of us dies and you all go through the influx together. Do you understand me?"

"What about you?" The words were barely out of Enna's mouth as another white troll burst through the tree line on the opposite bank of the river. It sniffed the bank, using its six eyes to scan the shoreline before spotting its prey and lunging into the river after them.

Rorax grimaced but didn't take her eyes off the troll. "I can't run, Enna. My best chance is to take this thing head-on, but we can't risk the horn."

Enna didn't move from her spot, so Rorax gave Enna a look out of the corner of her eye. "But if you don't start running in the next thirty seconds, Enna, I swear to Kään, I will tie you up and leave you as bait."

Enna jerked up straight. "I'll go get Briar."

"Enna, that's not—"

But Enna was already gone, disappearing through the trees.

Rorax gritted her teeth, focusing back on the river in time to see Serena and Mo finally reaching the bank. Stella and Isgra didn't have any Water magick to propel them, so they hadn't reached the shore yet and were still a few yards out. The troll was nearly halfway across the water, snarling.

Serena spied Rorax standing in the trees, and before her pride could stop her, she started to beg. "Rorax! Oh gods, Rorax help us!"

Rorax looked over Serena's shoulder at Isgra who was pushing out of the river, her face twisted in an ugly mask of panic and fear.

Rorax resisted the urge to put her hand to her ribs. She didn't trust Isgra not to use the injury to her advantage.

"We don't have a chance against it unless we can sever the connection to the obsidian circlet—the little black stone sitting in the troll's forehead. It will protect the troll from magick while it's still intact. You just need to make a slice across its forehead that's at least a centimeter deep."

Rorax looked around them. They were in the thick woods next to a small rocky bluff, not a very good location for openly taking down a troll.

"Isgra, set some of this brush on fire in lines twenty yards to the sides. We can't use magick directly *on* the troll, but we can use it to corral him. Let's see if it's scared enough of fire to stay in a box," Rorax commanded. Serena and Mo only had close-range weapons, but Stella had a full quiver of bows and arrows, and Isgra had some throwing knives.

The troll roared in fury. He was at least two thirds of the way across the river now, and she had maybe fifty seconds before it was on them.

"Isgra and Stella, climb the bluff and use your ranged weapons," instructed Rorax. "Serena, Itzel, and Mo? Grab some sticks. Make it into a torch."

They all did as they were told, too scared to argue.

As the troll pulled itself out of the water, Rorax noted that this troll was fractionally smaller than the other. It was covered in the same white fur and had a dark obsidian crystal on its forehead. The troll also gripped a long club in one hand.

Its six eyes carefully observed the ring of flames that Isgra had created, but in one move it sidestepped the blaze and rushed at the Contestars.

"*Fuck*," Rorax hissed. It barreled straight for Rorax, who was the closest. Itzel stepped forward and threw her torch at the troll before it got close enough to swing at Rorax.

The torch sizzled uselessly against the troll's wet fur, but the troll stopped its advance, growled in anger, and turned its attention to the Highborn.

There was a yell from the trees, and to Rorax's chagrin, Enna, Briar, Lily, and Mairi came running through the trees with their weapons raised.

The troll ignored the newcomers and hurled its club at Itzel. The club caught her body so hard she smashed against the rocks.

Itzel's skull made a sickening crunching sound, and as her body crumpled on the rocks, blood started to pool around her head.

Within a few breaths, Rorax felt the influx hit her, and the anger and the adrenaline coursed through her system as she took a breath in—right before someone tackled her to the ground.

Her rib screamed in protest, and the right side of her body throbbed in agony. But the pain snapped her out of her influx, and the red mist threatening at the edges of her vision dissipated almost as soon as it had come.

Briar, a small blonde from the House of Air, rolled with Rorax, her teeth snapping at Rorax's face and her hands grabbing for Rorax's throat.

Rorax tried to buck her off, but she could almost feel the jagged edges of her ribs rub against her insides and she stopped. Briar successfully wrapped her hands around Rorax's neck and squeezed, and Rorax gritted her teeth and arched her back just enough to jerk Glimr free. She threw her head to the side and used her connection to Glimr to smash its hilt against Briar's skull. With a loud smack of bone against metal, Briar's body went limp on top of hers.

Rorax shoved Briar away from her and deftly started pulling out every hidden knife she could find on Briar's small body.

Briar only had three knives left, and they were all too short to do any real damage.

Stella and Lily were swinging a sword at each other, but the other Contestars eyed each other and the troll with wariness. They were unsure who was the biggest threat or who they should attack first.

The troll took a slow step closer, and thankfully all the Contestars turned to focus on it, even Stella and Lily.

"Stella, Isgra, attack first from the front, then fall back. Mo, you step in from the back and get his attention with something showy. Then I'll throw the knives." Rorax barked the orders loudly, and they all moved to obey.

Isgra opened her arms in a circle, and a big ball of fire lit in the sky. It grew just a little as Mo blew into it, feeding it oxygen. The enraged troll growled, turning toward the flame. When it did, Rorax threw two knives.

One knife sunk deep into the soft flesh of the troll's uppermost left eye, and the troll flinched at the impact. The other knife nicked the hard brow bone and bounced off into the dirt.

"Fuck!" Rorax hissed as the troll roared with pain, then hurled its club at her. She dodged, throwing her body to the side to get out of the way.

Searing, ripping pain shot down her side as she rolled and came up in a crouch.

Rorax grabbed Briar's third knife as the troll threw its head back and roared again.

It started to charge her—a hurtling eight-foot mass of muscles, white fur, and an excessive number of eyeballs. The earth quaked under her feet as it advanced.

Rorax sucked in a breath and looked around. There weren't any trees or rocks to dodge behind.

In a moment of sheer, amazing stupidity, Rorax charged it back.

"Rorax!" Enna screamed in horror, but Rorax didn't stop.

When the troll got close enough, it reached its arm out to grab her. She gripped its wrist, swung under its heavy arm, and used her momentum and the troll's own weight to swing around its arm long enough to be able to drop it on its back. She heaved with every bit of strength she had in her, then shoved Briar's third knife into the second eye socket and used Glimr to manually slice the chord between the beast's obsidian circlet before hurtling herself away from the troll's body.

But she didn't get far enough away. The troll twisted around furiously and backhanded her across the torso. She flew ten feet before hitting the ground hard, and the troll lumbered to its feet and started toward her, its intent lethal.

She pushed up to her hands and knees, desperately gasping for air. "Magick!" she rasped out as Mo stepped in the way of the troll before it batted her away like a fly. Enna stepped forward, too, barely brandishing her sword before meeting the same fate. Stella tried to throw a knife, but she missed.

"Magick!" she rasped. "USE YOUR MAGICK!"

The troll was only three feet away now, showing her every single massive, sharp tooth in its mouth before it burst into flames.

Isgra must have finally heard her because her eyes were the color of bright coals as she stepped forward, holding her hands out toward the troll's burning body. Flames curled lovingly around her hand and all around her body, licking her face like a lover as she burned the troll.

If Volla could see Isgra right now, there was little doubt in Rorax's mind that she would have been proud.

The troll shrieked in agony, waving its arms desperately as flames burned away its white fur and sizzled its skin.

The smell made Rorax retch as she watched the troll flail around, desperately trying to put out the flames that now boiled its skin and charred it away.

When the troll finally collapsed to the dirt in a smoldering heap, she couldn't hold back the nausea. She bent over and vomited.

It was mostly blood, and seeing it made her woozy. The troll must have cracked another rib.

Blood trickled down her nose, and she wiped it away with the back of her wrist. Gasping, she pressed her hand to her side, and it came away bloody.

No, not another broken rib, one of the troll's claws had ripped a brutal line down her side.

"Fuck." She was losing a lot of blood.

Isgra and Enna ran to her side. Enna looked pale, but Isgra was still glowing with flames. "You're an idiot," Isgra snapped. "Climbing onto the back of a troll."

Mo and Stella ran to stand side by side with Enna and Isgra. "Shit." Stella eyed the injury.

Rorax knew it was bad. The blood was slowing, but not fast enough.

"Help her onto my back. The horn and the end are only over that ridge," Enna ordered the girls. Briar, Serena, and Mairi immediately knelt beside her, but Isgra, Mo, and Stella didn't move.

"No." Isgra shook her head, looking Rorax over with a triumphant grin. "This is a competition, and my biggest competitor is down."

Briar scoffed from her knees at Rorax's side. "Isgra, you're an idiot. That injury isn't going to kill her, and you can't kill her or you'll die. We either help her down the mountain or we just piss her off."

Rorax wasn't so sure the injury wouldn't kill her, but she grinned up at Mo and Stella anyway.

Briar snickered when Isgra immediately bent down to help Rorax onto Enna's back.

"Should we bring Itzel's body back to the castle?" Enna asked, and they all turned around to stare at the body crumpled at the base of the rocky bluff.

"No," Rorax rasped. "We'll have one of Lamonte's men come back. We need to get out of these woods as fast as possible. Get Lily up though."

Rorax jerked her chin over to where Lily lay.

Mairi bent down to help wake up Lily, and Rorax closed her eyes, desperately trying to cling to consciousness.

Chapter 54

Jia

Goldsteel holds its edge better than silversteel, and you have an ax, Kaiya, Cannon signed, his face unamused. ***It has to be you. You and Piers hack your way in through the back door, and Jia and I will come in through the front.***

"We might not even need to come in through the back," Kaiya grumbled, signing her fingers back to Cannon. "You could be done before I get in."

The four of them—Kaiya, the prince, Cannon, and Jia—had become the predominant hunting party for Sumavari's Books of Summoning. Ayres usually stayed at the castle with Rorax to train her and keep an eye on her. Milla didn't go on hunts unless it was absolutely necessary.

Jia thought it was strange they so openly put their prince in dangerous situations over Ayres, but maybe it had something to do with the power that oozed from Ayres. He felt like a powder keg ready to blow in the same way that Kiniera was with her Ice Magick.

They were good at what they did—not as efficient or as lethal as her Heilstorm unit had been, but over the last couple of weeks, they had successfully retrieved four books, which meant four unsummoned monsters. Jia wasn't sure how many of Sumavari's books there were in total.

The four of them were in the countryside of Death, having tracked the latest book summoning to a small winery just south of the City of Stars. The Lyondreans had rolled the largest barrel of wine, a giant tun, in the cellar over the back entrance to block it. If they wanted their ambush to work, they needed to cut their way through the barrel, and they needed to use Kaiya's ax to do it.

Hopefully we won't need you, but please hurry, Cannon said, his fingers flying, his dark brown eyes serious.

"Come on, Kaiya, if one of your precious little rubies pops out, I'll buy you new ones," the prince said, eyeing the rubies embedded deeply into the middle of the goldsteel of her ax.

"Please, Your Majesty, I embedded these rubies myself. It would take the strength of ten stars to remove them," Kaiya scoffed, flipping her handsome weapon back and forth in her palm before gazing lovingly at it like a mother would a child.

She blew a resigned breath out of her nose and smacked Piers's elbow lightly with the back of her other hand. "Fine, let's go."

Cannon and Jia moved to the front door the Lyondreans had bolted shut and waited for the sound of Kaiya chopping into the wood of the barrel at the back door. When the big, booming sounds started from the other side of the building, Jia froze the lock on the door, and Cannon used his shoulder to break the lock and shove his way inside.

There was a group of five winery workers, all tied up and sitting by the wall watching in horror as eighteen men, all armed and ready to fight, faced the back door and the source of the loud booming blows. Jia could sense all of them were

Ungifted except one, and the thrum of the power he held was significantly lower than her own and much less impressive than Cannon's.

She let two arrows fly, hitting two of the Lyondrean men in the back before they even knew what was happening. A third went down with an arrow to the eye as he turned around to face them. Jia could feel Cannon's Death Magick as it plowed into the four men standing closest to them, and Jia couldn't repress her shudder as their bodies dropped to the floor, their lifeless eyes revealing nothing but empty shells.

Jia shot another arrow, but a sword swiped it away as Cannon dropped another three men. Jia knew his magick was tapped, and they would have to fight the remaining eight by hand.

The survivors gaped helplessly at the men Cannon had plucked away, their fear palpable as Jia pulled her sword and small dagger free from their sheaths. It would be preferable if they could capture some of them alive to question. But Lyondreans were typically hell-bent on fighting to the death over capture, and this lot seemed no different.

When they saw Jia approach, one of them lunged, the others at his back. Cannon joined the fray, pulling half of them away from her.

They were decently trained, and Jia struggled.

She cut down one man when he tripped over a rope and stumbled into her path and then another. One of the soldiers thrust a spear at her heart. She managed to knock it away, blocking it to the side, before she twisted and thrust her knife in his chest with her other hand.

She dislodged the knife as the man collapsed to his knees and turned to face down the last man.

Jia danced, but he knocked the sword out of her hand. They both stared at each other in shock before he drew his sword back, preparing to swing at her.

She should parry, block, dodge. But Jia couldn't do anything besides stare wide-eyed at the sword. Gods, she was about to die, and even her reflexes didn't seem to care. She couldn't move a muscle, and so she closed her eyes in acceptance, and maybe even a little relief, waiting for the impact to end her life.

The sword slapped against her side and bounced off harmlessly.

Jia's eyes wrenched open to see the man's face pale with horror, his sword down by her knees, out of striking distance. By some act of mercy from the gods, or inexperience from this soldier, his sword had twisted in the air so the flat of the blade bounced off her armor harmlessly, but the impact still made her stagger.

She tripped and landed with a huff on her back.

Jia looked up wide-eyed at the man standing above her, his sword raised again, but before the blow fell, goldsteel and rubies flashed and blood sprayed everywhere as Kaiya's battle-ax cleaved the man from shoulder to navel.

Jia flinched back in surprise as his corpse collapsed with a vulgar thud at her feet.

Kaiya stood, breathing heavily, staring down at Jia with wild eyes, both of her hands wrapped around her weapon.

Kaiya ripped her ax out of the body, and Jia felt her cheeks heat as she slowly pushed herself to her elbows. "Thank you—"

Kaiya reached down and violently grabbed Jia by the front of her tunic, pulling her up to her feet before slamming Jia into the tun next to them, the wood of the huge barrel groaning in protest.

Jia gasped in surprise, wrapping her hand around Kaiya's wrist as Kaiya lowered her face to Jia's.

"What the fuck was that?" Kaiya hissed. "I thought you were a Heilstorm."

"I am," Jia muttered, trying to jerk out of Kaiya's grasp, her cheeks getting hotter.

"I've seen Greywood work, and she's never sloppy. I've seen knights drunk on a barrel of moonshine fight better than that."

Jia gritted her teeth, squeezing Kaiya's wrist tighter. "I am not Rorax."

"Evidently," Kaiya sneered, analyzing Jia from head to toe. "What unit were you in?"

"One." Jia forced Kaiya's fingers off her tunic. She pushed Kaiya back a step and tried to move away.

"I met Sahana Thorash when the House of Ice came to do their reparations in Surmalinn," Kaiya said, stepping in Jia's path, fire in her eyes. She shoved Jia's shoulder back. "She never would have allowed that shit in her unit. You wouldn't have taken a step out of Koppar."

Jia gritted her teeth and tried to turn away, her cheeks burning in shame. But Kaiya snatched her wrist tightly and yanked her back. Cannon and the prince had collected what they came for, a linen bag that looked like it held a massive tome inside, and were releasing the winery workers. All of them were silent and pointedly ignored them.

"Listen to me, and you listen real good, Frostguard. If you want to die, that's your business. But it won't be here, it won't be with me, and it won't be searching for the Books of Summoning with the House of Death."

"Why do you care?" Jia ripped her arm away, embarrassed and desperately needing to get away.

"For about a thousand reasons, take your pick. If you die on a hunt, the ramifications for my House will be severe," Kaiya seethed. "Not only will Greywood and Kulltoug skin me alive for letting anything happen to you, but you're General Frostguard's daughter. Ye-Jun Frostguard's sister. The same people who're currently overseeing the training of House of Death soldiers in Skavetsia."

Jia wrinkled her nose and was about to bite back a retort, but Kaiya cut her off. "Not to mention, Ayres and my queen won't be happy about it either. Tensions between Ice and Death are already high, and your king is one of the only things securing House of Death's borders against Lyondrea until our new soldiers are deemed fit for duty. So, as I said, if you want to die, that's your business. But not here."

"He wouldn't abandon the House of Death like that." Raengar was a good man.

Kaiya finally stepped back. "Maybe. Maybe not, but what about us, Jia? You have been hunting with us for over a month. We like you. You're the best person that's come out of House of Ice in a century. We don't want to see you die either, Frostguard."

"We? Or just you?" Jia snapped, her hands trembling and her voice shaking from both fury and hurt. "We aren't together; we aren't even friends. Fucking once doesn't make me yours, Kaiya. It doesn't make us anything. We're nothing."

It was Kaiya's turn to take a step back, a tortured look in her eyes.

Feeling bitterly triumphant, Jia whipped around and started to stalk away.

"It's not what the Torch would have wanted for you either. To kill yourself. To die for nothing."

Jia froze, as the familiar, agonizing weight of grief crushed her lungs.

"Did you think I wouldn't find out?" Kaiya asked, a note of bitterness in her voice. "Volla was a celebrity at the Tournament of Houses, and her burial pyre was lit in Morvarand for fuck's sake."

Jia gritted her teeth and battled back her tears. Gods, why couldn't she breathe?

"Clean it up, or I'm informing Greywood you're unfit and pulling you off the hunts. You're a liability."

Jia did nothing but grit her teeth as Kaiya turned and stormed out, slamming what was left of the front door behind her.

CHAPTER 55

AYRES

As Ayres approached the Northern Castle from the back of his horse, he had an opportunity to study the transfer dragons from his saddle.

Transfer dragons were slow and clumsy during a battle but massive enough to carry twenty-five men a piece. House of Ice had donated four transfer dragons to the Choosing for the Guardian to use, but they had countless others and more being bred every day in the Nest, a city close to the northern border of House Ice.

Apart from Deimos, the King of Ice's legendary war dragon, dragons had a lifespan of around 1,000 years. The dragons Ice had donated had seen war before, probably seen battle in the War of the Wings and the War of the Slaves, maybe more. All four of the dragons boasted long scars around their bellies and snouts, and one even had a long white scar through the membrane of one of its massive wings.

If the dragons were back, it meant only one thing—the Contestars were back, too. Ayres spurred his horse into a canter.

Most of the guards were either training or lounging around in the courtyard, but there was enough of a buzz to know whatever happened during the trials had been exciting.

Ayres slid down from his horse as soon as the young stable boy took the reins and found Captain Lamonte leaning against the castle wall, watching his men train.

Ayres charged over to him, bombarding him with questions as soon as he reached the captain's side. "What happened today during the trial? How many Contestars made it out alive?"

Lamonte looked up from his men and raised his eyebrows at Ayres's tone. "Concerned are ya, brother? It's nice to see you this morning, too."

Ayres schooled his features into an uncaring mask. "I just want to know if I should pack my bags tonight or not."

Lamonte scratched under his chin, narrowing his eyes at Ayres. "I dunno. None of us do. Only a few men went to collect the Contestars, and they're in debriefing with the Guardian."

Ayres turned on his heel and left his friend behind without another word.

Ayres knocked on Rorax's door, but she wasn't there, just like she wasn't in the courtyard or the library.

He went next to the House of Death meeting room, where he found Kaiya, Cannon, and Milla sitting around the table playing a game of cards.

"What happened?" he demanded, using his hands to speak to Cannon as well. "Where's Rorax? I can't find her anywhere."

At his tone, Kaiya frowned and Milla raised her eyebrows at him, giving him a little smirk. "You went looking for her?"

"Yes," he admitted.

"Why?" Kaiya asked, her frown deepening.

Cannon signed, ***She's fine, Ayres. She's in the Healer's Hall. She took a few hits from a mountain troll, but she survived.***

Ayres gaped at his friend. "A mountain troll?"

Cannon nodded and continued. ***The Guardian chose them to protect the horns. The Lowborns were the only ones to bring their horn back. A troll took out one of the Contestars, and they all went through an influx. But one of the trolls was close, and the Contestars seemed to focus on the troll during the influx and not each other. Rorax stopped herself before she killed anyone. She passed the test, then helped the rest of them get out mostly unscathed. The Guardian is furious about that, actually. Usually, the first trial kills about half of them. It was the House of Dark's Contestar. They decided to move to be Isgra's second House.***

"I don't know why anyone would want to be that cunt's Protectorate," Kaiya said, shaking her head as she laid down a card. "But anyway, Rorax killed the first troll, then disabled the obsidian crown on the second so Isgra could burn it to a crisp."

Marras save him.

"Piers is with her. Should we go check on them?" Milla asked, already standing up.

Kaiya scowled at her. "I was just about to win for the *first* time."

Milla shrugged with a grin and moved to the door. They all followed her to the Healer's Hall where Tressa and another healer were walking down the aisle between the two columns of hospital beds. When Tressa saw Ayres, she pointed over to the bed in the front of the room, immediately to his right where Rorax lay unconscious.

Ayres frowned as he moved around to Rorax's side. If it weren't for her small chest movements signaling her breaths, he would have assumed she was dead. Her skin was ghostly pale, her lips chapped and white. Her shirt was pushed up her abdomen to under her breasts, revealing two long gashes that had long black stitches crisscrossing the skin over her stomach and holding it together. She looked so small in this bed, so fragile, so *vulnerable*.

Something flared in his stomach, and a surge of unbidden protectiveness rose inside him.

Piers sat in a chair at the side of her bed. He saw Ayres's expression and smiled grimly. "If you think this is bad, you should have been here an hour ago. She looked even worse then."

Tressa came to stand next to Ayres with her hands on her hips. "We only have two healers here right now, and we needed every ounce of magick we had to replace the blood she lost. She came to us on her own two feet, walking, and on the verge of death. Aryes, when she wakes up in a day or two, you need to tell her not to push it. She should have asked for more help," Tressa snapped.

"She wouldn't even let me touch her," Piers said, his face morphing into a grimace as he looked over her wounds. "I don't think she trusted me to help her."

Ayres frowned. Piers wouldn't hurt her; none of them would. They had agreed to protect her. He remembered the first night she had an influx, how they had fought and the words he had bit out to her. Guilt niggled deeper into his chest.

"I'll talk with her," he told Tressa.

"Get her out of here when you can, Ayres," Tressa said, giving Rorax a look that reminded him of the scathing looks he, too, used to give her. "I don't want another House to kill her, but I don't want her in my hall." Tressa turned and walked away.

Ayres sat on the bed opposite Rorax's and leaned over to put his elbows on his knees. "What happened?"

"Those are from the trolls." Piers pointed at the long vertical cuts over her ribs. "She had four fractured ribs, a punctured lung that was slowly drowning her, and a concussion." He pointed to a scratch on the corner of her eyebrow.

"Marras," Ayres muttered, shaking his head. "I hope this is the worst of it. Has anyone been in to see her?"

Piers shook his head. "Only me, Jia, and Kaiya. She's been completely passed out; we shouldn't leave her alone for the next few days."

Cannon and Milla shared a glance from the foot of Rorax's bed that set alarm bells off in Ayres's head. "What?"

"We know what the next trial will be, Ayres."

Chapter 56

Rorax

"You've got to be shitting me." Rorax shook her head, looking panicked at Milla, Ayres, Piers, and Cannon in turn. Kaiya and Jia were in the library for their evening shift.

The corner of Ayres's mouth twitched as he bent down to tie his boot. "We're not."

"Sharks," Rorax said in disbelief. "You're telling me the next trial involves sharks?"

"It won't be as bad as you're imagining it," Milla said, trying unsuccessfully to console her as Rorax ran the bloodiest possibilities through her mind.

Ayres's smug little smirk grew wider. "Why? Are you scared, Pup?"

She scowled at him, hating the way the nickname grated on her nerves even more when he was the one saying it. "Yes. The trial takes place in the Cracked Sea. Did you know that the Cracked Sea is the most dangerous body of water on the continent?"

Ayres nodded.

"Well, it's not because those sharks like to cuddle."

Cannon snickered, but Ayres full-on laughed at her, making Rorax daydream about kicking him in the ass while he was crouched over tying up his boots.

"I should just wear a giant chum bucket to the next trial to make it easier for them. It'll be a faster death that way," Rorax grumbled, looking up into the sky.

Cannon snapped his fingers to get her attention. ***You'll be fine. The sharks are aggressive in the bay, but they will go after the least threatening meal. Use your knife to spill some shark blood, and they'll back off. They can smell blood in the water but don't like it if it's their own.***

Some of her tension drained away.

"I vote for the chum bucket idea," Ayres muttered, grinning as he unfolded his huge body to stand. He stared down at her with a small twinkle in his dark charcoal eyes. "But if you're not up for that, Cannon is right. You'll be fine."

She gave him a glare, telling him he wasn't funny. "When is the trial?"

Cannon's fingers flew. ***It's in three weeks. We need to train a few days a week until then in the lake. I want you to be able to defend yourself while treading water.***

Rorax cracked her neck, signing back, ***Let's do this.***

It had been five days since the trial with the trolls. Even though she hadn't been able to move much, they were still eventful days. Rorax had been bound for the first two, but on the third day, she'd received her first-ever suit of heavy armor. It was mostly a plain sheet of silversteel molded to her measurements; the only decoration was the House of Death's crest in goldsteel welded to the chest. It had been sunny when she got it, and Tressa had approved of allowing her to try it on and walk outside as long as she didn't pull any of her stitches. Cannon had her walk slowly around the arena until she'd collapsed, exhausted from her wounds, into a small patch of dandelions.

On the fourth day, the black salt box from Surmalinn arrived. The box was the same size as a wooden shoebox. The outside was wrapped in polished goldsteel with square blue emeralds scattered over the top, but the inside was made entirely out of tiny black bricks. Milla held the box out to her, and Rorax forced herself to put Glimr inside. "We decided that Ayres will keep it in his room to keep it safe. We will give it back for the trials that you might need it."

That morning, Rorax had been released from her healing restrictions by Tressa after another long and awkward healing session. Tressa's hatred for Rorax was palpable in the air. Rorax had gone to her usual library shift in the afternoon, and now they stood in the Contestars' Courtyard for the evening training session with Lamonte and his men.

Ayres and Rorax had started off sparring, and like usual, the lieutenant humbled her. She didn't understand how one could be so fast *and* so burly—only possible by centuries of training and perfect technique that Rorax simply didn't have yet. Training with Ayres without Glimr sometimes made her feel young and inexperienced in a way she hadn't felt in a long time. It exposed holes in her training that were impossible to see while she had Glimr bridging the gap. She had learned that Ayres had fought in the War of the Slaves, and most likely other wars, and Rorax wanted to absorb all the experience and knowledge he and Cannon could possibly give her.

During a break, Rorax closed her eyes to keep them safely away from Ayres and felt the warm summer breeze kiss her skin, enjoying the low hum of the others training, when one of the doors to the courtyard slammed open.

Rorax's eyes popped open as they all turned to look at Narlaroca stalking through the doors.

Ayres, Milla, Piers, and Cannon shifted closer to Rorax as Narlaroca pulled a knife from her belt, her anger palpable even from thirty feet away.

Narlaroca didn't pay Rorax or anyone else any attention; she remained focused on one thing, one person, and one purpose.

With angry, purposeful steps, she walked right over to where Serena sparred with Captain Lamonte.

Unease tickled in Rorax's chest. Serena had killed Narlaroca's lover in the Tournament of Houses, and Narlaroca was here for blood.

Rorax watched in horror as Narlaroca ducked under Captain Lamonte's practice blade, pushed him back with a hand to his chest, and turned to Serena to viciously stab her in the heart.

Serena stared horrified at Narlaroca before sinking to her knees, her fingers fluttering uselessly around the knife in her chest as blood dribbled from her mouth.

Narlaroca grabbed Serena's bloody chin and lifted her face up. "You killed my mate, and for that you will not live to see another day."

Serena's eyes went wide right before her body slumped to the ground.

Lamonte ripped Narlaroca back a few steps, away from the body, and the courtyard descended into chaos. Shocked gasps and screams echoed, and the soldiers surrounding the courtyard rushed for Narlaroca.

A burst of flames erupted into the sky as Isgra's influx punched through her, and House of Ice soldiers worked double-time to keep the stray blazes away from the other Contestars.

Rorax saw a burst of light magick, some water, and another burst of fire before the influx hit her so hard she took a staggering step back.

A hot wave of aggression and anger filled her to the brim, and Rorax wanted more. More power. More anger. More blood. A familiar red film covered her eyes, and Rorax gritted her teeth. "Ayres. Milla. An influx," she hissed from between clenched teeth.

Rorax's blood sang in her veins as her eyes locked on Briar from across the courtyard, a bloodthirsty grin creeping across her lips. Briar was easy prey. She didn't have Glimr to use, but she had other knives that would work just as well.

"Fuck," Ayres bit out next to her.

Rorax took one step toward Briar and was just pulling a knife out of the back of her belt when Ayres's body slammed into her so hard, she went flying backward onto the cobblestones.

She landed on her back, and he followed her to the ground, landing on top of her.

Rorax gave an unflattering grunt and immediately started fighting to push him off her, but Ayres fought just as hard to stay perched where he was.

"I've got her, Milla. Keep everyone else away," Ayres shouted from over his shoulder as he snatched both of Rorax's hands with one huge hand and pinned them above her head. He used his other arm to push down on her abdomen, effectively trapping her knives under her.

"Got it," Milla called as she, Piers, and Cannon all fanned out protectively around them.

Rorax snapped her teeth up at Ayres's face. "Get off me, you fucking bastard."

Ayres's lip curled over his teeth, and he pressed his arm harder to her stomach. "We can't let you kill her, or you'll die, you broody fuck."

The anger in her blood flashed to a boiling point. "Don't tell me what to do, you *useless mongrel.*"

She bucked her hips, twisted, and heaved—doing anything to try and use her feet to move him even just a few inches, but he didn't budge. She snapped her teeth up at him again, getting closer to his face than before.

"Motherfucker," he hissed, jerking his head back a bit to avoid her teeth.

The movement of his upper body forced his lower body into her a little harder, and with one tiny scrape of fabric against her core, everything changed.

She stopped fighting under him, panting heavily, staring up at him with wide eyes. The anger, hatred, bloodlust, and aggression of the influx in her soul changed, and suddenly it barreled into a different vein, evolving into something else that she couldn't stop. Hot need and electricity thrummed through her so hard she gasped.

"Are you done?" Ayres growled down at her.

He pressed his arm tighter against her lower belly, and she could swear it felt like he was putting pressure directly on her womb. Her core gave a needy throb. He felt so good, her back arched off the cobblestones to press harder into him.

Ayres, reading her movement as another escape attempt, pressed his body even more tightly against hers, trying to keep her contained, but this time the metal ridge of his belt nudged against her most private place, so close to her clit and right where she wanted him.

Rorax whimpered. Loudly. Gods, she needed more.

Her cheeks started to burn, but before she could stop herself, she rolled her hips against his, and this time he read the movement as it was. Need.

Ayres turned into a statue above her.

She rolled her hips again, but this time her clit hit directly against his belt buckle, and she *moaned*. Heat and pleasure raced through her nerves, making her nipples hard and her heart beat faster. It wasn't enough, not *nearly* enough through her clothes, but it was just enough that she did it again.

She let out a soft, involuntary noise, and indecision darkened his eyes as they shifted from their usual charcoal gray to liquid silver, dropping from her eyes down to her lips. She could see the want there, the hunger, but she could also see the indecision, and she wanted it gone.

"Ayres," she breathed.

"Fuck," he snapped as she wriggled underneath him.

She wanted his hands all over her body.

"What the fuck is going on?" Ayres hissed.

The throaty sound of his voice permeated through her skin, and she couldn't help it... she couldn't stop it. Her spine arched off the ground in reaction to his voice. Her breasts brushed his chest, and she wanted *more*. She wanted to feel her skin against his.

She groaned with raw lust and need, closed her eyes, and groaned again.

"Rorax," Ayres warned with a low growl.

Rorax rubbed her still-clothed core against his hips again. This time she felt his long, hard length under the leather of his pants against her before he jerked his hips away.

She whimpered in dismay. "Ayres, I need it, *please*."

Ayres closed his eyes and took in a deep, steadying breath.

Rorax wriggled under him, but he was out of reach everywhere she needed him. "Ayres."

Ayres opened his eyes slowly, his irises a simmering silver. He chuckled, low and dark, as he bowed his head to run his lips slowly from her chin to her ear. "Beg for it again."

Rorax stared into his eyes, wide and pleading, to make sure he was listening. "Touch me."

"I want my *name*. The next words out of your pretty lips will be my name, or I'll fill your throat with my cock. Beg for me again, Little Crow."

He lowered his head back down to her neck, biting his teeth into her throat hard enough to hurt.

Electricity shot straight from her nipples over her belly button to her core where even more need and wetness bloomed. She was out of control and on fire, and she needed more. "Ayres, fuck Ayres, *please*."

"Please what?"

"Kiss me."

He did. He moved his hand up, wrapped his fist in her hair, and crushed his mouth to hers. Every single cell in her body seemed to sing with pleasure and relief as the influx coiled around her body. She whimpered into his mouth.

The influx in her blood wanted more from him. More skin, more heat, more pain, more pleasure. She wanted *everything* from him.

Rorax bit his lip urgently, and it was like they'd been set on fire. He bruised her lips as his tongue battled with hers. He dropped his hips onto hers fully and rolled his hard length against where she wanted him the most. It caused her to respond, her back arching into him again.

He used his free hand to slide up her leathers to right below her breast.

Rorax bit her lip and tried to angle her hips up to his again, to get his cock against her once more. "Ayres—"

"Gods above, are you two dry humping?" someone above them muttered.

Ayres snapped his head back away from Rorax's and stared down at her in disbelief.

The influx's hold on Rorax snapped. The red mist that had covered her vision dissipated, but her face burst into a kaleidoscope of embarrassed pinks as she stared back at Ayres with round, mortified eyes. "Oh, my gods. I... I am so sorry."

The other Contestars were settling down, too. There wasn't any rogue magick flying anywhere, and no one was yelling or screaming anymore. Only Mo still seemed to be struggling against her Protectorates.

Ayres's shock dissolved into a smug, shit-eating grin. "Don't be, Little Crow."

He released her wrists and pushed himself up off her in one graceful move, and she scrambled up.

Milla looked like she wanted to burst out laughing. "What just happened?"

"I... I...." Rorax swallowed, tucking a loose strand of hair behind her ear. "I was influxing, but then when he.... I.... It was.... I was on fire. It was all I could think about."

"*What* was all you could think about, Rorax?" Milla asked, tilting her head, her smile getting even bigger.

"I think my belt scraped against her in a way that made her influx turn into lust," Ayres stated matter-of-factly, his voice still rough as he looked Rorax up and down slowly. The look of hatred and mistrust from the last influx was gone; it had been replaced by something hot and hungry, and even though Rorax was mortified, she was also relieved.

Ayres grabbed Rorax's wrist. "We will be back," he told Milla, Cannon, and his men before pulling her away and dragging her into the corridor that was right off the Contestars' Courtyard.

It was deserted, and as soon as the heavy wooden door closed behind them, Rorax tugged free of his grasp. "Ayres, gods, I swear I didn't mean to *attack you*."

Rorax rubbed her hands over her face, her cheeks hot with embarrassment.

"I'm glad you did."

That was unexpected. Rorax's head snapped up out of her hands. "What?"

Ayres's face was serious, even clinical, as he studied her. "When this happens again, if we can use lust to quell it, we're going to. I would rather touch you than have you throwing knives at the other Contestars or, worse, me and my people. If that's okay with you."

Embarrassment and the lingering trace of heat clogged Rorax's throat. But something else made her hesitate, too. Something like... guilt as Rorax thought of Raengar. Nothing sexual had ever happened between them, but she had always wanted it to, had always thought it would. Would he care when he found out about Ayres touching her? Kissing her?

This arrangement could potentially save people's lives, and Raengar wasn't here to help her with it. She only had Ayres.

Rorax didn't know what to say, so she simply nodded.

"Red is your safe word, for when you snap out of your influxes and you want us to stop," Ayres said.

Rorax nodded again, as she rubbed the back of her neck, her eyes falling to the carpet, feeling confused and guilty.

"Rorax, look at me." His voice was low and serious and maybe a little unsure, but not angry or disgusted, so she tentatively raised her eyes to his.

"You did well today, telling us when the influx started. We will get through this, okay?" His eyes were warm and charcoal. Safe.

Rorax felt a small smile pull her lips up. "Okay."

Chapter 57

Ayres

Ayres watched Rorax run footwork drills with Lamonte when he felt the pull. Just a short little tug in the back of his brain that signaled someone was summoning Death Magick. He closed his eyes and focused.

A big pull had come from the west a couple days ago, on the border of House of Death and House of Fire.

This one, this one was from the north—northeast to be exact.

Cannon, Kaiya, Jia, and Piers had left yesterday on a hunt for the books, and Milla was permanently stationed at the castle, which left him with....

He groaned, dropping his head back. It'd been a week since Serena had been killed, and Rorax had starred in a number of his dreams and fantasies. Her mouth opened for him.... Gods, he needed space from her. Ayres needed to be near her as much as he needed an arrow to the chest.

He peeled open his eyes just enough to look out at his Contestar, who was laughing, flipping Lamonte off, and wiping sweat from her face with the bottom of her shirt at the same time.

The tug felt small, just a small attempt. Perfect for two people, and she was all he had. He'd have to come up with some story he could give the Guardian about taking Rorax with him to train out in the forest. He sighed and trudged over to Rorax to give her the news.

Chapter 58

Rorax

"We are on business for the queen—"

"I don' care if you're the queen's uncle, the queen's donkey, or the queen's favorite tit. It'll be six coppers for the night, and everyone's gotta pay an extra two coppers a person if they're getting in past sundown," the innkeeper—a man with a belly so round, Rorax thought for sure there was a watermelon hiding under his shirt, and a beard bushy enough Rorax could barely see his eyes and mouth—informed Ayres with his hands on his hips. "That's the policies."

Ayres gritted his teeth. "*Four* extra coppers?"

"Five if you keep wastin' me time."

Ayres grumbled and pulled out the coins from his back pocket. Rorax could have paid, but there was something deeply satisfying watching Ayres get extorted by his own House. The innkeeper pocketed the money but pulled out a long, iron key from behind the counter and dropped it into Ayres's palm. "Third door up the stairs to the left."

They had ridden their horses until they were frothing at the mouth. Day and night for three days they traveled, swapping out the beasts for fresh horses where they could at rest stops or little villages on their way. They had to catch a ferry over the Pike River yesterday morning and were now somewhere between Nyson's Gap and the Old Volcano.

Rorax was anxious that they were taking too long, that they would arrive to see that one of Sumavari's pets had already been summoned, but Ayres reassured her that some summonings from the books of Sumavari could take weeks from the very first pulls of magick until the actual summoning, depending on how much magick needed to be absorbed.

Rorax turned and started up the stairs with Ayres on her heels. They were in Karduru, staying at the only inn in the village. They had camped every night before this one, but the stables would be closed until morning, and they needed to buy fresh horses, so Ayres had thought they should splurge on a real bed before they fought the Lyondreans tomorrow.

Karduru was barely a village. It was more of a small camp in the Jagamines that was strategically placed on a common trade route through this area of the mountain range. It was a dangerous road, so the village was fully equipped with not only an inn but a small barracks, healers' quarters, and a tavern that Rorax was incredibly tempted to spend the night in rather than in a cramped room with Ayres.

They said nothing as they climbed the stairs and used the key to unlock their room. Inside there were two beds, both barely twin-size. Rorax sat on the one farthest from the door and immediately pulled off her boots.

Ayres sat on the other bed.

"How far is the Old Volcano from here?" Rorax asked as she reached up and started to undo the war braids from her hair.

"It's a half day's ride from where we are to get to the base. Not too far from where they are pulling magick." Ayres pulled off his traveling cloak, giving Rorax a better view of the black, high-necked leather armor he had on.

Rorax cocked her head and squinted at Ayres, watching as he started to loosen the ties on his greaves. "Why do you always wear clothes that cover your neck?"

The fingers at his wrist paused, and his eyes flashed dangerously up to hers. "What are you talking about?"

"Your neck. You always wear armor that comes nearly up to your jaw, and every shirt I've ever seen you in is a turtleneck or something similar. Are you hiding your tattoos?"

"I don't know what you're talking about," Ayres snapped.

Rorax continued to work on her braids until her hair was in loose waves around her shoulders and down her back. "My Heilstorm armor is designed similarly to yours. I wanted to hide my Contestar mark. Don't bother trying to deny it, but you don't have to get defensive; I was just wondering."

Ayres narrowed his eyes at her and ran his tongue over his teeth. "I'm not hiding anything."

She had to bite her lip to keep from rolling her eyes. "Okay, Lieutenant."

Rorax unbuckled Glimr's sheath from around her waist as they continued to get ready for bed in awkward silence. It wasn't until the candles had been blown out and Rorax was snuggly under the covers that Ayres spoke again. "You were right. I wear high-necked armor to hide my tattoos."

Rorax looked across her shoulder to Ayres, her eyebrows raised. "Honestly?"

"Yeah."

"Oh... why?" Rorax scrunched her nose.

Ayres's voice was low when he answered. "I don't like them."

Rorax huffed a laugh into the night. "That's a pity."

"Why?"

Rorax debated saying anything before she rolled over to face him, even though it was too dark to see anything besides the faint outline of him in the night. "That's a pity, because I remember—the first time I saw them, you were shirtless and escorting a woman out of your room—I remember being jealous that she had gotten to touch them and thanking the gods that men could look like that."

Ayres's head whipped around to look at her, and there were a few beats of loaded silence before he rumbled, "Honestly?"

"I will deny it if you ever bring it up, but yes. I really thought that. It didn't matter though; you opened your mouth a second later and *quickly* reminded me that you're nothing but a Death-Born prat."

Ayres laughed under his breath. "Nothing you don't deserve."

Rorax smiled. "Maybe."

"Good night, Greywood. And... thank you."

"Stop staring at me," Ayres grumbled when he caught Rorax staring at him for the sixth time that day. She couldn't help it. She'd never seen anyone with enough death magick that it manifested in their eyes. It was beautiful.

"When you track the power, there's red in your eyes," she mumbled. His irises pulsed a brilliant ruby red that rimmed his pupils and made his eyes appear to glow. They were getting close, so he had been keeping close tabs on the magick today, making them constantly red.

Ayres nodded. "Whenever I use, or even *want* to use, my death magick, my eyes turn red."

"What other magick do you hold? Dark?"

"Yes. My mother held an abundance and passed down the ability to me and most of my siblings."

Rorax nodded, adjusting the reins of the palomino horse they had bought that morning in Karduru. "When you're angry, your eyes turn silver. I should know, I've seen it enough."

They were passing through the grounds of the Old Volcano, a huge dormant volcano that used to burn down the forest here regularly thousands of years ago, but now it only served as a famous landmark. They were riding their horses around the edges of a huge pit, where there had once been a lava lake that had drained away, leaving a cliff on all sides but one. Two large towers, built out of black lava bricks, emerged out of the forest and were on each side of an old lava bed. Rorax edged her horse closer to the edge of the cliff that overlooked the sunken ground to see what was at the bottom, but it was just filled with dirt. Not even any plants grew there.

She hummed, looking over the other scenery around them. Besides the barren pit and the two black, dilapidated towers, it was beautiful here. They were on an old cart path going through the mountains and were high enough in altitude that only tall pine trees stretched over the mountain as far as her eyes could see, creating a sea of evergreen pines.

"Where did you feel the pull come from?" Rorax asked.

Ayres closed his charcoal and red-streaked eyes, breathing deeply. When his eyes flicked open again, they were bright red.

He jerked his head to the side and pointed past the Old Volcano looming to the northwest of them. "They are a few miles north of here, but there's some kind of barrier around it. Something that muffles the magick." Ayres's forehead creased.

"Is that a problem?"

Ayres waved his hand in the air dismissively. "I don't think so. It just means they have an Elite with them, someone who's capable of muffling magick. There's another abandoned tower a few miles from here—Helfast, they used to call it. I would bet that's where they have their camp. I can't think of another structure anywhere in that area to use to hide, unless they took a home from a civilian."

"Isn't this Helfast?" Rorax asked, shivering as she passed under the shadow of one of the tall, black towers. "It feels like a place that could be named after hell."

"No, these are just the Volcano Towers. I can't remember which war with Wymeria it was, but Death used to use these towers as a little military base," Ayres explained. He pointed over to the tower closest to the base of the Old Volcano. "They used to have bunkers that connected to lava tubes where soldiers would live. The ground is still warm here, even if the volcano isn't active, and there are hot springs under the towers where they use to bathe. They used it until Wymeria attacked it and hundreds of soldiers died here in the lava bed as they tried to escape the tunnels. Marras likes to remember the places where her people have died, and war zones in Death seem to never be able to grow vegetation back properly."

Rorax shivered again. "Fitting."

"You said fifteen, Ayres. *Fifteen*," Rorax hissed as they laid in the grass, elbow to elbow, staring out at an encampment of soldiers. There must have been seventy... eighty of them milling around in front of Helfast, the crumbling tower, running drills and keeping a wary eye on the tree line.

"How does a force this size even get across the border?"

A dark shadow passed over Ayres's features as he studied the soldiers. "I don't know."

"Gods save us."

Ayres's jaw flexed. "Come on. There's always a back entrance to the old towers."

Helfast was not *just* a tower. It was a small fortress with walls twelve feet high built around it. They wouldn't be able to walk right up to the Helfast tower; they'd have to find a way over the wall first.

They crept through the woods to the back of the castle. Thirty men had set up camp in the area. There was still a patch of forest between them and the encampment though, and Rorax was eternally grateful for the small grove as Ayres nudged her with his elbow and pointed to a black grate.

"The back entrance into the keep." Ayres worked his jaw, clearly conflicted. "There are too many of them. We need to retreat and get reinforcements."

"What? No!" Rorax exclaimed.

Ayres looked around at all the men. He appeared hesitant, but there was an edge in his eyes that made him seem almost *eager*, which contradicted what he spewed at her. "No. We have to go back and get Cannon and Piers."

"Look at me, Ayres. We're doing this, and we're doing it now. If we leave, we risk them being successful in this summoning."

Ayres bristled, but Rorax pressed on.

"We risk them being successful in conjuring up whatever foul thing *your* ancestor created. So, no, Ayres, we aren't waiting. We go in, and we go in right now. I can take out half of those men before they even know they're in danger."

Ayres stared down at her, rolling his jaw. "You would cripple yourself if you did that. Even Glimr has restrictions, Rorax." They'd retrieved Glimr from the salt box before leaving.

"I wouldn't be crippling myself. I'd be *pushing* my limits," she snapped. "I have more than enough power to get me through the castle."

"And how do you know that castle isn't teeming with more soldiers?"

"Well, is it?"

Mistrust and anger made his mouth tight, but Ayres's eyes flashed red as he reached his magick out to feel the souls in the castle. "No, it's empty except for ten, maybe fifteen life forms."

"So, as long as we do this quietly and don't alert the soldiers training out front, this can be done."

Ayres narrowed his eyes, his indecision naked for her to see.

Rorax took another step closer to him and attempted to soften her tone. "I won't be able to rest, won't be able to sleep or eat, and will scarcely be able to *live* until every one of those books are found." She placed her hand on her chest. "So, I'm going in there—with or without you, Ayres."

Ayres looked over at the men again, and that same fleeting eagerness flashed over his features before he glared back down at her and growled, "*Fine.* But if you do anything rogue, unexpected, or try to get this book back to your Butcher King—"

"I will remind you that my *king* is currently stationed in Morvarand, fighting for *your* House, *your* land, and *your* people. So even if I were to bring the book back to Raengar, at least I wouldn't have to go very far to do it," she seethed, edging up on her toes to get in his face. She had to talk herself down from lunging for his throat with her teeth.

He snarled at her. "Raengar? You're on a first-name basis with the Butcher King?"

If only he knew.

They glared at each other for a long second before she turned away, summoning Glimr to her palm. "We don't have time for this. Go down into the tunnels and search the vaults. I will climb the tower and start from the top."

"Meet me on the middle floor. Helfast has its jail on the main floor."

"Understood." Rorax nodded.

She was about to turn when Ayres reached out and grabbed her arm. "Be careful. My queen will cut off my balls if you die up there."

Rorax smirked and pulled her arm away. "You, too. I won't carry you out of here."

They stepped out of the shadows.

Rorax let Glimr fly. At the same time, a burst of black magick streaked with red lightning catapulted toward the unsuspecting soldiers.

It took them less than thirty seconds to silently clear the camp of thirty men.

Ayres heaved open the grate to the tunnel entrance, and Rorax ignored the way his muscles flexed under his leathers.

"Scream if you get caught," Ayres quipped and lowered his body down into the grate.

Rorax rolled her eyes and crept closer to the wall. There was a massive tree growing close enough she *might* be able to make the leap from a long branch to the tower. She climbed until she was near the top and sent her knife at the necks of eleven guards lining the walls. They all dropped like potato sacks straight to the ground. Her power strained as she summoned her knife back. She'd only have a few more kills with Glimr before the magick she held would be used up, and she'd be forced to choose between killing the soldiers manually or passing out.

Rorax leapt from her tree branch to the tower, catching herself and dangling by her fingertips on the extruding wooden beam. She carefully hauled her body upward, so she was perched on the wood. Then she peeked in through the window. It was an old bell tower with a big bronze bell hanging above the one man in the room. He was slight and had sandy blond hair. He sat at a dilapidated desk with his back hunched, scribbling furiously on a letter. His sword sat propped against the doorframe behind him, and when she slipped in through the top window, she positioned herself between him and his sword, rendering him defenseless.

She landed on the stone floor in a crouch and looked up into his face as he scrambled from his seat. As he took in her white eyes, his face went pale. "Fuck. I... I know you," he croaked.

Rorax slowly uncurled and couldn't help the triumphant grin that crept across her face. "You do?'

"Y-You're the Spine Cleaver."

Rorax's grin split into a smile. "I always liked that nickname."

"More than the Pup?"

Rorax's smile fell off her face, and she pulled a knife out of her hair. "Why are you here?"

He put his hands up in surrender. "Helfast was abandoned almost four hundred years ago, but it is still strong, the foundations—"

"No," Rorax snapped, slicing the air between them with her knife. "Why are you in the Realms? Why have you and all your men started to crawl out of your reeking rathole?"

Rorax advanced a step forward, and the man scrambled back, hitting his desk with his hip and causing the contents on it—ink bottles, quills, rolls of parchment—to rattle and fall off the edge to the floor.

"The... the books. Sumavari's books. We need to summon Sumavari's pets if we are to stand a chance in this war."

"The Pit monsters aren't sufficient?" she snarled.

"No, House of Ice is too strong." A calm look of steely determination came over him. "The Realms need to fall. They have abused their ministry over magick."

"It seems that we are protecting it just fine," Rorax sneered as she towered over the man.

"The magick in Lyondrea is corrupted."

Rorax remembered the wolves in Lyondrea, how her knife could not puncture through any of the wolves' fur, and believed him.

Magick in Illus lived in the earth. The Gifted could absorb it, holding it within themselves before they put it to use, but any magick in the ground that was *not* used regularly could spoil, rot until the magick spawned monsters. The Realms, the most magickly concentrated country in the world, had priests and paladins that roamed the land to use magick. Rorax didn't understand why he and his men would summon *monsters* when they popped up anyway, uninvited and without any prompting.

"Then why go to all this fucking trouble?" she snarled. "Why not just *ask* for the Guardians' help to solve it? It's their job to protect everyone in Illus. Everyone down to the dogs are allowed to request a meeting with the Guardians."

The man gave her a sad smile. "Do you truly think it's that easy? That the lords of the Realms do not push their issues to the front of the line?"

"Then push *harder*."

The cowering man in front of her seemed to regain a modicum of his courage. "Do you think we have not exhausted every conceivable route before choosing this one? We have begged until our knees were raw and pleaded until our voices ached for an audience with the Guardians and have received *nothing*."

Rorax tilted her head. There was no lie in this man's face. "Why have they ignored you?"

The man gritted his teeth. "The Guardians and the Council of Houses in Valitlinn often turn a blind eye to those who do not reside in the Realms."

Rorax's brow furrowed. "So, you turned to the Pits? You think unleashing Illus' horrors back into the world will solve anything?"

It actually might, Rorax thought. And that terrified her. Between the Pits, Lyondrea's forces, and Sumavari's monsters, it might be enough to break them.

"We are *desperate*," the man hissed. "I warn you now, Spine Cleaver, war *is* coming, and the Pits are just the beginning. With or without Sumavari's pets, we will burn the Realms to the ground until there is nothing but a smoking rubble of ash and bones so we can rebuild it from the ground up." The man smiled, a smile of defiance and determination.

Then the man lifted his hand and a flash of a white pill passed over his tongue and into his mouth. Rorax leapt forward and snatched his hand away, but she was too late. Seconds later, the man's body seized. Rorax stepped back, knowing there was nothing she could do. He coughed up a fountain of blood over his breastplate right before his chest stopped moving.

Rorax stepped to the man's desk, looking over his letters and paperwork, but there was nothing to be found but a map of Helfast and a letter from a scout who had come to check out the location prior to the rest of the soldiers' arrival. She opened the top drawer of the desk, and there, on a leather cord, was a golden key. Rorax plucked it out and jammed it into her back pocket. She didn't know what it was for, but it was bad practice to leave keys behind.

She rummaged around the desk some more but didn't find anything else that seemed useful. She stared at the dead man for half a second, sifting his words around in her mind, before she turned and hurled herself down the stairs.

Ayres thundered down the steps and paused as he saw the crumpled body of a prison guard, Rorax's knife still embedded in his neck. She flicked out her fingers and the knife returned to its sheath at her back.

"Do you have the book?" Rorax asked.

He shook his head grimly. "It's behind a locked door. In a witch room."

Which meant he wouldn't have been able to open it without the key, no matter the amount of magick he held.

Rorax fished the mysterious key out of the pocket of her leather pants with a triumphant grin. "Got it."

Ayres's mouth went tight as he snatched it out of her hand.

"Good work," Ayres grudgingly praised.

Rorax opened her mouth to respond right as a bell started to ring, cutting her off with long, loud tolls.

"Fuck," Ayres hissed. "*Fuck*."

"Let's go."

They took two hurried steps toward the exit before Ayres suddenly froze, causing Rorax to barrel into him.

"Umph. What're you—"

But Ayres was already bent over, cooing at something—at *someone*—in one of the cells. A little girl, maybe five or six years old, with dirty pale cheeks and wide, scared eyes. She had dirty blonde hair and big blue eyes, looking up at them from where she had crammed herself in the corner of her cell.

The little girl's dirty blonde hair was curly, and her eyes weren't the same color as Volla's, but the panic Rorax recognized. The same helpless expression, the same hope in her eyes that Rorax might be able to save her.

Rorax looked at the lock. It was thick and would require precious minutes to open.

Ayres took a step toward the girl, and Rorax gripped his wrist to stop him, panic inflating in her throat. "Ayres. The book."

"You aren't going to even try to save her?" he hissed at her in the darkness, the faint glimpse of warmth in his eyes she'd seen a few times since the Selection was replaced with the more familiar cold, black hatred.

"Ayres, we can come back and get her after we find the book," Rorax demanded, a desperation in her voice that she hated. The soldiers from outside were undoubtedly ascending on them right now. They wouldn't be able to save her. They would fail the girl, and she would die.

Plain agony danced in his eyes, and he sliced his hand through the air between them. "Fuck the book. I'm getting her out, and you won't survive here alone. Let's go."

"If they're successful in summoning Sumavari's pets, we could be putting *thousands* of lives at risk. I would never be able to live with myself if we let that happen!"

"And I will never be able to live with myself if we leave her here!"

They stood toe-to-toe. They needed to move; she could hear the shouts of the men outside the gates getting closer.

"Do you honestly have no compassion in that cold, black heart? Gods above, Rorax," he insisted. "This little girl could die. Someone could come back for her. We're getting her out of this cage *now*."

Rorax gaped at Ayres before looking down with wide eyes at the little girl who was curled up and shivering in the dirt, watching them with eyes that held the same amount of panic as Rorax's own.

Her tongue felt like a lead brick in her mouth, and her heart was hammering against her ribs so violently she could hear it in her ears. Rorax wouldn't be able to save her, even if she wanted to. The gods hadn't built her for that.

Ayres tossed Rorax the key and shook his head at her in disgust, then spun to the girl's cell. Rorax caught the key in her palms, the weight of the warm metal suddenly feeling like an anchor to her soul.

Images of Volla and Sahana's broken bodies, of the thousand others that Rorax had been unable or unwilling to save, danced in Rorax's eyes as darkness laced with hints of red lighting looped around the bars of the cell. With a flick of his hand, the bars ripped out of the cement and flew across the room, and Ayres moved into the cell. Rorax could see his exhaustion weighing on his shoulders as unbuckled his belt and held it out to Rorax as he knelt beside the girl.

"Strap her to my back."

No, just run!

"Ayres," Rorax whispered, her voice cracking in panic. "We won't survive. We could be leading her straight to an even more painful death. We don't know if we'll be able to make it out of here. We're going to fail her."

"We can do this, Rorax." His black gaze narrowed. He studied her for a split second as he tossed the belt away and bent down to the child and carefully cradled her in his arms.

They ran out of the fortress together. Rorax slung her knife through the lock on the back gate, and they started to run.

The men that had been stationed in the front of the fortress came around the corner, and arrows started hitting the grass behind them. They ran in zigzags, and Rorax positioned herself between Ayres and the archers until the woods got thicker.

They ducked behind a massive pine tree, and Rorax took the opportunity to stop and breathe, putting her hands on her hips. They were still a five-minute run from where their horses were tied up.

Ayres offered up his hand to her. "Come on."

She stared at it for a beat, two, and then shook her head.

"Get her out, Ayres," Rorax said. "Get her out. I'm going back for the book."

"Rorax, get your ass over here," Ayres growled, his hand still raised in the air toward her.

She shook her head and took a step back. "I have to do this."

Before he could say anything else, she turned and slipped back through the trees toward the tower.

Chapter 59

Ayres

Ayres didn't look back as he sprinted through the forest. The second he was clear of the shield, he'd transferred himself and the little girl back to Karduru, gently shoved her into the nearest person's arms, and transferred back to the edge of the shield. He vomited into the grass, the transfer knocking the wind out of him, but as soon as he could collect himself, he started to run.

Rorax was going to get herself killed.

Rorax was talented. She trained from sunup to sundown almost every single day to be as good as she was. But even she had her limits, and they were about to find out if a castle full of highly trained guards was it.

Ayres ran through puddles of rainwater and long stretches of mud, weaving in and out of tall pine trees and underbrush, until he broke through the clearing of the castle. There was Rorax, sprinting like hell toward him. In her arms, clutched to her chest, was one of Sumavari's books.

There were at least fifty soldiers behind her, running after her.

"Run you fucking bastard, *run*!" she screamed, shoving the book into his arms as she passed.

Kill them, his magick whispered into his mind. The bridge on his back *throbbed* with power, recognizing the book in his arms as *its* own. His power begged to be unleashed, to kill the men running at him, but he wouldn't.

He didn't trust Rorax enough with the information, and he didn't want Kiniera or the new King and Queen of Ice to know that he had such an immense amount of power at his fingertips. He also didn't know if he could stop it, if he could *not* kill her when he unleashed it.

So, Ayres turned and sprinted after Rorax. She was ten paces ahead of him. They ran from the clearing and into the trees, weaving and dodging through the forest as arrows flew at them.

Kill them. The men were nipping at his heels. If they didn't move faster, he wouldn't have a choice.

Then the worst thing imaginable happened. Rorax slipped in the mud and fell to her hands and knees.

She scrambled to stand, and just as Ayres was about to pick her up with his free arm, she looked over her shoulder, swore, and shoved him to the side with a grunt.

Her blood sprayed over his face as an arrow pierced through her shoulder and then another through her side. She fell into him, her body jerking as three more arrows struck.

He picked her up with one arm around her waist, the other under her knees, and started to run. They were only a few minutes from the border of this gods-damned magick force field; once they were across, he could transfer them both to safety.

"Ayres," she coughed. It was nothing but a wet, broken whisper, and his heart lurched.

Kill them, kill them, kill them, his power demanded.

He chanced a glance down at Rorax's face. Her usually golden tan skin was deathly pale, and blood was trickling out of her nose.

Another arrow narrowly missed them and thumped into the soil.

Kill them, kill them, kill them, kill them. The soldiers chasing them were close. They would both die if he didn't do something soon.

Ayres bent and set Rorax and the book down in a patch of long grass against the trunk of a pine tree.

"Hold on, Little Crow," he murmured in her ear. Then he turned to face the men and released the ironclad hold on the gate to his power.

Ayres was not simply Gifted. He had been blessed and cursed with the ultimate power of Death by Marras herself.

He was the Death Harbinger. The magick passed down from his ancestors to him, tasking him with guarding the afterlife and keeping the magick of the bridge between this life and the next life intact. He carried it everywhere he went, as a set of inked lines down his spine, and with it he carried more power in his soul than anyone he'd ever met besides the Guardians. It was hard to control and even harder to stop, and it was indiscriminate with its victims.

The Death Harbinger was a myth, something that had turned into legend that the Sumavari family had kept hidden since Sumavari's War. It was a secret that could prove to be deadly to him if anyone found out what he carried. Heir of Death. That's what he was.

One soldier had stopped a few feet back, his bow and arrow pulled taut as he aimed at Ayres. Ayres's mouth tipped up in cold amusement as the soldier let the arrow fly.

The shot was true and aimed straight for his chest, but right before it hit him, Ayres detonated like a bomb, releasing the latch on his magick.

A sonic wave of red death rushed toward the men, incinerating the arrow and turning the men chasing them into nothing but bloody mist where they stood.

As the red mist floated to the earth, their souls trickled down Ayres's spine—down the bridge and to the afterlife—making him shiver in pleasure. Once the souls passed, he mentally focused in on the castle and plucked out the souls of the Gifted remaining there. Ayres noticed the weight on his own magick lift as the one who had placed the magickal barrier around Helfast passed on.

He felt around, but there were no remaining human souls to take, so instead he shredded through the life of the trees and the grass, felling the mice, bugs, and a small herd of deer.

"Ayres?" a choked, slightly gurgled voice came from behind him, and his power stilled.

He had forgotten about the woman. He could pull the life from plants and animals all he wanted, but there wasn't the same satisfaction in it as ripping out a human life. He had wanted to take her life for a long, long time. Rorax's soul was different than the others though, stronger. It would require focus to pluck her roots away, as if her soul had burrowed in and attached to an anchor he'd need to unravel to release.

Ayres turned to look at her, and his power hesitated. On second thought, maybe it wouldn't be that hard to pluck away her life. She looked minutes away from death. It wouldn't take any effort at all to make her tumble down the bridge now; she had minutes left.

However, something about the female's feeble strength snapped him out of the magick's control, just enough that Ayres could shove his gift back into its cage.

Rorax's hooded snow-white eyes watched him. Her skin was deathly pale, and blood trickled down her front.

"Neat trick," she gurgled, blood dripping from the corner of her mouth. Rorax sucked in a haggard, wet, rattling breath and closed her eyes.

He fell to his knees next to her and cupped her face. "Rorax, open your eyes."

She didn't. "The girl… is she safe?"

"Yes."

Relief seeped into her face, and she cracked her eyes open. "Thank you, Ayres. Find… all the books. Find my brother."

Rorax reached up and touched the edges of his jaw with her cold, blood-soaked fingertips. "I'm… sorry… Surmalinn… the Wolf…. I'm sorry, Ayres."

Her fingers fell away from his face, and she closed her eyes, her breaths shallow and slow, and the presence of her soul lingering at his neck made itself known. She was getting ready to pass on.

Fuck.

Ayres scooped her and the book up off the ground and transferred them back to Karduru, the magical barrier no longer holding them in place. There were healers in Karduru; it was a supply outpost for travelers.

He collapsed to his knees, dumped the book to the side, and laid Rorax on the ground. Rorax's chest had stilled, and her soul was now positioning itself to barrel down into the afterlife.

Two lifeless, snow-white eyes stared up at him, sparkling now even in death.

"RORAX," Ayres bellowed, grasping both sides of Rorax's pale face. "RORAX." He barely even noticed that his hands were covered in blood. He couldn't remember if it was his blood, hers, or the men from the castle.

He shook her roughly, but her head just flopped lifelessly in his hands.

At the top of his spine, Ayres felt the familiar sensation again, the push of her soul wanting to pass to the next life.

His stomach rolled, and Ayres reached back to clamp his fingers to the back of his neck, refusing to let her travel down the bridge.

No. No. Absolutely not.

Ayres looked up desperately and saw the familiar buildings and civilians who were either staring at him or were popping their heads out of their houses to see who was yelling.

"Healer! Healer! She needs a healer!" he roared.

Someone started running toward him, but the man saw her body, all the blood, and froze.

"H-Her wounds... I don't think I'll be able to...."

"Try," Ayres snarled. It was such a feral, lethal sound, the healer flinched away. "I will kill everyone in this useless village in less than thirty seconds if you don't."

The healer looked up into Ayres's glowing red eyes and gulped loudly before he knelt next to Ayres and started to work. Rorax's wounds slowly started to close. Her body was still warm in his arms, but that presence at the top of his neck only got stronger.

His teeth gritted together harder as his anxiety grew. His tattoos glowed, warning him that she was close to the edge. But he kept one hand clamped around his neck and the other gripped the back of her head, pushing whatever power he had left into her to keep her on this side of the veil.

"Come on, Rorax. Stay with me." She would slip down the bridge even without Ayres's permission if she didn't come back within seconds.

Through his focus, he felt someone slide in the gravel next to him. He glanced up and almost wept in relief as he saw the House of Life colors with the fluorescent green lunar month embroidered on the woman next to him.

Her hands started to glow as she pressed them into Rorax's chest. He could barely breathe as he watched and prayed.

Please come back. Please come back, Rorax.

Slowly, ever so slowly, he felt the trickle in his neck disappear.

There was a flash of blinding white light, and with a yelp, the House of Life healer fell back onto her behind.

A hoarse gasp ripped out of Rorax's mouth, and he jerked his gaze down to see two, perfect lips vibrating with breath.

Unbelieving, he looked up into the healer's face, desperately searching for confirmation. When she offered him a small, tired smile, relief made his throat unbearably tight, and he let the hand at the back of his neck fall to cup Rorax's face instead.

The Life worker's skin was pale and covered in sweat, and her hand trembled as she reached up and brushed a piece of hair out of her eyes. "She hadn't crossed over just yet." She gave Ayres a small, knowing smile. "It was like death was refusing her, holding her on this side of the veil."

Another healer had come to kneel next to the first and was working on areas in Rorax's body that Ayres didn't even know needed attention. A wound from where the arrow that had hit the artery in her thigh was closing. She had another wound in her thigh, but that one wasn't bleeding nearly as much. One arrow was still lodged in her stomach.

The second Water healer looked up when he felt Ayres's heavy gaze on him and jerked his head down in a nod. "We obviously need to take that out, but she's almost stable. When she is, we need to move her into the infirmary and look at your wounds, sir."

Ayres snorted as he eyed the second healer, watching as he pulled the arrow from her stomach and focused his energy on the gaping wound. Ayres's wounds were nothing more than shallow cuts and scratches compared to hers.

He couldn't feel them anyway, his relief was too strong as he watched Rorax take another breath. Ayres sent up a silent prayer to Marras and her Ice God, Kään, in blessed thanks—thanks and relief that his savior and his friend had survived.

Chapter 60

Rorax

Rorax was alive, and she was damned angry about it.

Her whole body shuddered in pain as shivers wracked through her. *Again*. Nausea rolled in her stomach, even though she had already emptied it into a chamber pot by her bed at least six times.

She'd successfully gotten the book and even helped save the little girl, but by the time they came out on the other side, apparently, she'd been dead. Or, more accurately, she had stopped breathing. There were only two healers and a Life Healer stationed in Karduru, and between the three of them, they had somehow brought her back.

Rorax shivered again and had to fight a roll of nausea the pain brought with it.

Ayres had been roaring as soon as they touched the ground for a healer to bring her back to her body. It would have been very thoughtful of Ayres if it hadn't left her half alive and in constant agony when she could have been peacefully *dead*. She had to grudgingly admit that, eventually, she would be thankful, but right now she wanted to kill him for it. She had never felt so awful in her life.

A soldier appeared above her, holding out a small bowl of soup.

"I already told you," she snarled up at him, ignoring the soup, "bring me the lieutenant."

The soldier ignored her snarl, since it was nothing more than an angry, raspy whisper, and placed the soup next to her bed. "Can I get you some fresh water?" he asked. Together they eyed an untouched cup of water already next to her bed.

"No. You can bring me the lieutenant's head," she snapped, wincing as she felt the stitches down her side pull painfully and her stomach roiling in complaint.

The soldier snorted and shook his head. He tipped the cup into her mouth, forcing her to drink. "No can do. The lieutenant is out cold, too. Can't strike a man when he's down, but maybe when he wakes up." The soldier winked down at her and set the cup on the table next to the other. She promised herself she would punch the soldier into next week when she got the strength to stand up.

The soldier's eyes grew warm. "You saved her, you know. The kid."

A growl escaped her, and she slowly sat up in bed, her head spinning. She poked the soldier in the chest. "I shouldn't have saved either one of them. Ayres *or* the girl. I could have died." And she would have sacrificed her brother to another lifetime of torment and captivity. If she died, Darras would have no hope of ever being free.

Shame and regret seeped through her. She thought for a moment about walking over to Ayres herself and slitting his throat, but she was already woozy just from sitting, and her stitches probably wouldn't hold. She would most likely bleed out before she even got there.

Accepting her only plan of action, she collapsed back into her bed. Her head was spinning so much she knew she wouldn't make it back to the chamber pot if she threw up again.

The soldier stayed for a moment, mumbling something unintelligible, before walking away and leaving Rorax to slide comfortably back into unconsciousness.

When Rorax woke up the next time, she felt much better. Her head was clearer. Her chest and stomach still ached where the three arrows had struck her, and her thigh still burned, but she no longer felt nausea climbing up her throat relentlessly.

She tucked her fingers under her shirt hem and slid her hand up and across her torso to find where her stitches had been on her stomach and the upper left side ribs. She found only smooth, unblemished skin.

"You're flashing me."

Her head jerked up and around so fast, her neck twinged. Ayres smirked from where he sat lounging in a wooden chair in the corner of the room.

She felt bad for the poor chair legs as she narrowed her eyes at his hulking frame.

In Rorax's exploration of her wounds, her shirt had ridden up to reveal the undersides of her breasts. She didn't bother to cover them as she glowered at him.

Ayres was in a sleeveless shirt he must have been wearing under his armor, and she could see every single muscle in his strong arms as they draped over the back of the chair.

"I am going to kill you," Rorax threatened.

His smirk grew into a grin, and she ignored the way it made her stomach a degree or two warmer.

"I heard from one of the soldiers that when you woke up the first time, you kept saying the only thing that could help you heal from your wounds was my severed head as a decoration on your bedside table."

Rorax finally tugged her shirt down and narrowed her eyes at him. "It's still the only thing that will help."

Ayres tipped his head back and barked out a laugh, making the thin gold chain around his tattooed neck glint in the candlelight. Rorax hungrily eyed his fully exposed neck and the trapezius muscles framing it. Gods, even his throat made her hot. He tipped his smiling face down, and it was so gorgeous it made her feel violent. What was happening here? Why wasn't he glaring and scowling at her? He seemed more relaxed than he'd ever been before. The angry, mistrustful glint in his eyes had softened, just a bit, and the soft feeling in Rorax's chest told her she liked this new development. She liked it a lot.

She turned her head so she wouldn't have to look at him. "Go bother someone else. I'm trying to recover."

She could almost hear his eye roll as he continued to grin at her. "No," he said simply. "Come on, Little Crow. We have things to do today."

Rorax groaned. Her body ached, and as she tried to reach for magick to pull her knife, she didn't have any. "I need more sleep."

"Nope." She heard the chair groan in relief as he stood up and took a few steps toward her bed. He tapped her calf with the back of his hand. "The Guardian has summoned us to the castle. We need to be there in six days."

She grudgingly opened one eye and peeked up at him. "Why?"

"Your next trial, Rorax."

She jerked her head around and looked at him with wide eyes. "What?"

The corner of his lips turned up, and his charcoal eyes were surprisingly warm as he stared down at her. "We've been at camp for a week."

Rorax blinked up at him.

A whole *week* spent asleep. She still felt like freshly chewed meat, she barely had enough strength to summon her knife sitting by her bed, and yet she was expected to participate in a trial? Anxiety pooled in her stomach, and she swallowed, her throat tight. She knew the risks when she'd offered to help Ayres, but to be so unprepared for the next trial left her unsettled.

Ayres sat down on the edge of her bed, but she was so distracted she didn't even think about kicking him off.

"Hey," he murmured, his voice lower and softer than she'd ever heard it. She eyed him warily. "You saved my life." Rorax opened her mouth to growl at him, but he cut her off. "You saved my life, and because of that, I won't let you compete alone and without any help. I'll call for the House of Death's top healer to come give you an overhaul, make sure everything is in the best shape it can be."

"Are...," she croaked. "Are you sure?"

Ayres's lips twitched. "Don't look so surprised. You are my Contestar. It's my job to help you."

She closed her mouth and narrowed her eyes.

Ayres hit her leg with his elbow. "Alright, Little Slug. Go take a shower. I could smell you from two rooms over."

"Little *Slug*?" Rorax grumbled. "I like Little Crow more."

He moved to stand up, but she reached out and gripped his arm.

"What happened... to the little girl?" Rorax's heart gave an uneven thump.

Ayres smiled at her again with that unfamiliar warmth. "She's fine. Her parents are from here, Karduru. They have been reunited."

Rorax let out the breath she'd been holding and sighed quietly in relief. "I expect answers on the ride home about what happened. There is no way I could have survived if we had traveled by ordinary means. If you have enough power to *transfer*, why didn't we just start there?"

Ayres looked down at the hand on his arm. "My magick... the more I feed it, the harder it is to control. It's addicting. And I... I did not want you to know. I did not trust you with the knowledge of just how *much* magick I hold."

"Why?" Rorax eyed him. "Are you the Death Harbinger?"

Ayres rolled his eyes and clucked his tongue impatiently. "The Death Harbinger is a myth, but if it was real, you would need to be part of the ruling family for Marras to give you the gift."

Rorax scoffed and released her grip on his arm to lay back against her pillows. He might not be the Harbinger, but her instincts told her he had even more magick than he'd shown her. "It's a gods-damned miracle I haven't slaughtered you in your sleep yet."

The corner of Ayres's mouth pushed up. "It's not too late."

CHAPTER 61

AYRES

Ayres studied Rorax from over the firepit as he twirled a branch in his hands. She was curled up with her back against the tree, her sleeping roll pulled up and tucked under her chin. Ayres couldn't help but think she looked small and vulnerable bundled up like that, but she also looked calm and serene, the gold of the flames highlighting her features, making them look soft and warm.

The memory of Rorax's panicked eyes in the dungeon of Helfast flashed in his mind again, for the hundredth time that day. Even in the most pressing of situations, during their initial battle, or when Narlaroca almost scalped her during the Tournament of Houses, he didn't think he'd seen any emotion on Rorax's features except unflappable confidence, bloodlust, or the easy comfort that currently graced her features now. The fear, uncertainty, and panic she'd displayed before getting the little girl out was so confusing and foreign, it still unsettled him. He couldn't shake the image away.

It was their first night out of Karduru, and they'd stopped early for the night. Ayres had caught Rorax sliding off her horse from exhaustion, and after she had fallen to the ground trying to get off her horse again, he'd forced her to sit and rest while he made the fire and set up camp.

"Before we arrived at Helfast, I was staring at you. You're the one staring at me now, Lieutenant," Rorax said, not bothering to move her colorless eyes from the burning coals of the fire between them.

"How are you feeling? Are you okay?"

Rorax huffed a laugh. "I had no idea you had a single sympathetic bone in your whole gods-damned body."

"You'd be surprised."

"I doubt it."

Ayres rolled his eyes but then became serious.

"Why didn't you want to save her? The girl? I've never seen you look so. . . *distraught* before."

Rorax was quiet for so long he didn't think she was going to answer him.

"I don't... I don't think I've ever saved anyone before. Never rescued anyone. Not on a mission like that." Rorax bit the inside of her cheek and sucked in a deep breath, as if the words weighed on her. "The Wolf never let me attend missions where we extracted hostages. Looking back at my time under her command, I was only allowed to attend assassinations or coups. I think it was part of her programming for me. It desensitized me toward death. I was even more violent, angry, and cruel than I am today. That day in the courtyard in Surmalinn was the first day I decided I didn't want to *hurt* anyone who didn't deserve it anymore."

Ayres cocked his head at her, narrowing his eyes. "You had to *decide* that?"

Rorax took another deep breath and looked up into the dark, starry sky. "Most of the time, I just want to let my control go. I *want* to brutalize anything and anyone in my way. I know I could take what I want by force. Sometimes I just want to stop trying so hard to be good and decent, especially when it's so much easier—more natural—to... not be." Rorax let out a heavy sigh and bowed her head, this time studying the broken sticks and dried pine needles at her feet.

Ayres's shoulders tightened. "You like killing?"

"No," she blurted too fast before she let out a small, defeated sigh. "And yes. It's powerful. Sometimes it feels like the ultimate victory, the ultimate power to stand above someone and take their life. I think what I like most is the recognition, to know that my prey knows who I am. I demand their respect and their fear."

A little shiver ran through her shoulders, and Ayres gripped the branch a little tighter between his hands, the bark rough under his skin. He suddenly had an urge to tell her how good killing had started to feel to him as well, how addictive it had become to use his power. He wanted to tell her how he had to fight the little roll of pleasure he got when souls ran down the bridge on his back, the release he felt when the life in their eyes faded and their souls moved through him and into the afterlife. He wanted to say those words so desperately, to admit them out loud to someone who so clearly understood. Instead, they stayed stuck on his tongue, making the muscle feel thick and useless in his mouth.

"But I know that feeling, that power"—Rorax looked up into Ayres's eyes, the clear white irises unguarded and honest—"it's not what makes me happy. It is a hollow victory, and it doesn't ever last."

Gods, how well he knew that.

She swallowed, rolling her shoulders, and looked back at the dark trees. The loss of that connection made Ayres resist the urge to go over to her, to grip her face into his hands and force her to look at him. "Love lasts, family lasts. So I chose that. I want that. A family." A tear rolled down her cheek. "A real one."

Ayres didn't say anything; he couldn't. She'd shocked him, repeating back to him almost the same inner thoughts, feelings, and battles that plagued him.

"That's what stopped me that night. In Surmalinn." She angrily scrubbed the tears off her cheeks. "One of your queen's idiotic family members begged me to save her life, but not his own. It reminded me of when it was my own brother begging for *my* life when Lyondrea kidnapped him. One of my only memories of my brother was when he told me to hide, and the soldiers looking for him beat him into a bloody pulp and dragged him away. I could have been dragged away with him, but Darras protected me." She scrubbed away more tears. "At that moment, the queen's brother, begging for his sister's life, sounded just like him. I decided that night I didn't want to fight to conquer. I want to fight to deserve Darras's sacrifice. I want to fight for love, for freedom, for family. The influx reminded me of how close I came to breaking, of who I would have become, who I was before that moment." She closed her eyes, and her head hung a little.

Conrad. The *idiotic* brother that had convinced Rorax to save his sister's life. Ayres had three brothers, the two others had been with him when the Siege occurred, so Ayres had no idea that Conrad had played such a huge role.

Ayres's mouth felt like it was made of sandpaper, but he forced himself to ask, "What did you do after you saved the queen?"

Her face hardened, but she opened her eyes and raised her head again. "I told my commander to leave the city. I told him that if he harmed one more civilian or soldier, I would rip his heart out and use his last moments to make him watch me eat it."

"Gods," he muttered. The tiny seed of respect he had for Rorax grew roots deeper in his chest.

"Then I confronted the Wolf in Surmalinn's town square." Rorax swallowed. "I killed her there. I killed the only woman I had ever known as a mother. Then it was over."

"*Mother*." The word rattled something in him. "The Wolf was that important to you?"

"She found me. Pulled me off the streets. House of Ice has a social program where orphans are enrolled in a Warrior Program. They are taught to fight and how to be soldiers to eventually work for House of Ice. She took me to them for a few years before she recruited me as her own."

Rorax paused for a second, then grimly said, "You need to know, Lieutenant, that I am a product of hers. The Wolf. Every single skill, all my control, everything I am, she sculpted. She molded me day in and day out until everything she saw in me was perfectly honed. I was built to be her weapon. To help her be a conqueror. To kill."

Rorax looked up at him, almost begging him to see her. To see into the darkest part of her, to see the influence of the woman he hated most in the world, to see the parts that he could have decided were too heavy, too painful to bear. She wanted him to understand all of her. And he did. And it frightened him.

He saw so deep inside of her that he saw parts of himself looking back from within her. Parts he had buried and locked so deep inside he hadn't even admitted it to himself yet. Not really.

"I understand, Rorax." More than she would ever know.

He tried to ignore the sharp breath she took as he stood, turned, and walked into the forest.

"I'm going to leave horse shit on your pillow every night for a week," Rorax grumbled.

"How thoughtful," Ayres playfully said back. "I love the scent of fresh manure first thing in the morning."

"You would."

Ayres bit his tongue, desperately trying not to laugh.

Rorax was stiff, uncomfortable, and still in pain from her injuries after being on the road for nearly a week. Every jostle from her horse had Rorax mumbling something like, "I'm gonna spit in his milk" or "I'm gonna stab him in his sleep for not letting me die."

Something about her being so grumpy made his spirits soar. Her little empty threats were strangely endearing, and with every teasing grumble he wanted to chuckle. She was cute when she was hurt and ornery.

It was late, almost midnight, and only a few guards were on duty to watch them as they brought their horses in through the gate. They took a sharp left once they were inside the bailey, toward the stables.

Ayres dismounted his horse, feeling the weight of her snowy gaze as he started to undo the bridle of his horse. She cleared her throat, and he turned around to see her cheeks going pink. He raised an eyebrow at her, and she gripped the leather reins in her hand a little harder.

"Lieutenant, will you... help me down again? Please?" she mumbled, keeping her eyes down on the leather reins she squeezed in her hand. "My thigh... I just don't want to fall into the shit."

Rorax had fallen when dismounting her horse three times already on the way here; her leg that had been struck with two arrows kept collapsing underneath her as she dismounted, the muscle too injured to support her weight on the way down.

Ayres eyed the flush on her cheeks, and something in his chest warmed further. "Of course."

He walked over and palmed one of her muscular thighs as she grasped the pommel and slid her other leg over her horse. He gingerly cupped the thigh that was still covered in gauze from where she had taken an arrow and slowly lowered her to the ground.

Ayres straightened, but for some gods-damned reason, he kept his hands on her, letting his fingertips trail over the leather on the back of her thighs... up... up... up, until they were inches from the rounded curve of her ass. He pulled his hands away from her slowly, using every fragment of his self-control not to knead his hands into the round muscle there.

"Thank you," she murmured, turning gingerly around to face him, before he could manage to take a step back from her.

Rorax's face was only inches from his, and the space between them suddenly felt electric. Ayres could see the tiny freckles sprinkled over her nose, over the tan skin of her face, and he could see the tiny sparkles in the white of her irises as her eyes darted down to look at his mouth before flitting back up to his eyes.

I have to fight every day to be good. He had never met a woman that had made him feel so seen before, and she hadn't even meant to.

"Are you okay?" he asked softly. His eyes flickered down to her mouth in return. Her lips were pillowy and pink; she held them just slightly apart, just open enough that he could slide his tongue between them. Marras save him, he couldn't remember ever wanting to taste anything more in his life. The kiss they had shared during her influx had consumed him for weeks, and he wanted *more.* So much fucking more he wanted it all. She had heated his blood to the point where he felt like he was going to come apart at the seams. Why was it that the one woman he should hate the most in the world was so fucking beautiful? The gods were playing with him, surely.

He forced his eyes back to hers, and what he saw there pulled his self-control so thin it threatened to snap like a worn thread.

"Yeah," she whispered, and he felt her breath against his lips. "I'm okay."

Ayres wondered what it would be like to feel her under him without them fighting an influx.

With his other hand, he started to reach down to her hip and was just about to pull her against him, so he could feel her completely, to feel how alive—how *hot* she was for him—when the stable doors slammed open.

Cannon, Piers, and Kaiya stormed inside the stable. All three of them froze solid when they saw Ayres and Rorax, all with varying degrees of shock.

"Marras save us," Kaiya growled.

Rorax stepped away from Ayres, her cheeks flushing, and Ayres had to reach up and grip the pommel of her saddle to keep his hands steady, to keep him from reaching out to snatch her back. Or to keep himself from punching Kaiya—Ayres didn't know which.

Something like cold water zipped down his spine. Ayres knew this kind of involvement with Rorax would be extremely complicated, but reality hit him as he looked at the shock and anger on his friends' faces.

What happened out there? Cannon signed, looking pissed off. ***We felt the tiny ripple and then the surge. We didn't hear back from you besides that shitty little bird that said you were alive.***

"We were worried," Kaiya snapped, folding her arms over her chest, shooting an accusatory glare at Rorax who just raised her chin slightly back.

"Stand down," Ayres bit at Kaiya. "Rorax was the one who got the book out. There were more men there than I originally thought. Way too many for two people. And I… took care of it."

Kaiya slid her narrowed eyes to Ayres. "Can I speak with you? Privately?"

Ayres rolled his jaw, *no* dancing on his lips, but instead he nodded. He turned to Rorax, whose cheeks were still pink. "Go to the Healer's Hall. Get them to work out whatever they missed in Karduru. I'll take care of the horses."

She hesitated, as if she wanted to say something, but then nodded once before turning away from him.

He moved over to his saddlebags, fished out one of Sumavari's books, which he'd wrapped in a white linen cloth back at camp, and handed it to Cannon. "Book five. Get this to the queen."

Cannon took it, and Piers came up to clasp Ayres on the shoulder. "I'm just glad you guys made it back. Both of you." He nodded toward where Rorax was walking away, then left Ayres alone with Kaiya, whose eyes were blazing.

As soon as the stable doors closed behind them, Kaiya waved her hand to where Ayres had almost kissed Rorax. "What the *fuck* was that?"

Ayres gritted his teeth. He didn't owe Kaiya an explanation. "What was what?"

"Are you and the Spine Cleaver *lovers* now? Are you going to let the *Pup* become the Guardian just because she has a nice ass and blinks her pretty fucking eyes at you?" she snarled, and Ayres's temper flared, remembering how Rorax had shoved him out of the way, taking four arrows for him.

"The House of Death would *never* accept her as the Guardian," Kaiya continued. "Not after what happened in Surmalinn. It makes me *sick*—"

"Stop." Ayres took a breath in, pinching the bridge of his nose between his thumb and forefinger, forcing himself to calm down. "Kaiya. Step back."

"What happened out there to justify *that*?" she hissed back.

"She saved my life. She saved a little girl's life. She got the book out *single-handedly*," Ayres rattled off. "And with her dying breath, she said that she was *sorry*."

Kaiya's brows knitted together. "Her dying breath?"

"She died, Kaiya. For nearly three minutes, after taking arrows for *me*, after saving my *life*." Ayres blew out a breath and rubbed his hand over his short hair. "She went back and got that fucking book out by herself."

"Was it a setup?" Kaiya asked, suspicion dancing in her eyes. "Did she orchestrate it to be like that?"

Doubt flared through him for a half second before it was replaced with a twinge of guilt.

"She died. Her last words were *'I'm sorry,'* and she was furious when she found out she was still alive." Ayres shook his head, knowing with every fiber of his being she had given her heart and soul to make sure they got the book back, to make sure *he* survived to keep up the work. "She had nothing to do with it; be careful not to ask again while you're in front of her."

Kaiya's doubts still burned in her eyes, but she slowly nodded her acceptance, trusting Ayres.

"Enna is progressing swiftly. She has a good heart. She's fierce, and she would be a better fit for the Guardian. For all the Realms," Kaiya said.

Something flickered on Kaiya's face, something Ayres couldn't identify, but he nodded anyway. "I'll come watch her this afternoon."

Kaiya nodded back at him, then slowly pushed open the double doors and walked out. Ayres stood in the stable for a few moments, wondering what the fuck was happening to him.

Chapter 62

Raengar

Raengar slid off the back of Deimos, dropping down onto the moss-covered stones below.

It was nearly midnight in Luxamal, the City of Poisons, but as he stepped to the edge of the landing platform and looked over, he could still make out the outline of the buildings in the city with the witch-lights and torches that illuminated the night sky.

Luxamal, one of the largest cities in the House of Foliage and home to the largest universities, was made up of numerous blocky, stone pyramids. Raengar had been there only once before, while his father had still been king. The university was infamous for not only its poisons but for its recreational drugs, and his first experience in the city had not disappointed him. Rorax had been with him, and they had tried one of the many exotic blends for the first time together. The memory made his chest ache. He had been receiving constant updates from Kiniera about how she was doing and her progress in the trials, but he was still worried.

"Welcome to Luxamal, Your Grace."

Raengar turned to find one of the female acolytes of the university, wearing a long moss-colored robe, standing behind him, eyeing Deimos carefully. Upon further inspection, the robe wasn't just moss colored; it *was* moss—a thick, dark green moss that wrapped over her. A thick braid of golden threads draped like a sash across her body, marking her as one of the high acolytes of the university. He had worked with her before, and he hoped she could help him now.

"I received your letter; I assume your journey went well," she said, her voice cold and her shoulders and back as stiff as a rod.

Raengar turned to face her. "You're still the one who heads the Luxamal Division of Poisons?"

The acolyte nodded slowly, but she was wringing her hands. "You said in your letter that this matter was of the utmost importance."

"It is. In fact, it's a matter of national security." Raengar pulled the four vials Jia had given him from the inside pocket of his cloak and held them out to the woman who made no move to take them. "Test these. There is a blocker in the blood, Waterlily Rine. I think it was made in this school and used against my soldiers."

The acolyte sucked in a breath and wrung her hands harder as she looked up at him with wide, terrified eyes. "Your Grace, I would... I would never have approved such a thing."

Raengar didn't need her to be any more terrified of him than she already was, so he tried to soften his expression. "I know. But I need to know who did. If it was the King of Alloy, this could provide the evidence we need to convict him in his upcoming trial."

The fear in her eyes dissipated and instead the acolyte eyed him warily. "I knew your father. I knew King Katalon. He came to visit me on many occasions, perched on this very same dragon, demanding poisons to kill his enemies."

The acolyte moved her attention to his dragon, who was watching them both with one lazy electric blue eye, and Raengar felt his blood pressure rise. "I am not my father."

"And yet they call you the Butcher King."

"Ah yes, the Butcher King. The people do whisper that name around their dinner tables and in their halls." Raengar took a step closer, giving the acolyte a poisonous smile. "But I could not have become the Butcher King without help. If I remember correctly, my sister was the one who procured the poison that helped kill my father. I wonder where it originated from. Under the Guardians' Laws, it is illegal to aid and abet in the killing of a king."

The acolyte's face went pale, and her mouth tightened into a frown. "You would implicate yourself with this."

"You must not have heard many rumors about me if you thought I wouldn't rather rot in jail than let *King Määr of Alloy* rule another day." Raengar smiled, but it was not kind.

The acolyte nodded hesitantly. "Despite my... reservations, I do believe we are on the same side, My Lord. The King of Alloy has proven to be a dangerous enemy to the free people of the Realms. I will find what we need."

"Good." Raengar handed the vials over to her before stepping around Deimos's side gently reaching up to unhook a cast iron cage that held a beautiful, azure blue hawk, its head tucked into his wing.

The acolyte gasped in girlish delight, pressing her empty hand to her chest. "I... I have never seen a Blood Hawk in person before, My Lord."

Raengar smiled softly as he reached into the cage and rustled the feathers of the hawk, who lazily peaked its head up at him. "This bird is named Gawain. Give me your hand."

The acolyte moved her hand from her chest out toward the bird. Raengar gently wrapped his fingers around the woman's wrist and brought her closer to the bird. "This might sting."

To the acolyte's credit, she didn't so much as flinch when the bird reached out and bit her finger with its long, deep blue beak and ran its slimy black tongue over the injury, tasting the magick in the woman's blood.

When the hawk looked up at Raengar and then lazily buried its head in its wing once more, Raengar held out the cage to the woman.

"This hawk is blood-bonded to me. He'll always be able to find me wherever I am, and he will not release the message to anyone but me."

"My Lord... but why did you have it taste my blood?"

"Because now, on my command, when I send *you* messages, he will release the message to you and only you."

The acolyte's eyes went wide with wonder, and she held the cage up slightly closer to her face. "Let us pray that this bird carries nothing but the best of news, then."

Chapter 63

Rorax

Two days after returning to the castle, and two days before the next trial was scheduled to start, Rorax found herself standing in the courtyard, her jaw twitching as Isgra's ass hit the ground with a string of loud curses. Again.

Captain Lamonte was attempting to teach Isgra how to use a round, wooden shield to block an oncoming spear while still managing to swing the shield and slam her opponent.

Rorax had seen Volla struggle with the exact sequences, and she'd had the very same elbow dip when trying to flip an opponent on his or her back. Rorax knew exactly what Isgra needed to change to help her.

It set her teeth on edge.

Isgra didn't deserve her help, her guidance. But she would have instantly helped Volla to her feet, telling her where she went wrong.

The same way Volla would have helped Rorax.

Rorax clinched her jaw as Isgra hit the mat again. Seething up at Captain Lamonte like a hissing cat, Isgra grumbled, "This is a fucking waste of time. We don't even *need* that sequence."

Rorax had to bite her tongue to keep the snort back. She didn't normally carry a shield during her missions, but when one was available, it was rare if she didn't use the technique at least once a fight.

Lamonte just shrugged down to Isgra, who hadn't yet moved to get off her ass. "The Guardian laid out yer training programs, no' me."

Isgra got up again but did the same thing seconds later.

Jia, who was standing next to Rorax, pressed her lips together and tried not to smirk at Isgra's grumbling.

Isgra pushed up onto her feet, but she stayed bent over, clasping her hands on her knees. She was breathing like a dragon. And Rorax knew, she *knew*, she shouldn't say anything to Isgra. But she had to try. For Volla.

Rorax took a hesitant step forward. "Isgra listen, Volla used to struggle with the exact same move. If you let me, I'll show you how our trainer at the time taught her to fix it."

Isgra's cheeks turned pink, and she straightened up quickly, her hands clenched. "Do not *ever* compare me with that bitch again." Then she sucker punched Rorax in the face.

Rorax jerked back, but Isgra's fist still smashed against her lips and teeth, splitting Rorax's upper lip open and sending blood down her chin.

Rorax stepped away as blood started to fill her mouth.

Instinctively, she reached up to grab a knife out of her hair. The second she pulled the knife out, hands like iron manacles clamped down around her wrists and wretched her back. Rorax turned her head to see Ayres holding her arms as he jerked her further away from Isgra.

Jia and Cannon filled the spots in her peripheral vision as they flanked her and Ayres on either side. No one else in the courtyard moved, but Rorax felt heavy gazes on her.

"Rorax, if you throw that fucking knife and you kill her, you die," Ayres growled low in her ear, gripping her fist still clamped around the hilt of the knife. "If she needs to die today, give the word. But *you* can't kill her."

Something warm lit in her heart at his words, even as she bared her bloody teeth at Isgra. "What the *fuck* is your problem?"

"My problem is that you and that whore," she seethed, pointing to Jia with a shaking finger, "keep looking at me with puppy dog eyes, and I'm done. It's pathetic."

Ayres's hand wrapped tighter around her own, but Rorax kept her mouth closed.

Isgra looked over the blood on Rorax's face with smug satisfaction, her eyes still hungry for violence. "Do not ever mention that filthy name to me again. She was honorless, worthless; everything she ever did she fucked up. Her death was the best thing that happened to me and my family. They were smart to have sold her to the House of Ice the moment she was born."

Rorax's hand twitched, and Ayres gripped her tighter.

Rorax decided right then she would be happy to trade her firstborn child for the opportunity to wrap her bare hands around Isgra's neck, to squeeze every drop of life out of her. It would be *incredibly* satisfying.

Rorax's chest radiated with anger; her jaw clenched so hard her teeth threatened to crack. If Ayres had not been actively restraining her, she would have plunged her knife into Isgra's chest and carved out her heart.

She spit blood into the dirt between them before smiling wide at Isgra. Isgra flinched slightly and took a step away from Rorax, seeing the blood that coated the enamel of her teeth.

Rorax could only hope she looked as unhinged as she felt.

"Volla was better than you. At everything. The gods chose the wrong sister when they chose you for the Choosing." Rorax cocked her head, watching smugly as Isgra's face paled. The blow felt good, but it wasn't enough. "Enjoy the next few weeks of your life, Isgra, before you either *get* killed or *I* kill you. Either way, you won't be leaving here alive. I promise."

Isgra swallowed hard, but her eyes started to glitter dangerously. "You don't know *anything* about my sister. She *abandoned* us. *Left* us."

"You just said your family, the Torviks, *sold* her," Rorax bit out.

"She was strong, had training; she could have come back," Isgra hissed. "But she didn't. Our older brother Fiske died in the war, and my parents *fell apart,* and I…." Her throat worked furiously. "I was left alone to grieve, to pick up the pieces. She *never* came back."

Something uncomfortable and hot rolled through Rorax. Volla had talked about inviting her older brother to her wedding not three months ago. "Isgra, Volla didn't even know your brother was dead."

"I don't trust a word that comes out of your filthy fucking mouth." Isgra spit on the tiles at Rorax's feet and took a threatening step toward her. "I've heard some interesting rumors about you, Rorax. Rumor is you're fucking both the prince and his lieutenant at the same time. A little bird told me the only reason the House of Death chose you to be their Contestar was because you're nothing but a *whore.*"

The huge hand moved from Rorax's wrist and clapped around her shoulder, dragging her back a few more steps as Ayres shoved her behind him. Rorax allowed him to move her, but peeked around Ayres's shoulder to see. The look he gave Isgra sent chills down Rorax's spine.

The promise of death sat naked in his silver eyes, the muscles in his jaw jumping, as he bent down to get in her face. "Say one more word, Torvik, and I promise you will regret it."

Rorax must have broken Isgra's self-preservation when she broke Isgra's nose the last time, because Isgra narrowed her eyes up at Ayres and sneered, nasty and spiteful, "Was it really that good, Lieutenant? I've heard rumors about your conquests, and I have a hard time believing that scum"—she pointed to Rorax—"is really *that* talented."

Ayres growled, low and furious, and it sent chills running down Rorax's back. In all the months of training with Ayres, she had never once heard him make a sound like that. Not even after she had stabbed him, and not even when they'd almost died infiltrating the castle.

"Ayres," Rorax warned, but he let go of Rorax and stepped toward Isgra, so he was only feet away from her. His whole body trembled with the effort to keep his temper in check.

"Ayres, step back." Rorax reached out and feathered her fingertips down his arm before gripping his trembling wrist. Isgra was an idiot, but she didn't deserve to die—not yet at least.

She tried to pull him back, but he took another step forward, pulling Rorax with him. The energy in the courtyard crackled with danger.

Rorax glanced over her shoulder to see everyone staring at them. The livid expression on Lamonte's face made it seem like he wouldn't mind watching Isgra die today. In fact, no one looked worried on the Contestar's behalf. The look on Kiniera's face made it clear that if Ayres didn't kill her, she might.

Ayres took another step closer to Isgra. "Torvik, if you so much as give Rorax another *frown*, I will tear your head off your shoulders. You might not have a twin sister or a brother anymore, but you have another sister and two parents that are *very* much alive." He gave her a violent look that sent another shiver across Rorax's shoulders.

Isgra sucked in a breath, and all the blood seemed to drain from her face as her gaze flickered to Rorax and then back to Ayres.

There was a beat of heavy silence before Isgra turned tail and hustled back into the keep without another word.

Even when people in the courtyard started reluctantly milling around again and Lamonte called for the next Contestar pair to step into the ring, Rorax still felt eyes burning into her.

Ayres's chest was heaving, and his fists were still clenched at his sides. He was so angry, she could swear the evening air seemed to be steaming off his back.

But her? She wasn't angry anymore. Isgra wasn't worth it. No, she was still mentally processing Lieutenant Jackass defending her. She liked it.

Her knees felt a little weak and her heart a little heavy. She had never expected anyone from the House of Death to ever stand up for her.

"Ayres?" Rorax asked, her voice quiet and a little shaky.

He didn't answer, just slowly turned his head to the side to stare down at her, still angry.

Rorax rubbed her thumb over her ring, trying to blink away her tears. "Thank you," she croaked. "And I'm sorry. You shouldn't have had to.... That was nasty." She looked away from him, wanting to say something else, but her chin trembled. She didn't trust herself to speak.

"Ror, don't," Ayres ground out as he slowly wrapped one of his arms around her shoulders. He pulled her into him, forcing her to stumble face-first into his chest.

His other arm came to the back of her head and gently pressed her face a little closer to his chest. After a moment, she leaned into him, wrapping her arms around his waist, too.

She didn't know what was happening. Lieutenant Jackass was *hugging* her.

The grief for the loss of her best friend and her commander she'd held at bay suddenly felt heavy, like an unbearable weight she could no longer carry on her own. So, she leaned into Ayres a little more.

Kään help her, it felt good to know Ayres thought she was worth defending. To know Ayres thought she might have some potential, that she had enough goodness, kindness, and value in her *worth* defending, despite knowing the worst thing she had ever done.

Damn. She was going to cry.

Rorax breathed in his clean scent and his strength, then bit the inside of her cheek hard and pulled away from him.

Ayres stared down at her, his eyes searching her face. Whatever he found there made a shadow cross over his face. "Are you okay?"

She wiped her eyes before any more tears could escape and offered him a watery smile. "Yes...." She paused. "I will be."

His dark gaze traced her face, and a little zing of electricity danced down and coiled around her nipples like it had in the stables two days ago before they'd been interrupted. She stepped out of his reach before she decided to run her hands over his chest or say anything she shouldn't. "Thank you again... Ayres."

He blinked down at her, like his actions surprised even him. Or maybe it was because she had finally used his first name. "You're welcome."

CHAPTER 64

RORAX

Rorax's eyes flew open, her mind lurching violently from sleep.

She was in her room, the night before the next trial, and someone was picking her lock.

If it was Jia, Rorax would already have a knife to her throat. If it was Narlaroca, then Narlaroca would be dead in moments. If it was Ayres or his guard... Kään help her, they were about to learn something tonight.

Rorax grabbed the knife she kept on her nightstand and nimbly rolled out from beneath her covers. The plain knife didn't pulse, warming her palm like Glimr would have. But Glimr was in the black salt chest in Ayres's room.

She padded silently to crouch behind the door, and eventually the lock unlatched and the door swung open. A woman's head with a familiar set of white-blonde braids peeked in, and then a lean body stepped through the doorway, taking a few stealthy steps closer to Rorax's bed.

Why the fuck didn't she just knock? Ayres, the prince, and his guards were all going to give her a raging migraine.

Rorax waited for a breath to see if anyone else walked in, and when she didn't sense anyone, Rorax silently padded behind Kaiya who was now at the foot of her bed. She reached around and pressed the flat edge of the knife against the smooth dark skin over Kaiya's throat.

"That's a kill," she hummed into Kaiya's ear. The woman jerked slightly in her arms and let out a low growl.

Rorax was just releasing Kaiya, removing her knife from Kaiya's throat, and stepping away when someone grabbed her wrist. She was yanked back a step, and a warm band as thick as an anaconda wrapped around her throat.

"That's a kill," Ayres growled down into her ear, his thickly muscled forearm pressed against her throat. He could have crushed her windpipe if he really wanted to.

She smirked at him. "Touché."

Ayres didn't look amused as he moved his arm from her neck, his dark eyes glittering dangerously as he glowered down at her. "Get ready to go. We're leaving in twenty minutes. We have the location for the next book; there was a small pull on the ley line. We don't need everyone, so I'm leaving Jia and the prince here. It's a day and a half's ride west of here," he said quietly.

Their bodies were so close, she could feel the heat from his skin permeate her bones. She remembered the hug he'd given her earlier, remembered how his hard chest felt under her cheek.

She had to shake her head. *Focus. The trials.*

"Can I leave?" She wrinkled her nose up at him. "The next trial is tomorrow."

"We got word they're postponing the trial." His jaw worked as he stared down at her. "House of Ice needs their dragons back to help transport troops. Death needs those troops to reach their destination, so we need to stay out of their way."

The trial was postponed? Due to Ice-troop movements? Why hadn't she heard anything about it?

"Rorax," Ayres clipped, pressing slightly into her, his voice low. "I don't think you heard me. Get ready—"

"We are leaving in twenty minutes," she clipped back.

His jaw worked as he looked from one of her snowy white eyes to the other, and she couldn't help it. He was too close. Too hot. Just like he'd been in the stables, when he had pulled her closer and all she had wanted to do was arch up and—

Just before she would have done something incredibly stupid, dark fingers reached around and grabbed Ayres's shoulder, yanking him back a step and breaking apart the tension.

"Come on," Kaiya snapped, giving them both a dark look before leaving the room.

Ayres blinked down at Rorax, and she felt a light blush cover her cheeks. She'd forgotten the woman was even in the room. She was getting soft.

"Twenty minutes, Rorax. We'll meet you down in the stables."

Twenty minutes later, Rorax met Cannon, Kaiya, and Ayres outside.

Kaiya was in a dark mood, and it seemed like the lieutenant was too, so the four of them rode together in almost complete silence for over a day, stopping only briefly to rest the horses, take care of their basic needs, and steal a couple hours of sleep. Ayres took the lead, directing them to where the next book was supposed to be located. When they reached their destination, they reined in their horses a distance away and crept on foot the rest of the way.

Ayres's appraisal had been correct this time. Only fifteen soldiers were at the makeshift camp, and several of them huddled around the book, reading through it, trying to figure out how to summon and command Sumavari's fucking monsters.

Ayres signaled for them to spread out, then gave the signal to attack. Rorax decapitated five of the soldiers before they even knew what was happening. Glimr seemed almost gleeful to be out of the black salt box and sang through the air at Rorax's command.

Kaiya, Cannon, and Ayres swiftly handled the rest of the soldiers.

During the battle, the book had fallen into a puddle of blood next to a dead soldier. It hummed happily in Rorax's hands when she picked it up.

Not caring that the book was dripping with blood, she shoved it into Ayres's chest, splattering the blood across his armor. "These books give me the creeps."

"Me, too." Kaiya grimaced at it as Ayres bent down to slip it into his bag. "They always make me shiver whenever I see them."

Cannon stood apart from the group, hands on his hips, his attention down on his feet. He looked troubled.

Rorax tapped her foot three times on the ground to get his attention.

Cannon looked up at her, his mouth pinched tight, when a roar—a painfully familiar-sounding roar—erupted in the woods behind them.

"*Motherfucker*," Rorax hissed, and Cannon's face went white.

A troll? he asked.

Rorax nodded and turned to Kaiya, who already had her battle-ax in her hand. Ayres was just pulling the backpack onto his shoulders. She used her hands to furiously sign at them as she talked. "That's a mountain troll. We need to run."

They nodded but made it only a few steps before the troll burst through the trees. It looked the same as its counterparts had during the trial—big, muscled, apelike with six eyes that ran in two rows back toward its ears. A black stone glittered on the troll's forehead, and Rorax wanted to scream. An obsidian circlet.

The troll had a sharp stick—a handmade spear—clutched in its hand that it raised above its head.

Then it lunged at Kaiya.

Cannon was there, shoving Kaiya out of the way, and the troll's makeshift spear went straight through his right shoulder and pinned him into the ground.

"Cannon!" Kaiya shrieked, fear and panic raising her voice. She scrambled to her feet and swung her battle-ax at the troll. It scrambled back to avoid the wicked edge.

Ayres's tattoos lit up, but the troll's obsidian circlet was still in place. It wouldn't do any good, not even from him.

"Ayres," Rorax snapped out, and his bright-red gaze locked with hers. "The obsidian circlet. It has to be cut before magick will work. Give me your belt. Transport Kaiya, Cannon, and the book away." Her gaze moved to the giant troll, who was swinging at Kaiya while barely dancing out of reach of her battle-ax. "I'll kill the troll."

"My belt?" he snarled.

"Now!" she snapped again as the troll took advantage of Kaiya's slowing limbs, backhanding her hard enough to send her skidding across the forest floor. With nimble fingers, Ayres whipped his belt off and pressed it into her waiting palm.

"Rorax, wait—" Ayres hissed, but she didn't have time to argue, and neither did Cannon.

She sprinted toward the troll, who had abandoned Kaiya and was moving toward Cannon. He struggled in vain against the wooden spear pinning him to the ground.

The troll raised its huge, muscular, fur-covered arm and made a fist with its hand, ready to crush Cannon's skull, when Rorax lunged.

She slammed into it and wrapped her legs and arms around the troll's arm. The momentum made them both topple over, the troll hitting the earth with a loud crash.

The troll pushed itself up on one elbow, but it was slower than Rorax, who had already gotten to her feet. The troll's head was at the same level as her hip from this position, and she took advantage to land a roundhouse kick right into its face.

One of the troll's eyes ruptured under her boot, and blood squirted out from the destroyed socket.

The troll roared in agonizing pain, pushing itself to its feet, one hand covering the side of its head where the bloody hole was.

It saw Rorax and bellowed an angry roar right in her face. She took a step back.

Out of her peripheral vision, she saw Ayres yank the spear out of the earth and out of Cannon's shoulder. The troll must have noticed, too, from one of its five other good eyes. It started to turn its big, ugly head toward them, but Rorax took Ayres's belt and cracked it like a whip against the troll's chest.

Immediately she had the troll's entire attention.

"Fuck," she muttered as the troll threw its head back in an angry roar before lunging at her.

He missed, but only by inches, as Rorax turned and *ran*. She ducked behind a tree, barely missing another blow. Then another, then another as she ducked, dodged, and rolled under the troll's sweeping, lethal arms. She brought the troll farther and farther into the pine trees, away from Ayres, the book, Kaiya, and Cannon.

The troll picked up a giant, club-like stick from the ground and started to swing it violently.

Sliding to her knees, she ducked under the troll's waving club.

As soon as it passed her overhead, she lunged to her feet, pivoted around, and sprang onto the troll's back.

The troll roared in savage fury as she wrapped her left arm around its throat and used her right hand to slice her knife across the troll's forehead, straight across the troll's obsidian circlet.

The troll roared again, this time in pain, and it reached back, grabbed Rorax's shoulder in its massive hand, and hurled her forward off his back.

Rorax flew. She made it at least fifteen feet before she landed hard on her shoulder. She tried to roll forward to lessen the impact, but something in her chest snapped, and she couldn't hold in an agonized cry of pain as her clavicle bone snapped in two.

Rorax struggled to her knees, glaring over at the troll who was wiping uselessly at the blue blood dripping down its face from the incision on its forehead.

"Eat shit, you ugly fucking bastard," she muttered as she hauled herself to her feet. Before the troll could regain its bearings, she threw Glimr with her good arm. She directed it to his neck with her fingers, and with the magick it usually took her to sever the spinal column of twenty gifted men, she severed the troll's head from its shoulders.

The head fell to the earth with a violent thump, the body collapsing right next to it. Rorax breathed heavily for a moment, her shoulder in complete agony, and felt her magick tap out as she summoned her knife back to its sheath.

She could feel her bone tenting up, bulging under the cover of her skin, the stretch there painful as she staggered to the nearest tree and collapsed at the base.

Sitting there, she leaned her head back against the rough bark and focused on breathing without aggravating her injury.

If Ayres didn't come back for her, she was going to kill him. She didn't know how long she sat before she heard a stick cracking.

She whipped her head around to find Ayres cautiously approaching the body of the troll, his sword gripped tightly in his hand. Relief filled her chest.

"Ayres," she coughed, pushing herself to her knees with her uninjured arm.

"Gods above," Ayres bit out as he sheathed his sword and stalked over to her side. His silver eyes widened as he took in her collarbone. "You killed it."

She huffed out a laugh before wincing at the pain in her chest.

"Come on. Let's get you to a healer." He squatted down next to her, so they were at the same level. They clasped forearms, and with a squeezing sensation that agonized her shoulder so much she almost blacked out, he transferred them back to the horses.

You saved my life, Cannon signed to her from his cot. ***Thank you.***

There was a thick gauze bandage over his chest, seeping with blood where the troll had speared him through. The healer had taken care of most of his internal damage, but the surface skin was only held together by stitches.

Rorax cried out in pain as the healer grabbed her arm, pulled back her shoulder, pushed her collarbone back into place through the skin, and started to heal it. "You're welcome," Rorax choked out through tears that pricked at the corners of her eyes.

"That was fucking dumb," Kaiya griped from where she stood guard over Cannon. Her wrists dangled over the top of her battle-ax casually. "But so ballsy I just might tell the story over my next campout with the guard. You know, it's truly amazing you don't look more like ground-up meat with how often you're visiting the healers, Greywood."

Her words were warm, but Kaiya's eyes were still cold and mistrusting as they watched Rorax struggle.

Rorax winced and gritted her teeth to keep from whimpering as she felt the fibers of her bone slowly weave back together.

Ayres sat next to Cannon, his eyes also on Rorax. "Thank you. I owe you their lives."

The healer kept going until Rorax's bone felt sturdy and his fingers were trembling. "That will hold but be careful. When you get back to the Northern Castle, make your way up to the Healer's Hall immediately," he cautioned.

Rorax nodded her thanks, rubbing her palm over her flat collarbone where it had been visibly broken only minutes before.

Ayres's eyes tracked her hand moving slowly over the smooth skin before his jaw hardened, and he fixed her with a glare. "You continue to surprise me, Greywood. You're tough. But the next time you want to do something that risky, I want to be told. You shouldn't have to do that alone. I could have—"

Rorax held up a hand. He was right. She needed to treat them more like her team and less like she was just a disposable guard who would do anything to preserve their lives. They would all have a better chance of survival if they acted more like a team, but she couldn't say that. She would never admit out loud to Ayres that he was *right*.

So instead, she leaned back and grinned up at him.

"You're just mad I ruined another one of your precious belts."

Cannon huffed a reluctant laugh, and Ayres just gave her a sardonic tilt of his lips.

CHAPTER 65

RORAX

Bafta was nothing more than a dust bowl.

On average, the House of Death was green and full of lush forest and grassy plains. Bafta seemed to have missed the message to grow any kind of foliage whatsoever.

Rorax sneezed before she could cover her nose, and dark brown snot shot out all over the arm of her brand-new dress.

"That's fucking disgusting, Ror." Jia grimaced.

"There is just so much dust in this gods-forsaken town," Rorax grumbled, wiping her arm off the best she could. "Jesus, Hella is going to murder me when she sees this."

Hella had whacked her in the shoulder with her little painted silk fan the last time Rorax visited the seamstress's shop with a smudge of dirt on the sleeve of her new dress, warning her to be careful with her precious creations.

The roads were all made up of bone-dry dirt—until it rained—and as carts and carriages went through the streets, plumes of dust kicked up into the dry air.

Not even the sporadically placed flowerpots throughout the city could make the buildings look any less dusty.

Jia glanced up at the small clock tower in the center of the village. "We have ten more minutes to get there on time."

"We'll make it," Rorax assured her, as they continued. She used her hand to wipe the sweat away from her neck. It was summer, and the heat in the middle of the days had moved from hot to sweltering. She spent her afternoons over the past few weeks in the library, hiding away from the sun as she searched for ways to get around the Choosing.

She was picking up a yellow, sparkly dress Hella had designed for her, and Rorax was excited about it. Today, for their trip into town, she wore a different dress, a long, pale blue gown with a medium length slit up her thigh. She had ample pockets for all her knives and could move freely in the dress. It was currently her favorite article of clothing she owned.

They crossed the road and started along the mostly deserted, long and narrow alleyway situated between buildings so close they provided some shade.

A dark figure turned the corner, and familiarity made Rorax's heart lurched in her chest. She froze, and Jia, who had been walking closely behind Rorax, knocked into her.

"Ror, what're you... holy shit," Jia whispered.

Karan Thorash—mate to one of the most influential Heilstorms in House of Ice history—was heading right toward them.

Nothing but cold, determined fury lived in the hard lines of his face; his eyes—gods his eyes—were so dark they were nearly black. They held nothing of the familiar warmth Rorax was so used to seeing.

A warning screamed in the back of her head.

"Karan," Jia croaked, and Rorax knew if she looked back at her comrade, she would see tears in her eyes. "Karan, oh my gods."

Karan didn't seem to hear Jia as he grabbed Rorax by her shoulder, turned her, and slammed her against the nearest wall. The back of her skull cracked on the hard wood logs of the building.

Rorax hissed as a sharp pain shot from the back of her skull. She had her hair blade tucked into her hair as she always did, and the force of his actions made one of the blades nick painfully into her scalp. She felt a cool press of a blade to her throat and had to fight to keep her temper under control.

"Where is Sahana? Where the *fuck* is she, Ror?" Karan hissed down into Rorax's face. "What did you do to her?"

Jia tried to reach up and grab Karan's hand away from Rorax's shoulder, but he shoved Jia away before gripping Rorax's shoulder even tighter. "Karan, stop! Rorax didn't do—"

He snarled, pressing closer. "Sahana lived for almost 600 years, and yet just a few years after she gives you a chance, after she saves you, she's gone?"

"Karan, I'm so sorry." The anguish in Jia's voice twisted something hot and painful in Rorax's heart.

Karan still ignored Jia, his fingers wrapping around Rorax's shoulder and collarbone so tightly she knew she would have bruises. His hair was longer and in worse shape than Rorax had ever seen it; the greasy black strands trailed all the way past his unshaven jaw.

Sorrow and guilt burrowed deeper into her chest, and Rorax sagged a little. "I don't know, Karan. I don't know where they took her body. Crax was working with a Lyondrean general; we think they…." Rorax had to swallow hard, her throat achingly tight. "We think they probably burned it."

"Don't fucking *lie* to me, Rorax," Karan hissed, pressing the knife tighter against her throat.

Rorax felt blood from her cut scalp trickle down her back at the same time as she felt the knife bite deeper into the skin at her neck. She had to press her eyes together and take two deep breaths in through her nose to keep from knocking Karan on his ass.

Jia took a tiny step forward, her hands out placatingly. "Karan. Calm down, and we will tell you everything we know. There was nothing we could have done. Rorax saved my life."

Karan didn't so much as glance Jia's way. His eyes remained fixed on Rorax, glittering with fury.

"Do not *play* with me, *Pup*." He spit the words at her, and Rorax's hold on her temper slipped another inch at the nickname. "Where is she?"

Despite being a hair away from knocking Karan into the next week, Rorax tried her best to soften the truth. "Sahana is *dead*, Karan. She died in Lyondrea."

"No, she isn't," he hissed, almost nose-to-nose with her again. "I can still *feel* her. She's *alive*."

Gods above.

Rorax's eyebrows furrowed and something dangerous—something like hope—sprouted in her chest. "You can... still feel her?"

Karan's fingers tightened around Rorax's shoulder even more, and he leaned until they were nose-to-nose. "Yes, you *vicious* bitch, I can still feel her. I know she's alive. So, I'll ask you again, where the fuck *is* she?"

Jia made a strangling noise, and a weight lifted in Rorax's chest.

Rorax grabbed Karan's wrist, wretched it and the knife he held away from her neck, and sideswiped his feet from under him.

He landed on the ground with a loud, solid thud. Jia already had her sword out and pointed at Karan's chest.

"What do we do?" she asked Ror, keeping her eyes on the seething man at her feet.

Rorax rubbed gently at her shoulder where Karan's fingers had been, her thoughts going a mile a minute. "We need to find Kiniera, and we need to send a letter to the king."

"Should we reach out to Eshaal?" Jia asked. Eshaal was the leader of the second Heilstorm unit and was overseeing the rest of the Heilstorms currently.

"Yes, definitely." Rorax moved her fingers to the back of her neck, touching where the silver tattoos of the Contestars was slick with blood from where her hair knives had cut the back of her head. "And we need to find out where the Hunter is. We have a job for that bastard."

Rorax looked down at the small splatters of blood now spotting the front of her dress and sighed. Hella really was going to kill her.

CHAPTER 66

AYRES

Ayres pushed open the door to the seamstress's shop, his eyes sweeping over the large, colorful room. There was a small reception desk at the front of the room, and behind that, rows and rows of fabric in different colors and patterns lined the walls.

As he neared one of the racks of fabric, he recognized one. Ayres reached out and rubbed his thumb over the black, sparkly fabric Rorax had worn the night of the Selection and during the Seksitan dance. It must have been his imagination, but his pants suddenly seemed a little tight.

There were two dressing rooms, and they were both wide open and empty.

Rorax told him she'd sent her leathers here to patch the holes where the arrows had struck her during their first hunt and to pick up a new dress, but she wasn't here. The shop was completely empty.

An ugly feeling niggled in his gut. She wouldn't miss training, and she sure as hell would never miss her afternoon ritual of going to the library. Something was wrong.

Ayres was just about to leave when a secret door, or maybe a door he'd missed because it too was covered in colorful bundles of fabric, shot open.

A woman not over five feet tall, barely a pixie of a woman, stormed up to him. Her curly blonde hair had come loose from the bun on the top of her head, and it bounced in ringlets around her pale face. She wore a fashionable but loud, red-and-purple-striped dress and red stiletto sandals laced up her ankles. "Where have you been? You're late!" she wailed impatiently.

He hadn't scheduled an appointment with the tailor, but Ayres still eyed the clock by the reception desk and frowned. "Late?"

"Late! Rorax Greywood passed the shop hours ago with a cut on her neck and blood running down her back!" the woman shrieked at him, throwing her hands up in exasperation.

Her large blonde bun rolled around the top of her head in a threatening whirlwind. "Her violet-haired companion was with her, and they were leading a man down the road at knifepoint. Rorax didn't even come to pick up her dress!" the woman shrieked again, pointing a small finger at a short, obscenely sparkly, yellow dress. "That girl loves her dresses. She could be hurt or in trouble, and you took a century and a half to get down here!"

Ayres ignored the woman's jabs as a cold fury settled over his senses. Had the man hurt her? Why was she bleeding?

The woman started tapping her foot, looking up at him like she was about to strike him if he didn't get moving.

"Which direction did she take him?"

She waved her hands in exasperation. "Probably back to the castle, boy! Seeing as she can't go anywhere else!"

The tailor was right, Rorax was limited by her Blood Oath with the Guardian unless she was with him or Cannon.

Ayres spun on his heel and was pushing his way out when the seamstress called after him.

"Make sure Rorax comes and gets her dress and her new lingerie tomorrow. I made it just how she likes it—with extra lace."

Ayres froze in the doorway. His whole body went haywire. He needed to go and find her... but lingerie? Extra lace on Rorax? Did she wear those things under her dresses? Her armor? What kind of fabric had she used?

His chest and neck felt hot, and he was breathing a bit like a dragon as he forced himself to turn around and face the seamstress. She gave him a saucy wink before snapping and waving him out the door.

"Shoo, boy."

When Ayres reached Rorax's room, he hesitated for a split second outside the door. Then he heard muffled voices inside, and when he heard a distinctly male voice, he burst through the door.

Jia was sitting on the edge of Rorax's bed, Kiniera and a man he didn't know were occupying the two armchairs, and Rorax stood in the middle of her room with her back to him. He took in the rivulets of blood streaking from the nape of her neck down to the small of her back, coloring her long blue dress in vertical stripes of red down her spine. As she whirled to face the door, his eyes zeroed in on the angry red marks on her collarbone and shoulder. And there was a cut on her neck.

A hand, a *man's* hand, had made angry red marks around her throat.

Somewhere in the back of Ayres's mind, he was surprised to see the man alive. Rorax could more than take care of herself—she was the Spine Cleaver for gods' sake.

But if she wasn't going to defend herself, he would happily do it for her.

Ayres's limbs trembled with the intense desire to reach out to his power and rip the soul from the man's body. He wrestled it down. Instead, he looked over to the man and said, "I hope you enjoyed your last day with breath in your lungs. I'm about to fill them with blood."

Rorax stepped in front of Ayres and placed a hand on his forearm. Ayres didn't look away from the filth sitting in the middle of Rorax's room. The man had the good sense to look alarmed.

"Ayres," Rorax murmured. She rubbed a thumb over his skin.

Ayres didn't look away from the man who sat there like a ghost, a fragment of one who had missed too many meals and seen too many things. His light brown skin seemed sallow and pale, and deep purple bags colored the skin under his eyes.

He looked familiar, but Ayres was too far gone to connect any vague dots in his memory. And the truth was, he didn't give a flying fuck how broken the man was or what had happened to him. He had laid his hands on his Contestar and hurt her.

Rorax rubbed her thumb over Ayres's skin again, and where she touched felt tingly and hot. She was trying to soothe him, and it was working.

"Ayres." Rorax pulled at his arm, and he reluctantly looked down at her. There was worry pinching her eyes, but there was something else, too. Something that gave her eyes an extra light. Gods above, she was beautiful.

"Ayres, this is Karan. This is Sahana's mate."

Chapter 67

Rorax

Rorax slid her hand down his arm and entwined her fingers into his, giving them a tight squeeze. She hoped he didn't break her wrist for touching him without permission.

She was shocked. *Shocked.*

Ayres, Lieutenant Jackass, who had threatened to kill her almost every day since they'd met, was here. Standing in her room. Looking for her because she hadn't shown up to practice. Defending her.

He was here because he had been *worried* about her.

If she didn't know better, she might have been tempted to walk across the room to her window to see if the sky was on fire, or maybe falling. Or that Hell had frozen.

Ayres had finally looked down at her, and she almost sagged in relief as his irises faded from their bright red color to silver. She could reason with silver.

He had taken one look at the marks around her collarbone, and his eyes had instantly started glowing red like glittering rubies, and his power pulsated through the room, strong enough for even her to feel. She knew that if she didn't explain to him who Karan was *quickly*, Karan would be a lifeless corpse on her floor in seconds.

Jia slid past Ayres to close the door behind him, and his eyebrows shot up a millimeter, as if almost shocked to see her. He looked back to Karan, then to Kiniera and back as if surprised that Jia and Kiniera hadn't killed Karan themselves in her defense.

"What's going on?"

"Just a little top-secret House of Ice meeting, Lieutenant. Nothing special," Jia quipped, her voice sickly sweet as she brushed past him to get back to her spot on the side of Rorax's bed.

"It's none of his business." Karan lifted himself out of his chair to come and stand toe-to-toe with Ayres, even though Ayres was nearly six inches taller than Karan and twice as burly. A spike of red reentered Ayres's irises, so Rorax squeezed his hand a little tighter. She threw Karan a dirty look. "Karan, step back," she ordered, scowling until Karan shuffled back at a few inches.

Then she turned to look up at Ayres. "Sahana is alive. Karan is here looking for clues. We're going to see if we can help him find her."

The red abated. She could see that he had a million questions rolling around in his head, but he gave her a simple jerky nod. Rorax pointed to the now empty armchair by the fireplace. "Take a seat."

Ayres prowled around Karan, giving him a look that promised violence, before sinking into the open armchair across from where Kiniera sat in its twin.

"As I was saying," Kiniera drawled, eyeing Ayres before looking up at Karan, "Rorax is going to send a letter to the king and to Eshaal. I'm going to send one to the queen, and Jia will be reaching out to the contact in Lyondrea. See if the contact, by some miracle, knows where Sahana is and if she's still alive. Until then, Karan, as I've told you, we do not have any answers for you. We presumed that she had fallen alongside Volla."

Jia stiffened next to Rorax. "Can you give us any more information? Any more leads to where she is?" Jia asked, looking down at the floor. "When Volla was still alive, I could feel her. Feel where she was generally through the bond."

Karan's hands curled up into fists. "No," he spat. "I already told you. I can't feel her. It feels empty, but not... not like...." He ran his hand through his hair.

"Not like she's been ripped out of your chest?" Jia didn't look up from the floor, her voice flat and dead.

Karan deflated with a long sigh. "No, not like that."

Rorax and Kiniera shared a brief look.

"She must be in a Lyondrea prison," Ayres grumbled.

Rorax turned her attention to the lieutenant. "Ayres, where did the Guardian find the Hunter? Where can we find him, and is it possible to hire him?"

Ayres nodded. "You can hire him, anyone can for the right price. I don't know where he is. He came to her when he felt her power crumbling. I'll ask her when she returns from Valitlinn."

Karan shot him a grateful look, but Ayres kept his eyes locked on Rorax. "If Sahana is in a Lyondrean prison... it's not good. They line the walls with power-dampening wards, which is probably why you can't acutely feel her. It's poisonous to the Gifted over time. You need to prepare yourself for the worst. At the least, prepare yourself that you might not recognize the woman you find, if you even do find her."

Karan snarled. "I will find her. I will."

They all heard what Karan didn't say. He'd either find her, or he'd die trying.

CHAPTER 68

JIA

The wind nipped at Jia's cheeks as she looked up into the dark sky. It had been raining off and on all day, and there were still clouds in the sky. Even the stars seemed to have been snuffed out tonight. The summer night air was cool, and she had come up to the battlements to get a breath of fresh air. She sat perched on one of the flat crenelations of the wall, sitting on the top.

Sahana is alive. The news that their leader had survived was both the greatest news of her life and, selfishly she knew, the worst. It meant Volla had gone to the afterlife alone. It meant that Volla had been the only one to die that night.

Jia brushed her fingertips down her chest. She had been up for over an hour. The phantom pains of when she'd felt Volla dying plagued her dreams almost every night. She could still feel the devastating pain of the knife piercing through her chest, and it made sleeping nearly impossible even though she was exhausted, weary down to the bone.

Jia was and always would be proud of Volla, proud of all her wife had accomplished and proud that everyone had loved her so much. Volla had made her happy, had seen into the darkest parts of Jia's soul and had loved every inch of her anyway.

But sometimes... sometimes Jia wondered if the pain of Volla's loss was worth the love.

"Frostguard."

Jia looked over her shoulder, expecting one of the Guardian's soldiers to inform her she couldn't be up here. Instead, Kaiya stood there, holding a witch-light up in her palm, her other hand on her hip.

"What're you doing out here?" she asked.

Jia blushed, and guilt sat heavy in her stomach. It had been weeks since the hunt at the winery, and every time Kaiya talked to her or looked her way, she felt the same things—shame and guilt. For a multitude of things.

With a casualness Jia didn't really feel, she shrugged one shoulder. "Looking for stars."

Kaiya had been cool with her since she had saved Jia's life at the winery, and tonight was no different.

"Are you okay?" Kaiya asked, looking her over clinically.

Jia didn't have it in her to lie, so she just shrugged again and turned back to the black sky.

"You're not going to jump, are you?"

Jia huffed out a bitter laugh and hunched into herself. She'd thought about it, about simply stepping off the side, but she didn't think the fall would kill her. It would be a waste of her time. And she didn't want to die, not really. She just wanted the pain festering and eating inside her to end. She wanted Volla back.

Kaiya was so quiet, Jia thought she had walked away, but when she turned to look, Kaiya was still there, staring up at the moon, too.

"Come on, Frostguard." Kaiya sighed, blowing out a deep, resigned breath. "I want to show you something I found last week in the woods."

Kaiya made her go change into something warmer; then they trekked through the dark forest, using only a small witch-light Kaiya carried in her hand. For nearly twenty minutes, Kaiya led her through the sparse underbrush.

"Where are we going?" Jia hissed as the underbrush scraped against her shins.

"Just trust me," Kaiya whispered back.

"I do. If I didn't, I wouldn't let you lead me blind to my imminent death," Jia grumbled.

Kaiya snorted. "We're almost there."

A few minutes passed, and Kaiya tucked the witch-light into her pocket. "We're here."

Jia took a few more steps around a large tree, then saw where Kaiya had led her.

A small patch of forest was... glowing. Bioluminescent moss spread across the forest floor, seeping out of a small pond in the center of the clearing and creeping up the trees. The moss glowed in different colors, mostly in florescent green but with purple and pink patches, too. It illuminated everything around them in a soft green and purple glow.

Jia sucked in a breath, pressing her hand against her mouth in wonder as Kaiya toed a patch of incandescent moss close to where they stood.

"This moss is an invasive species from House of Light. They had a mass removal of it a few years ago from this area of the forest since it was choking out the native species and messing up the sleep schedules of the nocturnal bats and other animals that live in this area, but they must have missed some. I found this a few days ago during my patrol shift."

"It's beautiful," Jia marveled, stepping forward, looking around at all the light, soaking it in.

"Yeah, I think so, too," Kaiya agreed, moving to the edge of the water and sitting down on the soft moss.

The moss cushioned her as Jia sat next to Kaiya, looking around in awe. They sat together for a long time in silence, admiring the moss and the way it illuminated the forest.

"Are you okay?" Kaiya asked softly after a while.

"Yeah," Jia responded.

Kaiya slanted her a look. "No, you're not."

Jia studied the way the moss grew at the bottom of the pond, absorbing the light. "I'm fine."

"Stop lying, Frostguard."

Jia let out a long sigh and finally looked over to meet Kaiya's gaze. Concern lived there in the warm color of her eyes, and something in Jia's heart softened. "Okay. You're right. I'm not fine."

Kaiya nodded, and a frown pulled down at the corner of Kaiya's mouth. "What happened?"

"Volla... my wife, she was killed protecting us on a mission in Lyondrea. Right before we came here."

Kaiya nodded. She had heard it before. "And Isgra is her twin?"

Jia let out a bitter laugh and faced the pond again. "Identical twin."

"Gods, I'm sorry, Jia." Kaiya grimaced and rubbed at the back of her neck. "I am gonna ask this, and I want you to be honest. Are you trying to get yourself killed on the hunts?"

"No," Jia answered quickly. Kaiya tilted her head unbelievingly, and Jia's shoulders hunched slightly. "I'm not. Not actively. But if I were to lose my life... I wouldn't fight it."

Kaiya grimaced.

Jia brought her thighs to her chest and wrapped her arms around her knees. "Kaiya, I hurt. There is no 'me' anymore. She's the one who died, and yet there isn't much left of me without her. I-I'm nothing. Nothing but an empty shell of anguish and tortured grief. I need it to end."

Jia reached up and wiped away a tear with her finger. Kaiya turned to face her more fully. "I didn't know the Torch while she was alive, but I know she wasn't the only one who loves you. Live. If only for them. Greywood won't make it out of this without you."

"She has others supporting her."

"If you think she can survive this without you, you're a damn fool."

Jia nodded slowly and forced herself to look Kaiya in the eye. She needed to talk about something else that had been plaguing her for weeks. "I don't want to discuss that now. I want... I need to apologize to you, Kaiya. For saying what I did. For leading you on, for putting Death in a bad spot because of my actions, because you're right. If I were to die on a hunt, my mother would not be pleased."

Kaiya nodded and offered her a small smile. "Thank you."

"I can't offer you anything," Jia said, the words like sawdust in her mouth. "I have nothing. I am nothing." She was only grief and drowning loss now. "But I would like to be friends. I know I said we weren't, but I would like to be. You and your people, they are extraordinary."

"I didn't bring you out here for that." Kaiya offered her a somber smile. "I know the last thing you need is a lover. But you do need a friend. This place... well, it reminded me of you, and maybe you need a reminder that there is still light and beauty in this world, even in the depths of grief, even if it's not as bright as you deserve. I know it could never match your loss, but I hope it helps... even a little."

"Have you ever lost anyone special?"

Kaiya shook her head. "Not like that, not a mate. But when Ice invaded Death, I lost my mother and my two siblings. I defended the Whitewood with everything I had to give, but in the end, it wasn't enough."

Jia's eyes welled with tears as Kaiya leaned forward, plucking up a loose piece of bark from under some of the bright moss and gently placed it in the water. They watched it for a long moment as it slowly floated away.

"My grief always reminded me of the sea. At first, I was drowning and everything around me was nothing but wreckage. Even if I did see something beautiful, it cut me because they'd never see it. Everything good and beautiful reminded me of what I lost, and I was drowning." Kaiya swallowed hard. "But somehow, I swam. Or floated. I found a reason to live even when the waves battered me and would try to pull me back under.

"I found Cannon and his friends a few months later through the army. I was beating anyone they set me against to spar, so they brought me to Cannon. He introduced me to the prince and to Ayres and the guard, and they kept me busy. Gave me a purpose. Then suddenly it felt like the waves weren't hitting as hard and were farther and fewer between. I started to feel I could survive, even though I had been uncertain for so long. I don't know what it's like to lose a mate, but hang on. Swim. Find something in the wreckage to float on. At the very least, give yourself the chance to find out if you will ever be able to breathe again."

The tears that had been collecting in Jia's eyes finally fell. *Give yourself the chance to find out if you will ever be able to breathe again*. Gods, she was going to sob.

Kaiya looked out to the water again, and Jia forced herself to cry silently. She basked in the light in the dark night that surrounded her—and in her grief and lost love. This woman saw her. Kaiya understood her and her sorrows in a way that not even Rorax could understand.

They remained silent for a long while as Jia fought for composure. Eventually, when her tears stopped and her throat unknotted, Jia reached out to brush Kaiya's fingertips with her own.

"Thank you, Whitethorn."

CHAPTER 69

RAENGAR

Raengar paced back and forth on the roof of the same angular, blocky pyramid in Luxamal that he had been instructed to land on the last time he'd come to the University of Poison. Deimos curled up like a cat nearby. The dragon was big enough that he took up most of the space on the top, and Raengar wished he had more area to pace—not that any more space would let him thoroughly work out his anxiety.

It was midnight again, and there was no movement beyond the flickering witch-light torches that lit the pathways between the pyramids that made up the school here. Raengar would have normally stopped to admire the beauty of the ancient city and appreciate the University of Poison's rich history, but right then his head buzzed with nervous energy and worry.

The high acolyte of the university was late. He would give the woman ten more minutes before he slipped inside and started searching the hallways for her himself.

Raengar got in a few more paces back and forth before the trapdoor to the roof finally creaked opened and the woman scrambled out.

Even in the moonlight, her face looked paler and pinched tighter than he'd ever seen it before, and it sent a warning shooting through his mind. Something had gone wrong.

"Hello, Your Grace. Thank you for meeting me here."

Raengar put his hands on his hips, rocking forward onto the balls of his feet in case he needed to move. "What news?"

"I... well...." The woman sucked in a sharp breath and looked back at the trapdoor from where she'd emerged. "We've lost three different lab samples. The blood."

Raengar had to take three deep breaths to keep himself from freezing her heart into a solid brick. That was Rorax's blood. Beyond that, Volla, his friend, had died to make sure Jia and Rorax got away.

"You... *lost them*?" He could barely speak through his fury.

"No, no, I mean, not *lost* them." She cowered, looking fearfully past Raengar to where Deimos was watching. "Someone has been removing them from our laboratories."

That gave him pause. "What do you need? Do you need more men to secure the building?" Gods, if Määr was behind this, he would fly to Kammath right now and decimate it. Deimos was donned in his starsteel armor. Määr wouldn't be able to do anything but watch in horror as Raengar's dragon froze his city into ruin.

The woman shook her head. "I have decided to run the samples myself in secret. I *will* find out what you need."

Raengar rubbed his hand over his jaw. "How much of the original blood sample do you have left?"

There was a heavy beat of silence. "Only enough to run two more."

Raengar resisted the urge to coat his ice over the woman's skin. She *knew*. She *knew* what was at stake here. Without more proof that the King of Alloy was working against the Realms, he could walk free. Raengar would never let that happen. He didn't have any evidence, but he knew in his bones that Määr had helped Lyondrea open the Pits, and it was almost inevitable that thousands would die to close them.

"Run one more, do it by yourself and do it in secret. If it fails, you will come to Koppar, and I will get you what you need."

The woman's eyes went wide for a moment before she nodded once. "I do not wish to leave my home, but I will do what is needed for the good of the Realms. There is someone very powerful and very insistent behind both this poison and these... mishaps. If it is the King of Alloy, I want him uprooted and burned out. He should have no foothold here in a place of learning."

Raengar agreed.

CHAPTER 70

RORAX

"Karan just left for Lyondrea," Kiniera snapped, ripping out the wooden chair that was across the table from Rorax and collapsing in it with an angry huff. "He knocked out two of my men doing it."

Rorax leaned back in her chair. She sat at her favorite table, behind the stalagmite pillar in the back of the library. Ever since finding out that Sahana was still alive *somewhere*, freeing herself from the Choosing took on a whole new level of urgency. It felt like the most important thing she could be doing.

Kiniera leaned forward across the table, her teeth clenched. "Karan is messing with my plans. He can't just go into Lyondrea like a rutting, angry bull. He'll get himself caught, likely tortured, and then, if Sahana *is* alive, she's going to murder us all if he gets hurt—"

Kiniera cut herself off. Her cheeks uncharacteristically flushed with anger, but her nearly colorless, pale blue eyes flitted up over Rorax's head.

Rorax turned around just in time to see Ayres strolling through the books toward her. He was dressed in his usual high-collared shirt, despite the heat, and Rorax hated how her core suddenly pulsed and felt heavy.

Ayres's long, tattooed fingers gripped the top of the wooden chair next to her and pulled it out. She ignored the heat in her stomach and squinted up at him. "Hi?"

Ayres nodded to the House of Ice emissary as he folded himself into the chair. The corner of his mouth tipped up as he pulled one of the books Rorax had stacked in the middle of the table toward him. "I'm here for my shift."

The Death guards had started taking shifts in the library since the Selection, and usually Cannon sat with Rorax in the afternoons.

Rorax's brows furrowed as he flipped open the book to the first page. "I thought it was Cannon's shift today." He usually took the midday shift with her.

"I traded him. I have the night patrol again," he said, ignoring her and focusing on his book.

Rorax raised an eyebrow at Kiniera, who looked between Rorax and Ayres with narrowed eyes before her gaze settled on Rorax questioningly. Rorax just shrugged.

"Let me know when you hear back from the king, Rorax, or if you hear anything from Karan." Kiniera's mouth pressed into a frown, and she pushed to her feet. "I'll see you later."

"I will," Rorax said as she watched her old commander walk away.

When she was out of earshot, Ayres leaned over and spoke in a low voice. "Kiniera gives me the creeps."

Rorax snorted a laugh and looked over to find Ayres watching her. "She gives me the creeps, too. She was one of my first commanders at the Military Academy in Skavetsia. Her 'I mean business' voice will always make me shiver."

"How long was she your commander? How old were you?" he asked, leaning back in his chair.

"From when I was seven to fifteen. They recruited me as a full-time Heilstorm when I was sixteen." Rorax looked down at the book open and forgotten in front of her. "For a few years after I was recruited, the Wolf wanted to singularly focus on me. Get me up to speed to the rest of the Heilstorms."

Rorax ran her fingers down the pages of her book slowly, feeling the words under her fingertips, remembering the near-constant training, the whippings, the fear… everything in the name of "preparing her."

"Those were the most intense training years I ever had. It makes the Contestar training feel like a light workout," Rorax said.

"The Wolf… she was the one who recruited you?" He sounded gruff.

Rorax nodded, still not looking up at him.

"She was the one who thought teaching you how to read was an unnecessary task?"

Rorax's eyes flew up to his, watching as he flexed his arms in anger.

"Who told you that?" But she already knew the answer.

"Jia."

Rorax felt a blush bloom over her cheeks. "I know how to read, but I didn't until a few years ago."

"Sahana taught you, right?"

Rorax nodded. "Yeah, right after… not too long after the Siege." Rorax peeked up at him from under her lashes, scared that she had ruined the moment, but he only had a thoughtful look on his face.

"What was the first book you ever read?" he asked.

A smile tugged at Rorax's mouth as she turned back to running her fingers over the pages of her book. "A book on poisonous plants."

Ayres laughed, and the sound wrapped around her like a warm blanket. "Why am I not surprised?"

"You shouldn't be." She laughed, too, and when she looked back up at him, he was smiling down at her, and for a single moment, they sat grinning at each other.

It had changed, this angry, vile thing between them. Now it felt… safe—almost warm, and an awful lot like friendship.

Her chest felt warmer than before, and Rorax had to look away. "Come on, let's study, or I'm getting Cannon to switch his shift back."

Ayres rolled his eyes but leaned forward over his book.

He came to study with her every day for the rest of the week.

CHAPTER 71

TRESSA

Ren was going to kill her. She knew it, and she looked forward to every single moment.

Tressa's back arched off the bed, and she screamed so loud there was absolutely no way the guards outside couldn't hear her. But she didn't care.

"Ren!" she whimpered as he gave her clit one last lazy suck before climbing up her body, biting at one dark nipple before finally giving her his mouth. She tasted herself on him, a taste she admittedly loved, as he thrust inside her with one sharp push.

"Fuck!" she cried into his mouth as he moaned. He had prepared her with three fingers first, but the stretch of his cock? Nothing could prepare her for how amazing he felt inside her.

"Gods above, you feel good," Ren breathed. He grabbed her hands and pinned them to the bed by her head as he snapped his hips in and out with strokes so deep, she felt him *everywhere*.

"Ren, gods, Ren." She whimpered again, her head rolling back and forth on the sheets until he gripped her chin.

"Eyes, Tressa. I want your eyes on mine or down here." He cupped the back of her head to tilt her head forward so the only thing she could see was him slamming into her, his cock wet with her arousal. Gods above, he was huge.

"Gods, Ren." She stared with wide eyes, the sight so erotic she felt her orgasm getting closer. "Your cock? *Fuck*."

Tressa looked up at him to see a smug little smile on his face. He pulled her long legs over his shoulders, and the new position sent her rocketing toward her orgasm. His fingers strummed her clit and her nipple in that perfect, *perfect* rhythm, and within a few more minutes, she was erupting.

"Ren. Ren!"

He released her nipple to grip her chin, forcing her eyes to stay on him the whole time as her pussy clenched and spasmed around him. He finally grunted, collapsing on top of her and breathing hard in her ear. Sometimes she really wished she had spent the time to develop her Mind Walker talents more. She would never feel confident enough to walk his brain, but to be in his head when he came? It made her hot just thinking about it.

Those grunts, the hard breathing sounds he made in her ear, made her so hot she clenched one more time around his length, and it made him groan.

She giggled, and he pulled back to see it.

At the sight of her smile, Ren beamed down at her, his eyes sparkling. He stroked the side of her cheek with his thumb. "You are the most beautiful thing to walk this planet."

Tressa's cheeks heated, and she bit her bottom lip. "I think we are going to have 600 kids."

His smile got even wider. "Why do you think that?"

Tressa ran her hands up the sides of his torso and then down his back, touching all the muscle and strength and reliability that was this man. *Her* man. "Because I can't keep my hands off you. I'm obsessed with you... or at least certain *parts* of you."

She clenched around him, and he groaned. "You cruel, wicked thing."

The smile on his face faded, and his features grew serious. "Tressa, I know you already know this, but I consider you my wife. You are *mine*." He stroked his thumb across her bottom lip, and something in her chest glowed with the *rightness* of this. Of him. "I already have the ring, your parents' approval, and the seal of approval from the Council of Houses. I haven't officially asked because you were mourning Roo. The minute you're ready, truly ready, just say the word."

Love, so much *love*, flooded her chest, and suddenly she was blinking away tears. "I love you, you know that?"

He grinned down at her again and pressed his forehead against hers. "I know."

Ren finally pulled out of her and rolled onto his side. He propped his head up on one hand and reached over and started drawing a pattern on Tressa's bare thigh. "I also need to tell you something I heard from Ayres."

That made Tressa's muscles lock up. It had to be about Rorax, or Ayres wouldn't have bothered. "What did he say?"

"Ayres brought Rorax on an assignment recently, and Rorax sacrificed herself for him and a little girl, saving them from a camp of Lyondrean soldiers," Ren said slowly. "He said something like they were all 'seeing her change.' I want to warn you, because if she continues this trajectory, continues to save Ayres and his soldiers"—Ren flicked his gaze up to Tressa's—"he won't happily stand aside for you to kill her."

Tressa was going to be sick. Slowly, she sat up and rolled herself into a ball, looking at her toes. "Rorax is a monster, a *villain*," she whispered.

She could see Ren nodding out of the corner of her eye. "I know you're hurting, Tress, and so far, what she did means nothing. But if it becomes a pattern...." He shrugged. "Who knows what Ayres will do."

Tressa sighed and looked down at Ren's chest. "The Contestars are leaving for the North this morning to head to the location of the next trial," Tressa murmured. "While they're gone, I'm going to ask around and see what Rorax has actually been up to." Ren saw pain in her eyes.

"I miss Roo so much, Ren. It's this gaping hole in my heart that seems to get bigger every day. I can't forget what happened to her. And why." She looked up at Ren with tears clinging to her eyelashes.

"I know, sweetheart, I know." Ren kissed her forehead. "When you want your revenge, I will be right here, ready to do whatever you need."

CHAPTER 72

RORAX

The sound of pelting raindrops against the glass windowpane woke Rorax. She forced her eyes open and noticed it was almost light outside. She looked around her room. Her brain felt fuzzy, and the sheets in the bed were damp and sweaty.

She was in a room, but she wasn't in *her* room.

The next trial would take place north of the Northern Castle, in the Cracked Sea.

It was a twelve-hour dragon ride to the Cracked Sea from the Northern Castle, so they were staying at the largest fortress on Jerickson's Road for a week to make sure enough of the Guardian's court, including healers, emissaries, and soldiers, could be brought to the fortress.

It had been their first night there, and they had celebrated hard.

Fuck.

Rorax was so late. Cannon and Ayres were going to scalp her. She stumbled out of the small feather bed, groaning. Her head throbbed, and the floor seemed to rush at her even as she tried to steady herself.

What had she been drinking last night?

The castle here was small but had battlements large enough to accommodate the Guardian's court.

The keepers of this castle had thrown a small party to celebrate the arrival of the Contestars, and the party had eventually devolved into a late-night poker session in the Great Hall with herself, the prince, Jia, Milla, and Kaiya. Elios and Allurah had even made an appearance.

Cannon shook his head at them and went off to bed. Ayres, however, had taken it upon himself to come into the hall to tell Rorax that if she was late for her training session in the morning, she would pay.

Rorax groaned. Whatever punishment Ayres and Cannon would give her would surely make her sore, and the next trial was tomorrow.

Her head throbbed, and she rubbed at her temples. The Death Prince had made her try a bit of his special moonshine he had apparently been brewing himself, his golden eyes glinting with pride. She couldn't remember much more after that. Maybe that was why she felt so shitty this morning.

Rorax tried to pull on her favorite fighting bra, but the bindings... her fingers... they shook too much to pull them taut around herself. She shoved the bindings back into the small bag she had packed and instead pulled out the easiest bra to put on, nothing more than a bralette. At least she would have a *little* support there.

She pulled on her fighting leathers, having to pull extra tight around her chest, and hauled up her boots. Her fingers were shaking so much, she ended up just tucking the laces in the sides.

She could stop and see a healer, but if she got caught trying to soothe a hangover, Ayres would never let her forget it, and her pride wouldn't either. Today would be a good lesson on how to fight even when you made terrible decisions the night before. She didn't remember drinking enough to feel this shitty, but her memory of last night was vague at best.

Rorax opted to leave her hair knives behind and instead swept her hair in a ponytail, forgoing her usual war braids as she grabbed her sword and left the room.

As soon as she stepped outside, she gulped in the fresh air, but it didn't really help. The rain was falling in sheets now, making it even darker than it normally was at this hour, but she could still make out Ayres, Cannon, and, surprisingly, Lamonte standing at the end of the bailey already sparring. A few other soldiers were out exercising as well.

Rorax steeled her spine as she stalked up to them.

Lamonte spotted her first and jerked his chin up at her. "Good mornin', sunshine. They were takin' bets on if you'd make it out this fine day," he said, all cheer and smiles.

Her stomach rolled, letting her know that it in fact did *not* want to be out this early. She gritted her teeth. "Morning."

Ayres put his hands on his hips. "You got that deep in your cups two nights before a trial?"

"It's tomorrow; I thought I would have time to work through it," she grumbled, swallowing down bile. "The prince had me try his moonshine."

Cannon clicked his tongue and signed, ***You should know better than to drink anything the prince makes himself.***

She couldn't argue with that, so she didn't.

Cannon sighed and signed again. ***I'm glad you made it. We will start slow—a one-on-one with Ayres, then we'll get some of Lamonte's men to reenact a siege scene with you.***

Rorax nodded and deposited her cloak next to the wall, pulling her blade out.

When she turned to face Ayres, his eyes went a little wide as he took her in. "What're you wearing?"

Rorax looked down at her fighting leathers, then back up at him with a tired grin on her face. She hadn't been able to bind her breasts down this morning like she usually did, and he had noticed.

His eyes lingered hungrily on her chest before looking up to meet her gaze. She could have sworn he was blushing, but she couldn't tell for sure through the rain, and before she could make a snarky remark, Ayres attacked.

They weren't even at it for five minutes before he knocked her on her ass.

Rorax got back up slowly, rubbing her backside with her palm as Ayres snarled at her again. "Pathetic, Rorax. You let a night of drinking render you utterly useless."

She snarled back at him, but her heart wasn't in it. She felt so hot, like her insides were burning up, and she desperately wanted to throw up. But she wouldn't do it in front of Ayres.

Kään save her, what was *in* that moonshine?

They began again. It took Ayres even less time to deposit Rorax back onto the ground.

Rorax lay there for a moment, feeling the blessedly cold cobblestones and rainwater beneath her cheek.

She slowly raised her head to find Kaiya, who had appeared across the courtyard, watching Cannon's hands as she wrapped her white braids into a ponytail at the top of her head. Whatever Cannon signed to her made her frown. Rorax thought Kaiya had likely had just as much to drink as Rorax, but *she* didn't look like she was on the verge of death.

"Get up," Ayres snarled from above Rorax.

She got herself up slowly on trembling arms.

As they began again, Rorax lasted for another few minutes before Cannon came over, called time, and started signing at Ayres to direct Lamonte's men.

Rorax ignored them and walked to the gate, stepping outside over the bridge so she could feel the breeze on her skin. The sky was ominously gray and cloudy, but she was thankful for the cold wind as it whipped her hair around her face. She closed her eyes and tilted her face up to the rain, sucking in deep breaths while she untied the top of her leathers so she could expose her neck to the rain. She was so hot, so hot.

"Heard you were a little hungover from last night," Kaiya mocked, stepping closer to her.

Rorax peeled one eye open and scowled at Kaiya from the corner of her eye.

Kaiya laughed and shoved her with her elbow. It was just a little, playful shove, mild compared to what the tall woman normally dished out, but the force of it sent Rorax reeling.

She stumbled over her own feet, tripped, then toppled over the side of the bridge and into the moat surrounding the small fortress. Her face smacked the water first, but she didn't care. Didn't care about the blood she could taste in the back of her throat from her nose or the yells she heard from above her. She didn't care about any of it.

The minute her skin hit the water, she felt instant relief. She sighed, releasing little air bubbles out of her mouth.

The water felt phenomenal against her skin. Her whole body relaxed, and for the first time that day, she felt like she wasn't burning up from the inside out.

Even as her lungs started to protest and burn from the lack of oxygen, she refused to surface, refused to move her limbs away from the liquid cold.

Just a little bit longer, she pleaded with her lungs.

Rorax jerked as something big hit the water next to her. A hand grabbed the belt at the back of her leathers, and she started to struggle.

No, not yet, just a little longer, please!

She felt herself being thrown up and out of the water, onto the bank of the moat. She spluttered and coughed up water, dragging air back into her lungs.

"Rorax, what the *fuck* is going on?" Ayres growled.

She didn't answer for a few seconds, trying to make sense of the question. "Nothing. I just.... I just need to cool down. And... and then I'll... I'll get up to spar."

"Kaiya! Go get a healer. Something's wrong."

Rorax pressed her cheek against the grass, feeling the cool blades and the rain hitting the side of her cheek, but it wasn't enough. She was still too hot. She wanted to feel that cool rain kiss her *everywhere*.

With hands she could barely feel, she started stripping. She tore at the bindings and ties that held her in her leathers, and she desperately tried to peel them away from her skin so she could feel the rain.

She opened her eyes to see Ayres's face above hers. "Water, let me get back into the water," she rasped.

Ayres gritted his jaw as he gripped the leather armor she'd just shed in a tight fist. "No, no more water for now. We'll go take an ice bath in your room." He jerked his head up and handed her clothes to someone she couldn't see as she turned her head to eye the moat forlornly.

"Take her armor and go get her another gods-damned shirt," Ayres commanded. "Then meet us in my room."

A shiver racked down her spine, and every muscle in her ached, even as it felt like her skin was on fire.

A cool hand touched her forehead, and she closed her eyes, leaning into it and groaning.

"Rorax," Ayres hissed, and even with her eyes closed, she could tell he was furious. "You're burning up."

She felt a palm slide under her shoulders and another tuck under her knees to lift her up. Her head rolled around on the back of his arm, making nausea crawl up her throat, so she used her arms to clutch around his neck. He jerked her up close to his chest. He must have taken off his shirt when he dove in after her.

She liked the warmth coming off him and burrowed deeper into his arms. Rorax worried for a moment he would tell her to let go, but instead he squeezed her tighter, and she relaxed.

She rested her chin on his pectoral muscle. He had the nicest pectoral muscles she had ever seen on a man before, and the thick sinew running on the side of his neck was ridiculously attractive.

His chest rumbled from underneath her breasts. "Thank you."

You're welcome, she thought, her eyes tracking up the golden chain that always rested against his tanned skin.

Without thinking, she pulled herself up slowly, opened her mouth, and let the tip of her tongue trace over the skin and his tattoos on his chest until she reached his collarbones where she bit the crook of his neck softly.

She pressed the flat parts of her teeth against the flesh and gently bit down there, tasting his flesh for a second before releasing him. The hands around her tightened factionally.

It wasn't hard enough to mark, just enough to claim. She sighed, resting her cheek on his chest. Ayres had the best tattoos of any man she had ever seen.

He grunted again.

He climbed the stairs, and when he reached the top, she moved her face into the crook of his neck, her nose and lips pressing into his warm skin.

She stayed that way until he deposited her onto a soft bed. Her eyes flew open, taking in the white sheets.

White was a dangerous color for a sick woman.

"If you puke in this bed, Rorax, I'll throw you into the chicken coop and make you sleep there for a week."

A faint smile crossed over her lips. He wouldn't do that to her.

Ayres grunted again, and she fell unconscious.

CHAPTER 73

AYRES

Ayres looked at his chest in the mirror, over the tattoos that covered his skin after he'd accepted the oath to be the Death Harbinger.

Only Marras knew how much he hated them.

Marras's body, donned in her usual gray robes, had been the first thing that appeared on his chest after he'd accepted the Death Harbinger ability from his father. In the following weeks, more black ink started swirled out around her, spreading her art on him farther and farther across his skin. The tattoos now claimed almost every free inch of skin on his upper body besides his face.

He hated them. Hated the skulls, the bones, the shadows, the beautiful faces, the flowers, the symbols, the soldiers on his back telling the world of Sakar Sumavari's demise in Sumavari's War—he hated them all. Ayres's prison of black ink covered almost every inch of his skin and told the story of past mistakes, warning him of what would happen if he failed in his duties.

His duties. *Death.*

Marras help him, it was fucking miserable.

But today, seeing how Rorax had reacted to his tattoos up close, hearing her say again that she liked them, seeing how it had made her nipples hard, the contrast of Rorax's little pink tongue against his tanned and tattooed flesh as she licked over the water droplets on his chest, sliding up his collarbone....

Ayres rubbed the back of his shoulders with both hands. *Fuck* that had been hot. Even half dead, Ayres had wanted that pink little tongue to stay on him. He wanted it lower, tracing the gutters of his abdominal muscles down until she was low enough to curl that little tongue around his cock.

She had the most perfect little body he had ever seen in his life. Rorax trained every day for hours, had been training for years like that, and the result was lean muscle all over her body that he wanted to put his hands on, to knead and touch. Her breasts, gods above, seeing her in just her wet underclothes today had given him just about a perfect view of her tits. He was going to think about her in his fantasies for the rest of his fucking life.

Without thinking, he lashed out and struck the mirror with his fist, breaking the glass. It cut deep into his knuckles, spreading crimson droplets over the fragments of mirror where it shattered.

He stared at his reflection above where he'd struck and seethed at himself with pain and rage.

Why?

Why was it *her* that made him forget his curse?

Why was it always *her* that made him like the parts of himself he usually hated? Why was *she* the one who had made him feel so seen?

Neat trick, she had said when she saw his power in Helfast. That's it. She had been a hair away from death at the time... but *neat trick*? That was it?

It made him sick that she had this... hold on him. A hold he couldn't shake. A hold that he wanted and craved. He wanted her attention. Somewhere deep down in him, he was looking forward to the next time a Contestar died and he'd have to pin her down and make her wet. He wanted to taste that pretty pink mouth again.

He stalked out of his bathroom, pulling a shirt over his head as he stood next to his bed that Rorax was currently passed out in. The healer had left an hour ago with the diagnosis. Rorax had been poisoned.

Pathetic. He had called her pathetic this morning, even after she'd woken up and come to training after being *poisoned*.

He ran a hand over his short, cropped hair. Ayres owed her an apology for a fistful of things, but the minute she opened her eyes, he'd tell her he was sorry and that he was an ass.

Cannon, Kaiya, and Jia had all just left to track another summoning. It was Ayres's turn to go, but Cannon took one look at his face and shook his head.

You'll be too distracted. Stay with her. Find out what happened, his oldest friend had signed to him.

Ayres didn't know what could be worse, being away without any word on her condition, or being here, stuck watching her, waiting, and wondering if she was going to survive.

And for the gods' sake, this was the fucking *Pup*.

It shouldn't even have been an issue. He should be thankful someone else was taking care of her, killing her off so he wouldn't have to at the end of this.

Kiniera had come to see Rorax as well, assuring him that the poison the healer had extracted from her veins was something Heilstorms built an immunity to in their hellish training. It'd been a substance Rorax had already been exposed to numerous times, so it wouldn't be fatal for her if treated correctly.

But Rorax still hadn't stirred. Hadn't even moved. She was barely breathing, and she laid there like she was dead, so still and motionless, like the soul had been ripped from her and—

Ayres wrenched himself out of his panicked thoughts and jerked himself to his feet. He moved to the empty fireplace and placed both palms on the mantle, leaning into them and forcing himself to take in a few steadying breaths through his nose.

Something was happening to him, something he didn't like, something he couldn't control, something that... scared him. *She* scared him. He was starting to *care* about her.

There was a soft knock at the door, and he recognized the light steps as Milla walked into the room.

"Oh my," she breathed, rushing to the side of Rorax's bed. "I just heard from Piers that she'd been poisoned."

Ayres flexed his jaw.

Milla looked over her shoulder at him. "Do you have any idea who did it?"

The reminder that not only had she been poisoned, but whoever poisoned his Contestar was still breathing, made more anger pool in his chest, and his grip on the wooden mantle got tighter.

"No. No one has any clue. She might know but hasn't opened her eyes since this morning."

"Oh," Milla mumbled. She took a few steps closer to Ayres and placed a hand on his shoulder. "Ayres, are you okay?"

"I'm fine," he growled, but he wasn't. He was so far from fine he wasn't even sure what that looked like for him anymore.

She squeezed his arm tightly. "Ayres, this isn't your fault."

His jaw felt tight. It was. It was all his fault. Rorax had been in his care for nearly three moons, and not once had she ever complained or been late to a training session. He should have known something was wrong.

"I'll talk to Kiniera, see if she has any leads. I want to work together with her on this. We will find out who did this, Ayres."

He nodded, finally releasing the mantle and standing up straight to face her. "Thank you."

Milla nodded, looking up at him with something that looked like pity. He smothered a snarl as she patted his arm.

"You're allowed to like her, Ayres. You know that, right?"

He blinked, not expecting those words to come out of her mouth.

She gave him a sad, knowing smile. "I'm just saying, if you want her to be with you after the Choosing, tell her."

Ayres ground his molars together as he glowered down at Milla. It was so easy for her to say such things. Milla wouldn't be the one killing Rorax at the end of this if they couldn't free her. It would most likely be him, and any feelings he had for Rorax would make that job even more difficult than it already was.

"Just think about it." Milla smirked at him before turning and walking out of the room without another word.

Chapter 74

Rorax

The little island sat approximately one hundred yards off the coastline, and from what Rorax could see, there was only one building on it. Even from the shore, she could see the golden dome on the top gleaming in the sun.

Rorax wished the building would catch fire and burn to flames.

She kept her eyes on that little structure as the Guardian erected a barrier between the bystanders who had come to watch the trial and the Contestars milling around on the beach. Her stomach rolled violently, and she gritted her teeth to keep from projectile vomiting all over the sand.

Milla and Ayres had both petitioned the Guardian for an extension on the trial considering Rorax had been poisoned the day before, but it was no use.

"She competes or she dies," the Guardian told them.

Now Rorax's only goals were to live through the trial and try not to hurl so much that she drowned herself in the process. No one except the Guardian and her men knew what they would have to do once they arrived on that tiny, gods-forsaken island, but Rorax's primary objective at this point was to survive the swim. She could figure out the rest later.

Red sparks erupted in the air, and the Contestars made a mad dash to the beach.

Rorax slowly jogged to the surf and dove in. Gods, the sea felt good against her skin as she ducked under a midsized wave and started to drag herself through the water with sluggish strokes.

Briar stroked past Rorax; the lithe blonde looked comfortable in the waves, slicing through the water like a gods-damned mermaid.

Despite the salty water, Rorax forced her eyes open. Ayres had sent Kaiya into the village close to the castle yesterday and gathered intel for Rorax as she lay recovering from the poison attempt. The bay was notorious for having aggressive sharks, and they'd found out the civilians there had been feeding them, trying to gather the sharks closer to the shore where the Contestars would be. She needed to be able to see an oncoming attack. Rorax might be able to fend off one or even two sharks, but no more. Not in her current state.

Her stomach rolled violently, but Rorax was able to hold it down until she reached the sands of the island before emptying her stomach.

When she finally looked up from her hands and knees, the other Contestars were already up and sprinting to the small, white, circular building with the gleaming golden dome.

"Fuck," Rorax muttered, pushing off on unsteady legs after them. She tripped more than once, the skin on her palms ripping open on the sharp rocks.

Briar and Mo made it to the building first, yanking open the white double doorway into the building. The rest of the Contestars followed them inside and disappeared into the dark.

The golden dome gleamed, almost blinding Rorax as she moved toward it. At the top of the dome sat a lightning rod with a tiny carved rooster on top, its head twisted around to look down at her, its plumes on the backend high and golden. The rooster was the of the sigil of Midhurst. This must be an old ruin dedicated to their gods.

Rorax flipped the rooster off as she half jogged, half stumbled after the others, pushing herself to move faster across the rocks.

The doors were a plain whitewashed wood, and the entryway was surrounded by an intricately carved stone doorframe. Rorax flinched as the cuts on her palm seared hot when she grabbed the doorknob. She jerked the door open, leaving a bloody handprint on the white wooden door as she slipped inside.

The other Contestars hadn't made it very far.

Rorax sucked in a breath, and her eyes went wide in wonder as she took in the interior.

Golden mirrors with intricately bejeweled frames hung on the walls of the building. About ten feet inside was another door, a rounded gate that had golden figures, symbols, words, and witch-wards carved into the surface. It was the most intricately carved piece of art Rorax had ever seen, and it too appeared to be made of solid gold.

None of the other girls seemed to feel the same sense of awe as Rorax. They were already arguing with each other about what to do next.

Stella reached out to touch one of the sculptures, but Mo slapped her hand away. "Don't touch that. I can feel… something."

"Just have Isgra melt the damn door," Briar hissed up at Mo, getting in her face and standing toe-to-toe with her. Mo glowered down at Briar with equal ferocity, her hands curling and uncurling into fists.

Isgra snorted from where she stood, watching the two women's standoff with amusement. "Are you two going to stare each other to death?" she asked sarcastically. "Even I couldn't melt this door down. I'd need the Guardian's power to do it."

Stella stepped back from the rose she'd been about to touch and focused on the metal barrier in front of her before chewing into her lips. "I couldn't bend it; it's just too thick."

"You shouldn't try either," Enna mumbled. "This is a temple. Most of the metal here has probably been heavily warded against raiders."

Rorax took a few silent steps inside until she was directly behind the group. The door had to be ancient, likely over fifteen hundred years old.

The figures were in the old Midhurst style: two-dimensional, full-body figures with crow's heads. The swirled script of an ancient language was carved into the background behind the figures. This area had been part of the Midhurst territory before Lyondrea claimed it during the Breach over three hundred years ago.

Mo snarled, her upper lip curling up over her teeth. "Can any of you read what the door says?" Her dark eyes landed on Rorax, and her snarl turned into a sneer. "What about you, *Pup*?"

Rorax contemplated feeding Mo her teeth, her eyes dragging up and down the Contestar sharply until Mo shifted away from Rorax and turned back to the door.

Rorax looked up at the largest figurine of a massive crow skull in the center, sitting at the very top of the arched door. The sockets seemed to bare down into her soul, and a shiver rolled down her spine.

She ignored Mo and turned to Stella. "Search the door and look for two things. Can you recognize any of the witch-wards in place here? And can you tell if every figurine is warded or just some?"

Stella nodded once and began to comb over the door, looking for wards. Rorax turned to Mo, who was from House of Alloy. "Can you feel what's on the other side of the door? Any more metal?"

Mo glared at Rorax, then shifted uncomfortably and finally closed her eyes. "There's a shelf beyond this. I can't see what's on it, but... a shelf. The door must be protecting whatever's on it. I can't use my magick on it; it must be blessed."

Rorax nodded as Mo finished her examination of the door.

"Done," Stella huffed, wiping the sweat off her forehead. "Enna was right, we shouldn't touch anything on the wall except for the snake in the middle."

She pointed to the center of the door, where a tiny little garden snake lay under a row of golden roses. Rorax reached out to the little snake hesitantly. According to Stella, only this little carving was safe, but how much did she trust Stella?

Maybe it was a handle or a knocker....

Rorax had to bite the inside of her cheek to keep from screaming when the metallic snake's golden body animated itself. It lunged out and coiled its long body around her wrist. Rorax tried to yank her arm back to safety, but the tiny snake was much stronger than it looked. It forced her wrist around until her hand was palm up. With its tiny golden head, it leaned forward and flicked its little tongue across Rorax's blood, still wet on her skin from where she'd fallen on the rocks on the beach.

Rorax felt a rush in her head, and before she could scream, her eyes rolled back and she was thrown into a vision.

Wherever she was, it was bright. She looked around and realized she was in a field of amber wheat.

Rorax looked up and yelped, then fell back on her ass as a huge snake towered over her, its pink tongue as long as her forearm, tasting the air.

Rorax scooted back on her hands, sweat breaking out over her forehead, her heart thumping furiously in her chest. The snake considered her with one golden eye, the vertical slit dilating as it took her in.

"You are unlllike any of the Contestarsss before," it observed.

The voice trailed down Rorax's spine, and she shivered as the snake moved its giant head around, taking in the empty field of tall wheat grass around them. "It'sss comfortable in here, in your mind... very roomy."

It was in her head? And what did it mean, there was a lot of room in there?

Rorax shuffled back a couple more feet before standing on unsteady legs.

The snake could swallow her in one bite, or one of its fangs could puncture all the way through her chest twice over, and there would be nothing she could do.

"I'm... glad you like it," Rorax rasped, wiping her sweaty hands on her pants. "Make yourself comfortable... but not *too* comfortable."

The snake hissed in what Rorax prayed was a snake laugh and not the sound of hunger.

"The air tastesss... like Ssshadowbell. Were you poisssoned?" The snake tilted its head as its tongue tasted the air around her again.

Rorax grimaced and nodded.

"I can sssmell that you have sssomething unsssavory in your sssystem." The snake shook its head and focused on her again. "Take the coin back to the Guardian and take the necklaccce on the ssshelf. It will help you with your transssfer of power. Look for the tablesss for the transssfer. Prepare yoursssself for the war. Dessspite your missstakesss, the godsss ssstill chossse you to fight, Roraxxx Greywood."

Before Rorax could ask any questions, or even blink, her head rushed once more and then she was standing in front of the golden wall once again.

The little garden snake took a few more licks of her blood before it raised its head and winked at her.

It looked over at the rest of the girls, standing there gawking.

It unwrapped slowly from Rorax's wrist, and when none of the other Contestars moved forward, it solidified into the carving once more.

"That was disgusting." Briar shivered, eyeing the snake like she was afraid it might reach out and lick her, too.

There was a loud groan, like bending metal, and the door slowly creaked open, sliding to the side on ancient hinges.

Just as Mo had told them, behind the door was a wall lined with golden shelves. The giant door had been protecting nothing more than a closet.

Rorax sucked in a breath. Lining the shelves were golden coins with snakeheads stamped on one side. Rorax had a sneaking suspicion a rooster would be stamped on the other side. The snake and the rooster were on the Midhurst crest.

"Mo? Any enchantments?"

The girl's eyes went unfocused for a split second before she shook her head. "I don't think so."

The doorway wasn't wide enough for more than one person at a time, so Rorax took a step forward and picked up a coin.

The coin felt heavy in her hand.

A snake's voice tickled at the back of her head. *The necklaccce, take the necklaccce, Contessstar.*

Rorax blinked down at the coin in her palm a few times before looking up. On the top shelf there was a golden necklace. It looked like a sunburst, no bigger than one of the golden coins.

Take it.

Swallowing hard, Rorax reached out and grabbed the necklace from the top shelf.

"Hey," Lily barked, "that's the only one on the shelf."

Lily took a step toward the doorframe, and a strong wind burst out from the room, forcing Lily back a step.

"Oh, fantastic, Lily, will ya look at what you've done!" Briar pointed a finger over to the entrance to where the two golden mirrors hung. The mirrors were dripping, like molten gold down the wall, where they gathered in a puddle. When there was no more molten gold flowing down, two robed and golden warriors rose from the pools of metal. Two priests with metallic golden robes covering their faces and long staffs. One of them approached and swung its golden staff at Lily. With a loud crack, the staff caught Lily on the back and flung her into the air hard enough that her head cracked against the wall. She collapsed in a heap on the floor, and the other Contestars scrambled back, getting well out of the way of the golden priest.

"*Ta ei pakkunud oma verd*," the figure growled. It stood over Lily, its staff pointing down at her still form.

The other figure stepped closer to Rorax and pointed at her with a bony, metal finger. It then pointed at the door, motioning for her to step out of the tiny room. Rorax stepped away from the shelf, and the wall slid back into place behind her. The figure pressed its staff against Rorax's shoulders and pushed, forcing her toward the entrance. Her eyes snapped up to Enna's.

Verd. The Guard who'd attacked Lily had said, "*Ta ei pakkunud oma verd*."

She didn't know what the rest of it meant, but verd meant *blood* in the ancient language of the very first Gifted. Rorax now thanked the gods for the countless hours she'd spent in the library and for Radashan's seemingly pointless books.

"Rorax!" Enna cried. She tried to get closer, but the figurine herding her to the door swatted her away, the sound of bone against metal loud.

"Blood," Rorax hissed to the brunette over her shoulder as the guard pushed her toward the entrance. "Let the snake taste a drop of your blood!"

Almost as one, the remaining Contestars leaped forward, bringing their knives out to give an offering to the snake. Enna gave her one more fearful glance as the guard threw Rorax out and slammed the door behind her.

She tucked the necklace and the coin into her pocket and took off running as fast as her legs could go. If Lily died and triggered an influx, it would be a bloodbath in that room, and Rorax had Glimr strapped to her back. She needed to get herself as far away as possible from the other Contestars.

Rorax only tripped twice on her way back to the ocean. The first time she avoided falling on her hands, but the second time she ripped her palms open again. She cried out, taking a deep breath before she pushed herself up; blood dripped down her fingers. When she dove into the water, the cuts on her palms stung from the salt, but the water felt incredible against her overheated skin.

Rorax again kept her eyes open as she began stroking through the water. The waters were not nearly as empty as when she'd swam out to the island.

A dark figure streaked past her on the ocean floor below, and she shrieked in her throat, but nothing came past her again. There were a few more shapes as she paddled by, but thankfully nothing approached her.

Rorax had never been so happy to feel sand under her feet as she did the moment she reached the beach. Her toes scraped across the granules, and relief washed over her so intensely she wanted to cry.

She pushed herself up from the bottom and half jogged, half walked to where the crowd waited for the Contestars' arrival back on the beach. The Guardian stood in front of the crowd, amusement glittering in her dark gaze as she held her hand out. "Did you bring my prize?"

Rorax fished the dripping coin out of her back pocket and dropped it into the Guardian's palm.

The Guardian grimaced, took a white handkerchief to dry off the coin, and held it up to the light, flipping it over between the snake and rooster head.

The coin then vanished from between the Guardian's fingers, and Rorax's chest seized. Was she going to have to go back to get another coin?

The Guardian gave her a soft little smile. "Your trial is complete; Majauss has called her coin back. Take a seat while we wait for the others."

CHAPTER 75

RORAX

Rorax took a few steps away from the Guardian and found Milla and Ayres grinning at her through the wall of solid air the Guardian had erected before the trial started.

Milla pressed her palm against the transparent barrier, beaming. "You crazy bitch. How did you do it? You got to the temple after everyone else."

Ayres wasn't smiling at her like Milla, but Rorax could see the satisfaction on his face as his eyes flitted over her body, looking for wounds.

"I got lucky," she told Milla. Sweat and salt water dripped down her neck, and exhaustion pulled at her limbs. Gods, she had never been so excited for a bath and some sleep in her *life*.

An ear-piercing scream came from the water behind her, and collectively the whole crowd turned to look.

Stella, Mo, and Isgra had reached the beach and were half jogging, half walking toward the Guardian. Briar wasn't far behind them, but Enna... Enna was still in the water, dark fins circling around her.

Lily was nowhere to be seen.

Enna screamed again, and Rorax took an instinctive step toward the water.

"Rorax," Ayres growled from the other side of the barrier.

The Guardian accepted the coins from the three girls before she turned and eyed Rorax, considering her with an amused smile. "No one from the opposite side of the barrier is allowed to enter the water. *You* could, I suppose, but you've already won. Would you risk your life for a competitor who would not risk her life for you?"

Rorax gritted her teeth, turning to watch as a dark fin inched closer to Enna.

Rorax had made a promise to herself, a promise that she wouldn't leave the Realms without an acceptable Guardian when the power passed from the current Guardian to its successor.

If Lily was down, that left Mo, Stella, Isgra, Briar, Mairi, Enna, and herself. She couldn't, *wouldn't* leave the Realms' protection to a House of Alloy citizen or someone beholden to them. Mairi was barely skilled enough to tie her own fucking boots, and Briar didn't have the moral compass strong enough to lead the Realms. And beyond all that, Rorax *liked* Enna. She was her friend.

Enna screamed in terror again, and without another thought, Rorax ran back, sprinting toward the water.

"Crow, get back here!" Ayres demanded from behind the barrier.

There was a loud crashing boom, and Rorax looked over her shoulder to see Ayres slamming his fists against the barrier. His eyes were silver and red. "Rorax!" he bellowed.

She turned away and took two more steps until she was knee-deep in salt water before a hand wrenched her back.

"Where are you going? You've already won," Isgra snarled down at her.

"Let me go," Rorax fought to keep her voice even, "or I will dislocate your wrist."

"She's already gone. Let her die, you fool."

For a beat, Rorax stared into the eyes of her dead best friend. The best friend that she couldn't save, couldn't protect. "No."

Rorax ripped her arm out of Isgra's grip and dove into the water.

She swam furiously, begging her body to find the strength somewhere within her.

She kept pushing, her limbs burning as the adrenaline started to fade from her system. When Rorax was close enough, she ducked her head underwater to see what she was up against.

It was a squid. A giant squid with teeth protracting from its tentacles, who was slowly nipping at Enna's legs and releasing her blood into the water. The sharks were circling so they could enjoy whatever the squid left behind for them.

Cold fear speared down Rorax's chest as she took in the blood staining the water.

Rorax thanked the gods that her knife, Glimr, was in its sheath on her back, and with a thrust of her arm, she sent it in a tight spiral through the water.

Her knife sank itself into the center of the squid, and its tentacles instantly released around Enna's waist. Black inky blood gushed through the water, mingling with the red, as the squid's body slowly floated away.

Rorax summoned the knife back to her and rose to the surface.

She gasped a breath into her burning lungs and reached forward to grip Enna's wrist. Rorax jerked her forward, and Enna crashed into her side. "Come on, swim. We have to swim."

"Sharks," Enna said faintly, slumping forward, her forehead thudding onto Rorax's shoulder. "Let me go, Ror. Get back to shore."

Rorax turned Enna around, wrapped her arm around Enna's stomach, and kicked her legs furiously under Enna's weight to keep both their heads above water. Rorax twisted Enna's hair around her fist and yanked her friend's head back so she could see her neck. Black veins were starting to twist up Enna's throat from under her clothes.

Fuck.

"Enna, I need you to breathe. Stay with me."

She whimpered against Rorax's shoulder as Rorax started to haul her through the water.

Rorax could see the Guardian's wall of magick on the shore, only because a black and red magick cloud was starting to create a contrast. Loud yells erupted from the beach, and she could hear Ayres's thundering voice the loudest.

Enna had become dead weight in her arms, and her breathing started to grow ragged against her shoulder as Rorax pushed through the water. The yelling on the beach became louder, and she saw Isgra and Briar follow most of the emissaries offshore and turn toward camp as Ayres and the Guardian continued to yell at one another.

Rorax's limbs started to burn, and she gritted her teeth. She used almost every shred of energy and adrenaline left in her system to move forward, trying to ignore her rising panic.

She and Enna were going to be fish food in about five minutes if she didn't figure out something fast. But she couldn't think. She couldn't think, and she couldn't breathe. Her chest felt tighter and tighter; her lungs were taking in less and less air as panic settled into her system.

Enna's face dipped under the water just as movement in her peripheral vision sparked a new wave of fear in her chest. A dark fin sliced through the water toward her.

"Enna," she sobbed, trying to shake her friend and swim at the same time. Enna's head only lolled to one side in response. They were going to die, and there was nothing Rorax could do to save them. She'd given everything she had. "I'm so sorry."

Enna didn't say anything, and Rorax summoned her knife into her palm one last time. She threw it at the shark.

The movement made them slip under the surface, and Rorax inhaled some of the salty sea in through her nose. She kicked up and coughed, trying desperately to expel the water from her lungs.

From beneath the water, Ayres's voice was muffled, calling out to her, but she couldn't hear him, and she couldn't comprehend what he was saying until it was too late.

The shark, with one bloody eye, still raced toward them.

The shark hit Rorax so hard it blasted both her and Enna clean out of the water.

Rorax's head hit the water first, her vision going dark for a moment before she was kicking again, breaching the surface and desperately inhaling air into her lungs. Enna floated a few feet from her, face down, her dark hair billowing out around her like an ominous cloud.

Rorax gripped her wrist and pulled her limp body toward her. She hauled Enna's head up with her arms while her legs continued to tread water, pushing them toward the shore. Enna wasn't breathing, so Rorax slapped her hard, and she jerked, convulsing in her hold, expelling some of the water through her nose.

The shore was close now, so close. She gritted her teeth and surged forward.

Enna struggled. "Ror, Ror, let me go. I can swim."

"No," she gritted out as she hauled them both closer. They must have been twenty yards from the shore when she saw it again, but it was so close, too close. A dark fin.

She couldn't do anything but try to push Enna toward the shore, and she screamed, "SWIM!" before the shark clamped its jaws around Rorax.

Rorax could barely feel the pain as three layers of serrated teeth plunged into her back, stomach, and hip. The shark jerked her around under the water. She tried her best not to inhale, but as it yanked her back and forth, she opened her mouth to scream, and the water rushed into her lungs.

Her mind immediately became fuzzy, and the pain in her stomach and hips went numb.

If she was going to die here, at least it would be like this, where the pain was almost nonexistent and she was almost warm. For a heartbeat, she let herself give up for the moment. She let herself flirt with the idea of slipping into the ever-beckoning comfort of death, where she would never be in pain and never lose anyone she loved ever again.

Take me, I'm ready. I have fought, and there is nothing more I can give, she thought as she slipped into the darkness.

Almost as soon as she made her decision to slip under, a hot beam of power shot through her.

Pure energy, rage, and adrenaline consumed every cell in her body. An influx.

Using the strength that the influx fused into her very soul, Rorax summoned her knife to her palm and started to hack. She sliced, stabbed, and plunged her knife into the shark's gray side until finally the shark jerked, making a small welp of pain, and opened its jaws.

She pulled her flesh off rows of teeth, screaming internally, and kicked away.

With blurry eyes, she watched as the shark swam off through the water, its blood trailing behind it, before she turned sluggishly toward shore.

So much of her blood was in the water around her she couldn't see, so she kicked directly up until her head breached the surface.

She coughed up water and blood, gasping in deep, desperate breaths. She looked around frantically and saw that in her struggle, the shark had thankfully moved her even closer to the beach. Rorax pushed herself as much as she could toward the shore. When her toes lightly scraped the sandy bottom, she used her legs to propel herself forward. The movement jarred her injuries, and she screamed internally. Her left side burned. Rorax's influx was fading fast, her body unable to maintain her strength for long. She got close enough to the beach that she could touch the bottom but she hadn't been watching the waves. She heard Milla shriek her name, and she looked up just in time to see a giant wave angling right for her.

"Ayres!" Rorax screamed as a wave crashed into her and smashed her onto the shore. She felt her nose crack under the sand, and everything went black.

Chapter 76

Ayres

Something inside Ayres snapped the instant Rorax screamed his name, seconds before a wave smashed her onto the shore. The Guardian's air wall was wavering under the pressure of Ayres's magick, but as soon as Rorax hit the sand, he shattered it like thin glass. The Guardian hissed in fury, but he was way past giving a fuck. Ayres turned to a healer, at the same time sending his magick out to Rorax's crumpled body on the shore, lifting her unconscious form out of the water and bringing her closer to him.

"Help her," he ordered a healer next to him. The healer went pale as she took in Ayres's red eyes but wisely gave a weak nod.

He turned to Milla, who was standing next to her, and rattled off orders. "Get any other healers you see on this beach and bring them over here." He pointed a finger at Rorax's body that was swiftly coming closer to him, floating on a black cloud. One of her arms was draped off the side, and blood was trickling down her arm and dripping on the sand. Her death wasn't tingling at the back of his neck like it had been that day at Helfast, but it would be soon. It was already a dark shadow on the horizon.

"The other healers are at Enna's side, trying to get the poison out of her body," Milla replied.

"Get them over here."

Milla opened her mouth like she was about to say something, but she thought better of it and rushed over to direct the healers at Enna's side.

The Guardian eyed Ayres cautiously, and he snarled at her, "Get that poison out of Enna's body."

The Guardian stiffened, as if being ordered to do anything explicitly offended her. But a deep, threatening snarl ripped out of him, "Now."

She flinched, a sliver of fear in her eyes betraying her as she turned away stiffly and did as she was told.

Ayres spun back to Rorax's body. Anger and fear threatened to choke him. Rorax's skin was ashen, and blood was dripping down her arms into the sand.

Ayres was at her side in a flash, ripping off his shirt and pressing the cloth into her side. Her shadow still hovered in the back of his mind, but thankfully had not gotten closer to the bridge. He bent down to whisper in her ear. "I swear to the gods, if you try to die today, I will bring you back to kill you myself."

Rorax stirred, and a faint smile traced over her pale lips. "I already said no to death today, Ayres."

For that, the gods knew, Ayres was thankful.

CHAPTER 77

TRESSA

Tressa sat on the sand on the beach, exhausted and in shock. She watched as Enna and Rorax's unconscious bodies were both carted off by her team of healers.

She hadn't believed her ears when a messenger came running, saying that the Death lieutenant had demanded all available healers report to the beach.

Ayres wasn't her boss, and she'd bristled at the command, yet she had still come running.

Tressa only brought six of her healers to the Cracked Sea, and it had taken all of them to clear the squid's poison from Enna and to stitch Rorax's flesh back together from the deep shark bite in her side.

Rorax had risked her life *again* for a fellow Contestar and had survived without even a scar to show for it. The facts weren't computing in Tressa's head.

Rorax was a monster. A *monster*. But what kind of monster would risk herself to save her fellow Contestars? These were the people who would eventually cost Rorax her *life* if she didn't find her way out.

Lily had died in the gilded shrine on the island. One of Majauss's golden guards had bashed in her skull, and the resulting influx had saved Rorax's life. The gods themselves *chose* to save Rorax today.

Tressa ground her teeth together and wrapped her arms tightly around herself, her nails digging into the back of her arms.

Hate coated her tongue as she jerked her gaze to the waves in front of her. She hated herself, hated the Choosing, and, most of all, hated Rorax for how the flame of loathing in her chest had flickered and sputtered when she saw Rorax pull Enna through the water. Gods, she wished she was powerful enough to use her Mind Walker abilities, to be able to look through Rorax's mind, see what she was *really* like.

She dug her nails into herself even deeper.

A pale, calloused hand reached down in front of her, and after a moment's hesitation, she took it, letting Ren pull her onto her feet.

He wrapped her up in his arms and pushed his face into the crook of her neck. "I can see every thought on your face right now," he murmured. "Whatever you decide to do, I'm behind you."

He pulled his face back from hers; the ocean in the background accentuated the copper tones of his unbelievably handsome beard and long hair.

Gods above, Ren was so beautiful.

Tressa nodded and pulled him into her again, needing his warmth. They stood that way for a long time, her wrapped up in his big arms, letting herself feel conflicted and angry down to her core.

The moment was ruined when footfalls in the sand made Tressa peel her eyes open.

Ayres approached with angry strides, and something about the way he moved or maybe the expression on his face triggered alarm bells in Tressa's mind. Without thinking, she shot her hand out and clamped it around Ren's wrist. She gave it a squeeze in warning.

She had never seen Ayres so angry before. Not at her.

Ren dropped his arms from around her and grabbed her hand, taking a half step forward, edging his way slightly in front of her and putting himself between them.

It made her chest feel warm, even knowing, in a real fight, they would both be dead in seconds if Ayres wanted them to be.

Ayres's silver stare nearly impaled Tressa. He stopped a couple of feet from them, and his eyes narrowed. "Were you the one who poisoned Rorax?"

Tressa's eyebrows shot up. "What? No!"

The muscle in Ayres's jaw flexed.

"It wasn't us, Ayr," Tressa insisted.

The reminder that Rorax had been poisoned and still chose to go back to drag Enna out of the water made the once reliable flame in her chest flicker again. Tressa grimaced.

Ayres's silver eyes flicked back and forth between Tressa and Ren for a second before he nodded his acceptance. Something tight eased in Tressa's chest.

Ren didn't relax though. "Would it matter if we did? The plan all along has been that she dies or she leaves, Ayres. She's a Heilstorm. A Unit One Heilstorm. She has killed *thousands*. Gods above, Ayres, she even laid siege against *your* city. It's not surprising someone wants her dead, and you were okay with that a couple of months ago."

Tressa watched as the same conflict that was plaguing her flitted through Ayres's eyes.

Ayres's jaw clenched a few more times as he stared at Ren.

Ren and Ayres were the same height, but the *power* that radiated from Ayres, that dormant *thing* housed in Ayres's bones, was enough to send a chill through Tressa. From the way Ren squeezed Tressa's hand, she knew Ren felt it, too.

"I've changed my mind. She has the potential to help us," Ayres finally answered, looking from Ren to her, then back again. "*No one* touches her without my consent. No one lays a finger on that woman, or they answer to *me*."

A little squeak escaped her lips before she could stop it, and Ayres's heavy but thankfully silver gaze fell on her again. "Not *one* finger, Tressa. Not one scratch, not one bump, not so much as a fucking bruise. Not until I decide this is over. Do you understand?"

Tressa swallowed thickly before nodding.

Ayres cracked his neck and took a step back.

Ren relaxed a bit, and Ayres must have noticed because something like guilt pinched at the corners of his mouth. He rubbed the back of his neck, rubbing at the tattoos there. He looked tired.

"Are you alright, Ayres?" she asked tentatively.

He nodded, dropping his hand back to his side. "I think so. I'm sorry. I'm just... angry. She was attacked, and we don't know who did it yet. She has me twisted into knots right now, and I don't know what to do."

He swallowed, looking over to where Tressa's healers had disappeared into the castle with Rorax's unconscious body. "I will talk to you both tomorrow."

Ayres turned and walked away, leaving her and Ren to gape at his back.

Ren blew out a breath and rested his hands on his hips, watching his old friend walk away. "That is not good, Tress. Not good at all."

Her eyebrows furrowed together as she kept her eyes on the retreating figure in front of them. "Why not?"

"Ayres talks about Rorax the same way I talk about you."

CHAPTER 78

AYRES

Ayres pulled in another deep breath of air, feeling the pressure in his chest ease with every minute he was there. Home.

Leaning against the doorway to the balcony, he watched Rosalie as she tipped her white, delicately painted watering can forward to water her carefully manicured pathos vines.

Kaid, Rosalie's eleven-month-old son, sat on a blanket a few feet away watching his mother with big, curious eyes. She hummed to herself as she worked, and occasionally Kaid would coo and chirp, blowing his lips out and waving his pudgy little arms around in excitement as he tried to imitate her.

Gods, it was adorable.

Kaid blew his lips out and cooed loudly again, causing Rosalie to look over her shoulder at the boy and laugh before moving on to the next thirsty plant. "Pretty close, Kaid. Maybe your uncle can teach you how to *really* hum," Ayres said.

Rosalie arched her eyebrow at Ayres before laughing. "You would be an awful teacher. You can't carry a tune to save your life."

Ayres gave her a sardonic smile and pulled in one more deep breath of air before he bent down and picked up the small, pudgy blond boy.

Kaid immediately wrapped one of his little arms around Ayres's neck, focusing up at him with those big blue eyes as he smacked his other hand against Ayres's lips.

Ayres laughed and blew a little raspberry against the toddler's baby soft skin.

"He looks so much like Eliza did when she was his age," Ayres noted, talking about Rosalie's first child who was currently attending the University of Koppar in House of Ice. Even though it was the best school in the Realms, none of the family had been very happy about seeing her leave. Only after the new Ice Queen and King had both taken a Blood Oath to promise her safety did Rosalie relent.

"I know, but thankfully he's a lot less fussy than Eliza was. He's getting so big; he has been trying to talk to me almost nonstop the past two weeks." Rosalie set her watering can down and plucked her son out of Ayres's arms, resting him on her hip. "You're going to be a talker, huh? Just like your uncle. Driving his sister crazy with all his incessant babble."

Rosalie turned to Ayres and gave him a mocking smirk. "I'm talking about Conrad, of course."

"Of course." Ayres rolled his eyes as Rosalie moved to the double doors of the balcony and deposited Kaid into a waiting nursemaid's arm. "Will you take Kaid to his father? Tell him I'll be up for lunch."

The nursemaid nodded and left, closing the door to the balcony behind her.

Rosalie came back and rested her hip against the railing, facing Ayres and crossing her arms over her chest. "No more distractions, Ayr. Tell me why you're here."

Ayres crossed his arms over his chest, too. "Can't I just come and say hello now and again?"

Rosalie uncrossed her arms and used them to grab on to the railing behind her as something sad flitted across her face. "You used to do that, you know. Before you… before you took on the Harbinger."

Ayres grimaced, and guilt pitted in the bottom of his stomach. "I know, Rose. And I promise, once the Choosing is over, I'll be around more. I just…." He blew out his breath and raked a hand through his hair.

"Resent me. You resent what I have here… what *you* gave me—a life, a family, a chance at something normal."

Ayres flinched, and he had to look away from his sister as guilt and self-hatred gnawed at his heart so painfully, he thought he was going to be nauseous.

"Ayres," Rosalie snapped, taking a step closer and grabbing on to his wrist. "Ayres, stop. It's okay."

She weaved her fingers through his and looked down at their clasped hands. Her pale skin was so different, so bright compared to his tanned skin covered in dark tattoos.

"Ayres, every single day I am thankful for you. For your sacrifice. Without you, my family would be nonexistent. Kaid wouldn't be here, and Eliza—" Rosalie cut herself off and swallowed thickly. "Without you, Ayres, my children would be dead."

Ayres swallowed hard.

"Do you want to know something that keeps me up at night?" Rosalie swallowed thickly again, her watery eyes moving up to his. "The fact that I would do it again, Ayres. I know that I would let you take my place over and over again for them, even knowing what you would go through, what you would have to see, and what you would have to do to protect us."

Her tears finally spilled over onto her cheeks, and her chin started to tremble. But she did not look away from him. "And I'm—gods, I'm so sorry, Ayr. I am the worst sister in the whole world; you never should have had to accept it. I'm the oldest. It should have been me. I…."

Rosalie broke down into sobs, pulling her hands away from his to cover her face. Without hesitation, Ayres wrapped his arms around his sister and pulled her into his chest.

She cried and sobbed, her whole body shaking. He held her until her body was still enough that she could hear him.

"It's been hard." His throat worked as he banished the image of the face of the young girl he had to kill a few moons ago as it flashed in his mind. Instead, he tried to focus on his nephew, on his beautiful niece, who was just as strong and free as her mother. "And even then, I would make the same choice, too. Knowing what I know now, I would take it on again. Again, and again, and again. There would not ever be another choice for me, Rose."

Ayres moved his hands to her shoulders and stepped back, lowering his body enough that they were eye to watery eye. "It's not easy, Rose. But it's worth it. You and your family are worth it every day to me."

She peered up at him through wet lashes. "Do you mean that?"

"I never say things I don't mean."

Rosalie sniffled and gave him a faint smile before she pulled him back in for a hug. "Thank you. I needed to hear you say that."

He patted her back, trying to soothe her until she finally let him go. She wiped at her puffy red eyes, smiling sheepishly. "I'm sorry. I'm a mess. What can I do for you, Ayres? How is Piers holding up, pretending to be the prince?"

She backed away as Ayres chuckled. "Piers makes a better prince than I do most days. No one even bats an eye, and I'm pretty sure Lamonte and Elios have just forgotten at this point about the ruse. He's a natural."

Rosalie gave a meek laugh, and Ayres leaned back against the wall.

"Rose, I actually came here because I need to know why you chose Rorax as our Contestar."

Rosalie blinked at him as she wiped a stray tear off her cheek and another sad smile crossed over her lips. "I'm surprised you made it this long before asking."

She turned around and started peeling her vines off the railing, gently lifting each one so she could peer underneath them.

Ayres cocked his head to the side as he watched her lift more vines. "What're you doing?"

"I'm looking for—ah, here it is." Rosalie pointed to something, and Ayres moved to see what she was pointing at. On the gray stone railing, there was a bloody handprint.

It looked so fresh that Ayres fearfully turned over Rosalie's hands but didn't find any injuries on either one of them. It must have been someone else's blood.

He raised his eyebrow at her. "I don't understand."

"Those are Rorax's handprints," she said slowly, lifting a leaf to the left to show him another dark handprint. "I don't think it was her *own* blood on her hands, but I think this was exactly the spot where Rorax decided what she was doing was wrong, where she decided that she needed to save Surmalinn. These handprints have been here for *fifty* years, Ayres, and I have tried countless things to wash or scrub them away. Now I think that Marras blessed them as a reminder. I don't know what exactly the reminder is for, but there must be a reason I can't wash them away."

Ayres's jaw flexed as he stared down at the dark red stain. He covered one with his own hand, and the stone felt warm under his touch.

Jia had called her friend *Surmalinn's Savior.* Maybe Marras agreed.

"There's one more thing I want to show you, and then I'll explain everything." Rosalie turned on her heel and led him through the balcony's double doors and back into the palace, winding through two hallways before she stopped in front of a stone wall. It was completely empty of decoration and paint, just the flat gray stone.

Ayres looked down at her like she had lost her mind, and Rosalie rolled her eyes and pointed to a thin hairline crack in one of the stones.

Her voice was soft as she asked him, "Do you know what happened here?"

Ayres shook his head even as his stomach clenched.

"Yansley, one of Rorax's men, almost killed me here. He picked me up by my neck and threw me up against the wall." Rosalie brushed over the crack with the tips of her fingers. "He told me he was going to rape me, beat me, and then kill me."

Ayres's vision tunneled for a moment, and his jaw locked up. If Yansley wasn't already dead, Ayres would pluck his soul out of his body and blow it apart before the man could even *think* about going down the bridge into the afterlife.

"Rorax plunged her knife through his heart before decapitating him." Rosalie looked up from the small crack to raise an eyebrow at Ayres. "I assume she's shown you her... *attachment*?"

Ayres huffed a laugh, remembering the spot on his calf where she'd sliced into him the first time they met. "Yes, I know that knife well."

Rosalie snickered and looked back at the wall one last time before looping her arm through her brother's and leading him back toward the balcony. "What she did was wrong. She was responsible for the deaths of hundreds of our people...."

They stepped back out onto the balcony where they could look out and see most of Surmalinn and all its beauty.

"But without Rorax, Surmalinn would be nothing but a pile of rubble," she finished, looking up at Ayres while he gazed out on the cityscape. "After learning what the Wolf did to Rorax, I hated Rorax even more just because maybe deep down I *didn't* hate her. At least... not as much as I did before."

Ayres didn't say anything, so Rosalie pushed on. "I can sense that you're going through the same dilemma. I don't *like* Rorax, Ayres. I haven't seen her since that night, and I don't think I'll ever be able to look at her without a reminder of the night we lost Mom and Dad... the night that Povelinn was razed to the ground. But if you have feelings for her, or maybe just have *conflicted* feelings about her, that's okay. You're not alone. But I've concluded that Rorax *needs* to have people in her life who love her and help guide her toward what's right. I trust Rorax, Ayr. In fact, deep down, I trust her almost as much as I trust you."

That comment had Ayres's head snapping to her in disgust.

Rosalie gave him a little shrug. "I was hiding in the shadows when Rorax killed the Wolf. It happened in the Main Square." Rosalie pointed out into the city, and Ayres followed her gaze to the giant clock tower that stood above the rest of the city skyline. The original clock tower had fallen the night of the siege, but a new one had since been erected.

"The Wolf was angry that her *creation* betrayed her. The Wolf called herself Rorax's mother, told Rorax she had been misled and lied to by others. But in the end, Rorax never doubted her choice and never doubted herself."

Ayres could feel his indecision about Rorax melting away every second they stood there together, looking out into his city. He could feel something new start to take root in his chest, something that was starting to feel a lot like trust.

"If anyone can choose to do the right thing after that much control and constant indoctrination from their own *mother*, I would trust them to remain uncorrupted under almost any circumstances. No matter what House of Alloy or Lyondrea throws at her, I believe she will remain a stalwart. I think there's something divine guiding Rorax's moral compass, Ayres." Rosalie looked up at Ayres with a faraway look in her eyes. "She is destined to have some bigger purpose. When I found out Cannon had won the tournament and she'd been chosen as a Contestar, it felt too much like fate for me to ignore it."

"She is looking for a way to free herself from the Guardian's magick; she plans to take her own life rather than become the Guardian," Ayres said.

"Has she been successful in finding anything to free herself yet?"

Ayres shook his head, and Rosalie gave him a sad smile. "Don't give her any false hope of freedom, Ayres. But give her something to stay and work for."

"Like what?"

"If you can't give her anything more, give her friendship. Give Rorax something to fight for, Ayres, and we might just make it out of this war alive."

CHAPTER 79

RORAX

Rorax crashed to the ground so hard her teeth clicked together painfully.

She rolled to her side, scrambling over the rain-soaked cobblestones of the courtyard to stand up, but it was useless. Cannon almost casually stuck his sword in her face, the tip inches from her nose.

Rorax looked up the blade to see the fucker grinning down at her.

She scrunched her nose, frowning as his grin stretched even wider. He sheathed his sword to free his hands.

Why don't you make yourself at home down there, Ror? the jackass signed. ***You're shitty enough at this that I've knocked you on your ass four times already.***

Rorax grudgingly smirked. Gods, he was arrogant. She picked herself up and wiped the water and rain from her face with her fingers.

The last two weeks had been relatively quiet. There had been no new attempts on her life, and the next trial wasn't until next week. Even the summonings had decreased in their frequency. Kiniera had launched a quiet investigation into who had poisoned her before the trial in the Cracked Sea, but the trail had gone cold, and there were no clues. Rorax could barely remember anything from that night and learned that Kaiya and the prince had blacked out drunk.

The downtime had left her a lot of time to read through the stacks of books Radashan found for her, though most of them had been fruitless.

The only thing noteworthy to happen was the Lowborn Contestars' magick had finally manifested. Well, *most* of the Lowborns.

The first evening in the Northern Castle, after all the Contestars and the emissaries finally made it back from the Cracked Sea, Rorax pushed her way into the Contestars' Courtyard for training to find the Contestars gathered. There was an excited buzz in the air, an energy Rorax didn't understand.

Rorax had scraped her hair into a ponytail and cracked her neck before really taking in the scene. Then she reeled back and blinked and blinked again.

Enna stood in the middle of the courtyard in front of Captain Lamonte, grinning up at the man as a flame danced around her palm. Magick. The Lowborns finally had enough pieces of the Guardian magick after Lily's death to start manifesting abilities.

She'd closed her eyes and searched within herself that night after Lily's death. But there was nothing. Nothing new, nothing alive. Nothing that begged to be released. No magick.

She opened her eyes again to see Briar, the small blonde Contestar, floating an inch above the ground. Briar focused down at her feet, and her hair waved in the wind she'd manipulated to help her levitate.

Someone had come to stand next to Rorax. Cannon.

Can you feel any magick yet? he signed to her.

Rorax shook her head, her eyes wide. ***No, I don't think so.***

A little furrow appeared between Cannon's eyebrows. ***It may have something to do with your knife. Maybe it's running interference.***

Rorax swallowed and nodded.

It had been over a week since then, and every day was getting a little harder for Rorax. Ayres still hadn't returned from his trip to Surmalinn, and the entirety of the Contestars' training sessions focused on helping the Lowborns with their newfound abilities. Rorax, the only Contestar who still had no trace of Elemental Magick, was excluded, left on the outside of their training. Instead, she worked on the side, running drills and training at hand-to-hand combat with Cannon. He seemed to be pushing her even harder after the Lowborns' manifestations.

Today, it was raining, and most of the Contestars had long since quit their training for the evening and gone inside. But she and Cannon stayed. He'd wanted to show her a training move that could only be performed in the rain, using the water to allow a fighter to slide more easily across surfaces and misdirect opponents.

Water dripped down Cannon's nose as Rorax squared up to him.

He slid his feet, kicking up water and making it look like he planned to move to her right before striking her left.

Gods, he was fast.

She lifted the guard of her sword just in time to deflect the blow, the edge of his knife centimeters away from her arm.

They did the sequence four more times, and she only missed once, earning a little scratch on her forearm.

Rorax couldn't help the triumphant grin that broke out on her face.

Cannon grinned back at her and gave her a small little bow. ***Very good. Tomorrow we will throw that move into a sequence.***

Rorax squared up. ***Show me.***

Cannon shook his head, sheathing his sword and patting his stomach before raising his hands to tell her, ***You're a madwoman. I'm starving. It's past eight.***

She grinned and signed, ***Chicken. But thank you. If they asked me to choose the most-talented swordsman on the planet, I'd pick you. I'm lucky to be your Contestar.***

Cannon grinned and clapped her on the back. ***Thank you. Asskiss.***

Rorax laughed, and Cannon did, too.

Hurry up, and don't train in the dark. It's the best way to get cut.

Rorax nodded and watched him walk away. She completed her sequences again. Then again and again.

She'd been honest about what she'd said to Cannon. He was the most vicious fighter she'd ever seen. What he had lost with his sense of hearing, he made up for in other abilities.

Without her knife, it would take a miracle from Ukuros himself for Rorax to best Cannon one-on-one. She looked up to him almost the same way she had looked up to the Wolf, but he was different. The Wolf had isolated her, played mind games with her, and made it so Rorax knew nothing else besides the Wolf. She was dependent on the Wolf because for years there had been no one else.

Even surrounded by people and trainers, it was her choice to respect and look up to Cannon. He was a good man.

Footsteps on the stones behind her made her twirl around, her sword raised.

Squinting through the rain, she could just make out Niels, the House of Alloy emissary. He was dressed in Alloy green; the silver Morningstar of House Alloy was embroidered into the front of his tunic, and the sight made her eyes want to burn. His hair was slicked back like it usually was, and it made his pale face seem even more pinched and harrowed than usual.

Rorax slowly lowered her sword when he stopped a few feet away from her. He pulled his hood back, and rain dripped down his face, droplets running around his tight smile.

"Hello, Rorax," he cooed, his oily voice sending alarm bells ringing in her head.

"Niels." Rorax greeted him with a tight nod, suppressing a shiver that wanted to crawl down her back.

"I was hoping to catch you alone to chat." He took a step closer to her, stepping further into her space.

"What do you want?" Rorax asked bluntly and raised her chin at him. She hadn't seen him fight before, and it was obscenely cocky, but something in her blood told her she could take him and still be on time for the orange sweet rolls that were sometimes served with dinner to still be warm.

"I heard that the House of Weather has decided to become Enna Mistvalley's third House."

"I heard." Cannon had told her earlier in the day that Lily's Protectorate had moved to support Enna, becoming her third Protectorate.

Niels said, creeping a step closer, "Tell me, Rorax. Why is that?"

"What do you mean?"

"Why would some of the strongest houses in the Realms throw their lot behind a *Lowborn*? A Lowborn from the House of Fauna? Why would they pick her over you?"

Rorax narrowed her eyes. "I don't know."

"A pity. Do you know how Claira died?" Niels asked. He cocked his head, his eyes slithering over her body, hovering over her breasts before sliding down lower as he took a step forward.

That had her attention. Claira was the Contestar who'd been murdered in her bed on the night of the Selection. Lamonte and his men had never found out anything about her murder. Immediately, her blood started to sing, thrumming in her veins and demanding that she reach out and force him to tell her what he knew about Claira's death. But she remained still as he stepped closer to her.

Niels's hands reached out through the rain and rested on her hips.

Rorax's jaw clenched so tight her teeth ached as he drew close enough she could feel his heat down the front of her body.

"How did she die?" she asked, fighting to keep her voice even. This man was delusional. He had to be if he thought he was keeping his hands.

Don't stab him, Ror. Don't stab him. He isn't worth it. Not yet.

"Her sponsor, Wolfmoon, is a bit of a sadist. Apparently, there was just too much pain coming from too many sources, and she couldn't handle it," he sighed, his fingers sliding up her sides before lazily coming to a stop right under her breasts.

"I wanted to give you a warning. The Alloy King is *unhappy* that so many Highborns have died, and yet none of the Lowborns seem to be going anywhere. The king gave me permission to recruit Dori, if I felt it was necessary, to help... *put down* the Lowborns if I need to. So you need to stop protecting them; I wouldn't want *you* involved with—"

With a short kick, Rorax swept his feet out from underneath him. He landed on his back and wheezed, the air knocked from his lungs.

She stepped on his throat. "How, *exactly,* did you think this conversation was going to end, Emissary?"

The surprise in his bulging eyes told her he'd thought this would end much differently indeed. She snorted. "If you even breathe in my direction again, I will pluck out your eyeballs to use as olives before I peel the skin off your floppy cock to feed to the crows."

His eyes bulged even more, and she gave him a cold, wicked smile. She increased the pressure of her boot on his windpipe. "Of all the rumors spreading around about me, Emissary, it seems you chose the wrong ones to believe. I'm not a whore, but I would be happy to spill your blood to paint the stones here crimson. It's my favorite color."

Niels whimpered underneath her, trying to shove her away from his neck. She didn't budge.

"I'm glad to know who was behind Claira's death. I will get that information to those who need to know. But remember this, Niels, besides the other Contestars, there are no laws in the Choosing that say I can't kill whoever the fuck I want, when I want. I would happily start my reign of terror with you and Wolfmoon."

"You wouldn't dare. The King of House Alloy would kill you," Niels choked out from under her boot.

She lowered her face closer to his, and her cold smile grew even bigger. "I have faced your king, and I was left unimpressed and unafraid. Your king is nothing to me, and you are less."

"Hey!" a clear, masculine voice boomed.

Her head jerked up, and Cannon was there, looking furious. She blinked at Cannon, shocked at hearing his voice for the first time, before an evil grin spread across her face at the words he was signing to her.

Tell him if he lays another finger on you, I will pull the life from him, his wife, and his parents and store them in a dusty jar for the rest of my life.

Niels was still struggling underneath her boot, growing more and more purple until she released the pressure on his neck, just enough for him to suck in a desperate breath.

His frantic eyes looked up at Cannon. "Do... do you... you know what he just said?" he wheezed.

Rorax chuckled. "He just said he will suck the life from your bones, the bones of your *wife,* and the bones of your family to store in a tiny jar for the rest of his life." She released his neck and squatted down to his level, speaking low. "When he's done, I'll make sure to prop your bodies up where you can watch them rot from your useless little jars."

When Niels let out a low whimper, she sneered at him before she straightened and stepped away.

Rorax didn't give another glance to Niels, who had started violently coughing, before she nodded her thanks to Cannon. They stomped back to the keep together all while she desperately tried to convince herself not to turn around and cleave her sword through Niels's skull.

Niels was a blubbering idiot, but she would need to wait until after the Choosing to kill him.

Despite his wretchedness, Rorax wanted Niels to remain as the House of Alloy emissary. If nothing else, he was predictable and dull-witted. Malleable, even.

Whomever the Alloy King sent to replace him could be a new and potentially lethal piece in the game, and if she killed Niels prematurely, the Alloy King could send someone to try and keep her in check. That was the last thing she needed.

The guards opened the door for them when they approached, and Rorax took her long braid and squeezed the water from it, dripping all over the carpet.

Cannon motioned that he was going to the mess hall. She needed to change into dry clothes before she was ready to eat, so she signed that she would meet him there.

Rorax walked up a flight of stairs alone, her boots squeaking loudly against the stone steps. She was halfway down her hallway when she noticed a hulking figure in her way, standing like a roadblock.

Ayres stood in front of one of the windows, looking out into the courtyard. Relief filled her that he was finally back from Surmalinn.

Rorax opened her mouth to greet him and say something smart-assed about him being late before she noticed the tense lines of his shoulders, his neck flushed red under his tattoos, and the tight fists curled up at his sides. His fists were so tight the dark lines of the skull tattooed there stood out from his flesh like ink on paper.

Rorax's stomach clenched, and she immediately took stock of the hallway. It was deserted and quiet. They were completely alone. That only made her anxiety heighten. If there was a threat, she wasn't locking onto it.

"Ayres, what's wrong?" she asked in a low voice.

Ayres's fury, his pure and savage outrage, was so palpable she could almost taste it. His head bowed fractionally lower, and a vein popped out in his neck. His body coiled even tighter at her words, but he still said nothing.

Rorax made sure her boots were quiet now against the stone floor as she prowled down the hall. She didn't stop until she was close enough that she could touch him, to tackle him out of the way of an attack if she needed to.

"Ayres, what's going on?" she demanded, her voice still low as she looked out the window to where he was staring. It was barely light enough out to see through the rain, and she couldn't make out any unfamiliar shapes in the courtyard below. There was nothing there.

She felt her hackles raise. Gods above, she wished she had her knife.

Her hand darted out, and she wrapped her fingers around Ayres's tattooed wrist. She could feel every one of his tendons straining under the pads of her fingertips.

"Ayres, tell me what's going on," Rorax demanded again, giving his wrist a soft tug.

The touch finally broke him out of whatever thoughts had him trapped in his head. He blinked down at her fingers, like he was surprised she was touching him before he heaved in a few labored breaths.

"What was he doing out there?" Ayres ground out, his jaw tight.

"Who?"

He finally raised his angry eyes to hers. They were bright red. She hadn't seen the red this close before, and her stomach flipped with both excitement and fear.

"Niels, Rorax. What... the... *fuck* happened out there?" Ayres growled, jabbing a finger to the window with the hand she wasn't holding.

She blinked, looked out to where he was pointing at the abandoned courtyard, and understanding dawned. The tension in her body released, a big breath of air whooshed out of her before her skin started to crawl at the memory of Niels's hands sliding up her sides.

Shit. Rorax looked back up into Ayres's face and raised an eyebrow at him. "What do you mean?"

Ayres barked out a sharp, angry laugh, his eyes still flashing red. "You're a *shit* liar, Greywood."

He took an angry step closer to her, and she let his arm drop to take a step back.

"Why *the fuck* did Niels have his hands all over you?"

A shiver of disgust ran down Rorax's spine, and his eyes narrowed. She avoided his question to look him up and down, taking him in. He was as muddy and wet as she was. He must have just arrived from Surmalinn, so he likely had not seen everything. But surely, he didn't think she had *wanted* those advances? And from Niels? The thought made her sick.

"Niels threatened me, and then was brave enough to lay his hands on me before I made it *very* clear that if he did it again, he would lose those hands right before he lost his life." Rorax took another step back and leaned against the wall. She kept her voice carefully blank.

"He also wanted to fill me in on the unfortunate demise of Claira that night of the first influx. Allegedly, Dori Wolfmoon murdered her, the House of Water emissary. *Her own* emissary. Claira apparently didn't get as lucky with her Protectorate as I did."

Rorax gave a sardonic snort, but his eyes darkened a shade, turning a deeper red, and suddenly it wasn't funny at all anymore. She swallowed hard as her heart started thumping in her chest. "What are you going to do?"

"Did he touch you without your permission?" he asked, his voice so low and lethal the little hairs on her arms rose.

Ayres bent fractionally closer to her face, so close she could see the dark eyelashes framing his still red eyes. She could see a faint scar just above his left eyebrow and a faint freckle over his lip. Kään save her, he was handsome.

She managed to suck in a deep breath, smelling the hints of balsam pines that always surrounded him. "Rorax, *did he touch you without your permission*?"

"Yes," she breathed, staring up into his face. Her heart was beating hard in her chest, dancing to an uneven rhythm she didn't recognize.

"And he threatened you?" Ayres asked, again coming fractionally closer to her face, igniting sparks of fire in her blood that made her hands ache to touch him.

"Yes," she said simply and watched with hooded lids as his eyes darkened into a deeper red, almost the color of blood. It ignited her fear in the most delicious way possible, forcing her lust and her fear to coil in the bottom of her stomach. It made her feel alive, and she needed to touch him, needed to feel him all over her. "Ayres...."

"I'm going to kill him." His growl was the same blunt angry one he used on her from time to time. The one that usually made her hackles rise, but this new protectiveness sent a shot of delicious heat between her legs. It was addictive.

Right before she reached out to pull him into her, he stepped back.

She blinked, and before she could come to her senses, he was already halfway down the hallway.

"Ayres!" Rorax yelled, "Ayres, stop!"

She ran after him, and when he finally stopped to look down at her, his eyes were a lighter red than before, thank the gods. "Ayres, don't."

He opened his mouth, probably to tell her he was going to eat the emissary as lunch meat every day next week, but she raised her hands to cut him off. "Ayres, I can *handle* Niels. I would rather have Niels here than anyone else the Alloy King has in his arsenal."

"Ror—" He didn't look convinced, so it was time for a new tactic.

"Besides, you wouldn't want to hurt yourself beating him into oblivion, Lieutenant." She took a gamble and stepped back into him, running her palms slowly up his abdominals over the light leather armor he wore, and gave him a flirty little head tilt.

"Ror…." He squinted his eyes down at her, looking from one of her eyes to the other, his jaw clenching. "What do you mean, *hurt myself*?"

"Tell me, Lieutenant, do you think women would still fawn over you if they knew you'd hurt any part of the legendary trifecta?"

Ayres's eyebrows furrowed in confusion, and the corner of his perfect mouth tipped down. "The legendary trifecta?"

"Your mouth, your fingers, or your…." She shrugged downward, and he watched, his eyebrows pulling together, as she vaguely gestured down below his belt.

She sagged in relief when his eyes changed back to charcoal, and he threw his head back and laughed.

Gods, that laugh. She felt those happy vibrations all the way to her toes as she studied the movement in his thick, muscled, tattooed throat.

Arousal hit her again like a brick, and gods she wanted to lick that throat. He dropped his head back to her, a smug, panty-dropping smirk pulling up at the corner of his mouth.

Ayres reached out and cupped the nape of her neck, sliding his fingers into her hair. He lowered his head down to hers so he could whisper in her ear.

"Ror, you only break things if you don't know what you're doing." He traced his nose down the curve of her ear, gently brushing over the fine hairs of her earlobe. She couldn't stop the shiver of pleasure that rolled down her back. "And to answer your question, women would still flock to me. Maybe even more so once they find out the only thing they'll be able to have from me are my cock, tongue, and teeth."

Ayres nipped her earlobe to emphasize his point, and she had to bite down her whimper, her knees just about giving out as all the heat in her body settled between her legs. She grabbed onto his biceps for support.

A part of Rorax hated it, hated him for forcing her body to have such a response to him. Her panties were wet, and her breasts felt heavy and full as they brushed his chest every time she took in a breath. She felt out of control, and if she was honest with herself, it scared her a little.

Ayres pulled his head back to investigate her face, and obviously pleased at what he saw there, he brought her face so close to his she could taste his minty, warm breath across her lips.

He was going to kiss her again, *thank gods*.

There was a cough behind them, and they both turned their heads to see Cannon smirking. His arms were folded across his chest, his eyebrows raised.

She stayed frozen to the spot as Cannon signed to Ayres. ***Sorry to interrupt, but we need to talk. The Alloy Court stepped out of line today.***

"I saw," Ayres growled. Rorax tried to take a step back, but his grip became imperceptibly tighter in her hair. The sharp new pain in her scalp spiraled a new shot of lust to her core, and a tiny whimper slipped past her lips. If he didn't stop right now, she was going to jump him in the hallway in front of Cannon.

Rorax gently tugged herself out of Ayres's grip, and he reluctantly let her go.

She had to support herself on the wall for a beat so her knees wouldn't buckle; then she turned to Ayres and Cannon. Ayres watched her with smug satisfaction, and Cannon struggled to suppress a laugh.

Rorax flushed and stood up straight, jabbing a finger at Ayres. "Don't kill Niels. I'm serious, Lieutenant. I don't want a new emissary when this one is such a fucking blockhead."

She moved her finger to point at Cannon before signing to him, ***We humiliated Niels today, however. We should be prepared for retaliation of some kind. Let Milla know.***

They both grunted their agreement as she turned on her heel and started to walk away.

"Rorax. Wait."

Ayres reached out and grabbed her wrist, pulling her back around to face him.

"I saw this in one of the stalls in Surmalinn...." Ayres used his other hand to reach back to his back pocket, bringing forth a long, white silk ribbon that lay draped across his palm. House of Death's colors, black and red, danced across the white surface in a delicate paisley pattern. "It... reminded me of you."

Ayres's cheeks blushed as she reached out and lifted the ribbon from his palm with gentle fingers. "Thank you, Ayres."

Gods above, he had thought about her, even bought her something *pretty*. Butterflies fluttered in her stomach, and she went warm all over.

"You're welcome," he said, his voice low.

Chapter 80

Rorax

"Radashan."

The little man startled behind his desk and squeaked up at Rorax, who did her best not to grit her teeth or scowl down at the librarian.

Rorax tried to rein in her impatience. "I am thankful for your help, and I appreciate the books you're giving me. They are extremely informative, but I *need* books on the Choosing, or any books you know of that can tell me how to transfer the power and get myself *out of here*."

The little man blushed and played with the leg of his glasses. "I-I have been giving you material to help you with the trials, Rorax. But I don't think there are any books on the transfer of power from the Choosing." He shrugged helplessly. "At least, I haven't been able to find any."

Rorax gave an exasperated sigh and rubbed her temples. "There *has* to be something."

She'd just finished a book Radashan had gifted her called *Ancient Felidra Clan Guide,* and while it was a fascinating read on the big cats that had been gifted with dragon wings, it had absolutely *nothing* to do with freeing herself from the Choosing.

"I'll keep looking!" Radashan promised, nodding his head rapidly. "I'll find something, I promise."

"Thank you," Rorax sighed, just as the library doors opened and Elios and Ayres stepped through.

Rorax raised an eyebrow at Ayres before moving her gaze to the grinning blond behind him. The emissary of Fire didn't know what they were doing down here. No one did. But Ayres jerked his chin in the direction of their table anyway. "Let me know what you find, Radashan," Rorax muttered, offering the small man a tight smile before following Ayres and Elios through the stacks back to her table.

Elios eyed the papers and books that were haphazardly strewn across the surface of the small table. "You two look busy."

Ayres didn't give her a chance to answer Elios. He eyed the charm resting against Rorax's throat. "Is that the necklace? The one Majauss gave you in her temple?" he asked, motioning at her neck.

Rorax nodded and shifted her hair away to expose the necklace more clearly. She wore one of Hella's dresses, a flowy navy blue dress that ended just above her knee. The spaghetti straps and a shallow V-neck showed off the golden necklace. She had hoped someone would recognize it and say something.

"Elios studied ancient artifacts at the University of Surmalinn and Koppar. I wanted him to look at it," Ayres explained as Elios took a step closer to her, leaning down to look at the golden charm.

He reached out a hand before stopping halfway. "May I?" he asked, looking up at her.

Rorax nodded. Elios picked the necklace up, his fingers brushing gently over her skin, right over the swell of her breasts. The soft touch made her blush, and her eyes darted to Ayres.

Ayres's jaw tightened as he looked at the color on her cheeks, and he folded his arms across his chest. The scowl he gave Elios made her heart heat and go cold at the same time. Not that she cared what he thought, but did he care that Elios was touching her?

Ayres's eyes looked like a safe charcoal color; she dared a small smile up at Elios as he brought the necklace closer to his face.

"Paiki's fires." Elios whistled low. "I haven't seen one of these... well, ever." His deep blue eyes flicked down to hers. "I know you received it in the temple, but explain the details again, please."

Gods, Elios was *so* beautiful. The deep blue of his eyes sucked her in, and she had to blink to regain her focus. "Uh... Majauss told me to take it. When I was in her temple."

The corner of his mouth pressed down. "Did she say anything else?"

Rorax bit her lip and looked over at Ayres, who gave her a nod. "She said it would help me with the transfer of power and to look for the tables for the transfer. She also said to prepare myself for war."

Elios's mouth tipped into a full-blown frown. "Tables for the transfer?"

Rorax shrugged as his attention went back to her necklace.

He dropped the necklace back against her chest and took a step back. "I think it's one of the Ukuros Amulets. It's supposed to help with the transition of power and should help ease the intensity of the influxes as well."

Ayres grunted. "It isn't anything that's going to poison or harm her, is it?"

Elios narrowed his eyes on the amulet again before he shook his head, his eyebrows furrowing. "No, I don't think so. But it's what Majauss said that intrigues me most. Tables for the transfer."

"Do you know what those are?" Rorax asked.

"Yes, and I am surprised that you don't know, Ayres."

"Why is that?"

"The Transfer Tables were destroyed by one of the old Sumavari kings. Raiv Sumavari. I would assume it's common House of Death history."

"Refresh my memory." Ayres crossed his arms over his chest.

"Transfer Tables are useful tools for more than just stripping or transferring power and holding ability. They can dissolve magickal links as well, such as Blood

Oaths and Mating Bonds. The legend is that apparently Raiv Sumavari destroyed the tables to force his mate to stay bonded to him."

Rorax and Ayres shared a confused look before Rorax turned back to Elios. "So, what is the necklace?"

"Legend says that there is one surviving table that Raiv commissioned from the last remaining Sovereign Witch before he killed her. It is a key, Contestar, a key to activate the table."

Hope and joy surged in Rorax's chest. "Really?"

Elios grimaced and took a look at all the papers thrown over the small table. "You're looking for a way out of this, aren't you? You're trying to free yourself from the Choosing."

"Yes." Rorax nodded. "I'm trying to free myself and the other women."

"Paiki's fires." Elios ran a hand through his golden hair. "This is all a legend, Rorax. It was before the Breach, nearly seven hundred and fifty years ago. If the table existed, it would have been long destroyed or forgotten—unless the House of Death has been holding out on us."

"I don't know of anything like that, but I'll write a letter to the queen," said Ayres.

Elios nodded. "Hold on to that hope, Contestar, because if Majauss really did give you this necklace, then I would bet there's at least one table that survived."

After Elios finally left them, Rorax flipped the page on a book about Guardians. Over and over the book made it clear that the Guardians were created by Ukuros to protect the *world*, not just the Realms, though the function of the Guardian had been twisted and manipulated into not much more than a weapon for the Realms to use to retain power.

"What are you thinking about?" Ayres asked, not bothering to look up from his own book from where he sat across the table from her.

Rorax ran her finger over her ring. She didn't want to talk about the Guardians. Any of them. "These Books of Sumavari... what exactly is held in them?"

"Monsters," Ayres quipped. "Bad ones."

Rorax rolled her eyes. "All this time, I thought we were out risking our necks for books that make butterflies. How bad is bad? Something I could handle?"

Ayres snorted and slowly looked up from his book, his gaze heavy despite the humor curling at the corner of his mouth. "Maybe some of them. Cannon said the last book they brought back was for one of Sakar Sumavari's lesser monsters—a shadow griffon, twice the size of a normal griffon, twice the teeth."

"What was the book that we brought back?"

"It was one of Sakar's warlords—the Laughing Dread."

A shiver ran over Rorax's shoulders. "I've seen the Laughing Dread's skull in the war museum in Valitlinn." The skull was massive. It had two bull horns stretching two feet to each side and no eye sockets. It's teeth almost the same length and width as Rorax's fingers, shaved down into sharpened points, and the plaque on the wall had read that the reason the warlord had been called the Laughing Dread was because the warlord didn't have any lips, so his teeth were constantly on display in a deadly smile. The warlord had been sentient though, had commanded a large force of Sakar Sumavari's forces.

"I've seen it, too. Apparently, it used to use sonar to see and move, like a bat. He killed hundreds of people in Sumavari's War."

Rorax sent a thankful prayer up to Kään that they had retrieved the Laughing Dread's book—a monster that she would not survive fighting one-on-one. "What about the Death Harbinger?"

The Death Harbinger was nothing more than a rumor, said to be one of the House of Death royalty, but Rorax had now met two House of Death princes and the queen. None of them seemed to have very much Death Magick at all. Maybe it was one of Sumavari's pets.

Ayres ran his tongue over his teeth, his eyes darkening further, but he shook his head. "That's just a rumor. The Death Harbinger is not one of Sakar Sumavari's creations."

Rorax hummed, and something Ayres had just said a few minutes before finally sank into her brain. "Wait, you said that the Laughing Dread was only *one* of Sakar's warlords? Kään help us, how many are there?"

Ayres sighed. "Twelve. One made to rule each Realm. The Laughing Dread was blind, made to rule the House of Light so that they could not blind him."

"*Twelve*? How many have we found?"

"Only two." Ayres's face darkened again. "When you pray at night, pray that we find the warlords over the monsters. The monsters we can handle with enough clever men. The warlords... the warlords could kill us all."

Rorax opened her mouth to comment, but the sound of numerous heavy footsteps made Rorax twist around in her chair. The Guardian's soldiers were coming through the stacks, heading toward them.

Rorax sprang to her feet at the same time Ayres pushed up from the table.

The Guardian pushed her way to the front of the pack and casually looked Rorax up and down. Niels stood behind them all, watching them with a triumphant sneer.

"Hello, Greywood," the Guardian said. "We have been looking for you everywhere."

"What do you want?" Ayres demanded.

"I have waited long enough. I've given Tressa permission to walk through Rorax's brain." The Guardian's yellow eyes ran the length of Rorax, and whatever she found made her lips purse in displeasure. "Meet us in the Great Hall in five minutes."

CHAPTER 81

AYRES

Ayres forced himself to take a deep, slow breath.

He was going to kill the Guardian.

He stared up at her as she sat on her throne above. He could feel the outline of her soul so clearly, and with one gentle tug, he could pull it out of her flesh and send her down the bridge. It would take him less than three seconds.

They now stood in the Great Hall, side by side. Rorax trembled slightly next to him, and he suddenly remembered why he couldn't just pluck away the Guardian's life. The Guardian was the anchor of the Contestars' fledgling power. A Guardian dying before their power was properly transferred had never happened before. It was untested and uncertain, and there was a chance the Guardian's death would kill Rorax, would kill *all* the Contestars, and that was a gamble he wasn't willing to take.

The Guardian eyed Rorax; both distrust and disgust were clear in her face as she pursed her lips. "We need to know why you aren't manifesting any abilities, Greywood."

Rorax shook her head, taking a careful step forward. "I don't know. I have tried, and I've searched in my head, but there is nothing. I can't feel *anything*."

The Guardian's lips pursed together even more. "Fine. Try and keep your secrets, Greywood. It will be more satisfying to pry them out of you."

The Guardian turned around and nodded to Lamonte who stood by the door.

Lamonte opened it wide, and Tressa came in, her head held high.

Memories of the last time he had seen a Mind Walker work made his chest tight with horror. During the War of the Slaves, he had a Mind Walker in his unit, and the Mind Walker had men and women from Umber screaming, crying, and writhing on the floor, begging for the Mind Walker to leave their heads. That Mind Walker had been precise and lethal, knew exactly which synapses and parts of the mind to investigate and control.

Tressa was a novice, a fledgling Mind Walker who was untrained, untested, and untalented in that art.

"No." The growl that erupted from Ayres was so harsh, even Rorax flinched away slightly. He whipped his head back to face the Guardian. "You're a gods-damned *fool* if you think I would let you do this."

The Guardian gave him a bored look and an exasperated sigh. "I don't need your permission, *Lieutenant*, to investigate a Contestar who might not be fit for the Choosing."

Ayres felt slightly panicked as he whipped his head back to Tressa, whose gaze was zeroed in on Rorax, her eyes burning with an intent that unsettled his stomach. If she wasn't careful, Tressa could sever synapses and cause irreparable damage. The look on her face made him think that damage may be her goal.

Ren had slipped into the hall behind Tressa and shot Ayres a warning look when he saw the fury in Ayres's face. Ayres snarled, baring his teeth at his old friend in his own warning.

Rorax looked between the Guardian and Ayres, then to Tressa and Ren, her eyes narrowing. "What is going on?"

Tressa stopped a few feet in front of Rorax, her face triumphant. Her long, black braids swayed across the fabric of her black dress, and Ayres had an urge to grab them in a fist and use them to haul her as far away from Rorax as he could.

"I am not only the High Healer of the Northern Castle but also a Mind Walker," Tressa said, her chin lifting a fraction of an inch. "I'm going to search your mind to find out why you haven't manifested any of your abilities yet."

The color in Rorax's cheeks drained, but she remained still, not showing any indication she was unsteady or scared. Brave little fool.

"Fine, but I want *him* gone." Ayres pointed at Niels, who was watching all of this unfold with a smug smile on his face. The fucking worm.

The Guardian sighed and flicked her wrist. "Fine. Guards, please remove the emissary of Alloy from the hall."

Niels didn't bother to protest, he still had that triumphant look on his face, and Ayres knew Niels wouldn't be far away. No, Niels would linger closely, hoping for the chance to hear Rorax screaming.

"Ayres, hold her arms down," the Guardian called.

Tressa shook her head. "No, I want her lying down."

The Guardian just nodded and waved her hand out, indicating that there on the cold stones was as fine a place as any to search Rorax's mind.

"Can we at least go to her chambers, to her bed—" Ayres started, but the Guardian cut him off.

"No, we are doing this here and now. Get on your back, Greywood."

Rorax shot a look of such cold disregard and hatred at the Guardian, it would have sent terror down the spine of anyone else.

She slowly lowered herself to her knees and then to her bottom before she laid out on the stones.

Rorax tugged on her dress nervously. She stole a look at Ayres, and that one miniscule show of vulnerability had Ayres's teeth on edge.

"Now climb on top of her and pin her down, Ayres."

He opened his mouth to tell her to fuck off, but she just raised an eyebrow at him. "Would you rather have another man on top of her to make sure she stays still?"

Ayres gritted his teeth before bending down and straddling her waist, pinning her arms to her side with his knees.

Tressa came around to her head, and Rorax watched her with uncertainty.

"Ror, look at me." Her snow-white eyes moved to him, and he tried to give her a soothing smile. "I am right here. The less you fight it, the less it hurts."

Rorax nodded and swallowed loudly.

Tressa pressed her fingers against Rorax's scalp, and a second later, her eyes clouded over, a milky veil over her usually dark brown irises. The same veil covered Rorax's eyes, covering the dark pupils and dark outer rings of her white eyes.

Ayres gritted his teeth, preparing himself for Rorax's scream… but it never came.

Only a heavy, stifling silence thumped in the air. Tressa's face screwed up in concentration, but Rorax's face remained blank.

Ayres looked up at Ren, who had taken a protective stance behind Tressa. But Ren looked as confused as he was, shaking his head.

Tressa shifted on her knees, moving her face closer to Rorax's, her fingers trembling, but nothing else changed for long minutes.

Ayres kept his mouth shut until a drop of blood started to trickle out of the inner corners of Tressa's eyes.

"Fuck," Ayres snapped. "Pull her away, Ren."

Ren moved to see the bloody tears on Tressa's face and didn't think twice about scooping her up and pulling her up from Rorax and the stone-covered ground.

Rorax's eyes flew open at the same time as Tressa hissed in fury. "How dare you pull me out. I was still trying to find a way *in*."

Ayres pushed himself off Rorax and helped her to her feet. She staggered and gripped onto his sweater to steady herself. She blinked rapidly, her eyes unfocused as she stared straight ahead into his chest.

She looked... dazed. The usual signs of wide-eyed, animalistic terror he had become so familiar with after a Mind Walker's interrogations were completely absent from her features. She just looked confused.

Tressa kicked her limbs until Ren released her, reluctantly setting her down.

She immediately marched back to Rorax, but Ayres put himself between them, pulling Rorax behind him so fast she staggered.

"That's enough," he bit down at Tressa, who snarled back. "Tell us what happened."

"I never found out *what's* going on. I never even got *in*! She"—Tressa pointed a trembling finger at Rorax—"blocked me."

A heavy silence hung in the air. Rorax gripped the back of Ayres's sweater tighter.

"Tressa, tell us what happened. Could you feel any of the power?" the Guardian asked. Her gray eyebrows were furrowed together tightly, and she appeared just as confused as the rest of them.

Tressa ground her molars together and nodded once. "It's there. It's... buried."

"What do you mean, *buried*?" Rorax rasped from over his shoulder, her voice hoarse.

Tressa's eyes flashed at Rorax with naked contempt. "I mean, it's... your power feels... like an underground well; it's still buried under your *wall*."

"Will she be able to access this power?" the Guardian asked. "Or will we need to eliminate her to extract it?"

Rorax's fists clung to the fabric of Ayres's sweater and gripped tighter. He resisted the urge to reach around and comfort her.

Ayres opened his mouth to tell the bitch she wouldn't be eliminating even the lint from his ass, but Tressa started speaking first. "She will be able to access it. It feels like an underground well. You won't see it until it reaches the surface."

The Guardian pursed her lips. "How soon?"

Tressa shrugged, moving her eyes to Rorax, shooting daggers at her. "I don't know, but it's close enough to feel through her barrier. I could tell you for certain if you make her move her wall."

Ayres bared his teeth at her, and he felt his power rumble to life in his back.

"Enough." The Guardian stood. "I am pacified. As long as she manifests her magick by the time we're down to the final three Contestars, Rorax will remain a Contestar in the Choosing... if she lives that long."

CHAPTER 82

RORAX

Rorax rolled her shoulders as she made her way out to the Contestar' Courtyard. She had heard the yelling before she even made it up the steps from the library. She squinted as she shoved the keep's double doors open, the sun burning her eyes.

Tightening the long strands of white ribbon holding her hair in two buns on top of her head, Rorax took exactly four steps before coming to a screeching halt as soon as what she saw registered in her brain.

Mo and Mairi stood toe-to-toe, screaming at each other.

"Shit," Rorax mumbled under her breath, looking back and forth between the women.

Movement to her side made her look up as Briar came and stood next to her.

"What's going on?" Rorax asked.

"They just found out that Mo knew Mairi's brother, or some shit. Mo had somethin' to do with Mairi's brother being sold off to Ostr in the slave market."

"Holy Mother of Kään." Rorax's attention turned from Briar to the two other Contestars who were still screaming at one another.

Briar looked up at Rorax with sad eyes and shook her head, folding her arms across her chest protectively. "But hey, I've been waitin' for you. I... I wanted to talk to you 'bout somethin'." Briar shifted her weight from foot to foot and tucked a strand of short blonde hair behind her ear. Her lips were pressed together tightly, making the scar down her face pull taught.

"What is it?" Rorax tore her attention from the screaming women and watched Briar warily. Usually the Air-Born Contestar was composed and relaxed. This nervous energy was unusual, and it put Rorax on edge.

"I heard that you were tryin' to find a way outta' the Choosing. To free yourself from the magick. That's why you an' your Protectorates are always in the library, tryin' to find somethin' to help."

"It's true." Rorax nodded, "I am."

"If you find a way out, do ya think that I could use it, too? If I come down an' help? I know that I wouldn' be much use as a Guardian, don' have the connections or the temperament, but I don' wanna die to prove it. I have family back home, a sister."

Rorax turned fully to Briar. "We could use all the help we can get. We would be happy to have you. We might not be successful, and we both might end up dead anyway, but it's better than nothing."

Briar nodded eagerly, her face and posture relaxing. "Me too, that's all I want, just a chance."

"My shift is during the day, after my morning session and before Contestar training. Come and find me then. The librarian will show you the way."

Briar's face cracked a small smile. "Thank you, Rorax."

Rorax spotted Ayres staring at her from over Briar's blonde head. He was leaning against a pillar as he raised his hand and summoned her with two lazy, tattooed fingers, motioning her to come. She gave him a flat look and was tempted to flip him off.

"Excuse me," Rorax murmured to Briar, stepping around her fellow Contestar and stalking over to stand next to him, keeping a wary side-eye on the women still screaming at each other.

Ayres lowered his head down to her ear. His nose bumped her earlobe, and she fought to keep from leaning into him. "You're late," he murmured.

She scoffed. "Not like anyone is getting anything done anyway."

"Mairi has a reason to be upset."

"I heard, what happened to—"

Rorax didn't get to finish her sentence as Mairi screamed bloody murder, pulled a knife from her sleeve, and sliced it across Mo's throat. There was a beat of silence as both women, and the whole courtyard, stared at the blood running from between Mo's dark fingers.

Then the screaming started, and soldiers rushed the two Contestars.

"Fuck," Ayres clipped, grabbing Rorax's arm and all but throwing her behind him. She staggered, tripping over her own feet, and watched from over Ayres's shoulder as Mo fell to her knees, her hands still gripping her throat.

Mairi's shocked expression faded into something like pure fury. "Die, you evil bitch."

In a surprisingly graceful move for Mairi, she twirled and gave a roundhouse kick to the side of Mo's head. Mo's neck made a sickening snap, and her body crumpled to the ground.

Ror's eyes rolled back into her head as pure heat, anger, and bloodlust punched through her chest, and a red haze came over her eyes.

She snapped herself to attention to see Isgra grinning over at her, longing and anger plain on her face, too. Rorax smiled right back and pulled her hair knives from her buns. Glee and excitement bubbled up inside her, and suddenly she was *desperate* to see the deep red of Isgra's blood dousing the stones, to feel its warmth across her palms.

Volla would never know.

Rorax took one step before a strong pair of hands gripped one wrist and then the other, pinning them together.

"Hey!" she snapped as Ayres ripped one of the ties from her hair, causing the hair of one of her buns to fall loose, and twisted it around her wrists. He ripped the knives out of her hands, tossing them to the ground. He picked her up and had her pinned against his chest before she could think of a way to slip out of his hold.

"For the love of Marras, Rorax," Ayres growled as she started thrashing in his arms, trying to break free. She wanted to see Isgra's blood splattered across the stones, and she wanted it *now*. She had been so patient for so long. She deserved it.

"I will tear you to shreds," Rorax hissed. She didn't know if she was talking to Isgra or Ayres. She thrashed again, but gods above, wrestling Ayres was like wrestling a bull. He was breathing heavily but was otherwise undeterred as he dragged her away from the chaos. "Let me *go*."

"Heads up!" a House of Ice soldier hollered at them as a huge ball of fire barreled toward them. It didn't make it far.

A wall of black, crackling with red energy that looked like lightning, rushed up from the ground, protecting them from Isgra's fire. The wall didn't so much as flicker under the pressure of Isgra's fireball.

Rorax snarled. She desperately wished she had her knife, or any of the magick being dangerously flashed around from the other Contestars. Ayres's arms pinned her limbs down fractionally tighter, and he dragged her in long strides toward the nearest tower.

Just as they reached it, Milla and Cannon burst through the doors, along with a handful of Death Court guards. They came to an abrupt halt when they saw Ayres dragging Rorax away from the fighting. Rorax saw them and snarled even louder.

"Mediate this shit," Ayres snarled, jerking his chin over his shoulder. "Don't let any of the Lowborns die, especially Enna and Briar."

They nodded and disappeared into the fray.

The hallway was mostly deserted, and he dropped Rorax from over his shoulder, wrapping one arm around her hip and simply dragging her along beside him.

"Let me go." Rorax thrashed against him, arching her back, kicking her legs, and then trying to headbutt him. He didn't even flinch, and the rage from the influx burned hotter through her chest.

If she couldn't kill Isgra, she would settle for Ayres. The arrogant fucking asshole. He was dragging her down the hallway, closer to her room when the influx hit its peak. Power surged through her veins.

Her back arched in a different way this time as the magick fused its way into her cells, her upper body straining against his wrist and forearm.

"Fuck," Ayres clipped, quickening his pace.

She started thrashing even harder in his arms until they got to her room. She scratched her nails down his forearm so he would drop his hand away, but she only succeeded in making him curse and slide his arm down her torso.

Then a different kind of electricity rocked through her.

His palm had slid down her chest and had inadvertently cupped her breast.

She took three heaving breaths before arching her back to press herself further into his palm.

He squeezed.

"Ayres." A moan ripped from her lips as all the heat, all the anger and aggression in her blood, flipped and barreled down into her core.

"What's your safe word, Little Crow?" Ayres's voice was gravel and lust against her ear, and it made her even wetter.

She opened her mouth but didn't answer, *couldn't answer*.

"Little Crow," he growled. "You don't tell me, and I don't touch you. What is it?"

"Red," Rorax whimpered, *desperate* for his hands to continue.

"Good girl," he growled as everything exploded.

She needed his skin on hers *now*, she turned to face him and all but ripped off his sweater, exposing his broad chest. He pulled her leather Contestar armor off over her head and stared down at her breast bindings.

"You weren't wearing these that day you were poisoned."

"No, I wasn't."

Ayres's fingers dipped into the top of her bindings and ripped it off. He stared like a depraved man at her heavy breasts, his pupils dilating. She squirmed, rubbing her thighs together as the raw, animalistic expression made Rorax drip down her thighs. He reached behind her neck and into her hair and jerked her face back to his so roughly, Rorax groaned into his mouth.

She hoped he fucked like he kissed—hard and hot.

Her nipples scraped against his chest, alarmingly cold over a golden medallion that hung in the middle of his pecs and then hot against his warm skin, tickling over the slight hair on his chest.

Ayres continued to kiss her as he picked her up and carried her to her bed. He laid her down on her back and only broke off the kiss to take off Rorax's boots and rip off her pants.

Rorax was completely naked under him, and she only wanted one thing, spreading her legs for him. "Ayres," she pleaded, "touch me."

Ayres smirked and gripped her hair, yanking it back so he could see her face. "Where do you want me to touch you, Rorax? I expect you to be *very* specific."

She didn't hesitate, spreading her legs a fraction wider. "My pussy. Please."

He slid his fingers down to her wet slit but didn't enter her or circle her clit. She rolled her hips up like she was chasing his hand, but he didn't so much as graze her again.

Her influx writhed under her skin, needing more, *demanding* more. "*Please*, Ayres."

He slid his hands back up her slit and used the tip of his thumb to hit the target dead-on. Bull's-eye. Her hips bucked, and he tsked in disapproval. "Rorax, I said I want to hear what you want."

Ayres switched his thumb out for another finger and started to work her clit until her whole body hummed and tingled, her legs writhing around his hand. "Aryes, please. I need to come."

"That's my good girl," he murmured low in her ear. He inserted two fingers into her, and her hips bucked again. "What do you want inside you when you come first, Little Crow? My fingers, my fist, or my cock?"

She let out a distressed whimper as his finger continued to swirl her clit, his fingers pumping steadily inside her. "Cock. Your cock."

"Beg for it then," he snarled, pinching her clit so hard she gasped.

"Ayres!" she cried. "Please, Ayres, I don't—"

He flipped her over onto her stomach, gripped the hair at the back of her head, and jerked her torso up, forcing her skull up to his shoulder. Her spine almost bent in half, but before she could cry out, he slammed his cock all the way inside her pussy, buried to his hips in one single shove.

She screamed.

Ayres chuckled darkly and used the thumb he had used on her clit to wipe away the tears that had sprung to her eyes, mixing her fluids across her cheek as she panted heavily. "I like seeing you hurt on my cock, Little Crow."

Ayres let go of her hair but snaked his hand under one of her arms, wrapping his tattooed hand around the front of her throat to keep her head pinned against his shoulder. He started to slide slowly in and out of her, torturously slow, forcing her to feel every single thick inch of him.

He reached around with his other hand and must have felt how wet she was, how stretched her pussy was around his cock, because he groaned in her ear.

"So wet for me, Rorax. What a perfect, sloppy cunt."

Ayres's thumb rolled over her clit in a deliciously steady rhythm, and she felt more tears threaten to fall from her eyes. She felt it become swollen and engorged, and then the tip of his thumb slid just under the small swollen hood of her clit....

"Ayres. Ayres, I—" And she came. Erupted. All the anger, hate, lust, and heat the influx had brought into her body detonated.

"Fuck," Ayres grunted as she squeezed around him. "*Fuck*, Ror. You feel so fuckin' good."

He didn't stop.

He continued to pump into her, rubbing his thumb right where she needed it.

Rorax's remaining influx preened in happiness, but her swollen nub ached in protest of the over stimulation. "Ayres, I can't. I—"

He growled, his breath hot in her ear. "You either say the safe word, Ror, or you take it. You take my cock until I wring every *single* last orgasm your body and your influx can handle."

"Ayres." His words made her womb clench, and he grunted, pressing harder on her clit.

Ayres breathed heavily into her ear as he stroked his cock deep into her, and hearing him there, feeling the sweat of his chest on her back, his huge hand gripping her throat... she was going to come again.

When he gave a sharp slap to one of her breasts, his rings stinging against her nipple, something new and erotic woke up inside of her stomach. She sucked in a shocked breath as the sudden pain of it made the influx inside of her writhe, and with it rose pure, ecstatic pleasure.

"Again," Rorax pleaded, just as he slid home again, and she *moaned*. "Ayres, please, again."

He didn't slow his pace as he laughed in her hair, the scruff of his chin rubbing the soft skin on the back of her neck, his fingers flexing around her throat. "My Little Crow likes pain, hmm? Well, you know what I expect you to do when you want something."

She bit her lip, her hands tightening around his arm. He stopped rubbing her clit to pinch it, and she almost came right there around his cock again. "Please, Ayres."

"Please?"

"*Please.*" She was way past caring about begging.

He did as she asked, slapping one and then the other with shockingly brutal strikes, and then she came again, screaming his name and coming so hard she saw stars exploding behind her eyes.

Vaguely she could feel his balls tightening and heard him grunting something probably filthy as he stopped thrusting into her.

Rorax couldn't hear him, though. Couldn't feel anything except for him filling her with his cum. It was so sexy she would have moaned, but she could barely even breathe.

Her mind had been obliterated.

She sagged against his arm still bared over her chest, keeping her pressed against him as he heaved in gasping breaths.

Rorax couldn't even sit up anymore. Every nerve in her body sang with a deep euphoric calm. Never in her life had Rorax ever fucked rough like that before. Never in her life had she *ever* had an orgasm that made her feel so... high.

Ayres released her throat and let her sink forward onto her bed. She nuzzled into her blankets and groaned in pleasure.

"Ror, did you hear me?"

"Hmm?" she asked.

Ayres huffed out a laugh on her shoulder, and she peeled open an eye to stare sideways at him. He had followed her down to the mattress and was hovering over her. He pressed his lips to her naked shoulder, and something in her stomach went warm.

Then he wrapped his hands around her hips and flipped her over, so she was staring up into his face.

"Don't move, or the next thing I'll be slapping is your ass, and I promise it won't feel *nearly* as good as when I slapped those pretty pink nipples."

Rorax scowled, but Ayres just gave her a smug tilt of his lips as he got up and off the bed. Rorax's still open eyes followed his perfectly sculpted body as he disappeared into the bathroom, returning with a wet towel.

Ayres knelt between her legs, lifting them up and spreading them apart.

She could feel his cum dripping down and over her pussy and down her ass, and when her pussy twitched at the thought of it, she had to admit that she *liked* it there in some raw, fucked-up way. It made her warm inside.

Ayres stared, his eyes molten silver, for so long she started wiggling her hips with discomfort. "Ayres?"

"Sorry," Ayres grunted, finally dipping the towel down to clean her up.

He wiped her down, taking his time to slowly clean her.

"Do you still feel the influx at all?"

"No." But she sat up on her elbows to look at him still kneeling between her legs. She shivered when she saw the dark hungry look still lingering in his eyes. "Thank you, Ayres, for keeping me safe. For keeping me from hurting anyone."

Ayres nodded, a shadow of a smile on his lips. "Of course."

"What will happen to Mairi?"

"She is dead. Most likely." He padded over to deposit the wet rag into her hamper and pulled his pants back on before climbing back into bed with her.

Rorax watched him carefully the whole time, shaking her head in disbelief. She had just had sex with *Ayres*. It was everything she had ever wanted it to be and more. She could still feel him between her thighs, and she hoped that feeling would never go away. She already wanted more.

If only Mairi wouldn't have had to die for it to happen.

She ran both hands through her hair. "I can't believe it, but I would have done the same thing if I ever found myself in her position." She shook her head again and looked up to see Ayres watching her, studying her hair draped out over her pillow.

Ayres met her gaze with a hard, determined edge. "I would have, too. I would've done things a lot worse for my siblings, especially for my sister. I would have torn the world apart for her."

A ghost of a smile danced on her lips. "You have a sister?"

"Yes."

"Where does she live?"

"Surmalinn," Ayres answered, looking away from her, a sudden edge to his voice.

Rorax swallowed. "Did she... was she there during the Siege?"

"Yes. She survived."

The high euphoric feeling in her heart deflated, and she looked from his face to the ceiling. There was a long silence as Rorax studied the intricate patterns carved into the wood of her ceiling. "If I don't find a way to free myself from the Choosing, Ayres, you should take me back to Surmalinn."

She blinked, and a fat tear trickled down the side of her cheek and into the hair by her ear. "Your people deserve their revenge."

Ayres slowly rolled so he was flat on his stomach, his silence charged, and she could feel that he needed a moment to separate what they had just done with who she was. They lay in silence for a heavy moment, and when he spoke again, his voice was harder, colder.

"Some of my people would slaughter you on sight if you stepped into Surmalinn again." Ayres let out a long sigh. "Some of my people lost everyone they loved and everything they owned when you and the Wolf came."

Rorax steeled herself before turning to look back at him. The warmth was gone from his features, and it made her chest ache with regret.

"But there are others... others who view you as Surmalinn's guardian angel." He scoffed a bit and rubbed his hands over his face, then sat up in her bed.

"Really?" Her heart felt a little lighter as her eyes traced over the tattoos and the muscles on his back. The four, thin, vertical lines that traveled all the way down his spine, along with the skulls, the roses, Death's most infamous monsters, and thorns.

Despite herself, her tongue peaked out and touched the top of her lip. She would lick those tattoos one day.

He turned toward her, but only far enough that she could see the profile of his face. "You have your own statue in the library. In *both* of Surmalinn's libraries."

Rorax's lips parted in a silent stun.

"They don't look like you... not really. The cowl you used to wear made it so no one really knew who you were or what you looked like until you came here." He shrugged and looked down at his hands. "One of my brothers thinks you're a gods-damned hero. He told my sister to name her daughter after you. Another thinks you should be dragged through the streets and killed. You are a polarizing topic in my House, in my own family even."

Rorax pushed herself back up onto her elbows. "And what do you think?"

The muscles on his broad back flexed. "I don't know."

Rorax nodded. That answer was fine. It was honest and expected, but then Ayres let out a cold, angry, bitter laugh that cut her to her core. "Well, I obviously don't hate you enough not to fuck you, even if you are a monster."

She stiffened, right before her heart crumpled in her chest.

"Don't tell anyone about this," Ayres said to her over his shoulder, and her heart cracked a little bit more at the loathing, disgust, and hatred in his voice.

Rorax could see it; Ayres hated himself. One of the best men she'd ever known *deeply* hated himself for what had just happened between them, for what *had* been happening between them. Even though he had every right to think that way, to hate her like that, his words made her feel like she was disgusting. Rotten and empty.

Anger bloomed amidst the devastation in her chest. When did she allow herself to feel so much? When had she allowed herself to turn into… this? This sappy mess? Three months ago, she wouldn't have given two shits about what the lieutenant of the House of Death thought about her, what *anyone* thought about her.

Now she felt like she was spiraling out of control, like he had just punched the air out of her lungs.

Did Cannon feel this way about her? Did Piers and Kaiya?

She would be naïve to think they didn't feel the exact same way Ayres did. She was simply a tool to them.

Rorax hadn't done enough, wasn't enough.

Though maybe no matter what she did, no matter who she saved, or who she became, she would never be able to outgrow or atone for what she had done. She would always be the Wolf's Pup.

Ayres shuffled, leaning forward to pick up his boots off the floor and bent over to start lacing them up. She watched him, feeling utterly defeated.

Tears started to drip down her face, but she refused to let Ayres see her this way, refused to let him see that his words had cut her so deeply.

So instead, she brushed past him, grabbed the first dress from her closet, and pulled it on, not bothering with a bra or panties or even shoes. Rorax just needed to get away from him, *now*.

"Ror, where are—" Ayres started to ask, but Rorax closed the door between them and did not look back.

CHAPTER 83

AYRES

Ayres scowled at the back of Rorax's head as he leaned over and braced his sweaty palms on his knees.

The twenty thousand steps to the Mountain of the Oracle where the third trial would take place had been long, grueling, and hot. The hike hadn't been made any more pleasant by Cannon and Milla shooting glares over their shoulders at him every twenty seconds. Even Piers gave him a few dirty looks.

Rorax had already climbed these steps. She had hiked out of camp almost immediately after the transfer dragons had dropped them off. She'd come up hours before them apparently, wanting to scout it out.

Even though he was as pissed as all hell at her, he couldn't ignore the sense of relief at seeing her in front of him, alive and whole.

Rorax had avoided him for the last five days, ever since Mo had been killed and Mairi died and they fucked through her influx.

When Rorax slipped out of her room that evening, she'd apparently been crying.

Milla and Cannon were coming up to her room to check on them and make sure they had both survived the influx and had seen her tears.

Rorax gave Milla and Cannon a long look, her tears falling even faster down her cheeks at the sight of them, before turning and walking away without so much as a nod.

Milla had stormed into Rorax's room where Ayres was still getting dressed, demanding to know what the hell had happened. He hadn't even finished the story completely when Milla let out a long, pained groan.

"Marras save us." She had thrown her palms up in exasperation at Cannon and started signing before pointing a finger at Ayres, spitting mad. "Our Death Harbinger's got a brain the size of a *walnut*."

Ayres folded his arms over his chest, trying to keep a lid on his already frayed temper. But Milla wasn't done.

"How do you *ever* expect her to prove to us that she's changed if you won't *let* her?" Milla hissed. "Did you forget, Ayres, how she saved your sister from getting *raped*? How she single-handedly called off House of Ice's *entire fucking army* and sent them packing? How she donated enough money back to Surmalinn to rebuild not only a *hospital, but a whole city block*? How she saved *you* from Lyondrean soldiers? How she saved Kaiya and Cannon from a *troll*?"

Ayres rolled his jaw but said nothing, his chest still swimming in indecision and regret.

"Let me just get this straight." Milla jabbed a finger into his chest. "You said to a woman who has feelings for you, '*Well obviously I don't hate you enough not to fuck you, even if you're a monster*,' in your mean voice and expected her not to be *hurt*?"

Cannon snapped his fingers, and they both turned to him. ***Tell me what you said again***, he demanded.

Milla repeated the parts of the conversation when she had been facing Ayres, and the crease in Cannon's eyebrows furrowed deeper and deeper with every motion until it was a full-out glower. When Milla was done, Cannon started signing more furiously than Ayres had ever seen.

You called her a monster? Do you really feel that way? Are you ashamed by what you feel for her?

No. Sometimes. Ayres blew out his breath and raked a hand through his hair before starting again. ***I care more... that my people will care.***

Understanding flashed through Cannon's eyes, but his posture didn't relax.

"If you aren't going to help nurture her, Ayres, then stay the fuck away from her. We have an opportunity to solidify a *powerful* ally here. Did you know the House of Ice King basically considers Rorax to be his little *sister*? Don't offer her a friendship, or more, if all you'll ever be is her enemy and her judge. Don't fuck this up for us." Milla's eyes were sharp as knives on him as she moved her red-tipped fingers in the words for Cannon.

Ayres recalled their conversation that night as Rorax turned to look at them when they approached her.

Rorax's face was blank and cold, every plane of her face empty of any of the warmth that had been slowly growing there for him, *for them*, the last few months.

Gods, Ayres wanted that warmth from her every single day, but... what would his people say? What would his parents think if they were still alive? Marras's love, she was part of the reason they were killed in the first place.

He gritted his teeth and pushed those thoughts to the back of his head, but the way Rorax's eyes grew fractionally colder told him that the same indecision and resentment was written right there on his face for her to see. Again.

Fuck.

"Hello, Rorax! What have you found out?" Milla asked too brightly, pushing a sweaty lock of red hair out of her face with a big smile.

Rorax turned to the emissary but did not smile back. "There are five different entrances on this side of the mountain. According to what I've read, the job of the Oracle during the trial is to burn out any corruption and weakness. If any of us have any negative intentions for the Realms that are inspired from an outside country or force, it is the Oracle's job to weed that out." Rorax paused and looked out over the mountain range. "The Oracle also looks for mental weakness. I fully expect at least one of the Contestars to die here."

No fear, no excitement, no emotion of any kind flickered on her face as she gave her report. Rorax looked just the same as she had when they'd all first met her. Icy. Locked up. Determined. Driven to one thing and one thing only, like the world could burn to hell, but she wouldn't even flinch if she accomplished her goal.

Ayres's chest burned again, and his hands squeezed his hips so hard he'd likely give himself bruises.

The thought sparked a reminder in him of all the bruises he had marked into her skin with his mouth. Ayres flitted his eyes over Rorax's neck to inspect her tanned skin, but there was nothing to mark the slender column of her throat.

No bruises. No whisker burns. No bite marks. Nothing. She had either covered them up or gotten a healer to wipe them away, to wipe *him* away. Either option made his jaw tight.

Footsteps approached behind him, and Ayres turned to see Lamonte and his men trudging up the hill.

"Ah, glad to see you're already up here, Contestar," Lamonte called out, smiling brightly at Rorax. She just nodded once to him, no emotion showing behind her impenetrable wall.

Marras save him, Ayres hated it. Hated her emptiness.

If Lamonte noticed their tension, it didn't show. He didn't miss a beat as he walked past and motioned for them to follow.

A wide stone staircase rose, then stopped on a wide platform. Snaking out from the platform, five trails disappeared in each direction up the mountain, and Lamonte picked the one in the very center. The trail went straight up for a while before it started to wind back and forth, but it wasn't long before the forest gave way to a large stone tunnel that led directly into the side of the mountain.

Ayres's stomach churned. The tunnel appeared so dark he couldn't see inside it for more than ten feet.

Lamonte turned to Rorax. "This is your entrance, Ror. When the other Contestars arrive, they will use different entrances. Your Protectorates will be waiting here. No one is allowed to enter the Oracle's Mountain unsanctified." Lamonte's dark eyes focused directly on Ayres while he said this. "Any who tries will die."

Ayres bit back a snarl and turned to Rorax. She had all her knives except Glimr. He wished she would have brought it today, even with the danger of killing another Contestar.

Rorax nodded and handed her cloak to Milla, who took it without question. She didn't bother glancing back at Ayres as she turned and took one step toward her tunnel and into the dark.

Ayres's hand snapped out and latched on to her arm, dragging her back a step. "Be careful in there, Ror. Sometimes it's not the Oracle who kills things that wander too far into the dark. There could be creatures who still live there."

She looked up at him with those blank, white eyes and gave him the same empty nod she had given Lamonte earlier. His jaw tightened slightly, but before he could say anything else, she shook his hand off her arm, turned, and disappeared into the dark.

Chapter 84

Rorax

White fire torches sporadically lit the walls of the tunnel, giving the shaft an eerie gray cast. Rorax followed the tunnel for what seemed like miles, fighting to keep her breath steady as she pressed on. She smelled damp earth and decaying foliage but didn't hear any noises or detect any creatures scuttling about.

Finally, after what felt like hours of trudging through the gray passage, the tunnel gave way to a cave—giant, dark, and unending. It was so impenetrable, she couldn't see her hand in front of her face, but she kept taking hesitant, careful steps forward. Where was the Oracle? She felt a faint stir in the air and detected soft movements ahead of her.

"Your energy... it is familiar to us. An old energy," the darkness in front of her whispered. The sound seemed to seep around her, surrounding her on all sides.

Rorax froze, and her heart started beating a mile a minute in her chest.

"What is your name?" the darkness breathed.

"Rorax Greywood," Rorax answered, taking a step back and looking around desperately for something for her eyes to lock on to. There was nothing, only blackness.

"We will forage through your memories, your thoughts, to ensure you are worthy to be a Contestar."

White, cold mist erupted on both sides of her, and before she could move, two sets of cold, slimy hands grasped her arms. Rorax could finally make out two shadowy figures on either side of her through the mist. She opened her mouth to scream, but before any sound came out, she felt the Oracle tiptoeing around her mind the same way Tressa had done weeks before.

A thrill of fear raced down her spine. She struggled harder. She didn't want to be forced through her memories. She didn't want to relive her training, the Siege.... She didn't want to see the Wolf.

Rorax squeezed her eyes shut and did whatever she could think of to push the Oracle away from her mind, but no matter what she did, she couldn't push the Oracle all the way out.

However, it seemed that no matter what the Oracle did, no matter where it went or how hard it pushed and pushed and *pushed,* it couldn't find a way into her mind.

There was a long silence as the Oracle continued to press into her subconscious.

"Let me in, *Pup*," the Oracle finally hissed from all around her.

At the nickname, Rorax felt a deadly calm steal over her.

"How do you know that name?" Rorax asked the darkness, watching the white mist writhe in frustration before her.

The Oracle didn't say anything, but the pressure increased around her head. It was going to crush her skull. She had been the one chosen to die today. But if the Oracle had ever seen inside her mind, it hadn't even given her a *chance.*

The unfairness of it all threatened to clog her throat. Someone must have told the Oracle who she was, what she had done, and now the Oracle was trying to kill her.

But if this was all the power the Oracle had, Rorax wouldn't be dying today.

Rorax wrenched an arm away from the slimy hands grasping her, grabbed a knife at her belt, and shoved it up into the misty face of one the shadow guards.

The misty shape grunted, then disappeared into a puff of black smoke. She swiveled and did the same to the guard on her other side, and it disappeared, too.

"RESTRAIN HER!" the Oracle screamed, the sound reverberating and echoing all around her.

Rorax turned and tried to sprint back the way she had come, but another shadow guard materialized in front of her. She slit where she thought its throat would be, and it, too, dissipated into a puff of smoke.

She sprinted, arms pumping, for the mouth of the tunnel. The cave had become lighter, or maybe Rorax's eyes had adjusted, but she saw the black hole, the abyss in the middle of the cave. She sprinted around it and headed toward the tunnel's entrance.

Rorax was only a few strides away, but a guard appeared next to her and slammed her head with the butt of a blade with enough force that she went flying.

When she hit the ground, Rorax landed close enough to the abyss that black gravel and rocks scattered from the impact and flew over the edge of the cavern, disappearing over the cliff and into the darkness.

Fear burned through her, and Rorax shoved her way to her feet.

Four more vaporous guards appeared in front of her, holding their swords, approaching closer.

She took a step back and felt the ledge behind her.

Rorax hissed.

"Let us in, or we will throw you over the edge."

"I don't even know *how* to let you inside," she snapped, speaking to the ethereal voice.

The Oracle was silent for a moment, as if thinking. "Just imagine pushing open one of the corners of your mind. Push it open, like you're lifting the shell of a clam."

Rorax looked over to where she thought the Oracle was. "I'll try to let you in if you vow you'll look at my memories first before you try to do me harm."

The Oracle paused, as if assessing the bargain and Rorax herself. "I so vow," it finally said.

Rorax spent the next thirty minutes pushing—pushing and pushing and *pushing* until some little corner at the edge of her mind seemed to agree to let the Oracle in.

The Oracle seeped into her consciousness gleefully, right before it dragged her through all her worst memories. Through her most brutal moments. Through her darkest deeds. Through the capture of her brother.

A sob, a true anguished sob ripped through Rorax, then another and another until her throat felt ravaged. She swore she could still hear the echoes of her brother screaming her name, so she covered her ears, desperately trying to block the sound, rocking back and forth on her knees.

Tears streamed down her face, and she couldn't stop them.

She grabbed her hair knife and slit open her palm, using her old technique to focus her mind, hoping the pain would help her sharpen her senses, but it wasn't real pain, and it didn't help lessen her anguish.

She just watched as the blood dripped down into the dirt. The same sound Sahana's blood had made when she'd died.

The Oracle stood above her, draped in smoke and gray rags. It didn't have any eyes, only a gray fabric that stretched over the open sockets where its eyes and nose would be, but it had a mouth. A mouth that was open and full of rotting teeth, laughing at her as her memories brought back the horror of Volla's corpse, lying in the dirt, staring lifelessly into the sky.

Rorax screamed, and the memories switched to a balcony—familiar and in nearly all her nightmares when she dreamed about the Siege of Surmalinn.

Rorax bit back a sob as she looked down, and even her bloody handprints were there, the dark red blood visible against the light gray stone.

"See how many you have been responsible for killing, Pup?"

The Oracle pointed an old, gray-skinned finger to a woman lying on the stones at Rorax's feet, her blood pooled on the ground under her cheek, her throat slit. Next to the woman lay a pile of bodies, but Rorax refused to look. She couldn't for fear she would break.

Rorax's throat burned, her heart *burned*, and she turned to the Oracle. "Is the tour over?"

"One more."

The scene changed again, and then Rorax was kneeling in the main square in Surmalinn. The giant clocktower above her was on fire and in danger of collapsing at any moment.

And there she was, stalking the Wolf on a street near the main square.

Rorax's heart lurched in her chest as she took in the Wolf's long, soft brown hair—hair Rorax had buried her face in as a child. The long, willowy limbs that had soothed as many hurts as she had caused. The lips that had taught her so many things about survival. Her old trainer. Her old caretaker. Her *mother*.

"You're wrong about this place, Wolf," said the Rorax in her vision spat. "There are no weapons here."

"They have lied to you, Rorax, and you believed them. You have been lost." The Wolf sounded sad, like she, too, was in mourning as she prowled around her. "This city must fall."

But something about the casual way the Wolf dismissed the city and the innocent lives there snapped something inside of Rorax now. She focused on the scene in her head and came to herself in the present. The Wolf had been wrong, and through Rorax's actions in killing the Wolf, she had saved *thousands*.

Rorax had had enough. She was done suffering for her mistakes.

She'd been the only person who could have stepped in during the Siege, and again she alone found herself in the position to protect the next Guardian.

Shakily, Rorax got to her feet, then drew her sword. She took in two ragged breaths before she turned and stabbed the Oracle.

The sword sank deep into the Oracle's fabric-covered body, and she must have connected with something corporal because the Oracle screamed. The flaming buildings surrounding them in her mind shuddered, and Rorax could feel the Oracle thrashing around her mind, desperately trying to find a way out of Rorax's cage. The Oracle in front of her shuddered in pain, so Rorax twisted the sword in its body until it screamed again, thrashing even more.

"LET US OUT," the Oracle finally screamed, once again the sound all around her.

Rorax smiled manically, going even deeper. "You tried to trap me here. You tried to *break* me. Without even looking into my mind first. You broke your vow."

She twisted her sword, dragging it down slightly, and the Oracle howled in agony.

Rorax cupped the back of the Oracle's lumpy, hood-covered head, and brought it closer so she could whisper into its ear. "If you don't let me out of this cave, I will kill you."

Rorax knew only a Blood Oath would protect her once she let go of the Oracle. "Do you have any blood?"

The Oracle snarled but finally nodded.

"You're going to take a Blood Oath. You are going to tell me what I need to know, what you *would* have and *should* have told me. Then I am going to let you go and you will leave me, unharmed and alive, to get out of this cave and to the safety of my Protectorate, and then you will confirm to the Guardian that I have passed the trial."

The Oracle nodded, taking in deep, hissing breaths. "Yes. Yes, we agree. Take our blood." The Oracle used one of its own dirty, cracked nails to slice into its palm.

Rorax slapped her bloody palm on the Oracle's gray blood that trickled out of its wound, and a shudder of magick traveled through Rorax's veins as the agreement settled into her bones.

Rorax pulled her sword out of the Oracle's shoulder, and the creature screamed again.

"Now let us out," the Oracle whined.

"Tell me what I need to know first," Rorax said through gritted teeth.

The Oracle hesitated for a moment before it trembled, and its voice seemed to fracture into more than one vocal sound—the volume of it amplifying as if thirty people were speaking to her simultaneously. "All roads that lead out of the Choosing are being closed to you, Contestar. The King of Alloy will betray you.

The Prince of Death is not who he seems. You will need the thorn of the sea. The Realms will fall without your blood. Do not release the Star."

The Oracle broke the bindings and staggered back, heaving in breaths.

"Is that it?" Rorax snapped.

The Oracle hissed in anger. "For now, that is all the Scribbler has shown us, now let us *out*."

Rorax narrowed her eyes before lifting the corner of her mind and shoving them both through.

As soon as she had released them both from her mind, Rorax twirled to face the Oracle, only to feel another butt of a blade hit her across the temple and have darkness swallow her.

CHAPTER 85

AYRES

Ayres paced back and forth, his hands clenching and unclenching at his sides.

Cannon stood at the opening, staring into the dark tunnel, his hands on his hips.

Piers and Milla were playing cards, sitting cross-legged on the trail, both shooting the tunnel nervous glances at every sound. When Cannon started snapping his fingers, Milla and Piers scrambled to their feet, and Ayres positioned himself at Cannon's back.

Something's coming, he signed, not taking his eyes off the tunnel.

A few seconds later, a tall figure draped in shadow like a blanket of thick black smoke appeared. Ayres drew his blade, and so did the others.

In one of its shadow-draped hands, the figure held Rorax's sword, dragging it through the dirt, tip down. In his other hand, he held Rorax's wrist, dragging her limp body along like a sack of potatoes.

Was Rorax alive? Ayres's chest seized, and he stopped breathing as sharp fear pierced his heart.

They were all at Rorax's side in an instant. Ayres ripped the skeletal, shadowy hand away from her wrist and pressed his fingers into her throat, feeling for a pulse.

When he felt that glorious, fluttering thump against his fingertips, he whipped around and pressed his blade to where the shadow's skeletal neck would be, forcing it backward until Ayres had the figure against the tunnel's stone wall.

"What happened in there?" Ayres snarled.

"*Calm*, Harbinger. The Pup will live."

Ayres didn't even react to the moniker *Harbinger* as his heart skipped a beat in relief.

"I asked you what *happened*," Ayres growled, pressing his blade harder into the column of bone he could not see through the shadows.

"I do not know," the shadow hissed to Ayres. "I followed my orders from the Oracle to bring her here unconscious but alive. The Oracle instructed me to inform you that Roraxiva Greywood is not to step foot on the Oracle's Mountain again or she will die."

Ayres stared at the shadow for a long moment before reaching into it and grabbing the specter's spinal column. He used it to throw the shadow back into the tunnel where it came from. It disappeared into a puff of black smoke.

Ayres turned back to Rorax, who was being carefully flipped over onto her back by Milla and Piers. Ayres's jaw clenched in fury.

A big bruise was starting to develop on the top half of her face, and her lip was split down the middle, blood encrusting most of her mouth and nose. But she was alive, and that was all that mattered.

Ayres had half a mind to storm into the mountain and pluck the life from the Oracle and every being in its domain. But he knew the law of the land. The Death Harbinger was not to abuse his power on the gods' creatures, and if he broke the Gods' Law, Marras would punish him for it.

"We need to get her off this mountain, *now.*" Milla turned Rorax's head to the side with gentle fingers, so she could get a closer look at the large bruise still forming on her temple. "I'm worried about this bruise. If there's internal bleeding, any blood left sitting on her brain for too long—"

Ayres had Rorax scooped up in his arms, cradling her against his chest, before Milla could finish her sentence. "Let's go."

Milla snatched Rorax's blade off the ground, and they left.

Rorax roused a bit as they ventured down the trail, and relief hit him once more in his solar plexus.

She peeled one white eye open and blinked up at him twice before closing it again. "Ayres," she breathed.

He bent his head closer to hers. "Shh, Little Crow. I've got you."

She swallowed hard as her head bobbed against his chest. "Let me ride on your back. It'll be easier for you that way."

Ayres consented and slid her around his shoulders until her front was pressed against his back, and he gripped the underside of her thighs, her arms holding his neck loosely.

"Thank you, Ayres. Your men must love you if you treat them half as well as you treat me, even if you hate me," Rorax whispered, her breath brushing the skin of his neck.

Her words made Ayres almost stumble on the flat path. He opened his mouth to respond, but she went limp before he could.

Your men must love you if you treat them half as well as you treat me.

Guilt and shame burrowed into his heart. Rorax deserved better than him. Deserved a Protectorate who wasn't so torn about her, who wasn't keeping so many secrets from her.

He hated this feeling—the slick, oily feeling of his lies.

Ayres hiked down until they met Lamonte, who was waiting for them at the trailhead at the top of the Mountain of the Oracle.

Lamonte looked over Rorax's body with concern. "Is she okay? What happened?"

"We don't know," Milla answered. She looked around to make sure she was out of earshot of all Lamonte's men before she lowered her voice. "One of the Oracle's shadows dragged her to the mouth of the cave and told us she was banned from the mountain."

Lamonte's green eyes went wide with astonishment. "What?"

"They knocked her unconscious, so we need to get her to a healer," Ayres said, stepping around a wide-eyed Lamonte. He started down the stone steps of the mountain.

As Ayres descended, he wondered how she would react if she ever found out that he was the prince, that he was the Death Harbinger. The decision to pass himself off as nothing more than an army man meant he could hide his identity and his ability.

The legends stated Death Harbingers were some of the most powerful and terrifying beings in the Realms, and they could rip the life out of any living soul.

His identity and ability were closely guarded by his family. Anyone who remembered the lore about the Harbingers knew that the Sumavaris had been the Death Harbingers for nearly 15,000 years. By claiming that Ayres was nothing more than a soldier, no one ever looked at him suspiciously or noticed his power went beyond brute strength and lucky genes. No one ever put the pieces together.

Living his life as an ordinary man had once felt so freeing. He'd cherished his freedom and anonymity and protected it for over 600 years.

Now it was slowly poisoning him.

He felt like the pillars of his character that he had devoted his whole life meticulously building were slowly eroding away. Loyalty, honesty, strength, family, and sacrifice.

Ayres let out a powerful sigh and tried to unclench his jaw.

Just a couple more months, and this whole thing would be over. For better or worse.

"Thank the gods," Ayres mumbled to himself, rubbing his thumbs in small circles over the soft spot in her knee.

He still wasn't sure if he wanted Rorax as the future Guardian of the North or if he would rather have Enna. He hadn't made up his mind, but until he was forced to decide, Ayres was on Rorax's team. He was her Protectorate. Rorax had put her life on the line for him and his friends more times than he cared to remember, and she'd helped him get one of the Books of Sumavari back. She deserved everything he could give her.

Rorax unconsciously adjusted herself in his arms and snuggled closer, pressing her lips against the skin on the side of his neck.

He hummed in pleasure at the touch before he could stop himself. *Fuck*, that felt good.

But she was his Contestar. His champion. His... friend.

So, beyond the things she had done to his people, whatever this *thing* was that was blooming to life between them, it had to stop. These *feelings* for her needed to die; they needed to float away like smoke in the air.

Ayres needed to force their relationship back into a tentative friendship.

Friendship was easier, less volatile. He would be able to maintain a friendship with her. He could control her influxes safely without fucking her every time.

Ayres didn't know what it meant that those words felt like a lie in his own mind.

Ayres carried Rorax all the way to the bottom of the Mountain of the Oracle, then carried her straight to the healer's tent. Thankfully, it was one of Tressa's healers and not Tressa herself. He wasn't in the mood to deal with her today.

As soon as he laid Rorax out on a cot, the healer went to work.

"How bad is it?" Ayres asked as the healer's fingers emitted a soft glow, brushing over the bruise on Rorax's temple.

"It's not bad, sir. Mostly superficial. She doesn't have any magick in her, but I will give her a flush to help." As the healer worked, the bruise under Rorax's skin disappeared and the split on her lip sealed closed.

"She'll wake in just a moment," said the woman. "I'll go fetch some more water."

After only a few minutes, Rorax blinked those pretty, sparkling, colorless eyes up at him.

"Hey," Ayres murmured as Rorax pushed herself up to a sitting position.

Rorax swiped the stray hairs away from her face and looked around the tent, confused. "What happened?"

"I was hoping you could tell *me* what happened, Little Crow. One of the Oracle's shadows informed us that you have been banned from her mountain."

Rorax rolled her eyes and leaned back on her wrists. "That dramatic old coot."

Ayres bit back a smile and squatted down so that they were at the same eye level. "Ror, what happened?"

Rorax poked the inside of her cheek with her tongue and eyed him coolly before she decided to answer. "It tried to kill me."

"What?" Ayres's breath caught in his throat, but Rorax just lifted a hand to inspect her nail beds.

"It was like when Tressa tried to find her way inside my head, but it couldn't find a way in. I eventually found a way to open my mind to it, but then... I trapped it. I closed the door on it and told it I wouldn't let it out without a Blood Oath that promised me safe passage home."

"You trapped the *Oracle* in your mind?" Ayres choked.

Rorax looked away from her nails and smirked at him. "Cool trick, eh?"

He just stared at her.

The Oracle was one of the most ancient and powerful creatures in all the Realms, one of the only creatures in the world with a direct line to the Scribbler, the weaver of fate in the Realms. "Did it *say* anything when it tried to kill you?"

The grin faded from her face, and she swallowed hard. "It showed me my past. Showed me all my mistakes. It reminded me why I would never be fit to become the Guardian."

Rorax looked to the ground and reached up to tug her hair out of its braid. It fell between them like a thick curtain so Ayres could barely see her face.

"It gave me a clue to where Darras is, and... it said that I would be denied the opportunity to rip myself free of the Choosing."

Silence fell between them, heavy and so painful. Ayres sighed. "I'm sorry, Rorax, for what I said after the last influx."

She tucked a long strand of hair behind her ears, a small, sad smile on her lips. She still didn't meet Ayres's eyes, and he wanted to reach out and tilt her face up to his so he could see exactly what she was thinking.

"I understand, Lieutenant. I understand how this *attraction* between us must be... conflicting for you." Rorax fingered the frays on the edge of the blanket for a moment before her beautiful eyes finally met his. "I know it's unsavory for you, but I... I'm asking you to continue. If I am going through an influx, I'd much rather have it *with* you than fighting or killing anyone else." Her gaze dropped back to the blanket. "It's okay if you don't want to, or if the idea makes you sick. I'll ask someone else."

The last sentence out of her mouth made Ayres's head rear back as an ugly, foreign emotion filled his throat.

Someone else? She would find someone else to help her with the influxes?

His jaw tightened. The thought of someone else's hands on Rorax made him sick, but would demanding that no other man touch her put a romantic claim on her he didn't want?

Rorax must have seen the indecision in Ayres's face. "We'd remain as... friends. I'd never ask you for something that you could not give, Lieutenant. The *situation* would only last until the end of the Choosing—when I free myself or when I die."

Marras save him, he hated it when she called him *Lieutenant*. He hated it even more when she casually talked about her death.

Ayres stared at her for a long moment, proud that his eyes only dropped to her unbelievably perfect mouth once as he made his decision.

He rolled his jaw and nodded his consent. "Okay. Friends. And I will continue to help you with your influxes as you have them."

Rorax blew out a relieved breath. "Thank you. I would ask someone else, since I… you made it clear how I make you feel, but I'm not sure anyone else would survive it. Survive *me*."

Rorax seemed to curl in on herself, and at that moment, she looked so small sitting there. She looked defeated, alone, and so *vulnerable* that his heart cracked.

"Rorax…." Ayres wanted to reach out an arm to wrap it around her shoulders, to seep his strength into her. He wanted to bring *her* back. He wanted to bring back the Rorax that would never yield, the Rorax with fire in her blood and venom on her tongue.

But before he could, she pushed herself up off the cot and moved away from him. "I am going to see if a dragon is ready to fly us home."

CHAPTER 86

RAENGAR

Deimos landed with enough force on the stones of the landing port that the birds in the trees even a half a mile away took frightened flight into the air. He'd flown to a city just on the outskirts of Venzor on Azaele's Island. Grunting with exhaustion, Deimos shook his giant head and stretched his blue, glittering wings out as Raengar unbuckled himself and slid off his back. They'd been flying for nearly five days straight to get here, leaving only ten minutes after Raengar had gotten a Blood Hawk message in Morvarand that said:

Someone has been in the fucking Pit. Come to Venzor to pick up the head of a minotaur to take to the Council of Bastards.

-A

The landing base for dragons on Pit Island was nothing more than a deserted ruin of charred limestone and sticks, but someone must have seen him fly in, because speeding toward them were two armored velociraptors. Dinosaurs would never survive the cold of House of Ice, or most of the Realms' turbulent environments, but here on the warm, safe, tropical islands of Azaele's they thrived.

Raengar recognized Ashwani and Layaz Kulltoug, each riding on the back of an armored raptor. They were pulling a giant dead moose carcass between them that had been strung up to their mounts. Moose were not indigenous to the island but had been introduced to help feed the population of carnivores.

Layaz grinned, threw a leg over her raptor, and ran to the side of Deimos with a huge grin on her face. "Now *here* is a real lizard," Layaz crooned, rubbing her hands over Deimos's ice-blue scales, each one the size of a dinner plate, as the large beast looked down at her with a lazy blink.

Layaz looked a lot like her sister, Kiniera, except she had barely a third of Kiniera's power, which manifested in a healthy glow in Layaz's skin and eyes. She was still pale, still had the moon white hair of the Kulltougs, but she didn't look nearly as gaunt as Raengar's spymaster. The younger Kulltoug would last approximately two seconds in a match with her sister but had more warmth in her little finger than the spymaster had in her whole body.

"We brought some food for Deimos," Ashwani called out as she unhooked the moose carcass from the back of the raptors, who both watched Deimos carefully with alert eyes.

The velociraptors yapped nervously as Deimos lunged forward and eagerly ripped apart the moose, nearly stepping on the raptors in the process.

"There you go, beasty," Ashwani cooed, happily watching Deimos eat his dinner.

Ashwani was the queen here. She was part of the ruling Ashwani family, but the islands technically belonged to the House of Ice.

In exchange for their taxes, the Azalea Islands received protection from the House of Ice army and their dragons, along with free infrastructure and education for the island people. There had been calls of rebelling, of stepping out of House of Ice influence, but Ashwani and her ancestors all fought vigorously for the good that House of Ice brought to their people, especially with Pit Island right next to them. It was a constant threat and a reminder.

Ashwani was tall, had light brown skin, and tight, curly black hair that grew wildly around her face. She was fiercely loyal and had an unflappable friendship with Raengar and Isolde. Raengar had known few people in his life as stoic and capable as her.

"It's good to see you both," Raengar said, tilting his head at Ashwani as she worked.

Layaz stepped away from Deimos to wrap Raengar in a hug. "I'm so glad to see you! I haven't seen anyone from home in *months*. It's amazing to be reminded that I'm not the only pale person on the planet."

Raengar smiled down at the girl as she stepped back. Ashwani had asked for one of the Kulltougs to take permanent residence on the islands to help her take care of her Blood Hawks. Layaz had stepped forward and remained on the sunny islands for nearly twenty years, not that her pale skin ever showed any hint of that.

"How's my sister?" Layaz asked.

"Good. Leading our Contestar to victory."

Layaz's nose scrunched in distaste.

"Here's the head," Ashwani unhooked a bloody, linen bag from the side of her raptor.

It smelled absolutely *foul*, and there were flies buzzing around the white linen, but Raengar took it and opened it with the enthusiasm of a kid getting a present on Winter Solstice. A minotaur head. Black fur and long black bull horns slid around on a bloody piece of armor emblazoned with the Lyondrean crest.

"I would take that to Koppar, get a witch to freeze it." Ashwani grimaced in disgust. "Oh! Take this, too."

Raengar looked up to see Ashwani holding out a rolled-up piece of parchment out to him. Her seal stamped on the front in wax. "My signed statement saying this head and that armor was found on Pit Island. You know what this means, don't you?"

Raengar took the piece of parchment carefully in his hand and nodded gravely. "It means we're going to war."

CHAPTER 87

RORAX

A loud knock at Rorax's door made her head snap up from the book she was reading in alarm. She eyed the clock on the wall. It was well past midnight.

She grabbed a knife off the coffee table next to her and padded over to the door. "Who is it?"

"It's Kiniera's advisor, ma'am. I have a message from the Ice emissary asking you to come to her room." There was a hesitant pause before the man on the other side of the door got closer and whispered to her through the crack. "It's about the fourth trial. We finally managed to find out what's coming next."

Relief made her heart skip a beat, and she whipped open the door. Kiniera's advisor stood there, his cheeks a little pink as he jumped back out of Rorax's space. He reached his palm out. "Here, she told me to give this to you."

Come to my room, now.

-K

Rorax's mouth pinched tight around the corners. The hasty, shaking scrawl was not the cool, perfectly neat handwriting Kiniera used in all her professional correspondence, or even the personal letters Rorax had received from her in the past.

"I'll be there in a moment," Rorax said to the messenger.

Kiniera's assistant nodded and turned away as she closed the door.

Rorax pulled on her boots. She'd been reading in a white, long sleeve, cotton dress that Hella made for her, and she didn't bother to change as she pushed out of her room, sliding her hair blades into her braid on the way out.

Rorax didn't knock as she pushed inside Kiniera's room.

"Felidra," Kiniera blurted as soon as the latch closed behind Rorax. "You'll have to make a four-person team, and you'll have to steal a chrysalis from a felidra."

Kiniera looked frazzled, like she had been running her hands through her wispy hair as she paced furiously back and forth.

Rorax blinked at Kiniera, the words bouncing uselessly around in her head. "What in the hell are you talking about, Kiniera?"

"Your fourth trial, Rorax. They want you to steal a chrysalis. From the felidra colonies."

As the words started to sink in, Rorax's chest felt tighter and tighter. "A chrysalis. They want me to steal a chrysalis. From a felidra."

They stood staring at each other in horror for a long moment until a knock on the door interrupted them, and Kiniera brushed past Rorax to open it.

"What's going on?" Jia asked when Kiniera closed the door again.

Rorax kept staring at the spot where Kiniera had been standing, thoughts swirling so violently in her mind, she was surprised she wasn't screaming them across the room.

"Ror?"

A four-person team. To steal a felidra chrysalis. One of the most dangerous creatures in the Realms. Without magick.

The walls were pressing in on her.

Rorax had seen a rabid felidra kill a small group of men in *seconds* before someone in her unit had put it down. She needed to bring four other people in with her. Only four? How was she supposed to pick a group who would essentially be sacrifices to a trial?

"Rorax!" A hand on Rorax's elbow made her head snap up, but she still felt like she was choking as Jia pulled on her elbow again.

"Ror, are you okay?" she asked as the corners of her mouth pressed down into a frown.

Rorax trapped a hysterical laugh in her throat and nodded.

"Go tell Milla and the lieutenant," Kiniera said, pushing her hand through her frazzled hair again. "I need to prepare Isgra and put a team together that consists of... the most *disposable* soldiers we have, since they most likely won't be coming back."

Kiniera strode out of her room without waiting for a reply.

"Come on. I'll go get Milla." Jia gave Rorax a little shove toward the door. "Go to Ayres's room, and we'll meet you there."

Panic started to flood Rorax's system as she climbed down a flight of stairs and two long hallways. She found herself knocking on Ayres's door, feeling jittery.

She tapped her foot and looked around the hallway, biting her lip. She was five seconds away from losing her mind and didn't want her meltdown to happen in the hallway.

When Rorax didn't hear any movement from behind the door, she knocked again.

Looking over her shoulder to the thankfully still empty hallway, she hissed, "Ayres, open the gods-damned door!" She heard a low curse from within, and it finally jerked open.

Rorax hurled herself into his room, tripping over his feet and staggering forward before hitting her forehead on hard, warm flesh.

"Gods, I'm sorry." She felt the blush bloom across her cheeks and was grateful it was dark in his room.

"Ror?" His voice was sleepy and sexy as he closed the door behind him. His scent of balsam and pine calmed something inside her chest, even as something else in her core quivered.

"I need to talk to you," she blurted before he could say anything else in that voice. "I know what the next trial is. We're going into a nest of felidra to steal a chrysalis. It's a four-person team assault. My sponsor has to provide my team."

Red lighting cracked across the room, and a small fire erupted in the fireplace, illuminating the space. She yelped, jumping to Ayres. She clenched his massive biceps and stared wide-eyed at the fire before looking up at Ayres who was watching her with a crease between his eyebrows. Her face flushed into an even deeper kaleidoscope of reds and pinks as she released him and took two steps away. "I'm sorry," she said again.

"Rorax," Ayres demanded, grabbing her shoulders tightly with his tattooed hands, "take a deep breath. Calm down."

She nodded, looking at the carpet and did as she was told, gulping down breaths of air and pushing down her nerves. When she felt like she was back in control, she looked up at him.

Ayres watched her with alert eyes and that perfectly proportioned mouth tight at the corners. "I've never seen you this spooked before. What the *fuck* is going on?"

"The next trial. We're supposed to infiltrate a colony of felidra and extract a chrysalis." The words felt like ash in her mouth, but Ayres didn't so much as blink at the news.

"How many people can be on your team?" Ayres's voice was steady, so unwaveringly calm that she could feel some of her own panic ease.

"It's a team of four. Jia was with me when we found out. She's telling Milla now."

As if summoned, there was a brisk knock on the door. Rorax sucked in her breath, forcing her panic away. Ayres stepped away from her to answer it, letting an angry Milla and a slightly pale Jia into his room.

Ayres closed the door behind them, and Milla put her fists on her hips and glared up at Ayres. "The felidra? Really?"

Ayres shrugged a shoulder at her. Milla huffed before crossing the room and collapsing into one of the two armchairs by the fireplace.

Ayres pulled on a shirt that had been draped over the end of his bed and turned to Rorax. "Can you recruit anyone for your team? Who do you want?"

"I don't want anyone," Rorax blurted before she took a deep breath and turned to Jia. Rorax didn't even have to open her mouth before Jia nodded.

"I'm your emissary. I'm on your team whether you want me to be or not," Milla said to Ror, looking both her and Jia up and down from the armchair by the fire. Then her head slowly turned to Ayres. "I am going to ask Kaiya or Piers to be the fourth."

Ayres snarled at her, baring his teeth, "Like hell you are."

Milla leaned forward and rested her elbows on her knees to match his pose. "Ayres."

Ayres glowered at Milla for a long moment before turning his dark charcoal eyes to Rorax. A clear challenge rested there. "It will be me."

Rorax shared a confused glance with Jia. Why wouldn't Milla want Ayres on the team? He held the most magick in the castle, besides Kiniera, or so she'd been told.

"Have either of you two ever fought a felidra?" Milla motioned to Jia and Ror with a flick of her fingers, pulling their attention back to her.

They both shook their heads. Felidra, with the bodies of big cats and the wings of butterflies, resided predominantly in the Jagamine mountains between the House of Death and Life. They thrived in the tall mountains there and in other small pockets around the Realms. There was a small group that lived in the House of Ice's southern mountains where she had once seen a rabid felidra, but nowhere else in the Realm.

"They're smart. They are fast and come in varying shades of sentience. We might be able to reason with some... or bribe some, but the majority will try and kill us on sight once we arrive out of loyalty for the pack. We need to cover our scents the best we can when we get to the hunting ground. We also need to pray that we don't get placed near the heart of felidra territory. We're fucked if the king of the felidra catches us," Milla said.

Ayres sat on the edge of his bed and rested his elbows on his knees, watching Ror. "Do you know anything else about the challenge?"

"We're supposed to steal a chrysalis. I don't know when"—Rorax furiously rubbed her finger over her ring—"or where the task is, or even if you will be in the task with me or just on the sides yelling at me."

There was a beat of heavy silence, and a weight of inadequacy settled in Rorax's chest. It was so heavy she couldn't breathe. She was dragging some of her only surviving friends into a deadly situation, all of them unprepared and blind, and she wouldn't be able to protect them with any magick. She took a shuddering breath as Volla's face flashed into her mind. A roll of nausea built up in her stomach, and her panic started to rise again.

"Kiniera might know more. She didn't give us much before she left to deal with Isgra," Jia said.

"Felidra are fast, lethal, and as smart as a whip. This will be dangerous but not anything we won't be able to handle." Milla stood up and stretched her arms above her head. "Come on, girls, let's get to sleep. We'll talk to Kiniera in the morning."

Rorax had Ayres's door open with trembling fingers a half second later, more than ready to bolt from the room, but Ayres clasped a hand around her wrist and pulled her back against his side. "Go," he ordered Jia and Milla, jerking his head to motion them out. "I'll walk Rorax to her room in a moment."

Jia raised an eyebrow at him, and Milla smirked knowingly. "Very well, Lieutenant. Don't keep her up *all* night."

"She could really use some relaxation though, and I've heard you're just the man to do it." Jia winked at Ayres before he growled softly, and they swiftly left the room.

As soon as his door clicked shut, Ayres turned and pushed Rorax's shoulders gently against the door, planting his palms on the wood on either side of her head. "Ror, look at me. Are you okay?"

It felt like a band was strapped across her chest, constricting her breathing as she panted. She couldn't look up at him. Her throat felt like it was full of cotton. Her ears were buzzing, and all she could think about was Volla.

Volla's face. All those dead soldiers. All that blood.

"Ror." Ayres's voice was low and soft, but it sounded like he was underwater. She shook her head and grabbed little fistfuls of his T-shirt with trembling fingers.

Volla. Sahana. The blood....

"Ror, look at me."

Rorax gritted her teeth as tears threatened the rims of her eyes.

Volla. Darras....

He released her, took her hand in his, and tugged her to the bed with him. He sat down and pulled her into his lap, wrapping her legs around his waist so they could sit chest to chest. Rorax pressed her eyes against the muscle on the side of his throat and tightened her legs around his waist, squeezing his torso closer.

Tears started to drip down her cheeks before she could choke them back, and she grabbed bigger fistfuls of the soft, white shirt he wore.

Her breaths were still shallow and way too short, her chest still tight and painful.

Her friends. She was leading her friends to their deaths. Again. And she didn't have the magick to help them.

"Ror," Ayres said softly.

An image of a dead Jia planted itself on the back of her eyelids, her throat ripped out by the teeth of a lion or a jaguar felidra. She tried to shove it away, but it wouldn't go.

"Ror, it's going to be okay. We're going to be fine," he said, rocking her back and forth, one arm a tight band around her middle the other rubbing circles into her back.

The fact that he knew Rorax's tears were not for herself but for Jia—for all of them—and the fact that she was going to have to put them at risk warmed her heart.

Ayres might still battle with himself whether he liked her or not, if she was *worth it* or not, but the fact that he knew her well enough to know she was terrified for the loss of the people closest to her without her having to tell him, it touched her somewhere so deep down she didn't even recognize it. And it cracked her in half, her emotions finally forcing a loud sob from her throat.

"What if Jia dies?" she whispered, wiping the mixture of wet snot and tears on the back of her hand behind his back. "How would I ever face Volla? What if you die? If Milla...." Another sob and then another, and then even more ripped through her, and she pressed herself closer to him, wrapping her limbs around him tightly and using his shirt to absorb her tears.

He let her cry in his lap, rocking them back and forth and absentmindedly smoothing her hair with his fingertips.

When her sobs finally stopped wracking her body and only silent tears remained, she whispered, "I can't let you come, Ayres. Any of you. I've already caused so much damage to Death and her people, they can't lose you, too."

The hand rubbing her back froze, and Rorax swore a little growl rumbled in the back of his throat.

"Ayres?" She tried to pull back an inch to look at his face, but before she could, he flipped her over. She let out a whoosh of surprised breath as she landed on her back.

Ayres held his weight up with his elbows pressed on either side of her face, holding his dark head so it hovered over hers, the cheekbones in his face softly illuminated by the fire light.

"We are going to be *fine*, Rorax. I swear to you that I will make sure all four of us come out of this alive. *We* are going to make sure we make it out of this alive." The way he said it, his unwavering faith in his ability—in *her* ability—made something steady inside of her.

He rubbed a tear away from her cheek with his thumb. "But as of this moment, I am done letting you insult me, Little Crow. No more."

"Insult you?" Rorax's eyebrows pulled together. "What are you talking about?"

"You really think that a little *cat* can kill me?" The arrogant bastard narrowed his eyes.

She scrunched her nose and squirmed a bit underneath him. "Felidra are *not* just big cats. Sharp teeth, venomous, flies, some have spiky tails—all things that could kill you, Lieutenant."

Ayres hummed and lowered his head until his lips were only inches away from hers. "Good thing my Contestar has a little magick knife to protect me."

"*Little* knife?" She rolled her eyes, ignoring how her heartbeat sped at his proximity.

Her body suddenly felt flush as the reality of her current situation hit her. She was in Ayres's *bed*. *Underneath* him. Lying right where he had been sleeping shirtless not twenty minutes ago. After a month of nothing but cordial space between them, her body was elated at the attention. "Maybe I'll let the felidra take a bite of you. Just a taste. You'll either die, or it'll decide we aren't tasty enough for the trouble. It's worth a gamble, I think."

A slow, hungry wolflike grin spread across his mouth, and it made her clench her thighs together. "What do you think will happen if I take another taste of *you*, Ror?"

She should say that him tasting her again would never happen. She *should* say that, after what he'd said the last time they were together, she didn't want anything to do with him. But instead, she smirked back at him and slowly started wrapping her legs around his waist. "I think, Ayres, if you take another taste of me, you'll finally understand the meaning of the word *addiction*."

"Who says you haven't already taught me the meaning?" he whispered. The words made her feel more wet and needy than she already was, but before she could say anything, he threaded his fingers through the strands of hair at the side of her neck and kissed her.

Gods, kissing him made her feel like she had been struck by lightning. She groaned into his mouth and deepened the kiss, opening up to him. She tugged his shirt up and slipped her fingers under the fabric, feeling the hot skin and taught muscles of his lower abdomen.

He groaned like he was in pain before he broke away from her. "Wait. *Fuck*. I thought I was supposed to be comforting you."

She wriggled against him, scrunching up her nose and scowling as she watched a muscle in his jaw jump through the dark stubble. "You *were*." Rorax pouted, her voice husky and straining.

"Was I?" He traced her lips with the fingers of his other hand before he brushed the tips of his pointer and middle fingers over her bottom lip and inside her mouth. Still glaring at him, she wrapped her tongue around his fingers and pulled them deeper into her mouth.

Ayres's dark eyes erupted into silver as he watched them disappear between her lips. He pushed them deeper, down into the smooth, wet walls of her mouth, and she sucked them harder, challenging him with her eyes.

"Fuck," he growled, his silver eyes glinting in the darkness as he watched her lips stretch.

She scraped her teeth lightly against the bottom of his knuckles, watching as his pupils continued to blow out. Ayres plucked his fingers from her mouth and trailed the wet tips down over her lips and chin before he clasped his hand around her neck.

"What do you need?" he asked.

"You."

"Say it, Greywood, say exactly what you want, word for word, or I'm walking you back to your room right now."

She ground her teeth together. "I want you to fuck me. I don't want to wait until the next influx." Rorax ground against him, feeling him harden under their clothes.

"The last time we did this, you ignored me for days," Ayres growled.

"*Last time* you were an asshole."

He grunted. "I also... I was rough with you, Rorax. You were going through an influx, and I thought that's what you needed at the time to get through it."

"I have never come so hard in my whole life," she assured him. "Even without an influx, it's what I want."

Ayres didn't say anything.

"If you *don't* give me what I want," Rorax growled, "I'll go find someone else who might be up to the challenge."

Ayres laughed darkly, the sound low and throaty and a little bit angry. "There is no one alive who could fuck you like you need. No one but me."

He pressed his body between her legs, keeping his tattooed hand wrapped around her throat so tight she could feel the cool metal of his rings against her skin. Ayres kissed her again, deep and hard. His tongue pushed its way into her mouth. He devoured her like a fucking animal, hard like his anger and hatred were fueling his lust. Kään help her, she fucking loved it.

She tried to push his shoulders back, to roll on top of him, but he gathered her wrists with his other hand and pinned them above her head, out of his way. A small part of her fought it—against the heat rising in her—but she had never had a man overpower her like this before Ayres, and *gods* she wanted more.

He broke away, nipping the skin down her neck so hard it burned. His hand skated up her side, brushing over the side of her breast.

She whimpered, and before she could stop herself, she arched her back into him, pressing her breasts into his palm, aching for more, needing more. "Ayres."

He paused at the junction of her neck and shoulder, his breath ragged against her skin. He rose just high enough to look at her, and fear lodged in her throat.

Ayres's eyes were bright red.

Her heart started to pound. "I...."

"Say. It. Again."

"Fuck me, Ayres."

Ayres jerked her up from the bed, stalked over to his desk, and set her down flat on her back. He fumbled with something over her head, and when she turned to look, she saw the black salt box with Glimr inside it. Ayres picked up her knife, hissing in pain as the metal seared his palm, and stabbed the knife into the wood of the desk, three feet above her head.

When she heard him fumbling with his belt, she started to struggle with her hips, a weak attempt at escape. He growled a warning as he ripped his belt out of its loops and used it to clamp her hands together at the wrists and securing them to her knife.

When he was done securing her to the table, he used his own knife and split her dress from her neck down to her belly button. He grabbed the fabric and ripped it the rest of the way down. His hungry red eyes inspected every inch of her swollen flesh, her breasts heaving with her desperate attempts to breath.

"Fuck," he growled, testing the weight of her breast in his palm. "You are perfect." He bent down and sucked one of her nipples into his mouth; then he went lower and lower, dipping his tongue into her belly button before lowering himself to where she wanted him. He licked over her clit first, making her hips involuntarily buck in his mouth before he slid down and gave her slit a long lick. He stayed there, devouring her and using his fingers to stretch her until he thought she was ready for him.

He pulled his cock from his pants, gave it a rough squeeze, and ran it over her pussy, wetting the length against her slit. Rorax tried to angle her hips, to get more, to feel more, but the instant Ayres felt her grind her hips, he pulled back.

"Ror," he chastised, "your orgasms are mine to give you; you don't get to take them." Shaking his head like he was disappointed in her, he raised a hand and slapped her pussy.

She yelped, hips jerking off the table. "Ayres!" He did it one more time, and she jerked again. She felt herself dripping down into the fabric beneath her, and he slapped her there one more time. She was going to come.

She wriggled her hips in invitation, in a silent plea, but nothing came. Instead, he pulled her hips to the end of the table, stretching her arms out above her almost on the verge of pain and pressed himself into her. He did it slowly, inch by inch, and with every second she tried to savor him until he was seated all the way inside of her. Gods, he was big. Her eyes watered as the opening of her pussy walls pinched in pain from his size.

Ayres groaned so loud, right in her ear, his breath tickling the little hairs on her ear and making her weep around his cock even more than she had been. "*Fuck*, you feel good, Ror."

He lowered his hand between them and rubbed her clit as he started to move in and out of her with hard rolls of his hips. Ayres raised his head to look into her eyes, and she felt a trill of fear. His eyes were bright red.

The man fucking her ruthlessly into the table held Death Magick in his blood that was close enough to the surface to see. Ayres wanted to fuck her as bad as he wanted to kill her, and something about that made her heart beat faster, made the adrenaline thrum in her veins, and made her feel absolutely fucking alive.

He rubbed her slit harder as she leaked out from around him; she could feel herself dripping onto the table below.

Ayres stroked her higher and higher until she knew she was going to tumble into oblivion. His arm snaked under her back, keeping her spine curved off the table so she was forced to keep her body pressed against his.

"I'm—" She choked before she started panting out breaths. "I'm gonna come, Ayres."

"Keep those pretty eyes open, Rorax," Ayres growled. "I wanna see you come on my cock. I want to see what I've earned."

She forced her eyes from rolling into the back of her head and kept her eyes connected with him as she came, her walls squeezing and fluttering around his cock as he came inside of her.

"Marras, fucking save me, Rorax." Ayres panted in her ear. "Are you alright?"

"Yes," Rorax breathed back. "That was.... I feel...." Kään save her, she couldn't even speak. Her mind felt like it was in a cloud, like the strings holding her to her body had been cut and she was about to float away. She had never known such pleasure.

Ayres looked to be in the same state as her, his forehead pressed against hers. He didn't even look like he had the strength to stand.

He eventually straightened, looking down at Rorax with lazy, lusty eyes. He brushed a thumb over her nipple, causing her to moan softly again, before he pulled out of her. He brought a warm, wet cloth to clean her up. "Come on, I'm hungry."

Rorax's hands were still pinned above her. She looked down at her naked body, but it didn't even have a scrap of her dress left on it.

Ayres seemed to read her mind. He smirked and reached up to untie her wrists, placing her knife back in the black salt box before he turned to his dresser. "I'll give you a shirt."

Ayres tossed one of his white, long-sleeved, linen shirts at her, and she pulled it over her head. It rested midthigh and covered all her important bits.

He didn't bother with one for himself as he grabbed her hand and led her from his room and down into the deserted kitchen with sure, steady strides.

When he opened the door, Ayres immediately turned to her, lifted her up by her hips, and sat her down on the nearest countertop.

She looked around the tidy, empty kitchen that was lit by a dying fire. "What are we doing down here?"

"Making up for last time." Ayres added a log to the fire before he strode to the pantry and opened it. He rifled through something before pulling out an orange sweet roll. He held it out to her. "Here."

She gently took it from him, careful to make sure none of the citrus-flavored frosting fell away.

Ayres rummaged through the cold box, a box that Ice Witches runed to keep food chilled, and pulled out a glass jar of milk. "Do you prefer warm milk or cold?"

"Warm," she whispered, watching as the lieutenant of Death put a small pot of milk over the fire for her.

When he deemed the temperature hot enough, he pulled it off the fire. "Give me a mug from the cupboard behind you."

Rorax turned and pulled down a mug large enough for the contents of the pot. He poured the milk and handed her the warm mug. "Eat."

She nodded and took a bite from the roll in her hand.

He washed and returned the pot as she sat there, watching him as she chewed. When he was done, he returned to her side and tucked a long strand of hair behind her ear. "Are you feeling better?"

Rorax took a long drink of milk, and as she felt it warm her from the inside, she nodded. "Much better."

"Good."

Ayres waited until she was done before taking the mug from her hands and setting it to her side. He wedged her knees apart and stood between them, cupping the sides of her face in his hands, forcing her to look up at him.

"Now listen to me, Ror. I won't let you, Jia, or Milla die up there. Do you remember when I let my power go, that time when we'd gone to fetch Sumavari's book? I will slaughter the whole colony of felidra to ensure our survival. You don't have to do this alone."

Rorax's eyes burned, and she had to press her lips together to keep a sob trapped in her throat. She reached up and wrapped her hands around his thick wrists, fighting the tears that wanted to spring from her eyes.

His face got imperceptibly closer to hers, his eyes searching like he could see every doubt written right there on her soul. "Do you trust me, Rorax?"

Sitting half-dressed on the kitchen counter with a man who had saved her life numerous times, and would probably do so again, there was only one answer.

"Yes," she whispered. A tear fell from the corner of her eye, and he wiped it away. "I trust you, Ayres."

He cupped the back of her head and pulled her head forward, resting it against his shoulder.

"What's happening right now?" Rorax asked, thinking about the last time they'd been together. *I don't hate you enough not to fuck you.*

Ayres sighed into her hair, guessing the direction her thoughts had gone. "I'm sorry. That was cruel."

"It's okay."

"No, it's... it's not okay. You have proven at every possible opportunity that you deserve a chance to redeem yourself. But you won't get a chance if I don't give you one. It won't be easy, and sometimes... sometimes I'll still be angry, Ror, and I think I'm entitled to that... but I'm trying."

"Okay," Rorax whispered. A chance. That was all she could ask for.

CHAPTER 88

RORAX

It was early. So *damned* early. If after the war with Lyondrea ended and she somehow managed to survive it, Rorax was going to sleep in every day for the rest of her life.

Rorax laid back in the bleachers of the arena, her elbows up on the risers behind her, watching Ayres and the prince do their early morning workout. It was almost erotic the way Ayres's muscles moved under his deeply tanned, tattooed skin as he tried to lay bruises down on his friend.

Jia was lounging next to her, mostly inspecting the fletching on her arrows, but sometimes watching the men train below, albeit with about a third of the enthusiasm as Rorax had.

Jia and Rorax had finished their own workout a half hour earlier but had decided to watch the men for a bit.

"Technique research," Rorax claimed to her fellow Heilstorm, but at this point, Rorax had to admit to herself she wasn't researching much of anything besides the male anatomy. Her core still ached with the ghost of Ayres's cock inside her, and her fantasies had gone wild. Last night, after she'd finished her sweet roll, he had walked her back to her room, leaving her only after her lock slid into place.

Now Rorax *should* go take another bath and go immediately to the library, but the idea was about as appealing as a splinter in the eye. She was exhausted, mentally and physically, and she was getting tired of sitting in the dark, dusty library. Her hopes of finding anything useful dwindled a little more every day, and it took more of her willpower to linger down there. If she was about to die, she wanted to spend her remaining moments in the sun.

"Enna wants to come sit with us," Jia murmured, her gaze locked on something down below. Rorax followed Jia's line of sight where Enna stood. She was hesitating at the foot of the arena's steps, her nervous glance flitting from one Heilstorm to the other.

Rorax caught Enna's eye and jerked her chin, motioning for Enna to come over. Enna visibly swallowed before slowly walking up the arena steps to greet them.

"Hi," Enna breathed. She tucked a long strand of hair behind her ear and stood there for a long, awkward second.

"Take a seat, Firebreather," Jia drawled, "or walk your sweet ass back down the stairs. You're blocking my view."

Enna frowned but immediately plopped down onto the bench next to Rorax.

"Is it true?" Enna asked, her innocent brown eyes wide and slightly disbelieving. Rorax didn't say anything, waiting for the woman to elaborate, but Jia beat her to it.

"Greywood is a lot of things, Firebreather, but a mind reader isn't one of them," she mocked, making Enna's light brown cheeks blush.

"Relax, Jia," Rorax admonished, keeping her eyes on Enna and trying to make her features friendly and comforting. "Is what true, Enna?"

"Is it true that they're training me so hard and you've saved me so many times... so that you can give me the throne to be the next Guardian of the North?"

Jia snickered at the same time as Rorax's eyebrows furrowed in confusion.

Hadn't Elios already told her the plan? Hadn't he and Kaiya been preparing her?

"Yes," Rorax confirmed slowly. "It's true."

"Oh." Enna's big brown eyes went huge with bewilderment, and she leaned back in shock. "*Oh*. It all makes so much sense now. But... why?"

"Because can you imagine Isgra being the new Guardian? She'd have everyone in the Realms enslaved and making her wine or carrying her around within the week," Jia snorted.

"A week?" Rorax scoffed. "I have more faith in her than that. She could do it in an hour."

Enna watched their back and forth as they chuckled darkly together before Rorax turned to give Enna her full attention. "I want you on the throne because I think you're the best. Out of all of us, you are the kindest, most aware, one of the bravest, and one of the most educated. You're smart, and you will care about what's best for the Realms and her people."

Enna swallowed hard, like she had something stuck in her throat. "What about you?"

Rorax's face darkened. "I'm not worthy."

Jia made a displeased grunt from behind Rorax. Enna just looked long and hard into Rorax's eyes; a deep crease formed between her eyebrows until she finally gave Rorax a short nod. "Okay."

Jia stood abruptly from her seat. Rorax looked up at her from over her shoulder to see a cold look on her friend's face. "Before that though, we need to find a way to free Rorax from the Choosing, so she doesn't have to die to give you the throne. So, if you'll excuse us, we have things to do."

Jia turned and started stomping her way down the stairs.

"Have I done something to offend her?" Enna asked as they watched Jia's purple ponytail swish behind her as she descended the stairs.

Rorax sighed. "She's scared I won't find a way out of the Choosing."

"Would you really die, if sacrificing yourself was the best thing to do for the Realms?"

The note of disbelief in Enna's voice made Rorax turn back to the Contestar, her mouth tight. "Yes."

"Of course. But I guess... I guess it's surprising. Coming from...." Enna bit her lip, and color bloomed over her light brown skin.

"Coming from the Pup?"

"Yeah."

"I would do anything for my home, for my house, and for my family." Rorax meant it now more than ever as she looked from one of Enna's big brown eyes to the other. Rorax pushed herself up to follow Jia, who was now waiting for her at the bottom of the stairs.

"Come on," Rorax said, motioning for Enna to follow. They descended the stairs in silence, and as Rorax hit the grass on the ground floor of the arena, she looked up to see Ayres walking toward her. He was still shirtless, and she couldn't stop her eyes from hungrily drinking in every inch of exposed, tattooed skin.

Gods above, this man was beautiful.

Ayres stopped in front of her, and Rorax jerked her gaze up from the deep gutters of his abdominal muscles to his face. He gave her a little smirk, and her cheeks started to burn.

"I saw your workout with Jia. You're getting faster in your armor," Ayres said.

"Thank you, Lieutenant."

He stepped closer, filling her senses with him as he whispered in her ear. "How long do you think you were staring at me today, Contestar? The full hour I was down here?"

Rorax's cheeks burned even more, but she still rolled her eyes, not bothering to hide a small smile curling up the side of her mouth. "I have *eyes*, Lieutenant. You not wearing a shirt and expecting me not to look is like bringing me something sweet and then expecting me to share it."

Ayres smiled down at her like she was absolutely adorable.

Not a grin, or him brandishing his teeth threateningly at her.

A full-blown, happy smile.

Bright, unfiltered joy and admiration shone down on her, and his smile felt like the sun was caressing her, or like she was a blind man seeing colors for the first time.

"I didn't know you could smile like *that*," Rorax muttered, slightly awestruck.

Of course, that only made his smile pull at the corners even more, this time with smug satisfaction.

"It seems that I am a man of *many* talents, Ror."

Gods, the straight white teeth, the light stubble framing those lips....

Ayres winked at Rorax before he turned and walked off the arena field, starting the trek back to the castle.

"Holy shit." The unadulterated awe in Jia's voice made a laugh bubble up in Rorax's throat. "Holy *fucking* shit, what was *that*?"

Rorax tore her gaze away from Ayres's retreating ass to look at Jia from over her shoulder. She pressed her lips together and raised an eyebrow as if asking her *what?* But Rorax knew. She fucking *knew*.

"The first and last time I saw a penis, I threw up," Jia said, starting to fan her slightly pink cheeks with her hand, her gaze still focused on Ayres. "One smile from that man, and my ovaries just gave the signal that I might need to give cocks a second chance. Gods, he needs to give out warnings before he flashes that thing. He could decimate civilizations."

Jia continued fanning herself.

Enna grabbed Rorax's arm, and they stared at each other for half a beat before they were both bent over at the waist laughing.

"What? Am I wrong?" Jia asked, which only made Rorax laugh harder. Because no, she was not wrong, and gods it felt good to laugh.

CHAPTER 89

TRESSA

"You have been released from your post." The Guardian pulled the top off a crystal decanter and poured a generous serving of amber liquid into a glass. Her movements were slow and casual, like the words she'd just uttered weren't threatening to upheave Tressa's whole life.

It was late; usually Tressa would already be in bed by now snuggled into Ren's side, but tonight the Guardian's men had summoned her to the Guardian's chamber.

Surely Tressa had heard wrong. The fourth trial was in two days, and the Contestars were expected to steal from a colony of *felidras.* The Contestars were going to need her magick now more than ever.

"But the trial... the Contestars?" Her words felt jumbled and clumsy in her mouth as her brain floundered around the Guardian's incomprehensible words.

"You will stay through the fourth trial, but you are to head home to your mother by the end of the week."

"That...." Tressa swallowed hard. "That wasn't the agreement."

"No," the Guardian snapped, finally turning around to face Tressa, her yellow eyes as sharp as broken glass. "The agreement was that you would be here, serving as my primary healer until the end of the Choosing in exchange for my soldiers defending your border and my support for your family. But *apparently* your mother doesn't need my protection anymore. She broke the agreement."

The words made her feel like the floor was falling out from under her. "*No.* No, you're wrong. My mother wouldn't do that." Tressa's voice shook as shock and fear rolled down her throat and into her stomach. "She knows we won't survive."

The Guardian sneered and pointed to a letter that had been left opened on the table. "Read for yourself."

Tressa tried to keep her hands from shaking as she picked up the creamy envelope. She read the letter inside once, twice, and then a third time just to make sure she had truly read it correctly.

Send my daughter home and get your soldiers out of my Realm. Our agreement is over.

-Abebe Eluvan

Queen of House of Life

Life Magick was a beautiful, wonderful thing. It was by far the worst magick when it came to defense. The Guardian's men were the only thing securing the border between Lyondrea and the House of Life. The Guardian's support was also the only reason other potential ruling families hadn't challenged her and her mother for the crown. As much as she hated the Guardian, her support was the only reason Tressa, and her mother were still alive.

"I'm so sorry. She is still grieving over the death of my sister. She doesn't know what she's saying," Tressa said, hating how she sounded so close to begging.

The Guardian smirked at Tressa, that maternal figure completely absent now.

Instead, a foreign, cold thing lay behind the Guardian's eyes that made a shiver run down Tressa's spine.

"I don't care. The agreement is over. Pack your things; you will stay through to the next trial, or until the next team of healers I've hired arrives, and then you will be on the first wagon home."

Tressa opened her mouth to argue, to ask what had changed, and maybe even to plead for her to change her mind, but the Guardian waved her hand in the air to cut her off.

"The decision has been made." She turned toward her soldiers at the entrance of the room. "Escort the princess back to her quarters, or to the mess hall. Just somewhere away from here."

Two of the Guardian's soldiers came up and grabbed Tressa's shoulders. She struggled against them, but they were stronger. "You can't do this. You *know* we won't survive."

The Guardian shrugged as she moved her attention to the small water fountain bubbling up in the center of her room. "I will leave this world in a few months, and I will not be the one to feel the fallout of your mother's idiocy."

The soldiers dragged Tressa away, not caring that she was kicking and screaming the whole time.

Chapter 90

Rorax

Rorax had just climbed out of the bath when there were two hard knocks on her door. She pulled it open to find Ayres standing in the hallway. His jaw was ticking, which wasn't unusual, but he had an orange roll wrapped in a napkin in his other hand, and that *was* unusual.

"I'm here to check on you and your nerves, and to talk more about the felidra strategy." His eyes slowly looked her up and down, his scowl deepening.

"Do I need to start a charity drive in the nearest village to get you your own pair of pants? Do you even *own* pants? Do you always open the door like this?" Ayres grumbled, his eyes skimming over her legs.

The V-neck green silk slip she had on covered her ass, three inches down her thigh, *and* covered all her most important bits. She loved it; it made her feel feminine and almost girly. "I own as many pants as you do shirts. Maybe, between the two of us, we really should start a fund, see if we can get a complete outfit. Even the shirt you have on right now is *extremely* questionable."

She raised an eyebrow, and he grinned. Ayres *technically* had a shirt on, but it was one of those white, sleeveless cotton shirts he wore as his base layer under his armor. It was skintight and was slightly see-through. As Rorax looked him up and down, she could see every single inch of the pectorals, laterals, and thick covering of tattoos that made up the deeply intoxicating combination that was Ayres's torso.

She had a sudden inclination to lick him.

Ayres's mouth tipped up at the corner. "Fair point. But only around you. I don't like to show outsiders my tattoos. You seem to like them though."

"Like them?" They made her feral sometimes because she liked them so much. She rolled her eyes at herself and at him and waved him in with a lazy hand. "Come in, Lieutenant. Make yourself at home."

He ignored the two armchairs next to the burning fireplace and instead walked over to the made-up bed and plopped down on it, the wooden frame groaning under his weight as he spread out on the plain brown comforter.

Rorax walked past him and into her closet to her box of ribbons. "Any new information about the trial tomorrow?"

"No." Ayres let out a heavy sigh, and she heard the frame groan even louder as he adjusted his body on her bed. "Nothing. I just stopped by Kiniera's room to confirm. There haven't been any reports, and not even any rumors. Whoever the Guardian is trusting with the information about the trials has it carefully locked down."

Rorax's fingers brushed over *his* ribbon. It was red, white, and black, the colors of his House swirling together. She wanted to wear it. It was her favorite ribbon, but she didn't want Ayres to know that. It felt too... intimate. Instead, she plucked a long, plain black ribbon from the box.

"Does Lamonte know anything?" she asked, walking out of her closet and tying up her hair in a ponytail on the top of her head. Rorax took one look at Ayres on her bed and had to prop herself on the doorframe to keep her dignity intact.

He was stretched out, his boot-covered ankles crossed as they dangled off the end of her bed. His biceps were bunched up by his ears, and his huge fingers were weaved together behind his head. Rorax eyed the muscles and the incredibly detailed tattoos over his biceps.

Ayres, the largest, most savagely dangerous man she had ever met, was sprawled out on her bed like he owned it. Like he *belonged* there. He looked so damned beautiful doing it, she had to cross her arms over her chest to hide her nipples. She didn't trust her knees to support her weight across the room, so she stayed where she was.

She could picture him sprawled out every day on their bed, watching her with those hungry eyes as she got ready to sleep while preparing himself for his overnight guard duty or getting ready for bed himself. They had fucked last night, and it was something she wanted more of. *He* was something she wanted more of.

A flicker of regret brushed through her. If she won the Choosing, it was likely he wouldn't stay with her. He would probably go home to Morvarand. But if she lost… she would be dead, and he would eventually find himself sprawled out on another woman's bed just like this.

The thought made her irrationally irritable.

Ayres had been staring at Rorax's ceiling with a pensive look on his face, but his eyes flicked to her, and he caught her scowling. "What?"

She forced a half-assed smile on her face and shrugged. "Nothing, you just look… comfy. It's cute."

"Cute," Ayres drawled, rolling his eyes. "I *am* cute, Ror. More than cute."

He was. So much more.

Ayres gave her a smug, knowing grin before jerking his chin to her bedside table where her orange roll was waiting for her. "I brought that for you, Ror."

"Oh! I forgot," she exclaimed, jumping over and snatching it up, then holding it like a precious object in both palms. "Thank you."

Ayres just nodded and watched her as she slinked into the bathroom to eat her roll, so she didn't have to share it. Once she was done and had licked the last of the frosting off her fingers, she brushed her teeth and was just combing the last tangles out of her still-wet hair when she heard the bed creak from the other room.

Ayres stalked into the bathroom, and she looked up at him as he appeared in the mirror behind her.

He got close enough that she could feel the heat at her back and smell his scent—balsam pines.

"The toilet is over there," she breathed, pointing to a door over her shoulder with her brush. "If that's what you're looking for."

Ayres didn't move a muscle, and mischief glittered in his eyes. He slid his muscular, tattooed forearms and hands on either side of her to rest them on the white granite counter, caging her in.

"Are you going to tell me what all that in the arena was about today?" He reached up and brushed the wet hair off her shoulder.

Rorax turned and glowered up at him, not realizing her mistake until she saw that those perfect lips were less than a foot away from her own.

Stop, stop, stop. Get it together. Get your shit together, Greywood, she thought.

Rorax licked her lips, using everything in her to keep her glower steady. "I have no idea what you're talking about."

A muscle in his jaw jumped as he watched her tongue slide over her top lip. Silver began to swirl in his eyes, and it made her heart thump in her chest.

"The prince told me you were up there watching me for nearly the full hour."

Gods, he sounded so smug.

Her smirk immediately dropped into a frown. "That snitch."

Ayres tipped his head back and laughed—a loud, booming sound that made her very soul arch in pleasure.

"You were both training without a shirt on, and the prince is hot." She smirked at him and leaned back on her palms.

The laughter fell off that handsome face like a rock in water, and a splinter of red broke through the dark color of his irises.

She had to bite her lip to keep from grinning. Jealousy looked good on Ayres.

He hummed, studying her face for a beat before leaning his head down to hers. He nipped her ear and dragged his teeth along the sensitive skin of her lobe slowly.

He whispered as his left hand slid up her side, so it was even with her breasts, "I can feel whenever your eyes are on me, Ror. They are like a brand. Hot...." He used his fingers to pull down the straps of her nightgown, leaving her nearly topless. Ayres's eyes burned as he swiped a thumb across her nipple. "Heavy...," Ayres continued in a whisper. She tried to arch into him, her heart like a drum in her chest, and her breasts heavy and tingling with need. Gods above, she had never wanted anything more than she wanted this man. He cupped both of her breasts in his hands and squeezed gently until she moaned. "Claiming."

She felt the stubble of his beard move against her cheek as he started to slowly step back, but her body screamed in protest.

She jolted forward, gripped his hair, and jerked his face down to hers. He was so close she could feel his breath tickle her lips, and her stomach coil in excitement. He was right there and on the brink of losing control, his eyes silver with red fractures.

"Are you going to kiss me?" he asked, the corner of his mouth tipping up in a shit-eating grin.

"No." She was sitting, almost fully exposed on her bathroom countertop, lying through her teeth.

"Why not?" He leaned down and bit her ear again softly.

She whimpered, moving her neck to give him more access to her. "Ayres."

He growled at the sound, and in a split second, he lifted her off the counter, twisting his fingers in her hair tightly. "Not an answer."

She hesitated, knowing exactly why she *shouldn't* kiss him. They had agreed to be platonic about this, agreed to be physical to help her through her influxes, but now she wanted it more, wanted him inside her again. He had broken their agreement last night, had kissed her with so much force she had been surprised her lips hadn't been bruised this morning. She didn't know how he felt about it, but it wasn't her job to figure out his feelings.

She had only felt this kind of want for one other man, and he wasn't here.

So, when Ayres kissed her again, she kissed him back. Roughly.

One of his hands gripped her hair while the other slid down her back to her hips and jerked her an inch forward. She wrapped her legs around his waist and clamped his hips to hers. He moaned in her mouth as his tongue touched hers once before claiming her.

Dear gods, this man knew how to kiss. She was so hot. Too hot. Sparks of pleasure skittered through her blood, accumulating in her core, soaking her panties.

One of her hands gripped his shoulder as the other waded through the short, silky strands of hair. His hair wasn't long enough to grip, so she softly scraped her nails against his scalp.

He must have liked that because he pulled her hair, and her lips parted from his and her head tipped back. He trailed slow kisses from her earlobe, down the side of her jaw, to her throat. He slid his hand from her hair, down her hip, across the bare skin on her thigh, and cupped the back of her calf, almost engulfing it completely.

Then there was a knock at the door.

No! Rorax screamed inwardly as Ayres returned to her mouth hungrily. Her lips opened under his as the knock sounded again. Then again.

Ayres broke off the kiss, his breathing haggard as he growled under his breath.

"Don't fucking move," he ordered, reaching into his pants to adjust himself before moving to the door.

Rorax couldn't hear what was said over her panting, just the low rumble of Ayres's voice.

He stalked back into her bathroom, planting his hands back on either side of her on the counter. "There's been some news. The fourth trial has been postponed."

She blinked at him, willing her brain to move faster. "Why?"

"Same reason as last time. Ice is moving more troops through Nyson's Gap, and they need the transfer dragons again." Ayres looked down at her body with hungry eyes before shaking his head and standing up straight. "Kiniera also summoned us both to her room. The messenger said it's important."

Rorax groaned as Ayres stepped back to give her space. "She wants both of us?"

Ayres nodded as he pulled his shirt back over his head. "Her assistant didn't seem that surprised to see me in here."

Rorax shook her head as she adjusted her bra and pushed herself off the counter. "Kiniera knows everything."

She padded through her room to her closet and changed into her fighting leathers… just in case.

Kiniera, who always looked tired and exhausted, looked absolutely wrecked as she ushered Rorax, Jia, Ayres, and Milla into her room. The walls were covered in ice, but the floors and the table had been cleared for them.

Kiniera looked thinner than the last time Rorax had seen her, and the ever-present dark circles under her eyes were unusually prominent under her skin. Rorax was surprised she hadn't collapsed under the weight of her power.

"I received news from both the current leader of the Unit Two Heilstorms and from my source stationed in Lyondrea," Kiniera said once everyone was situated around her table. "The House of Ice has officially obtained information that confirms Lyondrea is not just trying to open one Pit, but four total—three on Lyondrean soil and the other on Pit Island. We were also able to get a pair of eyes on the first, and we've confirmed that it has been opened."

Rorax's jaw dropped. She had to repeat Kiniera's words over to herself three times before they made sense. "The Pits… you found them. For certain?" Rorax asked, and her old mentor nodded.

"We found them, and Raengar is currently in possession of undeniable evidence."

Everyone sat in stunned silence for a moment before Milla jumped to her feet. "We need to send maps to our queen and to the King of Fire."

Kiniera made a placating gesture to her fellow emissary. "I've already sent Blood Hawks with copies to the capital cities of Weather, Fire, Death, Light, and Fauna—the only Realms we could confirm are not under the influence of the House of Alloy."

Only six. Only six Houses remained unpolluted and untouched from King Määr.

So few.

Rorax eyed the tension in Kiniera's shoulders. That wasn't the end of Kiniera's news. "What else did you find?"

"One of the Pits is already functional. That's the one we were able to get eyes on. There's a rumor the second and third are only weeks from being activated." Kiniera slid her eyes to Rorax. "Scouts from Azaele's Island have reported movement from Pit Island. Lyondrea apparently sent a ship full of men who tried to activate it again."

Rorax's whole body turned to ice.

"*Fuck*," Ayres hissed from next to Rorax.

"House of Ice is sending men to help fortify House of Death's front lines and help contain what is leaking out of the only active Pit. But we are now no longer able to send the large contingent originally negotiated with the Death Queen. If the island is activated and we lose control of the Elus River...."

Kiniera didn't have to finish the sentence. If the House of Ice lost control of the opening of the river, the twelve Realms would fall. The River of Elu, one of the only safe methods of drinking water and transport, was under the protection and jurisdiction of Ice. It was an unnatural river, controlled and filtered in through the sea and pushed out through the continent by magick.

"And who exactly are you sending to aid us?" Milla asked from the head of the table, her lips pressed tightly together.

"In addition to *our king* fighting on the border for your people, we are sending the Frost Dragons and six companies of men." Both Rorax and Jia stiffened and made worried eye contact across the table as Kiniera continued. "That's why the trial has been postponed for a week. We need to move those men across the river uninterrupted. The House of Death desperately needs them."

Ayres rubbed a hand over his head. "We need to get this bloody Choosing over with. We should be over there trying to help them close the Pit."

Milla nodded. "They can't be allowed to open the second or third Pit, or we're fucked."

"Successfully opening the Pit on the island would be equally catastrophic. Since the end of the Island Rebellion, we have not had any soldiers stationed on Azaele's Islands." Kiniera continued, "All of the House of Ice fortresses have been reclaimed by civilians or the sea. We are utterly unprepared for a large-scale conflict there. And there are no guarantees that the Kingdoms of Wymeria and Umber would not press their advantage if the House of Ice was fighting a war on two fronts already. We might be able to handle three fronts, but the House of Ice will fall if they are faced with a war on four fronts."

Ayres cursed under his breath and scrubbed his hands over his face.

"As soon as Enna becomes the Guardian, we will head out to the Pit and see what we can learn," Rorax said. "The fact that we even know where the first one is, it's progress."

Kiniera nodded slowly and stood up. "Go to bed. Tomorrow we can reconvene to go over the details then."

Chapter 91

Rorax

The next day turned out to be normal, when Rorax wished it would have been anything *but*. She went through the motions—early morning training, her session in the library, and now Contestar training. But her mind was spinning.

They had finally found the Pits. The Frost Dragons were currently flying to the House of Death in aid. Lyondrea was trying to unleash what was on Pit Island.

The knowledge that she was *here*, eating sweets and wasting time, and *not* in Lyondrea suddenly seemed to punch her in the gut. She could already be out formulating and executing a plan to destroy the Pit. Instead, she was *here*.

Rorax stood against one of the walls of the courtyard, watching as Lamonte and a tutor from House of Fire helped Enna perfect her whips of fire, when movement caught her attention from the corner of her eye. Cannon had gone completely stiff, the tendons straining in his neck as he rocked back on his heels.

When his muscles relaxed, he jerked his head at Ayres, who was standing across the courtyard from them.

Stay here and focus on what Lamonte is saying. This will eventually pertain to you.

She nodded absently and watched as Ayres and Cannon disappeared through the doors that led to the guard's side of the bailey.

Rorax waited for a moment, looking around to see if anyone else was watching. When she didn't see anyone's eyes on her, she turned and followed them. She didn't see them immediately, so she crossed the courtyard to the stables, cracking the door open just enough so she could listen to their conversation.

"You can't go alone," Ayres growled. "I don't care if there are ten or ten thousand. Conrad will be arriving at the castle tomorrow, and I have to be here. I won't risk you going alone, so wait for Piers and Kaiya to get back."

There wasn't an audible response, and Rorax rolled her eyes at herself. She couldn't eavesdrop on a conversation through the Language of Hands.

She padded inside and leaned against a stall silently. Neither one of them noticed her. Ayres and Cannon were in a standoff, almost toe-to-toe as Cannon signed up at him with flying fingers. ***...could be too late. It's a small one, only a group of maybe five. I'll be fine.***

Rorax took a few steps forward, sensing a golden opportunity to get away, to get out of the castle and away from her thoughts and to finally be useful. "I'll go."

Ayres jerked his head over to look at her, and Cannon followed his gaze.

The darker male frowned at her. ***What did you say?***

"I said I'll go." Rorax moved her fingers, talking at the same time. "Jia should stay here until the Frost Dragons arrive. Her brother is in the unit, so she needs to stay."

Ayres's jaw flexed as he stood there, looking back and forth between them before settling his dark eyes on Rorax. "I'll approve it only if there are less than twenty men there, Rorax. *Twenty.* If it's like last time, where there are more men than expected, you are to *come home*. I want your word on this, both of you."

Rorax opened her mouth to argue, but Ayres set his jaw and folded his arms across his chest. She shot a glance at Cannon, who signed, ***I give you my word.***

She gritted her teeth for a minute, but finally nodded. "I promise."

Ayres's jaw went tight for a moment, and his eyes narrowed on her face right before he accepted her oath. "Be safe."

Rorax watched as Cannon carefully wrapped one of Sumavari's books in a linen cloth. This book was thinner than the one she and Ayres recovered a few months before, but the way Cannon's face had paled when he looked inside to read which monster the book was for, told Rorax it was just as deadly.

There had been exactly fifteen men, just as Cannon predicted, holed up in an abandoned house protecting the book. The soldiers had kidnapped and sacrificed the farmer who had lived there in hopes that they could use his blood to start the summoning process. Thankfully, they'd been unsuccessful. Rorax and Cannon had buried the poor farmer in the ground beside the house before getting on their horses and starting the six-day journey back to the castle.

On their first night, after they set up their campsite and started a fire, Cannon took the time to rewrap the book more carefully. The sight of the familiar blood-red book, the golden trim flashing in the firelight like it was winking at her, sent a shiver down her spine. The contents of that book could kill thousands.

Cannon placed the wrapped book in a small leather backpack, then tucked it into his sleeping pack. He looked more comfortable in these woods than Rorax had ever seen him. He was glowing almost and relaxed. They were still in the mountain range on the border of Fire and Death, south of the City of Stars but north of Povelinn. He must have grown up somewhere nearby, or just spent a great deal of time in these mountains; he was completely at ease.

He plopped down on his sleeping bag on the opposite side of the small fire from Rorax and signed, ***I'll take the first watch.***

She nodded. They sat for a long moment before Cannon snapped his fingers, getting her attention. ***How long have you been a Heilstorm?***

Rorax considered Cannon. Her instincts and habits were to deflect and evade all personal questions, but she caught sight of the nearly black, ten-pointed star right below his left ear. The dark scar, raised slightly off his skin, was the only thing left of the mark carved crudely onto the dark flesh on the column of his neck.

Her fault, her mistake, her sin.

Rorax sucked in a steadying breath and steeled her spine. ***I'm one hundred and sixty-six years old. I was recruited officially when I was sixteen; it's all I've ever known.***

Cannon blinked in surprise. ***166? You're just a child.***

Rorax rolled her eyes. She'd sent more souls to the afterlife than most people would in six lifetimes and had seen enough to make her feel old enough to be one of the Elder Elites.

Who recruited you?

Rorax cracked her neck hesitantly before answering him. ***The Wolf.***

His face paled, and Rorax scrambled for another topic.

How long have you been working for Ayres? Rorax asked her mentor.

It's been a long time... around 400 years? I've been in his army for nearly 600... and part of the prince's personal guard with him for only 60. We're cousins, but he is practically a brother to me.

Rorax blinked, thinking of Piers's golden eyes. ***I didn't know you were cousins. Did he recruit you because of your magick? I've been told that you hold a lot.***

Cannon nodded. ***My magick is the reason I've also been well trained. The House of Death can't risk having anyone walking around who can't control their powers. Some Gifted hold enough magick to pluck people's lives away like they would pick a ripe strawberry. So, the training regimen in House Death is strict. It isn't nearly as intense as a Heilstorm's, but it's rigorous.***

Rorax watched the flames for a bit before steeling her spine again and turning back to Cannon. There was one question that had been burning in the back of her mind since she'd seen the star on Cannon's neck. ***Who did that to you? Who gave you the star on your neck?***

If they were still alive, she would kill them. Or deliver them to Cannon.

Cannon studied her for a long moment, the fire reflecting off his black eyes almost looked internal. He said nothing, just continued to stare at her, the question hanging heavy between them.

Just when Rorax thought he wasn't going to answer, his hands started moving. ***Yansley. Your top commander during the Siege. It was right after you broke through the wall. I was one of the only men stationed on the wall that night in Surmalinn. I killed half a dozen of his men with a single thought, so he branded me forever to remind me of my 'folly.'***

Rorax held his gaze, even though his stare felt like it was melting her insides in a boiling pot of shame and anger.

I love my life as it is, but he took… so much from me. If he wasn't already in the underworld, I wouldn't rest until I put him there. Bitterness swept across his features, and a tendon strained his jaw.

A shiver wracked through her shoulders. Yansley. The coarsest, most bloodthirsty male she had ever met.

Rosalie told all of us how Yansley died. I am thankful to you, for protecting our queen, he signed.

I'm sorry I could not have waited for you to kill him yourself.

He shrugged. ***I put my hatred past me long ago.***

Have you been blessed by the Goddess of Alloy? she asked next, not wanting to talk about Yansley anymore.

Some of the bitterness in Cannon's eyes softened, and he looked amused. ***You might be one of the most unapologetically nosey people I have ever met.***

Rorax smirked but didn't bother denying anything.

Cannon sighed and nodded. ***I went with a handful of the newly deaf soldiers to the Life Temple and then Alloy. The Life goddess could not heal the wound due to the black salt, but the Alloy Goddess gave me and a few others the gift to be able to feel vibrations in the Alloy around us; it helps us mostly in combat, to feel who's around us.***

Rorax grinned. ***That's amazing. Watching you in the Tournament of Houses was incredible.***

He nodded, but the smile wasn't completely full-fledged. ***It helps. Because of it, I'm never taken off guard.***

He sighed, a muscle straining in his jaw again. ***Ayres won't let me fight in any wars though or go to the front lines with my men. During the War of the Slaves, I was stationed in Surmalinn. Ordered to wait and watch as my friends and my men went to war. My ability gets muddled when I'm surrounded by too many bodies; it gets difficult to differentiate.***

He picked up a twig between his fingers and snapped it, aggravated. Rorax found a new subject. ***Congratulations on your Tournament win. It was impressive***.

He cracked a thin smile that relieved the tension building between her shoulder blades. ***Kaiya was angry with me for weeks after that.***

That made Rorax smile, too, and she leaned back in her sleeping bag. ***I'm sorry. For what happened at Surmalinn. If I could change everything, I would.***

Cannon stared at her for a long, tense moment before nodding at her. ***Thank you.***

Povelinn is close by, right?

Yes. It's about fifteen miles south of us.

Can we stop by there tomorrow?

Cannon was quiet for a long, tense moment, his dark eyes analyzing her face. ***There is nothing there except for smoldering ruins, Rorax. It's nothing more than a grave. That city will not give you the absolution you seek.***

I still want to go, Rorax signed back.

Rorax... Cannon reached out and snapped another twig between his fingers. ***Ayres did not agree to this.***

I need to see, she signed to him. ***I need to see what happened there. I'll deal with Ayres.***

Cannon sighed and scrubbed a hand over his face in exasperation. ***I'll show you where the ruins are, but I won't go into the city.***

Cannon hadn't lied or exaggerated.

About anything.

There was nothing left of Povelinn but ashes and burned-out, crumbling structures.

Rorax walked around the ruins, stepping carefully down the cobblestone path that used to serve as the main road in and out of Povelinn, taking everything in.

Marras must have cursed the very ground here. Nothing lived.

After forest fires, the ash of the trees and plants added nutrients to the soil, making it easier for new growth. Here, it was like the ashes chained and strangled every new semblance of life, constricting everything to remain in the same state of decay. In every direction she looked, there was nothing but black soot and the jagged ruins of buildings.

As she toured what was left of the city, the black dust she kicked up with her steps smelled to her like fear and betrayal. The Wolf and the House of Ice had left nothing standing—nothing but rubble, desolation, and complete destruction.

Rorax stopped walking when she made it to the city center. She'd already had to stop and vomit three times on her way, but as she stepped into the square and eyed the ruins of the temple that once stood there, the bile in her stomach threatened to rise again.

A cool breeze kissed Rorax's cheeks and ruffled her hair as she crossed the empty square and stepped carefully into the temple ruins. The sides and the back wall of the temple had both collapsed in the fire, but the statue of Marras still stood; the white marble was streaked and stained with soot and what looked like blood.

Marras's hood was drawn low over her face, her arms extended in welcome, as if she waited to embrace all who looked upon her form.

Rorax had never prayed to Marras before, and though it was dangerous to pray to the gods without knowing how they preferred their devotions, Rorax fell to her knees at the feet of the statue.

She looked up into Marras's beautifully haunting marble face for a heartbeat that felt like an eternity, and her guilt, her shame, her grief came to a peak, boiling under her skin so turbulently there was nothing she could do but cry.

Her sobs shook her so violently she had to lean forward to support herself on her hands. "I'm sorry. I'm… I'm so sorry," she cried. "I should have stopped her. This… this never should have happened."

Rorax stayed there, crying at Marras's feet, remembering all the signs and clues, but she was too slow to understand until it had been too late. Rorax's blind faith in the Wolf had allowed her to be built into a monster. She was going to sacrifice everything to make it right, but her choices and decisions were something she feared she would never be able to atone for, and she would always see the blood that covered her skin. She stayed there, kneeling before Marras until the sun moved to the center of the sky, until she had no more tears to give.

She thanked Kään and Ukuros, and any other god she could think of for giving her the handful of people she had who loved her back in Koppar. They'd brought her back from the darkness. Her soul would have been even more frayed, broken, and blood soaked than it already was without them.

"Forgive me." Rorax looked up into that soot-streaked, beautiful face once more. "Help me to protect them now."

There was no answer and no movement beyond the soft breeze that danced through her hair, so she pushed herself up off the ground and slowly walked back to Cannon.

CHAPTER 92

JIA

Jia stood at the edge of the battlements, watching as the familiar blue and white war dragons circled the Northern Castle, preparing to land on the grounds. The four much larger transfer dragons chained at the base of the castle rumbled and roared happily at reuniting with some of the dragons they'd grown up with.

Jia kept her eyes to the sky, looking for one dragon in particular. Skydancer. She was a handsome white dragon with a proud set of long, twisted horns that always pointed to the sky.

The great beast would sometimes nuzzle her like a cat and rumble a deep purr as she rubbed her nose against Jia's stomach, even though the tip was larger than Jia's whole torso. Skydancer was the fastest dragon in the House of Ice's arsenal, the fourth largest war dragon, and Jia's favorite dragon in the world.

When her brother, Ye-Jun, had bonded to Skydancer, Jia had started sneaking into the dragon hold in Koppar to toss the dragon venison cubes or calf tongues, which were Skydancer's favorite.

When she became a Heilstorm, she chose to forgo a dragon—choosing instead to fight alongside Volla.

Jia clenched her teeth, trying not to feel the ache in her chest, when she caught sight of the great white dragon at the end of the train.

Jia abandoned her spot on the wall and blindly ran through the corridors, barely seeing anyone or anything in her haste. She made it outside, moving to where the massive white war dragon had landed, and then she heard someone call her name.

"Jia!"

There he was, in his saddle. Ye-Jun. As tall and powerful and as safe as she'd always remembered. She didn't speak and barely reacted as he dismounted his dragon and rushed to her side. He cupped her face with the second-most familiar hands in her life and raised her face to his.

"Jia," he said, searching her face with purple eyes identical to her own, undoubtedly seeing the desolation she wouldn't be able to hide from him. "Talk to me."

Her face scrunched up as she desperately tried to hold her pain inside.

"Tell me what's wrong, what happened with the Torch? I've only heard rumors."

The moment he asked, everything inside of her crumpled. She couldn't do this. She couldn't pretend anymore that she was okay.

She wrapped her arms around Ye-Jun's neck, displacing his hands on her face, and sobbed into his chest. He patted her back and did not tell her not to cry.

"Where's your room?"

"This way." She stepped back, wiping her nose on the back of her sleeve, and led him to her room, avoiding prying eyes as they walked through the corridor.

Ye-Jun sat on the end of her bed and opened his arms. "Come here."

She sat next to him, pushed her face in the crook of his neck again, and cried. For the first time in months, Jia felt wholly and utterly safe, and she became completely undone.

Rorax was her friend, but she had always been Volla's friend first, and she was here, fighting for her life and trying to escape from the Choosing. She didn't have time to grieve in the same way Jia needed to.

But Ye-Jun was her brother, and he was loyal to her, first, foremost, and forever. Her blood. And she was going to soak up every ounce of comfort he could give her.

Ye-Jun rocked them back and forth, rubbing her back gently. "I didn't even know you two were together."

"I... I didn't want to tell you," Jia admitted, blubbering over her words. "I didn't trust you to keep the secret from Mom. If she knew, she would have had us separated, and we wouldn't have been able to be in the same unit."

Ye-Jun didn't bother trying to lie to her, just continued to make soothing motions down her spine.

"She asked me to marry her the day before we left for Lyondrea, a few days before... a few days before—" Jia choked on her tears.

Ye-Jun held her tighter, letting her sob into his shirt. "I'm sorry, Jia. Volla was a good solider and a good woman. I never got to see you together, but she is exactly the type of woman I would have wanted for you."

Jia wiped the tears from her eyes and smiled. "Me too."

When the tears finally stopped, Ye-Jun asked, "How is Rorax?"

"She is... alive." Jia laughed humorlessly. "She spends her time training and looking for a way to free herself from the Choosing. She's also been fucking the lieutenant of Death to help get her through the influxes. It helps."

Ye-Jun stilled beside her. She knew Ye-Jun and Rorax didn't have romantic feelings toward one another, but he still cared about her deeply. The king, on the other hand....

Ye-Jun released a long sigh. "I have to tell Raengar."

"He isn't going to be pleased, but I think it's safer for everyone if he finds out when he can't legally come here to kill the lieutenant."

Ye-Jun laughed humorlessly. "This situation is an absolute clusterfuck."

Someone knocked on the door. "The Guardian is asking for you, Commander."

Ye-Jun grimaced and released Jia. "Let me get this over with, and we'll talk some more later."

CHAPTER 93

RORAX

It was dawn on the seventh day when Rorax and Cannon finally made it back to the Northern Castle. The morning was cool; the sun's light was gently dipping its fingers through the trees, and the birds were out chirping loudly, telling the world that it was time to rise.

Cannon hadn't said anything when Rorax emerged from Povelinn with red and puffy eyes, tear tracks cutting through the thin layer of soot that covered her skin. He had met her with a somber grimace and patted her back gently. They made camp just outside of Povelinn, close enough that she could still see the outlines of the ruins illuminated in moonlight as she sat next to the fire Cannon had built for them. That was days ago.

Rorax's horse made it past the last bend around the edge of the clearing surrounding the Northern Castle, and the castle came into view. The only thing she could do was look around in awe.

Cannon whistled as his horse pulled up next to hers, and together they sat, taking in the fifty or more Ice Dragons—war dragons specifically—sporadically sprinkled throughout the clearing. They also watched the men and women who wore fluffy, fur-lined coats and light blue, leather armor bearing the unmistakable crest of the House of Ice Frost Dragons on the chest.

The soldiers milled around, setting up camp, starting fires, and still undoing the tack from the dragons. They must have just arrived.

Cannon nudged her with his elbow; he gave her a concerned glance that she saw out of the corner of her eye.

Rorax snapped out of it and tossed her reins to Cannon as she slipped off her horse.

Take the horses around the long way back to the stables, Rorax signed to Cannon. ***Be careful, most horses don't like dragons. Tell the stable boy I'll tip him extra if he takes care of mine for me.***

Cannon's brow furrowed, but before he could sign anything to her, she turned and took off at a sprint, leaving Cannon staring after her.

Rorax ran across the lawn toward the tents. She passed dragon after dragon, all of whom did nothing other than give Rorax lazy glances as their handlers washed their light blue scales or undid their tack. She searched wildly over the creatures and men, looking for one man in particular, but she couldn't see him.

Once she got to the center of the tents with no sign of her old friend, she stopped and asked for directions from a gruff man she vaguely recognized. He told her that Ye-Jun had been one of the last to arrive, but he had already gone inside with his sister. She turned on her heel and all but ran to the castle.

When she finally got to the mess hall, she slammed open the doors so loud that everyone inside looked up from their food and stared at her, but she was too busy scanning everyone's faces to care. Until she spotted him.

Sitting next to his purple-haired sister, grinning up at her with that cocky, shit-eating grin she secretly adored so, *so* much, was Ye-Jun Frostguard.

Rorax ran to him.

Ye-Jun uncurled that long, lethal body from the wooden bench and held out his arms just in time for Rorax to slam into him, wrapping her arms around his neck so tightly she was probably choking him. He wrapped his arms around her waist and lifted her feet off the ground.

His arms squeezed her as tightly as she held on to him, and he laughed into her hair. "My, my, my... Rorax Greywood is a *Contestar*. You and my little sister are just *full* of surprises, aren't you, Grumpy?"

Rorax's eyes were wet as Ye-Jun set her on her feet and pulled back to take in her face.

Gods, she was so happy to see him, her chest felt like it was going to burst.

After feeling nearly hollowed out after her visit to Povelinn, it felt like a gift from the gods to have him here.

Her oldest friend—not counting Raengar and Isolde—was here.

Rorax reached up and squeezed his shoulders, grinning like an idiot into Ye-Jun's ridiculously beautiful face.

Like his sister, Ye-Jun had been blessed with some of the most beautiful genes the Realms could give. His silky black hair was half up, half down, the top pulled back, but the bottom half of his hair draped down to the middle of his chest. Despite the two hoops on either side of his bottom lip, Ye-Jun also had two eyebrow piercings. One in each eyebrow that sat above the same purple-colored phoenix eyes that Jia had. He also had the same square jaw, straight nose, and the same perfect skin.

He was a head and a half taller than his sister though, almost as tall as Ayres.

Jia stood up from the bench, hovering behind her brother and looking around the hall. "I hate to ruin the moment, but we should take this upstairs."

Rorax looked around and realized that everyone in the mess hall was completely silent and openly staring at them. She felt one gaze that always seemed heavier than the rest and turned her head to find Ayres's silver eyes already on her, boring holes right into her soul.

Why were his eyes silver? Was he angry? Her eyebrows furrowed for half a moment before she turned back to Ye-Jun and Jia. "I've been traveling by horseback for days, let me go take a bath."

"Meet us in Kiniera's room," Jia said. "We have a lot to discuss."

Rorax played with the hem of her dress, standing outside Kiniera's room.

It was stupid. *She* was being stupid, but she felt... *shy*. Ye-Jun had been one of the first people to see her as more than just the Wolf's weapon or *the Pup*, one of the first to see her as a *person*, and yet he had never seen her dressed in anything besides her leather armor. She had on a long, silky black dress, one of Hella's creations, the ribbon that Ayres had given her in her hair... and she wanted Ye-Jun to notice *her*.

Not in a romantic way. Yes, she had lost her virginity to Ye-Jun over a hundred years ago, but it had never been *romantic* between them.

Rorax just wanted him to *see* her, recognize the same change she felt in herself.

With one final steady breath, she lifted her hand and knocked on the wooden door.

Jia opened it and stepped back to let Rorax inside.

Like always, Ye-Jun didn't let Rorax down.

"Holy shit, Grumpy." Ye-Jun whistled the second she stepped into the room, eyeing her up and down slowly, like a man appreciating art. "Kään save the men who are stationed here. I wouldn't be able to keep my hands off you for all the gold in the Guardian's treasury. Gods, I forget that you're a woman under all your bullshit, Grumps."

Rorax rolled her eyes but grinned at Jia's brother.

"Sit down, you two," Kiniera drawled from her table, like she was bored with them already.

A giant map had been spread out in front of Kiniera, detailing the House of Death border with Lyondrea. Rorax and Ye-Jun moved over to the table and took a seat as Kiniera pointed to a spot on the map just south of Morvarand. "The king wants you to meet him at the base of the mountain here first."

Rorax's spine straightened. "Raengar is still fighting on the border?"

Kiniera simply nodded and moved on. "Once you are there, you'll receive more direction. The Guardians have obviously not officially declared war against Lyondrea, and Raengar is forbidden to cross onto Lyondrean soil uninvited until then. He will most likely have you on overhead watch duty, or maybe even ask you to try and scout the Pits from overhead."

"Death has dragons at their disposal, why haven't they used them to spy already?" Jia asked.

Kiniera shook her head. "They cannot go to the same altitude as the Frost Dragons, and Lyondrea has dragon arrows perched at the border just waiting for them to try. Raengar had them stand down because Death can't afford to lose a single dragon."

Dragon arrows were long and spear-like and could be shot from giant crossbows built into the ground; they were capable of piercing the scales of all but the oldest and largest dragons. The only dragons who could fly high enough out of the arrows reach were the Ice Dragons. The cold atmosphere never affected the them, nor their riders, since only the soldiers with the strongest affinity for Ice Magick were chosen.

Ye-Jun hummed his understanding.

Rorax eyed the map. "How many men are crossing the river right now?"

"Five thousand freshly trained Death soldiers and seven thousand veteran Ice soldiers, plus one hundred of my men on dragon back," Ye-Jun said. About a third of the total Frost Dragon force. "That should be more than enough to hold them steady for now, at least until the Choosing ends and we can send the new North Guardian."

"It has been mostly quiet on the front lines. Raengar has only had to deal with small-scale skirmishes, but they are becoming more and more constant," Kiniera said. "He hasn't made any contact with any more Pit monsters. The Pits have either stalled out, or they are trying to keep it hidden for as long as possible while they gather their strength for a full-scale assault."

"Is Death still the weakest link of the four border Houses?" Rorax asked.

Kiniera nodded. "Weather has made their border nearly impassable for a large-scale army. There is a constant lightning storm there. Fire has the manpower to keep their borders *mostly* secure, but Death... Death still has not fully recovered from the assault."

Rorax's throat went dry.

Ye-Jun rubbed his chin with his palm. "What about Alloy and Foliage?"

"Alloy would be a massive problem if they open their borders to a Lyondrean army. Our spies there remain active and have not reported any movement, which is encouraging. Foliage would be an issue, but the border they share with Lyondrea is mostly swamp land. It would be a long and treacherous journey to run an army through there. If I was the one planning a war on the Realms, I would march my army through here." Kiniera pressed her finger against the map at the lowlands between the High Queen's Mountain and the beginning of the Jagamine mountain range. Right where Raengar was currently stationed.

Rorax frowned.

"We're moving out tomorrow morning. I don't want the king there alone any longer," Ye-Jun said, his lips pressed together in displeasure just as hard as Rorax's.

"None of us do. I'm just thankful you're getting to him before anything serious happens," Rorax said.

Ye-Jun stiffened, and his eyes clouded over with white, a common enough occurrence. Ye-Jun was an Elite, with the power to see the immediate future. Ranging from thirty seconds to minutes ahead, it made him nearly impossible to kill on the battlefield and an absolute nightmare to play cards with.

"Come on, Rorax, I think I need to get you to bed," Ye-Jun said with a smirk.

CHAPTER 94

AYRES

Ayres gripped his playing cards so tightly in his hands they curled under the pressure.

Since Kiniera had informed them that the fourth trial had been postponed due to troop movements across Nyson's Gap and that some of the freshly trained House of Death soldiers were coming to stay at the Northern Castle with the Frost Dragons, he knew there would be a possibility of him seeing his brothers.

Ayres had three: Erich, Conrad, and Talon.

Rosalie was the oldest out of all of them, but Ayres was the oldest male.

Erich, the second-oldest son, had been forced to expose his identity to gain the trust and support of House of Ice. But no one besides their sworn men knew that Talon, Conrad, and himself were the other House of Death Princes. The secret had been carefully guarded by his people.

Talon, the youngest and most mischievous of all the Sumavari brothers, had been training in the House of Ice under Commander Ye-Jun Frostguard for the past five years. Talon looked like Ayres but with a thick beard and long, shoulder-length hair that was half pulled up into a bun—a hairstyle that Ayres suspected was copied from the commander.

Conrad, who was blond like Rosalie and their mother, had flown in on a different man's dragon. Ayres's heart had given a thankful squeeze at seeing his younger brothers alive and whole again.

What Ayres *hadn't* known or expected or been very pleased about was that Commander Ye-Jun and Rorax were friends. *Close* friends.

His jaw locked so tightly the little voice in the back of his head warned him not to crack a molar. The image of Rorax sprinting into the commander's waiting arms and then beaming up into his face with pure, unadulterated joy felt like it had been seared into his retinas, into his soul. His chest hurt, and he felt *angry.*

Ayres was more than just angry, but he refused to identify that ugly thing filling his chest and squeezing his lungs as *jealousy*. He wouldn't.

"What's wrong with you?"

Ayres slanted a look across the table to a pair of eyes the exact shade of dark charcoal gray as his, only set under golden blond hair. He grimaced sheepishly at Conrad and threw his cards face down on the table and rubbed his hands over his face.

Gods, he was pathetic.

Two of the three men he loved and missed most in the world were sitting right in front of him in the flesh, alive and well, playing *cards* with him even, and here he was brooding like an undisciplined pubescent boy—trying and failing to get a woman out of his mind.

Marras help him. Ayres needed to sort himself out.

"Nothing," Ayres clipped. "I'm fine."

"Good, because it's your turn, and it has been for the last five minutes," Conrad griped.

Talon, a few years younger than Conrad, eyed Ayres over his cards with a knowing smirk. "It's that little House of Ice girl who's on your mind, isn't it? Your *Contestar*?" Talon crooned.

Ayres shot Talon an unamused glare before picking his cards back up off the table and picking a random one to play.

"Who cares? Ayres has a new woman every week," Conrad sneered, the tendons in his neck tightening as he played his card.

"It has *nothing* to do with her. It's your turn, Tal," Ayres grumbled through gritted teeth, and Talon's smirk got even bigger.

"You know, while I was in Koppar, I heard an interesting rumor about their beloved commander, Ye-Jun." Talon dropped his gaze down to his cards, tilting his head as he considered them. "I heard from his men that one of his crowning achievements was that the commander was a regular in one of the Heilstorm's beds. After their little display in the Great Hall, I guess I know the rumors were true. They're probably together right now getting *reacquainted*—Ayres, where the fuck are you going? It's your turn next!"

Ayres was already at the door, yanking it open and storming into the hall.

He didn't stop until he was at Rorax's door. He listened for a moment, but when he didn't hear voices or, even worse, any of her sexy little whimpers, he knocked on the door, hard. He rested his hands on his hips, trying to suck in deep, calming breaths.

Gods, no one before in his life had ever twisted him into a knot like this. He felt wild, off-center, and for some gods-damned reason, his instincts told him the only person in the world who could help ground him was behind this flimsy wooden door.

The lock flipped, and Rorax swung the door open. Her room was empty except for her. His breath whooshed out of him, and the tight thing that had been squeezing his chest, making him feel absolutely crazy, eased fractionally.

Rorax blinked up at him in surprise before taking a step back and gesturing inside. "Ayres? What are you doing here?"

He brushed past her. The fireplace illuminated the whole room in a warm glow. An open book sat draped over the arm of one of her chairs, and the ribbon he'd given her lay next to it, like she had pulled it free of her long strands while she'd been curled up reading. Good.

"Ayres, are you okay? What's going on?"

He stared at the ribbon for a long second before finally pulling his eyes away to stare into hers. "Are you fucking Ye-Jun?"

Rorax's lips parted, and her cheeks went bright red. "I... no. Not anymore. I.... We used to be, though, used to be *involved*."

Ayres stared at her, wrestling with anger and *jealousy* in his chest for so long that she rubbed her finger over her ring as she tucked a piece of hair behind her ear. "Ayres, it was years ago. He's one of my best friends now, and he always has been. That's all there ever was between us. Friendship. Trust."

Rorax's eyes were so wide, so open and *earnest*, he believed her. That *thing* in his chest eased some more but didn't completely disappear.

He reached around and grabbed the ribbon still draped across the arm of her chair.

"Hey, that's mine! Ayres, you can't take it back just because you found out you weren't my *first*. I saw a girl coming out of your room once, and I haven't stolen any of *your*—" Ayres crossed the room, snatched Rorax's wrists and tied them together with his ribbon.

The anger on her face completely dissipated as he bent and picked her up at the waist before turning and dropped her on her bed.

"Ayres," she breathed his name as he moved over her, her pupils dilating as she watched.

Ayres bent his head down to her ear to growl, "I don't care if you were with him a hundred years ago or ten minutes ago, Ror. From this point on, if he puts his hands on you ever again, I will rip out every bone from his body."

Rorax slanted him a look. "Ayres, Ye-Jun is my *friend*. Don't hurt him. But... you shouldn't worry either. I wouldn't want him to touch me, not like you do."

That was enough for him. Ayres hooked his fingers on the band of her panties and slowly dragged the lace down her legs, pushing her dress up, and spreading her legs apart. Her pussy glistened in the firelight, and he bent his head down to run his tongue up her slit. Gods, she tasted fucking good. So good he wanted to taste her every single day.

Rorax's hips started undulating under him as he sucked her clit into his mouth, and he moaned as she slipped her fingers into his hair, gripping the short strands tightly.

"Fuck, Ayres," she whimpered. "Right there."

She ground her pussy against his face until she came, and then he fucked her, slow and sweet. In that moment, she sure as fuck felt a lot like his.

When Ayres eventually dragged himself back through the hallway, back to his room where his brothers still sat, bickering amongst themselves, Talon looked up and gave Ayres a knowing smile. "You look like you just got fucked."

"Your talent never ceases to amaze me," Conrad deadpanned, his arms crossed over his chest as he looked Ayres over, "and disgust me."

Chapter 95

Jia

Jia laughed in Ye-Jun's face as he grimaced at her in mock desperation. "*Fuck*. They don't have *any* Whitleherb here?"

She shook her head. "Trust me, I have been searching since I arrived."

Ye-Jun grunted in mock devastation as he twirled Jia out on his arm before pulling her back into him and dipping her low.

Having Ye-Jun here was a boon to her morale; she felt alive, happy even. Between Ye-Jun being the Frost Dragon commander and her own duties in Koppar, she and her brother hadn't had so much uninterrupted time in years, and gods it felt amazing. No one could alleviate pain like a sibling, and Ye-Jun always radiated with so much love and light that she couldn't remain in the shadows if she tried; just being around his glow was healing.

The Guardian had called for an impromptu ball to be held in honor of the Frost Dragons' arrival. There had been some grumbling from the men and from some of the Houses, but now that everyone was properly drunk, all were enjoying themselves thoroughly. They were halfway through the night, and Ye-Jun had already asked her to dance several times, making an already spectacular night even better.

As their dance slowed to an end, Ye-Jun stepped back and patted his pocket. "I might have brought something a little extra for you, if you want it. It's Lemon Whitleherb, your favorite." He winked at her, and she smirked. Of course, Ye-Jun would never leave home without being prepared.

"No," Jia shook her head. "That's okay."

"I'll be on the balcony if you change your mind." Ye-Jun gave her hand a squeeze before he slipped through the crowd.

Jia turned, a small smile on her face before she stopped short. Her stomach dropped to the floor as she stared in horror from across the room.

Kaiya Whitethorn was cupping Enna on the back of her neck, bringing her closer so she could whisper into her ear. Whatever Kaiya had said made Enna grin from ear to ear.

Why were they so close? It made Jia grit her teeth so hard, the tendons in her neck strained.

Then Kaiya pulled back and kissed Enna, slipping her fingers higher into Enna's long black hair and pulling her into her embrace. White-hot fury ripped its way through Jia's system.

Betrayal, thick and hot, clogged her throat and made her hands curl into fists.

Enna was her enemy. Her number one obstacle to making Rorax the next Guardian of the Realms. Kaiya was supposed to be her friend, her ally. She had pulled Jia out of some of the darkest days of her life, and now *this*?

Jia made a mad dash to the edge of the dance floor. Kiniera would be there, in the darkest corner. Kiniera rarely left the shadows, where she could watch everything and everyone, and she did not let Jia down tonight.

Like clockwork, the spymaster was there, her long blonde hair half up and half down, black lipstick coloring her dark lips.

"Do you see them?" Jia seethed, pointing behind her to Kaiya and Enna, who were still locked together on the floor.

"Do I see... who?" Kiniera drawled, looking out over the floor with lazy, pale blue eyes.

"Kaiya Whitethorn and Enna Mistvalley. *Together. Kissing,*" Jia hissed from between her teeth. "The House of Death is betraying us."

Kiniera slid her eyes over to Jia, so slow and lazy it made Jia want to hit her. "Kaiya Whitethorn has overseen the training of Mistvalley since the Selection. They have been lovers for... oh, I don't know, a couple of months? I think Whitethorn bedded her not long after the first trial."

"The first trial," Jia seethed. Gods, she was so angry her hands were shaking. "You didn't think to warn us? Why is she training her?"

"House of Death made the arrangement after the Death Queen chose Rorax to be their Contestar. House of Fire didn't bring anyone adequate to train Mistvalley in hand-to-hand combat, and Whitethorn is an excellent mentor." Kiniera shrugged and took a long drink of wine. "They are all fools though. Mistvalley is so abysmally uncoordinated, it would take a miracle from Ukuros himself to get her physically where she would need to be to wield the Guardian's power with any authority. It might take years. Yet they still cling to the belief she is the best choice for the Guardianship."

"What do you think?"

Kiniera's eyes sharpened. "Doesn't matter what I think. I have orders from the king."

Jia could have throttled the spymaster right here in the Guardian's ballroom. "I'm asking you, Kiniera. What's your opinion on Enna becoming the Northern Guardian?"

"I would snap her neck with my bare hands before I would let that happen."

"Then why let them train her?"

"One reason is because the House of Death still hasn't come around fully to the idea of Rorax becoming the Guardian. It makes them feel better." Kiniera rolled her eyes and swirled her wine in her glass absentmindedly. "The biggest reason though is because Rorax herself hasn't accepted the inevitable yet. She was born to be the Guardian of the Realms, yet she still thinks she is destined for a life of self-pity and grief." Kiniera rolled her eyes again, and this time took a long gulp of her wine.

A shock went up Jia's spine. "Do you really believe that?"

"Which part?" Kiniera asked, closing one eye and tilting her head. "Though I suppose it doesn't matter. The answer is yes to both."

"You really think she was born to be the Guardian of the Realms?"

Kaiya nodded. "I always believed that Rorax was shy. She was always in the shadow of some great leader, the Wolf, then Sahana. But over the past few months, she has proven to be shrewd, calculating, and emotionally in-tune more than I ever thought possible. Combined with her knife, I have been underestimating her."

"So, you're playing the long game, then?"

Kiniera nodded again, this time with a mean little smile. "Glad we could get you all caught up."

Jia slanted one last look at Kaiya and Enna before she turned and left the hall.

CHAPTER 96

AYRES

Rorax winked at Ayres and stood on her tiptoes to whisper in his ear. "I am going to go follow Jia, make sure she is okay. I'll be back in a minute."

"I'm going to go get a breath of fresh air. I'll be on the balcony overlooking the Contestars' Courtyard. Find me there when you get back." Ayres brushed his lips over her temple as she nodded before she stepped away and slipped out of the Great Hall.

Ayres took a glass of champagne off a waiter's tray as he made his way down two flights of stairs to where the overlook was. He tipped back the glass, draining it completely. The courtyard was deserted but was still lit up with torches. The castle was beautiful in the evening. He wouldn't mind spending time here with Rorax if she became the Guardian and made this her new home if something happened to Enna.

But gods, what if something *didn't* happen to Enna? What if they couldn't find a way out for Rorax?

The door opened behind him.

"It's nice to officially meet you... *Lieutenant.*"

Ayres spun on his heel to come face-to-face with Commander Ye-Jun, the leader of the Frost Dragon brigade. The commander was almost as tall as Ayres was but was leaner. His long hair was half pinned away from his face, the piercings in his eyebrows and bottom lip glinting in the torchlight.

Ye-Jun's purple eyes glittered as he studied him, and Ayres had to admit it left him feeling unsettled. Ye-Jun was one of the most powerful men in the Realms. He not only held an impressive amount of Ice Magick, but he was an Elite—one of the few people in Illus who held magick that wasn't one of the twelve major elements sections. His magick let him see into the future. Ayres didn't know how far in advance he could see, but Talon had reported that it made him nearly impossible to defeat in one-on-one combat. He was also a dragon rider *and* the son to General Frostguard, the highest-ranking officer in House of Ice's army.

Ye-Jun pulled a joint from his pocket, used the stone wall to light a match, and lit up the end. He breathed in a long pull as he smiled wickedly at Ayres over the glowing ember. As the smoke hit the air, Ayres recognized it immediately. Whitleherb. He was surprised it wasn't anything stronger.

"What?" Ayres snapped.

Ye-Jun's eyes tracked over him so slowly and deliberately, Ayres didn't know if he wanted to snarl or fidget. "I was just noticing how uncanny the resemblance is between you and your brothers."

Ayres couldn't stop his eyes from widening, and the smirk Ye-Jun gave him confirmed that Ayres had given himself away. "Talon has been training with me for years, and if he were to cut his hair, you two could be twins. Tell me, Lieutenant, does the Spine Cleaver know that you're a Prince of Death?"

Ayres startled and looked around the courtyard, confirming that no one was outside with them or standing within earshot of their conversation. "No. Not yet. How do you know?"

"I saw it last night." Ye-Jun tapped his temple, his purple eyes flashing. Ayres sized up the commander, and the smile on Ye-Jun's face grew even wider as he slowly blew out a lungful of smoke through his nose. “It’s humorous that you think *I’m* your biggest rival.”

“What are you talking about?”

Ayres’s brows furrowed in confusion, and Ye-Jun took a step closer to him. “I took Rorax’s virginity, *Lieutenant*, did you know that?”

Ayres stopped breathing. He had to look away, focusing instead on the railing beside him, on the worn stones, and on forcing deep breaths into his lungs so he wouldn’t reach out with his power and shred Ye-Jun’s soul.

“But you should know that Rorax came to *me*.”

Ayres’s eyes flicked back to the man in front of him, and Ye-Jun smiled with all his teeth. Ayres couldn’t tell if he was brave or just wanted to die.

Ye-Jun flicked the ash off his joint with tattooed fingers. “She came to me because she trusted me. We were friends, we were always stuck together on the same fucked-up missions from Katalon, and… she knew I had some *experience*. There was someone else who came later for her, and *he* is the one you should be concerned about.”

Marras save him, he should have kept his damn mouth shut. “Who?”

Ye-Jun didn’t look away from Ayres’s hard gaze as he shrugged a shoulder. “She’ll tell you, if she thinks you deserve to know.”

Ayres looked back at the commander as he took another drag, eyeing his face and seeing nothing but honesty and a little smug satisfaction.

Ye-Jun continued. “I wouldn’t say that Rorax is like my little sister, because she has *the most* fantastic tits I’ve ever held, and I wouldn’t hesitate to taste them again if she ever offered.”

Ayres bit into his cheek so hard he tasted blood.

“But I will say she’s still family, and I would do anything for her. She’s one of the best friends I’ve ever had.” A shadow passed over Ye-Jun’s face as he took one last drag from his joint and smashed it under his boot. “You better pray to all your gods, Lieutenant. You’re gonna need them if you’re courting Greywood.”

Ye-Jun moved to take a step around Ayres, giving him a pat on his shoulder. Ayres reached out to grip Ye-Jun’s shoulder, stopping the commander from walking away, and leaned in close to him. "If you ever talk about Rorax, her *tits*, or *tasting* her ever again," he leaned in closer and whispered, "I will cut out all of your organs and feed them to your dragon."

A corner of Ye-Jun's mouth lifted, and his eyes glittered dangerously. "I can see why she likes you."

Ayres opened his mouth to snarl something else when Ye-Jun stiffened next to him.

Ye-Jun's purple irises, which were the exact same shade as Jia's, clouded over with white. Not like Rorax's eyes, where the iris itself was white, but like a veil that descended over the entire eye, covering everything.

Ayres watched in awe. He had heard about this, knew that the commander was an Elite and had glimpses into the future, but had never seen it in action.

Ye-Jun started laughing, something wicked and disbelieving, and the clouds covering his eyes gave way to purple. "You fool. You should have told her your identity sooner rather than later if you'd planned to keep her, *Prince*."

The commander's words skated up Ayres's skin like little shocks, anxiety curling around in his throat. "What do you mean?"

"If you run, you might be able to intercept Rorax from seeing your brother giving your *decoy* a goodbye kiss," Ye-Jun snorted loudly.

Ayres's mouth went bone dry. "Where?"

"Stables."

Ayres turned and ran, pumping his arms and pushing his limbs to carry him faster through the hall and down two flights of stairs.

He slammed both double doors open, startling the horses closest to the entrance. Rorax came in at that moment through the side door. She saw Ayres and opened her mouth to say something, but a sound in one of the stalls caught her attention. A moan.

Before Ayres could even think, Rorax was across the room, looking for the source. She froze as if made of stone. She blinked. Then stared at Piers and Conrad kissing desperately as if it was their last moment in this fucking terrible world.

Chapter 97

Rorax

Rorax had never thought of herself as mentally slow before, but she couldn't comprehend what she was seeing, no matter how many times she blinked.

This particular horse stall was empty except for a Death Prince kissing… the Death Prince.

Rorax stepped back.

Piers was shirtless, and Conrad's hands were roaming over the exposed flesh as he sucked Piers's tongue in his mouth.

Brothers. They were brothers. Weren't they brothers? No wonder they were hiding in the stables, incest was an egregious sin in the Realms.

She took another step back.

"Conrad," Ayres barked from somewhere on the side of her.

The two men in front of her sprang apart, panting.

Piers made a strangled noise when he saw her, but she didn't look away from Conrad's glare as the blond man wiped over his lips with the back of his wrist.

He stared back at her, his lust dissipating and disdain replacing it in his dark charcoal irises.

Charcoal.

The same color as....

She took another step back, and it was almost like she could feel the puzzle pieces come together in her head. The prince she had come to know here at the castle had golden eyes. Flashy, beautiful, golden eyes.

"Rorax," Ayres snapped. "Look at me."

She could hear Ayres's footsteps getting closer, so she dashed the opposite way, turning to face him.

"Do not fucking touch me," she bit out at as his hand reached for her.

Ayres stopped moving, but she felt his power ripple slightly around her.

His power. His endless, dangerous power. The black mist and the red lightning. The way his tattoos glowed and moved. The long, vertical lines running down his back....

Gods above. She must be blind.

"*You're* the prince," she snarled at Ayres. "Not Piers. That's why everyone follows *your* command and is worried about *your* safety."

Ayres looked like he was made of stone. Right before she had died defending him in Helfast, his power had surged and *all* the men chasing them had died.

"You're the Death Harbinger."

No one moved a muscle for a long moment as the silence hung between them.

Then Piers chuckled from the stall where he still stood half naked. "Damn, she's good."

From the corner of her eye, Conrad scowled at him, but Rorax's eyes were pinned on Ayres.

He was breathing hard, indecision and anger, and... something else was warring on his face. "Rorax, come here."

She took another step back and bared her teeth at him. "If you have lied to me to get to some unnamed goal, I will kill you."

CHAPTER 98

AYRES

Ayres could see the old pain, the old scars the Wolf had given her so clearly in that moment, and it made his chest ache.

Guilt, shame, and regret sliced him across his chest so deeply he was sure, if he looked down, he would see his blood dripping from his heart. "Rorax, no. Stop. It's not like that. It's *not* the same."

"No. No, it's not the same. I'm not burning down the biggest city in your Realm or butchering thousands of innocents just because you asked me to. *Yet.*" She laughed bitterly, and the sound almost made Ayres drop to his knees. "You lied to me, Ayres, just like she did. You *all* lied to me, and I am so *sick* of the people I trust deceiving me."

"Listen to me, Ror." Ayres took two steps forward, his palms offered to her. "I didn't do this to hurt you. This had *nothing* to do with you. I was doing this a long—"

"I. Don't. Care," Rorax spat, the freckled skin of her nose scrunching in anger.

Marras help him, he wished she weren't so fucking beautiful.

She turned on her heel, furiously striding away from him, her long black hair flipping over her shoulder, trailing all the way down her white dress to the top of the soft curve of her ass.

Ayres lunged out and grabbed her arm, and with a sharp *push* of his power, he transferred them down the ley line into his favorite cave.

As soon as they touched the ground, Ayres swayed on his feet at the effort of it, his head spinning violently.

Gods he hated transferring.

Rorax used his momentary wave of exhaustion to wrench away from his hold on her arm. Her heels caught on the rocks, and she tripped, landing hard on her hands and knees.

"Fuck," Ayres grunted as she moved her hand a fraction and left a small streak of blood on the rocks.

The situation was quickly getting away from him. He felt like he was trying to wrestle water. "Rorax, here." He offered her his hand, but she flipped over onto her backside and scrambled away from him, leaving bloody smudges on the stone from her palms and getting the back of her white dress dirty.

Her white eyes were wide and panicked as she quickly looked over the cave.

Ayres's stomach tightened, all too familiar with people looking at him like *that*. He fought the urge to avoid her frightened eyes, to nurse his disappointment and shame in private, but he couldn't. Ayres stood transfixed, unable to move, until the expression in her eyes switched from panic to wonder. She took in the waterfall and the pond, enchanted to be so still, it perfectly reflected the stars above them through a hole in the ceiling of the cave.

The moon was nowhere to be found in the sky, letting the stars shine so bright you could see each one.

Ayres didn't say anything as he watched her. If Rorax felt genuinely threatened by him, nothing would have been able to distract her from the threat.

She wasn't scared of him, not really. That nugget of truth sparked something small, something warm, and something that felt dangerously like hope in his chest. Ayres kept his eyes pinned to her as he murmured softly, "I can do a lot of things, Ror."

Her head snapped around to glare at him. She stood, and Ayres felt a pinch of self-loathing when he saw the blood trickle down her calf from the cut in her knee.

"Take me back, Ayres," she hissed.

"I can't. We need to talk about this first." Ayres tightened his arms around his chest and forced himself to look unaffected, even though he felt scared and raw. Gods, he didn't want to lose her. "Piers, Milla, and my whole guard could be affected if this came to light. Piers could lose his head for impersonating a prince."

"I won't tell anyone," Rorax snapped. "I still need a Protectorate. It's too late to change now."

"You could ask Kiniera to be your second House," Ayres pointed out. "I want a Blood Oath from you, and then I will take you back."

"No," she growled. "You don't deserve *anything* from me, Ayres *Sumavari*."

"I can't risk my guard."

"You're just going to have to trust me." Rorax turned her back on him.

Did he believe her? Did he trust her enough to risk the lives of his guard? Of his best friends and family?

No, he had too much to lose to trust her.

"You agree to a Blood Oath, or I kill you. Right now. Right here." Ayres felt his power rumble, begging to be released even as his heart begged him not to.

Rorax raised her chin, her eyes spitting fire and brimstone at him. She opened her mouth, then closed it, too angry and hurt to speak.

It was this or death. She didn't have a choice. She reached over and ripped a knife out of Ayres's belt, then sliced a cut open on the inside of her arm right below her elbow.

"Do it, you reeking, traitorous bastard," she hissed.

A drop of blood trickled over the thin scar of the Blood Oath she had made with the Guardian. Inwardly, Ayres winced as Rorax deftly flipped his knife and handed it to him. Ayres took it, slicing open his finger. He pressed the blood to hers. "Do you swear on your life, Roraxiva Greywood, that you will tell no one who I am and what my abilities are?"

"I swear," Rorax responded with gritted teeth.

"And you swear to never release the true identity of Piers Olufsen?"

Rorax's jaw flexed. "*I swear.*"

With the words, Ayres pushed a bit of his magick into her, sealing the oath.

Rorax jerked away from him and smashed herself against the wall of the cave, getting as far away from him as she could get. Horror and disgust etched into every line of her face.

Fuck.

Ayres took a step away, but she charged him until they were chest to chest, angry tears filling her eyes. "You forced me into another Blood Oath. I feel *violated*, Ayres Sumavari. Violated down to my soul, my very blood." Her angry tears dripped down her cheeks, and every single one of them shredded into him.

Fuck. "Rorax, I—"

"Take me *back*," she demanded, more tears slipping down her cheeks. "*Now.*"

Ayres shut his mouth and looked into her eyes before he nodded. He loosely took hold of her arm, then transferred them back to the castle.

As soon as they arrived, she ripped away from him. "Do not touch me *ever* again."

Rorax wrapped her arms around herself and tried to flee, but then she was in the hands of another man.

Conrad.

Conrad threw an off-balance Rorax against the wall and placed his blade against her neck.

"I told you if I ever saw you again, I would slit your throat, you wretched bitch," Conrad seethed into her face.

Ayres had forgotten the pair knew each other. Conrad had been in the castle the night of the Siege in Surmalinn. And while Conrad had tried to protect Rosalie and failed, in the end it had been *Rorax* who had been Rosalie's savior. Ayres let out a low warning growl, wondering if Ye-Jun had seen all this transpiring in his vision.

"Do it," Rorax spit back to Conrad. "Kill me. Right now. You were a coward then, and you're a coward now."

"Let her go, Conrad. We've promised to protect her," Piers said, his mouth pressed into a tight line.

"He could kill me. Promises and honor apparently don't mean anything to Death without blood to secure it," Rorax hissed, the words cutting into Ayres's heart a little deeper. Ayres reached out and grabbed Conrad's arm and viscously yanked his brother back from Rorax.

"If you touch her again, I'll tear your arm from your socket," Ayres growled.

Rorax blinked at him, heartbreak and confusion seeping into the planes of her face, before she turned her back and ran down the hall. Ayres had a sinking feeling as he watched her run away from him, that she was leaving him for the rest of his life. Despite what she had promised last night, she would never be his again.

When Rorax disappeared around the corner, Ayres sank to his knees and stared at his hands, at his blood mixed with hers, and tried to ignore the indecision and regret roiling around in his chest.

CHAPTER 99

RORAX

Rorax puked in the toilet. Barely making it to her room, she hurled everything that she'd eaten for dinner that night straight into the ceramic bowl. Ayres Sumavari's blood was now linked to hers, controlling hers, and she was going to kill him for it. Slaughter him in cold blood.

She was sick and tired of other people's blood controlling her.

Rorax would be tied to Ayres until he relented, pulled the magick back, and severed the connection. She instinctively wanted to take a blade to her arm and shred the skin there until every drop of his was out of her system. But she knew it didn't work like that, which was a damned shame.

CHAPTER 100

RAENGAR

Raengar watched as the Frost Dragon riders banked their beasts, slowing their dragons as they circled the air before landing systematically in the clearing around them. He was casually leaning against a tree, but the tension beneath his skin made him feel like a tinderbox waiting to explode.

When Ye-Jun and his dragon, Frostflight, landed, the commander slipped off and immediately came to clasp Raengar on the arm.

Ye-Jun grinned, and the piercing in his eyebrow glinted in the sun as he looked Raengar over. "Your Grace, trying out a new lotion?"

Raengar grinned back and resisted the urge to rub his hand over his blood-soaked face. "It's been a long day."

The border skirmishes had picked up in intensity. The monsters hadn't surfaced yet, but there were more soldiers than ever, and it had been a massacre. Raengar had lost only a couple of men to arrows, but Lyondrea was losing men by the dozens now every day. He didn't know how long Lyondrea could sustain this pace and didn't know what they would do when they became desperate.

"Tell me, how is the Choosing going? What's going on at the Northern Castle?" Raengar didn't need to ask about Rorax. Ye-Jun knew Raengar well.

The smile on Ye-Jun's mouth fell, and he reached up to tug on one of his tiny hoop earrings. "You didn't even wait for five minutes."

A muscle in Raengar's jaw flexed. It was a miracle he'd waited this long.

Ye-Jun crossed his arms over his chest and studied Raengar from head to foot. "Do you have any weapons on you?"

Raengar cocked his head and narrowed his eyes. "Why?"

Ye-Jun squinted back. "Rorax is... excelling. Kiniera didn't want to say anything in front of her, because Rorax isn't on board yet, but Kiniera fully expects Rorax to assume the Guardianship."

"What do you mean Rorax isn't on board?"

"Rorax has recruited the whole House of Death and convinced Kiniera to have all the ancient libraries searched for information on how to free themselves from the Choosing."

Raengar stared. "She... wants to free herself? She doesn't want to be the Guardian?"

Ye-Jun scratched his chin. "After what happened in Surmalinn, she doesn't feel worthy."

Raengar felt his temper flare as hot as the New Volcano. The abuse Rorax had endured—*been* enduring when they found her—was some of the worst kind imaginable. It was a miracle and a testament to her strength that she hadn't come out of the crucible more twisted than she was. In Raengar's opinion, no one deserved a safe and peaceful life more than her, and one day he was going to give it to her.

"Also, there is something else you should know." The hesitation in Ye-Jun's voice made Raengar narrow his eyes in suspicion. "Rorax has taken a lover."

Raengar would kill any man who touched her. He stared for a long moment, trying to rein in his temper before he growled, "*Who*?"

"Ayres Sumavari."

A surname almost as infamous as his own. Sumavari. A Death Prince.

Raengar rolled his jaw, trying to refrain from turning the tree next to him into an explosion of ice shards.

Raengar had never met this prince. House of Death was famously private with the identity of their heirs. Raengar had only ever met Erich—the general of House of Death's army—and Rosalie Sumavari, who at the time was the crown princess, and who was now their queen.

"That's not all, Raengar," Ye-Jun said carefully. "He's the Death Harbinger. I saw it in a vision."

Raengar went blind with rage. He could vaguely feel ice crawling up his wrists. Gods, Rorax never made it easy. Now he was going to have to find a replacement Death Harbinger for after he killed him.

Chapter 101

Rorax

"I am leaving for a summoning."

Rorax looked up from the book she had been buried in. Ayres was standing across the table from her, gripping the back of the chair and watching her with wary eyes.

She forced a blank look on her face, even as anger and fear spiked its way through her chest. He was abandoning her. *Now?* "The felidra trial is tomorrow."

Ayres's jaw clenched, and he rubbed a hand over the back of his neck. "I know. But Cannon and Piers are already gone. I don't know when they'll be back, and the summonings are in two separate directions."

"You're going alone?" A new fear, a different fear, that Rorax wished she could smother, spilled like cold water though her chest. "No. Take Kaiya or wait a day. You can't go alone."

Ayres studied her face, agony spilling from his dark eyes. "You haven't spoken to me or even *looked* at me in *two weeks*, Rorax."

Would you even care if I didn't come back? The unspoken question lingered between them. Her heart ached in her chest. Ayres had been trying to speak to her, to touch her, to even get her to *look* at him for nearly two weeks with no results.

Rorax was too exhausted. She was tired of the people she trusted most keeping secrets and hiding who they were from her. And she was still angry. *So* angry. Angry that Ayres hadn't told her the truth and angry that she hadn't *seen* it, hadn't noticed that she had been fucking the *Death Harbinger*. Angry that he had threatened to kill her and had forced her to accept the oath, and, most of all, angry at herself that she had fallen so deeply under this man's spell that she missed him almost as much as she missed Volla even as he lived and breathed right in front of her.

Rorax forced those thoughts away and crossed her arms over her chest, leaning back in her chair. "Take Kaiya. Or Milla. Hell, you could even take Jia. But you *can't* go alone, Ayres."

He was the Death Harbinger, but he could still die, and if he did, it would be catastrophic to his House.

"You need a four-person team tomorrow to help you through a felidra den."

"I'll ask Kiniera to fill in. You can't go alone."

Ayres reached up and pinched the bridge of his nose with his thumb and forefinger before dropping his hand and blowing a long breath out of his nose. "I'll bring Kaiya."

"Okay, I'm glad that's sorted," she said before bowing her head back down to her book.

Ayres stood there for a few beats before coming over to her side of the table. Slowly, he kneeled at her side, and she forced herself to look at him.

He had dark circles under his eyes, but his gaze was cold and angry. "How long are you going to keep this up?"

Rorax cocked her head at him. "Keep up what, Ayres?"

His eyes narrowed into slits, and the muscles in his tattooed throat strained. "You haven't spoken a word to me in *two weeks*."

She resisted the urge to spit in his face. "Until you remove the oath, this is our new normal. I would suggest you get used to it."

"Be safe tomorrow, Little Crow. I'm sorry... I'm sorry I won't be there." His mouth tightened, and something almost vulnerable glittered in his eye.

Be safe, Harbinger. Come back to me. The words were on the tip of her tongue, but instead Rorax only nodded to signal she had heard him before she turned away and went back to her book.

CHAPTER 102

RORAX

"Your fourth trial is simple. Lead your team into one of the five dens of the felidra. Find a chrysalis, pick it up, and carry it out of the den. Once the chrysalis has been placed securely on this pedestal, you will be finished with the trial."

The Guardian pointed a wrinkled finger at a thick stump that was the same height as her knees.

Rorax rolled her shoulders back, watching the Guardian announce the rules before they hiked up to the colonies. There were five separate dens in this part of the mountains, and whoever pulled the longest straw had first choice of which den they went to.

Rorax stood in a line, shoulder to shoulder with the other four surviving Contestars—Stella, Enna, Briar, and Isgra.

She looked over to her team where Kiniera, Jia, and Milla stood, also attentively listening to the Guardian. Jia stood with her long, silver hunting bow strapped to her back. Kiniera had a long, ice-covered scythe gripped in one hand, her Ice Magick causing frost to creep up and over her fingers and wrists, climbing up slowly toward her elbow. Milla had matching goldsteel katanas that rose over her shoulders. Rorax prayed the woman knew how to use them.

As the three of them stood together, panic threatened to break out of the box where Rorax had so firmly locked it away before she forced herself to return her focus on the Guardian.

"We are going to pull sticks to see who goes first," she said, just as Lamonte stepped forward, his hand wrapped around a fistful of smooth sprigs. "The Contestar who pulls the longest stick will decide which den and which order she wishes to compete in first."

Rorax's shoulders tensed as Lamonte offered his fist out to her. If she pulled the shortest, she was all but dead. Being the only Contestar unable to use magick to defend herself against the felidra was a *massive* disadvantage, and one of the only ways she would be able to make up for it was the element of surprise.

Rorax reached out with slightly shaking fingers and pulled the one closest to her. It slid against the smooth, brown skin of Lamonte's hand. Not the longest stick, but not the shortest either.

Fuck.

Enna, Briar, Stella, and Isgra pulled next. Briar got the longest stick, then Enna, Rorax, Stella, and finally Isgra with the shortest.

Rorax was placed right in the middle; the felidra might not know exactly what was happening by the time she arrived. She might have a chance. Might. If the gods were with her and she was unfathomably lucky.

Rorax closed her eyes and breathed in a long, slow breath, trying to calm her heart that was thrashing against her ribs with anxiety. She tilted her face up to the sky. She wanted to feel the sun on her face and the wind in her hair before she went and died in a cave.

Rorax turned to her team, but someone grabbed her wrist and yanked her back.

"Take this." Briar held the longest stick in the air, right in front of Rorax's face. Her face was set with determination; her scar pulled tight across her features.

Rorax squinted her eyes at the blonde in suspicion. She didn't think Briar was trying to sabotage her, but Briar also had the best positioning out of all of them. "Why?"

"You know as well as I do that whoever gets the longest fuckin' stick has the highest chance of makin' it out of here alive," Briar said slowly, like she was talking to a child.

Rorax nodded. "So why are you trying to give it away?"

"Just take it."

Rorax's eyebrows pulled together. "Why?"

"My magick manifested on time, like it should've." Briar raised Rorax's wrist and shoved the long stick into her hand. "Yours is late. You'll be a sittin' duck out there at third place."

"I've got the best team. Their magick makes up for what I lack. Take it back," Rorax said, trying to snatch Briar's hand.

"No."

"Take it."

"I will not." Briar held her hands up and took a step back.

"Briar, don't be thick." Rorax could feel everyone's eyes on her as she snarled, but she didn't care.

Briar tucked a lock of short, white-blonde hair behind her ear and pointed a stiff finger at Rorax's chest. "You're the best chance we've got of gettin' us outta the Chosin' in one relatively whole piece, once you find a way to get us outta this magick. You've gotta be alive to make that happen, so yeah, I'm givin' the long stick to you."

Rorax gritted her teeth and wrapped her fist around the little useless piece of wood as a flush of inadequacy ran through her chest. "What if I can't figure it out? What if you die out there, you stubborn cow?"

"Then you'll keep tryin'." Briar's face was calm and determined, and so, *so* trusting to someone who might not deserve it. "Maybe one day that effort will help future people get themselves out of this nightmare. I believe in you to at least make that happen, Rorax. So, take this bloody stick and go get a chrysalis."

"Try not to kill any of the felidra," Kiniera muttered as they prowled through the forest. "The felidra have long memories. We want to be in and out of this as quickly as possible."

"What happens if we accidentally *do* kill one?" Milla asked.

"They remember," Kiniera drawled. "They will bring other felidra to familiarize themselves with your scent, and they will attack on sight for the rest of your life."

Milla frowned, adjusting and tightening the straps holding the katanas on her back. "Marras help us."

"I'm not sure even the gods would help us against the felidra." Rorax sighed. She had chosen the closest den, and they were almost there. Rocks and trees held the signs of nearby big cats. There were long scratches in the bark and rocks and the occasional skeleton of the giant moose that heavily populated this area of the Jagamines.

Rorax climbed over a giant boulder, her leather armor gently scraping the surface as she fell to the other side of it. Milla dropped down in the dirt next to her.

"We have an incoming target," Milla snapped, pointing a finger into the air where a giant felidra was flying straight toward them.

The earth shook as the felidra landed in front of them only twenty feet ahead and stretched out its giant wings from its back.

Felidra were a lot like their griffon cousins. The big body of a big cat and wings that stretched the length of three full-grown men. The difference was that griffons heavily populated the Jagamines in the south instead of the north. Felidra hadn't evolved an eagle head, keeping all their feline features, and instead of feathery wings of their griffon relatives, their wings were leathery and dragon-like. Felidra technically had four wings—one giant set and a smaller set attached right under the first layered over the top set on their back.

Aesthetically, the bottom set of wings made felidra resemble a butterfly when they were fully exposed. Functionally, the extra wings made them more precise in their aerial movements than either dragons or griffons.

The felidra that faced them now had the body of a snow leopard, his wings blue and black. It curled its upper lip over large canines. "You are moving too close to a nearby felidra den," the felidra said.

Rorax stepped forward, her palms outstretched, trying to placate the big cat. "I am a Contestar of the newest Choosing. I was tasked to collect a chrysalis and return it to camp."

The leopard snarled again. "We have lost many of our cubs to the Gifted. Countless."

"If I do not complete this task, I will die."

The felidra obviously didn't care. It didn't even hesitate as it pounced.

Jia sliced her hand up in the air, and a pillar of ice sprouted from the ground, knocking the oncoming felidra off course and sending it careening to the trees on the side. It recovered quickly and lunged at Milla, who drew her katanas out just in time to block the claws arching for her neck. Milla rolled away at the same time a vine of ice wrapped around the felidra, spreading over its short white fur with quick ropes, anchoring the beast to the forest floor and enveloping it, even as it struggled. The felidra roared once before ice muzzled it.

Rorax turned to Kiniera, who had her arm outstretched toward the felidra. Ice covered her fingertips, and her normally pale blue eyes were a deep turquoise as she used her magick to control the beast.

The felidra was breathing hard in a furious panic, and even though it couldn't open its mouth fully, it curled its lip over its sharp canines in a promise of death when it broke free of its cage.

Kiniera ignored the cat and turned her back on it once it was subdued, facing the mountain. "We must be getting close. We should hurry. He will melt through that fast enough."

They continued to climb, further and further until they came to a cave. It looked natural enough; the only marker that gave it away was a series of crude runes that had been etched into the side of the mountain above the cave entrance.

Rorax stepped lightly, silently prowling over the large granite stones that made up the entrance of the den and keeping a lookout for any guards, but there were none. It was deserted outside. She led the way to the entrance of the cave, and when she didn't hear or see anything from within, they all slipped inside. The cave simply led to a tunnel wide enough to accommodate four felidra abreast and lined with witch-light sconces. Smaller passageways led away from the main tunnel, but some instinct deep inside Rorax told her to stay on the main path for now. Felidra wouldn't likely keep their young near the entrance of the cave. No, they would be deep and protected.

Rorax glanced back at Kiniera and pointed to one of the smaller passages leading away from the main tunnel. "Fill these."

Kiniera studied the hallway and grinned. "Good idea, Greywood."

Kiniera held out her hand palm down, her fingertips pointing to the dirt, and as she raised her hand, a two-foot-wide wall of ice filled the entrance of the hallway. As they moved past, Kiniera filled in the different branches of the cave's hallways with thick blocks of ice.

"Should we spread the magick so Kiniera doesn't burn out?" Milla asked, looking over her shoulder at Jia. "Don't you hold Ice Magick?"

Kiniera snorted, and Jia shook her head. "I only hold enough magick to conjure four or five of those barriers without issue."

"I hold enough power to fill this whole damned cave with ice and still have magick left over," Kiniera said flatly, simply stating a fact. Power was never a source of pride for Kiniera. Rorax had always sensed that there was something about holding so much magick that caused Kiniera emotional turmoil, but she had never known why.

Milla looked at Kiniera with new interest.

"What if the chrysalises are through there?" Milla asked, placing her palm against one of the barriers.

"Then I remove the ice, and we search inside," Kiniera said as she finished one hallway entrance and then turned to the next. "Until then, very few felidra have the strength or the magick capacity to blast through this much ice. It will keep us from having to fight an army to get out."

They continued down the main tunnel until it led them into a room that looked like a crude throne room. There was a cast iron chandelier bolted to the ceiling, and in it were witch-lights, enough to cast the room into a bright glow. There was a stone chair large enough to fit a *massive* felidra, and on the steps leading up to the throne were three armored felidra soldiers waiting for them. A panther was crouched on the right, on the left was a snow leopard, and in the middle was a tiger, all equipped with massive, colorful wings.

"I thought I could smell something foul," the one on the left grumbled, the white snow leopard, shaking out its long fur as it hungrily assessed them.

"Ring the alarm," the tiger said to the panther. "Get the king back here, now."

"And scare away our dinner?" the snow leopard cooed, baring its sharp canines. "I don't want to share."

It crouched low, its golden yellow eyes bouncing from one of them to the other as if deciding which of them it wanted to make his lunch. Rorax crouched low as well, getting ready for a fight.

Before it could pounce, however, a large ice barrier erupted from the floor, arched over the felidra, and touched the wall behind them, trapping them inside a bubble of ice. There was a roar of outrage, and the sound of three heavy bodies as they hurdled themselves against Kiniera's magick unsuccessfully.

"They are making too much noise," Rorax hissed. "They're going to alert the whole cave we're here."

"We don't have time to fight them," Kiniera snapped. "But they must have been guarding the throne room for a reason. There weren't any guards stationed anywhere but here. Find out why."

"I'd bet a gold coin that's why," Milla said, pointing over their shoulders to the back wall, behind the backside of the throne, where a narrow passageway was hidden in the shadows.

"Good eye," Rorax praised as they jogged across the room, ignoring the sound of the felidra trying their best to claw through Kiniera's ice.

They passed through the doorway and through a short hallway into a large holding chamber. The room was filled with rows and rows of stone tables holding nearly thirty chrysalises containing the unborn felidra. They were the size of large loaves of bread and came in various colors—green, blue, black, brown, gray, spotted, orange, and red. All different and all eerily beautiful.

Jia whistled, and Milla gasped in delight, and even Rorax felt tongue-tied. She had never seen a felidra chrysalis in person before, and they were beautiful.

"Grab one, let's go," Kiniera growled, snapping them all into focus.

Each chrysalis was placed on beautiful, embroidered quilts, and Rorax ran her fingers over the stitching as her eyes swept over the different colors and patterns of each chrysalis. She looked around the room until one caught her eye. It was the exact same size as the others, the same shape, but this one was black with a golden band running over the middle.

"How about this one?" Jia stepped closer to one up front that was draped in a golden blanket, but Rorax threw an arm out to stop her and shook her head.

"No, this one... this is it." She tipped her head down to the black-and-gold-wrapped cocoon. Jia just shrugged as Rorax moved over to it and gingerly slid her hands over the smooth surface.

"Great, you've got it. Let's go, Greywood," Kiniera snapped.

Rorax carefully picked it up and tucked it in the crook of her arm like a sack of flour.

They ran out as fast as their limbs would carry them out of the cave. The felidra were all alert now, some having heard the distress sounds of their comrades. Almost all the passageways that had been blocked by Kiniera had the sounds of snarling, roaring, and digging coming from the other side as they ran past them. Rorax's heart pounded in her chest like thunder as she sprinted for the way out. They were so close to the exit now she could see the light from the outdoors.

She had never been so thankful to feel the sun on her face as the four of them streaked out, but they didn't make it five steps outside before a horrifying roar sounded from above. It was so loud and angry it vibrated in Rorax's chest, and all the birds resting in the trees surrounding the cave flew from their perches. She didn't dare look up as she curled her arms around the chrysalis, clutching it tightly to her chest.

A giant moose carcass dropped from the air and landed behind her, spraying her back with blood and decay.

A felidra landed on the ground next to her, and the force of the wind from the impact sent her flying. She twisted her body in the air to shield the chrysalis's fall with her body, grunting in pain as she landed mostly on her shoulder and skidded over rocks on her back until she slid to a stop.

She scrambled upright and ran a trembling hand over the surface of the black chrysalis in her arms, feeling for damage. It didn't have even a scratch on it.

"Release the chrysalis, or your comrades die."

Rorax whipped her head around, and the air in her lungs turned to ice as thick as Kiniera's walls.

Twenty feet away from her, Jia lay face down but struggling. One single black claw, the same length as Rorax's hand, curled around Jia's neck. Panic seized her throat as Rorax's gaze slowly tracked up the muscular limbs of the largest felidra Rorax had ever seen. Her whole body went cold with fear.

Full-grown felidra were usually around the size of the Umber's famous desert elephants. But this felidra was bigger. *Much* bigger.

Jet-black, short fur covered the entire panther-like body before meeting the giant, gold-and-black wings that were fully extended. The dragon-like wings were so overwhelming and so beautiful that Rorax had to take a staggering step back. This felidra's wings were colored black and shimmering gold, the design on them reminding her of the monarch butterflies around the Realms.

The felidra snarled, bringing Rorax's attention back to its lethal, snarling face. "I am Kaslikar the Third, King of the Felidra, and the chrysalis you are holding is my firstborn heir."

Kään help her. Rorax felt like she might faint; her arms and knees went weak, and for a moment the world around her blurred. Rorax had fucked up. Jia was going to die. She had chosen the wrong chrysalis. With a frantic glance around, Rorax saw that Milla was in a similar predicament, a long claw holding her throat on the ground. Kiniera stood, her Ice Magick swirling around her. Kiniera stared at Rorax and gave her a small shake of her head to confirm that her magick would not be fast enough to save Jia, or that she thought that using her magick on the king was a terrible idea.

The king crouched its feline body lower, its ears pressing into the back of its head, its golden eyes tracking her with lethal intent. "If you drop the chrysalis or cause any damage to it, I will slaughter you, all four of your comrades, and the entire camp at the base of the mountain."

Rorax forced a breath into her lungs, forced herself to stand straighter, and leveled a look into Kaslikar's golden eyes. "If you kill them, I will *crush* this chrysalis."

A growl erupted from behind Kaslikar from a felidra Rorax couldn't see.

"Let. It. Go." Kaslikar used his other paw to rake his claws down Jia's side. She screamed in agony as it cut through the surface of her flesh across her ribs, causing blood to run from the short wound. It was only four inches long, but with one more long swipe down her side, her intestines would be spilled.

"Stop. STOP," Rorax shrieked.

Rorax summoned Glimr and poised the tip to jab up into the chrysalis.

Kaslikar's golden eyes went wide, his paw stopped, and his tail whipped in agitation behind him. "A Sestera Blade."

"Glimr is bound to me." Rorax pressed her knife against the smooth skin of the chrysalis and saw Kaslikar stop breathing. "Gods, I don't even *want* this fucking chrysalis," she hissed.

"But you have come here to steal it, nonetheless," Kaslikar snarled, his upper lip curling up over his long canines, his whiskers fluttering.

Rorax ground her teeth. "I was to steal it on a trial for the Choosing. I had no choice."

Kaslikar lowered his giant head until it was in her face, his hot breath blowing the strands of her hair away from her face, smelling of blood. "The Choosing?

The Guardian had her Contestars *try and steal from me*? I should kill you and your companions right now."

Rorax tightened her limbs. "Do it. Kill us all. But your unborn son will follow us into death."

Panic flashed in the golden pools of Kaslikar's eyes.

"Let me get back to my camp. Let me lay the chrysalis at the Guardian's feet, and then you can have it back. The rules are that the Contestar needs to lay the chrysalis on a stump next to the Guardian, and then my trial is over, and I will have no further use for it."

Kaslikar's eyes flashed, and his tail twitched again behind him. "That is all?"

"That's it. Let us fly on your back to return to camp. I will lay it down, and then you return home with it."

"None of the Gifted have been on a felidra since the War of the Wings." Kaslikar snarled down in her face. Kaslikar considered her for a moment, his golden eyes flashing back and forth from her face to his unborn child, before he snarled, turning back to his men and giving them a nod of his head.

"I will give you each a felidra to ride to accompany you back to the Contestar camp. Your soldiers will stay in the air until we touch down."

Rorax nodded. "Then you can scoop the chrysalises off the Guardian's stump before anyone touches them."

"You ride with me. If there is even a shadow of deceit, your soldiers will die."

Rorax nodded her consent, staring at the very scary pool of blood that was starting to accumulate under Jia. "I understand. Let's go."

Kaslikar bent down, and Rorax wasted no time.

"You trust me on your back?" Rorax asked as she swung her legs up and over Kaslikar's giant back.

"You would not survive the fall if you were to kill me in the air, and I *will* make sure my heir arrives safely," Kaslikar snarled, and with one powerful thrust, they were airborne. "Do not drop my son, Contestar."

Rorax clung desperately to the king's short fur, her thighs pressed into the sides of the big cat, feeling the muscles underneath her work to keep them all in the air.

Rorax looked over her shoulder to see Jia, her unconscious body slung over the back of the yellow, spotted felidra.

The flight back to camp was short, and the soldiers scrambled into defensive positions until Kiniera flashed her magick down on them, signaling it was them.

As soon as they touched down, Rorax slipped off the king's back and sprinted to the Guardian's stump. The Guardian was standing over the stump, watching carefully with yellow eyes as Rorax gently placed the chrysalis on its surface.

Rorax looked up at the Guardian who was looking behind Rorax at the small contingent of felidra that she had brought with her. "Roraxiva Greywood, you have hereby completed your fourth trial successfully."

Relief made her limbs heavy as she turned to the nearest soldier. "Get Jia Frostguard to the nearest healer's tent. Now."

A ripping sound came from behind her, and Rorax looked over her shoulder to the chrysalis just in time to see it break open and a tuft of black hair pop out of the top. The chrysalis cracked again, and a head, small and covered in slime, strained out its fibrous constraints. Rorax jolted as a pair of two clear, golden eyes pierced into hers.

Rorax felt something inside of her shift.

The vertical slits in the middle of the cub's golden irises dilated in the sudden bright light, and it tilted its black head to look at her more fully. Familiarity rang in her head and in her soul, causing her to take a staggering step back. She *knew* those eyes.

Rorax opened her mouth, but before she could say a word, a giant silvery head nearly the same size of Rorax's whole upper body moved in front of her and pressed hard against Rorax's chest, forcing her back a few more steps.

Rorax didn't see the cub again as its mother gently grasped her son in her maw and lifted him away.

CHAPTER 103

RORAX

"Enna just got back to camp with her chrysalis, alive and all in one piece."

Rorax blinked away thoughts of golden panther eyes, her shoulders sagging in relief as Milla crossed through the healers' tent. She sat next to where Rorax was perched on the edge of a cot, sitting opposite an unconscious Jia. The healers were carefully stitching the skin together where the long claws had raked through Jia's side.

Milla watched the healer for a moment before turning her body to Rorax. "Rorax, that was the most reckless thing I've ever seen, and I've been friends with Ayres and Cannon for over 500 years."

The reminder of Ayres was unwelcome and painful, but a slow, proud smirk found its way across Rorax's mouth anyway.

"She's all done," one of Tressa's underlings said when the stitching was done and wrapped. "Tell her to be careful, and to change the bandages out with fresh ones tonight."

"Thank you," Rorax said. "I will wake her, leave us please." The healers bowed and left the tent, leaving her and Milla together alone with an unconscious Jia.

"I'm sorry about what Ayres did, Rorax. Truly. We wanted to tell you who he was but...."

Rorax looked up at Milla, and they stared at each other for a long moment. Rorax studied the lines of regret and sorrow etched in Milla's face before nodding slowly. "I believe you."

"Do you think you'll be able to forgive us?"

"I think I can forgive you, Cannon, and Piers. But Ayres...." Rorax's stomach curled as she ran her fingers over the leather where the horizontal scar was on her upper arm where Ayres's Blood Oath was. "I don't know."

Milla shifted forward in her seat. "It's dangerous for us to tell anyone who he is. If that information ever gets into the wrong hands, they could use it—use *him*—as a weapon."

"I understand, but Ayres and I... after we...." Rorax swallowed a painful lump in her throat. "After *everything*, he didn't trust me. He felt like he had to force me into a Blood Oath."

"And that upsets you? Why?"

"Because I don't know what else I can do to prove to him that I've changed. That I'm not the Pup. I don't want to have to die for him, *again*, for him to feel like he can trust me."

Milla studied her hands in her lap. "I'm sorry, Rorax. He trusts you. He does."

"Not enough." Rorax gritted her teeth and rubbed her thumb furiously over her ring, wishing she could have Glimr back. She felt on edge. Milla had thrust the Black Box into Rorax's hands the minute they arrived back at camp, and Rorax had grudgingly slid Glimr into it, suddenly feeling naked. Isgra would be fine; she had that blue inferno that always raged just under her skin. But Stella? Briar? The gods would decide if they survived or not. Rorax got up and sat next to Jia, gently shaking her shoulder.

Jia's eyes peeled open, and she groaned. "Gods, I feel like death."

Rorax's laugh was tense, but something in her chest eased as Jia pushed herself up.

The three of them left the healer's tent and moved to a waiting tent. Enna, Elios, and Kiniera took up three out of the ten chairs that had been set up in a half circle in the middle.

Enna looked up at Rorax with bright eyes and a smile. "You survived!"

"Barely," Kiniera smirked. "Rorax asked the King of the Felidra for a ride on his back."

Enna and Elios's jaws dropped open at the same time, and Enna's eyes went huge. "You're serious?"

Kiniera snickered and nodded her head. "He gave her one, too."

"I picked the wrong chrysalis," Rorax said, sliding into one of the chairs.

Jia gingerly slid into the chair next to Rorax. Milla sat in front of Rorax, leaning her back into Rorax's knees as she looked over her shoulder at her with a hopeful but hesitant look on her face. "Braid my hair please, Rorax?"

"I still have blood on my hands," Rorax warned, but Milla waved her off.

"It will blend right in."

Rorax snorted, and with only a moment's hesitation, she got to work, sectioning out Milla's long wine-colored strands.

"Do you miss him?" Milla asked.

Rorax's fingers froze in midair, and Milla peaked over her shoulder to offer Rorax a small smile.

Rorax went back to braiding. "Ye-Jun and I decided to be just friends a long time ago, Milla. You can bed him if you'd like. Just know that, eventually, I might hear every detail of your sex life in *excruciating* detail."

Milla reached over and pinched Rorax's leg. "Ayres, Ror, I meant *Ayres*. You might as well not try and deny it. You have been moping for over a fortnight now."

Rorax opened her mouth to lie, but Jia—casually cleaning her nails in the chair on Rorax's left—piped up. "She wore the ribbon he gave her in her hair today."

Milla and Enna laughed out loud, and Rorax scowled.

Jia just smirked, not bothering to look up from her knife.

"It doesn't *matter* if I miss him or not. Until he removes the Blood Oath, he is dead to me," Rorax snapped, feeling defensive.

That shut them up. Everyone was quiet for a moment, with nothing but the sound of silky strands sliding over each other between Rorax's capable fingers, until Milla asked, "Is being connected to him really that horrible, Ror?"

"He threatened my life to do it. So, yes, it's that horrible." Her words were bitter and angry, and the familiar, tumultuous feeling she always got when she thought about the Blood Oath made her stomach roil. She wanted Ayres, he had been her friend, and now... now it felt like everything they had built was nothing more than smoldering ruins.

She didn't have time to lament it more.

Furious, lethal heat flashed up Rorax's back and seeped into her chest. Her head jerked up to see Enna staring at her, her usually serene features twisted up in fury.

"Milla," Rorax clipped. "Milla. An influx."

Milla took one look at Rorax's face before scrambling to her feet and shrieking, "GUARDS!"

Rorax slowly stood, crouching forward to lean on the balls of her feet, needing to throw herself, needing to wrap her hands around Enna's pretty little throat to squeeze the life out of it, when Jia's body slammed her to the ground.

Jia rolled, but Rorax rolled harder and threw a punch, and Jia's lip split open.

"*Fuck off*, Ror," Jia hissed as blood started streaming down her chin.

Jia headbutted Rorax, narrowly missing her nose.

Rorax raised her hand to punch again, but her hand was seized and wrenched back behind her back. Rorax struggled as Milla dragged her backward off Jia, but Jia lifted herself off the ground and threw herself at Ror's other arm, latching on. Milla and Jia stretched her out, pulling her in a tug of war. They held her like this, immobile with her arms stretched, like a little puppet on their strings, dodging Rorax's attempts to lash out with her teeth or her feet until Rorax felt the anger receding back into her mind.

Slowly, ever so slowly, she relaxed.

"You back?" Jia asked.

Rorax nodded at her friend, breathing hard. "I'm back."

"Good." Jia quickly dropped her arm and gingerly fingered her side. "Hell, you popped one of my stitches."

"I'm sorry," Rorax said.

Milla dropped her other arm and almost as soon as the anger left, worry sank in.

"Where is Enna?"

Milla jerked her thumb over her shoulder. "Kiniera has her iced in the tent."

Rorax and Jia shared an amused look.

They went back to the tent to find Enna now sporting a split lip where Kiniera had had to elbow her in the face. Her clothes were sopping wet, and Rorax grinned.

"Did she pin you in an ice cube?" Jia asked, grinning.

Enna's face turned sour. "I was a solid block of ice all the way up to my neck."

Jia and Rorax both chuckled, feeling her pain.

The smile slowly faded from Rorax's face. "I wonder who just died."

Jia and Kiniera didn't look bothered, but Enna's expression went bleak. "I hope it's not Briar."

Kiniera left the tent to see what she could find out from the others, and as they waited to hear more, Rorax paced at the mouth of the tent, praying, even though she didn't know who she was praying for.

Rorax didn't know and couldn't decide who would be worse.

Isgra was her best friend's sister, her last tie to Volla, no matter how much Isgra hated her. Briar was her friend. Gods, she prayed it was Stella.

Suddenly, the tent flap was ripped open, and Kiniera stood in the opening, her face grave. "It's Briar. She is in the medical tent. She was hit. She's... she didn't make it, Rorax."

Rorax pushed past Kiniera and ran. She ran until she threw open the tent flap, and there she was. Briar. Her skin cold and gray, a garish contrast to the red blood crusted thickly around a vicious laceration on her throat.

Rorax didn't even make it all the way to Briar's body before her muscles denied her and she fell to her knees in the middle of the tent.

As she stared at the body, her breath came faster and faster. Her mind started to buzz as agony and anger crawled up her chest, burning inside her lungs, inside of her chest, and up her throat until she couldn't contain it anymore. More heat and anger and *power* thrust through her.

She could almost hear it as the barrier in her mind cracked. The wall that had been holding her magick back could no longer contain her.

Rorax threw her head back and screamed, trying to relieve the pressure and the *heat* in her chest, and like a dam bursting, her magick ignited. Flames, a column of pure, hot fire spewed out of her mouth. It felt like a volcano had erupted inside her, and all she could do was throw her head back and let it flow.

More, more, more. She wanted it to consume her.

The column grew, twisting and breathing and growing hotter in a kaleidoscope of different-colored flames as they rose to the ceiling of the tent, threatening to set it on fire.

More, more, more, more, more.

She felt another influx hit through her body, and her scream intensified. She was going to burn up, she was going to burn everything up, and gods above, she wanted it. She wanted it to hurt, to scourge away every shred of pain and regret and failure that was still inside her. She wanted to burn *everything*; she wanted to be hollowed out and emptied of everything so she could start again, *try* again.

Rorax stayed there on her knees, urging her flames hotter and bigger until something in the back of her head twinged in a familiar complaint, but she did not stop.

Sweat poured down her spine, but she did not stop.

She didn't stop until something cold and hard smacked into her temple, and she was forced to tumble into the darkness.

Chapter 104

Rorax

"Nope. Not tonight, Rorax." Piers plucked the empty bottle out of Rorax's hands just as she turned to smash it against the wall.

She didn't mind. Piers had been babysitting her ever since she had stumbled, already drunk, from her room for the Final Three Ball. She was on the balcony of the Contestars' Courtyard, having convinced Piers she needed some air.

There were only three Contestars left. Stella and Briar had both been cut down by the felidra today. She had no idea what the castle could possibly be celebrating when inside she felt so dead and lifeless.

Rorax swayed on her feet, swallowing the last contents of her glass down before she pulled on the string in her mind that called her fire, and a little flame lit at the end of her pointer finger.

"Fire. I can fiiiinally do it, Piers."

Piers grimaced but nodded. "Very good, Ror."

Piers and Cannon were waiting for them at the castle when they arrived. Ayres had stopped for an extra day to run an errand, probably to take care of one of his princely duties. Rorax was excited for Ayres to be back; she was so excited to show him what she could do.

As soon as the thought came, she clenched her teeth against it. That was at least the tenth time tonight that she had thought of *him*. He'd only been gone for a few days, and there was an ache in her heart that just wouldn't *leave her alone.* Even though Rorax had finally manifested her magick today, she felt even shittier than before. She hadn't even known that was possible.

Jia and Kiniera had gone to bed a long time ago, both needing rest after all the magick they'd used today.

"Rorax, come on. We have to go back to the Great Hall. The Guardian's about to give a speech."

She let Piers guide her down the empty corridor. Rorax had long ago shed the heels she'd worn to the party, but even barefoot she still staggered back to the Great Hall.

Milla was standing outside the doors, tapping her foot, and visibly relaxed when she saw Rorax.

"She's about to start," Milla said, opening the door to the front of the room where the Guardian stood in front of her throne. There was a gleam in the Guardian's eyes that Rorax had never seen before, and even inebriated, the cold glitter made her hackles rise.

"Thank you all for coming tonight." The Guardian smiled, a full and slightly threatening display of her teeth. "Tonight, we celebrate. We celebrate the fact that we are finally down to our final three Contestars."

Rorax felt eyes on her as there was a murmur around the room and a small, polite clap.

When the clapping died down, the Guardian continued. "But tonight, I also wanted to spend this time remembering the sacrifices and the glorious things that I have done in my eight-hundred-year reign as Guardian of the North."

Piers and Milla shared a look, and the murmur of voices grew louder.

The Guardian looked around the room with an arrogant, wicked smile on her lips. "I have defended this country, defended the magick in the Realms, and defended its people. I have fought and bled and loved for the Realms, for every single one of you. I have sacrificed everything. Now it is time to repay that favor. Kneel, all of you."

There was a confused murmur from the crowd. Never had a Guardian asked them to kneel before. Kings rarely even asked that from their subjects.

"Kneel. *Now*," the Guardian hissed to the room, the temperature plummeting as Ice Magick kissed Rorax's skin. Slowly, people around the room start to kneel. Milla and Piers shared a concerned glance before slowly sinking to a knee.

Rorax was about to bend her knee with the rest of the crowd when something silver caught her eye. Tressa, in a silver dress, was bowing to her knee but staring with defiant daggers in her eyes in the Guardian's direction. A few rows behind Tressa, Isgra and Enna kneeled as well.

Briar and Stella should have been here tonight to celebrate. Mo and Mairi and Roo and Serena, all twelve of the Contestars should be here to celebrate.

Suddenly, her knees felt stiff and brittle, as if they would snap if she tried to bend them. Milla tried to grab Rorax's wrist to tug her down, but Rorax jerked her arm free and drunkenly stumbled forward toward the Guardian.

"Rorax!" Piers hissed, but Rorax staggered forward on unsteady feet.

A hand clamped down on her wrist, but Rorax yanked herself free. "No."

"Let her go, Prince," the Guardian said, eyeing Rorax with hunger. "I want to know what the Spine Cleaver has to say."

The Guardian watched her, and Rorax felt her own foreign power roil under her skin in response before she could repress it. She shivered but took another step forward. "I will *never* bend a knee to you."

Whatever the Guardian had been expecting Rorax to say, this wasn't it.

The Guardian's chin jerked back fractionally. "What did you say?"

"Why should we bow to you? You didn't find a way to *free* us," Rorax hissed. "So, I will not. I will not bow to a woman who has sentenced eleven innocent girls to death because she wouldn't spend the *time* to find a way to undo the magick that binds us here. I will not bow to a Guardian who released her magick in the middle of a potential war and refused to go to the front lines to defend the

Realms. I *refuse*," Rorax hissed between her teeth, slicing her hand through the air.

The Guardian's eyes were a vision of pure and lethal hatred, and her chin lifted a fraction. Power started to vibrate the very air around Rorax. "That is *rich* coming from a Heilstorm who has sat idly by to watch *hundreds* die."

"Sat idly by?" Rorax laughed bitterly. "I did my job. You are the Northern Guardian! It's your job"—she jabbed a finger into the Guardian's chest—"your duty, to protect the people. To protect *all the people* who live in this *world*. You not only failed the Realms, but everyone, and you continue to fail us through your inaction," Rorax seethed. "Lyondrea is starting a war because *you* couldn't be bothered by them."

There were loud gasps from the crowd. Everyone in the hall stayed low to the floor, kneeling, but in a quick glance over her shoulder, Rorax saw Milla and Piers looking up at her in utter shock.

A flicker of surprise danced across the Guardian's gaze. "You dare to speak to me thus?" Her voice was a promise. A promise of violence and bloodshed. A promise of Rorax's death if she continued down her path.

Rorax didn't care. She had found a worthy outlet to project her own burning self-hatred, and she was going to use it.

"I refuse to kneel in the dirt for a Guardian who has left this shit for us." Rorax had to grit her teeth to refrain from spitting at the Guardian.

The Guardian cocked her head, and her pale-yellow eyes traced over Rorax slowly. "You will lose everything if you do not gain restraint and direction, Greywood."

"Your Guardianship, I have nothing left to lose." Rorax snorted harshly, opening her arms welcomingly. There was no way she could touch Darras in Lyondrea, and Jia could handle herself.

The Guardian's thin mouth turned up a bit at the corners, her head remaining cocked as she studied her again.

"Not even Jia?" she asked softly with feigned concern. "Not even the precious House of Death Protectorates?" Her eyes flashed.

"You wouldn't hurt them to get to me."

The Guardian made three tsking noises with her tongue before she started to circle around Rorax like a shark. She stopped right before Rorax, her eyes flashing, her posture straight and queenly. Even in her withered and slightly broken state, she still towered over Rorax, but Rorax held her chin high and did not back away.

What's your name?

Rorax Greywood.

What does that mean?

It means fear has no room here. No space to grow into the cracks and splinters of your heart.

The Guardian reached to cup Rorax's chin, and her sharp fingernails bit down into Rorax's skin. She squeezed so hard Rorax felt her skin split underneath her nails. She did her best not to flinch or yelp as her blood stained the Guardian's fingers. Rorax kept the Guardian's gaze, but tears from the pain started to well even without her permission.

"You often seem to forget, Rorax Greywood, who you stand before. What I am capable of. How far the reaches of my power can go. You have but a mere fraction of it." The Guardian's eyes glinted in pleasure as she watched Rorax's blood drip down her hand, but her voice did not change from the even, peaceful, lethal tone.

Rorax narrowed her eyes slightly and finally lost the fight to her tears as they slowly slipped down her cheeks.

"Your friends are alive, but they will not remain so if you continue to be so wild and unyielding. I respect your courage and your bravery, but your blatant disrespect and disregard will get you nowhere." The Guardian squeezed Rorax's chin even tighter, her icy nails penetrating deeper into her skin. Rorax felt them connect with her bone, and she couldn't stop the whimper that escaped from her lips. Blood and tears now flowed down her face, down her neck, and into the fabric of her white dress, staining the front crimson. The Guardian pulled Rorax's head closer to her, aggravating Rorax's cuts and scraping along her jawbone. She swallowed back the bile crawling up her throat, effectively cutting off any screams.

"I would kill you," the Guardian murmured into her ear softly, eerily maternal, "but unfortunately, the Guardian is strictly prohibited by the magick to kill any member from the Choosing. I would die, too. And the Death Harbinger seems to have favorited you. But that doesn't mean I won't hurt you and those you love. Make smarter decisions, Greywood."

The Guardian jerked her head away from Rorax, her yellow eyes glinting in dark pleasure.

"BLACK SALT!" The Guardian barked out over her shoulder at her guards.

There was a murmuring in the crowd, and a guard scrambled out of the hall, returning with a small bowl of black granules. Rorax's breath hitched as the Guardian raised her free hand and gazed lovingly at the ice nails protruding from the tips of her fingers of the hand that wasn't holding Rorax captive. They elongated from short, sharp claws to lethal blades, each six inches long.

The Guardian made a show of licking the side of the ice blades emerging from the tips of her fingers before dipping it into the black salt granules. Rorax tried to jerk her head back and out of the Guardian's grip, but she was in too deep, and the only thing Rorax accomplished was a deeper, tighter hold into her flesh.

Tense energy and murmurs filled the room as the crowd watched the Guardian, uncertain of what to do.

"If you apologize, Greywood, and fall to your knees begging for my mercy, I will grant you a reprieve," the Guardian lovingly purred.

Rorax snarled through her tears, and on complete impulse, she jerked her head back and headbutted the Guardian as hard as she could.

The Guardian's nose gave a sickening crunch, and immediately blood started to spurt out of her nostrils. She spluttered, and hot blood that was not her own splattered across Rorax's face.

The Guardian jerked her head away, but instead of being angry, a soft, loving look passed over the Guardian's face as she took in her shards that were still embedded deeply into Rorax's jawbone.

"That was a mistake, *Pup*." The Guardian's sinister grin sent another shiver of fear shooting violently down Rorax's spine, and she didn't even have the chance to scream before the Guardian started to swing.

Rorax's eyes peeled open through the dried tears, but she couldn't see anything in the darkness. She didn't need to see the blood that coated her skin to know it was there. She could smell it, the smell of rust and iron clogging her nose. She could feel it, too; there was a sticky sheen of it on her skin.

Rorax gritted her teeth against a roll of nausea and did her best to take a deep breath through her nose.

She cried out as her back gave a sharp, painful throb in response to her movements. She raised her palms to push herself up, but wherever she was, it was too smooth and slippery for her wet fingers to grip. As she tried to lift her torso, her palms slipped out from under her, and her face smacked hard against the cool, smooth surface.

She let out a moan of pain at the impact on her cheek and went limp again as she closed her eyes, resigned to her fate.

A door somewhere opened, and there was a feminine gasp. Rorax tried to open her eyes again, and this time there was enough light that she could see the smooth, white surface of a tub.

"Ror... are you okay?"

Her body had been dumped into a tub, and she was sleeping face down with her cheek pressed to the slick, ceramic surface. At least it was cool against her burning cheek.

"Rorax?"

Her eyes flicked up.

Striding in from the open doorway was Milla. Next to her were Piers and Jia. All three of them gaped at her with wide, frightened eyes.

Rorax tried to nod her head, but the muscles at the top of her back screamed.

She sucked in a breath and tried to push herself up again. Her elbows shook violently underneath her weight, and her head started to spin so fast she had to lower herself back down.

"Milla, can—" She swallowed painfully against her dry throat as tears started to track down her nose and onto the surface of the tub beneath her. "Can you help me get out of the tub please?" Her voice was pitiful—small and demoralized—and she hated it.

Milla pushed a lock of red hair behind her ear and rushed to the left side of the bathtub. "Of course, of course. Piers, will you grab her right side?"

Piers nodded and silently moved to the side of the tub, ready to help Milla tug her out.

"Don't touch her. I've got her."

Rorax's whole body froze in recognition before collapsing again, her limbs weak from the sheer relief.

Ayres.

Ayres was back, and he was here in this bloody room. With her.

A sob broke through her lips, making her body sing in agony. She looked up into his face, trying furiously to blink the tears away. "Ayres."

Jia, Milla, and Piers took a fast step back so that Ayres could squat down next to her. "Gods above, Ror." He pushed a strand of hair matted with blood behind her ear. "It's even worse than I expected."

Comfort, clear and calming, ran like a balm over her frayed nerves at the sound of his voice. It made more tears trail down her face, but this time it was different. These were tears of relief, not pain or fear. It was going to be okay. *She* was going to be okay. Ayres had come back.

Another relieved sob bubbled out of her lips.

"Ror, I am going to have to jostle you, and I might have to place my arms across the cuts on your lower back. It's going to hurt, but I will do my very best not to aggravate the skin. Okay, Little Crow?" He moved his hand from her ear to cup the back of her head.

Rorax saw Jia and Piers look at each other from the corner of her eye, but she didn't look away from Ayres's charcoal and silver eyes as she nodded.

"You're not going to attack me?" he asked, smiling tightly as he edged closer.

Rorax laughed softly, wiping away a single tear from her good cheek. "No, I promise. I couldn't even if I wanted to."

Ayres nodded and ever so gently he lifted and folded her into his arms, one arm carefully lodged under her lower back by her shoulder blades, the other under her knees.

She had to bite her lip so she wouldn't scream as sharp, agonizing pain erupted from her cuts. Ayres shifted her body, so she was clinging to him monkey style, her core pressed against his abs, her ankles crossed behind his back. She wrapped her arms around his neck and buried her face into his skin on her good cheek—letting tears flow freely down her face.

Ayres turned to Milla, Piers, and Jia with Rorax in his arms. "I'm taking her upstairs into the prince's quarters. The bathtub is bigger so we can fit in another body in there with her to wash the wounds. We can't leave her here like this. She can't defend herself and would be easy picking for Isgra and her hoard if they come looking to increase their odds in the Choosing. I'll spend the night with her tonight to make sure nothing happens."

"She can sleep in my bed when she's done with her bath," Piers offered. "The bed is only a few steps away. I can sleep here in her room."

Ayres shook his head, his whiskered face catching the few strands of her hair that weren't matted in blood. "People will be looking for her while she's down. Find somewhere else. Sleep on Milla's floor, with Lamonte, or in my quarters."

"Tough choice, Piers," Rorax muttered against Ayres's neck, barely coherent in his arms.

Rorax smiled to herself against Ayres's neck as Milla informed Piers there was no chance in hell he could sleep in her room.

Rorax's vision started to darken, and she closed her eyes against it.

Ayres gently shook her. "Rorax. Rorax, stay awake for me, baby."

She tried to respond, to make a sound, but the blackness was getting stronger. She needed to sleep....

"Go get Tressa," Ayres ordered one of them. "She is still losing too much blood."

Rorax didn't remember anything else until Ayres set her down into the prince's bathtub.

She caught sight of a dark, feminine hand pushing Rorax's bloody hair away from her face. A soft voice was saying her name, asking her questions, but Rorax couldn't hear her, like her ears were under water.

The voice climbed into the tub and settled behind her; the hand gently pushed away some bloody hair again.

Someone began cutting away what was left of Rorax's dress, carefully patting away the blood. Rorax could feel magick attempting to heal the angry cuts.

Rorax's skin had looked like filet mignon before Tressa started healing it. From the side of her breast and over her back to the other breast was completely shredded, all the way down her back from armpit to hip. Muscles, tendons, nerves—anything that was there was severed or sliced.

Rorax could feel everything begin to knit back together. Everything would eventually heal, except her skin. It would scar from the black salt. The vertical and horizontal cuts made her flesh look like a one-colored checkerboard.

Tressa managed to cover the biggest gashes with a thin, hot, angry layer of skin.

"I'm sorry, Rorax. Your tattoo... it's ruined. All my healers left the castle two days ago. I'm the only one here, and that's all I have to give you."

Rorax opened her eyes and turned to look at her, her back muscles screaming at the effort. "Thank you. I am so lucky and blessed that you were willing to come to my aid, Tressa. I am grateful."

Tressa just blinked at Rorax and left to find her a shirt and some bandages to cover the smaller cuts she hadn't been able to get to. Rorax collapsed against the side of the tub until Tressa returned.

Ayres entered once Rorax was ready to be moved. Rorax's head rolled over his shoulder and pressed into his neck as he picked her up and rested her in the gigantic bed.

"Thank you," Rorax mumbled. He might have responded, but as soon as he pulled the covers over her, she was asleep.

Chapter 105

Tressa

Tressa's hands trembled over the flesh of Rorax's back, healing the deep slashes across her skin, trying to block out the words that were ringing in her mind.

"I will not bow to a woman who has sentenced eleven innocent girls to death because she wouldn't spend the time to find a way to undo the magick."

Rorax was right. Through her inaction, the Guardian had failed them, and Rorax was as much a victim in this as Roo had been.

Fuck.

The anger and the hatred that had been building in her stomach and chest for months sputtered. She desperately called out for it, needing it to help her crawl out of her own pit of regret and grief, but it was gone.

Ayres gingerly brushed his hand over Rorax's head, the movement affectionate and loving, and for the first time, Tressa didn't feel betrayed by his actions. She understood them. Rorax Greywood used almost every moment of her waking life fighting for a better future—for herself, for her friends, for the Contestars. Her unyielding focus and never-ending efforts were admirable.

Tressa dared to admit that she respected Rorax. *Liked* her, even.

The Guardian might not have killed Rorax, but she hadn't been that far away from it either. And with all the black salt, Rorax would have scars of this night for the rest of her life.

"Is she gonna be alright?" Ayres asked.

"Yes, she is going to live," Tressa soothed.

"Thank you... I know that you harbor ill feelings toward her—"

"I was wrong, Ayres," Tressa blurted, surprising them both. "What she's doing... trying to free the Contestars from the magick? It's... admirable. Roo would have wanted that. I'd like to think she would have tried to free them all, too."

"I think she would have," Ayres agreed.

Ayres ran his hand over Rorax's hair again, and a dark shadow passed over his features.

"What's wrong?" Tressa asked.

"I... care about her," Ayres admitted, like Tressa was trying to drag the words out of him.

Tressa smiled at her old friend. "I know."

"I know I said we would kill her at the end of this, if she made it to the top three...."

A part of Tressa still wanted to; a part of her wanted to stop healing the violent gashes and tear out Rorax's throat instead. But after what Rorax had said tonight, Tressa hesitated. If Rorax could find a way to stop future Choosings, or make them less violent, Tressa would support her. "Is she going to try and become the next Guardian then? I would support you if you made that decision."

Ayres frowned. "No, I don't think so. She hasn't changed her mind about it."

Tressa's eyebrows pulled together. "Why not? She unlocked her magick today. She would be a boon in the war."

Ayres blinked at her, like this possibility had never occurred to him before. "She thinks Enna would be a better Guardian than her."

Tressa hummed. She'd thought that before. Now she didn't know what she thought.

Ayres sighed, shoving his hand through his hair. “She won’t even look at me right now.”

“She will forgive you.” Tressa smiled and nudged him with her elbow. “If you decide you want to choose her, House of Life will wholeheartedly support your decision, Ayres. She would be good for the Realms. She’s strong enough to handle it.”

“Thank you,” Ayres said, stroking Rorax’s hair again. “She has to survive all this first though.”

“She will, Ayres.”

Chapter 106

Ayres

Ayres knocked on the wooden door so hard it shot sharp pain through his knuckles. He waited for half a beat before breaking the lock and throwing it open. The Guardian's chambers were large, and Ayres had only ever seen one room. She had a welcoming space that had a small fountain in the middle of it decorated with marble statues of old Guardians. A couple of tables had been pushed against the walls that were scattered with papers, and large plants sprouted out of their pots by the windows, now growing up the walls with long vines.

Ayres had always thought this room was a perfect escape for the Guardian—on normal days. But this was not a normal day.

The Guardian was halfway across the stone floor, and she stopped midstep and bowed her head slightly when she saw him. "Hello, Prince."

A growl ripped out from his lips before he could stop it. He stalked over to her and bared his teeth. "If you fucking touch her again, I will rip out your throat and then feed the pieces to you."

A shadow crossed over the Guardian's face, and her lips pressed together. "I did not intend for my actions to go as far as they did."

He stepped closer to her and snarled, forcing himself not to reach out and throttle her. "Nothing was left intact on her back. You left her in *ribbons*."

The Guardian took a step away from him and lowered her gaze to the floor. "Ayres, please understand—"

"No, you understand me." Ayres barely recognized his own voice as it deepened into a lethal, aggressive purr. "If you touch her again, if a single scratch from you mars her skin again, I will not hesitate to obliterate *everything* that you are."

A snort-like breath ripped out of the Guardian's nose, and her blue eyes finally flickered up to him. "So, she is the one then?"

Ayres ignored her, his teeth gritted so hard his jaw throbbed. "Do you understand me, Guardian?"

There was a pregnant pause as the Guardian studied him with wary eyes, noticing the faint glow of his tattoos and the muscles straining in his neck before nodding once. He doubted she feared death in the slightest, but he had nothing left to threaten her with besides violence.

Ayres flashed his teeth at her again and turned toward the door.

"This competition needs to end swiftly, Prince. If Greywood is the one you all want to choose as your next Guardian, then we need to move into action immediately," the Guardian said, ignoring his dismissal.

Ayres froze and slowly looked at her from over her shoulder. "The Choosing is still in motion. I do not know if Rorax is the best choice."

"May I offer you a suggestion then, Prince?" One of the Guardian's eyes twitched. "Make your choice between Roraxiva and Enna. Isgra would simply become the next Vadik, and the Realms will not survive another Guardian like him."

Vadik, the Western Guardian. Cruel and arrogant, Vadik was rumored to be *deeply* loyal to the House of Alloy.

His brows furrowed. "Isgra is nothing like Vadik."

"She will be." The Guardian turned away from him and moved toward the fountain in the middle of her room. She slowly reached down and skimmed her fingers across the glassy surface of the water. "Oxana is the only one now with the power to push Vadik back, and she was never one to deny him anything."

A dark shadow crossed over her face before she pulled her hand back from the water and straightened.

"I am losing my grip on my abilities and my sanity more and more with each passing day, Prince. The magick is starting to rule me, not the other way around. The force tethering me to this world is no longer strong enough to subdue the power of the Guardian and is becoming unstable. It's deteriorating and becoming difficult to control."

Ayres raised an eyebrow at her and looked her up and down, looking for signs that she was losing control. "Do you need to tie together?"

The Guardian shook her head, not looking up at him from the surface of the water. "Unfortunately, our tying ceremonies have become obsolete. They are no longer effective."

A strange, tight sensation started to creep across his neck. "What do you mean it's no longer effective?"

The Guardian looked up at Ayres and narrowed her eyes. "I mean, Prince, that if this competition does not end very soon, Roraxiva's back will be the *least* of the destruction I inflict upon the Realms. I would say I have another month, two at most, before this body succumbs to the power."

CHAPTER 107

RORAX

Rorax jerked straight up, her nightmares fading into the back of her mind. She looked around the room with wild eyes before the muscles in her back seized up, trying to protect the still shredded tissue there. She cried out in pain.

"Hey, hey. You're alright, Ror. Relax," a deep, velvety voice commanded. There was a fireplace lit in the room, and in front of the flames, a big body rose from a makeshift bed on the ground.

Rorax would know that body anywhere.

She was panting and sweaty, situated in the center of an overly large, four-poster bed, with nothing but a white sheet surrounding her waist. Her upper body was completely bare, but she didn't care. It was Ayres.

She bit her lip and rocked forward, willing the sharp pain to fade and the tears to stop.

Ayres hesitated on his way over to her before situating himself on the side of the bed.

Her eyes filled with tears as the skin on her back seared again in pain. She clenched her jaw and tried to blink them away. "Fuck, that hurts."

"How can I help?"

She looked up at Ayres. The corners of his mouth were turned down as his dark, charcoal eyes scanned her face.

This man. This man had once been a symbol of comfort and strength to her. He had protected her, advocated for her, saved her life, and had become one of her most trusted friends.

Looking up at him, Rorax's heart broke.

"Ror." His voice was thick and hoarse as he reached out for her, but then thought better of it and let his hand fall uselessly to the bed next to her.

She closed her eyes, forcing herself not to lean into the touch as tears started to track down her face. "Safe. Being with you was where I used to feel *safe*. But now...."

Tears clogged her throat, and her voice sounded more broken than it ever had before. He had lied to her.

"Ever since you made me take the Blood Oath, I don't want to know you, and it feels like something fundamental—something deep inside of me—has shattered. It's broken. I-I'm broken." A sob ripped out of her chest so painfully that her back seized up again in protest, and gods, it was like her whole body was on fire.

"Ror, fuck. I'm so sorry." He tried to pull her into his chest, but she pushed his hands away the best she could.

"Stop, please, Ayres. Go get Jia, *please*."

Ayres's hands froze. He looked tortured, and his throat worked with words she thought he was going to say, but eventually he nodded and silently left the room.

Chapter 108

Jia

"Marras save me, Piers, it was a good shot, but it would have been sad if you'd missed it," Kaiya said, also signing with her fingers.

Jia tried to cover her smile as she tossed the rabbit bone of the leg she'd been eating into the fire.

"Horseshit, Whitethorn, that shot was incredible," Piers insisted, also using his fingers to speak, his eyes so wide and earnest it almost made him seem like a little kid, not like the six-hundred-year-old immortal that he was.

"Yeah, you're a gods-damned prodigy with a bow and arrow," Kaiya deadpanned, rolling her eyes. She threw her bone into the fire, too, and wiped her mouth with the back of her hand. "If you take six hundred shots, hopefully you'll make at least one."

"I thought it was cool, Piers." Jia smirked. "Just not cooler than my shot."

"When you put an arrow right through her eye socket? Gods, that was perfection." Piers laughed, his golden eyes flashing in the fire as he smiled contagiously at Jia.

No, perfection was when Kaiya slapped the tall male with the blunt side of her ax, and he fell into the fire, Cannon signed enthusiastically. A horrible way to die, but he would have been a pain in the ass to cross swords with. He was even taller than Kaiya, by six inches.

Piers laughed, and Jia's smile grew. It really had been perfect timing.

Jia smiled across the fire at Cannon, and Kaiya pulled the blanket around her even more tightly.

Jia was just close enough to the fire to feel its warmth against her skin, but for the first time in a long time, she felt warm inside, too. Both her heart and soul felt content, happy even. She wasn't whole or complete by any means, but maybe for now that was okay.

It was all thanks to these people, these random Death-Born guards who made her feel like she was part of them. She might have lost her old family, her favorite family with Volla and Rorax and Sahana, but here, they had made a new family, somehow. Through the pain and destruction House of Ice had caused them, they had become close. Jia felt the beginnings of belonging. Even though the love of her life was dead, she had found new love. A different sort of love. One that didn't set her on fire, but one that warmed her bones and soothed her soul. For now, that was enough, and Jia knew she would do anything to protect it through the coming storm.

Maybe even kill Enna Mistvalley.

Chapter 109

Raengar

Raengar gripped the small piece of paper in his hand tightly. The woman had asked him to meet her in a nondescript butcher's shop at the edge of a small town. She had the results and knew exactly who had ordered the Waterlily Rine to use against Unit One. Whoever had ordered it was powerful enough that she felt she needed to flee the university for safety.

It may have been foolish, but Raengar trusted the woman. He did not, however, trust anything about the situation. It would be *so* easy for this to be compromised. Raengar should have left a soldier there to keep eyes on it, even if the woman had ferociously denied him.

When Raengar got to the butcher's shop, he paused. There was a light on in the hut, a small little candle, and through the window he could see her standing, facing away from him.

Sweat trickled down his back, and his instincts prickled. Something wasn't right.

Raengar pushed forward anyway, opening the door. The woman turned to him and let out a muffled scream. She stood with her hands bound in front of her and a fabric gag in her mouth, her eyes wide with fear.

Raengar looked around for a threat, and only when he looked up did he find his attacker.

A man, haggard and homeless, was perched on a beam above him, watching Raengar with crazed curiosity.

"So, it was the King of Ice meddling in our affairs," the man said, his head cocking to the side sharply, like a bird's. "I would recognize the thump of that dragon-demon's wings anywhere. I told them it was someone powerful."

The man swung down and dropped to the floor, positioning himself between Raengar and the door. He was frighteningly skinny, dressed in nothing more than rags and dirt, but he had a bloody, rusty, wicked ax tucked in his waistband. "You're early, usurper. I haven't even started on her yet." The man pulled the ax free and motioned to the woman with the dark blade.

Raengar's lip curled over his teeth. "What do you think you're doing?"

"Destroying evidence against my king." The man smiled, showing off the five rotting teeth he had managed to keep in his skull, his greasy, chin-length hair swaying back and forth. "Time to die."

Without any more words or taunts, the man swung his ax down with surprising speed, and Raengar barely had time to duck under the blade. He stepped to the side and had to duck again as the haggard man swung at him with crazed belligerence. Raengar pulled his sword free, just in time to block a blow that would have lobbed off his head.

"I've heard stories about you, Butcher King."

"Who the fuck are you?"

"I am Rivey."

Rivey ducked a blast of ice Raengar sent his way, almost folding his spine in two before popping up like a long reed. As he straightened, a silversteel necklace that had been hiding in his shirt peeked out, the clean silver sharply contrasted against the dirty skin of Rivey's emaciated neck. Without thinking, Raengar reached out, fisted the necklace, and ripped it off the little man's neck.

It had House of Alloy's sigil of a Morningstar stamped on the front. King Määr had sent him.

Raengar threw the necklace on the ground. "Your king sent you to die, Rivey."

Rivey smiled, once again showing off his rotting brown teeth. "I will not die here. I have killed too many before you to die here and promised my king I would return to kill for him again."

Rivey slashed his blade and sliced at Raengar's stomach. Raengar lurched back, just barely in time, and Rivey's blade sliced open the top layer of Raengar's leather armor.

Raengar used his proximity and backhanded Rivey across the face with enough force to send him sprawling to the floor. But almost like a spider, Rivey rolled to his feet. From his dirty waistband, he pulled two knives and threw them both at Raengar. Raengar blocked one with his sword and iced away the other, but he was unprepared for the third knife that Rivey sent plunging into his right shoulder. Raengar roared his displeasure as Rivey lunged and landed his fist to Raengar's face, splitting open his bottom lip.

"I expected more from the Butcher King," Rivey taunted, dancing on his toes and flashing his disgusting teeth again. "You are a legend in my House, a hero—"

Rivey's voice choked off as he gasped, his fingers fluttering over his chest and his mouth opening and closing like a fish gasping for air as Raengar straightened up to his full height, towering over Rivey as the man's heart froze into a solid block in his chest.

Raengar sneered at Rivey and reached down to grip the man's jaw in his hand. "Go to hell."

Rivey's eyes went wide as Raengar pulled the knife from his shoulder and used it to slice the man's neck. Rivey's body fell to the floor.

Raengar moved to the woman and pulled the cloth out of her mouth.

"Gods bless you," she gasped as Raengar sliced the rope from her hands with Rivey's bloodstained knife.

"Are there more men?"

"No. No, it was him. He killed them all." The woman's voice choked up, but relief splintered through Raengar.

"Do you have the results?"

"I—yes." The woman reached into the deep pocket of her robes and with trembling fingers, she held up a small roll of paper.

Raengar snatched it, ignoring the throb from the wound in his shoulder and the smears of blood he left over the pristine parchment.

At the words he read, a smile spread over his mouth, and muscles he didn't even know were tense relaxed. Thank Kään. This would be more than enough to put Määr in a cell and enough to convict him of conspiracy against the Realms.

CHAPTER 110

RORAX

Six targets.

Six darts of ice.

Six bull's-eyes.

Rorax smirked when she saw where she hit each target, and that smirk grew into a smug smile when Cannon gave her an impressed whistle.

Very good, Greywood, Cannon signed**. *Now do it with earth.***

She did as she was told, slinging six sharp darts of earth toward the targets made of straw and wood that they had haphazardly arranged in stone stands, collecting another six bull's-eyes to brag about.

The Elemental Magick that she had finally uncracked wasn't that different from the magick she was already used to with Glimr.

The hardest part was filtering through the new strings of additional magick she felt, flipping through them until she found the right one she wanted to use. The best part about magick was how it manifested in her eyes, overlapping the white iris with the vibrant colors of the rainbow.

The grueling practices she'd subjected herself to were slowly becoming second nature. She was the best with short bursts of magick—magick that felt like she was simply throwing her knife around. Ice and earth daggers, balls of flame, a dagger of darkness, small bursts of lightning—any kind of magick she could fashion into a weapon, Rorax excelled at. Anything she wanted to grow or summon for her pleasure—blossoms or ice sculptures or beautiful light shows bursting from her fingertips—were much harder.

A full moon cycle had passed since Rorax had finally accessed her magick. It had been one of the most challenging and strenuous times in her life. Working on only a few hours of sleep, Rorax would rise before dawn and not return to her bed until well after midnight.

Rorax knew her magick would leave her once she found a way to free herself from the Choosing, but while she had it, she wanted to feel it, push her ability to the maximum, find out what she could do. She wanted to know what it felt like to have so much *power* at the touch of her fingers. It was addicting.

Rorax would never admit it out loud to anyone, but she also used this time as a distraction from Ayres—or more like Ayres's absence.

Ayres no longer came to the Contestars' training sessions. He never came to their study sessions, and he barely looked her way when she managed to catch a glimpse of him in the mess hall or around the castle.

Rorax had forgiven him for lying to her, for hiding who he was. Here at the castle, he was just a man. He wasn't the Harbinger or the Prince of House Death; he was just a man.

Everyday people still sneered at Rorax, whispered behind their hands calling her *the Pup*, looked at her with fear, like she wanted to slaughter the whole castle and was just biding her time. And so Rorax understood him. If Rorax could go back to her blessed, wonderful anonymity, she would. Her heart ached for it.

Rorax was hurt that Ayres had not trusted her with the truth and still furious he had forced the Blood Oath on her. Both *reasonable* things to be upset by. Both things she deserved an apology for—something that could easily be fixed. But the apology never came. Not after a full cycle of Rorax waking up before dawn, training until her muscles failed, and searching through books all day, and falling into bed late. He had been avoiding her relentlessly.

Jia, Lamonte, Piers, and Cannon trained her magick through the day, and Ayres never appeared during any of them. He had completely abandoned her.

Rorax hated—*hated*—that she had all the attention in the world, and yet she still felt alone without him.

Her heart gave a painful jerk, and her mouth twisted.

Cannon snapped his fingers, and she looked over at him, hating the pity written all over his face. ***Are you okay?***

Rorax nodded and forced her features to appear neutral. ***I'm fine.***

Cannon gave her a look that told Rorax her lie was as flimsy as a wet noodle. She blew out a heavy sigh before straightening her spine.

Rorax felt her pride crumble away as she asked, ***Where is he?***

Cannon pursed his lips, tilting his head to the side. ***He is holed up in one of the old, abandoned librarian offices.***

Why?

Cannon folded his arms over his chest and shrugged, the red bands on his biceps flashing in the sun. ***No one knows. He gave us orders to focus on you and to stay out of his way.***

The way Cannon's eyes pinched tight in the corners made Rorax think that something was wrong. ***Is he okay?***

Cannon nodded slowly, but his uncertainty was clear. ***Yes, but if you wanted to check in on him, I wouldn't stop you.***

CHAPTER 111

AYRES

Ayres ran a hand over his head, his fingers combing through his freshly washed hair. It was getting long, falling over his ears and forehead.

He would cut it, but he remembered when Rorax had fisted it the last time they were together, pulling on it ruthlessly—deliciously—as she ground her pussy against his face.

Ayres groaned and scrubbed his hands over his jaw, letting out a long sigh. His muscles and his bones were stiff. He was exhausted, emotionally and physically.

Ayres had been in the shitty little abandoned office—with abhorrent paintings of hot-air balloons the last librarian had hung all over the walls—nonstop for almost a month.

He was hiding from his friends, from his people, and, most importantly, from Rorax, only leaving when there was a tug on the ley lines, for his workout during the time he knew Rorax would be in the Contestars' Courtyard, or if he needed to take care of a hygiene problem.

Ayres's eyes were sore, his fingers were always constantly covered in ink, and every lead he had so far was going cold.

He was so, so tired.

Ayres was searching, desperately searching, for a way to get Rorax and her friend out of this *fucking* Choosing, but every single day it looked more and more helpless.

Neither he nor any of his librarians at home in Surmalinn or Morvarand had been able to find anything. Not a *shred* of evidence. Kiniera had informed him that House of Ice was having similar results. He had even sent a raven to Merosa, the Witch Queen who resided in the Salt Stone City of House of Fauna, but she didn't have any information for him either.

When his ancestor, Raiv Sumavari, had destroyed the evidence of the Transfer Tables, he had been very, *very* thorough.

Rorax choosing to champion these women was going to be her destruction when she couldn't save them, and nothing he was doing was helping.

It was utterly, utterly useless. *He* was utterly useless.

Ayres picked up the crystal decanter he had brought with him that was full of whiskey and pulled a long swallow down his throat.

The burn going down was exactly what he needed.

When the bottle was empty, he turned and hurled it against the wall, and it shattered, glass spraying everywhere. Watching it shatter against the stones was the most satisfying thing he had seen all cycle.

Ayres ran his hands through his hair again, his shoulders drooping.

He was going to lose her. Rorax was going to die if he didn't find *something*. The fifth trial was coming up; he had a little over a month left. Rorax would never agree to Enna's death in exchange for hers. She would kill herself before agreeing to that, and he didn't know what to do. He didn't want to lose her, but Enna was still the chosen successor they had all agreed upon.

The door to the lost librarian's office slammed open, and something in his chest soothed as Rorax, in all her furious glory, burst in.

Gods, she was beautiful. Her wavy, long, black hair was billowing around her shoulders, draping over her chest, and begging for him to wrap it around his fist and force her into him so he could breathe her in, or maybe force her to her knees so he could fuck her mouth.

Gods that mouth....

She slammed the door behind her and stormed toward him. "Where the *fuck* have you been, Ayres?"

CHAPTER 112

RORAX

Rorax's chest heaved in angry breaths as she glared at Ayres, trying to keep any evidence of her hurt out of her eyes. He was standing there, looking as beautiful and deadly as ever. His hands were on his hips, and he was standing in front of a pile of shattered glass. Why was he here in this shitty little office? Why wasn't he with her?

Ayres rolled his shoulders, like he was trying to shake away the tension coiled there. "I'm working, Ror."

The meaty part of his palm rubbed his forehead. He looked tired, drained, as if he was not getting nearly enough sleep. But that wasn't why she was here. She wasn't here to care; she was here to get answers. His eyes roamed the length of her body, as if drinking in the sight of her, savoring it, and it made her anger hotter.

"Have you been avoiding me, Ayres?"

His eyes and mouth went hard, but he said nothing, and it caused Rorax's heart to pinch.

"Are you punishing me for being angry about finding out you're the *prince*?"

A muscle in Ayres's jaw jumped. "What? No, of course not."

She bared her teeth at him, feeling her fledgling power screaming to unleash it on him, to hurt him the same way she was hurting.

Before she did anything rash, she turned toward the door, wanting—*needing*—to get away from this man. Rorax's hand was almost at the handle when a wall of black shadow and red lightning cut in front of her, zapping her fingers away.

He wasn't letting her go.

Rorax's heart leapt at the implication, which made her scowl with anger at herself for her pitiful hope. Ayres bit out a low laugh at the look on her face as he moved toward her. Every single slow step he made had a predatory intent that made her instincts urge her to flee. There was nothing between her and the Death Harbinger's power but a long black dress she had put on before coming here. For the first time since she had met him, she could actually feel it—the hint of power that everyone had mentioned to her before now. The amount of power that he must hold was almost unimaginable, like Kiniera's.

Rorax pushed her fear down and rolled her tongue over her teeth, wanting to punch that smug grin off his face. "I'm sorry I disturbed you."

He stopped in front of her, making a little tsk, tsk, tsk sound with his tongue. "Don't lie, Little Crow."

Despite her instincts telling her it was a bad idea to provoke the Death Harbinger, the very, *very* short leash she had on her temper snapped in half.

She tried to punch Ayres in the face, but he turned a shoulder away from her, and her fist sailed right past his head into the waiting air. He took her fist, twisted it behind her back, and shoved her face-first into the wall so hard the picture frame above her rattled.

"I've missed this." Ayres's eyes were fixed on where he had one of his powerful thighs pressed between both of hers to pin her against the wall. Her dress was riding up and had bunched in the middle of her thighs. He leaned closer until his lips brushed against the sensitive skin of her neck right above her thrumming pulse. "I've missed you." He nipped her earlobe with his teeth.

Fuck. Her body jerked before a paralyzing, erotic current shot through her, straight to her core. She hated the little wet spot she could feel blooming there.

Rorax grunted and turned her head away, so the back of her head was in his face. His nose tickled the strands of hair on the back of her head as he breathed in her scent, and it made her nipples tighten under her dress.

She hated him. Truly.

Her back arched involuntarily, and part of her wanted to persuade him—wanted to beg, bribe, threaten—*anything* to convince him that having her spread out before him where he could put tongue, teeth, and fingers in her was the only thing he could do for the rest of the day.

Rorax chanced a glance up at him, finding his gaze was silver. It would only take one push—one more small little arch—to snap his control, and he would take her, right there.

She maneuvered out of his grasp and stepped back toward the door. "Let me out."

Ayres ignored her and instead rested his fist against the wall where she had just been standing. He closed his eyes and pressed his forehead against his fist, as if he could still feel her against him there. He looked like he was both longing and in mourning, like *she* had left him, like *she* had put this barrier between them.

Gods, he was infuriating. Rorax glowered at him from across the room, her hands balling into fists so tight she could feel her nails threatening to pierce her skin. "I'll kill you."

Ayres turned, slow and predatory, his eyes trailing to her. He grinned, showing all his teeth in more of a snarl than a smile, and before she could blink, he was on her. Ayres kissed her hard and fast, his arms encircling her and hoisting her up from the ground. He slammed her against the stone wall so hard she cried out in shock.

Taking the open opportunity, he started to kiss down her neck.

"You don't want to kill me, Little Crow. That's not why you came to find me." His right hand simultaneously pulled the low neckline of her dress and bra down, releasing her breasts. She had to wrap her arm around his neck, one hand gripping his shoulder so hard she was probably going to leave bruises. The other hand was at his wrist, pulling it closer as he kneaded one of her breasts and pinched a nipple roughly. She whimpered into his mouth and arched her back greedily, pressing herself more fully into him.

"Ayres," she whimpered, "I need more."

He laughed darkly as he released her nipple and used that same hand to shove her dress even farther up her legs, so it rested above her hips. His belt clinked against the zipper as the button of his pants came undone, and she felt a rush of excitement. He moved her panties to the side with his fingers and pressed inside. She rocked her hips on him, riding his fingers for a moment, showing him how wet and ready she was, how much she desperately wanted this, before his fingers disappeared and she felt him guide his cock inside her.

He slammed his full length into her. There was a twinge of delicious pain, and she screamed his name.

"Fuck, Ror," he clipped out, gripping both of her knees in support so he could watch his cock slide in and out. "I have been waiting for days to be right"—he pulled all the way out of her—"here." He slammed back in.

She rolled her hips, and Ayres lowered his head to her shoulder and started to pump faster and faster into her, so hard that the paintings on the wall rattled and threatened to fall. The combination of the positioning and how big he was resulted in him rubbing against places she didn't even know *could* feel good.

She was going to explode; she was going to kaleidoscope into a thousand pieces, and she was going to love every second of it. "Ayres," she whimpered. "Ayres, I'm going to come."

He gritted his teeth, pumping harder as her walls grew tighter and tighter.

She screamed his name again, her fingernails digging into his shoulders, grabbing fistfuls of his shirt as she came. One of the paintings fell off the wall as he continued to stroke into her, and she came again, one orgasm rolling into the next. She came so hard she saw stars.

His eyes were redder than she had ever seen, except for during her first hunt in Helfast when he had saved them, and she loved it. Loved that she could make him lose control, that she could push his buttons so hard that he could snap his precious self-restraint.

This was Ayres Sumavari, Death Prince and Death Harbinger. He had to have a legendary amount of discipline to be able to keep his power in check. And yet she, Roraxiva Greywood, was the only person on the planet she knew who could make him shed his discipline like a snakeskin.

"We're not done," Ayres snarled as he lifted her away from the wall. With one arm around her waist, the other at her hip, he turned to the desk.

He pressed his mouth to hers, his tongue reaching in to stroke hers, and in one swipe of his arm, he cleared everything off the desk.

Still rock-hard inside of her, he dropped her onto the surface. He lowered his head to her neck as his cock slid out, pumped inside of her, withdrew, and then, as he drilled into her again, he clamped his canines onto her skin and bit.

Her body tensed as pain sent a jolt of electricity through her. It was immediately replaced by pure, unfiltered pleasure that made her see stars. She gasped out his name.

His teeth released the flesh of her throat and pulled away so he could watch her fall apart.

She couldn't move. She couldn't do anything but breathe, whimper, and beg for more as he fucked her and used his thumb to rub over her clit. Ayres growled, and at the sound, her eyes rolled into the back of her head, and she came again. Hard. Harder than she ever had come before in her whole entire life.

Waves of pleasure coursed through her blood, and she felt detached from her body, floating away in a balloon of pure ecstasy.

Ayres thrust inside of her once more before collapsing onto his elbows on either side of her. His dark eyes were hooded with satisfaction as he looked down at Rorax, almost nose-to-nose with her. She smiled softly, feeling so whole and relaxed and happy to have him back right here, connected with her, looking at her like she was everything is his world, his sun and stars.

She completely forgot that she was still angry with him, until he opened his fucking mouth again.

"I *was* avoiding you, Ror," he said, swallowing hard, squeezing his eyes shut and breaking their connection. "Because this… you… I can't think about anything else when you're near me except how much I want you. Yet, I can't find any relief when you are not with me. I *ache* for you. Always."

Just as Rorax opened her mouth to say something snarky, Ayres opened his eyes and reached up to pluck one of her hair knives free.

Rorax could barely believe it when Ayres gently sliced into the scar where he had done the Blood Oath before slicing into his own thumb. He set her knife on the desk and lowered himself to his knees in front of her, looking up into her eyes as she sat up to watch him. "Roraxiva Greywood, I release you from your Blood Oath."

She winced when it felt like her cut had been zapped but didn't look away from his face.

"I should have done that long ago." Ayres stayed on his knees as he reached out and grabbed her boot-clad ankles dangling off the side of the desk. "I am sorry, Rorax. Forgive me. For everything. I should have told you who I was after you took those arrows for me on your first hunt, or after you saved both Cannon and Kaiya's life and took that troll on by yourself. And most importantly, I should never have forced you to take the Blood Oath once you figured it out. I am sorry for always making you feel as though you still have something to prove to me, even after you already have. Time and time again."

Rorax forgot to breathe as he rose to his feet and cupped her face in his warm hands. He tilted her jaw up to him and looked from one of her eyes to the other. "You are enough, and you have done enough to earn my forgiveness, my protection, my friendship, and my loyalty."

Rorax's lip started to tremble, and he pressed a thumb gently into her lower lip.

"You have to survive this. I don't want to live in a world where you're no longer in it," he said, his gaze moving over her face, the soft expression on his features reminding her how Volla used to look at Jia. "So, yes, I have been avoiding you,

Rorax. You're right, and I'm sorry for that, too. I just... I just needed some space to try and focus."

Ayres released Rorax's face, and he stepped over to the desk he was using. She watched as he moved to the pile of books and papers he had flung off his desk, picking up a few and looking them over as he ran a tattooed hand over his short hair. "I have been trying to find a way to release you and Isgra from the Choosing. I swear I've searched through almost every book and scroll in this whole gods-damned library, but...." He looked back up at her and grimaced, eyeing the tears that had started to fall from her eyes. "Ror, what's wrong?"

Rorax quickly brushed the stray tears off her cheeks and swallowed the lump in her throat. "You've been here for the past month... researching?"

Ayres put his hands on his hips, looking over the stacks of paper forlornly. "Not successfully, Ror, but—"

Rorax launched herself from the desk and threw herself into his arms, burying her face in his neck. Relief swept through her like a wrecking ball. He hadn't abandoned her. He had been throwing all his energy into saving her life.

She sagged, and Ayres tightened his arms around her waist, squeezing hard. "I am with you, my Little Crow."

CHAPTER 113

RORAX

"I've been instructed ta stay righ' here. Good luck, Greywood." Lamonte stopped on the edge of the cluster of small buildings, a dilapidated and crumbling village, folding his arms over his chest as he looked down at Rorax.

The transport dragons had dropped the necessary people for the trial a few miles south of the border, and from there, Lamonte had been Rorax's guide from the camp to here. The Guardian had given the three remaining Contestars very clear instructions. *"Harpies have infiltrated some of the small villages on the border. Your task is to identify and kill the harpies in your given village. Bring me a head so I know the job has been completed."*

Rorax gave him a nod and turned to the village. Harpies were foul creatures. They took pleasure in killing, and the males were known to rape their victims. They usually left nothing standing. Rorax had seen many villages turned into nothing but ashes after a visit from a harpy.

Using the Life Magick, she sent a pulse through the village. Maybe... four forms? Three?

Rorax could smell the rot, the decay from all around the village, seeping into her nose. She crept forward through the underbrush surrounding the village until she stepped on something soft that crunched under her boot. Rorax looked down to find a severed hand. Flies buzzed angrily around the removed appendage, and her stomach roiled. The smell of decay wasn't a mystery anymore, and as she looked closer at the land around her, she noticed several chunks of flesh and appendages that had been carelessly discarded.

"Disgusting," Rorax grumbled as she crept forward and pushed her way inside the first cabin where the closest energy signature was.

It turned out there were two energy signatures.

A woman standing at a stove pulled a small child behind her, both scared and skittish upon Rorax's intrusion.

"Hello, harpy," Rorax drawled, pulling her sword.

The woman didn't say anything, just looked wildly around the kitchen for an escape.

"You and your clan just killed a small contingent of the Guardian's men, and you slaughtered this entire village. How do you plead?"

"Not guilty. It's not true," the harpy shrieked.

"I stepped on a severed hand just outside," Rorax snarled.

"*Lies.* We would *never* do such a thing." The harpy pulled the child to her side, and Rorax's upper lip curled.

"We did it," the child sneered at Rorax. "I would do it again."

The harpy hissed in outrage, but Rorax didn't have time for this.

In one fell swoop, Rorax decapitated the harpy, the humanistic head falling to the floor with a wet thump.

The child blinked at the decapitated human form on the floor twice before it snapped its eyes up to Rorax. The young harpy didn't have the same control of its glamor magick its mother had. Its irises switched between the humanlike chocolate brown to yellow with vertical-slitted pupils.

With a loud, inhuman screech, the harpy started to shift. Even though it was still not full grown, it towered over Rorax by a foot. The smooth, childlike skin of its upper body gave way to flesh-colored scales while its legs were covered in brown feathers. Wings erupted out of its back, and claws grew out of its hands.

Rorax threw Glimr, but the harpy swatted it out of the air, hissing in pain as the blade cut into its taloned hand.

It screamed again, the jaw distending past what was human, showing its rows and rows of sharp, long, needlelike teeth.

Rorax swung her hand, and a pick of ice shot from her palms and rammed right down the harpy's throat.

The harpy dropped, its blue and black blood splattering across the wall behind it.

Rorax turned and exited the hut to find two other harpies already waiting for her in their full forms, claws and wings out.

"Contestar," the tallest one purred. "We speculated if the Guardian would send her disposable lapdogs after us."

"Harpies always talk too much." Rorax pulled Glimr close to her face, watching as the black harpy blood dripped down the blade and onto her fingers, seeping into the horizontal lines of the skin on her knuckles. "But you never tell me what I really want to know."

"Which is what?"

She dropped her blade away from her face to focus on the two oversized birds. "What are you doing here? I thought your home was in Wymeria's mountains."

"Koleti has allowed us to expand our borders." The harpy gave Rorax a cold smile. "Expand our menus."

"Oh? Have you been speaking to him? Or was this a decision based on delusion or bloodlust?"

The harpy smiled, showing its sharp rows of teeth, but said nothing.

Rorax forced her frustration down. "Tell me, who is Koleti communicating with?"

"Wouldn't you like to know?"

"Has Koleti agreed to help Lyondrea win the war against the Realms?" When the harpy said nothing, Rorax gritted her teeth. "Tell me, or your demise will be so painful I'll have you begging me for death for days."

The harpy looked Rorax up and down slowly, focusing in on her eyes. "If my death was destined to be brought upon by you, *Spine Cleaver*, it was always destined to be painful and slow."

The harpy lunged.

Her talons ripped long gashes around Rorax's arm as Rorax spun and set it on fire. The harpy screamed in pain, causing enough of a distraction as Rorax spun and hacked the harpy's head clean off with her sword.

She turned in time to see the other harpy bend to lunge, but with her Death Magick, she reached out to feel his soul and *pulled*. With what felt like a subtle *pop*, the second harpy dropped to the ground.

She stared at it for a moment, breathing heavily before she walked over and toed the harpy's taloned hand carefully. It was dead.

"Nice work." Rorax spun to find Lamonte leaning against one of the posts of the hut, watching her with those beautiful green eyes. "Most new Contestars are frightened of their new Death Magick."

"I have never been scared of death," she said before she turned, lifted her sword, and chopped the harpy's head free.

CHAPTER 114

JIA

Jia looked up from a scroll she'd been assigned to read as Milla and Cannon hurried through the stacks of books toward her. Something about their stiff gait and serious demeanor made Jia's stomach tighten with trepidation. Kaiya sat across from Jia with her back to them, but when she heard them approaching, she twisted around.

"Enna failed to kill her harpy," Milla snapped.

Jia blinked. What?

"What did you just say?" Kaiya asked slowly.

"Enna didn't kill her harpy. She said she couldn't. She wanted to 'save them,'" Milla explained, quoting Enna's words with her fingers.

As Milla's words sank in, relief made Jia's limbs heavy. Thank Kään. She could stop pretending that she thought Enna would be the better Guardian over Rorax. She could start pushing people toward Rorax. Because Rorax *was* the better option. It was no longer just an opinion. With a Pit War looming over them, she was the *only* option.

"Where are they?" Jia asked.

"Rorax and Enna are in the Great Hall with the Guardian now."

"This changes nothing," Kaiya snapped, pushing up from her seat.

Jia stood up, too, her hands curled into fists at her side. "This changes everything."

Jia was vibrating with anger and the now solidified knowledge that Enna would never be the Guardian. She was going to use this, take every inch this blunder allowed her.

"She is still the better choice than Rorax," said Kaiya.

Gods, but that wasn't true, and now Jia had proof. "Enna can't protect us," Jia hissed, coming around the table and looking into Kaiya's cold brown eyes. "Rorax can."

"You don't know that." Kaiya reached up and pushed Jia's shoulders, rocking her back a few steps.

Jia shoved her back viciously. "Yes, I do. Don't touch me, Whitethorn."

Kaiya took one step closer, her beautiful face twisted in anger. She was in Jia's face before Milla wrenched Kaiya back a few steps.

Milla squeezed between their chests, forcing them both back with a hard push. "Stop it, both of you. Until we hear from the Guardian, we don't know if Enna is disqualified or not. Until then, nothing has been decided."

"And what if she has been disqualified?" Jia asked. "That leaves us with the option of Rorax or Isgra."

Milla rubbed circles into her temples. "If Enna gets disqualified, then we move forward with Rorax. Isgra is under Alloy influence."

A muscle in Kaiya's jaw popped as she glowered down at Jia. "She hasn't been disqualified."

"Even if she hasn't, do you honestly still believe she's the best option?" Jia asked, raising her arms in exasperation. "She couldn't kill a harpy. How is she supposed to defend your people in a Pit War, for Kään's sake?"

Kaiya looked like she was about to breathe fire, but Jia didn't have time to argue with her. She turned to Milla. "We need a protection unit on Rorax at all times. This just escalated. Rorax's safety needs to be a priority. Alloy will be coming after her harder than ever."

Jia should just kill Enna. She should just put a shard of ice straight through her heart and save everyone the dilemma. She wasn't conspiring with Rorax, so the magick wouldn't kill her. And then Rorax would have Ice, Death, and, at the very least, Fire, Weather, and Air at her back as well. Maybe even more protection once Kiniera got fully on board and started using her connections.

More footsteps approached the table, and almost like Jia had summoned her, Kiniera and Ayres joined them.

"I am renouncing Isgra as the House of Ice's Contestar and naming ourselves as Rorax's second House. It's time," Kiniera said, coming to a stop in front of Milla. Jia sagged a bit in relief. After the deaths of Stella and Briar, their Houses chose to back Isgra and Enna. Both had all the protection a Contestar could want. As it stood, Isgra had Ice as her head House, with Alloy, Dark, Light, Water, and Foliage as supporting Houses. Enna had Fire as her head House with Life, Air, Weather, and Fauna. Rorax had only Death.

"I can put a soldier on her." Kiniera turned to Jia. "You go. You'll have the first watch when Rorax returns. Her situation has changed, and she'll receive the news better from a friend than she would from one of my other soldiers."

Jia nodded her agreement, feeling Kaiya's hot glare on her back. "Done."

Chapter 115

Rorax

A short dragon ride later and Rorax returned to the Northern Castle with the harpy's head in a blood-soaked linen sack. When she stood in front of the Guardian in the Great Hall, she pulled the head out and rolled it to the Guardian's feet, next to the head that Isgra had already returned.

Dark, coagulated blood flicked up onto the Guardian's dress and cheek, and the Guardian flinched, her lips curling. "Tell me, Contestar, did the harpies say anything useful before their death? Or was it more of their useless drabble?"

"They said that one of them had been communicating with Koleti, who gave them permission to 'expand their borders.'"

A disgusted smile crept over the Guardian's mouth as she toed the head, pulling the jaw down and revealing the rows of the harpy's long teeth. "I am not sad I will be passing this Koleti issue to someone else."

Rorax resisted the urge to fist her hands at her sides as a feeling of indignation and abandonment rushed through her chest. "What will need to be done?"

"Someone will need to visit Koleti's temple in Wymeria, remind him that the Guardians *allow* his creatures a small foothold in Illus, when they really all belong in Hell."

Rorax cracked her neck and didn't look away from the Guardian.

One day, Rorax was going to kill her.

The Guardian had apologized to Rorax, had sent her a short note mentioning her regretful "outburst," but it wasn't enough. It had taken her nearly the full two weeks to completely heal her back, even with nearly constant treatments from Tressa. The amount of black salt the Guardian had used had lodged deeply into Rorax's muscles, and it had taken Tressa a long time to completely heal the wounds. They had multiple sessions where Tressa had to reopen Rorax's skin to dig any remaining dark granules out. Worst of all, her matching tattoo of the Ice Dragon she had gotten with Raengar and Isolde was almost unrecognizable with how her scars now sliced it up.

Once they had completely removed the dark substance from Rorax, Tressa had left for home, traveling back to the capital of the House of Life with another apology that she could not do more for her.

The Great Hall doors heaved open behind her, and Rorax turned on her heel to watch Enna push through.

Rorax looked her friend up and down. There were no visible injuries on her, and she was completely empty-handed.

Why was she empty-handed?

Had the harpies left her village before she'd even arrived?

The Guardian rose from her throne, her mouth pinched and her yellow eyes sharp. "Where is your harpy head?"

Enna stopped walking when she was alongside Rorax. She gave her a hello nod before turning to the Guardian. She swallowed hard but kept her back straight as she answered. "I decided to spare them."

The Guardian blinked in confusion. "You... decided to spare them."

"The harpy had *children*, four little girls and a son. So, I spared its life in exchange for its immediate departure," Enna said. "I can go back and ensure that the harpy followed its word. There must be another way besides mindless slaughter."

The silence that followed was thick, and Rorax's stomach dropped. Enna had failed her trial. What did that mean?

"Mindless slaughter. You mean to tell me that you… let it live?" the Guardian asked in disbelief.

"Yes, I—"

Rorax could see the Guardian tremble in rage from where she stood, nearly fifteen feet away.

"THAT HARPY," the Guardian shrieked, her voice so loud the windows around them shuddered and groaned, "SLAUGHTERED THAT ENTIRE VILLAGE."

The Guardian took one step forward, her fingers flashing between human digits and claws as she grappled for control of her power. Rorax fought the instinct to pull Enna behind her back when the Guardian's fingers started to grow long nails made of ice.

"There are a lot of *creatures* that should inspire your pity, your *mercy*, but a harpy is no better than a lizard. It feels no love or warmth, has no sense of *community* or *sentience* beyond its own survival. It lives off the Gifteds' magickal blood, and it will continue to hunt our people until there are none left." The Guardian raised her hand. She was still trembling, and Rorax could see the effort it took her to turn away from Enna and not attack her on sight. "Get this *mongrel* out of my sight before I rip her to shreds. In fact, I want *all* of you out of my sight. Get out."

There were some unhappy murmurs, but eventually any of the bystanders that had been milling around in the hall filtered out.

Rorax turned to leave as well, but the Guardian erected a wall of air where Rorax tried to move, effectively blocking her way. "Not you. I must speak with you, Greywood."

Guards shuffled forward and led Enna out of the hall. Once the doors were closed behind her, the Guardian relaxed a fraction and turned to Lamonte. "Find the harpy and its pups and put them down."

Lamonte nodded once and disappeared out the hallway with his men.

The hall was empty when the Guardian turned to Rorax and pointed one claw-tipped finger at her. "Ready yourself."

Rorax could barely breathe. "What do you mean?"

"Before a Contestar can become the Guardian, there will be a vote on whether the Council of Houses accept her. Enna has failed this trial. Some of the Houses will not vote for her because of this."

The words clanged through Rorax's chest.

"What does that mean?"

"It means you need to ready yourself, Greywood, because my recommendation that Isgra Torvik is unfit to be the Guardian may no longer be enough."

Rorax pushed out of the Great Hall and let her feet guide her back to her room.

Ready yourself.

Enna had failed the fifth trial. She had not been able to look past the surface of the harpies' glamour and do what needed to be done. She had not protected the surrounding villages from a potential attack.

Ready yourself.

They needed to do something, to stage something. *Something* to prove to the Council of Houses that Enna was still worthy. Rorax turned the corner to the hallway of her room.

"Hello, Rorax."

Rorax froze midstep and snapped her head up to find Niels standing outside of his room.

"Niels." Rorax looked Niels up and down impatiently. "What do you want?"

"I wanted to congratulate you on a job well done."

Rorax huffed out a laugh.

"I also have a message for you. There is no subtle way to say this, but the Alloy King would rather spill the blood of thousands of the Realms' soldiers than see the Spine Cleaver as the Guardian. He commands that you step down, or he will hunt you down. Torture you. Poison you if he has to. He is willing to start a war over this, Contestar."

Rorax opened her mouth to respond, but movement distracted her.

Jia slipped out of the shadows behind her, two lethal-looking ice spears in her hands, and stepped subtly in front of Rorax. "There is now a witness to your threats against the House of Death's champion. Death has every right to call for blood against Alloy."

Niels snarled. "Death would never survive a war against Alloy. They would crumble in days."

Jia's smile turned poisonous. "Tell me, Emissary, how long would Alloy survive against the House of Ice?" She turned her head to Rorax. "A week? Maybe two?"

Rorax grinned. "A few days *maximum*."

Niels's snarl all but melted away. "They have no claim."

Jia turned back to Niels, her wicked grin growing. "They have *every* claim. Ice is Rorax's second House."

Niels huffed his cheeks and scurried away.

Rorax rubbed her hands over her face. "You should have claimed a kill just then. I didn't even know you were there."

Jia grinned as her weapons melted into water in her hands. "As your new security unit, I'm trying not to slack on my first day."

"My security unit?"

"As a new potential Guardian, your Protectorates want a new security team on you. You'll have coverage now every day."

Irritation flickered in Rorax's chest. A new potential Guardian? She hadn't consented to this. They hadn't even discussed what had happened with Enna yet or deliberated the ramifications, no decisions had been made. "On whose authority?"

"Ayres and Kiniera."

Rorax rolled her jaw and pushed past Jia.

Ayres, Kaiya, and Piers were in the library for their shift when Rorax pushed open the doors, Jia on Rorax's heels as Rorax led her through the stacks and stalactites to her table.

"I have a security unit on me now?" Rorax snapped as Ayres looked up to see her.

Ayres stretched his hands above his head before lazily uncurling himself from his chair as Rorax stomped her way over to him.

Ayres opened his mouth to answer, but Jia cut him off.

"Niels threatened to kill Rorax if she didn't step down. Threatened to poison her and threatened that the Alloy King would hunt her down and torture her."

Ayres's head snapped up to Jia's, his jaw hard, his eyes bright red. "He said *what*?"

A shiver ran down Rorax's spine, and she moved to put herself in front of Jia, to silently tell her to shut the fuck up, but Jia just wrapped an arm around Rorax's shoulders and shoved Ror back to wedge her way in front. Rorax scowled at the back of her head.

"Niels blatantly and openly threatened Ror in the hallway right outside of the Great Hall," Jia said to Ayres.

"Niels isn't a threat," Rorax ground out between her teeth to the back of Jia's head. "He is a *mongrel*."

"He is a threat, and he's about to be an example." Ayres stared down at Jia for a long moment before he nodded. "Thank you."

Jia smirked. "Ror is very excited about our new arrangement."

Ayres looked up at Ror with a resigned sigh. "Get used to it, Little Crow."

"What do you think you're doing?" Rorax hissed at him. "Enna is still our primary focus until the Guardian disqualifies her."

Ayres sighed and sat back in his chair. "We need to think about what this means for the future of the Realms. I don't think Enna is the best choice for the Guardianship anymore."

"Well, *I am* sure she is the right choice. And it's *my life, my Choosing*."

Jia stiffened next to her, and Ayres looked up at her with mournful eyes. "We have a lot to think about. Until we hear back from the Guardian, you will have a guard at your side at all times. I'm not taking any chances. Understood? We can talk about it then."

"Niels is dead."

Alarmed, Rorax stared wide-eyed at Jia who had just picked the lock and came to sit at the end of her bed. "What?"

"Niels is...." Jia yawned, stretching out on Rorax's bedspread. "Ayres beheaded him in front of the whole court."

Rorax bolted from the room and down the hall. She threw open Ayres's door without bothering to knock.

He was sitting on the edge of his bed. He was shirtless, and his golden chain around his neck glinted in the warm light from the fireplace. His pants were undone but still around his hips while he fiddled with a knife in his fingers. He looked up, startled as she slammed the door behind her.

"What the fuck did you do?" Rorax ignored how her body suddenly ached for him, ignoring his glorious torso with all the swirling tattoos, and glared at him.

He let out a long sigh, dropping the knife on his bed behind him and buckling up his new belt with lithe fingers before calmly looking at her. "Good morning, Rorax."

"I asked, *what did you do*?"

"I killed him." Ayres put his hands on his hips and smiled a cold, devilish smile at her that nearly derailed her anger.

"Why?"

He hesitated. “Niels threatening to kill you in a hallway full of people is unacceptable.”

“You just pitted me directly against the House of Alloy,” she snapped, shoving a finger at him.

Ayres leaned in closer, his heat invading her space. “If you, for one second, believed you weren’t already pitted against them, you’re a fool. It’s a matter of your security, Ror, to make sure that everyone here knows any threat against your life is a threat Death and Ice will take *very* seriously.”

Rorax gritted her teeth.

“However,” he said, running his fingers through the short length of his hair, “we need to run things by you. Communicate with you. And I’m sorry for that. Next time, you’ll be informed.”

Exasperated, Rorax turned to go. Ayres caught her wrist and tugged her into him, looping an arm around her waist and kissing her before she could pull away.

CHAPTER 116

TRESSA

Tressa pushed open the doors to the tavern, ignoring all the faces that turned and looked her way.

She had her eyes locked on one woman, who sat at the back of the room in a secluded booth surrounded by her five personal bodyguards.

Eluvan Abebe, the Queen of House of Life. Her mother.

Tressa walked straight back to the booth, nodding at familiar guards before standing in front of her mother.

Her mother's black curly hair was short, to show off the twisted crown of goldsteel donned on top of her head. She was draped in a long golden gown that had the green lunar moth of House Life embroidered on it. She looked beautiful, but something in her mother's brown eyes betrayed her grief.

They stared at each other for a long moment before her mother fell on her, a blubbering mess of tears and snot, looping her arms around Tressa's neck and dangling down as if her legs could no longer hold the woman up. "*Tressa... Tressa*, my girl. Home, where she belongs," her mother sobbed.

Tressa was thankful that her skin was dark enough to cover her embarrassment as she looked over her shoulder and saw the whole tavern had turned to stare at her.

"Momma... Momma, shhh. It's okay." Tressa ran a hand up and down her mother's back in soothing strokes as she continued to tremble in Tressa's arms.

"I'm just so glad you're *home*. I couldn't live one more day with you away from me. It... it felt like you were *both* gone," her mother sobbed, and guilt filled Tressa's chest.

Tressa hugged her mother more closely and kissed the top of the head. "I missed you too, Momma. I love you."

"Sit, please."

Tressa sat.

"Tell me about Gimren; you have seen him, haven't you? He's there at the Northern Castle. Has he proposed yet?"

Tressa's mouth tipped up slightly, but she shook her head. "No, Momma, he hasn't proposed. We wanted to wait until after the Choosing."

"Well, you're done with that now, so tell him to propose anytime." Her mother looked at her. "Is that Heilstorm monster still at the castle? Maybe her head could be a bridal gift."

"Rorax is as much a victim of the Choosing as Roo," Tressa said, keeping her voice calm.

Her mother took her napkin and wiped the frown on her mouth. "My own daughter is so foreign to me."

As her mother moved, something on her finger flashed in the candlelight. "What is that, Momma?"

Her mother just shook her head, putting the napkin back on her lap. "We can talk about that in a bit."

"Is that a *ring*?"

Her mother didn't answer. She just grabbed her glass of her wine with the hand that didn't have a giant diamond sitting on the middle finger and took a long swallow.

"Mom," Tressa snapped.

"Tressa, do not speak to me like that," her mother snapped back.

Tressa recoiled, like her mother had slapped her across the face, before she leaned forward, pressing her palms against the table.

"You will tell me where you got that ring *right now.*" Her mother flinched, and even to Tressa, her voice sounded foreign and hard.

Movement caused Tressa to look out the window. A pair of men walked past, and the sun caught the silver mace etched on the chest of their plate armor. The green metallic edges of their armor shone so brightly it felt like Tressa might go blind as she stared. There was only one House that used that color of green on their armor, only one House that had a silver Morningstar as their House sigil.

She forgot how to breathe. Her lungs burned, and her heart stopped beating in her chest as she turned back to her mother in shock. "You *wouldn't.*"

Her mother's mouth pinched. "Tressa, you don't understand."

"What did you promise him?"

"Who? I-I didn't promise him anything, I—"

Tressa slammed her hands on the table. "*What did you promise him, Momma?* The King of Alloy doesn't do *anything* for free."

Her mother's gaze fell to the table as she started to fiddle furiously with her wedding ring that she hadn't taken off once in the five years since her father's death. "He gave us soldiers to help secure the border and vowed he would protect us and threaten anyone who might think about challenging us as the ruling family of House Life... in exchange we must use our vote in the Council of Houses to sway them against his trial."

Tressa's heart crumpled smaller and smaller in her chest with every word. "*Momma*, what were you thinking?"

Tears started to slip down her mother's cheeks, and Tressa's heart deflated even more.

"I was thinking that I miss my family. That I missed my only surviving daughter and this was the only way I could get you out of your servitude at the Northern Castle and get you home." She wiped her cheek with the back of her wrist. "I was thinking that they were going to send you to a god's awful war after the Choosing. I was thinking that I was already so alone... and that I... I wouldn't be able to handle it if you left me, too."

Tressa's mouth snapped shut. She pushed herself away from the table.

She needed some air, and she needed to get out of this gods-forsaken tavern. She turned but only took two steps when something else caught her eye through the same window.

Tucked under the arm of one of the soldiers was a familiar book. A book that was one of a set she had once seen in the library in Surmalinn. A blood-red book with gold trim and the Goddess of Death, Marras, on the front.

Tressa's whole body froze into a block of ice.

One of Sumavari's books.

A thousand thoughts tracked through her mind. Shit, shit, *shit.*

"Do you see that?" her mother whispered.

Tressa could do nothing but gape at the soldier, who mercifully didn't notice her staring, as he tucked the book in the back of a saddlebag and mounted his horse.

Her mother turned her face to look up at Tressa, the same fear and shock in her eyes that was currently burrowing into Tressa's heart.

"What have I done?" she asked.

Tressa bent down on the side of the table and pressed her hand over her mother's. It was shaking and cold, so she squeezed it tightly. "I have to go, Momma. I must warn Ayres and the House of Death. But then I am going to come back, I *promise*. We will figure out what to do. Together, okay?"

Tears streamed down the queen's face, but she straightened her shoulders and nodded. "Go."

CHAPTER 117

RAENGAR

Raengar ignored the gasps and the outraged shouts as he made his way to where he knew the Council of Houses held their meetings.

The guards knew better than to interfere and did nothing besides stare at him in shock as he burst through the doors.

House of Alloy was on probation until after King Määr's trial was over, so only eleven of the twelve kings and queens that made up the Council of Houses looked up at him from where they sat.

The King of Water stood up, spluttering, as he looked horrified at the frozen, mangled head dangling from Raengar's fingertips. "What in the hell is going on?"

Isolde stood from where she sat as Raengar slammed the head of the minotaur on the table and set the scroll with the test results from Luxamal next to it. Isolde looked smug and triumphant as she turned to face the King of Water. "Your Grace, that is the head of a minotaur, a Pit monster recovered from Pit Island. You asked us for proof that the creatures live. Here is your proof."

Raengar held up the paper with the results and the history of purchase. "This is the University of Luxamal's report on the samples of Jia Frostguard and Rorax

Greywood's blood from the Heilstorm mission that was betrayed—the mission that was ordered, approved, and prepared by *this* Council was betrayed. It shows proof that the blocker used in their attack was ordered by King Määr."

The Weather King whooshed out a breath of relief. "Thank the gods."

"This is enough proof to convict King Määr of treason," King Tulek of Fire said, rubbing his hand over his jaw thoughtfully.

"More than enough. Statements and witnesses have signed their names below, and all are willing to testify," Raengar said, standing straighter.

"And the Pits?"

"At least one has been opened. Go home and prepare your armies. We are going to war."

Chapter 118

Rorax

"Are you boiling… a leaf?"

Rorax peaked over Jia's shoulder to see the long green leaf in the water.

Jia snorted, not bothering to turn to look at her. "It's a reed leaf for my zongzi. Ye-Jun sent them to me so I could celebrate the Ice Dragon Festival, even though I won't be at home. I'm making them early. He also told me to tell you good luck."

Rorax sniffed the air, and her stomach grumbled. "By chance did he also remind you to share?"

"Of course not. Ye-Jun shares as well as you do." Jia gave her a flat look over her shoulder. "But I'll take pity on you if you help me wrap them."

Rorax moved to Jia's side eagerly. "The festival isn't for another few months. Why are we celebrating early?"

"I need to," Jia said, her voice slipping from congenial to angry and short.

"Why?"

Jia ignored Ror as she lifted the long leaves out of the pot with metal tongs and laid them on a plate.

"Fold the reed like this to make the bottom into a cone." Jia demonstrated; her tone short. "Then fill the cone with rice and meat, then wrap it all together."

They worked silently as they filled the leaves. Then Jia briskly showed Rorax how to tie the zongzi together with string.

Jia carried the plate and led Ror up to the roof of one of the towers, sitting with their legs dangling off the edge. She didn't say a word to Rorax as they silently ate their food, wouldn't even look at her.

When Rorax was done, she set her plate on the ground and leaned back on her wrists. "Are you going to tell me what's wrong? Or do I have to guess?"

Jia's lips turned down at the corners as she wiped a stray kernel of rice out of the corner of her mouth. "You should already know, Ror."

"Well, I don't," Rorax snapped, looking over at her with tired eyes. "So, enlighten me."

Jia took a big bite of her last zongzi before she finally spoke, her eyes trained on the mountains in front of them. "I need to talk to you about something."

"I gathered that," Rorax said flatly.

Jia's purple eyes slanted a look at Rorax, and she puffed out an angry breath. "Kään help me Ror, why are you such a sarcastic bitch all the time?"

Rorax's jaw went slack, and Jia exploded out, "Gods, I can't even look at you right now without wanting to punch you."

Rorax reeled back. "What?"

"Back in Lyondrea, when Crax had me strung up on her torture table, it looked like you were going to walk away from Volla and me. It looked like you were going to abandon us for the opportunity to find Darras. I was hurt, but deep down I understood. I believed in your right to choose your family. But now—" Jia's voice broke, and she raised a fist to her mouth just as her chin started trembling.

"Jia... I—"

She held up a finger. "Stop. Shut the fuck up and listen to me, Ror."

Rorax's jaw snapped shut.

Jia sucked in a deep breath, straightened her spine, and leveled a withering gaze at Rorax. "I wanted to talk to you to let you know I won't be working for you at the library anymore."

"Why?" Rorax narrowed her eyes. "I know I should have been down there with you more. I didn't mean to give you a bunch of shit to do then abandon—"

Jia cut Rorax off with a slice of her hand through the air, looking like she was itching to break Rorax's nose. "Rorax, I'm not mad you asked me to read some motherfucking books."

Rorax's brow furrowed, and unease started to pool in her stomach. "I'm confused."

"I'm mad that you are blatantly and actively planning for someone not nearly as capable or as qualified as you to be the Guardian of the Realms while the Realms are at WAR." She yelled the last word at Rorax so loudly, Rorax's whole body flinched away. "It's nearly impossible to advocate for someone when they won't even advocate for themselves. You refuse to open your gods-damned eyes and see that the Realms not only wants you, but it also *needs* you."

Rorax was glad she had finished all her zongzi because she would have dropped them off the side of the tower. Her mouth fell open to speak, but words failed her as she gaped at her friend.

Jia wasn't finished.

"I am *so fucking angry*, because we all deserve a Guardian who will make sacrifices for her people. Who is willingly be selfless and do what needs to be done. When it was just my life on the line, I couldn't do it. I wouldn't dream of asking you to give up searching for Darras. But now? Now that hundreds of *thousands* of lives are on the line? I can't even *believe* that I have to ask you."

"We... we all agreed that Enna—" Rorax began to protest, but Jia cut her off again.

"*You* always said that Enna would be a better Guardian, and in some ways, you're right. Enna would have been a better diplomat. A better role model for the citizens. A more graceful and charismatic Guardian. But gods above, Rorax, open your eyes!" She laughed bitterly, exasperated like she was trying to talk sense into a petulant child. "We don't need a *diplomat* right now. The Realms are looking another Pit War right in the eye, and they need a Guardian who's strong enough to turn the tide." Angry tears started to form in Jia's eyes, and her chin trembled again as she wiped the tears away with her fingertips.

Rorax couldn't do anything but stare as Jia dragged in a deep breath. The air was starting to taste like evening. The sun had set, and everything was descending into shadows around them, and Rorax wished they could have even five more minutes of light.

After a few moments, Jia gently grabbed one of Rorax's hands off her lap and wrapped her soft hand around it. "I know you never wanted this, Ror. That you never wanted the responsibility or the weight of being the Guardian. I know that the only thing you've ever wanted was your family and your freedom." Jia sniffled. "But, Rorax, I'm asking you to choose us. Fight for this new family we have made here. Fight for the Realms."

Rorax didn't know what to say. "I.... Jia, I don't know how you can even ask me."

Jia narrowed her eyes. "What do you mean?"

"After everything that has happened?" Rorax's bottom lip wobbled. "Isgra was right, Jia. If I couldn't save my best friend.... I am so sorry. I should have acted earlier that night; I should have fought harder. Volla.... We could have—"

"No," Jia cut Rorax off as she reached out and cupped Rorax's face almost reverently. "Ror, there is nothing you could have done."

"Jia, I don't know if I can save the Realms. I couldn't save Volla. I couldn't save Briar. Sahana is in prison right now. Darras is probably right next to her." A sob ripped through Rorax as Jia held her face, the sound full of pain and rage. "Why couldn't I save her? What if I can't save Enna? Or Isgra?"

Rorax let out another loud sob, her shoulders shaking with tears.

Jia released Rorax's face and clasped one of Rorax's hands, making a sandwich out of Rorax's palm with her own. "Listen to me, Ror. You couldn't save Volla, but I got to say *goodbye*. I got to tell Volla I loved her and that I was so proud to be her wife. Crax didn't get to kill me, and because of that, I got to say goodbye.

I wouldn't have had that goodbye without you, Ror. Crax would have taken it away. Think about it, Rorax. Think about becoming the Guardian. For me... for Volla."

Rorax pulled Jia into a hug, and they sat there crying together until Rorax's tear ducts were swollen and painful.

Rorax let her go and wiped her nose on her sleeve. "I got snot in your hair."

Jia made an amused grunt. "That's so nasty. You're disgusting, Ror."

A little watery, pitiful laugh burst out of Rorax as Jia gripped her hands again. "I know this is going to be painful, but in order for the Realms to stand, you *have to* become the Guardian."

"I don't—"

The door to the top of the tower opened, and Rorax turned to look over her shoulder to see Ayres poke his head around the door, his eyes locking on her face with a concerned grimace. "Are you okay?"

Rorax nodded as he pushed his way onto the tower and picked her up from the ledge. She wrapped herself around him monkey style, her legs around his waist, her face buried in his neck.

"Should I send Kaiya or Milla up for you?" he asked Jia over Rorax's head.

"No, I want to be here alone for a bit."

"Are you going to go to the Great Hall for dinner?" he murmured to Jia.

"No, I'm not hungry. We just had some food. Thank you though, Ayres."

Rorax looked at her friend from over her shoulder, saying softly, "You should eat some more."

"I will, when I'm ready."

Rorax nodded before laying her cheek against Ayres's shoulder.

He slowly carried her to his room. They were about halfway there when they passed one of his men. "Go find Emissary Garrison and tell her to bring Jia Frostguard a hot meal and some wine. She is in need of a friend. Bring a meal to my room after you find her and some of the cook's orange rolls," he ordered.

"I'm not going to share those, you know," Rorax mumbled against his neck.

"I know." Ayres ran a hand over the back of hair.

Rorax squeezed her limbs around him even harder, and his hand moved to rub his big palm up and down her spine. Slow tears started to drip free from her eyes and onto his black sweater.

"What were you two talking about?" Ayres asked.

"The Choosing."

"What about it?"

Rorax cuddled closer into him. "Jia… she wants me to become the Guardian rather than Enna."

"Oh, I see." When they got to his room, he grabbed a shirt from his drawer and sat with her in his lap. He tugged at her shirt, so she lifted her arms as he gently removed the material up and over her head. He reached behind and slowly removed her chest bindings and bra.

Ayres's eyes latched on to her breasts for an instant, a brief glint of hunger in his gaze, but he didn't give them a second glance as he grabbed his shirt and slid it down over her torso. When he was done she snuggled into his massive body.

They sat in silence as she slowly cried into his sweater, and he rubbed her back softly until there was a knock on the door. He gently moved her from his lap and moved to the door. "Take off your pants, Ror, get comfortable. We have a lot to talk about."

Ayres returned with her food just as she was done pulling off her leathers.

Ayres watched as she eyed the plate with a side of three orange sweet rolls and smiled. "I hope there's enough of those there. If not, we can get more."

Her heart ached because it was so full.

Fight for this new family we have made here, Jia had asked.

Rorax ate in silence for a beat before asking him, "What do you think I should do?"

Ayres rubbed his hands together. "I know that Enna is important to you, Ror. She's an amazing woman." He looked up into her eyes, his gaze unyielding and certain. "But you need to consider the ramifications if she becomes the Guardian and cannot do what we need her to do."

"That wasn't the agreement I made with you, or with her," Rorax protested with a shake of her head.

Ayres scooped her off the bed and sat her back into his lap, so she was straddling him, sitting chest to chest. "Would you be up for a new deal?"

Rorax blinked in confusion. *A new deal? What would that mean?*

"We think… we think you should become the new Northern Guardian of the Realms when the time comes."

Rorax turned into a statue made of confusion and anxiety in his arms.

"You don't need to make a decision today, or tonight, or even for another month, Ror, but you *do* need to decide." Ayres tucked a strand of hair behind her ear. "Whatever you decide, it's your responsibility, your choice, and your consequences. So, make sure you choose the one you will be able to live with, because you *will* live, Rorax. If I must burn down the bridgeway to the afterlife to keep you with me, I will."

Rorax huffed a wet laugh against Ayres's neck and placed a kiss at the junction of his shoulder.

Then something happened, something soft and distant nudged at the Death Magick chord she now held in the back of her mind. She was dismissing it just as Ayres's arms tensed around her. She jerked her head back to look up at him. He had that *look* on his face.

"Was that a…?"

Ayres's eyes were alert and wary. "A summoning. A large one. Someone is using death magick."

"Why could I feel it?"

"That must be part of your new magick," Ayres said, studying her face, his mouth going tight in thought. "You must hold enough magick now to feel the ley lines when they get pulled hard like that."

"That means the other Contestars can feel it too." Rorax frowned.

Ayres shrugged. "They wouldn't know what it means; it feels like nothing more than an itch if you don't know what it is."

"Do you want me to come with you? To help you find the book?"

Ayres shook his head and ran a thumb over her cheek. "No, Cannon and I will go. You stay here with Jia and think about what I've said. Okay? Consider the idea of becoming the new Guardian of the North."

Rorax thought of Enna and reluctantly nodded. "Okay."

CHAPTER 119

RORAX

Rorax used a shield to bat away one of Jia's oncoming blows and then twisted to block another. The morning dew made the grass slick, and as Jia landed both swords on her shield, the impact made Rorax skid back an inch.

Rorax cursed under her breath and took a step forward, gaining back the ground she'd lost and used the shield she had borrowed from Lamonte's training collection to take a swing, trying to move on the offensive.

It didn't work. Jia slapped the shield to the side, twirled, and pressed the top of her blade to Rorax's chest.

Rorax gave a flat look to the blade before looking up at Jia's smug smile. "I hope a bird takes a shit on you this morning."

Jia laughed, dropping the blade away from Rorax to wipe her sweat away. "You're getting better with that thing. If you ever had to go one-on-one with just a shield, at least you'd have a chance."

Ever since their talk on the tower, Jia had been normal and, thankfully, hadn't brought the topic of the Guardianship up again.

Rorax laughed, too, and opened her mouth to say something smart-ass, when a sharp, panicked whinny made her jerk her head around.

Tressa, on a large white stallion, was galloping through one of the narrow, arched entryways to the arena, heading full speed toward them, her blue dress billowing out behind her.

"Where are Ayres and Cannon?" Tressa demanded as she slowed her horse next to Jia. The animal was sweaty and frothing from the mouth with exhaustion.

Jia and Rorax shared a nervous, uncertain look. "They're... gone," Rorax said, "and they probably won't be back until the end of this week."

"*Fuck.*" Tressa squeezed her eyes shut and bit her knuckle between her teeth.

When Rorax saw tears slip down Tressa's face, the sense of unease in Rorax's stomach grew into thick knots. "Tressa, what's going on?"

"My mother—" Tressa's voice broke off before she tried again. "My mother has allowed the House of Alloy passage into our Realm. I saw a platoon of soldiers carrying a Book of Sumavari. There were too many of them for me to get it back alone, and it could be anywhere by now."

Cold ice speared into Rorax's chest. "Where?"

"Leluvar, five days ago. I don't know where they are now."

Almost like it had been summoned, Rorax felt the little, tiny pull of Death Magick at the back of her skull.

It was in the complete opposite direction from where Ayres was right now.

Rorax swore before she turned to Jia. "Go get your bow and get ready. We need to send a Blood Hawk to Ayres, and then we're leaving."

Following the pull in the back of her mind, Rorax led Jia through the woods. They had pushed their horses through the night, stopping to steal fresh ones from villages along the way. Five days later, and they were getting close.

She felt the pull getting stronger and stronger as she got closer to the summoning point, and with every step closer, her stomach tied in tighter knots.

They had just passed through Karduru, the town full of healers that had saved her life on her very first hunt with Ayres. The little girl she had saved lived here with her parents.

If the Lyondreans were successful here, that little village would be one of the first to be attacked with whichever of Sumavari's monsters were conjured.

No matter the cost, Rorax was determined they wouldn't be successful.

Rorax pulled her horse to a halt when she felt them getting close. They were nearly on top of the summoning. "We walk from here." They dismounted from their horses and continued silently through the underbrush until it cleared away. Rorax sucked in a sharp breath as she took in the view. She knew where they were, she had passed by here before with Ayres.

The Lyondreans were using the Volcano Towers for their summoning.

Two tall dark towers on either side of the clearing—one on each side of the now empty lava lake. They were simple and made of lava brick. Ancient, dilapidated things that looked weathered and beaten down but still stood firm against time.

Rorax felt a sharp pull toward the one closest to Jia and her.

"That one," Rorax said, pointing to it. "There are five soldiers in there."

Jia pulled the bow from her back. "Do you want to sneak in or bust through the front door?"

The pull at the back of Rorax's neck strained like she had never felt before. "Burst in. We don't have time to wait."

They crept over to the side.

When Rorax felt the presence by the front door move slightly away, she gave the sign. Using a small battering ram made of ice, Jia busted open the fragile door. The five soldiers inside yelled in surprise until either an arrow made of ice sank into their hearts or Glimr cut their throats.

They killed the soldiers in less than a minute, and when they reached the top of the stairs, Jia wasted no time to kick open the door.

A red circle had been painted on the ground in blood. It was glowing, and there was a man standing on the inside of the circle, directly over the body of a woman whose throat had been cut; her blood had been used to make the summoning circle.

A strong Alloy soldier erected a wall of stone between them, and Rorax used her own Alloy Magick to slice the barrier in two.

"Stop!"

The man's eyes went wide as he paused within the circle, and before Rorax could stop him, he slammed his hands palm first down on the floor.

Rorax grabbed Jia and lunged to the side, covering her friend with her body just as magick exploded.

The whole top of the tower was ripped off and exploded into nothing but rubble and dust, smoke filling the air.

Coughing violently, her ears ringing, Rorax pushed herself to her feet and moved herself into what was left of the doorway, staggering.

The man in the summoning circle had been thrown so violently his neck was twisted at an awkward angle from his prone body. In fact, all the men who had been in the room looked unnaturally still, and all the energy signatures were gone.

"*Fuck*. Are you okay?" Rorax turned to Jia, who slowly moved herself up to her elbows, nodding.

Rorax stepped over the broken barrier of earth and bent to pick up the red and golden Book of Sumavari from the ground. She wiped the dust off with her arm as Jia stepped to the edge of the tower to look out at the grounds.

Whatever she saw there made her choke. "Ror."

Unease prickled at the back of Rorax's neck as she stepped next to her friend.

Below them, clawing their way out of the crusty ground, were undead soldiers. Hundreds of them. Mangled and gory, most of them nothing but decomposing skin dangling on armored skeletons.

Kään help her.

"Come on, let's go." Rorax turned and sprinted, running down the stairs, stepping over dead soldiers and not stopping until she skidded to a halt on the edge of the cliff.

Draugr. Undead soldiers.

Ancient generals from Wymeria and the House of Death had chosen the site of an old volcano to fight, and now they were being called again to war using Death Magick.

The only advantage Rorax had was they were all at the bottom of the old lake that had only drained from one side, making it so there was a forty-foot cliff on all sides of them except one. For them to escape, they had to go through that one side. If she beat them there, she could design a way to funnel them, and hopefully she could hold them off until Ayres and the guard got there.

As the draugr ripped themselves out of the earth, Rorax pulled the ribbon out of her hair, tying it around the book's cover tightly before thrusting it into Jia's arms.

Jia took the book, her eyebrows furrowed in confusion until she looked up and saw the expression on Rorax's face. "Oh no. *No.* If you think I'm letting you fight them alone, you're insane."

"That book needs to get to Ayres as fast as you can get it to him. It can't stay here, and *those* things can't get out, or they will move straight toward Karduru." Rorax pointed at the herd slowly starting to move toward their escape. She needed to get down there. "I can handle them. Ayres is close; I can feel him. Get that book to him, Jia. That is the most important thing you can do. For everyone."

Rorax pulled her sword out of its sheath and summoned Glimr to her palm. It warmed under her skin, like an old friend saying hello, and Rorax squeezed it a little tighter.

She was ready.

She was meant to be here. In this moment. Protecting the House of Death.

All the pent-up violence and anger from the last few months simmered under her skin as she eyed the dead army. She wanted to be unleashed.

Jia swallowed thickly as she watched Rorax get herself ready for battle, tears lining her eyes as she looked down on the draugr army. She threw her arm around Rorax's neck in a brief hug. "Sakar Sumavari was an absolute fucking bastard," Jia muttered into her hair before she turned and sprinted toward the direction of her horse.

Rorax tightened the grip on her blades and let herself feel that bloodthirsty rage for half a beat before going to meet the army head-on.

Chapter 120

Ayres

Ayres and the guard turned a corner on the wagon path that led straight to the Old Volcano and nearly ran into Jia, who was pushing her horse, galloping fast toward them, away from it.

Ayres could feel the book. It was there, with Jia.

Jia pulled the reins to stop her horse so sharply it caused the animal to rear up in protest. When the horse settled, Ayres saw that Jia's eyes were wild and bright with fear, and tears streaked down her face. "Ayres, *gods*, Ayres, hurry. She's back there. They summoned a draugr army."

"Where is the book?" Even if this was Rorax's friend, Ayres didn't know if he trusted this woman enough to leave her with one of the Books of Sumavari, or if he believed her enough to know it all wasn't a giant trap for him and the guard. Jia lifted her shirt, and there it was, the red-and-gold cover gleaming in the twilight sun.

Splattered with blood and tied around the book in a double knot was the ribbon Ayres had given Rorax.

Ayres's heart gave a painful, panicked squeeze as he reached out and yanked the ribbon off the book. "Where is she?"

"At the ruins of the old volcano, two miles. Hurry, Ayres, she's there and she's fighting them all alone." A little sob of panic burst out of Jia's mouth, and she had to look away from him, pressing her wrist against her mouth.

Ayres looked over his shoulder to Milla, Kaiya, Cannon, and Piers. "Go," he commanded them. "Hurry. There is one more book there, and Rorax is alone."

His four guards pushed their horses forward as Ayres focused upon Jia again. "Jia, listen carefully to me. This book needs to get back to Surmalinn or thousands of people's lives will be at risk. Do not stop, do not wait, do not talk to anyone. We will get Rorax out of this alive. I promise you. Focus on the book."

Jia took a ragged, steadying breath. "Go, I can do this." Then she spurred her horse back to a breakneck speed.

Ayres caught up to his guard in time to see Piers, Milla, and Cannon disappear into a short, squatty tower. Kaiya stood frozen, a giant battle-ax dangling in her hand, at the edge of the cliff.

"What are you doing?" Ayres battled his irritation at Kaiya's hesitation, but as he stepped onto the ledge next to her, he froze, too.

Rorax was there, shooting ice picks and knives made of earth, decapitating the draugr apparitions left and right like she was felling dominos, using fire whips to corral and control them and using thick walls of black darkness to section off the soldiers around her to thoroughly mow through the rest facing her.

She was a twirling black blur of lethal majesty.

Never in his life had he seen someone move like *that*; never had he seen so many different magick types being worked so symbiotically as weapons.

Rorax flipped a section of earth over, squashing at least twenty-five draugr warriors. She pivoted, sending vines to support her dark wall, before holding her hand up to level a small section of soldiers with loud, crackling lightning. One soldier broke through, charging at her, but she skewered him through with a large shard of ice.

A flaming arrow streaked in the sky, hurtling toward her back.

Ayres's heart squeezed. He opened his mouth to scream her name, but before he could, the arrow stopped moving three feet from her and dropped to the ground.

He sagged with relief.

Of course.

Of course, she was thorough enough to remember an air shield. They had drilled into her time and time again that, when you were in the middle of a battlefield, you needed someone at your back.

She was out there alone because she knew she was powerful enough to be that person for herself.

"Marras above," Kaiya whispered.

Ayres looked over at Kaiya to find tears streaking down her dark brown skin.

Ayres hadn't known until Kaiya looked up at him, her dark eyes glimmering with grief and sorrowful acceptance, and the truth struck him like a bolt of lightning. Enna Mistvalley, Kaiya's friend and lover, would never have the opportunity to become the new Northern Guardian of the Realms.

In another world, in another lifetime, Enna would have been the perfect Guardian to rule with a just and gentle hand. She would have looked over the Realms with the same care and charisma that she looked over her friends with.

But on the brink of destruction, the Realms didn't need a just and gentle hand. They needed a protector. A warrior.

They needed that brutal, true, ferocious heart beating in the middle of a battlefield, facing hundreds of draugr soldiers all by herself so that she could buy her friends enough time to find the Books of Sumavari.

Rorax Greywood was destined to be the next Guardian of the Realms.

The door to the tower behind them burst apart as Cannon and Piers barreled through.

"We got it!" Piers panted, holding a leather-bound book up for Ayres to see. "We're here."

Ayres turned to Cannon and began to sign furiously. ***Take the book, take my horse, and ride to Surmalinn. Do not stop for anything. Meet us back at the Northern Castle.***

Piers thrust the book into Cannon's arms. He snatched it and sprinted away to Ayres's horse.

"As for the rest of you—" Ayres gave the two remaining members of his guard a bloodthirsty smile. "—to the Spine Cleaver."

Chapter 121

Rorax

Rorax almost cried in relief when an arrow flew by her head to kill a draugr soldier she had missed with her ice picks, stabbing him square between the eyes and dropping him to the ground before a black wall—a black wall streaked with red lighting—erected all around her, pushing the closest draugr soldiers more than twenty feet away.

She took in a ragged, thankful breath and bent over to rest her hands on her knees.

Ayres was here. Ayres was *here*.

Rorax swiveled her head around to find him charging toward her, and gods above he was truly, amazingly glorious.

His black battle armor went all the way up to his neck, his glittering black longsword peaked up over his shoulder, and in his other hand he had a shortsword already covered in black draugr blood. His eyes were bright red, and his intense features were focused on her. He looked every inch the beautiful, lethal Harbinger that he was.

"Took your sweet time," Rorax drawled when he got close enough, wiping at a drop of blood and sweat that was coming out of her nose.

Ayres's skin around his bright red eyes crinkled with amusement as he studied her from head to toe. Dark scruff had grown back on his face around his perfect mouth that tilted into a smile that was nothing but pure devil. "I was enjoying the show, Little Crow."

Rorax huffed before standing up straight and cracking her neck. "Did you get the other book?"

Ayres nodded. "Both books are on their way to Surmalinn as we speak."

Good. Rorax twirled her knife in her fingers. She could hear soldiers around her and suddenly felt eager to get back into the fray. "Break is over, let's go."

Ayres cocked his head and gave her another analyzing look over. "How close are you to a burnout? My guard and I can handle it from here."

As if to confirm his words, Kaiya let out a battle cry nearby, and the sound of falling draugr followed.

"I could use the practice." Rorax took in a few more deep breaths, feeling the heaviness and the slight ache in her limbs. She was going to feel like death after this. "I have another thirty minutes in me. If I decide to test myself, maybe more."

A wicked smile crossed his lips again as he reached back and pulled his longsword out from over his head. "We can have this done in twenty."

Rorax smiled back. "Then lead the way."

CHAPTER 122

RORAX

"Gods, I want to get home. I *desperately* want to get this filth off me. It's *disgusting*," Milla complained, looking herself over and shuddering.

It had taken less time to clear the battlefield than Ayres predicted, but it wasn't a moment too soon for Rorax. They combed through the soldiers, beheading and hacking through the bodies of their ancient heroes, and only when they confirmed that every draugr was once again dead did they finally start making their way back to their horses. Rorax had to drag herself.

She had overdone it. She had gotten all the practice she wanted, true, but she had also come dangerously close to completely tapping out toward the end. Not only were her magick reserves running on fumes, but her physical reserves were almost gone as well. All her limbs and muscles were smarting, warning her they were close to failure, and her whole body *ached* with exhaustion. Rorax somehow got to her horse, groaning as she pulled herself up.

Only when she was firmly seated did she allow her pride to inflate inside of her chest. She had single-handedly held off an entire draugr army—an admittedly small army, with less than two hundred half-wit soldiers, but she had done it.

"Are you okay?" Ayres pulled his horse next to her gray Garron and looked over her with knowing eyes. Despite the warmth of pride in her chest, her body was starting to feel cold and feverish. Even holding the reins of her horse felt like a huge task. If they had to ride hard for any reason, she was going to fall off her horse.

Ayres must have been able to see her exhaustion because he didn't wait for Rorax to answer as he reached over, wrapped one arm around her middle, and plucked her up and out of her saddle. He dragged her over to him like she weighed nothing and settled her in front of him, her back pressed against his chest.

Ayres looked over at Piers. "Guide her horse back; she's dead on her feet."

Piers nodded.

"Thank you," she murmured to them, resting her head back against Ayres's shoulder as he wrapped his dark cloak around her tightly.

"How do you feel?" Ayres asked. He ran the meat of his palm down the length of her left leg, pressing down hard and massaging the aching muscles in her quad. She moaned in pleasure as he did it again, kneading over the ache.

"Like shit," she breathed. "That feels so good."

Ayres huffed a laugh in her ear and did it again, rubbing the muscle.

"You were impressive out there," Ayres muttered. "I've never seen anyone hold off an army single-handedly like that."

Rorax moaned again as he transferred his reins to his left hand to rub his right palm down her opposite leg. His fingers rubbed deliciously hard into the flesh there. "It felt good to... release. To see what I could do."

Ayres hummed in understanding.

"I'm sorry about leaving without you. I know one of your cardinal rules is to never leave without backup."

Ayres's fingers stopped kneading, and she felt his jaw flex against her earlobe.

"I was furious with you. Furious that you didn't wait for me, furious that you went in alone with only one soldier at your back. My instincts were screaming at me to lock you in a room, to keep you safe and out of harm's way, but...." He sighed as if the words were heavy, like every syllable said cost him something.

Rorax felt her insides tighten as his breath hit the sensitive hairs on her ears and neck. "There are very few people in the Realms more powerful or more qualified to fight this than you, Rorax." He pulled his arm tighter around her. "And if I want to keep you, I must let you. If I try to keep you safe but leashed, I'll lose you anyway, and it would cost hundreds of people's lives in the process."

Ayres sighed. "I know it won't be easy, and I know I'll have to come to terms and accept the fact that the woman who is *mine* is also one of the most powerful beings in the Realms—in the *world*—but I will trust you to know your worth to the Realms, to decide which risks and which missions are worth it, and to trust that you won't make any brash and unruly decisions with your life."

Something hot and bright and happy burned through Rorax's chest.

"That being said"—Ayres reached down and gently pushed his thumb in the soft flesh under Rorax's chin, forcing her to tilt her head up to look at him—"your fledgling magick abilities were untested going into battle today. I'm grateful to have both books back, but taking on a draugr army by yourself falls under the classification of 'questionable decisions,' Little Crow."

Rorax scowled. Ayres grinned down at her and lowered his voice so no one could hear him. "However, I've never been so hard going into a fight. For the next hundred years, when I *tend to* myself, I will use today as my material."

Rorax grinned up at him, and he smiled back.

"It won't be like that in a month or two, though once I release my magick to Enna," said Rorax.

The smile on Ayres's face fell away, and his mouth pressed together in a tight line. He stopped his horse, and his eyes flitted up past her to his guard.

"You three go ahead. Rorax and I need a moment," Ayres commanded Kaiya, Milla, and Piers. Kaiya gave Ayres an almost grieving look that Rorax didn't understand, but none of them said a word as they kicked their horses farther down the path and out of earshot.

All the cheekiness that had lived in Ayres's face was gone, replaced by somber seriousness that made Rorax uneasy.

"We need to talk," Ayres murmured, looking down at her with charcoal eyes so dark they were almost black.

"About what?" Rorax asked hesitantly as she snuggled deeper into his chest.

"About the conversation you had with Jia the other day."

Rorax's insides went cold. "About... the Choosing?"

"Yes." Ayres sighed, reaching up and rubbing the back of his head.

"What about it?"

He studied her for a long, heavy moment, contemplating his words. "When we find the way to release Contestars from the Choosing, we need to use it to release Enna," Ayres said in that voice that was commanding, unmovable, unshakable, and never-endingly steady. "Rorax, you know as well as I do that Enna would *never* have been able to do what you did today. She would never be able to fight in the same capacity as you did. *You* are the Guardian the Realms need, Rorax. You. Not Enna. Not Isgra. *You.*"

His eyes were so hot, so sure on her face, that Rorax had to drop her stare onto the hands in her lap.

"You handle the magick better than anyone, you *wield* it more comfortably than any Guardian before you. Even when your magick fails, your body is trained enough to carry on the fight with Glimr and the rest of your weapons."

Rorax shook her head. "It doesn't matter. Enna—"

"Do you really think Enna could have done *that*?" Ayres released her hips to gesture with his arm to the direction of the Old Volcano where she had fought the draugr. "We both know that even on her most bloody, ruthless day, Enna would never have the reckless abandon and skill to be able to do that, Rorax. And as the Guardian facing a Pit War, you are going to face so much worse than that."

Rorax swallowed hard, thinking of the look of grief and understanding Kaiya had given Ayres. "Have you told Kaiya?"

"Kaiya doesn't need to be told. She already knows. I know. Jia knows. Kiniera knows. Hell, Rorax, I think we *all* know. Including you." Ayres's voice remained unmovable and as steady as his eyes.

"This is still your choice, Rorax, but if you chose to abandon the Realms... well, it's the *wrong* choice—a choice that could leave millions dead."

Rorax finally found the gumption to look back up at Ayres, and they were silent for a long time, silently communicating.

"You were born to be the Guardian, Rorax."

"After everything I have done, how can you still think I'm destined to become this?" Her voice was small and pitiful, telling exactly how she felt inside. Small. Stained. Unworthy.

Ayres cupped his hand around her face, bringing it up to his. "The Guardian role aside, Rorax Greywood, how can you still think you are not enough? Have you not bled enough? Fought enough?"

"I don't know," she whispered. "I don't know if it will ever be enough."

"Then let me tell you. As the firstborn Prince of Death, the right-hand of Marras, heir to the Harbinger of Death, and a son of Sumavari, you have done *enough, Rorax*. Forgive yourself, because I have forgiven you already. *We* have forgiven you already."

"Conrad will never forgive me."

"No, and there will be others who have lost too much to forgive, but the majority of my people, the queen, Cannon, me... and even *Marras herself* has forgiven you." Ayres brushed the hair out of her face tenderly. "Rorax, you've been fighting your whole life. If you decide to keep fighting for us or not, you have absolved yourself of your sins, and you can rest in peace that you have earned."

Tears, thick, hot drops slipped down her face. "Do you mean that?"

Ayres cupped the sides of her face with his hand, wiping the tears away from her skin. "I do."

Rorax pressed her fingers to Ayres's chest plate, over the tattoo of Marras marked in the center of his pectorals. "When we stopped in Povelinn, I asked her... I asked her to help me keep you and your people safe."

Ayres wrapped his hand around hers, squeezing it tightly. "You make me feel safe, Rorax. Not just physically, but...." Ayres's throat worked. "I trust you, completely and in all things. When Jia, a Heilstorm and a daughter of an *Ice general* rode by with one of Sumavari's books, I was going to pry it from her hands, but...."

Ayres released her hand to dig in his pocket, pulling out her ribbon. It was blood speckled and dirty, but nothing had ever made her heart glow in her chest more than this gesture. She reached out and rubbed her fingers over the silk. "Thank you, Ayres."

CHAPTER 123

RORAX

Jia leaned against the railing, looking Rorax's filth-covered body up and down with a raised eyebrow. "You look good for a woman who just took on an undead army all by herself."

Rorax snorted, looking down at her gore-encrusted fighting leathers. It was dusk, and Rorax and the guard had just gotten back from the ruins around the Old Volcano after a two-day journey. Their company had stopped at an inn last night on the way back to the Northern Castle. Rorax and Ayres shared a room, but they didn't discuss anything more all night. He had just rubbed out her muscles and kissed her sweetly until she fell asleep in his arms. She had been too exhausted to even take a bath.

They had just arrived back at the Northern Castle when Rorax spotted Jia standing on the balcony watching the Contestars' training session and came up to join her.

"I always look good, Frostguard." Rorax gave her a sardonic tilt of her lips and moved past her to stand at the railing overlooking the Contestars' Courtyard. Isgra and Enna were down there, training with Lamonte. They were having a competition to see who could grow a vine faster than the other up the side of the castle wall, through an obstacle course that Lamonte had drawn in chalk on the wall.

Rorax watched Enna focus on the foliage in front of her, Lamonte by her side, yelling instructions.

You are the Guardian the Realms need, Rorax, Ayres had said to her. *I have already forgiven you.*

Isgra's vine crossed the finish line before Enna's, and she thrust her arms into the air in victory. The motion was so familiar, so *Volla*, it made Rorax's heart crack. In the ache, a moment of clarity rushed through her fast enough it nearly took her breath away.

If Volla Torvik, the Torch of Valitlinn, knew what was at stake. she would have already kicked Rorax's ass to Lunalia by now.

"Jia, go get Kiniera. Tell her I have something we need to discuss."

Rorax waited for the sharpshooter to tell her to fuck off, but she must have sensed something was happening because she slipped away into the tower without a word.

Rorax stared down at Isgra, her gaze locked on the face that was identical to her best friend who she had not fought hard enough to save. She would not willingly lose anyone else. She would fight tooth and nail. She would lie and cheat, fight dirty and scrappy. She would give everything the gods had given to her.

The large wooden door to the north tower opened, and Kiniera's steps sounded behind her, but Rorax couldn't tear her eyes away from Enna and Isgra on the ground. Every second she spent staring at Isgra, her resolve grew and steeled itself until it was an unyielding demand in her heart.

What's your name?

Rorax Greywood.

What does that mean?

It means that I will fight with everything I am to protect those that I love.

"Rorax?" Kiniera asked.

Rorax raised her chin and straightened her shoulders. "I need you to send a Blood Hawk to the king."

"Oh?" Kiniera smiled, something in her voice sounding vaguely triumphant. "And pray tell, Rorax, what should I tell him?"

Rorax slowly turned to face the spymaster. "Tell the king that I demand a Heilstorm unit go searching for my brother. I *will* find him. I cannot leave Darras to a future of more captivity and torment."

Kiniera raised an eyebrow, a knowing smile on her pale lips. "Anything else?"

"Tell him that if he will provide me that, then in one month's time, I will be by his side as the Northern Guardian of the Realms."

Atonement of the Spine Cleaver Character Guide and Glossary

Contestars

Highborns are born with high quantities of elemental magick in their blood. Lowborns have little elemental magick or none at all.

Briar - Lowborn

Claira - Lowborn

Enna (En-nah) - Lowborn

Isgra - Lowborn

Itzel - (It-sell) - Highborn

Lily - Highborn

Mairi (Mary) - Lowborn

Mo - Highborn

Roo - Highborn

Rorax (Roar-Axe) - Lowborn

Serena - Highborn

Stella - Highborn

Heilstorms

Sahana Thorash (Sa-ha-na Thor-ash) - Founder of the Heilstorms. Commander of the first unit. Wife and mate to Karan Thorash.

Volla Torvik (Vol-la Tore-Vick) – Second-in-command of the first Heilstorm unit. Wife and mate of Jia Frostguard.

Rorax Greywood (Roar-Axe) - Third-in-command.

Jia Frostguard (Gee-ah Frost-Guard) - New recruit. Wife and mate of Volla Torvik.

House of Air

Allurah (All-er-ah) - House of Air's emissary at the Choosing.

House of Alloy

Narlaroca (Nar-lah-row-cah) - A fierce citizen of House Alloy.

Niels - The House of Alloy's emissary during the Choosing.

House of Dark

Lamonte (Lah-mon-t) - Captain of the Northern Guardian's guards.

House of Death

Ayres Sumavari - Queen Sumavari's younger brother.

Rosalie Sumavari - The Queen of Death.

Kaid Sumavari - Queen Sumavari's son and her second-born child.

Eliza Sumavari - Heir to the House of Death's throne and Queen Rosalie's firstborn.

Conrad Sumavari - Queen Sumavari's younger brother.

Talon Sumavari - The Queen of Death's youngest brother. Currently training with the Frost Dragons.

Erich Sumavari (Erik) - The Queen of Death's younger brother and general to her armies.

Milla Garrison - Spymaster for House of Death and their emissary during the Choosing.

Piers Olufsen (Pierce Oh-loof-sen) - A member of Ayres's close guard and a red herring prince.

Cannon Musa - A member of Ayres's close guard. Was fighting during the Siege of Surmalinn and lost his hearing during the battle. He later becomes Rorax's close friend and mentor.

Kaiya Thorne (Kai-yuh) - Most commonly known as Kaiya Whitethorne due to her part in defending the Whitewood forest in the House of Death.

House of Fauna

Merosa - Queen of the Witches. Places the witch-rune on the back of Rorax's ear to help Rorax hide her eyes.

House of Fire

Elios Delgata - House of Fire's emissary at the Choosing.

House of Ice

Raengar Carbore (Rain-gar Car-bore) - The King and co-ruler of the House of Ice, Son of King Katalon the Corrupt, and Rider of Deimos Ice-Born.

Isolde Carbore (Is-old Car-bore) - The Queen and co-ruler of the House of Ice, Daughter of King Katalon the Corrupt, and rider of Frostlight Goldhorn.

Kiniera Kulltoug (Kin-yee-air-ah Cult-ow-g) - Spymaster of the House of Ice and emissary for House of Ice during the Choosing.

Ye-Jun Frostguard (Yee-June Frost-guard) - Commander of the Frost Dragons.

Tag Norvakson (Tag Nor-vak-son) - Steward of Koppar and Raengar's second-in-command.

Sahana Thorash - Leader and director of the Heilstorms.

General Frostguard - Mother to Jia and Ye-Jun Frostguard, General of the House of Ice armies, supervisor to House of Ice reparations.

Layaz Kulltoug (Lie-az Kulltoug) - Ambassador for House of Ice currently stationed in the Azaela's Islands. Kiniera Kulltoug's sister.

Eshaal (Ee-shawl) - First-in-command of the second Heilstorm unit.

House of Life

Tressa Abebe - Head healer during the Choosing and House of Life's first princess and heir to the throne.

Roo Abebe - House of Life's second-born girl, she was sacrificed to find Rorax during the Choosing.

Gimren (Ren) Norvakson - House of Life's emissary during the Choosing and Tressa Abebe's lover.

Queen Abebe - The Queen of House Life and Tressa and Roo's mother.

House of Water

Dori Wolfmoon - House of Water's emissary during the Choosing.

Center House

The Northern Guardian - Galadis (mostly referred to as the Guardian in AOTSC)

The Western Guardian - Vadik

The Eastern Guardian - Oxana

Radashan (Rad-ah-shan) - The librarian for the Northern Castle.

Gods

GODS OF THE REALMS THAT ARE MENTIONED

Kään (Cah-n) - God of Ice

Marras (Mar-ras) - God of Death

Kuu (Coo) - God of Life

Paiki (Pay-kee) - God of Fire "Paiki's Fires"

Asepp (Ah-sep) – God of Alloy

SOVEREIGN GODS THAT ARE MENTIONED

Ukuros (Oo-koo- rose) - the Supreme God/Supreme God of the Realms

Majauss (May-ouse) - the Protector God

Koleti (Cole-eti) - the God of Monsters

Cities Mentioned

Koppar (Ko-par) - Capital city of the House of Ice.

Morvarand - Capital city of the House of Death.

Skavetsia (Skah-vet-see-ah) - Major city in House of Ice, location of one of the largest military academies in the country.

Bafta - Small town outside of the Northern Castle.

Surmalinn (Sir-mah-linn) - Major city in the House of Death.

City of Stars - City where Stars are mined.

Leluvar (Lel-oo-var) - Capital city of the House of Life.

Underground Market

Angelo - The king of the underground market.

Hella Wellbrok - Seamstress in Bafta, works for the King of the Underground.

Glossary

A.R. - An acronym standing for After the Rip. When the Gods landed on Illus. All years are counted from that event on.

The Choosing - Deadly competition where the Gods choose a potential new Guardian.

Contestar - One of the twelve people chosen to compete in the Choosing.

Goldsteel - A golden-colored metal that is immune to Alloy Magick.

Guardians - There are three Guardians that lead Illus. They rank even higher than kings in the social structure of Illus due to the immense amount of magick they hold.

Illus - Name of the planet.

Silversteel - A silver-colored metal that is immune to Alloy Magick.

Stars - Clumps of crystalized magick that are found in the earth. Come in various sizes. Small stars can be used to make potions and weapons more virile; large stars are extremely rare, much more violent, and are usually used in war as a weapon of mass destruction.

Starsteel - Steel that is infused with Stars.

Rathmore Venom - Venom from snakes that originate in Rathmore. With the right dose, Rathmore Venom can give the user a psychedelic effect and feelings of euphoria. The wrong dose can act as a rage stimulant. Moderately addictive.

Sakar's warlords - The seventeen warlords that were transformed from men into monsters. About half of Sakar Sumavari's books raise these warlords from the dead.

Sestera Blade - A blade that can be moved and used by the mind.

Shadowbell - A dangerous kind of poison grown in the House of Fauna and the University of Luxamal.

Starsoot - Drug made of the soot of burned Stars. Incredibly dangerous. Makes the user temporarily able to hold more power. Highly addictive.

Waterlily Rine - Blocks those who have ingested it from being able to use their magic. Highly effective, tasteless, and extremely expensive.

Witch - Those who hold magick that can only be applied to things using wards and witch-runes. For example, Ice Witches apply runes to silversteel boxes to create cold boxes in order to store food.

Witch-Rune - A technique a witch uses to apply her magic. For example, an Ice Witch must apply a rune to a cold box in order for it to be used to keep food fresh.

Whitleherb (Wit-el-herb) - Recreational drug that calms the senses and relaxes the user. Some strains have psychedelic effects. Slightly addictive.

Acknowledgements

I am immensely proud of this book. I started it on October 18, 2020 while I was locked away in quarantine during COVID, and I never would have imagined it would become such an amazing project.

At its peak, *Atonement of the Spine Cleaver* was 225,000 words. An extremely ambitious project for a debut author. I would not have completed it without a handful of people in my corner.

Foremost, I would like to thank my mother. She self-published a book before I did and has been patiently and expertly guiding me through the steps. She's been my greatest cheerleader, my greatest supporter, and was the first one to say "you need to take this seriously." I never could have finished this without her, and can never thank her enough.

I would also like to thank my dad, who is "cooler than anyone else." He's been a continuous driver and an undying supporter of all my creative endeavors, and I am so lucky and so thankful for his support and love. He is the most prolific reader I know, and I will always be thankful for his example. Also, Dad, thank you for reading A Game of Thrones with me, it's been so much more fun with you!

The next person I would like to thank is my brother, Nick, who has helped build worlds with me before. We spent years as kids playing with toys and creating stories together, and without his past ideas and his past love for fantasy, this world I created would only be half as interesting.

To my editor, Jennifer Murgia, who convinced me to write the Jia POV and who was continually patient with me through at least seven months of editing; thank you for all of your hard work. I am so thankful to have found you!

To Virginia Cantrell who did another round of copy edits for me, THANK YOU. Your work made me even more confident in Atonement of the Spine Cleaver than I thought possible.

And finally, to my readers: thank you so much for giving this book a chance. I appreciate you more than you know.

About the Author

Atonement of the Spine Cleaver is F.E. Bryce's debut novel. Bryce has always been an avid epic fantasy consumer and is excited to bring her own story to life. She lives in Utah with her two lovely dogs and is either watching the newest epic fantasy movie or taking her dogs for a nice long hike.

Connect with her on Instagram: @f.e.bryce.writes or shoot her an email at febryceauthor@gmail.com

Printed in Great Britain
by Amazon

42617727R00435